HEX

A NOVEL OF LOVE SPELLS

DARIECK SCOTT

CARROLL & GRAF PUBLISHERS
NEW YORK

HEX

A Novel of Love Spells

Carroll & Graf Publishers
An Imprint of Avalon Publishing Group, Inc.
245 West 17th Street, 11th Floor
New York, NY 10011

AVALON
publishing group incorporated

First Carroll & Graf edition 2007

Library of Congress Cataloging-in-Publication Data is available.

ISBN-13: 978-0-78671-764-4
ISBN-10: 0-7867-1764-5

9 8 7 6 5 4 3 2 1

Interior design by *Ivelisse Robles Marrero*
Printed in the United States of America
Distributed by Publishers Group West

To the memory of my godmother,
Shirley Waldrum

Acknowledgments

I have been wonderfully fortunate to have the emotional and practical support of my partner, Stephen Liacouras; the indefatigable enthusiasm he has brought to this novel from its earliest beginnings, and his willingness, through draft after draft, to read and contribute thoughtful, invaluable comments were gifts I'm continually amazed by. Ty Blair's extensive comments on an early draft were also invaluable. I am very grateful to Lucy Jane Bledsoe, Beth Mende Conny, Ian Duncan, Gabrielle Glaser, Lisa Moore, Dionne Scott, Cilla Smith, and Timothy Wager for their comments on drafts, advice, and generally helping me to feel it was worthwhile to finish this project. Regarding the latter this novel might have foundered altogether, lost to the diffidence and despair that—alas—so often accompanies my forays in the world of publishing, but for profound support and guidance from two beacons of light: Shari Carlson and my fellow singers in Studio 300; and Phyllis Pay and my fellow practitioners at the Intuitive Energy Center. Attentive comments from Sharon Holland (who attended a reading of a portion of the novel I gave at the University of Illinois, Chicago) editors at Tor, and Chip Delany (my idol) were timely and vital. Much gratitude is due also to my editor, Don Weise, who provided *Hex* exactly the right pair of eyes and the home it needed.

I have relied a great deal on two excellent layman's guides to theoretical physics and cosmology by Michio Kaku, *Hyperspace* (Doubleday, 1994) and *Parallel Worlds* (Doubleday, 2005), and on Paul Davies' *About Time* (Touchstone, 1995). As a committed fantasist I have ruthlessly ignored and otherwise mangled the sound science of both men's work when it suited the story to do so, but their books were invaluable guides nonetheless. Elaine Brown's *A Taste of Power* (Pantheon, 1992) and David Hilliard's *This Side of Glory* (Little, Brown, 1993) were similarly inspirational (and somewhat similarly loosely handled vis-à-vis pesky facts) regarding the Black Panther Party.

Prologue

On the night of August 20, 1953, shortly after nine, with nearly everyone else onboard sleeping away their exhaustion as the *Roan* lists contentedly at dock, Verity Gapstone rises quietly so as not to disturb Credence, whose small, warm body is tucked beside her in bed. She watches her son for a moment. He stirs a little, but then sinks again into the bright virgin dreamworld of the almost-nine-year-old.

On the small half-moon desk that abuts the wall of her cabin, she spies *Hex*. Its red dye swims up like a buoy tip from the dried-blood brown that floods the darkened room. She lifts the porthole cover a couple of inches to let in a splash of oyster light. *Hex* lies heavy in her hands—heavy, but something makes her fingers tingle as they caress the leather (she can't help stroking it, petting it). Expectation? It is her emotion, surely, her imagination only that makes the bound manuscript seem, in the shadows of the short hall as she creeps past the Roses' cabin and past Lin's, like a living creature. Verity takes *Hex* up to the dining quarters. The table is empty, the dishes cleared. She switches on a small lamp—its illumination is weak, the letters on the page miasmic, oily, seeming to flow up to her eyes out of memory rather than through sight. The blackness and grayness beyond the long windows starboard and port side have a more powerful presence than the book, even though all she can really see are shapes, outlines: the black Caribbean softly gurgling, a narrow strip of gray shore mounting upward from the sea, and then, abruptly, Libertytown, squared and triangle-topped shadows humped and bleeding into one another. Looking at Libertytown without being able to make out more than its sketch, it's as though the island village were either entirely alien, set down like a playhouse on top of sand and grass for the amusement of some ancient divinities, or—just as likely—as though it were a completely natural outgrowth of the native vegetation as it crawls toward the beach: an autochthonous city. The island calls to her.

But no. The book is present, real, what the words describe is true. Verity sets to work on the final corrections.

"Why is it important to get all the *love* spells right?" Atalanta had asked Verity weeks ago when the Roses had first hired her to emend their manuscript. Atalanta Rose's voice has a very limited tonal range; most of her words barge through the begrudgingly parted corner of lips otherwise compressed in a grimace, and almost everything she says trails a low growl not unlike a cat's complaints. At the time Verity hadn't yet learned that Atalanta's disdain is universal, and so, offended, she'd refused to answer the question, and Atalanta, taking umbrage at Verity's offense, refused to repeat it. Now, with things softer between them, Verity wishes she had answered. Verity could tell Atalanta that though of course you cannot summon love, you can't command it, nor even its constituents, lust or admiration or need, a love spell is effective insofar as it aims its arrows at the heart of magic itself: connection—the connections running invisibly, like spider's web threads spooled from a common center, between each thing, between seen and unseen, between would-be lover and yet-to-be-loved. Verity could tell her that she herself had come to this truth through hard trial, through losses that had broken her heart, broken *her*. Her husband, David, lost to fire; her aunt Plennie, lost to wind; her parents, to murder and illness—all still with her. Not as ghosts, or some angelic communication. The true remaining presence doesn't involve a visitation, any addition to the world we know. It has rather to do with something already *in* the world, something that *is* the world. Something always darting away like a shadow moving beyond the scope of peripheral vision: not so much gone as merely missed. You simply miss seeing what's there.

Verity could advise Atalanta to cultivate a discipline of observation. Simple things. Obvious things—because if you can't observe the obvious, you'll never achieve an understanding of the more elusive realities. Try a negative credo first: not to bask in the sunlight without searching the sky for traces of the moon. Not to follow the ramble of butterflies through a meadow without holding in your thought and forcing to your eye the visage of the crawling, fuzzy, earthbound creatures they were and—somewhere—yet remain. Not to smile at a young brown couple as they emerge from a basement afloat on the notes of jazz saxophones and walk the pavement lost in the heat of ardor without noticing the child that waits between them, and noticing, too, the babes they themselves once were, wet with the gloss of afterbirth. Not to pass by the old site of the auctions without seeing naked African bodies displayed like fish in a farmer's market stall, without seeing the skin around their mouths balloon as fingers rummage over their gums, without hearing the pipe music they jiggle to, without seeing blood trickle from the tail of a whip gripped in the seller's hand. In all things notice. Notice what's missing. And call it back, if you can.

Verity herself had learned to live by that creed, and healed her brokenness by it. When her father died two years ago, Verity had linked herself with him for eternity with a silver chain that clasps Verity's wrist to his. No one can see the chain. The ignorant would call it imaginary. But Verity's certainty of its existence is unshakable. Afterward, when she would feel a tug at the tip of her finger, or notice, as if from far off, her wrist leap from its resting place on her lap and swing toward the window where the moonlight crosses the front of her house in New Orleans, when she would want to walk down one street but find herself turning down another, she would know: the dead are not dead. It is only our failure to perceive them that makes it seem so. They are merely Missing.

Verity could tell Atalanta this truth, and that under its light love spells are the best spells, the only truly real spells. Because a love spell trains our attention on what is there; it works because all it need do is reunite what was never truly sundered. Verity would say this, if Atalanta were awake now, and she would tell Credence, too.

And maybe it would soften the blow. If she doesn't come back. If it *looks* like she doesn't come back.

Corrections done, notes completed; she's finished in an hour or less. At the end, when it's really come to it, she hesitates. She'll need to take pages from the book, that intuition seems clear to her, but how many? She decides, impulsively, on eight, and rips out eight pages (none of the pages that she corrected, of course), tearing slowly so as to mitigate the noise and so that she gets as much of the page as she can.

She goes back to her cabin and places *Hex* on the desk in the position she found it. Atalanta and Aden will be looking for it, once they find she's gone. As Verity dresses, Credence makes a small noise, almost a hurt noise, or maybe a little moan of fear, a half-syllabic mew that comes and goes quickly but that burrows straight into her stomach. His face is turned away from the cabin door, away from her. She steps around the bed, looks at him, can see the ripples passing through the skin of his eyelids. Verity strokes his back lightly. If he wakes, would that mean he should accompany her? Would it be safe for him to? If she's right, yes. If not . . . but Credence doesn't wake.

Verity returns to *Hex*, opens it, and writes a message on the title page. She lifts it again. Her fingers don't tingle. The book is quiet now, dead. An omen?

Then out into the night she goes. She takes a flashlight, and when the captain, who isn't asleep, asks her where she's going, she tells him she's taking a little walk on the island. It isn't long before she finds the main road that leaves Libertytown and travels east, and she walks along it, fearlessly, though it is dark and she is alone, sure of her mission and its inviolability.

When she reaches the eastern beach, she's not sure she's at the spot she was before—this appears to be a small cove, and the longer stretches of shore north and south are hidden from her. But it's adequate for the purposes of her experiment. She slips off her shoes and walks along for a while, letting her soles nestle in the sand that has not yet lost all the day's warmth. The sea is a black sheet rustling on the line, its half-glimpsed wrinkles catching then casting away the living moon- and starlight. Verity bends low to look at the gently sloshing water of the cove, as if there is something laid across the surface that she might be able to read, as if there were a spirit swimming in the depths that might be trying to reach her.

In the shifting light—a cloud slipping past the moon, perhaps—a bit of the water jumps. Flails, as if thrashing in its own dream. Likely it's a fish or a frog, but Verity imagines there is a mermaid using the cove bottom as her bed, the sea as her quilt, and she delights in the young-girl silliness of her imagining. As she basks in pleasure, she realizes that she has already bridged the gap between worlds, that already a missing piece of herself, the child she once was, has floated back across the ether and lives again in her body.

For a moment, before it fades, she spies two small whirling pools in the water, each fat at one end and narrow at the other. Two great teardrops joined at the hinge from which they fall from the eye. Like an eight, lying on its side. The sign of infinity. She was right then, in her choice of number.

Verity unhooks her rings from her ears. They were a birthday gift from David. With some difficulty she folds the eight pages from *Hex* into eight very crude paper boats—they're more like the paper airplanes her recalcitrant students at St. Michael's send flying when her back is turned, but they'll do, she hopes. Verity puts one earring in one boat, and the other in another, and in the six others drops shavings of David's hair she'd found on the dresser top after she'd been told he'd died, and that she's kept these two years.

She moves uncomfortably out into the cove, thankful that the water's not as rough as it was on the open beach in the morning. She whispers with what she hopes is the force of sorcery to the eight paper boats as she sets them in the tide. *May you float until you find them*.

Quietly she calls the great goddess of the New World Yorubas, Yemanja of the sea. She calls Petbe the Requiter, lightning-eyed god who rises up from the black abyss. The names of gods are nothing, she knows. She and Lin and Atalanta and even Aden have agreed that divine names are just fetishes, practically a case of mistaken identity, since what you're really calling is the whole Universe. Call by whatever name, and It will come: hiding in a mask, veiled in a sign, the God-force waits for your summons like some great hulking she-bear crouched down behind a trio of beautiful roses too lovely to pass without picking.

Verity Gapstone waits, on the edge of the sea, with the rock-strewn white sand behind her and its drowned cousins beneath her bare feet, the waters of the cove tickling and slapping her calves.

The air is a bit cool, a bit heavy, but the water is balmy. After a while, tired, with nothing happening (but she knew it wouldn't, the nothing that's happened proves nothing, what is to happen has yet to occur, she can feel it if not see it, coming from over the edge of the world; push off the doubts!)—Verity sinks down into the sea, lets it soak her pants and panties, push her shirt against her belly, lets it enfold and claim her. Like old Aunt Plennie's baths back in Jacksonburg.

Is it only the mind's deception, its restless quest to make sense of things that require no sense in order for them to be real, that brings Plennie's baths so strongly to her memory? For it's too right, in a way, too cleanly circular, to lower yourself into the water and in that single movement and its simple sensations to perceive time folding backward on itself, since, in a way, it was Plennie and her tub that brought Verity here.

Verity lived four years in her husband David's hometown of Jacksonburg, Mississippi, and the entire time, though immersed in raising their young son and surrounded by David's relations, she never ceased to feel like a visitor living out of her luggage. There was an implacable alienness about Jacksonburg, an almost living, irascible hostility to being known. In the end—once it had killed David and Plennie—she'd just surrendered to it, stopped waging the campaign to find her own anchorage among its steep hills. She'd never really perceived the connecting threads between her life and the lives of Jacksonburg's folk, that's for sure. Perhaps it was the town's truly hideous poverty, the way navigating a dirt road inevitably brought you face-to-face with a heap of trash, as though garbage could be your only destination; the sudden gaps between homes, even in the botched little downtown, where small meadows thick with tangled weeds and dotted with soupy puddles thinly veiled in olive green would spring up; the rats that dared play hide-and-seek games in broad daylight; the mean, pinch-eyed old folks sitting up smoking pipes on porches that dropped off the edges of shacks like lower lips in a pout. And the women on those porches, always giving her the what-a-bitch eye. (And she knew why they did: they didn't like Verity's looks—her height and willowy body, her high yellow color and Indian cheekbones, her dark black hair too much like a white woman's to avoid the appearance of deliberate flaunting.)

She was not much loved there, except by David's aunt Plennie, who was in her own way as much an outsider as Verity, and who, more importantly, possessed a home that boasted comforts unknown to many others in town, including the modest row house Verity and David shared with David's brother and sister-in-law.

The close quarters of the Gapstones' two-story row house troubled Verity but didn't dishearten her. The lack of hot running water, however, occasionally gave birth to rhapsodic fantasies of divorce and single-motherhood. It seems silly to Verity now that she complained so much then. The wood-burning cast-iron stove in the kitchen was equipped with a reservoir attachment that held water in its metallic cylinder, and since the stove was almost always hot—just as the kitchen was almost always busy, its walls seeming to plump with the steam issuing trainlike from its ever-busy pots, as Verity and David's sister-in-law Cissy labored to keep three small children, themselves, and two grown men fed—the water in the reservoir stayed perennially warm. All you had to do for a hot bath was dip bucketfuls out to pour into the round tin tub in the bathroom that everyone shared. But before she married David Gapstone, not since earliest childhood had Verity been required to trundle back and forth between the kitchen and the bathroom to ensure the comforts of warm-water bathing, or grasp a tin tub by the handles like some trash barrel and haul it out to empty it at the end of every bath. For about five days out of seven Verity could accept these tedious additions to her life with what she then imagined was a healthy measure of good-wife stoicism. But there were limits to the warmth thrown off by the fire of marital love: and David's peculiar nonagenarian aunt Plennie, owner of a pleasant, clean, modern home, had beautifully enameled hot-water spigots, and a luxurious white porcelain tub inlaid at the bottom with designs of fishes and wavy tide lines of polished jewel.

When David introduced Verity to his aunt, Plennie Davenport had shaken Verity's hand and said, "Look like you need a bath." Verity—admittedly rather sweaty and out of sorts from the long climb up the hill to the woman's house, which presided like a castle on the eagle's-eyrie edge of arguably the humblest of Jacksonburg's humble neighborhoods—shot a glance of bewilderment and ignited outrage at David. David gave her a reassuring, amused smile. "Come on and have one on me," Aunt Plennie had said. "Make a old lady happy."

The promise of the porcelain tub stifled any qualms roused by Verity's insulted pride. She had been in Jacksonburg for a week, and it had been rough going. While David occupied himself playing with Credence and the dogs in the backyard, Plennie drew her new niece a bath, efficiently and gracefully moving her tiny frame around the capacious bathroom, testing the temperature of the miraculously abundant running water by rolling up her sleeve and dipping in an elbow.

And then, after the first few minutes, when Verity's sulky wariness had completely dissipated in the glory of a warm liquid caress that felt like the new birth of baptism, Plennie entered the room carrying a scotch-and-soda, sat down on the chair where Verity had draped her clothes, and—her gaze directed forward, parallel to Verity, as if admiring the craftwork of the tiled backsplash on the wall—she started talking. Telling stories.

Verity, aghast, had sunk into the tub like a hippo so that the crazy woman wouldn't be able to see anything below Verity's nose through the suds and wavy distortion. She remained submerged, pushing against the upward lift of the water, at length forced to soap herself as best she could underwater, wondering what kind of insane family she'd married into, until Plennie, evidently satisfied—satisfied without Verity offering so much as a word in conversation, mind you—rose from the chair and left Verity to pat down her puckered skin with a towel and get dressed. Afterward, David couldn't explain to Verity why Plennie had offered her a bath; she'd never offered him one. "She may thought you really needed it," he'd said with a laugh. Verity frowned—but only with the muscles around her mouth. The rest of her body was now loose and labile, content with itself.

So Verity went back for another visit, and then another, until hers became a weekly pilgrimage. Every week Plennie offered a bath; Verity sank down in the tub; Plennie told stories. Eventually it was probably the odd company as much as the lulling buoyancy of the bath that brought Verity up out of the water, let her sit there in the tub with her breasts alternately half-bare and submerged according to her own whim and luxury.

Plennie's stories were odd, not the sort Verity would have expected an old woman like her to tell. They weren't about her past or the gossip of the day or about her family history or the predations of white folk or the upkeep of her garden. Plennie seemed rather to be working out some obscure philosophical theorem.

"I been thinking about it," Verity can hear Plennie saying now just as she would often begin then, the rasping sigh of Plennie's words almost mimicked by the sough of the gentle surf, lapping her body, wrapping its arms around her legs and torso. "Last time we talked, I started to tell you about the ships." ("Mmhm," Verity would have murmured—and murmurs now, drifting off into play with her toes in the water.) "But I couldn't have told you everything, because nobody knows the whole story. There were many ships, hundreds and hundreds of them. As many, maybe, as seven fleets of a thousand ships each that made the crossing." (Plennie loved to make up numbers, Verity found.) "Some of these people were escaping plague and war. There was a nasty plague back in those days, on the other side of the water. Some of them wanted fortunes, wanted land to rule. Or freedom to commit crimes they couldn't get away with back there where they come from, and for some that meant freedom to worship, for others freedom to murder and rape. As we know, many came with captives, indentured servants they treated like cattle, slaves they treated worse than cattle. 'Course no one says the exodus happened all at once. We do know the crossings happened for more than three hundred years before commerce came to a halt.

"Now most of these ships passed through powerful storms that run like a curtain across the sea, storms that would swallow up whole these little squalls everybody get so excited about here. Now the thing is—" (Plennie enjoyed pausing at key points, to take an elongated sip of whatever new cocktail had caught her fancy.) "*Most* of the ships passed through. But lots of them didn't. Many got lost. And this is a riddle nobody has an answer to: many passed through the curtain, but many got lost. Some that got lost in fact passed through, but landed on shores and in countries they didn't intend. And many that passed through were lost forever.

"So what ships landed where? Who was lost, and who was found? Our ancestors made the trip, so we think we are the found ones. But are we? Maybe we're lost, here. I don't mean the usual: that we're lost because this country was never really our home. They been telling us that since the first. I mean, when you make that long, long trip over, and you get somewhere, ain't it true that just like where you come from is only a idea in your mind because you no longer there, that you don't *really know* where you *arrived* is exactly where you (or them taking you) set out to go? Maybe they just *telling* you that you made it. Maybe they made a mistake and want you to make the same mistake, so they don't end up losing you, too. Maybe *you* got lost, and you just don't know."

"Mm," Verity intones, docked and becalmed in something akin to sleep as she remembers.

Verity feels the wind pick up, hears the water groan in protest. She remembers, too, a dream she had once when Plennie was talking, one of those slips of dream that prey on the tired body and come so quickly it's as if it's been waiting for hours to visit, as if it's perched on the inside of your eyelids to swoop down the moment they stay shut. In the dream—which she sees again now behind her shut eyes, dreams again now, bathing at the edge of the sea—the water in the tub transformed itself into an expansive, rippling body, a vast sea sundering the shores of far lands, curtaining travelers from their intended destinations. Out of the bay between the mountains of Verity's knees protruding from the water issued white scuds of soapy foam, like a fleet of boats bobbing out to the ocean. The water of the sea dark like wine, the sky above the mountains of her knees black. She looked toward the horizon and saw lightning arch down to the water. In the passing brightness there was an image that stayed with her when she rose back above the surface of the dream, and that she now recalls:

a line of ruffled high cloud, and a blade of light that struck the water and sped toward her. As if the clouds were the hilts of a knife aimed at her throat. As if the clouds were a grin, and the light a taunting tongue.

"Verity!" (A voice shouting her name.)

Verity opens her eyes. Lin is there at the cove, touching her wet warm shoulder with a cold hand.

Verity's frightened surprise—how could Lin have found her, in the dark, with so many little beaches, so many places she could be? had Lin followed Verity from the yacht without Verity knowing?—falls almost as quickly as it rises. Lin has been her guide in the worlds of the unseen. Lin knows things.

Eyes wide in the dark, Verity feels stinging whips of salt spray across her bare arms and face. The harsh wind seems to have arisen from nothing, to have shot up, volcanic, from some deep recess. She feels the heavy night air on the Caribbean island combust, she sees lightning (Petbe's eyes?), hears thunder.

The dream in Plennie's tub. She remembered it, she saw it again, and it is happening.

Verity has to speak twice to be heard. "I wondered if you'd come."

"All you had to do was ask, heifer!" Lin shouts.

"It was part of the experiment not to," Verity manages to say.

"Huh," Lin grunts. "I like the way you decided to do this."

Verity answers at the top of her lungs. "Will you say the word with me?"

Lin gets down in the water with her and together they shout it as loud as they can. "Ablanatanalba!"

Then, as the rain, instigated by mounting wind, mushrooms into a storm, the two women stop trying to speak and hold one another.

Tonight, August 20, 1953, Verity spreads one arm out wide

and hooks the other around Lin's waist, and she digs her buttocks in and plants her feet as they sink into the sand. She wants to make her body report the openness of her mind and spirit. She wants to be as wide and empty a vessel as a human being can become.

The rain burns her skin, and Lin is an indistinct shadow next to her, glimpsed through slitted eyelids crusted with salt. She hears a crack—*shoopiterr!*—and the wild lightning burns an image on her retina: fulminating clouds. Black woolly tangles of rapidly spooling string across the breadth of heaven.

Then dark.

Verity stares into the night that defies all sight, the darkness that yawns and bellows, holding her in its mouth. The tide swirls up, dashes itself against her neck, her face. Verity perceives, without being able to see, a heaviness descend upon her from above. Panicked—no, no, not *this, this isn't what I asked for*—she struggles to rise, still holding on to Lin, whom she can barely feel, so cold are her hands, so wet is her flesh.

The heaviness, the presence, the blackness, falls with the force of a hammer stroke and the crush of a thousand arms gathering her in. *Shouldn't my neck snap?* she thinks. *Shouldn't my spine be crushed? Why are my thoughts still here?* And: *Will David and Plennie and Daddy receive what I give?*

Her scholar's mind, active to the last, wants to categorize what saturates and overwhelms her senses, bursting them apart from within. *It can't be only a storm. . . . Is it a ship? A fleet of invading ships?*

But she never sees what it is.

Part 1
Apparitions

Miami, Florida
late September, the present . . .

1

South Beach dance club, long after midnight

It's all about the look at Redemption, a place with a mock cathedral ceiling and black and vermilion draperies that sway from flying buttresses and settle upon the dance floor like the trailing capes of monarchs in triumphal procession. In the faux nave, glistening half-clad boy toy performers sidle their taut hips and asses, flashing here and there a thatch of evenly cropped pubic hair and profiling through phosphorescent swim trunks their bouncing genitalia. Three curvaceous silicone-augmented women (not the usual gender of performers at the club, but tonight's special, after all), wearing nothing other than adhesive glowing circles that cap their nipples and thongs visible only when bombarded by infrared radiation, cavort wildly among the boy toys. They all whip stole lengths of bright cloth around their bodies and twirl them in the spotlights, and the troop of them appears to be gyrating in whirlpools of pink, blue, orange, green, red.

Langston watches from a narrow balcony that hangs like a sheer cliff's edge above the wide sunken dance floor, and to his appreciative eye the swirl of the performers' colored tails seems answered by the movement of the various tribes below him: the hordes of big-bosomed shirtless golden and caramel gay boys and slinky big-bosomed gay girls, the slender-armed straight white girls in brief silk slips with hair flying, and their white boy companions gloriously tattooed and parading their unworked hairy chests, the would-be ghetto-gals with nappy neon-blond naturals and scowling polo-shirted brothas who swore they'd never set foot in the place, the tall, leering, maniacally drunk Eurotourists.

Lights beamed from far above on the ceiling and from narrow glass-covered shafts that tunnel into the floor streak around the room. Langston swoons in the sea of effects. He has a penchant for dreaminess and for the world not as it is but as it should be. To Langston the ceiling is a night sky blooming with white stars hidden and then revealed by passing dark masses of clouds lit from within. Below him the magnificent bodies surge in and out of a swirling pattern: they become a nest of snakes, undulating, slithering against and beside one another. They are a dragon, Langston decides in awe, they are the pinioned wings and scales of a dragon and the sweat on their bodies makes the dragon glow like a second moon.

For a moment he can't decide whether the pleasure is keener standing above watching or if it would be better joining them. The music decides for him. On so many nights in such clubs merely a deafening and intermittently exhilarating backdrop for the more compelling dramas enacted on the floor, tonight the beat seems to exert a steady magnetic force. Descended from his perch to the pit, Langston finds himself being pushed by the shifting crowd into Azaril, who's moving in that strange not-quite-on-the-beat shoulder arms hips groove of his. Azaril's eyes seem to liquefy as he and Langston both fall sway to the rhythm. Langston stares: he begins with the legs—Azaril's big legs are bare, but surely not cool because the hair on them is almost like an animal's, and because of that there is something feral about his being even though he has tried to mask the lupine in him behind a dour pair of glasses—and then Langston lingers at Azaril's head, the thick, thick black hair in rich, tangled kinks and curls, the Technicolorbrown eyes. The sun-christened iced-tea coloring of his face and arms. Azaril's loose white short-sleeved T-shirt can't contain the overflowing froth of his chest hair.

The sight—the dark skin and black hair, the white shirt—is like an ignition. Langston shoots Azaril a riskily lascivious look, imagines he sees some dim reflection of ardor hidden in Azaril's little smile. Of course the magic of the evening—and the narcotics in Langston's system—throw his perceptions askew. Langston finds his mind dithering and dilating, as though a great magnifying glass and a pair of supernatural scissors were editing the pages of his experience from moment to moment, and now Azaril the Glory and the Mystery looms large. Azaril is half black, half Palestinian, a lineage so unlikely to Langston that it is an enticement, a seduction in itself, drawing him forward into the deep chambers of some underground crypt, each recess darker and more heavily scented than the one before.

But Azaril explains so little of himself. Maybe he has nothing to tell. When Langston first met him one year ago, in the back row of a cramped, lopsided Berkeley movie theater where the floor was slick with popcorn butter drippings and crushed Raisinets, and you had to be careful not to set your Coke down for too long lest it begin to slide and tip all over your neighbor's foot, Azaril was sitting two seats to Langston's left, loudly scribbling with a number 2 pencil in a notebook. He put the pencil down from time to time so that he could scratch obsessively at the scruff of a nascent goatee, which, in the ensuing year, he's not yet found the nerve to let grow. Langston was feeling prickly and vulnerable, aware of Azaril's every move. He leaned over to ask Azaril a carefully rehearsed question, but got sidetracked when he took his first direct look at the cute scruff surrounding very cute lips that looked engorged with collagen. In the package with this lose-yourself-in-my-lips mouth there was a goofy, apologetic smile, ingenuous as a six-year-old boy's. "'M I disturbing you?" Azaril asked. "I write loud"—an almost preposterous admission that simply slew Langston, it was so kind and so abundant with laid-back California social ease. Langston could only shake his head and give back a loose, inarticulate smile, he was so thrown.

After the movie ended, though, Langston was ready to whip around before the credits were finished to ask Azaril what he was writing. Despite an outbreak of sweat under his arms and in both the front and back of his underwear, Langston was able to confirm easily enough that, as he'd hoped, they were in the same modern cinema class, held Tuesday and Thursday mornings in a cavernous lecture hall. Langston asked Azaril if he liked the class, and Azaril said yes, it was a nice break from his demanding studies in genetics, though he probably shouldn't be wasting time he should be spending in the lab. Langston smiled through this pleasantry, then—abruptly, as if forced to shout a warning to prevent Azaril from falling into a pothole—invited The Beautiful One to have coffee. Azaril hesitated—perhaps contemplating the number of hours he'd logged in the lab, perhaps calculating the likelihood that Langston had enough temerity to think he was going to get some. Then, ambivalently, he agreed. Langston, observing every facial tic, every shift of movement, scanning for signs that his fondest hopes might be realized, had assessed Azaril's response as that of a shy, inexperienced boy responding to an invitation for a date. *Ah, he's only twenty-six, so he's just recently come out*, Langston concluded. Later, at the café, with the idea planted in his imagination that he was going to lead this hot young thing into the promised land, Langston talked and talked and talked, laughed and chuckled and smirked and flashed winning smile after smile, reaching across the table from moment to moment to lay his palms across Azaril's bare arm.

When they parted, Langston told Azaril he'd had a delightful time talking with him. He was about to suggest some other, more intimate rendezvous, when Azaril replied—with that heart-melting apologetic smile—that while he, too, had enjoyed the chat tremendously, he'd screwed up, since now he was late to meet a woman he was dating. Langston had immediately felt a constriction in the sinus cavities behind his eyes—an all too familiar feeling, since Langston does have a thing for straight boys.

And maybe that's all the mystery there is, really. All it takes to compel Langston to work strenuously at building and maintaining a friendship that constantly tortures him, and all it really ever took for Langston to feel slightly, stupidly in love.

In love. Not quite knowing where his body is, Langston takes a minute or two to really step into the music, to move with the hum and throb of the beat, align the pulse of his blood and the firing of the nerve cells in his muscles with it. Langston pulls his lips into his mouth as if bearing down with determination and begins to go. His heart vibrates, he finds his arms rising on the current of the music and his hands floating above his head, as if the tips of his elbows were antennae through which he receives the applause of the universe: he is The Diva, untroubled by foolish crushes, the quiver of his voice sends waves across the heavenly void, it kindles the constellations and gives them shape and name, arranges dust and asteroids to ring Saturn—

After the wave crests, Langston and Azaril drift off through the press of bodies to the floor to the patio outside, a bare concrete lawn bordered by tall, thick walls painted black. The walls have a sinister medieval bearing, they're like pincers closing in.

But any real danger of claustrophobia is diminished by what you see when your eyes inevitably draw upward: trails of fire skirt the lower edge of the glowing half-moon, hot blues and wintry reds as rich as cherry Popsicles, chariot racing amid the towering gray clouds.

It's been like this for six nights, but it still awes Langston a little. All that color in the sky. Darkness that's never dark for long, at least not the deep, steady dark of space or even the milkshake haze of billions of city lights, but erratic, brilliant, violent light. More like a Marvel Comics Silver Surfer sky, lit up with the blazing coronas of purple and orange triple stars, the exhaust of rogue comets. Miami these days is an ancient astrologer's dream—or nightmare—with the heavens in turmoil and the chaos of the spheres reflected on Earth. As above, so below: Langston sniffs the sweet musk of hashish and the salt sea flow together on the air, and scans across a wash of bodies heaped one upon another in every cranny of the patio, elbow over his shoulder, arm around her neck, ringed toes lightly tapping ringed earlobes in tandem with the bass—the sound is like a heavy footfall: heavy feet that skip and alight as if they were ballet toes: rushing speed and languorous dawdling at once, amid a frenzy of heavy silhouettes. The galloping music haloes every moment with thrumming sound, echoing even in the brief dreams of catnaps, making the muscles of sleeping bodies twitch, urging, prodding folks to rise up again and dance.

How strange: that Langston's and Azaril's (and Damian's, though he's nowhere to be found at the moment) low-key hurricane season vacation has been so transformed, become an impromptu Miami Mardis Gras. That so much easy, lazy joy and so much fire in the sky should be the result of one man's death.

It's three hours till dawn. By 10 A.M. Fidel Castro will have been dead for exactly six days.

Azaril can't keep looking up. He drops his eyes and tries to focus on something solid, but he can't. Is it the 24 or the E or the X or whatever? He's swimming in some kind of scary, giddy stupor, thinking about Langston and him, and how they're feeling so connected and how weird it is, and how it's like sand granules, the way pieces rub against one another, chafing, but there's something good and right about that chafing, about that coarseness—

All of which evaporates as Azaril catches sight of Damian: Damian's broad shoulders and slim hips and almost femininely protruding butt, padding softly toward him and Langston. The clashing lights of the club follow Damian out into the humid night, draping him like a cloak. That *has* to be the E X, that *can't* be real—but maybe it is. With Damian, anything's possible. Just watching Damian's smile dig muscular corners at the bottom of his Nefertiti-like cheekbones instantly sends a warm boozy clarity spreading through Azaril's body. He seizes up in embarrassment for a moment, afraid his bladder's just opened and he's pissed on himself.

Damian emerges from the club with three people following him. One of them he tugs along playfully, with a finger hooked though the hoop that swings from the guy's ear. Reynaldo's the guy's name, Azaril manages to remember. Reynaldo with the hoop earring stumbles as Damian pulls him, laughing. And it really is a funny sight, because Reynaldo is so much more substantial than Damian, with jutting rounds of muscle tattooing a ridged design on the skin of his sleeveless shirt, and biceps and forearms that look like they could crack a skull between them.

Langston thinks it's like watching a girlish nymph lead a burly centaur across a meadow with only a rope of flowers as a bridle. Azaril, churning inside, thinks Reynaldo's lips look indecently damp.

"What are you on?" Azaril says. His voice is loud and hearty with a fraternity-boy chumminess that makes Langston cringe.

"Nothin much. You?" Damian is as content and at ease as Azaril obviously is not. Langston wants to hug Azaril and protect him. But he doesn't dare.

Azaril smiles. "Some Ecstasy blend and some somethin-somethin." Azaril has told Langston that before this trip to Miami he has never indulged in more than a hit or two of marijuana.

"Naughty boy," Damian replies benevolently.

Langston sinks with resignation as he observes the proud glow on Azaril's face. Azaril's behavior is disgusting. Langston notes the other two members of Damian's entourage hovering silently behind like Second and Third Wife. But then he himself can't help feeling a sharp pleasure sprinkle over his head like the water of blessing as Damian leans down to greet him in a deep bourbon and baritone voice. "How you doin, baby?"

Langston kisses Damian on the cheek, presses against sinew and a thin sheath of silk shirt and silk pants, catches a whiff of the slightly coconut flavor of Damian's cologne mixed with a lamina of sweat. Langston starts reintroducing himself to Reynaldo, but before he can form the L on his tongue, Reynaldo says, "Langston Fleetwood, we met before," and then enfolds him in a hug that lingers longer than necessary for courtesy.

This is the Ecstasy, no doubt, casting its spell of indiscriminate good feeling over all like Glinda the Good Witch giving a benediction with her wand. Then again, X isn't supposed to help your memory, so it comes as a surprise that Reynaldo remembers Langston at all. They met briefly two days ago, in a café walk-by moment so befogged by hot sun and cocktails that it might as well have happened in a Dalí world at the bottom of a swimming pool. Despite playing doggie on a leash, Reynaldo looks very casual and cool with his black sideburns, his wide hands pushing into the pockets of his nylon cargo shorts, and his dark low-cut widow's peak, like a ship's prow edging toward his smooth forehead. Reynaldo smells freshly laundered, a bit like a mountain meadow. Langston catalogues the total effect—porn star body, cinnamon and sugar Latin beauty, jet hair, scent of the north woods—and imagines Reynaldo incongruously cast in a sex flick set in an Alaskan cabin, bearishly bringing a great ax down upon a supine log while his bloated eel-like penis spills from the button fly of red long johns.

The other two camp followers are introduced as Angel and Angela Heredia. They are twins, and though Angela is a tiny bit taller, their legs are identical: hairless swimmers' thighs sleek like sharks' bodies, and calves that seem constantly in flex. They hang back and nod a greeting, their hands glumly clasped behind their backs as if preparing to read a list of nominees from a teleprompter. No doubt the twins resent not having a place of prominence at Damian's side; and probably they're feeling a little baffled at the lack of self-respect that keeps them there, miserably hanging on.

Langston sympathizes. Of all of them, he's known Damian the longest, though their relationship is strained, having been cleaved by a long interregnum. Ages ago, Langston and Damian lived an ocean away in Germany, where their fathers were stationed on tours of military duty; they were classmates in junior high school. There are few moments in the biographies of North Americans more wretched than junior high school, a kind of torture chamber in which you are made to examine in funhouse-mirror detail your various facial and psychological zits, and taught to perfect an array of self-flagellation techniques that will make you a usefully compliant citizen. But Langston looks back upon that strange time sandwiched between childhood and teenagerdom with a sad, sweet longing. When Langston sees

Damian today, he sees and feels him as he was back then: Damian the popular boy, the athletic, smart, good-looking, has-his-pick-of-the-girls boy, who descended from the empyrean to gather Langston up to dwell on high with him among the exalted. Langston knows too well what makes Reynaldo and the Heredias and Azaril and the others Damian's hungry disciples. It's the moments he gives you: a small smile meant only for you; a cock of the head beckoning you away with him to a secret rendezvous; the dreamy yet utterly earthbound way his eyes hold yours as he listens while you talk and talk and keep talking, because his patience seems infinite and in his presence you feel free to expand, you feel exultantly free to take up the whole room if you want. Damian moments are so good, so much more than you think you have any right to expect. Damian moments are so deep—and yet so narrow, no wider than Damian's smile. So hard to let go when they pass. And they always do, because Damian always goes away.

It's been a quarter of a century since then—Damian and Langston met again by chance only a year ago, in Sproul Plaza at Berkeley, and Damian didn't even recognize Langston at first—but Langston still feels the ache of that Damian feeling when it was new: like the skin's surprise at the warmth of the Caribbean sun after a lifetime's Finnish chill.

Poor Azaril is all caught up in it—which of course must be doubly horrible for him, being a (so he says) straight boy.

"Haven't seen you for like two whole days, bro," Azaril is saying. "Where you been, man?"

(God, it's so tiresome, that "man" mess, the fake street grammar—)

Damian shrugs, eyes taking in the hordes sprawled around him. "Ah, Rey here and me . . ."Then Damian grabs Reynaldo's thick neck and pulls possessively as he lunges forward to take a kiss—sloppy tongue, twists of the head, soft bulges in the cheeks. In a voice so thick and lascivious it makes Langston tremble, Damian finishes up with an answer from the corner of his mouth. "We've been, you know, getting to know each other."

Langston observes Azaril's face fall then struggle quickly upward again into the light. As always when his boy is in need, Langston plunges in to the rescue. "Aren't they 'sposed to be passing around free drinks on the hour?"

Angel and Angela perk up immediately. Damian—you can almost see his ears go erect, like a dog's—breaks off from fondling Reynaldo, and right away they're all beelining for the bar.

Azaril trails a step behind Damian and his three wives of the moment, his head dipping between his shoulders as he takes slow, pigeon-toed strides around and over the bodies sprawled across the patio. Langston slips his hand onto one of Azaril's big rolling shoulders and offers a consolatory smile. He leans in to say something—but whatever it is, sweet or funny or wise, it gets lost in the welter of music.

Langston feels a twinge of a headache as he quickly sucks down his drink. Azaril joins him on a kind of pew with one of the Heredia twins—ah yes, this must be the male twin, Angel, though it's not easy to tell. Angel has stars painted at the corners of his eyes, and long hair, and long nails clearer than water; he acknowledges them with an ethereal declination of his chin. Azaril nudges Langston and points at something, but Langston thinks he's calling his attention to the passing trays of complimentary Brie and martini glasses of mojitos that the manager has donated as her contribution to the citywide celebrations. The three of them accept liberal helpings of both and settle back to take in the scene as it slowly begins to wind down.

On a solitary platform set altarlike near the center of the floor, a cage holds a dangerously thin drag queen, slight as a feather, who spins around in her dominatrix leather lace-up skirt and marches with her booted feet wide apart, rocking her pelvis forward while swinging the tresses of her auburn wig and her planet-sized ball earrings to the raucous beat. Over and over she makes the same move: spin, march, rock, swing, an inexpert choreography not unlike heavy-metal thrashing, completely out of sync with the statuesque formality with which she descends from the cage, batting eyelashes as big as butterfly wings and hand-fanning her prettily oval cocoa-colored face. "Did you see?" Azaril speaks near Langston's ear. "He—she—slipped on the last rung of the ladder and broke her heel."

Langston stirs, unsure why this development should be of note to Azaril but always willing to work up some interest on his boy's behalf. "She all right?"

"Looks like. She's up, laughing and sashaying on over to the bar."

"I'm glad she came down," Langston says. "She's horrible."

"Aren't those two girls over there beautiful?"

"Huh? Oh. Mmhm. I like that one's hair. . . ."

"They're so gorgeous. You never meet women like that in the real world."

"That's because they're probably not anatomical women. . . . Az, don't you think this is, like, insane?"

Azaril pauses. "Aren't gay clubs like this usually?"

"Not that. In fact they're not usually like this. This whole mix of people, I mean. What are we all celebrating? It's not right."

"You mean Castro?" Azaril sets his drink between his legs, scratches his stubbled cheek. "My thing is, it was gonna happen eventually. Cuba couldn't stand up forever against the American empire. I'm not exactly happy, but you know, you can't read about how he treated your people—the gays—and feel too upset about it." Azaril's hands become fists. "You know what I'm saying? Marxism just isn't the right philosophy for people in the

Americas, especially people of color. It's from Europe, it is not African or, or Native, or even Latin."

Langston's already dissatisfied with the conversation. *The gays*. What a grotesque noun. He never knows how the possessives and nominatives will be parceled out in these political conversations with Azaril: sometimes they're "our people"—interesting, given Azaril's being half-Arab and not even raised around black folks—and then other times it's "your people," generally meaning some gerrymandered amalgam of gay men, lesbians, transsexuals, drag queens, bisexual guys (but not the girls), teenage girls with a similar interest to Langston's in pop icons and TV shows, New Age-y psychic-hotliner astrology buffs, and foofy lit-crit academics who don't do work with "real people." "Well, anyway," Langston says, just to end it, "now Cuba can finally get some American money, and those crazy right-wingers won't have anything else to scream and plot assassinations about."

"Right!" Azaril agrees with passion. "Cuba libre!" he says loudly to Angel. (In the melee of sound, Langston hears, "Oo eeb!")

Angel gives him a lethal glare, stands, and walks away toward the bar.

"What's up with the Herediaseses?" Azaril says.

"Shit." Reynaldo shrugs. He's appeared beside them. He's not with Damian. Interesting. "Angel's suspicious. Ha! Suspicious as fuck. A lot of us hate it when non-Cubans start talking bout this shit. People worry it's all a hoax. God damn, man. Those *cabrones* want Castro's head on a pole, hanging like a fish to spit at, like fucking Mussolini's body. Then they'll be happy. Not before." Langston thinks there's something of the brooder in Reynaldo. Something simmers inside that hard musculature that seems built for violent action—for hurling a javelin, maybe, or cutting through sinew and bone with a broadsword. Still, he's sweet in his gruffness. Almost roly-poly. "Here, drink this shit, man. It's got some kinda lemon in it."

Langston complies a trifle nervously (a trifle excitedly—*Look at this man's arms*) (a trifle hopefully—*Why's he offering me a drink? Does he like me?* He's *gay, at least*—).

Azaril asks, "Will you go back?"

"Prob'ly, yeah. To visit. Everyone will. Hey, you like it, that little tiny tiny limón taste? Good, huh? Where the fuck did Damian go?"

Langston peers at Reynaldo over the rim of the glass. The alcohol disorients him; he sees the top of Reynaldo's head growing from the rounded edge of the glass, Reynaldo's body a smudge awash in liquid the color of muddied lime. "So you're really into Damian, huh? He's that hot?" He laughs to cover the stupidity of his question.

Reynaldo scowls a bit. "It's not about that. I mean, yeah, but—whatever. I just, I dunno. I like him." He abruptly turns to them with a scrutinizing gaze. "I never did get the scoop on what's up with you two. Boyfriends? Or just having fun?"

"Oh, no," Langston says quickly, soberly. "We're not even—we're not dating." He can't get the words "Azaril's straight" out of his mouth. "We're just friends."

Reynaldo waves the glass in his hand at their heads. "Don't fucking say that. Just friends. There's nothing *just* about friends. People always act like they wanna be more than friends, like friendship is nothing. I hate that shit. I can't stand people fucking saying that. Sometimes you can become friends so fast, and it's so *exciting*. Like falling in love. Till you can't even tell the difference. I don't even know, man, if Damian is my friend, or—whatever."

This has a slight disorienting effect, as if the music had suddenly changed tempo. Azaril looks at Langston, in appeal, it seems, to Langston's superior judgment on matters of homo friendships. At that moment a woman screams through the speakers, *I'm addicted I'm addicted I'm addicted*, and Langston suddenly feels deeply warm, oozingly moist, like a sponge sopping with hot water. Something he's taken tonight just kicked in—the perfect excuse to ignore Reynaldo's discomfiting ruminations. Mindful of his manners, Langston gives Reynaldo a high-society lady smile, lets the palm of his hand roll down Azaril's tight chest by way of farewell, and gets up. His steps curiously rabbitlike to him, he parts the nearest dancing threesome (two blondie babes and a tall Stetson-wearing black guy with serious pecs) as if flinging open the gates of his estate, leaving the Young and Confused soap opera behind.

Five minutes later

Langston sits on the floor against the wall. Legs and midriffs and big feet in glowing shoes and tanned torsos swirl around and above him, thick and wet like snowflakes in a storm.

Langston wants to know what the bartender put in his drink—his fourth since he stepped through Redemption's doors. A Sandman cocktail the barboy called it, with his kiss-me lips cocked in a wily half smile. Langston loves it, loves feeling like he's whittled down to his essence, emptied of intestines and vessels and the silliness of blood and semen, loves the state of being a consciousness whose thoughts are electric surges. At any moment he'll crack like a whip across the sky. . . .

I DESIRE love—beyond all thought and reason!

The weird thing is the way that the diva's words disappear as soon as they're uttered, the sound of her voice flees into the dark canals of his ears like water down a drain, and it's gone. For a second even the memory of sound is impossible.

Langston's head pitches forward and his body rocks as if he

were on the deck of a ferry, and all about him is impenetrable black. But he can still see. Langston has a vision while draped in the blackest of black, and the darkness is a blank screen on which his sight beams like a projector's light, the darkness is an unseen sea on which the island of his vision floats, up and down, up and down in the lapping waves of black.

At the bottom of a big hill, fat as a moon fallen to earth, stands a tall woman, the reddish undercoat of Native heritage simmering beneath her high yellow color, a single strand of gray running snakelike through her black hair pulled tightly back from her skull and bound in a braid running down between her shoulder blades. Her hair feels too tightly bound to her skull, there is an ache at her temples and behind her eyes, and her hand is being squeezed so tightly by the little boy beside her that she could cry. Maybe she will cry; the desire to wail tosses savagely within her, but she can't quite drag it forth. The devastation around her looks like the wake of war: fires burn among piles of heaped timber, a child claws at one mound screaming for her mother. Above, in ascending layers up the slope of the hill, lie bodies of men and women entangled with one another, their necks curiously twisted so that she can see the bones poke through the skin; and farther up, water gushes from a gash in the road, sends rivers down toward her; and farther up, a group of folks—family? neighbors?—walks repeatedly back and forth across the barely discernible outlines of the unpaved street, surveying the ruins of their homes, shaking their heads. Some hug one another, blankly smiling with tears slipping down their cheeks. And at the top of the hill, to the left, a freshly painted house, long as a ship it seems, with a row of bedroom windows reflecting the sun of a southern exposure and a pretty screened-in porch: it stands proudly like a queen astride the summit, as marvelously well made as a locomotive car.

This time: this time when she goes up the hill, she'll—

The same woman elsewhere. There is another human shape huddled close to her. The white floor of a long, weirdly shaped narrow room stretches behind her—no, this is a beach, she's standing on sand now. Her legs are cut off below the knees in black water. The world suddenly splits open (lightning rivers across the scene)—Langston gasps when the wall of water advances upon him. The sky and the two women get wiped away as if they were merely stains by vigorous fumes of mist and huge tongues of water lashing down toward him, curling into fists. He feels the savage, rapier thrust of the wind, the water falls—

There is no water wall anymore, the air is clear, the clouds have fled. From shadows of gun gray and sea-sad blue, the open sky turns a burning white. Langston squints in the brightness. The hole in the sky, wide as a whale's mouth, goes blue. It is like the leap of gas flame in a dark kitchen. Smell of burning, like hot combs singeing hair. A man appears. Is he on fire? He stands before the mouth that devours the sky, and his back is turned so that his face is hidden. All Langston can see are the heavy topographic lines of the man's back muscles as the man spreads his arms upward in an expansive gesture of welcome.

Two figures reveal themselves at the man's feet—blip, blip, they appear—and they squat like apes, looking upward. One is big, one small, both of similar color, both male. Reynaldo! The smaller one bobs on the folded hinge of his knees, with a lace-up leather skirt riding his slender thighs and his ball earrings bouncing. The drag queen in the cage?

Suddenly the man above them—his attitude like that of a liberator modeling civilization for the ignorant—shouts, and the effort to speak flings his head around, over his shoulder, and at last Langston can see: a broad face deeply grooved like the man's back, and the slightly Benin cast of a forehead and chin that bear a vague familiarity, as if the face were a disguise for another face Langston knows well.

It's Damian. Damian shouts, and what he shouts are the words: *Oh fuck this time it's gonna kill me.*

Damian points to an empty blue breach in the black heavens.

Some time later

Someone is shouting.

"Langston! Langston, wake up!"

Langston opens his eyes and squints at Azaril looking down at him. Damian is there, his naked torso a canvas of soft velvet skin and supple lines of muscle. Towering up above Langston, Damian's folded hands and gently furrowed brow and eternally collegiate physique give him the aspect of a rave Buddha. He is numinous.

Langston's visions collapse, bubbles banished with a pinprick.

Langston smiles up at Azaril and Damian looking down.

"You're OK, you're OK," Langston hears himself saying to Damian as he feels his body lifted and his weight come to rest in the strength of Damian's arms. "I was having this wild . . ." he starts to say, but it is clear that neither Damian nor Azaril hear him or know he's speaking as they hoist him between them and arrange either arm around their shoulders. They move toward the smoky light of the open exit door.

"You OK, man?" Azaril asks, looking at him now as they emerge. Langston drinks up this tender concern with a powerful squeeze of Azaril's shoulder and a nod. They pause, adjusting as they inhale gasoline fumes and the sea—a faint freshness, too, as if it may have rained: pleasingly invigorating after the hours of smelling the sweat of human bodies.

A flower of crimson and gold comes to noisy, violent birth above. They stop and look up, then keep going. As they walk,

Langston tries to join in the soft laughter and bonhomie of post-revel accounts: what was seen, what and who was done. Damian is saying something about where he was, something about the drag queen, and Azaril seems titillated. Neither Reynaldo nor the Heredia twins' names are spoken. Langston tries to join in, tries to laugh, tries to break in and tell them something about what he felt, what he saw. Nothing comes out. The presence of the woman with her child, and the dream version of Damian cling to him, sharp, unshakable. He can't hear them, but he can see them clearly enough, and they block out all other sight: their three faces taut and creased in silent shouts of alarm and warning.

Wessex House Hotel, first daylight

Langston and Azaril return to their room and dash to the windows to pull down the shades. As soon as Damian gets in, they'll stuff a towel at the bottom of the door, though there is nothing they can do about the room's vibrating yellow walls. "Why did we choose an Art Deco hotel?" Azaril grumbles, scratching the rough hair on his chest.

Damian taps briefly on the door before entering—a peculiar civility on his part, but then he hasn't been in the room much. He, too, squints at the unwelcome radiance of the room.

"Did I hear you talking to someone in the hallway?" Langston asks.

"The woman a few doors down, in 351. Mrs. Gillory," Damian says.

"That pale woman? She's odd," Langston comments at the same time that Azaril says, "At this hour?"

"Some people do their sleeping while the moon's up," Damian replies nonchalantly. But Langston catches, or thinks he catches, something deliberately mysterious in Damian's manner, as if he's editing facts that might be of interest. Of course, with

Damian's catholic tastes in sexual partners, the old woman's probably just another trick.

"'Night," Damian says as he begins to undress.

There are two beds, one nearer the door, the other nearer the windows. When the three of them first arrived in the early evening a week ago, Langston had entered the room, glanced briefly through the tall windows at the blue and gold late-sun sky stretching away beyond sight, and then moved eagerly toward the beds, feeling a frisson of childish fear and excitement about how the sleeping arrangements would be settled, as if the three of them were on a high school sports team the night before an away game and he was the closeted ultrabutch, hiding his hard-ons. How thrillingly awkward: three men of differing sexual persuasion. Two queen-size beds.

So far these little moments of bedtime etiquette meltdown have been the highlight of Langston's trip. All during the flight from California he had been quietly grousing about Damian's last-minute decision to join Langston and Azaril on their trip, cutting his eyes at his old friend and making tart comments (until he noticed Azaril looking at him quizzically). Miami was, after all, ostensibly a professional destination, at least for Langston. There was a conference of new classical studies scholars being held at the University of Miami where he was to give a (rather hastily cobbled together) paper. It had taken weeks to convince Azaril to come along, and only after Langston offered to pay two-thirds of his ticket (and to accompany Azaril to an infamous strip club) did Azaril agree. Langston guesses that Azaril was actually delighted to take a break from his tedious research on abstruse questions about the mitochondria of stem cells, but being straight he needed the armor of plausible excuses in order to keep his heterosexuality pure and inviolate while letting a homo pay for his trip to a homo paradise. The addition of

Damian to the delicate balance of Langston and Azaril's relationship had been a colossal blunder on Langston's part. Langston and Azaril had been walking down Telegraph to the apartment building they both live in when they met Damian emerging from Amoeba Records with a sack full of CDs. Langston—driven, no doubt, by a desire to show Azaril off to Damian—blabbed about the trip. Damian seemed impressed in all the ways Langston might have hoped, but the victory proved Pyrrhic. Turned out Damian and Azaril had met before, *and* Damian had some frequent-flier miles he needed to redeem, so—why not? it'll be *fun*—Damian said he'd come along with them.

It was just the kind of presumption you might expect from Damian, barging in where no courteous person would assume there was even a shred of an implied invitation, especially given that Langston and Damian are practically ex-friends who almost never spend time together anymore. Langston could have told lies designed to let Damian know he wasn't welcome. But, startled by the fact that Azaril and Damian knew one another—though only from a brief meeting, they said—Langston grinned bravely and went right along with the idea, pretending that there had in fact been an implied invitation, and consoling himself with (1) the hope that Damian would be his usual unreliable self and forget, (2) the realization that the hotel room would be cheaper split three ways, (3) the hope that maybe exposure to other homosexuals would be useful for bringing Azaril out of what Langston hoped with all his heart was a closet, and (4) the sense that maybe Damian's self-invitation was really about the two of them making up and getting close again after all these years.

Consolation tally: Damian didn't forget, to Langston's wonder; what Langston saves by paying a third of the room rate does in fact add up now that they've decided to stay on a bit longer because of all the Castro craziness; and—weighing very heavily in the equation—there's been the unexpected bonus of the bed situation. On the first night, Azaril, as if stepping into the role of gentleman chaperone to two licentious female cousins, insisted on sleeping in the stuffed armchair. He gallantly assured Langston and Damian it was more luxurious than his futon back in Berkeley. Langston and Damian's lack of demonstrative appreciation must have been chafing, however, since a few hours before morning, Langston woke groggily when he felt the mattress tilt and found Azaril slipping in bed beside him—sans the long shapeless T-shirt that made him vaguely resemble a housewife dressed up for Saturday morning tennis lessons. Despite the fact that Azaril hugged the edge of the bed and seemed vigilant in the deepest somnolence against becoming entangled with his friend (Langston inched over as much as he dared), Langston had spent the rest of the morning waltzing through half-asleep fantasies: that this bed was their bed in their home, that they were lying together exhausted, having rutted like pigs at the height of estrus through the night, and that when they awakened, Azaril's arm would be cast casually over Langston's chest, his arm hairs tickling Langston's nipples. . . .

Nobody said anything the next morning. Damian, with characteristic smoothness, behaved as if Azaril and Langston had been in bed together from the start.

The next night they'd come back to the room much later—Castro's demise was announced that afternoon—and Damian wasn't there. Langston was too tired to feel defeated by circumstances and spread himself out on the bed they'd shared, assuming Azaril would shelter himself in the other. But just as he'd dropped into sleep, he felt a warm hand shove him over. Opened one eye, saw Azaril—this time in leg-hugging black boxers that seemed to plump his buttocks like a pair of pillows. "Damian might be back," Azaril had said.

And so it's been the nights since, the nights that have become late mornings and middays in disregard of the sun's clock; and with the slippage of each unit of hours, with each piece of daylight they lose to pay for wandering the Miami night sampling one party after another, Azaril's physical reserve has been slipping, too: feet have nestled in the hollows between the bedmate's legs, arms have been carelessly flung. The two of them have drawn closer, though nothing's been said. Last night (or yesterday morning), Langston, after a showy bout of pillow fluffing and arranging the bedspread, dared mumble—"Come to bed." Azaril, in the armchair watching CNN reports of Miami "chaos" and "eerie calm" in Cuba, lazily and wordlessly complied.

For Langston it's been Eden: everything he could realistically hope for. Almost.

Tonight, after securing their vampires' den from sunlight, Damian mumbles, "'Night," and then—Langston's brain can't come up with an equation that describes the confluence of forces that bring this cosmic event to pass; it's almost as if their thoughts are in synchrony, their bodies bound together by a common electrical pulse—Azaril, Langston, and Damian all at one moment seem to lose the will to keep standing and collapse together onto the bed farthest from the window: Damian's bed, which has lain undisturbed for the last three nights.

Damian lies in the middle; they are pressed against one another on the mattress. No one is moving.

Langston is fully awake, his exhaustion gone. He feels trapped lying on his back, afraid to move lest he disturb the miracle.

Damian scoots down to the bottom of the bed and leaps up. Langston blows a sigh of disappointment, of relief.

Then he sees Damian stripping. Shoes off, socks off, sweaty pants (somewhat resistant while being worked down the thighs). Followed by sweaty shirt and sweaty underwear.

Damian walks around to the nightstand side of the bed, where Azaril appears to be already snoozing. Gently he begins rolling Azaril off the bed. Azaril sags as if under the weight of a particularly cumbersome dream, and Langston freezes in terror and hope: Azaril's face skirts dangerously near Damian's pubic patch. Another drunken head bob and Az's lips will be trailing slobber over the length of Damian's dick and he'll swing down till his forehead presses against Damian's high-riding testicles, the edge of his big broken nose'll be digging into the moist hair-clotted ravine beneath (Langston can't actually even see the path between Damian's balls and his hole, but just now he thinks he can smell it, he believes he could slip the tip of his tongue between his lips and taste it on the air, the smell of musk and heaven)—ohmigah, is Damian getting hard? Langston could swear it's thickening—

But abruptly Azaril slots upright. His mouth, compressed at the moment when it might have made contact with the goods, now hangs open. He gazes at Damian like a child awakened by his mother. Damian responds in kind, his fingers deftly unbuttoning Azaril's shirt and unlooping his belt, undoing Azaril's waist button, unzipping Azaril's jeans.

Azaril stands beside the bed in a hunchback-assistant droop, wearing disappointingly blouselike white boxers. Damian catches Langston's eye and motions for Langston to get up. Langston dumbly obeys. Then Damian rolls back the spread and the sheets and gives Azaril a gentle pat on his rather nicely defined rear deltoid. Dutiful Azaril crawls in and acts as if he's soundly in REM even before his head reaches the pillow.

Damian motions to Langston again. Langston looks back blankly. "Get in," Damian whispers—in deference, presumably, to Azaril's vital beauty sleep needs.

Langston sheepishly doffs his clothes, deciding after a moment of dithering to match Azaril's modesty and keep his rather uncomfortably damp underwear on (he wonders how he looks in them, and whether Damian approves or disapproves). Then he climbs in.

A threesome at last, Langston realizes. It's humiliating. Any man worth his balls getting into bed with two people after whom he either lusts or has historically lusted should be hyped up with testosterone in such a moment, ready and eager to drop trou and jump bones and shoot repeat loads. But Langston lies in bed as if suspended, like an actor in a Hong Kong action flick astride the air with only wires to keep him in place.

He collects himself enough to slip his undershorts off beneath the sheets. Then he watches Damian crawl on his hands and knees over the sheets between them, crouched, with everything dangling freely. It's wonderful, of course. How could it not be? Not just Damian's dick or his body or his gorgeous face or the swirls and eddies of color that flow across his back in the form of a dragon tattoo; but the whole of him, Damian's entire aura, unfettered somehow, appears before Langston and burns away the sting of his self-consciousness, as if Damian were revealed for the first time in the fullest of his divinity, as a presence of scorching, soothing heat.

Damian turns briefly away, then tucks himself under the sheet and encloses them both in his embrace. Silence rolls over them with the sheets.

Langston clings to his corner and turns away.

Throughout the night he's aware of the heat of Damian's body beside him, and of the lisping breeze of the air-cooler vent running its fingers over his back or stomach as he turns and tosses. The darkness in the room, the stillness and quiet broken only by Azaril's sleep-sighs—real ones this time—fill Langston with sadness and a terrible clarity: this small room, its muted hidden colors, its plush but cold furnishings, describes the breadth and limit of his world, and everything that lies here with him in silence, everything undone, unseen, inert, everything he cannot dare and is too afraid to feel, is his life.

"You're both so beautiful," Damian whispers at some point, as if he has been quietly lying there, watching them with the perfect night vision of cat's eyes.

But both Langston and Azaril are asleep by then.

Some seven hours later, Azaril carefully drops his bare feet to the rug, rises, and tiptoes around the bed. He peeks for a blinding half second around the blinds, allowing an opera of greedy afternoon sunlight to trumpet and blare off the walls. As the blinds swing hurriedly back into place, he looks over at the bed and appraises Langston entwined in sheets that pool around his radiant brown buttocks. The sight makes Azaril rear back a little, and he's surprised at the shock he feels. What if Langston sees him looking? He leans in to check. No movement. Good. Azaril darts into the bathroom and shuts the door.

But Langston is awake. And Langston is waiting: for the rapid squishing sound, like boots in the mud. Is he thinking of me? Langston wonders, but doesn't want to risk hoping. Or is it just a morning habit? Then the faucet comes on, and a stream of water racing against drain and gravity makes it hard to hear (but not difficult to imagine) that little cry.

Langston lies still with his eyes shut tight. He reaches out to his left, but feels only the afterglow of Damian's presence.

Rapid knocking cracks the quiet of the room. "Hey!": a loud whisper.

More knocking. It stops. "Hey, Damian!": an outburst.

Azaril calls from the bathroom for Langston to get the door.

"Get up, nigga, it's important!" thunders from the hall.

A choice of words that brings Langston to uncomfortable attention. He slips free of the sheets with regret, unsettled by that inevitable sense of time vertigo, his body's knowledge that it's late in the day, several hours past noon, when his mind wants to believe he's awakened to a fresh morning.

"I'm coming," Langston says as he pulls his shorts on.

No sooner has he unlatched the door than Reynaldo shoulders past him into the room and comes to a dramatic halt, throwing his hands angrily in the air. "Shit. Is he in the bathroom?"

On cue, Azaril comes up behind Reynaldo, hastily tucked and with a T-shirt on, but (*oooo*) still sweaty. Reynaldo eyes Azaril, and glances helplessly through the open door of the bathroom. He doesn't find what he wants to find, and his body seems to shrink. "Oh, fuck." His head falls into his hands and he presses his fingers against the bone beneath the skin of his forehead. "How long's Damian been gone, do you know?"

"I have no idea," Langston says. "What's the matter?" His nonchalance is false. It's like his body already knows what's happening; his stomach is quickly tightening and his breath is growing short. He remembers his vision on the dance floor, the fearful look on Damian's face. And Reynaldo—Reynaldo was in the dream. Threatening? Helping? Langston doesn't know for sure. Azaril thinks it's sort of funny, imagining that some kind of lover's spat has brought Reynaldo to their room all tight-faced and out of breath. "Damian left at around eleven, twelve maybe," he says to Reynaldo with an amused huff. Langston looks at him sharply. Azaril shrugs. "He said he was going to a demonstration."

Reynaldo gives a short, agitated moan, like a man who has bet his mortgage on black and just watched the little ball scoot sideways into a deep red pit. He sags onto the bed. "Then something happened to him. Bad. He might be—he could be hurt."

Langston doesn't hear what Azaril says in response.

Of course, Langston thinks. *Of course this would happen again.*

2

Later, dusk

Driving to meet the drag queen in Little Havana, Langston and Azaril pass Reynaldo's cell phone back and forth between them, attempting to decode the digitally reproduced sounds of a recorded message:

"Hey, whazup, Rey, you're not here buuuut I wish you were—hear that?" Damian's voice, though somewhat distant. Followed by the thumping of drums, brash and insouciant, there must be several drums playing, it's enough to make you start swaying in your seat, but this only lasts a moment before a piercing scream breaks through, joined almost immediately by other cries. A few drumbeats trail off, overwhelmed immediately by indefinable noises, almost like static but without the sharp electronic crackle, more a kind of quickened, excited white noise—the blurred sound of hundreds of voices, Langston guesses. The blurry static washes over what is probably Damian saying—in an alarming weakness of tone—"Wait!" And then there is a jolting boom that sounds like a stone wall fell over.

A chorus of distraught cries suddenly very near the phone. Then the whine of a siren, its forlorn note of warning struggling in the background. Followed by a long silence, empty of all but the dim rustle of unused phone time, before the message ends.

Azaril's just finished dialing Damian's cell phone number again. Langston looks at him. "Same thing. 'The number you are trying to reach is currently unavailable. Please try again later.'"

"You called the hospitals?" Langston asks Reynaldo.

Reynaldo looks harassed. "I called the local hospital. If he was one of the people hurt at the demonstration, he shoulda been there, and he wasn't. Police didn't have anything on him, and it's too soon for them to call him a missing person. If you wanna call other hospitals—"

"Shh," Azaril says, reaching forward from the passenger seat to turn up the radio.

The woman's voice, practiced in its soothing, up-slope down-slope cadences, fills the interior of the car. "Miami police are still trying to determine the cause of the explosion that panicked a crowd of five thousand attending a rally in Little Havana earlier today. At least six people were seriously injured, most of them trampled by fellow demonstrators who ran from the rally site when a combustion of unknown origin blew out one of the speakers during a performance of the *salsero* band Arenas Libre. Witnesses report that a plume of fire shot up almost thirty feet in the air, then went out almost as soon as it erupted. The performers' stage was severely damaged in the blast, but the band members were unhurt. The demonstration, billed as a gathering for people who wanted to celebrate the commitment to social justice of the Cuban Revolution but condemn the dictatorship's abuse of human rights, was not licensed by the city. Organizers claim that they wanted to make a statement against what they see as the, quote—ghoulish orgy—unquote, taking place in the celebrations all over Miami since the report of Fidel Castro's death." Another voice breaks in, somewhat hoarse but precise in its Anglophonic enunciation. "We just wanted people to know that there's an alternative, that not everyone thinks it's appropriate to run around getting drunk and dancing because a man died—a man who had his flaws, but was in many ways a Cuban patriot like many of his enemies. Somebody didn't like that message and blew us up, and the authorities are doing nothing. We call on everyone to stop the madness!" The woman's voice returns. "The mayor's office released a statement saying that this latest incident only underscores the need for citizens and visitors, whatever their politics may be, to attend sanctioned rallies where police protection can be guaranteed, such as the one held two days ago at the Orange Bowl. Celebrate safe, the statement urges. Elsewhere, vandals were caught attempting to steal some of the items on the altars set up around Freedom Tower, which at last count numbered one hundred forty-eight—"

Reynaldo shuts the radio off. "That's the same shit," he says. "This time they got the audio from the organizer. Whatever. Those people aren't even Cuban, and probably not even from Miami, just like more than half the people acting like idiots out here." He appears to say this to them by way of instruction, as a defense against the impugning of his people's and his city's reputation. Neither Langston nor Azaril challenge him with a different view.

They rumble through the streets of South Beach toward the causeway in Reynaldo's father's car, a long, galumphing vehicle lifted up on elephantine wheels that looks to Langston like a cross between an SUV and a hearse. Through the tinted windows it's shocking to see how calm South Beach has become in the span of a few hours. The police, like armored beetles, swarm the streets, and the revelers, perhaps finally exhausted, have retired to hibernate. Kinder, gentler tourists come out of hiding, and levelheaded early-evening shoppers flop-flop on the smoldering concrete in their sandals.

Langston watches the passersby, noting their presence without distinguishing them. He's a picture tube, they are a flickering succession of signals he receives and reflects without understanding. His brain feels locked, seized. Reynaldo has told them that last night before leaving the club Damian had said he was going to the demonstration the next morning. Curiously—and somewhat insultingly, from Reynaldo's point of view—Damian was planning to go to the demonstration with the drag queen they'd seen dancing so terribly in the cage. Apparently Damian had met her and the two of them hit it off last night. ("I do not fucking understand males who get so fuckin interested in these she-males," Reynaldo complains. "If you want a woman, why not get a real one?") The drag queen, Miss DeShon, invited Damian to brunch at a café in the city, and from there they were headed to the rally.

"I know one of Redemption's managers," Reynaldo's reassuring them again. "She gave me Miss DeShon's number, so I called her, and she said she was glad I called cuz she was concerned about Damian and didn't know what to do, and then she asked me to meet her on Calle Ocho, and then she hung up."

"That sounds—fishy," Langston worries. "If DeShon's concerned, why didn't she tell you what concerned him? What if she's done something to Damian—kidnapped him, or robbed him—and this is, like, a setup?"

"Don't be such a drama queen, Langston," Azaril says energetically. "Damian's just lost his cell phone or it's not working or something, but he's no lightweight, he can take care of himself. I'm sure he's fine." He's trying to be the soothing voice of reason, but Langston shoots him a glowering frown. Obviously he's unhappy about that drama-queen bit, which Azaril had thrown in consciously, figuring it'd be taken as affectionate and fraternal (or sororal). Azaril rolls his eyes. Those nasty disapproving looks Langston gives can be terribly wounding, and the vulnerability Azaril feels makes him furious.

He wonders in an inquisitional way how he ended up spending so much time with gay boys and bi boys. You become friends with one, you're OK with that, it doesn't mean anything, in the final analysis a guy is a guy, but then it's like there's a beachhead or something, and whole armies of them come to land. Azaril has tried to keep a lid on it, to just act like nothing is happening. But it's been hard, traveling with Langston and Damian both, what with Langston supposedly being Azaril's best buddy, and there being some kind of history Damian has with Langston. Neither fesses up, though, and then it gets complicated, because Langston sometimes gets moody over the idea that Azaril supposedly has more in common with Damian than with Langston. Azaril's been trying to make it up to Langston, make an effort to focus on him. What if Damian ran off because *he's* jealous, either of Azaril himself or of Langston? Maybe it has something to do with what happened last night, with the three of them in the same bed—which Azaril doesn't even want to think about. The whole thing gives Azaril a queasy feeling, as if he's stepped into the midst of some bizarre MTV gay reality show, with two mustache-twirling villains plotting to take his homosexual virginity or something.

"Look," Azaril says.

A great angular white cruise ship, bristling with globes of light that sway like hammocks in a breeze, lies docked and glimmering in the water along the causeway. So massive is it that it dwarfs everything around it. In the fast-spreading darkness of evening its bulk dominates even the sea. The slant of prow and stern bends in a faintly evil smirk, as if the hull were merely a thin white skin beneath which coils some antediluvian reptile, its arsenal of teeth and claws momentarily sheathed.

"We should've just gone on a cruise." Azaril turns to look at Langston in the backseat.

Langston gives him a forced grin. Azaril's words are an apology—it's always this way with them, nothing can ever really be said, it must always be deciphered—and, partially comforted, Langston burrows back down into himself as they cross over into Miami proper.

Reynaldo, perhaps feeling left out of the unspoken communion, turns on his MP3 player. A frenetic, trippy dance mix, similar to what they danced to toward the end of last night, flows through the speakers. Langston looks at Reynaldo coolly bobbing his head, once in a while elegantly lifting his shoulder to the beat, and he remembers for the first time since he awoke Reynaldo's place in his drug vision—Reynaldo crouched at Damian's feet, looking up with an expression shining with beatific adoration. He tries to decide what this might mean, but something about the dark interior of cars and loud music seems always to put him to sleep, and soon his chin is bouncing gently against his clavicle.

Amid the flotsam of his strange car-ride dreams Reynaldo keeps appearing, and Castro in shorts like a UPS delivery man's, and the drag queen's there, too, her face as beautiful as a masque and covertly malefic like the queen in Disney's *Snow White*.

Calle Ocho, around 9 P.M.

By the time they reach parts of the city that Langston and Azaril vaguely recognize from their various forays during the last several days, the night has deepened. A massing of clouds obscures the face of the half-moon, while its lunar glow rings their playfully morphing edges with a ghostly penumbra. The heavens seem now at their blackest and most beautiful, a grand sable mourning gown draped over some grande mourning dame who boasts depths wiser and more mysterious than the sea. There is an expectant quiet in the car (except for Reynaldo's player, still blasting away like a NATO bombing), as they take a turn and begin to cruise through the quiet, seemingly deserted environs of the neighborhood.

The population on Calle Ocho is surprisingly scant. Across the street, two tourist couples who have come to sample the spice of Cuban culture content themselves in gawking at nothing as they walk slowly along a line of dry cleaners, closed cafés, and laundromats. There are three or four other people strolling farther down the block. The modest brown street could be a two-lane road in a suburban neighborhood in Ohio.

They drive for several minutes, until Reynaldo pulls the car up along a curb. "I think this is the address."

Azaril lets the window down and leans out. "It's one of those, uh . . ." SILVIA'S arches in blue letters across a high, wide glass window that wraps around the corner of a two-story building. Inside, shadowy but easy enough to make out, there is a long counter with stacks of packages wrapped in brown paper behind it, and several rows of colored candles and the various likenesses of the saints arranged in a tall, orderly display cabinet against the far wall. To the right stands a dark, narrow door.

"It's a botánica," Reynaldo says. "They sell herbs and candles and paraphernalia for Santería."

"Oh," Azaril says. He doesn't mean to sound ominous, but as he opens the door and steps onto the curb, the syllable seems to float from the interior of the car and hang in the quiet night air. They step out of the car and the doors resound harshly as they close, but there is no swift answer, no echo in noise or movement, from anything else on the street. In the absence of sound, their senses seem to inflate the space around them to take up the slack: the distances between objects, between the sidewalk and its counterpart on the other side, between the squat, brooding old station wagon double-parked behind them and the hydrant on the corner, seem to stretch and lengthen, become somehow fraught and unsettling.

Langston feels as if they have trespassed upon a sacred space, that they will be punished.

"So where is he?" Azaril asks impatiently.

"She," Langston corrects him. "You call drag queens *she*." He's about to explain when something he sees makes him catch his breath. A clump of darkness peeking out from the far corner of the botanica—it had looked like a shrub, or maybe a small trash bin—suddenly grows and detaches itself from the wall and moves swiftly toward them.

It takes a brief moment for their eyes to adjust, though the street is well lit and the moon's face shimmers benevolently overhead. The fuzzy shape resolves into a slender man wearing a delicate blood-colored mesh T-shirt that displays his delicate midriff, the top of his skull and ears enlarged by a pair of headphones and a skinny iPod bulging at the hip of his low-riding thigh-hugging jeans. Before anyone can say anything, he emits a burst of off-key scat singing.

Reynaldo steps forward protectively (riling Azaril, who thinks he should do it). And then, with dramatic timing he's perfected stomping in leather skirts on top of massive speakers all over Miami, the man comes to a hard stop and removes his headphones as if lifting a tiara from princely locks. He extends his hand for what might be a kiss or a shake and tilts his sharp chin at Reynaldo. "I recognize you. Seen you around, on Twelfth Street beach. In some clubs. Don't they call you Ray-Ray?" His drawl is broad and flat.

Reynaldo's very slow to answer. "My name is Reynaldo. You're Miss DeShon?"

"Miss DeShon is a stage personality. She appears when paid, or occasionally at her own pleasure." His eyes slide toward

Azaril and Langston. "You didn't tell me you was bringin somebody. Who are you two? Where you come from? Who sent you?" Miss DeShon's color in the moonlight is deep and burnished, and his cheeks are broad and high. His eyebrows are shaven off, and his chest flat as if covered by a thin layer of flesh stretched as tight as saran wrap. The hair on his head is straightened and pulled back, except for shaggy wisps that cluster at the top of his forehead.

He is, Azaril decides, handsome, even striking in a funny way. Part Diana Ross on a diet and part Dickensian street urchin. "I'm Azaril Shahid-Coleman, this is Langston Fleetwood. We're both friends of Damian's."

Miss DeShon appears to ignore this. "My, but you do got some pecs on you, huh?" Pause. "And legs. And even the ink spot is cute!" He seems satisfied with this assessment. "Who sent you?"

Reynaldo tenses and looks as if he might get violent. "Look, no one sent us. We have a mutual friend—Gina Lorenz, at Redemption, she gave me your number—"

"Oh, *Gi-na*!" His thin arms rise exultantly and he rocks backward on his heels, throwing his crotch (revealingly outlined in the tight jeans, Langston notes) forward. "Well, all *right* then, any friend of Miss Lollobrigida is to absolute certainty a friend of mine! Excuse my rudeness, you never know who you talking to these days." His eyelashes flutter.

Langston, as if breaking from some kind of trance, steps forward (the air doesn't feel right to him: it feels heavy, like the clouds are about to break—and there's a haze, a haziness in his eyes). "Miss . . . DeShon," he says, extending his hand for a formal handshake. "You do know our friend Damian, right? Damian Sundiata. You were with him today, at the rally on Calle Ocho. We're concerned—that something might have happened to him there."

Miss DeShon puts a finger to his lips. Langston senses that he's weighing whether or not to be cautious. "Oh, so . . . you two are the ones Damian said was *traveling* with him. I thought he said his friend was named Langley. Used to be a Langley Wallingford on *All My Children*, that's what keeps messing up your name for me," he muses. "You must be the ones with him last night at the club! Did you catch my performance? I thrive on constructive criticism, tell me what you really thought. My actual name is Quentin, by the way. Quentin Manuel Morgan Shaw." His tone implies a curtsey.

"Look—"

"Oh, now, Ray-Ray, don't let your thong dig too far up yuh ass. I asked you here for a reason. Just ain't much reason to rush. Not at this point, 'cause really, it's all over." (Reynaldo glances at Langston in alarm.) "They sealed off the area where the stage was"—Quentin gestures up the street, and they can see a block or so away and off to the left yellow tape and the dim outlines of a stage—"but this is where we were when it happened. I figured maybe I'd come back here and find something. And, lo and behold."

Abruptly he slings the wide leather band of a voluminous black bag toward them; it seems almost to materialize out of the darkness over his shoulder, and Langston flinches, thinking for a moment that Quentin's going to hit them with it. Quentin smiles broadly, showing two rows of small, almost catlike teeth before he unzips the bag, rummages through it, and then produces a thin metallic device, an oblong shape the size of a child's palm with two short sleek arms jutting out on one side.

"What is that, a taser?" Azaril asks. Langston thinks he's spooked, too.

Quentin hands it to Reynaldo, who grabs it roughly. He reads aloud, "Motorola." He sighs and his shoulders fall. "Is this . . .?"

"Iss all that's left of that fine ass boy's phone." Quentin nods. "Least I think it is. It's hard to remember exactly."

"Wait a minute—" Langston raises his hand as if to give Quentin a traffic cop's stop command. "I'm confused. Would you tell us what happened, please? Tell us the whole story."

Quentin makes a flourish in the air with his hand. "Oh, the *whole* story! You want some dirty details." It is scarcely possible to tell if anything the man says is in earnest or in jest. Langston detects in Quentin's manner a newly expansive note of enjoyment: the triumph of interview. "Well, all right, Miss Girl. Less see. First off, Damian came up after the performance last night. I had already spied out his fine semibald head and his sexy body earlier from my lookout up in the ho cage, but he was all up on some cracker model-type doin Lord knows what snuggled up in one of the naves. I guess that was you, Ray-Ray. So I was promptly through with him and I didn't pay him further notice until I saw him skip out the door with Ray-Ray, and I was like, whatever. Then not a half hour later my show is finished and I'm out my wig and enjoying my complimentary libations at the bar and receiving my plaudits and admirations, when I turn around and see he's back, sitting on a stool next to me and looking me in the eye. I was going to serve the attitude he deserved for walking out on my performance with that cracker. Excuse me. Cuban cracker. But Damian had this, like, shadow on his head, new hair growing back—which I find arousing—and then them little gold rings on his nipples, and this string of pubic hair like ivy crawling up out his pants and up to his outie. And dripping wet, absolutely *wet*, because he got caught in a little rain shower coming back into the club. Even so, my judgment was, he still deserved to be dissed, but before I could put my nose in the air, he reached around his back and gave me a rose. A rose. Isn't that sweet? 'For your stunning performance and extraordinary beauty,' he said. And y'all must all know that smile of his."

This earns a somewhat grudging nod of assent from Reynaldo, an involuntary one from Langston—who turns, too late, to see how Azaril has reacted: nothing, a stone straight-boy face.

"After that, Miss Maria Shaw's child was not going to let this fine brotha be one who got away. He said some such blah blah blah about his *friends* and how he had to get back to them. And I was like, who cares about them?" He smiles, but now only Langston does him the courtesy of a strained little chuckle. "Just kidding. He told me how smart you was, Langley. Langston. He said y'all was friends back in high school—"

"Junior high school."

"Mmhm—well, he was high, so he coulda said high school. I do possess among my attributes a sharp memory. Anyway, he talked and talked and we just had a good old time off by ourselves—we had to step out of tired old Redemption, you know, to really *connect*. But then he had to get back to you all, so I invited him for brunch, and he said he couldn't do *that*, either—and let me say I do not usually take two refusals in a row—but he wanted me to join him at this counter-demonstration rally or whatever around lunchtime down to Calle Ocho. I wasn't feelin it, but when a brotha like that wants something, well, you just know you happy to be in the service again, you know what I'm sayin?"

Reynaldo turns his shoulder to Quentin and says in a loud voice he obviously thinks is a whisper, "Let's go. This is bullshit."

"So Damian and I went to Calle Ocho," Quentin continues aggressively. "We listened to these boring ass speeches by all them skinny white boys with goatees and all the dykes and stuff, we hung out, had some drinks and some coffee, flirted, watched the males. Then, I will never forget it, we were in the crowd and moving our necks and gettin all up into this salsero band. He made a call on his phone—which I didn't like—but he was holding my hand, so that was working, and it was gettin real hazy all of a sudden, and I said to him, it's gon be *hot*, baby, it's gon be a day you can smell like fresh bread baking, like the sun roasting the city. My Damian liked me saying that and while he was holding the phone he kissed me on my cheek: perfect."

Azaril and Langston exchange glances. Reynaldo looks furious.

"And then, child—all hell in a handbasket. We heard some big, like, rumble, louder than the music. I expected to look down and see the earth opening up like it do in California. But it was some kind of explosion, 'cause when you looked up at the stage where the band was playing, there was a fire burning like crazy behind it. I mean like a big fire, a tall fire. Smoke blowing out *fast*. People screamed, the band just stood there, folks started running. We had to run, too, 'less we wanted them crazy ass Cubans to run us over. It was a hell of a time just getting back this far away from the stage, with people sprintin and other people standin there gawking like it was some car accident they wanted to see. I fell down, scraped my knee. Damian picked me up. Then we stopped right here, 'cause I was already out of breath. I looked back at Damian—and as God is my witness, as I was looking at him, he disappeared."

"You lost Damian in the crowd?" Azaril asks.

"I lost him, but not in the crowd. He was holding my hand. And then he wasn't holding my hand. His hand, it just, like—melted. My palm where his hand was got cold. And he wasn't there. He disappeared."

Reynaldo turns slowly to give Langston and Azaril a long look before he says to Quentin, "Uh huh."

Azaril's wondering what Quentin was high on. "He must have just slipped away from you. Maybe—I don't know, the explosion upset you?"

"All I know is that he disappeared," Quentin says stoutly. "There, then not there. That's the best I can come up with. He might as well have dissolved right into the window of that shop." Quentin points to the dark pane of glass that stands four feet wide and tall.

They peer at the window.

"Come on," Reynaldo snaps. "So what, he ran away?" He looks to Langston for input, but Langston's squinting off into the middle distance. "You don't believe this, I hope."

"Um, I just wanna see if there are—clues, or anything." Langston trails off. He doesn't want to tell them that he's examining the surroundings for any resonance with his vision: Does the sky look in any way similar? Does Quentin himself look anything like the way he looked to Langston in that strange half-world he stumbled into on the floor of Redemption?

Azaril makes a loud sniffing noise. "Does anyone else smell that? Like something's burning . . ."

"I don't believe anything he says," Reynaldo says to Langston. "For all we know, DeShon mighta got Damian involved in like a fucking drug deal gone bad or something." He stops short. "I smell it, too."

"Could you give me that faceplate from Damian's phone, Reynaldo? I mean, if it really is Damian's phone . . ." As the earpiece touches Langston's fingers, the haze lying over everything suddenly clears. The street is bright, the lamps pulsing with sharp, colorless light. And then Langston recognizes the smell: burning, the burning of hair, of meat. Human flesh? The same stench that floated through his hallucination.

The wind picks up, and they can all hear a loud, wet sound off in the darkness like a large balloon popping. "Uh oh," Quentin says. "Sounds kinda like it did at the—"

It comes at them like a rogue breaking from the herd; later

they'll wonder how they failed to hear it until it was right in front of them: a moving wall of noise becoming more and more dense. A mob, a storm wind of sound and fury, thunderous and heedless. Perhaps as many as a hundred people, they run as one, their feet unseen in the crush of galloping legs and the thicket of bodies, all chaos focused into a single, grasping thrust forward. Not five feet beyond their reach speeds a desperate lone runner.

"*Ayudame*! *Ayuda*!" the runner cries, but he's not stupid enough to wait for rescue, as his knees pump high and his arms strain to pull him away. He is a tallish fellow, in green fatigues and nice solid boots, with a bushy beard and a very familiar face.

Fidel Castro.

Reynaldo gets off a "What!" and Quentin yells, "He's doing Castro drag!" and Reynaldo says, "They'll kill him!" while Azaril surges forward with, "We have to help!" and Langston screams out, "Az!"

But when Azaril goes, he goes. The guy in Castro drag (he's doing a good job; you can't tell the difference) streaks past them, close enough that they can hear his ragged exhalations, like sizzling pellets cast upon the asphalt. Langston sees Azaril try to get between Fidel and the mob, waving his arms and shouting like a fool, but no sooner does he see this than Azaril is swallowed up, completely engulfed in the moving limbs of the horde. Langston almost screams, but catches himself, stuffs the shriek of horror back in with his hand over his mouth; he ends up making a sound like someone expelling water from their windpipe. He moves after Azaril, but Reynaldo's large hands yank him backward by his wrist. Reynaldo pushes back against the botanica's gate and holds Langston tightly, brutally to his body. Langston squirms without effect; Reynaldo, with that big bodybuilder physique, is far too strong for him. But Quentin clings to Reynaldo's side, pressed flat on the gate like Christ on the cross to avoid being swept into the crowd. With three fingers he tugs tightly on Reynaldo's black T-shirt.

After the mob passes—Langston looks, the last of them is twenty yards away—they're still holding one another, arms and hands strained, their jaws and brows wired tight. Everything is crisp and clear, like the air after the passage of a storm. The hood of Reynaldo's car is dimpled in three places and one side-view mirror seems slightly ajar. Detritus is scattered over the pavement. A half strand of faux pearls lies a few feet from them, a fallen pack of Marlboros smashed flat, a watch chain without a watch, and somebody's Discover card, chipped at the corner. Quentin marvels at one cup of a 36B black bra speared by the branch of a small tree while the strap and the other cup dangle, swaying.

The two tourist couples they'd seen earlier are gone, ingested, it seems, by the mob.

"I'm calling the police, you hoodlums!" A portly woman wearing a diaphanous scarf over her hair and knotted at her ample chin leans out on the sill of an open window above SILVIA'S—perhaps Silvia herself. "I mean *you*, you bastards!"

Quentin gives her the finger, and Reynaldo says something rather coarse in high school Spanish.

Suddenly aware of themselves, the three release each other, and Langston bounds immediately into the street. Off in the distance, beyond a long row of variously damaged automobiles, the mob is converging upon a single point.

"Where's Azaril?" Langston asks, bewildered. He turns to look at Reynaldo for help. Then he looks back into the distance, he looks at Quentin. "Where's Azaril? Does anyone see him?"

"I think they got him," Quentin says.

Langston whirls on him. "You—! This is your fault!"

A couple of paunchy guys with camcorders on their shoulders and press IDs bouncing from the clips on their shirt pockets run by, thirsty hounds panting and grinning.

"You have to come with me. We have to find Az," Langston pleads with Reynaldo.

Quentin hears sirens. "I say we get in y'all's car, and get the hell out of here," he says.

Langston is going to strike Quentin, that's his plan, except that Reynaldo at that very moment spies a shadow separating itself from the writhing dark mass of shapes down the block. "Is that Azaril?"

Langston bolts. "Az! Az!"

It is Azaril, he knows it, it must be him—the hair, you can tell by the shape of the hair, those lumpy curls, and the walk—although he's walking too slowly. Langston knows he is behaving hysterically, but if it is Azaril, then even hysteria isn't good enough. Langston sprints toward him, almost collides with him, and only then really sees his face, when he has his body wrapped up in his arms.

"Are you all right, are you all right, are you—?"

Azaril, except for a couple of bruises on his arms and the feeling that his skin has just been scoured in an automated car wash, is fine. Physically, that is. He hangs limply in Langston's arms and responds to Langston's fierce relief with a wan pat on Langston's shoulder. He pries himself loose, looking over Langston's head toward the mob: black stick figures that look from a distance like characters in a primitive cinema cartoon, with their exaggerated, spasmodic movements.

"Are you OK?"

Azaril shakes his head. "Those . . . people. Do you know what they're doing? Can you hear them? They are ripping that man apart. They are *ripping* him apart, piece by piece. With their hands. Their bare hands."

Years of training make Langston think irrelevantly of Euripides. “Should we get you to a hospital?” he says, not liking the haunted slack of Azaril’s lower lip.

“It was so easy,” Azaril says as Reynaldo and Quentin draw near. “You’d think it wouldn’t be so easy to just—rip a body apart like that. They’d grab hold of one piece of him and another group would pull on the other—it didn’t seem real. People grabbed both his arms by the elbows and planted their feet against his ribs. An old guy had a checkerboard in one hand, and a, a foot in the other. There were Cubans, and I swear there were, like, frat boys. I think there was a big group of Haitians. It didn’t seem real. . . .”

They all hear the sirens. “We need to get up,” Quentin warns.

Instinctual dread of gun-toting men in blue makes them all click into action—all except Azaril, who appears drained of energy but doesn’t protest as they herd him into the backseat. Langston urges him to put on his seat belt, queries whether he feels anything broken or twisted, and asks, “Did anyone attack you?”

Azaril doesn’t answer. Quentin climbs in the front beside Reynaldo. When the car starts, Quentin barks directions from the passenger seat. “Take a right here.” Reynaldo glances at him but obeys. They run a yellow light and speed off, a heartbeat or two before two squad cars and a police van come barreling through the intersection.

“Where’s the nearest hospital, do you know?” Langston demands of no one in particular.

Azaril pulls Langston’s hand from his brow. “It took lots of them to do it.” It’s as if he’s reciting. “The blood came out funny. I’d think it would shoot up like a fountain. In the movies it would. And they just kept at it. They passed parts of him back and forth like it was a football game. I’ve never seen people more insane. They tore his arms out of his sockets. Because he looked like Castro.”

"I think it *was* Castro," Quentin says.

"Oh, that's ridiculous. That's just ridiculous," Langston snaps. He waits for Reynaldo's confirmation, but Reynaldo doesn't say anything, though he does seem to darken somehow; his eyes, reflected in the rearview mirror, become molten with intensity. Langston, exasperated, taps Quentin on his head. "Where are you giving Reynaldo directions to?"

Quentin looks back at him patronizingly. "Well, Azaril looks like he could use some rest, so I figured we'd better just go kick it at y'all's hotel."

Reynaldo's sour laugh is full of hostility, but since this plan seems a sensible enough thing to do under completely unreasonable circumstances, Langston relents.

Azaril shuts his eyes to rest, and then opens them again because of the images that come immediately to his mind. He's grateful for Reynaldo's loud music. Its relentless volume bludgeons the terror and vertigo of the evening from his consciousness, its swift, metronomic, echoing beats mass and crackle like whips of lightning through him, bringing sensation back to his numb body, making him feel, if not quite alive, at least lively: as if he's become a dark gaseous cloud borne on currents of wind.

3

Back at the hotel, almost midnight

Reynaldo wants to crash in their hotel room, too; he's sick of driving and doesn't want to have to go all the way back home tonight. The brazenness of this, almost an announcement rather than a request, irritates Langston, and he gropes for a way to respond in the negative. Then Reynaldo adds, "If Damian comes back, I don't want to hear about it by fuckin phone, I want to see him myself"—and again Langston recalls Reynaldo's presence in his vision, and Quentin's, too. He sighs. "OK."

At the hotel Quentin seems quite merry, holding the door open for Azaril, complimenting the Wessex's choice location, striding along with his bag looking ominously plump and well stocked. How is it, Langston wonders, that he's been the target of so many uninvited guests lately? His aunt Reginia would tell him that the universe is a marvelously intricate lattice in which all things are connected by etheric, vibratory strands, and in this unimaginably efficient little corner of said universe, very little is truly coincidental: if you keep finding yourself among clowns, she's told him, either you yourself are a clown and don't know it, or the clowns have something important to tell you.

They're greeted as they trudge into the lobby by night desk

attendant Luisa de Lascaux (she's part Nicaraguan émigré, part French journalist—unless of course the name is a fake). The lobby is bustling despite the late hour, with various folks milling about in the vague trouble-seeking manner of houseguests who creep downstairs to raid the refrigerator after the hosts are asleep. Luisa gives Langston and Azaril an indulgent smile and starts to ask them where they have been and what they have been doing. This is sales patter: in the past several days she's sold them K, X, and two postage stamps of acid. The debauchery of days past—only hours past, really, though it seems longer—embarrasses Langston, so he waves at Luisa and keeps walking, though he wonders if perhaps he should ask whether the hotel keeps a nurse or paramedic on the premises who can take a quick look at Azaril. Azaril ignores Luisa, grumbles something to no one about the noise, skips the elevator, and bounds up the stairs. Reynaldo pays Luisa the courtesy of a slightly more attentive greeting as he passes.

Luisa is heartened by this and smiles back, cautiously, while Reynaldo continues on his way. She describes herself as a "big gal"—puzzling when you see her slim upper body and gentle shoulders behind the check-in counter, understandable when you look below to her hips and her humpy good-time derriere that must surely have been imported from west Africa. Many men are quick to express their ardent responses to Luisa's combination of sylph waist and lioness lower depths, and for a moment she thinks this is what Reynaldo has responded to, and what Reynaldo wants (even if he is walking with a buttload of fags). Not that he'll get it: not without a wedding ring and/or a six-figure salary. Possibly—though she doubts it—Reynaldo could fit the bill. She's considering how much longer she should wait before it's the right moment to drop by their room, just in case they need a narcotic to cap the evening or go to sleep, when the phone buzzes and 351 lights up on her board.

On the third floor, Langston considers and then rejects the idea of crashing with the rest. Beds get sorted quickly: Reynaldo and Quentin in one, though they both seem to find the idea unappetizing, Azaril collapsed in the other, with a sliver of space left for Langston. He's tired, too, but feels the need to take a few moments to decompress.

"Try not to fucking disappear," Reynaldo growls when Langston makes his excuses. Langston wishes Azaril had said it. And isn't that awful? The boy's traumatized and Langston's still looking to wring an extra declaration of love from him. "Naw," Langston answers, "last night Damian mentioned talking to the woman down the hall. I think I'm gonna go ask her if she's seen him. Long shot, but . . . I'll be back in a minute."

As he shuts the door behind him, he hears, "Help! Help!"

It is a woman's scream coming from around the hallway's bend, followed by a curious, pipy barking.

Before Langston can make sense of it, a little wheat-colored dog with floppy ears and a narrow snout, yipping and moving as fast as his little feet can carry him, makes the far corner and gallops down the hall. Langston recoils, thinking the dog is going to bite him, although it's just a little guy, but a dog in a hotel like this, the sight cracks Langston's frame of reference, somehow—and the dog flies past him.

An elevator bay lies at the end of the hall; its doors slide open. The dog ducks into it and is gone.

A man from the hotel staff, a big German guy by the name of Wilhelm, comes huffing up the stairs. He stops, looks at Langston, who looks at him, and then he looks at a woman who stands catching her breath halfway down the hall. She is a strikingly blond and strikingly pale individual in a blue bathrobe.

Wilhelm, whose own native pallor is covered by a lobster tan, strikes a befittingly dignified pose and clasps his hands behind his back. "Ma'am?"

The woman's mouth has been partially open. It closes and opens again, and then she becomes animated. "I don't know how to tell you this, but there is a *dog* in this hotel, it was in my *room!* It took the elevator!"

Wilhelm scampers toward her. "My God, did it bite you? Are you well? Has the room been damaged?"

The woman winces and puts her hand up so that Wilhelm can only get so close. "Oh, I'm *fine*, really. It didn't do *anything*. Except bark." She nods cautiously at Langston for corroboration. "But go see about it, please! It may have gone down to the lobby! Don't let it get out in the streets! I'll help as soon as I get dressed."

Unsure, Wilhelm wavers for a moment before he turns, and with an air of considerable reluctance he trots back down the stairs.

In the silence, the woman and Langston are left looking at the expanse of the hallway carpet and the splashy blue-and-green Deco walls. Langston's cooking up a suitable introduction when someone opens 339's door from inside. Langston glances hopefully, sees Quentin's face wearing a sneer and a questioning look on it. More sharply than he intends, Langston says, "It's nothing. Close the door." He does not want his moment with the woman disturbed. But now she's headed away from him, presumably back to her room. "Mrs. Gillory?" Langston ventures as he begins to go after her.

She wheels toward him and her tone is sharp. "How do you know my name, motherfucker?"

Langston feels the air go out of him for a second before he answers. "Uh, it's funny, I was actually coming to see you." She looks blankly at him. "A friend of mine met you. Damian Sundiata? He told me your name."

"Oh," Mrs. Gillory says. She appears to relax, though as she takes in the fact of him standing there near her, she gathers up the neck of her bathrobe. She looks like a silent-movie star, powdered to the gills. "I do hope my—the dog—didn't disturb you. It is very late, I know. Even in all this." She punctuates with an expansive wave of her arm. Langston doesn't know if "all this" refers to the hotel or to the Castro revelry.

"No, the dog—I wasn't even asleep," Langston answers. Captured in her strange, almost unblinking gaze—her eyes are a strange color he can't make out—he doesn't quite feel able to start plying her with questions about Damian. "It's just that I was taken by surprise. Do you have any idea how that dog got in here?" Soften her up with some relevant chitchat, he thinks, though something in him, a tiny light, flickering at the bottom of many-fathomed depths, tells him that the subject may be important. "It seemed a little strange. For the dog to get into your room, I mean."

Mrs. Gillory snaps to him as if she had forgotten his presence. "What?" Then she blinks, her lips curve on one side, and she begins a low, slow laugh. "As a matter of fact, you know—yes. It *was* strange. The oddest thing, actually. This won't make sense—though somehow, young man, I've a feeling that it may make perfect sense to *you*"—Langston instinctively rears back from her sudden shift—"But I was just *furious* with Alan-Michael—my husband—he's very well known, perhaps you've heard of him, do you read? He was a reporter for the *Times*—never mind. We were arguing, you see—and we can get very vicious, nothing untoward, of course, married people do do that—and I actually *thought*, that *dog*, he is absolutely canine! I could have throttled him. I turned my back on him, because I never wanted to see the son of a four-legged mongrel again, and suddenly—" she smiles. "Suddenly that crazy little dog came out from under the bed. Or from *some*where. And my husband was gone. Isn't that odd?" She shakes her head as if to say, Lord, what people will do, then moves toward the open door of her room.

Langston ponders this, his heart racing. "Should I go help the hotel guy find him? Are you concerned that something might have happened to him?"

"Oh, he'll come back. I just have to make sure they don't take him to the pound or grind him up into horse food or something." Mrs. Gillory waves bye-bye and slams the door to 351.

"I meant your husband," Langston says to the door.

His mind whirls. Damian disappearing, the Castro lookalike torn to pieces by a mob—which is ridiculous, of course, though the way things seem to be going, the unlikelihood of it doesn't convince him it isn't true—and now this strange woman and her disappearing husband and materializing little dog.

He wanders down the hall past Mrs. Gillory's door, around the corner where the soft-drink and ice dispenser squat inelegantly amid the ebullient color of the walls and carpet, then farther down another wing, wincing as his feet ache in his shoes. Langston wants Azaril to be with him to sort it all out and steel his courage to ask Mrs. Gillory further questions. He should go back to the room and talk to him. Instead he lolls about indecisively, wandering the corridors. There always seems to be some risk his conscious mind can't name and that his more rational faculties refuse to esteem when it comes to really going and asking Azaril for something: asking Azaril to do something with him, to be with him. Is this Mrs. Gillory lead important enough to disturb Azaril? This degree of agonizing makes no sense if it's true that he and Azaril are "just friends," nor does it avail Langston anything if his overall project is to seduce sexually sleepy Azaril to open the closet door (as he fancies it in his bolder moments). But it's difficult to fix his mouth in just the right way to ask, Langston finds. There's always the chance Azaril will say, "No way," or, "That's stupid," with that curt tone of voice like a sheer drop-off at the edge of a cliff: straight-boy privilege, object-of-desire privilege, just say what you will and say it any old way at all because the salivating queer boy will probably swallow it without responding, in the desperate hope that he will someday be permitted to swallow your divine semen.

Since the matter makes his stomach go hollow, Langston marches back to his wing of the hotel. Better to brave the dragons lair, instead.

Langston raps hard on 351.

"Hm?"

"Mrs. Gillory?" Langston croaks—all that unexpressed emotion breaking free—and then resumes in what he likes to think of as his hypnotic tone. "It's Langston Fleetwood, from 339."

There is no reply. Langston knocks again, more loudly.

Then his fist strikes air as the door opens in a silky rush, noiseless and frictionless. Mrs. Gillory fills the emptied space, a tall, tight white-fleshed fleshy body in a black low-cut taffeta gown and black heels. She appears to be ready for a prom for fifty-year-olds.

"My young man. I was getting dressed. Do come in." She seizes his wrist.

The door is shut (and locked: he hears it) behind him.

Langston's senses reel. The smell of the room, a peppermint-candy perfume smell, so powerful that he could stick his tongue out and taste the flavor of the air.

"If this isn't a good time . . ."

"Oh no no no. I do not turn away lovely young men who come to my door. I have an upbringing to uphold." She cannot possibly be serious, but it is somewhat convincing, the way the pale blond tresses, like winter sunlight, fall across her shoulders, and the way her oddly dark eyelashes lower. Her eyes shift, or seem to, between a kind of blue and a tawny pink.

Mrs. Gillory places her long finger at her chin. "What exact African stock are you, dear? Ibo? Hausa, perhaps? You *are* very lovely. Are you one of these models the photographers come here to go gaga over? You cannot possibly be from this benighted country. Such midnight in the color, like—mm, like a primeval moment before the Word and Genesis, I should think." Her hand still grips his wrist, and she pulls him farther into the room, green where his is yellow. "Oh, don't *worry*. I am not a predator. I do not *stalk* young men."

Since her back is partially turned to him, he sees the muscles in it ripple with the movement of her arms. Quickly, in and out, recalled and then forgotten, he recognizes the image of the man's back—the dream Damian—from his vision.

She lets his wrist fall. "No, I do not stalk. I simply have an interest in things *africaine*. Right, Oscar, baby?"

As one of her hands dances high in the air, a little reddish brown, narrow-snouted dog leaps up from the floor behind the bed and turns around and around on its hind legs, yipping. "Good Oscar, good Oscar," Mrs. Gillory sings, and keeps the dog turning.

"The dog!" Langston exclaims. "They found him that fast?"

"Yes, lurking about the lobby restroom. The *women's* restroom, mind you."

Langston scrutinizes the dog. Is there a trace of resentment and maleficence in its black eyes as it spins for her pleasure? "He doesn't look like an Oscar."

Mrs. Gillory drops her hand and looks directly at Langston. "Do tell. Well, dear, he is a dog, and I am his master, so I name him whatever I want. Look more closely. Can't you just see him, green and grouchy and yarny and rooting through the garbage?

Osscarrrr!" The dog, panting and settled back on its haunches now, bares its teeth and growls.

"He doesn't seem to like the name," Langston observes. He feels confused about what he's planned to say.

"And I doesn't seem to care," Mrs. Gillory retorts. Langston grimaces. "You lie down and shut up, Oscar. Or I'll go for my *leash*."

The dog shakes its head with almost human irritation before it lies down.

"Why aren't you out celebrating the fall of Mr. Castro and the final triumph of Western civilization, Mr. Fleetwood?"

Langston, watching the dog, finds a sense of renewed purpose. His voice is light and calm. "Can I ask you some questions, Mrs. Gillory? If you don't mind?"

Mrs. Gillory holds his gaze for a moment, reading it, perhaps, then throws back her head. Her laughter is sharp and shrill. "Questions?"

He stumbles a bit, trying to regain the courage of his hunch. "I only wanted to know, because I'm curious. . . ." He decides to soften her up first. "I, um, had this idea—are you by any chance a psychic, Mrs. Gillory? Paranormally gifted, maybe?"

Mrs. Gillory appears to find his question intriguing. "I'm told my grandmother was . . . loony, possibly in a kind of psychic way. And I do have an affinity for her, they've always said so. Oh, you would have adored my grandmother! She was a *hoot*. She had a love for collecting exotica. Which was unfortunate for her. She was lost, flying over an ocean, or perhaps in the Himalayas. No one knows the true story." She pours water from a bottle into a plastic cup. She doesn't offer any. "But since I also feel an affinity for *you*, my beautiful young man with the primeval cheekbones and midnight brows, I will say this: I have always had a feeling that I could *do* things."

She bends toward him. Her tone is like his, calm and light, insinuating. "Do you understand?"

Langston tries to hold his ground. But the way she looks at him, her eyes somehow inhuman, and the dog sitting there staring at him with its small, black, animal eyes, the smell: there's nothing to help him keep within the bounds of sanity. "Is there a connection between your husband and—did you turn your dog—I mean your husband—into a dog?"

Mrs. Gillory looks at him steadily as she plays with her hair, flipping swaths of it from side to side across her face. Finally she sighs. "Mr. Fleetwood, that is a very silly notion, isn't it?"

She sits down on the bed, slips off one of her shoes, and rubs the stockinged foot round and round on the dog's soft head. "Now come! Enough about canines and their mysterious origins. Tell me about yourself. What do you do? And why are you here, in Miami, at this hotel? There was a famous black Union soldier, in the Civil War, a Christian Fleetwood, wasn't there? He escaped from a Virginia farm before the war, tried to volunteer for the army in Ohio, I believe, and he was turned away, so he went to another town, passed as white, joined the local brigade, and a couple of years later managed to slaughter a heap of Confederates before he was finally found out. The story is never quite clear on this point, but I have always wondered, how *did* they find him out? They say he was wounded. Did someone have to help him urinate, maybe, and recognized the goods for what they truly were?"

Langston winces at the crimson smile that lifts one corner of her mouth halfway across her cheek. "I'm surprised you've heard of my ancestor," he says diplomatically. "It's not exactly the sort of thing most people know."

The dog squeals beneath Mrs. Gillory's toe, but she holds it down. "I have an interest—"

"In things *africaine*," Langston finishes for her. He begins to move slowly back, a step closer to the door with each pause between sentences. "To answer your question, I'm a grad student at Berkeley. I came here to give a talk at a conference, which unfortunately pretty much came to nothing because of all the chaos after Castro's death. Two people on my panel discussion didn't even show. Anyway. My friends and I have been on vacation all week—and celebrating," he adds, not sure whether her comment about the triumph of Western civilization was meant to be taken seriously. "But something happened recently, and I thought maybe you could be of help. I mentioned Damian Sundiata to you when we met. Our friend?"

"Ah, Damian!" She purses her lips extravagantly. "Yes. He's quite something, isn't he? Almost as beautiful as you." Langston blushes. She actually appears to notice, and smiles knowingly. "I thought Damian quite the cad at first. He rather *suavely* introduced himself to me at the bar downstairs. But he was really very sweet. And then I had the thought that he was being evangelical with me, telling me that 'someone' or some 'higher power' or something of the sort had 'brought' him to me. Of course I don't have much truck with the evangelicals. They are a plague upon this country from my point of view, and really from the point of view of any intelligent person if you ask me—oh, but I do hope that when you say something has 'happened' you don't mean anything's gone ill for Damian!"

"Well . . ."

"Because that would be awful. Because you know we really *talked* and afterwards I felt so much better. I have the feeling—I'm sure everyone says things of this nature, and it's miserable to be trite, but there it is—I do have the feeling that we knew one another. Have known one another."

Langston nods impatiently. "He said someone sent him to you?"

"Less some*one*. More some*thing*."

"But why? You never met before. Why did he approach you at the bar, single you out?" As soon as he's said it, he knows he shouldn't have.

Mrs. Gillory's eyes and lips narrow down to slits. "Some men like women, you know," she says.

"Oh, no, I didn't mean—! Did he say anything about—his plans, or anything?"

She shrugs, evidently insulted or bored, or both. "Nothing I can recall." From the nightstand drawer she removes a gold-plated cigarette case and draws a slender white cigarette from it.

"I'm intruding. I should go." He begins to move decisively toward the door, but then feels the urge to ask, "Will you be leaving Miami anytime soon?"

"I've extended my stay indefinitely. Why leave? Everything of interest is happening right here, right now." She picks the dog up into her arms, pushes its head against her breast, and tries to hold the cigarette to its mouth. It twists, helplessly, in her grip. Langston watches, remembering her hand on his wrist.

"Don't let me keep you, Mr. Fleetwood."

Behind him the door lock trips, or he hears a sound that makes him think so. The door, he sees, is slightly open, not closed as he'd thought.

"I shall call you in the event I begin to manifest psychic powers," Mrs. Gillory says, and lights the cigarette in her mouth with a match she strikes on the bottom of her other high-heeled shoe.

Langston nods vaguely. "OK. Good."

"What is the PhD in, by the by?"

"Uh, Ancient Civilizations is what it's called," he mutters.

"Ah. The classics. Well well." The dog is cringing, actually whimpering, pressed and held to the tall woman's bosom. Mrs. Gillory waves bye-bye and Langston before he can think to move finds himself in the hallway, his hand on the doorknob, absently, as if the hand is not his own. He tries the door and finds it shut tight and locked.

"Ah-ah-*ah*, Oscar," he hears. "*Bad* boy. Now Mama has to get her *leash*."

Through a window at the hall's eastern end Langston sees a sky of darkening mauve, and the white fattened bulb of a moon just past half sinking toward the ocean. He quivers violently, overcome by a sharp chill.

Langston passes quickly back by the room he has paid for. He's about to go in when he hears Quentin's long, high Halloween cackle.

Langston retreats to the lobby.

The lobby is a small labyrinth of comfort zones, with soft night-lights beaming over angled cubbyholes, and cul-de-sacs of huge, fluffy couches facing one another beneath the dark fronds of tall green plants and dainty palm trees. Langston will choose a secluded corner, lie flat on his back with his face to the ceiling fans, drape one of the chenille throws over him for a cover, and then pass the waning hours of the night in a numb doze.

Try as he might, though, he can't duck past the reception desk without Luisa spying him out. "Langston! I thought you were headed to sleep!" Luisa lies.

Langston slows but keeps walking. "Things got a little funky up there. I figured I could get a little peace and quiet down here." He sounds plaintive.

"I'm sorry," Luisa says. "At least things are finally quieting down a little. Most people'll probably even go back to work tomorrow."

"Yeah, hope so," Langston says noncommittally.

"People may go back to the jay oh bee, but I wouldn't count much on no rest."

Langston briefly checks his step to take in the speaker's face: brown and parched, hair like the matte on a wet rat's back, and thin lips supporting a mustache that verges on the Hitlerian. The man perches at the corner of the reception desk and is leaning avidly over it as if it were a bar. Probably trying to get into Luisa's pants. He's short, and his shape resembles a balloon on a long stem, with a round, broad-shouldered topside and a scrawny lower body. His thick throat muscles pulse at the open neck of an oversize white button-down shirt. "Cain't rest," the man says emphatically, getting into the swing of a speech Langston feels he probably ought to avoid, "not when these ghosts are about. Miami'll be a city of haints 'fore you can say National Guard. Right, duckie?"

Luisa rolls her eyes at him and gives her focus to Langston. "Did you hear? About Castro?"

Langston comes to a full stop. "What do you mean? He's dead. Right?"

"Conceivably not," the scary man says. He has the pages of a newspaper laid out before him. "An old widow babe in Coral Gables yesterday—she wishes to remain anonymous; let us call her Rhapsody Blue. Yesterday Rhapsody came out to her ever so fine and well-tended backyard garden, said redoubt being carefully secluded from the riffraff, and what did she see? Old Fidel himself, that's who, on all fours like a dog and sniffing at her bed of African marigolds. Now, if you are a widow and a woman of substance such as Madame Blue, what do you do in such a predicament? You duck in, you call the cops, and then you invite the Maximum Leader of Cuba into your breakfast nook overlooking said garden for tea and a lecture on the evils of the communistic lifestyle. Lo and behold, Senor Castro is very gracious. He accepts that wrong has been done as well as right committed. He tells a long story that begins with the joys of revolution back in the dawning days of the postwar world, moving on to an account of a delightful swim he shared with Connecticut Senator Lowell Weicker—indicating his love of peaceful coexistence—and concludes somewhat irrelevantly with an envious paean to the martial grace of Brazilian capoeira."

The man's voice is strained—he smokes too much, clearly—but his rhythm is sensual, almost incantatory. "Rhapsody Blue the old widow babe is delighted, wants to know who this well-spoken and passionate felon really is before they lock him up. Why, Fidel Castro, madam, says he, and kisses her hand despite its forest of unseemly age spots. At this historical moment Miami's finest arrive at the door. Said sentries, both essentially rookies, enter, see Fidel. He bolts—through the window of the breakfast nook. Glass shatters over the grass of the well-mown lawn. Rhapsody the widow babe screams, and you get some rookie gunfire to rip up your Sunday-afternoon quiet. Castro bleeds, but quick as you can say Grounds for an Unnecessary Use of Deadly Force Lawsuit Against the City, our favorite dictator dives into the soil bed of the widow's garden. And makes the getaway. But!" The man points at nothing—the gods, maybe. "No trace of the body can be found. However, half the African marigolds are dug up and yanked like bad plumbing. Three witnesses to these facts, presumptively sober: the two rookies and Rhapsody Blue. Four witnesses, we learn later, since nosy neighboress Mrs. Alvarez, who just turned fifty, was looking from the window that looks over old babe's garden and she saw exactly what the cops and the widow saw. Except, unlike them, she swears it was the real Castro. And says she should know because she met the man personally forty years ago, and never forgot him."

Langston moves closer. "When did this happen?"

The man smiles humorlessly and holds up a copy of the *Miami Herald*. "Yesterday, September 14. As I said. 'Course, nobody can get confirmation from Cuba that the Maximum Potency's corpus delecti is safe and lying unmoved in state. Anyway, Rhapsody Blue's report don't sit especially good with a story told by the Beauvais family—mama, papa, three kids, all of Haitian persuasion, who call police two hours after the incident in Rhapsody Blue's garden to say that a man looking like Castro waved their car down on some deserted neighborhood road and asked them directions to the nearest public library. At this time they inquired of the gentleman as to why he was dressed up like Castro. He tells them that Haiti was the place of the first true people's revolution in the hemisphere, and that they must honor its memory. Off he then goes into an alley."

Luisa plays with the phone cord. "Isn't that wild? And then on the news tonight I heard there was a sighting in Little Havana—"

"Is there any explanation for all this?" Langston interrupts. "From the authorities, I mean?"

The man shrugs. "There's talk that a big, bad sorcerer magus type has been summoning demons to descend upon our fair city."

"The authorities say *that?*"

"Who in the Sam hell are the friggin authorities? People say that. People around town, who have lived here a good long time and know their left ball from their right."

"I don't believe it," Luisa says imperiously.

The man flicks his eyes at her and draws himself up (making his legs' contact with Earth even more tenuous) and begins declaiming, making sure to enunciate each consonant. "I'll tell you what I believe. Plain and simple. It is all over. There's a hole in the ozone of history, and ghosts and phonies of yester ages are streaming in. The modern period of man's push for perfectibility is coming to a crashing close, and we will soon commence burrowing down into the dark, dark depths of *unreason*." He hitches his belt and smiles amiably at Luisa's small bust (boyish, the way he likes them).

"Can I see that?" Langston points to the newspaper.

"Buy your own," the man says and hastily folds it under his armpit. "Enough jabber. When you gonna give up some sugar for Daddy, Lu?"

The phone rings, and with the receiver in one hand Luisa turns so that she looks directly at Langston. She gestures secretly back toward the man. HE'S CRAZY, she mouths, and scrunches up her face to highlight the Z. Brightly, she says, "Wessex House. How may I help you?"

Langston nods wearily at her. He glances over at the Hitlerish man; the newspaper is now firmly lodged under his arm, and he is glaring at Langston with blind hostility in rheumy, killer-for-hire eyes. Perhaps the lobby won't be the most restful location for the evening. Luisa is still talking on the phone, and she is writing quickly on a pad, so Langston, when he catches her eye, mouths to her DO YOU HAVE ANYTHING FOR, and then he steeples the fingers of his hands together and holds them at a tilt beside his head and closes his eyes. Luisa keeps speaking, but she flips a page on her pad, scratches out a word and a numerical figure, and holds it up to Langston.

She's overcharging him, but it's obscenely late and he's too desperate to argue.

At 1:57 A.M., Langston gingerly opens the door to his room.

What he hears is the hiss of quick hush-hush whispers, and what he sees are two shapes scrambling on the nearest bed, a flash glimpse of Reynaldo's hairy butt and the codpiece curve of Quentin's fat-at-the-base-skinny-at-the-head erection.

My God, Langston thinks ruefully: *Men*.

At least the two of them have the decency not to giggle. He shambles toward the bathroom to give them some time to finish whatever ridiculous act they've started—but not before taking a hard, long look at Azaril, whose bare back rises and falls on the other bed and whose soft snore seems entirely authentic.

Langston emerges from the bathroom ten minutes later, washed, naked—he's slept nude beside Azaril once, why not twice?—with two capsules swimming down the length of his esophagus. The shapes of Reynaldo and Quentin lie unmoving and separate. Langston slips quietly into the bed with Azaril, lightly brushes Azaril's toes with his own, and soon drops off to sleep.

Awakened by the shift in weight on the bed and the tingle across the knuckles of his toes, Azaril turns over, scratches, repositions, and repositions again. Finally he rises.

One-quarter of his consciousness still afloat in porous sleep, Azaril waddles to the bathroom in a fugue. He was dreaming something. Already he can't remember what. An adventure of some kind. He can still see the picture of a jungle stream lying black like flowing oil between banks of thorny bushes, and steam rising in clouds off the water. He was in a boat. His father was with him. Though Azaril has never actually met his father or even seen a picture of him. In the dream his father looked like—dream faces are so indistinct, they're not even faces so much as expressions or feelings wrapped up in the smudged outlines of a face—in his dream his father *felt* like Damian.

When Azaril leaves the bathroom, his head is fuzzy. He feels drunk. He steps noisily and quickly toward Damian's bag, makes out its blob left half-unzipped on the cushions of the tiny love seat shoved against the wall. In the dim light—is it growing lighter outside? he feels a sense of panic—Azaril thrusts his hand inside, rummages blindly, and pulls free a sock. He holds it up to his face. It's a dark-blue dress sock, specked with tiny stitched gold stars. Fuzzily, mindlessly, he inhales. Then he wraps the sock around his wrist, climbs into bed, shoves his hand under the pillow, and once his heart slows down, falls again into deep sleep.

4

The same day, midafternoon

Morning arrives at 3:00 P.M.

Langston makes his way around and through the archipelago of Azaril's clothing on the floor. He knocks at the door of the bathroom and asks for what seems like the fifth time for Azaril to hurry up; he can't hold it much longer. Azaril mumbles something as the shower comes on, and Langston considers barging in now that the toilet is free, but he knows Azaril won't stand for it, that Azaril would rather clench his bladder to the edge of peeing in his pants rather than unzip at a public urinal and so he'd be furious if Langston violated one of his primary taboos by whipping it out in front of him. Langston suspects there's a particular fear Azaril has of being in the presence of Langston's penis, his *gay* penis—as if the sight of it would make his heterosexual self crumble Semele-like into dust.

He looks again at the note on the pillow of the other bed. The sheets have been nicely tucked in, and the comforter and chamois evened out and smoothed down with the dowdy fastidiousness your pushing-fifty-and-still-unwed second cousin Sally might display in a protracted visit to the guest bedroom. Reynaldo, or Quentin?

We went out for lunch, the note says. *Back by 5, 5:30*.

It is too soon out of bed for Langston to consider the implications of this—from one undesired roommate to two new ones—what on planet Earth could Reynaldo and Quentin see in each other?—he will need to get going by four o'clock in order to make it to Aunt Reginia's house on time, is it possible Damian's really in danger, it's certainly possible that they just wouldn't have heard from him for this span of time, but with Quentin's story and his vision—my God, is that Azaril's underwear?

Blue bikini briefs, carelessly tossed to the floor, lying twisted inside out. Thin as a ribbon. Silky, almost, small and tight and not at all comfortable, one imagines. Langston picks them up by the elastic with thumb and forefinger. No, not comfortable, but sexy. Designed to give the viewer pleasure, not the wearer: an instrument of seduction, or a prize for the successful seducer. Unless the viewer *is* the wearer, and the viewer likes seeing himself with a silky bulge and his olive butt cheeks hanging out? Or maybe Azaril bought these for dates with that girl Alana, that smug, apple-faced Irishy woman he used to date. Do straight guys buy sexy underwear for dates? Langston digs the idea, it goes along with his fantasies about virile Italian studs who wear gold chains around their necks and have black hair all over their chests and around their belly buttons and swagger around the bedroom in underwear just like this, and get their wives and girlfriends pregnant all the time, they're so hot and he-man and full of spunk.

Langston brings the briefs closer to his nose just as the bathroom door swings open and a plume of steam blusters out like an angry genie. "Told you I'd be done in a sec," Azaril says, emerging in a towel. Langston, terrified and yet thrilled that he might have been caught, that something might finally begin, rises and freezes in a half-stand, half-sit as he quickly drinks in the sight. The expression of Azaril's voice and face are hard to read, but since nothing in it remotely suggests fury or surprise, Langston—sifting through relief and disappointment—guesses that Azaril doesn't notice his briefs conspicuously draped over Langston's toes.

Langston makes for the bathroom with an urgency that has nothing to do with his bladder. Defiantly, though, he keeps the door open as he relieves himself.

"You didn't get an answer from this Gillory woman if she'd actually *seen* Damian or whether he'd told her anything about his plans?"

Azaril's earnestness and focused sense of priority make Langston feel ashamed of himself. "I was too distracted. The way she was acting—she threw me off." He hasn't yet said anything about his suspicions concerning Mrs. Gillory's husband and her sudden adoption of a suddenly appearing dog. Already he's thinking that his guess was ridiculous: she spooked him, that's all, and of course he has been taking drugs his system isn't used to.

"You should go back and ask," Azaril says. "Or you want me to do it?"

"There's no time to do that right now," Langston says hastily as he steps into the shower—he peeks out the door: yep, Azaril's back is turned to him. "We're gonna be late for dinner at my aunt's as it is."

There's a pause. Langston, his senses prickling, hesitates before turning the knob of the showerhead.

"I don't think I'm going." Azaril's voice seems to travel from far off—the consequence of keeping his back turned, and of the whine of apology that thins his otherwise resonant tone.

"Oh, come on, you have to go, she's expecting you!" Langston pleads, knowing full well that his aunt, with her peculiar caginess and abrupt bouts of misanthropy, would probably prefer that he not bring Azaril along. As the water streams down over him, Langston starts selling loudly and rapidly: he tells Azaril that his Aunt Reginia is a fabulous cook, that she has a spectacular house, that Azaril would find Aunt Reginia fascinating because she knows so many things and she's traveled widely, and the Mediterranean is her favorite region of the world.

"Huh," Azaril grunts.

"Oh, definitely," Langston shouts. "She loves the Mediterranean countries. She has pictures from Moorish Spain, Sardinia, Naples, Tunis, the Mani, the Turkish coast, of course Egypt, Israel she enjoyed, too. Lebanon."

"Lebanon?"

Langston had thought Israel or Egypt would be the hook, but if Lebanon works, then Langston can work Lebanon. He turns the water down low and flings open the shower door. "Oh, she *loves* Lebanon. Well—she went there a long time ago. You know, they used to say that Beirut was the Paris of the Middle East, so maybe it was back then that she traveled there. She's raising two sons now, so she hasn't really been out of Florida for about twelve years, I think." He holds back before casting the most important bait: "Also, this may sound kind of weird, but I think she could help us find Damian."

"How? Is she a detective?"

Ah: got him. "She's . . . kind of a medium, or a spiritualist. She's not very public about it, but she's developed a very good reputation. The police call her in to help them. She's worked with them on a few big cases."

Langston waits while Azaril digests this. "You actually believe she has psychic powers?"

"I do," Langston says. "Psychic sensitivities, anyway. She's read all kinds of stuff accurately for people in my family. According to her, and I think I pretty much believe this, everyone has the basic intuitive sensitivity that people call psychic power. The rest of us tend to ignore it. She pays attention to hers."

"If that's true, you should go into a trance and find Damian for us," Azaril says. The jocular note in Azaril's tone makes Langston hopeful. Maybe he ought to tell Azaril about what he saw on the dance floor at Redemption.

"Ahight, I'm in," Azaril says, sounding almost cheerful.

Langston gives himself one last vigorous soaping and rinsing, and steps out of the shower, feeling good. Sometimes he worries it's an ugly thing he's engaged in with Azaril, and that the attention-giving, ego-stroking, fear-soothing, goal-assisting superfriend he is to Azaril is just a highly orchestrated performance, having no genuine motive but—what? To fuck him. And not even for good clean lustful reasons, but to fulfill a more sinister agenda hatched in the dark corners of his unconscious, an agenda entirely analogous to—if not exactly the same as—that of any repulsive old perv padding after young smooth skin. He's only older than Azaril by a decade, but still. Sometimes Langston fears that he wants to capture Azaril, to take and consume him. That he is, on some psychological or psychic level, a predator. But in moments like now the guilt is entirely gone, and he can believe that what's between them is meaningful and perhaps even sacred, that some destiny with deep unfolding purpose has drawn them together. It's because he and Azaril are so much better in privacy, without others around (Damian especially). Their rhythms are more closely synchronized, their moments of opening up and closing down, of reading the other's needs and being read, flow with grace and surefootedness in closed rooms: like a dancing duo that becomes clumsy when the cameras roll or the judges are watching, but that in practice, in their private studio, astonish themselves with the precision of their timing.

Or like a couple, who don't get along in groups but can be everything to one another in the cloister of their bedroom.

"Hey!" Azaril calls.

Langston emerges, hoping that the vision of him dripping wet with a towel barely wound about his waist in all his slender beauty will make Azaril gasp in surprised ecstasy. "What do you need?" Langston asks (too high, too girly—he'll be mortified when he plays the scene over in his head a few seconds from now).

Azaril turns and regards Langston with an inscrutably thoughtful gaze—as if, perhaps, he doesn't even see the body in front of him. "What happened to the drag guy and Reynaldo?"

Langston shrivels. "They're . . . out. We'll leave them a note and the key at the front desk with Luisa."

Now Azaril is looking at him carefully, there is a long pause—a flint of hope strikes anew in Langston's chest—and then Azaril smiles and shakes his head. "You gay boys," he says as he passes back into the bathroom carrying a shirt and pants but no underwear, and locks the door.

5

Aunt Reginia's domain, Key West, evening

Langston's Aunt Reginia—Reginia Jameson Wolfe, to peers and those not her kin—would not be pleased to hear her nephew describe her as a "medium," and she would take particular umbrage at the notion of being called a "spiritualist." She is not satisfied with the usual labels for her kind of work, and prefers in professional settings to be addressed as Mrs. Wolfe, doctor of divinity and secular oracle. Her clients come to her solely by referral and see her by appointment, in a small, brilliantly sunny flat exactly three miles from her home. There Mrs. Wolfe soothes them with a tall cup of tea and a raisin scone before sitting down to gently hold their hands while she reveals to them the terrifying truths of their lives. At the conclusion of the reading, she offers a white cotton handkerchief as a complimentary gift for those who leave in tears. For these services Mrs. Wolfe charges astronomical fees. She hates to pimp her gifts, but a woman has to eat, she has two sons, and she's very jealous of her leisure time.

Azaril's nerves begin to twitter once they turn off Highway 1 onto White Street and find their way to Aunt Reginia's house. As a general matter it unsettles him to have to meet the families of his friends, and in Langston's case it makes him feel all married or something. He can hear the rubber soles of his suede tennies brush over the pavement of the sidewalk as he joins Langston, who is unlatching the gate in the four-foot-high chestnut-wood fence.

"Cute neighborhood," Azaril remarks, and then pokes his head inside the gate to see just what a psychic's house looks like.

Aunt Reginia's home is long, with two cottagelike wings on either side of a larger two-story central domicile that crests in a high, steepled ceiling. The color of the paint is undistinguished, chestnut like the fence, with sorrel highlights. As much of it as you can see clearly, anyway: the yard is terribly untended, sticky moss hugging one side of the house, low tree branches sweeping half-shaded narrow windows, shrubbery pushing against the walls, grass too long, and a jumbled-up garden off to the left with some pretty white lilies sharing soil with two vines of tomatoes on sticks and one lone stalk of white corn. The look would be slightly creepy, except that the scientist in Azaril reassures the rest of him that looks can be deceiving.

The sky has mellowed into the slurred color of ice cubes listing in a glass of Lillet, and the spreading early evening shadows play games with depth perception. They have arrived a tad late.

Azaril stops short, gasps, points. "Lang, watch out!"

But Langston keeps walking. He has already seen it—a brawny, yellow-and-black-striped snake, slicking between the green stalks of the garden. "That's Morningstar. He's OK."

Maybe Langston's part of a whole family of witches, Azaril thinks, and—his eye warily on the snake—he follows Langston cautiously to the front door.

Langston rings the bell a couple of times. After a moment they can hear some fumbling going on with the lock, and then standing there in the doorway is a tall woman, a shade heavy maybe ("stout," Langston's mother says in her sister's defense), almond brown in color with a wide, pleasant face neither young nor old. And that same dignified demeanor and ease of bearing you can see in portraits of Langston's mother ("Them Jameson girls are like that," everyone says), and, at times, in Langston himself.

Langston and his aunt smile and laugh to see each other, and as they step forward into each other's hugs, say almost in unison, "Well, now, let me take a look at you."

Langston is a bit disappointed, truth be told. Aunt Reginia's hair used to be a big, elegant arrangement of beauty-shop-perfect cascades, peaks and comin'-round-the-mountain swirls. Back in the day, a light frost of blond gave her 'do's elaborate propriety a wild-woman edge. Back then, Langston was as proud of his Aunt Reginia's hair as she was. As a boy moving from army base to army base, he liked to show new friends his picture of her on the porch of the house she used to have in Miami. It is with a pang of hurt that he snuggles close to find that the once-grand arrangement has been subjected to an austerity regime. Peaks and swirls have given way to a tight, cropped, salt-and-pepper natural cut low over the dramatic curve of her skull. She is wearing a blue cotton shirt with shiny buttons and a comfortable pair of flared black twill pants.

For her part Reginia thinks her nephew looks alarmingly gaunt. If she were the kind of good stout southern matriarch who watches hawklike over the health of her kin, she'd usher the boy inside for instant fattening, whip up some cornbread and peach cobbler, stick a catheter in his arm, and force-feed heaps of it to him—but she isn't that kind of woman. It's this heroin chic thing, and all that so-called partying the young people do in South Beach that explains him looking this way, she decides clinically: oh well—children will be children.

"This is my friend Azaril Shahid-Coleman," Langston says and steps aside.

Azaril smiles uncertainly and Reginia extends her hand, but

then she says, "Ah, hell, might as well give you a hug, too," and pulls a startled Azaril into her chest.

"Nice to meet you," Azaril mumbles, straightening himself.

"Sorry we're late," Langston says.

"Oh, don't worry," Aunt Reginia says over her shoulder as she closes the door behind them and leads them through the foyer. "I'm not making anything fancy, and I kept the ingredients waiting for you two to come help me cook. I was going to make gumbo, but that mess takes too long and I get tired trying to turn southern every time somebody comes to visit. Come on down with me to the basement. The boys are down there. They couldn't wait to eat, so they ordered pizza."

"How old are they now? It's been, what? Four years since I've seen them?"

"Yep. You Fleetwoods don't come down here to see me as much as you did when you all were children, and since I don't travel like I used to, seems like none of you get to see my boys grow up, except on Kodak. Until you called me a couple days ago, young man, I haven't even talked to you since March."

"I know, I know, I get busy, lazy . . ."

"Do manage to keep up with Zuli, though, since every time I look up, she's on the news."

Langston winces. It is commonplace among the Fleetwood side of the family to footnote every *Langston, honey, so good to see you!* with an adoring reference to his older sister, Zuli: code for, *She's doing* so *well, and what's this—your seventh year in your p-h-d in what was it again—archeology?* Aunt Reginia, being a doctor herself and, more importantly, a Jameson (the Jamesons do not think much of the Fleetwoods, and vice versa), has till now spared Langston this torture, but evidently the awe-of-Zuli-sniffle has blossomed into a full-scale contagion, against which in-law rivalries no longer provide prophylaxis.

"Oh," he says unhappily, "what's Zuli in the news for now?"

"Prosecuting those Sudanese terrorists, child, haven't you heard?"

"Wow." That's Azaril, in reference not to Zuli's high-profile legal assignment, but to Aunt Reginia's surprisingly uncluttered and commodious living room—the polished white oak slats of the floor and the soft, creamy decor, and the far wall, a bright pyramid of white-framed windows that embraces a pair of French doors at the pyramid's base and crowns at the zenith of the ceiling steeple. Beyond the doors and through the windows, there is a small, grassy courtyard, clipped, meticulously tended, and boasting a harmony as distinct as the tumult of the front yard. "Cool."

"Oh, yeah, isn't that nice?" Langston says, mostly to avoid talking about Zuli. "On either side of the courtyard are the wings, and you circle around to the kitchen and dining room on the other side of the courtyard."

"When was this house built?"

"Nineteen eighty-seven," Aunt Reginia answers. "Most of it, anyway. The central part and half of one of the wings were already here. I had the rest built for my boys, before they were born. Little did I know they'd spend most of their time down in the basement with the TV. And I'm supposed to be able to see the future." She holds open a door onto a descending stairway for them, and smiles at Azaril as Langston ducks his head and steps onto the top stair. "You know, I believe if I locked this door and didn't let them out, they wouldn't know the difference, long as Domino's delivered. Sometimes I'd rather have my children do an experimental course in psychotropic drugs than let them watch that television."

Langston knows that the mention of drugs is aimed in his direction.

The narrow stairway and its severely slanting ceiling deposit them upon the gray floor of the basement. For a den of iniquity it has little to recommend it—it's rather like a wide cement cell, with a large musty rug, a floral-patterned love seat, a coffee table, two end tables, and two lamps that are currently out. The room's strongest illumination comes from the high wattage of what might be the biggest television in the Caribbean, which has colonized an entire wall.

"Gabriel, Michael! Y'all can't say hello?" Langston yells to the two figures on the love seat.

One, a round-headed, handsome fellow (handsome, yes, but teetering on the edge of obesity, Langston notes), glances over his shoulder, then jumps up. "Whazup, yo?" he says with a voice deeper than his age, and he stumbles over the foot of the love seat to go hug his cousin.

For Langston, this casual *yo*, a mere fling of a word, feels like a welcome from Saint Peter at the gates. He hugs Gabriel fiercely.

Back on the love seat, Michael is more focused, or perhaps more hostile. "Lang," is his contribution, along with a brief bob of the head. He is far slimmer than Gabriel, darker and richer in complexion, and as Michael's left arm dangles behind the couch, Langston can see lean adolescent sinew.

"What happened to my hug?" Langston says, and he thinks everyone can hear his voice tremble.

"Oh, you haven't been around for quite *some*," Aunt Reginia says as she moves past Azaril. "Michael here has informed me that he does not do hugging anymore. These two sprout some curls below the navel, and it's become so I have to hold them up against the wall by the neck and slap them three times to get a 'Mama, I love you.'" But she says this with unmistakable pride, and she beams to see Langston together with her sons.

Gabriel goes to sit back down, and Langston asks, "What game are you watching?"

Gabriel and Michael, engrossed in the larger-than-life events on the screen, can't summon the will to get their tongues moving before Aunt Reginia answers. "Football tapes, my dear, from last year's season at the high school. They are learning the strategy of the game. I told them to take up something useful, like marksmanship or fencing. Something that might help in a pinch in the coming Race and Technology War."

Azaril, who is somewhat hurt that he's not been introduced, says, "What race war?"

Reginia looks at him, her amused expression softening the withering glance he sees Michael shoot him from over his shoulder. "You mean, *which* race war. But I said Race and *Technology* War—although it could just be a New Sexual Revolution and Health Care War to go along with the Terrorizing Terrorists War. All of them at once. I don't know. In my meditations last week I thought I got wind of something. Signs, portents. Tectonic shifts, planetary alignments, ominous geyser eruptions, entropic surges. Then I sat down in front of the damn TV and saw some Lena-Horne-makeup-wearing fake Indian in a bad Hollywood movie talking about how he feels 'nature' rising up against us. And got the chills. Who knows what it means? Something's coming. Maybe just the rise of a Democrat with some Gott-damn backbone. Of course this is all in psychic time," she adds cryptically.

"Really?" Langston says. "I was just talking to this guy last night who was saying that something huge was happening. He said that there's this hole in history, and that, basically, all of modernity is coming to a violent end."

Aunt Reginia shrugs. "I wouldn't put too much into that kinda trash prediction. Sounds like a sermon or a fund-raising letter, not a reading. You can put that fire and brimstone treacle right up there with, 'You will meet a tall, dark, handsome stranger.'"

"But, what do you think's been going on, then? There've been a lot of very strange things happening the last couple of days," Azaril says excitedly.

"For example?"

Langston interrupts. "For example, I don't know if you read this in the paper or not, but there have been reports that Fidel Castro has been seen, in several different locations: on a roadside by a Haitian family, in a woman's garden—"

"Oh, yes, mmhm, I did read that," Reginia says. She cocks her head and tugs on her earlobe. "And there was supposedly another one of these Castro sightings in Little Havana, too, last night."

"Yes!" Azaril exclaims, and everyone in the room stares at him. "We were there! Langston and me!"

"You saw this creature? Did it look like Castro?"

"He looked just like the Castro I've seen in magazines and newspapers, yes," Azaril says. He shakes his head in consternation. "Not that much of him was left when the mob was through."

"Huh, yeah, I guess not. 'Course, just like the other sightings, by the time anybody official got there to examine the evidence, they couldn't find anything, no body at all. Funny."

It seems to require all the self-control Azaril can manage to keep him from jumping up and down and pounding his fists in the air when he hears this. "But I saw the man! I saw them tear him apart! I saw his flesh, his skin practically—*torn* from his face! The blood!"

Aunt Reginia maintains her slightly ironic, distracted air. "Yes, but whose blood? Can you be sure you saw the man's blood, not someone else's? The newsfolk certainly didn't report finding torn-off body parts. These may-God-forgive-me-for-profanity 'journalists' would break away from a story about California sinking into the Pacific to show us some fresh body parts. Don't let it trouble you, sweetie," she says—this as she comes out of her contemplation of the ills of yellow journalism to take note of Azaril's extreme agitation; instantly she begins to think of him as being a little sweet and cute, rather than just a vessel of testosterone driving her favorite nephew crazy. She puts her hand on his shoulder (not an entirely idle or meaningless gesture, when one is a secular oracle).

"Listen, this kind of violent hysteria is just business more or less as usual in Miami. Every time you look up, there's a brush fire: the 1982 riots, the '89 riots, tourists gunned down, Versace offed like some Mafia hit, little Elian, Hurricane Andrew, Hurricanes Frankie, Johnny, and Luigi. And the Mariel Boatlift! Lord God. And don't even mention the stolen election. That's why I had to move out of there. The place wears on your nerves. That blood you saw could be the ghost of blood, the echo of somebody's corpuscles and hemoglobin bubbling up. A volcano eruption from the past. People die or get hurt in as ugly a way as they have as often as they do around here, sometimes it's like pieces of them get seared into the soil. Like a brand. What you saw could have been that kind of manifestation. Anyhow, that's my working theory."

"Do you mean, Mrs. Wolfe, that I may have had a psychic experience?" Azaril says. "That what I saw wasn't physical reality?"

"Well—I wouldn't say exactly that, now. Not without knowing more. Sometimes psychic reality is more true than what we call physical reality. In which case, what difference does it make? If you saw the blood and the flesh, Azrael, you saw the blood and the flesh."

"Az*a*ril."

"Oh. Sorry."

"Ma. Ma!"

Reginia's mouth very slowly makes a downward turn, and her eyes do not leave Azaril and Langston when she frostily answers, "Michael."

"It's hard to concentrate, Ma."

"Ohhhh," Aunt Reginia says, and her eyebrows lift almost to her hairline. "Forgive me, Lord. The man has spoken. Neither age nor wisdom count, for when the man speaks, we jump. Langston, Azrael. Let's continue our discussion in the kitchen, so as not to disturb the master of the house," she says, and begins to walk up the cramped stairway. "And don't you come up there asking to be fed, Michael Wolfe, because as rude as you've been, I'd feed the mice my mother's milk before I'd let you enjoy another fruit of my labor."

"Ma."

"I'm serious."

"Sorry, Ma."

"Yes, I know you are."

When they reach the hallway and shut the door behind them, Langston whispers to Azaril, "I told you she'd talk your ear off. That psychic reality stuff . . ."

"Oh, no. I like it. She's great."

The kitchen, like the front yard, living room, courtyard, and basement, is a doorway onto yet another galaxy in the Reginia Jameson Wolfe universe. This time Azaril sees the ethos as being of a kind of shaggy nobility. It's large—very large—with long windows draped in curtains like a Victorian-era dress filtering the amber light of dusk, discolored water stains and peeling paint where the walls merge with the ceiling, a grandfather clock in the corner opposite an unused fireplace with family photographs on the wrought-iron mantel, a tiered antique sideboard with pristine china plates displayed on the open top cabinet and half-open lower drawers bulging with dish towels and cutout recipes, a voluptuous industrial stove sporting six eyes, a spotless steel sink, and a Corian counter backed by a slender mirror and decorated along its length by five wide-mouthed bowls of bright red peppers, emerald jalapeños, lemons, onions, and eggplant, respectively. In the center of this vast expanse is a vast table, where, along with a loaf of homemade potato bread (one slice has been cut—Gabriel's doing, no doubt) and a sleek bottle of *primitivo*, there is an open jar of jam and three paperback books in a skewed pile.

"Don't mind the mess," Aunt Reginia says, and gathers up pens scattered on the face of the table. "My kitchen is my work-room. We built a big study, but Dilbert used it all the time, and when he ran off I couldn't bring myself to go in it anymore."

"Dilbert is . . .?" Azaril asks.

"My ex-husband. You talked to him recently, Langston? You or your father?"

"Um, well . . . Dad may have . . ."

"Oh, forget it. I don't want to know. What on earth are these doing here?" Scowling, Reginia pulls out a chair that has been pushed flush against the table, and lifts a plate, ringed with pink prawns and a dollop of aioli dressing in the center. "Gabriel!" she thunders. "I told you the shrimp was not to be touched! Did you think you were going to hide it up here in a chair? Don't lie to me! I can feel your touch all over the plate!" She makes a noise of disgust and offers the plate to them as if handing them a soiled diaper for disposal. "Here, Langston, Azrael. To snack on while you help me cook."

"What are we making?" says Azaril.

"Risotto. Langston, could you chop up some celery—it's in the fridge, the bottom, no, child, lower—and get the carrots and the parsley, too—right. Chop all that up and put it in that pot on the stove with the broth in it, then simmer it. Azrael, could you take two of those onions from the bowl over there, chop them up, fine? You don't cry when you chop onions, do you? Both of y'all wash your hands first, now."

Langston gives Azaril a wry look. "And what, may I ask, will you be doing, Aunt Reginia?"

"I will be supervising the cooking and checking the recipe, smart-butt. He sounds just like his mother, Azrael; have you met her? And when the moment arrives, Miss Thing, I'll take my sixty-plus-year-old body over to the stove and actually do the cooking. You two are my sous-chefs, I am the master chef. Get it?" Both she and Langston laugh.

"But I still want to know what you think," Langston says from over at the sink, scrubbing his hands. "Do you think these Castro sightings and all the strange stuff is related to what you've been sensing in your meditations?"

Aunt Reginia, seated at the table and bent over a cookbook, flippantly flips a page. "Oh, don't ask me questions like that, Langston. I can't explain everything that happens under the sun. I'd have to think more about it. I swear, if I was a lawyer, everybody in the family'd be trying to have me take their neighbor to court, and even that would be easier than having to read every little event in the world for you, your mother and my cousins and auntees and uncles. Lord help me, even the Fleetwood clan comes sniffing around, too, trying to get readings on real estate deals. I have said, I do not have a tap into the mind of God. Does your family treat you like this, Azrael? Asking you whether DNA is responsible for their arthritis or the decline in American SAT scores, or some such?"

Azaril, handling the onions, hesitates. "Well . . . I don't really have much family."

Reginia looks up from her recipes and holds him in her gaze. "Oh, yes. That's right."

"I still have to press you, Aunt Reginia. I think what that old guy told me last night may not be entirely trash. Maybe these Castro apparitions are, like, cosmic symbols. Like, of the final death of communism. And then when you consider that communism is part of the whole project of the rational alleviation of human suffering—I mean, these days all we have left is rampant capitalism and fundamentalist religious zealotry. So you *could* argue everything will be reduced to a cycle of predation and survival, saved versus heathen, ultrarich versus ultrapoor. You *could* argue maybe we have reached the end—"

Reginia shuts her cookbook over one hand. "Langston, first off, there is no reason to believe that what happens in front of your face and in your newspaper says anything at all about where the *world* is going. The presumption that the U.S. and all her colonies are at the leading edge of human development is just silly."

"Exactly," Azaril chimes in—to Langston's considerable irritation.

"Second, even if America were all that mattered in the world as we know it, the thing you have to understand is that the forces that truly move this world simply do not operate that way. Even taken as a whole, humankind's little systems and little ideals and passions are not the primary engine of the universe. Capitalism, communism: they just happen to be the instruments, the tools human beings use for the greater spiritual work none of us really understand. (Although I do happen to understand a great deal of it.) The universe would no more arrange for symbols of the death of the Enlightenment et cetera to stumble around Miami than it would send a comet to commemorate the high Nielsen ratings of the telecast of *Roots*. History—the history of ideas, the history of politics, all history as we learn it, is nothing, when it's seen from the perspective of the true power of the universe. You see what I'm saying? I don't mean that these things aren't important to us, in our little lives. Of course they are. But in the end, my dear, there is only the infinite consciousness of the universe, which you and I can barely begin to understand when we talk about time and its unfolding, but which we'll likely never fully grasp." The book slaps against the table as she flings it open again, apparently pleased with herself for having brought a satisfactory end to the conversation.

"There's some significance to the fact that it's Castro we're seeing," Langston maintains. He has nicked his thumb trying to slice a stubborn carrot, and is now intermittently sucking on it.

"Well, it is always marginally possible that I could be wrong." She shrugs and smiles sheepishly. She busily dashes off little notes on a piece of paper. "You know, I did a reading of Castro once, back in 1974. Well, not of *him* precisely, but of some of his effects. Somebody who'd worked for him or close to him—it was all a bit mysterious—brought me an old cap, buttons off a uniform or something. I couldn't read much, really. Of course, the FBI or CIA or somebody who spies for a living got wind of it, and came and ransacked my house without a word or a warrant. They've got snitches everywhere. They wanted to question me, but I avoided them."

"Avoided them? How did you get out of it?"

"Oh, it was easy to get them off my back. All I needed was the name of the agency contact down here, vicious, cold little fellow, one of the exiles. Men like that, their crimes stand out in plain sight with 'guilt' in red neon lettering right on their foreheads. They want everybody to know what they're up to, even if their lives depend on secrecy. They crave attention. With them, you don't even need more than a name—unless of course they've got extra psychic protection. He didn't. After I got tired of the agency tailing and harassing both me and the strapping young thing who was then my live-in man, I picked up the phone and told the snitch as kindly as I could that I knew who that woman was he slept with, and what kind of information he was giving her, and don't think I won't let Colonel CIA or Special Agent FBI know all about it *and* the bribe. You see, he worked for the Russians, too. Never heard from the James Bond set again. They do still tap my phone every once in a while. Soon as I figure it out, I start calling Langston's mother and saying nonsense words like *hoogabooga lapmelikme poosiepowher ogabavadoon*." Azaril breaks into a wide smile at the suggestive way her tongue moves. "That stops 'em real fast—probably think I'm casting a porno incantation on 'em. Isn't that a laugh."

There's quiet for a moment while Langston alternately chops and sucks his thumb, and Aunt Reginia peers at the pages of the cookbook and jots down her little notes. Azaril watches both of them while slicing the onions. Reginia, crazy though she probably is, has made Langston's stock rise considerably.

"That's enough, Langston," Reginia says without looking up from her cookbook. "Just put them in the pot and turn on the heat. Azrael—there's a big bottle of olive oil in that cabinet you're standing right in front of. Get that, pour me a few tablespoons in the skillet, and you can start sautéing me those onions. On medium heat, about five minutes."

"Excuse me," Azaril says. "Can I first—where's the bathroom?"

Langston answers. "Back down the hall, second, no, third door on your left. Right, Aunt Reginia?"

"Mmhm. Soon as you pass by the living room." Now she looks up. "Don't get lost. And hurry back."

Azaril gets the uncomfortable feeling that it behooves his safety to take this advice seriously, and darts out of the kitchen.

"So . . . what do you make of him?"

"Do you think you could ask me something about my life or something, Langston Hughes Fleetwood? Ask me about how my lilies are doing, how my businesses are panning out."

"We talked about that on the phone! Stop teasing me! I told you I'm crazy about him. I'm not asking you to do a reading, because I'm family, and you don't want to read family because people choose their families for a reason and you don't want revealing our stuff to interfere with you learning your own stuff."

Reginia speaks the last thirty-five words along with Langston as he recites them in bored singsong, substituting you's for I's and me's, and punctuates the end with, "Precisely!"

"All I want is a first impression," Langston pleads. "Come on, Aunt Reginia. Please. You're so accurate. No one is ever as helpful as you."

"Do you think that flattery mess is supposed to move me? I've got two boys downstairs, I don't need to be needed." She tries to look mean and fails. "Oh, all right. Lord."

She closes the cookbook, pushes it away. She shuts her eyes for a moment, then opens them quickly, flinching, as if singed by a sudden blaze. Then, quickly, she releases a huge, relieved sigh. "I'll say this much. That boy has been up, down, and around the cradle of civilization for the last four thousand years. Eridu to Kish to Ur. A sailor for—well, the image I got looked like right around eighteenth dynasty in Egypt. Got another picture like a hoplite in Sparta or someplace. Assassin for an emperor in Byzantium. A Seljuk warrior. King's man, every time, always killing for his master, forever running his sword through somebody's entrails in his master's name. Downed in battle. He's Palestinian, you said? I guess it's kind of like the Yoruba say, you get born as your own descendants. Or in this case, near about.

The universe got him, though, this time. He ended up here, of all places."

Langston stands before the open pot. The steam leaves beads of sweat on his forehead. "That's . . . interesting. Especially given the fact that I study a lot of that history. But the stuff about being a king's man—I don't get that."

"I think I do. Unfortunately. Poor thing."

"What do you mean? Is there danger facing him?"

Reginia gives the impression of a professor who's finally lost patience with a simpleton student. "No more *danger* than the usual, Langston. Look, I said I would not do a reading. You wanted first impressions, there are your first impressions. Now go measure out three cups of the arborio rice—lower cabinet, right side, make sure, now, it's not the long-grain rice, you want the arborio. The measuring cups are in the left-most top drawer."

"You won't tell me anything else?"

"No, Langston! And once you get the—oh, Azaril. You're back already."

"Cool bathroom. I like that tile."

"Oh, the limestone. Yes, that is nice. One of Dilbert's inspirations. Do you know one of my so-called colleagues was over for dinner, went into that bathroom, and came back gabbling on about how he 'felt' that very limestone had sunk to the bottom of the sea with Atlantis?"

Azaril laughs.

"As if the stone could be *that* damn old. Now, why don't you step over to the fridge for me, sweetie, and on the second tier you'll see a blue glass bowl with some foil over it. Bring that out, that's the chicken we'll put in the risotto. And then maybe you could slice up one of those bell peppers for me, bite-size chunks. Is no one going to rid me of these meddlesome shrimp? I see y'all haven't taken a bite yet. It's from a good seafood store."

Langston finishes with the arborio rice, sullenly paces over to the table, and picks his way around until he finds the prawn that looks the juiciest. He will be nursing it for a minute or so. Azaril, on his way to the fridge, grabs three prawns by the tails, swabs them in the aioli dip, and downs them before he gets to the other end of the kitchen.

"Do you have your restaurant send you over food sometimes?" Langston asks to butter Aunt Reginia up.

"Not since I lost my chef to a higher bidder in Miami and the legislature passed that law denying health care to illegal immigrants—that means half my workforce could be spreading microbes in the food. I wouldn't touch the stuff. The place still has a good atmosphere, though."

Azaril is rinsing off the knife he has been using. "Has Langston asked you about our friend Damian yet, Mrs. Wolfe?"

"No," she says, and casts a look toward her nephew. "Why would he ask me about your friend?"

"He disappeared," Azaril says eagerly, "and we haven't been able to find him. The last person we know to have seen him claims that he disappeared into thin air."

"We last saw him late Friday night—Saturday early A.M.," Langston rather glumly puts in. "Saturday around noon he was seen by someone he'd been hanging out with. They were on Calle Ocho together, and Damian skipped out or 'disappeared' or something. It's possible he'd been in and out of the hotel room while we were gone, but we haven't seen him, yesterday or today."

"Have you called the police?" Reginia says, as she scoops handfuls of chopped bell pepper from Azaril's cutting board and drops them into a wok. She spoons some of the onions out of the shallow pool of olive oil in the skillet and adds them to the peppers. "Although I guess it hasn't been more than seventy-two hours, so he doesn't fit the missing persons report requirements yet, if memory serves me."

Azaril stops chopping. "We figured the police wouldn't be much help. You know, with all the craziness in the city, and the weird things, they'd have other priorities."

"Huh, you may be right." She asks some questions about the condition of the hotel room when they found it, then falls silent, her brow creasing above the black rim of the wok. Azaril watches, half-expecting that she's going to start chanting some mumbo jumbo. She looks up at him suddenly. "I'd say it seems more likely that your friend was injured in a mugging than that he ran off or disappeared into thin air. I'd figure him to be laying out in an alley, unconscious. Weirdness and craziness doesn't mean that the same-old same-old takes a holiday to make room for it." Her laugh is humorless.

It unnerves Langston to see the alarm in Azaril's face. "Since it's been a while that he's been missing, Aunt Reginia, and we haven't begun to seriously pursue the possibility of foul play, maybe you could, if you can, try to give us a clue. It's possible that this is an emergency."

Langston is prepared for a tart response, though he guesses that Reginia, mercurial in mood and occasionally in principle, has suddenly taken an interest. "Tell me what you know," she says, and she listens quietly while salting and peppering the sizzling mélange of onions, peppers, and chicken strips in the wok.

Langston listens, too, because Azaril does most of the talking, stopping from time to time only to check that his version of the facts matches Langston's. Langston grunts and nods, mostly. He has the perverse desire to challenge Azaril about a crucial fact, just to mess everything up. If his eyes were like mood rings, they would bit by bit tint a darker and deeper shade of jealous green.

When the story is done, Aunt Reginia is holding a measuring

cup of arborio rice in her hand, poised to pour it into the skillet. Her hand does not move. "Say your friend's name," she says mildly. "Say it three times, slowly, then say it three times again. Both of you."

Langston is reluctant. Azaril, eager, begins, and Langston, seeing Azaril's eyes widen and his mouth begin to frown when he notices Langston isn't helping, joins in, a syllable or so behind. Langston feels himself shaking, Azaril hears himself singing. The chant, the hymn, the psalm—it sounds like one of these as they say the words, the vibration of the name in their ears growing, spreading, becoming tentacled, stronger, and stranger than they had any reason to anticipate. It's as if the broiling heat of Damian's name in their throats sweeps the walls and rattles the grandfather clock in the corner. It makes their eyes film over, momentarily toppling the foundations of perception, so that what is close to them seems to retreat, what is far swings near.

When they stop, unaccountably breathless, they expect a thunderclap and perhaps a flourish of arctic wind or a flurry of fiery hail. But there's only the sound of the vegetables and chicken, hissing as they wilt in their juices.

"Damian Sundiata," Reginia repeats. The cup of rice is still in her hand. "But that's not his real name."

"No," Langston says. "He changed it. It used to be Damian Garrow."

"I didn't know that!" Azaril says.

"Shhh," Reginia admonishes him. Then, suddenly: "Oh, shit. I've burned the damn onions. Why, why under heaven and earth can I not get my mind and fingers together to cook a simple meal? Good Jesus! Damn, damn, damn!" She bends over the stove and starts furiously digging with a spoon at the onions in the wok. With an edge in her voice that they hope only has to do with the onions, she says, "Boys, I tell you what: I don't know where your friend is. Couldn't get a fix on him. Which is odd. I'm usually damn good at that sort of thing. But the hit I get is that it's all connected in some way. Damian 'disappears,' and the Castros show up and vanish. You're present or linked to at least part of both events. That's too much coincidence to be coincidental. Now the fact that I can't even get a regional or hemispheric drop on this Damian could mean that he's under psychic cover—which I doubt, because he'd have to know his way around for that to be the case. More likely it means something else is going on . . . something—"

Azaril almost shouts over her. "What?!"

Reginia slides him a look that causes silence to prevail for a few moments. "*Something*," she says at last, "that's more *general*, something having to do with the phenomena we've been talking about tonight. Like your friend—like the Castros—might not be *here*. They might be in one of the other places. Which surprises the heck out of me."

Langston finds himself raising his hand. "I don't under—"

"See," she says quickly, "these Castros everyone keeps seeing could very possibly be Castros from parallel realities."

Azaril squints. "Like *Star Trek* . . .?"

"It's not so very far-fetched," Reginia says. "There are scientists who claim that the fact that gravity is relatively weak compared to forces like the nuclear force or electromagnetism is an effect of the presence of parallel universes. They could be crackpots, but who knows? And we do know for verifiable laboratory-tested fact that photons have been shown to tunnel through barriers they shouldn't be able to move through, and that they even move faster than the speed of light for a flash, and that's not supposed to happen either." Langston and Azaril stare dumbly. "No, really. Theoretically the particles of energy that make up a parallel Castro could end up here, running like a fool down Calle

Ocho. 'Course it should take longer than the life of planet Earth for phenomena like Castro tunneling through the weak barriers between parallels to occur, but still . . ." The funny looks on their faces begin to irritate her. "Do either of you understand anything about quantum cosmology?"

Langston looks querulously at Azaril, Azaril at Langston.

"Good Lord, do they teach you children anything in those colleges these days? Look, this is the most basic stuff . . ." Maintaining her focus on the disaster in the pan, she launches into a theoretical account of the birth of the universe that has them wagging their chins in a mixture of total incomprehension and delighted surprise at their brief match strikes of understanding. They do manage to put together a fuzzy picture in their minds—the effect, perhaps, of knowledge gained by intravenous psychic transmission. Get a picture, Reginia says, of bubbles of concentrated light, sometimes thickly clustered, sometimes far-flung, tiny half globes and quarter globes. Think of a view of streetlamps and house lights in a densely populated city, beaming from the steep slopes of a row of hills at night. See that, she urges them, and there you see a not unreasonable model of the universe entire, which is to say all of everything that can be, all the universes: a glorious latticework, a jeweled netting. All these bubbles, which from your view are lit rooms shining through windows and moving car headlights and metal surfaces that reflect the light that passes over them, are, from a divine point of view, each a universe. Ours is some thousands of millions of light years across, and others are mere baby universes: tiny, tiny, tiny, almost infinitely more tiny than the smallest globule of drool on the corner of your lip. A huge number of these small bubbles appear and disappear with a swiftness that makes your slipperiest thought seem like a redwood tree by comparison. But under certain conditions, these baby universes, these little bubbles, could suddenly expand—like the Big

Bang, the super-heating, dimension-cracking conditions of which led our own universe to spread out in search of *lebensraum*.

"According to this theory all that can exist does exist at least in some way," Reginia says, "from possibilities of infinitesimal probability to the things so highly probable they pass for what's real: the gravitational pull of planets, the shoes hurting my damn feet, Newton tossing his apple or whatever. The real, though, is only what ends up being the most probable—for reasons we don't know except that it has something to do with consciousness itself."

She starts in on Heisenberg then—we can never be sure where a particle of energy is or what its velocity might be, because a particle isn't a discrete little pinprick so much as it's a wave, a material graph of the possible: on some level it will be and is everywhere and every-when; particles of energy are the fundamental constituents of reality; they're what we and everything is. "So just as on the macro level, on the slope of the hill I asked you to picture, there are all sorts of possible universes, on the micro level there are also all sorts of possible heres and nows, lots of possible windows and houses."

Reginia stops to search their faces.

"Yeah, like in that movie . . ." Langston mutters.

"Yes, but it's a genuine theory, a better explanation of reality on the large scale than all your capitalism and fundamentalism hoogabooga," Reginia insists. She tries again: "Think back to those lights glowing on the hillside and zero in on one house. Imagine because of a trick of the angle of view, or because of the way the air is moving or because you're high or whatever"—small wheeze of disgust— "that the image flickers, you see it giving off emanations: so that for just a moment you see surrounding it, haloing it, ghost images of the house, hundreds of them, more popping up every second. These *exist*. They are parallel, quantum realities created by each divergent choice made—each different position along a spectrum of possibility—of each particle of physical being. If a photon is observed to move off in one direction rather than the other, the possibility that it could have moved off in the other direction must happen, somewhere some-when in quantum space-time, because everything that can happen does. If a giraffe strips the bark of one tree rather than another, the same effect."

Langston feels moved to rescue his aunt from being considered a loon. "This is interesting, but . . . you don't mean—"

Azaril jumps in. "You mean Damian's somehow—in a different house, or something? He's not in Miami? Or Florida even?"

"No!" Reginia jabs the spoon at Azaril. "But that's a decent start. Unlike my nephew, who should know better, you already have a solid idea of how gathering knowledge from intuition rather than the five senses works. Remember what I said about psychic time? That colleague of mine, Eric, who figured the limestone must have come from Atlantis—Eric by the way is a pretty eminent oracle—got that idea because the vibrations he picked up gave him the idea of *very old* and *sunk into the sea*. Which happens to be the definition of limestone, more or less, so it wasn't exactly Eric's finest moment as a psychic reader, but you see what I mean? Atlantis popped up for him because Atlantis figures in his personal idiosyncratic dictionary of archetypes as a synonym for old and sunk into the sea, among other things. He probably watches too many Disney movies. Now, if I read someone and see she has a family issue, and I get a picture of the Romanovs in a gray photograph, that don't mean she's the missing Anastasia or Catherine the Great reincarnated. It does probably mean the family is very insular and sheltered, unaware of its peculiar outmoded ways and the enemies around it. Although"—she raises the spoon into the air to punctuate—"we mustn't get over-dazzled by our rational explanations. The first thing you gotta understand about physics, cosmology, and really all the sciences of the out-there and the in-here," she taps her chest, "is that it would be ridiculous to suppose we know very much. Compared to what we don't know, what we do know is like a snap of your fingers. The muckety-mucks at Harvard and Berkeley like to tell you what can't be. What they mean is that whatever it is, they don't have the tools to measure it or the theory to explain it. Is your Castro a mass hallucination or a bundle of energy that tunneled between parallel universes? No reason both can't be true."

"Which means, in Damian's case?" Langston asks. He hopes his tone doesn't betray the fact that he's trying hard to temper exasperation.

"It means your friend is *caught*. Snatched. Snatched to somewhere that I can't pinpoint. Feels to me like Damian is *between*. Profoundly between. To me the picture comes up as being caught between the breaks in probability that separate parallel universes. Caught, or suspended, like somebody on a cross—'course we know where that imagery comes from, we can't get away from it in this culture—but it feels almost like this Damian is crucified. Azaril might think of it as being caught outside the house. No reason both can't be true. The important thing is, whether he's caught between the infinite forces present at the Schwarzschild radius that would fuse a body into something smaller than an atom in considerably less than a millisecond—or he's trapped in a drug fugue because he ingested a tablet of something intended to tranquilize pachyderms—or two thugs have him between them pulling on either of his arms until he rips apart: your friend is in trouble. You need to go get him."

Langston feels his stomach clench. "He's in danger?" He hears himself sputtering and knows it's because he's trying to hold back recognition rippling through his body. "But how could we, how could the police 'go get him'?"

Reginia shakes her head. "Not the police. You. Especially *you*, Langston. I do find—Michael! Miiiiichael!"

When Michael arrives his breath is short, and his eyebrows are drawn down low. He does not speak but waits, arms folded, for Mother's command. Reginia's rinsing off her spoon and doesn't look up. "Baby, go back down there and get me that box of your father's things. The big carton, not the shoebox. You know where that is?" Michael knows where that is; he grimaces, turns on his heel, and goes.

"You're both males. Can anyone tell me why that child always comes to me with his face scrunched up like he just put his nose in a dog's behind?" Reginia sighs, as she leaves the sink and takes the cups of rice to spread out over the surface of the skillet. "I was about to add, that I do find your friend all over you, Langston. When you said his name, pieces of you lit up—red, a splash of purple. Know what I mean? I was looking for him, but I kept finding *you*. Come here." Langston hesitates, then walks over to her. "Closer, child. Right. Here . . ." Reginia points to Langston's stomach, a half finger's length below the sternum. "Here," and she points to the center of his chest, where his heart beats. "And here," at the apple of his throat. "It's like his scent is on you. These could be blockages of some kind. I'd have to do a proper reading."

"What about me?" Azaril asks. "You find him on me?"

Reginia pauses and squints at him. "Yes. Some. But not as much."

The door to the kitchen opens, slowly, and Michael leans in, his arms full with a hefty and much-dented brown carton. "Where you want it, Ma?"

"There should be a book on the top, Michael. Take that out

for me, please, and place it on the table. Then you can take the box back to the basement. I don't want that man's paraphernalia clogging up my workroom." She adds sweetly, "Thank you, sweetie."

Michael coughs as the dust rises from the interior of the carton; it seems, for a moment, as if his hair, skin, and eyes have gone gray. The book he unceremoniously abandons on the table is heavy enough to make a very loud noise when it falls, and it causes the slicing knife to skip on the breadboard.

The book's cover is a dull red, and faceless, without word or symbol. "Can you believe that carton and a shoebox—with a pair of shoes I bought him, thank you very much—is all that man left when he took off? These musician types, they travel light. 'All you need is your art and a plate of good southern red beans,' that man said. With his cornpone Alabama ass. Good red beans and his piano, which he had crated up and sent to him in Japan. Never date a man from Alabama! They get messed up over there, dealing with all those hateful white folks. When he skipped out of here, he left this book behind. He used to say it brought him good luck. Then again, when his music wasn't coming together for a long stretch, he'd complain it laid a curse on him. I call the thing *Hex*, which, I believe, was to be its original title."

Langston leans over the table to look at it. "What's it about?"

"The story as Dilbert told it to me is that a couple of children of the old-money American aristocracy in its high autumn—one, Aden Rose, a ne'er-do-well, and his wife, Atalanta, the daughter of a crazy classicist who gave her 'a man's education'—decided to become anthropologists after the Great War, and selected the religious 'superstitions' of the so-called primitive as their field of study. They hadn't a lick of training, but being rich and pampered, they had plenty of cash to squander and, I must say, a healthy dose of chutzpah. Interviewed a bunch of people, paid them, I guess, mostly charlatans who claimed to have in their possession the occult secrets of darkest Africa. Some of these folks actually had the Roses writing down spells where you sing what amounts to a chorus of 'Dixie' backwards and sprinkle salt in a doorway on the night of a full moon to summon a demon—just out and out foolishness like that. Still, after a couple years of travel on both sides of the Atlantic, up and down the Caribbean, plus the obligatory stop in New Orleans, they put together a manuscript which they snookered the publishing house of Harcourt, Brace in New York into buying. The manuscript is the very thing you now have in your hand.

"The Roses spent more than a decade collecting all their fake junk, but in the end the manuscript wasn't published. The Roses had a vanity press print it up for them, and what you see before you is one fruit of that determined effort. Somehow this bound copy of the manuscript found its way into the capable hands of a conjure woman in New Orleans. You may not know about conjure women, Azaril, but the women and men of conjure were practitioners of certain kinds of knowledge passed down from the West African faiths native to the slaves, knowledge which they transformed to meet the new circumstances, and disguised to avoid the persecution of the white folks. Conjure is a cousin to vadoun, obeah, Santeria, all that."

"I know something about that stuff," Azaril says—somewhat defensively, Langston thinks.

"Good on ya, sweetie. Now, this conjure woman, a Miss Verity Gapstone, her signature's somewhere in the back of the book you have in your hands—Dilbert never found out much about her but turns out she had a scholarly inclination as well as a store of knowledge, and she set about to correct the mistakes in the text. Either because the Roses asked her or for her own purposes, I guess. Wrote all over the margins of the thing, crossed out this, that, and whatever. She didn't finish, 'cause the emendations stop about halfway through. Anyway it passed its way down by Lord knows what paths to someone else, a gentleman to this day only identified as a dapper, dignified, nappy-headed Negro—these are my ex-husband's words—who so loved the way my ex played his jazz piano that he gave it to him as a gift. This was in the early '70s."

"This guy gave Uncle Dilbert a marked-up book as a gift for playing so well?" Langston interrupts.

"Sounds fishy to you, too, huh?" Reginia says. "Well, Dilbert said how he guessed the book had some personal significance to the man—maybe he was somehow connected to the Roses. Anyway Dilbert had all kinds of creatures runnin around after him giving him gifts all the time—girls, women, some men, too. Frankly I don't think it was always just for his playing."

"You think the man was homosexual?" Azaril asks.

Langston rolls his eyes at the word, and Reginia eyes Azaril so shrewdly that he begins to blush. "I have no idea," she says, as if she has exactly the right idea but refuses to communicate it. "Langston's uncle kept the gift all these years, but left it with me when he ran off. And when he finished packing up this box, he said, 'Give this to old Langston sometime, he might appreciate it.' Who knows, maybe 'cause of the—sexuality connection. I wasn't in the mood to pay his final instructions much heed at the time, and in fact I may have said something to the effect of fuck you, write a will. But evidently what he said found some room somewhere in my head, because our conversation tonight reminded me of it. So—Langston, that's yours. Enjoy."

Langston murmurs his gratitude. Already he's transfixed by the book. He holds it, caressing it, running his index finger along the ridges of the pages and over the rough red cover.

Azaril is puzzled. "But, does this have anything to do with Damian? What should we—what should Langston do with it?"

"Do with it? Baby, don't ask me. Spells, incantations, incense, and goat's blood at the crossroads under the dark moon, feeding the Loas, all that hoopla—no sister. That is faith stuff, and faith stuff is the root of sorcery stuff, and sorcery is not my bag. Oh, I can talk the talk. I can speak the language of the profession. I respect the belief behind the ceremony. What works for you, works for you. But for me, when it comes down to it, give me the now, the down-to-earth."

"But you're a psychic, Mrs. Wolfe. That's not exactly down-to-earth," Azaril says. He adds hastily, "Not for most people, anyway."

"I don't like that word, *psychic*. I'm a *sensitive*. It's not easy to explain. But, since you're here with my nephew and he thinks he loves you—or something—I'll tell you how it is for me. First off, though, I want you to take that measuring cup over there, Azaril, no, the glass one, and ladle me out a half cup of the broth—oh, but first strain out the vegetables with the colander! Then you can pour the broth back into the pot. Right. OK. Give me the cup, and just stand there ready to give me another half cup when I ask for it."

Reginia begins to arc her wooden spoon through the swarm of rice and across the bottom of the skillet.

"From the first day it came, I just knew. Knew it. Saw it, heard it, tasted it, smelled it. In the days of my girlhood, being prone to do girlish things, I'd tell what I knew out loud and not stop to think about it. Like when my wild, beautiful mother used to have me sit at dark tables in juke joints while she danced and did her young-woman thing. Now, your mother hates me to tell stories about your grandmother like this, Langston, but it's the truth, Mama was a wild one. Well, one night we were at the joint and I started screaming—girlish, silly, as I said. Mama came over to shut me up because even in the juke joint a scream might be something to remark upon, and I tell you when she asked me what was wrong I looked at her like she was crazy. 'Mama, who you looking at?' (I thought I was so grown sometimes.) 'Did you or did you not see that man with the big belly and little legs all up on Miss Larsen open his mouth on her face and breathe fire all over her? The smoke's so thick I can't see if she made it out, and if it's choking me, it's about killed her!' Well, Mother dear, the wild thing, told me to hush and gave me a drink, and went back out onto the dance floor. When I saw Miss Larsen again after the smoke cleared, she was bones and a worn robe of skin, and a big hideous skull on a stick neck, grinning like a Cheshire.

"Next day Miss Larsen and this big-bellied man were married, and in a year she was dead: he took everything from her. Money, sex, house, food. Sex. Left her dried up with nothing. The neighborhood scuttle was that she died happy because until and beyond the moment she passed, Miss Larsen believed that man loved her. Her family wanted to bury her like a good Baptist, but he had her cremated. Another half, Azaril. You know what I'm telling you? I saw it, no different from if you look over and see a painting on the wall. Nothing to it. Nothing spooky or out of this world, no gods nor trolls nor kittens of Beelzebub or any of that yin-yang, just it's there and you'd have to be closing your eyes not to see it. You know?"

Azaril affects a look of comprehension. Indeed he has understood, at least some of it, but it was the part about Langston loving him that makes him stand now without the full weight of his two feet on the floor, swaying like a hammock in a stiff breeze. Langston, surprisingly, is so engrossed in what his aunt is saying and in the way the book seems to make his palms tingle that he tags the *love* word, locks it and files it under FUTURE WORRIES and lets it go, so that he can get back to business.

"As for that book, now—! That book is all about magic and mumbo jumbo. I've read it, I understand what I can, I told you what I could tell you. But I don't mess with it. You shouldn't, either." Reginia flicks an impatient finger at the book, and she sees that in Langston's hands it is no longer dusty or frayed, but glowing, radiant, cherished, like a poltergeist that has made its peace, a minor forest god at last appeased. This troubles her a little. "Not that that'll stop you."

"There is, then, a connection between Damian's disappearance, the Miami stuff, *and* this book," Langston says confidently. The heft of a book in his hand grounds him.

"I don't think that thing will give you much *direct* guidance as to what's going on, especially not what's happening in the city," Aunt Reginia avers. "But the reason it came to mind is that I put the fire that lights up in you when you say Damian Sundiata's name together with the little bit I can pick up when I fumble around with *Hex*. I don't want to get too technical. You always sound like a fool when you get technical talking about this stuff, and I don't like that glazed-eye look people get. But everything in the world, everything in the universe, whirls and spins and spirals. And everything spins and whirls in its own unique way. But then some things spin similar to other things. Family members, for example. It's all about vibration, and if you consider superstring theory—well, anyway. There is a vibration I pick up from that book—and a strong one—that feels a lot like the way you light up when you say Damian's name. Similar spin."

Langston's mouth drops open despite himself. "You mean Damian used to own this book?"

Reginia frowns. "Not Damian, not likely, no. Too young. Probably more like a relative. His daddy owned it at some point, maybe. That would make more sense. The book's got masculine vibrations all over it. I reckon old Verity Gapstone musta been pretty butch herself. 'Nother half, Azaril. My hunch—but it's a strong hunch, so maybe I should say my almost for certain ninety percent sure belief—is that you track down Damian's daddy, then you'll track down Damian. They are connected, and connected right through the text and margins of *Hex*. And somehow—I couldn't get technical with this hunch if I tried—these Miami apparitions are in some way, probably indirectly, involved."

Langston—moved by impulses he would under ordinary circumstances instinctually crush, but now, with *Hex* in his hands, he feels he can trust—chooses this moment to reveal what he's seen to them. He condenses what he guesses about the drugs influencing him at the moment of his vision, and tries to repress the fact that he was lying on the floor of a club at the time, thinking this an unconvincing locale for oracular insight (but Reginia keeps asking questions). Both Reginia and Azaril listen in respectful silence as he tells them, in as much detail as he can recall, about the sky, and Damian, and Quentin and Reynaldo.

"What was it you heard him say?" Azaril demands when Langston's finished.

Langston can't look at him, feeling overwhelmed by guilt. "Um, I don't remember for sure, it was—an expletive, and then, 'I think it's gonna kill me this time.' I would have mentioned it before, but you know, I just thought it was—you know, being drunk and all . . ."

Reginia makes a scoffing noise. "Drunk, hmmp. Sometimes the right combo of drugs are a good working tool. You know about mushrooms and psilocybin and all that, I presume. What I'm interested in is the 'this time' bit." Reginia frowns. "That fits, though, doesn't it? If *Hex* has any connection to this, and Damian's family has a connection, there could be something recurring or habitual in the phenomenon: families, books, they're always about repetition. Magical phenomena, too, for that matter. You recall any strange things like these Castro apparitions happening around Damian in the past?"

Langston draws a blank—though he suspects there's something he's not remembering.

Reginia shrugs. "Anyhoo, my baby has had a vision! Isn't that cute. I knew you were caught up in this. Damian got snatched, but when it happened, he threw a line out to you. Now," she inhales, long and deep. "Boys, you have worked me *over* this evening, so Langston, you finish the stirring. When you can see the bottom of the pan while you stir, pour more broth in. It needs about ten more minutes, and that, my sweetlings, is when we eat. I hope y'all don't mind the taste of burnt onions. I don't plan to go through this all over again."

6

South Beach, around 10:00 P.M.

The plate glass window of the restaurant is framed by massive curtains as soft and lazy as loungewear, and the low illumination that circulates like cigarette haze above the round tables gives the environs a laid-back, summer-evening-on-the-veranda feel. In this milieu you are invited to live out the sensual clichés of southern gothic: walk to the restroom in a slow, hip-swinging sashay; fill your hand with a snifter of Jack Daniel's or a chalice brimming with mint julep, and watch your dinner partner's succulent, wet lips through heavy-lidded eyes.

Reynaldo and Quentin have choice seating at the window's northern edge. Quentin's head lolls against the curtain, his right cheek massaged in furrows of carmine crushed velvet. Indeed he does handle a slender vial of mint julep in his slender fingers, and his contentment with the state of things is such that every now and again he emits a low, furry purr. Reynaldo, glassy-eyed, sucks the taste of cranberry chutney off his finger. They have scarcely spoken a word for thirty minutes, being beguiled by the window sights and by the food, two plump, pearly white catfish encased in a savory crust of cornmeal.

This late-evening somnolence is broken only by the occasional appearance of their waitress, a six-foot-tall drink of liquid with a winsome little smile and graceful arms and hands that glide in and out of their sight like snatches of dream. She leans across Reynaldo to replenish his water. The tiny hairs of her forearm brush ever so slightly across his nose as she straightens. They both feel it. "Sorry," she says, quietly and with more of that dreamy charm.

When she has again disappeared, Quentin (stroking his slick, much-stroked head of hair) says, "You got all the bitches after you."

Reynaldo—his head was turned away, watching her ass take a turn around the corner of the bar—slowly comes to consciousness and finds himself peering through wisps of ether at the face of an alien entity. "What?"

"Mm, yeah" (smiling, purring). "They don't walk past the table without looking twice."

"That's disgusting—the way you call them bitches, like that's just their natural name."

"Oh, please. I *admire* bitches. I look up to bitches. I believe in and kneel down and pray to Our Mother Goddess Bitch, Life Herself. I don't mean disrespect by it."

"I see. And are you a bitch? Are you OK with somebody calling you bitch?"

Quentin, working Miss DeShon, takes up her fork. "Oh, no, I did not say I was no*body's* bitch. I didn't hear the word *bitch* coming from your lips last night."

Reynaldo's glassy expression flattens and hardens, becomes a sheer, arctic shelf. "No, because the word was *itch*. I had one, and I used you to scratch it."

"Mmhm. How 'bout I reach across this table and scratch you for real."

"Anyway," Reynaldo says. He could go further still with this, but he doesn't want to. It might get too good to him. He has noted this, that since Damian disappeared nothing makes him feel stronger or more brilliant, sharper or more razor-edge clear than teasing Quentin, needling and pricking him. It might get so good he'd never want to stop. In the interest of saving his immortal soul he heads off in a different direction. "I have something serious I need to discuss with you."

"Ew. Can't you relax? Would somebody get this ho a drink, please? He doesn't shut up unless you put something in his mouth."

"You don't really know anything about Damian, do you? It's a big made-up story."

"Look, every godfatherfuckin word I said to y'all was true. Every word."

"You can be honest with me, Quentin. What is it you really want? From Langston and Azaril, or from Damian—assuming you actually even know him?"

Quentin purses his lips in a certain way—a move that mimics his mother, Miss Maria Shaw, which, if Reynaldo knew her, might alert him to his peril. He says loudly, "Gaw, just cuz I sucked your dick till you came in my mouth last night doesn't mean you own me and shit."

This little missile is timed to perfection and detonates precisely on target, just as the waitress arrives with tonight's dessert menu printed on two slivers of purple crepe paper. Reynaldo sees her and blushes. He glares at Quentin in wrath while the waitress's smile dries and cracks like mud on the desert floor—but only for a moment. This time she keeps her eyes and arm hairs to herself, thank you, and she doesn't even look at Reynaldo when she replaces his empty plate with the menu. "Specials are on the board," she says with bright dismissiveness.

Reynaldo watches her go. He looks back to Quentin, whose grin is the visage of innocence. He wants to be angry, but a laugh finds its way out of his throat. "You sick motherfucker," he says warmly.

"You bitch." Quentin laughs, too, and beneath the table strokes Reynaldo's shod feet with his bare toes.

A boom of thunder shatters the air. For an instant the restaurant heaves, as if thrice a bull's bulk has just been hurled against the walls.

"Unhand me, lout!" someone shouts, the voice a piercing counterpart to the thunder's heft.

"I was just trying to help!"

That is the maître d'. His plaintive entreaty falls on deaf ears. He wants to catch her or delay her somehow, as she is clearly quite dangerous, but he cannot move, pinned and hog-tied to the spot by some rogue strip of gravity. Helplessly he watches while she moves free and unfettered like a blade over ice, like a phantasm out of nightmares. She is a tall, terrible, beautiful woman whose shoulders look to be wider than Gibraltar. The restaurant's patrons forget their meals to gawk, but they cannot see her very well, or else there is some veil over their perception so that they cannot see her all at once. She appears to them in pieces: clothing like battlements on a medieval tower—an all-black wrap of indeterminate material and volume that falls from her neck to below her elbows, a jet black long dress somehow skin-tight and yet tightly Puritan, capped with black-heeled boots. And then that demon's face: a veritable mess of snow-blond hair, albino eyes with a Medusa stare to freeze marrow into stone, and an open mouth, red red red as a Weimaraner hound's.

"Mister Fleetwood!" this apparition cries, and damn if it doesn't start thundering again.

"Mister Fleetwood!" Suddenly she is before Quentin and Reynaldo, and she slams one hand down on their table so that it pitches to and fro. Reynaldo's glass, pretty but regrettably fragile, splits in a meandering ream from rim to stem.

"You are friends of Mr. Fleetwood?"

Reynaldo, his hands to his ears, finds the courage to answer. "Fleetwood?"

"*Langston* Fleetwood!"

Somewhere back there in the world, the restaurant manager bites clean through the edge of her fingernail while her bartender dials the police.

"Yeah, yeah, Langston, we know him . . ." Quentin says, over the Klaxon ringing in his head.

"Shhh!" Reynaldo admonishes him, and kicks him under the table.

"Where is he?" the woman demands.

"He's out," Reynaldo says defiantly. "He'll be back when he gets back."

The woman holds him for a moment in her eyes. "Ah. Capital," she says and smiles, almost sweetly.

The air seems to move again, and everyone in the restaurant gulps for breath. The woman bends closer to the table. Her breath reeks. She whispers, as if suddenly overcome by the need for decorum. "I was concerned that he might have departed. My name is Roan Gillory. Mr. Fleetwood and I are well acquainted. I am very fond of Mr. Fleetwood, as you, being his friends also, will surely understand. (And be certain you *are* his friends, my pets; I would not take kindly to his enemies.)"

She directs a discerning look first at Reynaldo, who drops his eyes immediately, and then at Quentin, who cannot match her and drops his gaze to Reynaldo's spilled water, spreading like a plague and seeping into the cotton tablecloth. "Do give Mr. Fleetwood a message for me, won't you? Tell him I must see him at once! I don't care what hour he returns, he must come see me immediately! Do you understand? Tell him just that!"

She turns to leave, but then casts a glance back over her shoulder. "Be *certain* to give him the message."

Diners scurry from Mrs. Gillory's path, each under his, her, or its own power. Wind thrashes against the plate glass window. When the mod, youthful manager reaches to open the door for Mrs. Gillory (the customer's needs always come first), a zephyr whisks her off her feet and drops her to the floor. Just as the door swings behind her, she reaches into her bosom and flicks a wad of hundred-dollar bills from her fingers. High into the air the little bundle vaults, and then at the zenith of its flight explodes and falls apart. Twenty green bills drift to the carpet. "For your damages."

It takes a few minutes for the dust to settle. Someone suggests calling the police, and someone else curtly asks what the hell good that's gonna do; the bartender says, Hello, I called them, and then someone else mentions that the world has gone crazy, didn't you hear that Castro was seen tonight on a balcony of the Radisson, playing the ukulele? Another fellow shakily demands the drink he ordered before the visitation, which (once the manager gets back up and puts some lotion on her knees) serves in a small way to make everyone start feeling on top of things again. The tall-drink-of-water waitress starts collecting drink orders at her tables, but she steers clear of table seven, where the two nasty queens are sitting.

Quentin looks in alarm at Reynaldo. "Who is that crazy vampire-looking bitch?"

"*W*itch," Reynaldo corrects him wearily. He stares blankly at the door to the restaurant, disoriented and yet incongruously calm, aware of, grateful even, for his solidity and coherence, like a lone unscathed survivor of tempest and flood who stands on dry ground, surrounded by devastation. "I guess we'd better get our check and get back to the hotel," he says.

On the Key, late

The clock edges 1:00 A.M. when Langston and Azaril find themselves again amid the muddle of Aunt Reginia's front yard, their bellies and senses gorged with food. Gabriel and Michael have already paid their respects and retired for the evening—or rather they were forced to, since this is a school night—and so now it is the three adults, lingering on the doorstep.

Langston carries his gift. It has not strayed far from his reach throughout the evening, and more than once already he has been caught checking out of the conversation to peruse the book's pages. Aunt Reginia presses him repeatedly to her bosom in farewell hugs, and also presses bills into his palm amounting to one hundred and fifty dollars.

Langston protests.

"It's walking-around money, sweetie. Take it and shut up," Reginia whispers. She smoothes over the trickle of tears on her cheek with the back of her hand—she dislikes partings—and then abruptly steps off the walk and reaches into the weeds. "Have you met Morningstar?"

Azaril has been standing by awkwardly, and when he sees the snake he is taken aback and makes a face. Reginia holds out her arms and allows the snake to investigate her.

"Wow," Azaril says. "You've got that thing in hand."

"Yeah. But he's getting old," she says, and suddenly she sounds very old. "Starting to slip on me." She bends to let Morningstar free in the grass. "When are y'all planning to go back to California?"

"Our tickets are for return on Tuesday, but it only costs seventy-five dollars to change them, and the way things are going . . ." Langston replies.

"You might need some more money, then."

"Aunt Reginia."

Reginia is rooting around in the pockets of her pants. "Here, this'll make it an even three. Take it. You might need it."

"Aunt Reginia, you know Mom doesn't like you to—"

"You are not a child anymore, Langston. You can choose to accept or reject gifts without Mama's approval, can't you? And this cash isn't for free, now. You have to do me two favors in return. One, call me to let me know what's going on with all this. At *least* until the thing's settled, I expect to hear from you every couple days, minimum. OK?"

Both Langston and Azaril nod, though neither has any clear idea of how they're going to go about settling anything.

"Second, listen very carefully to what I'm going tell you: you are investigating a disappearance, and I am telling you that disappearance is a *condition*. It is a *state*. Of existence. Black folks in this country been appearing and disappearing and most of all being disappeared since they disappeared from Africa. I hope I don't have to spell this out for you. There is both a physical and a metaphysical component to everything that happens under the sun and moon. And look over your shoulder. You can count on pursuit."

"What do you mean?"

"Certain folk come sniffing when power gets worked like it's working now with these Castros running around. Jackals. Witches, warlocks, werewolves."

This is more than mildly alarming to Azaril. "Werewolves?"

Langston, however, is dispassionate in reply. "OK, Aunt Reginia. Thank you. For the dinner and the advice. And the book! We'll be talking."

"It was great to meet you, Mrs. Wolfe."

"Fine, fine, my pleasure, my pleasure. You not too drunk,

now? There's plenty of room in the boys' wing, like I said. You'd have your privacy."

Azaril wonders what exactly she means by that, but in any case there is little need to respond, since the issue has already been twice settled in the last hour. Langston has had only two glasses of wine, so he'll drive; they really should get back and see if there's any news on Damian, and to make sure Quentin hasn't absconded with everything in their hotel room (that part was supposed to be a joke). Reginia isn't satisfied, so she'll stand there on the doorstep until she sees the car pull away without hitting a lamppost.

Langston is very quiet once they close the gate behind them. Good-byes are trying for him, too, especially where his mother and Aunt Reginia are concerned.

Azaril is drunk, in a mild, sloshy way. "Do you ever get the feeling that you're a well-cut piece in one very strange and humongous puzzle?"

"What do you mean?"

"I mean, it's very weird, how all that fell into place. The book, the connection with Damian, your aunt. Us all being here together. That dream you had. At a time like this, with all this craziness happening."

"It could be coincidence. Or my aunt could have planned it. She's a Capricorn. They like to run everything."

"What about that werewolf shit?"

"I wouldn't go too crazy over the stuff she said, Azaril. She is gifted, but I'm sure you noticed that she's a little—abstract. I didn't understand half of what she said. She probably meant the *idea* of werewolves, or something. I don't know if I buy the idea that we're the keys to finding Damian. I could go along with the idea that his father is involved. He was—unpleasant, when I knew of him years ago."

"Do you think he was the one who gave your Uncle Dilbert this book?"

"That would be a wild coincidence. But nah. Sergeant Garrow was not dapper and not likely to be handing off gifts to male jazz pianists."

Azaril mulls this over. "Well, you said she's worked with the police before. I say we at least try to locate Garrow. Hey, you never asked her about Mrs. Gillory!"

"Oh, yeah. That's strange, that I forgot that."

"Hmm."

But Langston has other things on his mind. He complains that the cash is spilling out of his pocket and that he must tighten his shoelaces—and worries that his manner gives away how premeditated his actions are. Azaril doesn't seem to take anything amiss, so Langston hands him the keys and bids him go on ahead.

"You want me to take the book?" Azaril asks, feeling a spike in his curiosity since he hasn't been able to look at *Hex* for most of the evening.

"I got it. Go on, I'll catch up." Langston slowly kneels to the asphalt.

When Azaril is a yard and a half away, Langston drops his shoelaces, flips open *Hex* to the page he's dog-eared, and whispers, "I love you."

It begins as a query rather than a declaration. Yet it sounds good, it has a ring to it. It feels fine on the tongue, like wine. "I love you," he says again, quieter, using the words like a prism, to encase, to beatify and dangle like a Christmas ornament the surprising joy of it, this profound thing that he (maybe) feels. "I love you," he says, louder now: the third part of the incantation should be the most powerful and deeply felt, the book says.

But it feels to Langston as if he has spoken into a void; Azaril has vanished (Azaril has stepped into the car), and the darkness of the night smothers the sound of Langston's voice, the darkness holds it, and then scatters it, like petals on the wind.

Then he gets in the car, and they drive off.

~

(Later this night four bodies will lie in slumber, a snore here, a kind of tribbling noise there, a tiny spasmodic sigh. Langston will wake suddenly. His open eyes will burn and glow, slice through the darkness like the klieg lights of a police helicopter. Then, a panther in hunt, he'll move beneath the sheets he shares with Azaril, rising up upon his hip and elbow. He'll hover above Azaril's body, an apparition. "I love you," he will say again, and sprinkle the stubble from his razor gently over Azaril's head: the completion of a potent incantation, or so Langston hopes.)

Room 351, Wessex House

At about the time Langston and Azaril drive back onto Duval Street and head north, Mrs. Roan Gillory paces by her window overlooking a narrow street that leads to the beach. A few revelers pass to and fro; they shake maracas and have bells tied to the rings that pierce their navels and make a joyful racket. Mrs. Gillory might ordinarily be annoyed, but not tonight. She wishes that she, too, could be as carefree, that she could pierce every pierce-able piece of her flesh and take the beaches by storm. A bit of pain and a dollop of drunken debauch might do her good. Something to remind her of the flesh. Something to prove, even if it is a lie, the intransitive nature of reality.

There is nothing real anymore in her world. It is all ruins.

It is not pleasant to have a husband to whom one can refer metaphorically as a dog, but such griefs are not unknown to many women in the world. It doubles, no, trebles the unpleasantness to be somehow responsible for—in some thoroughly inexplicable way—*turning* one's husband into a four-legged, floppy-eared, cold-snouted, tail-wagging creature. This, surely, is a cross that no other woman in all history has ever had to bear. She does not want to live in a world where the line between thought and reality is so blurred, particularly when, once done, the deed can't be undone. Roan hadn't wanted such finality: teaching a Cro-Magnon like her husband a lesson is one thing, but the Alan Michael Gillorys of the world do have their uses, and it is frightening to think they might all, through some slip of her tongue, some momentary upsurge of bitterness, suddenly lose everything that makes them useful.

She lights a cigarette. How would that other Roan have handled it? No doubt she would never have found herself in such a position. No, the other Roan would have married better, done better, been in every way better. She was the very Bitch of Perfection.

The golden years of Roan Gillory's youth, the stretch of time between the ages of five and eleven, are lost to her, yanked by the roots out of the world we share into a realm of mystery whose secrets reveal themselves fitfully and mischievously, in places and at times when their reality can't be satisfactorily verified: in these moments Roan Gillory sometimes beholds scenes, snippets, played out before her eyes in which she is a participant, and that are so vivid, so fully detailed and weighted with gravity that they must surely be the visitations of memory. Or are they hallucinations?

The latter question—whether she is mentally ill—has been checked and rechecked for years, but neither neurologist nor psychiatrist has been able to truly settle the matter. Roan, her mother, her husbands, have all been assured on several occasions that, according to the best that science can determine, she is fully functioning, more or less stable, and certainly sane. At the very worst she is prey to occasional episodes of such minor duration that they do not qualify for any certain diagnosis. "All we can say," the doctor of the moment has now said innumerable times, "is that whether these visions are recovered memories or something else, they are an apparently benign consequence of the slight changes in her brain function that occurred due to the accident."

The Accident. Of which she has no memories, not even the tease of one. Having absorbed in her voluminous and eclectic encyclopedia of knowledge a smattering of basic Hindu teachings and an acquaintance with both Tibetan Buddhist and ancient Egyptian Books of the Dead, Roan Gillory came to the conclusion years ago that The Accident was a failed attempt by the cosmos to usher her on to her next existence. In lieu of her eternal soul's through-the-white-light passage to a new body, direct access to the person she was prior to 1953 has simply been denied; it is as if the angel of death, angered by his unexpected failure, now buzzes in her ear like a hornet, drowning out the sounds of her former life. In grander moments, when she is boring her family and friends once again with the claim that she "can do things," Roan muses that the part of her brain that might have been occupied holding on to dead memories has now been freed for other, more effectual activities. "I don't mean to be megalomaniacal," she has been heard to say, as coughs and fits of lint picking suddenly erupt around the room, "but I daresay that what happened to me was very much in the nature of a resurrection."

This theory annoys her mother, Anne, a well-educated woman with an empiricist's disregard for fancies of any kind. Anne is tiny, but she gives the impression of having been fashioned from the more durable elements of the earth. All iron and calcium, Anne was so clever concerning matters of the material world that at sixteen she had the foresight to eschew her parents' wild ways (they were busy gallivanting halfway around the globe in search of *magic*, of all things). She decided to save the dwindling family fortune by marrying into the very old and very rich Ansleys. "Generations of Yankee trading money and a fine railroad-and-banking robber baron fortune to top it off," Anne is still heard to remark on occasion—often while guiding you by the elbow on a stroll through her capacious gardens and speaking in a whisper that percolates with high-pitched giggles, as if she recognizes the vulgarity of any imputation that she researched the Ansley finances before reeling Roland Ansley in on her well-baited line, and yet craves the praise her hard-nosed stock trader's mentality is undoubtedly due. For a woman of Anne's temperament and substance, her fourth child Roan's bad luck is something of an affront: God's intention was surely not to resurrect Roan, for there is no such being and resurrections are merely mythological; and thus Roan's so-called Accident is, in Anne's estimation, the thinly traceable result of an obscure failure of Roan's will and foresight.

"Imagine a child who wanders off on the very day of her eleventh birthday, with all her little friends gathering at the camp to celebrate," Anne Ansley can still be heard to say on occasion. "A child who without any care or heedfulness in the world crosses some treacherous road, and is struck by a truck—a *truck*—being driven by some foreign drunkard who hadn't any business being there anyway! Far out in the Adirondacks even, in the very heart of nowhere, with not a hint of traffic anywhere to be seen, she managed to take leave of her senses and find the one penniless drunkard careening around on that one misbegotten road! At midday! Imagine!" In the last decade, the rueful tone with which Anne used to tell the story has lost its former bitterness. She speaks of The Accident now in an almost amused manner, as though the proven success of her other children has allowed her to regard Roan's misfortune as an intellectual puzzle that she's free to peruse at her leisure, like books about the history of China.

While innocent bystanders at the Ansley home either cringe at these revelations of family history or take venomous glee in them, Roan takes little umbrage. Like her mother, she, too, finds herself among heaped puzzle pieces when she tries to make sense of The Accident, though her perspective is considerably less detached. "And before, she was such a lovely child," Anne frequently adds, and it is the puzzle of that pronoun *she* and the genuine aura of admiration that colors Anne's manner when she speaks it that unseats Roan, that makes her feel that she might collapse in on herself in the middle of the after-dinner room, become smaller and smaller until she's no more than a proton, wiggling around the nucleus of an atom far vaster than the reach of her comprehension.

Who was she, that lovely girl, the girl Roan really was and is still supposed to be? It was Anne who began to call Roan's youth the "golden years," a term which was meant as a reproach, and which Anne defined by conjuring images of that other Roan's industriousness, her obedience, ladylike social grace, and sensitivity to the feelings of others.

"You were happy, Roan," Anne will say.

Roan, silent, defeated, wonders: Was she? *Was I?*

Then why throw it all away on an unpaved back road where the slope is so steep even an adult can't see above its crown and one is hidden from whomever is climbing the other side?

Only something powerful, something mighty before which one ought to bow down in awe could have mandated so complete a calamity. For when eleven-year-old Roan, her broken bones healed, emerged from an eighteen-day coma, she was not the Roan of old, she was a new being entirely, a girl who seemed to have lost many of her inhibitions in addition to her memory. She had been transformed into a copy of the original Roan, a creature as dark as the other Roan was golden.

It ought to have been clear that there was trouble in the offing when upon her arrival home from the hospital, Roan greeted her second-cousin-once-removed Edmond, who was among the welcome-back party. Anne, at first pleased to find her daughter's social graces intact, became alarmed when she saw the strange smile on Roan's face as Edmond spoke. Cousin Edmond, always a boor, began in his usual tactless way to detail the myriad ills which beset him, working himself up to the point of having tears well in his eyes as he lovingly complained of how he could no longer write letters by hand or stroke his cats or set his records on the phonograph because of his advanced arthritis. "Your arthritis!" Roan bellowed. Several heads turned. "It must be painful being so decrepit. The muscles just cramping up, becoming twisted and gnarled like old tree roots. As if they were shutting down, closing in on themselves. As if your whole body were some decaying, useless old thing about to die."

Roan's father, Roland, attributed his daughter's faux pas and sudden maturity of expression to lingering effects of The Accident, an excuse that managed to shield the family from the truth for a time (though Edmond henceforward did not accept invitations to Anne and Roland's homes, and indeed he died of a stroke not two years later). But no one could have predicted then how irrevocably Roan's behavior had been changed. After her return from near death, Roan embarked upon what from her bewildered parents' perspective was a life of serial misadventure.

Roan began to curse (of course Anne did as well, but never in public and so inventively). She insisted that her birthday no longer fell on August 21 but on September 9, the day when she recovered from her coma. She kissed her grandfather Aden's young valet-in-training on the lips—he was a Negro, you know—and she kissed him in front of everyone, she practically threw herself at him, she dived off the prow of the boat on the lake where she'd been fishing with her cousins, swam to the shore, and without even drying herself stomped up the stairs of the main cottage and into the sitting room, where she planted a very wet pair of lips on the young Negro's mouth, and kept them affixed there while the neighbors who had come for supper stared. (The Negro valet was henceforward not welcome at Camp Ansley.) On a trip to Paris sponsored by her girls' school, Roan snuck off from the other members of class to purchase and smoke what she was told was opium, and then went to see a Vietnamese psychic, who promptly told her that since the age of eleven her body had been occupied by an incorporeal alien from another galaxy.

Were it not for the fact that she was a crackerjack student who breezed the top scores in classes ranging from analytic calculus to Russian literature, Anne might have had the girl committed. It was even suggested by one of the Ansley brothers-in-law that Roan be given a lobotomy—not a mean lobotomy or a bad old-time lobotomy, of course, but a modern, newfangled lobotomy intended only to take the edges off her willful personality and prevent her from capsizing into lunacy. Present during this discussion was Roan's grandfather Aden, who adored Roan. Aden decked Roan's Ansley uncle (a man half his age) on the spot, employing a bastard version of martial arts capoeira that he'd picked up slumming in Rio. (Henceforward neither of Anne's parents was warmly welcomed at the Ansley cottage in Newport.)

Yet even Roan's doting grandparents failed to suspect the desperation in which she lived each day, the fear in her that was never fully quieted. The fragmentary visions of her former life taunted her, nagged her, settled in her bones like an insatiable ache.

In these brief flashes of sight Roan can never see the girl she used to be. She has no recollection before age eleven of ever staring at herself in the mirror or into a watery reflection. In each memory, whether of a bucolic scene in which she sits on the edge of the dock at Camp Ansley with her toes in the warm August water watching mosquitoes dance around the splotchy flesh of her legs, or whether she recalls listening with her back turned while her mother shouts at her father again, trying to stifle rage, Roan sees only pieces of herself: her skinny arms or thick ankles, the shadowy protrusion of her nose and a pouting lip, the grubby tomboy's fingernails, blond hair almost as white as snow blown into her eyes by the wind.

For a long time Anne plied her with photographs, as if the old Roan in glossy black-and-white could work magic and return her true daughter to her. But the pictures made Roan unhappy. She looked like that girl, only older; there in front of her own eyes lay a picture taken on the morning before the day that the small truck, slamming to a halt, struck her and sent her flying several feet down the hill. But somehow Roan couldn't manage the trick of the mind that would identify that image with herself. She needed the memories she could not summon in order to imagine, as those of us more fortunate are able so readily to imagine, that the two-dimensional image of a body whose cells we have long since shed and regenerated is continuous with the body we inhabit now, and that memories of the past, as hazy as they are, as pocked with half-truths as they become, belong to that image, are centered in that image.

Roan feared she might be insane, and fearing insanity she feared both being alone with her madness and being in the presence of people who might realize how crazy she was. She fervently hoped that something, anything, could bring her under control. As a direct consequence she found herself marrying Arthur Debenham Berry, a disastrous creature of her mother's invention. Without much hope Anne Ansley in May 1967 had traveled up from the north shore of Long Island to attend her daughter's Smith graduation. Anne participated gaily enough in all the commencement activities and barely batted an eyelash when Roan showed up at the Phi Beta Kappa ceremony barefoot. After Roland had showered Roan with graduation gifts and Roan's siblings were gathering for their departures, however, Anne pulled Roan aside. "There is a young man I think you should consider marrying," she said. Roan burst out laughing, but Anne had expected this, and she marched on bravely. "You've been mentioned to him as a prospect. He is a businessman and comes from a good family. Not the best family, but you ought to be very satisfied that any man of means and repute will consider you at all. You know what I mean."

Though Roan laughed again, the laugh was tinny, and its hollowness was the sound that Anne, canny in her assessment of her daughter's weaknesses, had been patiently awaiting. She pressed her advantage, and, with her considerable skills in procuring marriages guiding the way, Roan and Arthur met, were in due course affianced, and wed.

The marriage lasted three years. Arthur was a Daddy's Boy, intent in his every deed and posture to re-create the perfection of his father, who had in all the years of Arthur's life treated him with doting contempt. Arthur did not quite know how to be with women, or perhaps he had no real interest in women other than to reflect his father's apparent interest in them (his father saw a great many prostitutes, whom he gratuitously referred to as "strumpets"). When not lapping at his father's heels, Arthur spent time joking and working (in that order) with the boys in the executive suite of his father's corporation or with his large coterie of hypermasculine friends.

As luck or ill fortune would have it, Arthur's best friend from his college days, Alan Michael Gillory, was an ambitious reporter for the *New York Times*. Black Irish, loud, pugnacious, with shiny eyes like iridescent black beetles and satiny weeds of ebon hair sprouting from the open collar of his shirt and across the backs of his moon-colored hands and knuckles, Gillory impressed his colleagues with his terrierlike refusal to let any story go without making it into a sensation. His lithe, animal presence and his faintly evil smile were what tended to impress his colleagues' wives. Gillory had a great many opinions and he bellowed them often as he prowled the newsroom and the Berrys' living room—and, within ten months of their first meeting, he aired his opinions in private audience with Roan, as he strutted naked, like a hairy, belligerent animal, around the bedroom she and Arthur shared.

From Roan's perspective, it was inevitable that she and Alan Michael should tryst, inevitable that Arthur should discover them with the bedsheets wound about their limbs and sweat glowing on their brows and underwear tossed willy-nilly against the antique mirror and on the windowsill, inevitable and desirable that there should be a great operatic scene and death threats and scandal and that her mother should refuse to speak to her (a vow Anne kept for a month). The divorce was dramatic and made the pages of *Vanity Fair*.

Roan would have liked to have just lived with Alan Michael rather than marry him, but a little voice kept telling her that she needed to tie him to her somehow. She needed him. She was drawn to him, not so much for the carnal sway he held over women, as for what critics called his raging ambition and what she herself knew to be some more basic quality of his being truly and deeply disturbed. Alan Michael's mania reflected Roan's and in it she hoped to quell or douse or simply manage her own fire. They loved one another intensely for as long as they were able, and when that was done, Roan saw to it that they hated one another intensely for as long as they could accomplish that. Both states were to her one and the same. The sex, for instance, didn't change either way—indeed, she was never so satisfied as when they made love in anger, and sex was thus unveiled as what she knew it truly was: a savage contest of will and power. In between fights and ecstasies she toyed with the idea of starting up a career, but she never managed to get much further than treating these ideas precisely as toys, taking up and rapidly discarding various forays into photography, dance criticism, and campaign fund-raising much as a six-year-old in need of Ritalin therapy might handle her Christmas gifts. With Alan Michael, Roan's life was not satisfying, but it was diverting: her visions and her fears, the inexplicable sensations of deep ill ease, of being out of place, that at times overtake her did not cease, but they abated, and she was freed from giving them her constant attention.

Just in the past year or so things have taken an unhappy turn. Last winter waves of heat began to run through her body, like the coils of an electric cord wrapped tight around her legs, like a pair of burning arms pressed against her back and around her breasts. She often feels she's running a fever, but the thermometer almost never shows it. In the tub she washes gently if at all. She fears—she knows; she cannot know; her fear is ridiculous, and it is inexorable, she cannot escape it—that soap on her body will rub away not only dead skin but the thin, overheated outer layers of her being, and in the end nothing fleshy or tangible will be left but a bodiless blob of fiery electric energy. As a consequence she has adopted a European hygiene schedule: two baths a week and heavy dousing with perfume.

A week ago she invited herself along for Alan Michael's little trip to Miami with full knowledge that he was very likely going to see one of his sweethearts, a falsely sweet twenty-five-year-old model from Tennessee who once reached the finals of a reality-show competition. Roan was thankful for the girl. She needed a fight. She arrived prepared to read the riot act and throw a riot, too.

And she'd done it; it was all going along swimmingly. Screaming at Alan Michael, she had achieved that distracted, almost meditative out-of-body state of pure, untrammeled rage. She was in a kind of hot boiling bliss, searching about for items to throw at him that might leave a sexy scar if they glanced across his face—when she felt something horrible. Another strange sensation, as if suddenly a bubble had forced its way through the wall of her chest. As if high winds or the airless equivalent of winds were whipping about her, the skin on her face pulled back like hair being yanked from behind, the air in her lungs and throat sucked away. A heart attack? I am having a heart attack, she thought. But as her body began to tilt toward the floor, the thought came to her that new and frightening though this sensation was, nevertheless it arrived carrying a certain blithe confidence, an equable composure, as if it were a freshly bathed and perfumed monk come to dole out last rites to the slain on a quiet battlefield. It was peaceful and rather old, this feeling; it had the air of being pedigreed.

An experience, she knew as her sense of balance left her and she crumpled to the floor, that the other, truer Roan had known well.

She couldn't make sense of it—not with Alan Michael there to watch and ridicule, that sixty-three-year-old fool still looking at life through the slit of his penis, that dog, that *canine*. She shut her eyes, she prepared herself to just go, she had decided she would put on capri pants and go run along the beach, ghastly as the prospect of being an old woman doing such a thing would be. And then she found a dog staring up at her from the floor, its button-black eyes wide as if transfixed, its tail erect and still.

Now the visions, the terrifying, ungovernable sensations that everyone has known would one day destroy her—her mother has warned her many times, her late father, bless his soul, whispered his fears to her on his hospital bed, Arthur hoped he would live to see the day it happened—now they've all come back, no longer a tide, but a flood.

Was this feeling what drove the other Roan to do what she did, that morning she wandered away from the cottage to step out into the street? Or is this feeling the stirring of power, the odd incalculable shift in cosmic forces that brought the truck to her, brought it from the other side of the universe to the roadside in order to make her what she is today?

Roan doesn't want any more deaths, any more resurrections. She won't have it. She has told God more than once, and she means to be heard: "I simply will not have it!" she vows.

Alan Michael Gillory, stroking his testicles with the soft pads of his paws, can only look doleful in reply.

7

Wessex Hotel, much later

Langston and Azaril arrive at Wessex House 339 a couple of hours after Reynaldo and Quentin have returned. When they open the door, they feel rather than see a ragged pallor hovering in the room like a cloudy mist, growing more wan and gray with each of Reynaldo's long sighs.

Reynaldo cocks an eyebrow and lifts his hand in a weak gesture as Azaril bounds into the room, but otherwise he doesn't move. His worldview has been given something of a jolt, and he's out of sorts. He had considered Damian's "disappearance" just a silly queen's bad joke, at best an elaborate narcotic hallucination. Castro on Calle Ocho he was sure would be explained in time, it would *have* to be, and none of them had been close enough to see what really happened, anyway. But Roan Gillory, that's another matter. He saw that. He was there. For the past couple of hours—while Quentin lolls on his back on the comfy bed channel surfing (his eyes skittering back and forth as if following a ball in a tennis match) and every so often rises up to forage in the minibar like a grizzly bear casing an abandoned campsite—Reynaldo has been drumming his fingers on the table and sinking deeper into a mood.

"Ohmigah, swee*ties*! He*llo*!" Quentin finds himself leaping to his feet as he greets the two returning truants. He is *immensely* relieved, he says; if only he had a string of pearls at his neck to clutch.

"I see you didn't find Damian," Reynaldo mumbles, now that he's raised his eyes from the tabletop.

"No, but wait'll you hear this!" Azaril says. Before they can say a word, the story spills out of Azaril, rather haphazardly, owing to the alcohol still slaying his brain cells: the way he's telling it, it is impossible to follow the stuff about Langston's stomach lighting up, for example. But what Azaril lacks in clarity he makes up in animation. Langston hangs back, offering a few nods of assent; he worries that both Azaril and his aunt will come off as candidates for an asylum.

Reynaldo and Quentin—most especially Reynaldo, from whom Langston, with a swirl of surprise, recognizes he desires the most and expects the worst—don't laugh or roll their eyes or cut dubious glances at one another, or even smile. "So Damian being gone, the Castro sightings, all of it might have something to do with Damian's father and this book?" Reynaldo says. It looks as if a smile is fighting with his better sense.

They both want a look at the book, to which Langston agrees, though reluctantly.

The words that leap out at Reynaldo as he thumbs the pages confirm his nagging fear that he is out of his depth, but at least it's begun to be clear that there are depths to plumb. None of the random spells and folktales he comes across make any sense, but the way the book feels resting in his palms does: not quite at rest, but as if gently, gently pulsing. Quentin gets a different sensation: he is curious, and reads random paragraphs, searching for something—exactly what, even he can't say—and he thinks he almost hears wind, the hot, moaning wind that a lost traveler might hear in a desert or on a lonely heath.

"But that's not all!" they hear Azaril saying. "Lang actually knows where Damian's father is! We can contact him!"

"I *think* I know," Langston corrects him. "When I was visiting Yale a couple of years ago, I saw Damian's father once—totally out of the blue, in the gym with a bunch of people he was leading around. I don't think Mr. Garrow recognized me, but I was sure it was him. And then I found out he was working in the athletics department, doing PR or something. I didn't talk to him or anything, but Damian confirmed it, when I asked. That was almost two years ago, though. He could be long gone from Yale by now."

"We can call and find out," Azaril says.

"It's a little late in the night to do that," Langston says.

"But you buy this," Reynaldo says, looking to Azaril.

"Completely," Azaril replies, so firmly and free of doubt that Langston wonders whether the spell he's working on has already begun to take some kind of effect—or whether it's just that Az will clutch at any reed of hope if it means finding Damian. But that's just his jealousy taunting him, of course.

"And I guess since it's your aunt, you believe it, too," Reynaldo says to Langston. Langston nods. "Well, I guess I can believe it myself, then." He pauses. "You need to go down the hall and see Mrs. Gillory, Langston. Like, soon. Real soon."

Langston flops to the bed in horror only partly feigned and listens gap-mouthed as Quentin and Reynaldo—Quentin more emphatic on every detail than Reynaldo—recount the incident in the restaurant. Langston sees no recourse but to whine. "It's almost four o'clock in the morning."

"Doesn't matter," Reynaldo says. "Nobody's sleeping in this town these days. Either you're up or you're passed out to the point where nobody could disturb you if they tried. I got off the phone from my mom like an hour ago. Ordinarily she's in bed by nine."

"And besides, Mrs. Gill or whatever say she want to see your ass as soon as you got here," Quentin adds. "'Do you *understand?* Tell him just *that!*' Crazy-ass heifer."

Azaril stays to hear the whole story told again, but Langston doesn't. The scared, dazzled expression in Reynaldo's eyes looks exactly the way Langston felt when he first went to Mrs. Gillory's room. He retrieves *Hex* from Quentin—maybe it will provide some protection, he thinks—and leaves.

If Langston allowed himself to believe, he might give in to it, admit it. He might think: yes, it *could* be so. Magic. For days now, there have been all around him glimpses and glimmerings of the ephemeral, of magic, like the dust of crushed dandelions carried on the breeze, catching here and there a spark of light that makes fragile particles visible to the eye. Dance-floor visions, sightings of the dead, colors blossoming in his own body that he can't see, but if told they're there he can nevertheless feel. If he allows himself to imagine, it's not even ridiculous. His aunt Reginia is a psychic; she sees things others don't see, right? The lack of acceptable explanation for a phenomenon in no way means that the phenomenon doesn't exist. OK, maybe he hasn't had enough sleep the last few days, and certainly he's been a tad indulgent with drinks and drugs. But there's no doubt—he cannot stir up enough doubt to disbelieve—that the woman rooming a few doors down the hall from him has done—or is doing—something that brushes against those tiny psychic antennae of the brain that alert us to the presence of the uncanny.

He tries to resist the shudder that runs through him. He summons his intellectual training. The sensation of the uncanny, Herr Freud tells us, is merely the confusion of repressed memory, the return of some dim childhood feeling once familiar but now recollected in a time and place alien to its origin, so that the feeling is rendered strange, unsettling; it is the sense of being at home and finding one's cozy home unhomely; it is a disturbance that smudges the line between what we believe is inside and what is outside; it is—

It is the feel, the real, inescapable *feel*, right now, this very minute, of Mrs. Gillory's pale hands creeping over his, their muscular grip, their weight pressing down, the light trickle of sweat in the grooves of her palm running cold across the veins on the back of his hand. And the smell of that awful, sweet, sweet smell.

Room 351. Mrs. Gillory's door is a sky blue, a sky as it looks when the fiercest of the sunlight has begun to retreat and the darkness in every color grows richer and more secret, the blue of gloaming or of balmy cloud-swept late afternoons—very unlike the murky sea-bottom green of her room's interior, which immediately immerses you in the wafting flow of a mermaid's world as you enter.

Langston hovers at the blue door, taking diver's breaths to try to calm his palpitant heart. He tries to envision gnarled, mighty roots flowing from the base of his spine to the core of the earth. Knocks.

Summoned from within by a low, incomprehensible word almost as soon as his fist touches the door, Langston once again crosses the threshold of room 351.

He steps into a chasm of fantasy, a breach in good sense, logic and the laws of physics. He cannot see Mrs. Gillory, not just yet, because his eyes are drawn to the spectacle of a jungle ensconced in a hotel room.

Dark soil like wet coffee grounds lifts the floor almost a foot above the level of the hallway. His feet pad over a carpet of ferns layered as if they have been falling to the ground for seasons, and he navigates tall weeds thick as cables that sprout monstrous broad-spanning flowers. Palm trees, thin spears of leafy bamboo, and a startling triad of green big-leaf maples with shaggy, moss-mantled branches like the arms of gibbons dominate the landscape—roomscape—and far above Langston's head the trees twine together and strain against the ceiling in a futile push upward toward the sun. Small, plumed birds feathered in a vibrant spectrum of the primary colors trade nonsense syllables and test orchestral arrangements from amidst the upper planes and take inspection swoops over Langston's head. Langston drops into a protective crouch after a hooked beak chances rather too close to his left eye. He watches a flock of mango and magenta butterflies rise from a flush thicket of yellow flowers to swirl around the trunks of the trees in patterns that remind him of the boys in the nave of Redemption, caressing their sweat-slick physiques with bolts of silk. Below the sounds of the insects buzzing and birds calling to one another, Langston believes he can discern a consistent white noise, like the warble of a brook making its way over a bed of smooth-worn rocks. This is off more or less in the direction that the bathroom should be.

There's no turning back, of course. The door is shut, its outlines having faded into the Amazonian night. Space has lost its meaning: in some corner farther away than any corner of any decent room should be, Langston sees a queen-size mattress, upended and leaning against a wall of darkness like a windblown tree against the face of a cliff. In the triangular emptiness beneath lies Mrs. Gillory's dog, taking shelter from the fulsome tropical heat, his snout upon his paws. He, too, seems to have expanded, with legs, teeth, and body twice the size Langston recalls. This inflation may well explain the smell—not the cloying candy smell of yesterday, but like massive dog droppings baked to maximum pungency by sunlight and doused by showers of expensive perfume. It is sweet and disgusting and horrible.

The reasonable response would be to panic, but reason no longer seems the wisest option. Langston feels like a sponge, ready to absorb whatever he makes contact with. Instead of *Shit this is crazy this is dangerous I need to hop a plane and get the fuck out of here no no no this cannot cannot be*, his mind says, *Cool*, it's like a video game come to life, and he's almost about to get lost in the fantasy made reality, wondering whether there will be a noble horse swifter than the wind for him to ride—or perhaps Tarzan will come swinging down all sweaty and hairy and horny from some secret sentry spot up among the leaves?

Then he spies Mrs. Gillory off in the distance.

She is not the towering giant Quentin is at this moment describing back in 339. She is haggard, and she appears to have shriveled where all else has expanded. Her pale face is more ashen than Langston remembers. The green kimono that shrouds her body makes her neck and face look diseased. She lies huddled upon a bed set in the middle of a clearing ringed by a semicircle of modest shrubs sparkling with damp blueberries.

"Ah, my dear, dear Mr. Fleetwood," she says and rises to sit and wave him in her direction. She speaks as if drugged. Her eyes do not meet his; instead she looks steadily at his chest. She sneezes loudly, followed quickly by an ugly wet cough.

"How good of you to come. I fear—I fear I made rather a spectacle of myself when I found your friends. Lesson learned: it's best I don't leave the room. One cannot predict the consequences. I become—something else. Some desperate and dark creature. Perhaps the id running wild. But I did need you, Mr. Fleetwood. When I couldn't locate you, after I called and called your room and that buffoonish Teuton Wilhelm said he hadn't any notion where you'd gone to, I simply panicked." She gestures at the room, helplessly. "Things have gone mad."

Langston holds *Hex* to his chest with both arms crossed over it like a schoolgirl in gray-and-navy uniform, or like straps over the breastplate of a suit of armor. There is a need for limits, for the definitive, when one is confronted by chaos and impossibility, so having picked up a trick or two from his father, he frowns heavily and speaks in a tone of no-nonsense demand. "What the hell's happened here? What's all . . . How did this . . .?"

Mrs. Gillory leans over upon her knees and holds her face in her hands. "That is what I desire you to tell *me*. Oh, yes, I admit, I turned my husband into a dog, I certainly did. I didn't mean to and could not possibly have anticipated that I would do so—that I *could* do so. But it happened, and well, at first I did not wish to ask questions. I assumed either that I had gone mad or that really I had inherited some peculiar sorcerous gift of my grandmother's. I reasoned it out that Alan Michael wasn't actually a dog, but that I had somehow caused him to *believe* he was a dog, and then convinced you and the hotel staff as well, and I thought that it would all just sort of fade away once I stopped being angry with him. Well, you see how it has come out. If these are 'psychic projections' or some such twaddle, they do begin to have the tenacity of the real. Meantime all of what you see here, my little corner of Sumatra, sprung up when I was napping. And I can't make it go away. I think it's still *growing*. Those weeds weren't there when I lay down to rest. Oh, Mr. Fleetwood! I am accustomed to oddities. But this! I have developed powers, of all things. You said you were an expert on the paranormal. You must, must help me!"

Langston looks about him. A tiny bird, the size and color of a green opal set in a wealthy woman's ring, dives down at his head from some unguessed height, then swerves aside. "I didn't say—Mrs. Gillory, I'm not an expert. I couldn't begin to—"

Mrs. Gillory shrieks, throws herself back flat upon the bed, and kicks her thick-calved legs in the air. "Oh, *Mr.* Fleetwood! Please! I beg of you! I am in terror, the very mouth of terror! Its teeth imprison me. They are like razors, can't you feel them?

They shall shred and devour me, if you don't help." She concludes with a horrendous sneeze.

Langston responds to her desperation by instinct, like a mother to the wail of her infant. "If I could help, I would . . . I just don't know how. Lots of very bizarre things are going on out there. Castro resurrections, my friend Damian disappearing into thin air—did I tell you that? What's happening to you might be connected. Maybe my aunt Reginia could help. She's already helping us find Damian—and she gave me her husband's spell book, which she thinks is connected to his disappearance. It's actually full of incorrect spells, evidently, although even if it wasn't, I don't see how it could help with, with this kind of thing. Oh, I don't know, Mrs. Gillory. It's tired and I'm late."

"I don't care about the hour, or Castro or Damian or whoever! Oh! In everything, in everything I am betrayed, everything I attempt, every goal I set, always, always, always *this*: God, mocking me! Tormenting me!" She is standing now, suddenly taller it seems, her fists clenched at her sides. "Look here. You must help me! You will help me! Hand me that fucking book! Now!" Langston hears something twang through the air—like sheets of metal clashing against one another—and looks down to see leaves lift from the ground and buzz around his ankles. Lightning? A storm? "*Please*, Mr. Fleetwood! If your aunt believes this book can help you find your friend, then perhaps something in it could be useful for me as well. What is it exactly, a catalogue of paranormal phenomena?"

"Not exactly . . ."

But she has pried the book from him before his sentence concludes. Langston is afraid she might damage it, the way she seizes the cover and rips it open. If nothing else, she's sure to screw up the thing's aura, or something. "Be careful," he says sharply.

Mrs. Gillory doesn't answer, but the dog growls listlessly on her behalf, with the enthusiasm of a postal clerk.

Langston stands by unhappily; maybe he ought to take the opportunity to run?

Mrs. Gillory's fierce, pale scowl begins to crack.

"What?" Langston demands.

"My dear boy!" Mrs. Gillory exclaims. The edge falls from her tone, and all at once she becomes a being of smiles and sunny disposition. "Didn't I say you would help me? We are *fated* to one another. Oh, I knew it was true, the very moment I saw you," she says, wagging her finger at him. "Something in the voice and those eyes of yours—some resonance. Oh, it's clear now. You are my savior."

"OK," Langston replies in what he hopes is a soothing and helpful tone.

"This book, this little foolish thing. It is known to me. Well known. I have a copy, in rather better shape, without all the high school yearbook scrawl, in my home. My mother's home, to be precise. Aden and Atalanta Rose, the authors, were my grandparents."

For some reason Langston feels as if he has been slapped. "You're kidding," he says, knowing she is not.

"Yes, my loony grandmother and her poof husband. The only sure marriage is with a poofter, you know. Even Mother said so. In such arrangements, everything is laid out, there is no question of fidelity and no question of jealousy, either. Ah, my grandparents were dear people, the dearest. They sent me gifts and letters from abroad. They were always traveling. I didn't see them as much as I would have liked because of that, and then when they chanced our way—well, my mother and her parents did not get on. Grandmother died without her daughter there to comfort her—disappeared, actually, as I told you, on one of her airplane joyrides. Shortly afterward, Grandfather got involved in some sixties nonsense and was killed."

Langston, keeping a hawk's eye on what she's doing to his book, murmurs condolences.

"Yes, it was quite dreadful. He was strangled and knifed by someone, we never knew who. The police said his former valet did it, but there was no proof, and even Mother didn't believe it, that man was so very sweet. The poor valet was apprehended and died in custody. The brutes. I remember he was so *tall*. The valet, I mean. Dadda Rose was not an imposing figure, physically; one wondered whether any other homosexual would have him. Of course," she sighs, ignoring the look of horror on Langston's face, "the real murderer was never captured. Nineteen . . . seventy, I think it was. Yes."

She is turning the pages from the top with her fingers, and gazes past the faded typewriter's print as she speaks. "You've seen the book before?" Langston asks. He looks at *Hex* skeptically now, as if it has betrayed a promise.

"Yes. Mother inherited their effects after they died—everything they owned was kept in an absurd vault, you know, because they hadn't a proper home anywhere in the world. She and I went through everything, piece by piece, and Mother told me all about the Great Lost Manuscript of Dadda and Mamma Rose. And now you've returned another copy to us! How delightful!"

Langston doesn't like the sound of that pronoun. He's got more than half a mind to pop her one, grab the book , and make a break for it. His legs tense—lean slow-twitch muscle fibers, best suited to cross-country treks rather than power sprints (unlike sister Zuli, who cleaned up in the hundred meters at state), but they might do the job. What would Mrs. Gillory do if she caught him, though, that's the question. And then of course it's not nice to hit a woman. But if she's a demon witch, is she a woman per se? Langston's fingers itch, right at the top.

Mrs. Gillory smooths the rumpled spread on her bed and sits. "Now, Mr. Fleetwood, you must tell me everything your aunt told you. And the whole story about dear Damian, too. He discorporated into thin air, you say? Don't fret. Such things happen. Tell me, then. Spare nothing. I shall listen, patiently."

She's just about glued *Hex* to her lap, and she's moved farther back from him. Langston notes a row of little anthills following roughly the path from the door to his feet, and fat red ants cruising around on six-legged patrols: new growth, apparently, because they weren't there when he walked in. He can almost feel their antennae brush against his ankle. Are the ants a threat? Does she know he's thinking about grabbing *Hex* and leaving? Mrs. Gillory grins redly at him, and Langston suddenly has a keen memory of sitting down to play in an anthill when he was four. He starts talking.

When he's finished, Mrs. Gillory sneezes. Otherwise she's a picture of newfound serenity and health. "Oh, I remember some of those stories," she says. Langston isn't certain what she's referring to, nor is he certain to whom she is speaking, so quiet is her tone. "Certainly this 'dapper, elegant Negro' your uncle met—that is precious, what a precise and precious description!—certainly he would have been the valet. You know, my father would go on about Dadda Rose, to tweak Mommy I believe. He would say that Dadda Rose had a thing for black homosexuals. During the twenties Dadda Rose dragged Mama Rose all around Harlem . . . yes, actually I remember Dadda and Mama Rose talking about it a couple of times! Laughing, talking about the good old days—drinking, likely, those two could drink. Their favorite club had a very beautiful name—the Ubangi! And they went to drag balls in the Savoy Ballroom!" She laughs. "Black poofters! Can you imagine my grandparents? Ah—family history." She gives Langston what he takes to be a look that means something significant and poignant has passed between them. He's dumbfounded, of course, but responds with an expression of keen interest, thinking that if she continues, at some point she'll begin to make sense.

"They took such joy in those stories, in their madcap lives. Think of it, to look back upon the past with something other than regret and disgust . . . Well. And here the two of us are today, together! Isn't it perfect, isn't it the proof of God, that our family histories are sewn together along the same seam?"

Mrs. Gillory rises to her slippered feet with an air of perfect satisfaction and begins to bustle about the bed, searching the copse of blueberry shrubs for something. "As for Damian—well, I've done a bit of disappearing of my own in my day. Parents often have something to do with it. There is no rational sense to these things, but unquestionably your aunt is quite right. Go you must. Search out whomever and whatever you must to locate Damian. Take along *Hex* if you wish, my dear. I feel very strongly that in helping him you will help *me*. It cannot be coincidence that we should meet, that you should come, like a beauteous black Greek, bearing the gift of this book. Surely your path and mine are linked together."

Langston falters, taken aback. "But . . . you know, actually, I was just planning to call Mr. Garrow—that's Damian's dad—"

"No, I don't think that will do at all," she says in the manner of an investment counselor pointing out the error of selling too soon. Having drawn the conclusions she desires to draw, it's as though her earlier desperation were entirely conjured away, as if the fauna rioting around her were no more discomfiting than the buzzing of a few houseflies. "You have to *go*. You can't conduct these kinds of investigations from *afar*. What if he points you right to Damian? What if he doesn't know anything, but someone else he knows knows? Your aunt said, *find* Damian's father and thus find Damian. That's exactly what you must do. Bring your friends. You will undoubtedly need help. Will $10,000 help you on your way? I'll write you some of those credit card checks." Her hand claws toward the satiny evening purse on the dressing table beside a giant Venus flytrap.

Langston is aghast. "Ten *thousand* . . ."

"I am very wealthy, Mr. Fleetwood."

That much he had figured, but then why stay in this hotel? "I like Art Deco," she says. Is she reading his mind? "And"—she coughs noisily—"I like young, hard bodies."

Langston stands motionless as she hands him the book and a small pile of checks. "Cash those at any bank. And be back here within ten days. Otherwise I shall have to alert the police, the FBI, private detectives. All those professional lynchers."

Downstairs, Luisa's eyes light up when she sees colorful Visa checks between Langston's long ebony thumb and the waxy red cover of a book as he slowly walks into the lobby. Langston smiles, a little sadly, she thinks, although what she sees may be no more than weariness. He orders an ample supply of Vicodin painkillers ("liveliness pills," he calls them), sedatives, E, K, and a bit of speed. Luisa, though delighted, of course, cannot conceal her surprise, but Langston assures her that the order is a cache for four. He doesn't doubt that Azaril will be game for this mess his aunt has gotten him into, and surely Reynaldo and Quentin, too, will come along. The Hardy Boys always took Chet, the chubby coward, on adventures with them, didn't they? Reynaldo's not chubby, but he's muscular, and Quentin's a drag queen ghetto boy who seems a bit cowardly, so that updates

Franklin W. Dixon's fifties entertainments right into the new millennium.

Langston cashes one of Mrs. Gillory's checks and marvels at the faces of currency denominations of which he has had, until this moment, only theoretical knowledge. He looks at the pills in a plastic bag, twists them up as if they were a bag of Halloween candies—the promise of easy peace, of blissful forgetfulness, ecstasy-to-order. He probably won't even take them, but the look of them there, in a packaging of glistening air, is soothing, a steadying counterweight to the acute fear that keeps spiking from his intestines to his lungs.

8

The next day, sundown

In the west an orange, perfectly round halo is poised above the Miami skyline, and if you travel outside the city limits or have a view unbroken by house or building, you can see great lengths of reddish pink cloud angle toward the sunken sun like burning jet trails, or like the scarlet entrails of heaven, maybe. Langston, Azaril, Reynaldo, and Quentin gaze upon the sight while riding the currents of the upper air in a jet headed north to New York City's JFK Airport, from whence they will make their way to New Haven, Connecticut, to meet Damian's father, Mr. Garrow.

In the sky time moves differently—actually, Langston knows, a microsecond or so faster, because at thirty thousand feet the plane is freer than earthbound mortals from the manacles of planetary gravity—but to Langston's perception time seems suspended in air, simply because most of the things on the ground aren't present: the buildings and shops, the buses and the BART schedules, the people you have to coordinate with to make meetings and movies, everything that gives time its seemingly inescapable solidity. Reynaldo and Quentin sit together in the middle tier of cramped coach-class seats (Quentin made a strong case for going first class with Mrs. Gillory's cash, but Langston vetoed the idea). The two comb through the pages of newspapers.

The frenetic way Reynaldo attacks turning the pages of *USA Today* suggests something of how caged he feels, how caged he always feels in small, tight spaces such as this, and signals the incessant questioning that plagues him as he pretends to read, like, *Why am I doing this?* and, *How can I even believe the shit they're telling me?* and, *Why am I sure*—but only in a shaky, slippery way, that tidal comes-and-goes kind of clarity—*that finding Damian means finding out something important for myself? Well, after all, it's a free trip*, he tells himself as he settles down to take a look at column-length bite-size stories that say "House Republicans Challenge Reports of Castro's Death" and "Mourning in Many Latin American Capitals" and "Spanish Government Calls for Lifting Sanctions."

Quentin enjoys better luck and a more luxurious mood, making his way with slow relish through *People*'s special feature "Heartthrobs of Yesteryear: Marlon Brando, James Dean, and Montgomery Clift." He oohs over the glossy photographs and movie stills. They're so exciting, he tries to tell Reynaldo, mythic even, in part because their images are so beautifully staged. That turn of the head for the profile, this costume, so gorgeous—but also they're beautiful because in black and white they lie upon the page leached of color, seeming in their incongruity with the colors of life to represent some other, godlike dimension of being, where face and form are no more than a pleasing shroud, mere corporeal envelopes for all the religious pleasures and soulful anguish of desire. He tries to say exactly what he thinks, but the words don't come out as he would like them to, and Reynaldo merely gives him an irritated squint of incomprehension and a roll of his eyes.

Across the aisle, Langston builds memorials to his Miami sojourn in his thoughts, obelisks and pyramids and circles of Cyclopean stone that hold solid and unshakable the exquisite recall of little things: his sultry recline upon a bench in the open afternoon sun, the tart kiss of lemon juice in cool seltzer upon his tongue at a late-morning breakfast, the brown body of the man whom he would have as his lover, in brief black trunks, rising from the foam of the sea.

Azaril is dead asleep. He sleeps with his head tilted forward. Langston thinks this is cute. Then Azaril's head, responding to the call of his private dream, suddenly tilts further, so that it hangs suspended over Langston's shoulder, delicately balanced. If Langston were to shift the tendons of his frontal deltoids, Azaril's face would swing like a derrick straight into Langston's crotch—an idea that snaps Langston right out of his reverie. This is how they would be if they were together always: if Azaril abandoned his apple-faced Irish chick and the pretense of heterosexuality, if he got over his peculiar schoolboy straight-guy crush on Damian, if the couldas wouldas and shouldas were all aligned just so, Langston and Azaril could play out this scene every time they boarded a plane or took a train, on one of their many overseas trips, say, where they'd be shuttling down-continent on the train from Calais to Florence. Maybe the love spell is kicking in? The possibility—dim, to be sure, the spell could easily have been one of the fakes—thrills Langston, and it worries him, too. Not because it would mean that he's capable of working magic; this is a prospect of which Langston has no fear, since, like his patron Mrs. Gillory, he has long held the conviction that under the right set of circumstances he could *do* things. It's the more prosaic possibility that concerns him: the thought of what it might mean if Azaril really did come to love him, and they became—*gulp*: boyfriends.

Langston has a terror of a particular scene: two lovers at the close of an evening, after the TV clicks off, when the sounds of cars on the street below their window rise up to fill the space the TV surrenders, and lonely night buses rattle by, ferrying scattered passengers in their illuminated interiors like bats revealed by a camper's flashlight in a cavern, and it's as if a curtain has been drawn down upon the stage of the day. The two lovers have only each other left. And they lock hands and plant a peck on each other's lips. "I love you," they say, but the words, like the glancing kiss, are an abstraction, a brisk and efficient renewal of musty old vows, an indifferent promise of future togetherness. Their minds are busy with tomorrow's unwanted duties, the tedious robotic details of having to check the dryer to see if the clothes are done, and to remember to fold them so that they don't get wrinkled. Langston abhors this—the routine of everyday love. Not that he's naive; he knows that the brick and mortar of relationships consists of the everyday. But he's romantic. He wants love to be something that's always palpable, always trembling in his body, flooding the five senses as well as thc clusive, all-important sixth. He wants love to be disorienting, uplifting, revelatory—he wants it to be a mystical ecstasy rather than a religion. The satisfactions of requited love he barely understands; it's the intoxication of being in love, of being overwhelmed from within that he honors, that he wants to arrest and hold like a quantum physicist struggling to stop a streaming photon in its tracks.

Azaril releases a loud, clogged snore. A thin thread of drool connects the opening of his mouth with Langston's shirt. This only makes Langston want him more. The stewardess—her name is Patsy: she has the sturdy, somber look and manner of a grief counselor—perhaps in response to the snore, perhaps even in quick, barely conscious psychic recognition of the deep bond between the two men, gives Langston a sympathetic look. Langston hastily covers his lap with his hands to hide his incipient erection and smiles back.

He is being very foolish, of course, very reckless with his feelings. Things are bound to come to a bad end. After all, this has happened before. It's all about repetition, Aunt Reginia warned, and it's really sick, it's cruel, the way the universe cleverly manipulates events so that the same things that hurt you before cycle back in fresh disguises. The way, depending on how you look at it, Azaril could be what Damian was to Langston twenty years ago; and the way Damian plays the same part in Azaril's life as he played in Langston's.

The year was 1981. When Langston first met Damian—and the first time Damian disappeared.

Gray skies brooded over Ansbach, West Germany. There, alongside primeval forest and the castles of medieval princelings, lay one among scores of U.S. Army bases that pocked the German landscape and provided lodging and refuge for armored divisions, tanks and tank drivers and tank strategists, alert to what all believed to be the eternal Soviet threat. The morbid paranoia of this task was reflected not only in the sky that watched it getting done but in the daily routines of the soldiers and their families, who led lives that often seemed no more than tiny frozen ponds, anxiously awaiting the thaw of a belated summer.

"A rat trap," Langston's mother pronounced disgustedly of Katterbach Kaserne, one of Ansbach's three major encampments, where junior officers and NCOs and their wives and children clustered in three- and four-story works of indifferent brick and plaster: by all appearances, a kind of low-income housing project in a suburban setting. In view of the alternatives, though, she probably oughtn't to have complained. Langston's father was a lieutenant colonel with the judge advocate general, and so his family lived in their own duplex with their own little yard at Katterbach's border, just above a steep drop-off into rock and forest and winding road, and at a discreet distance from the three-story projects of the plebeians.

Langston shared his mother's disgust, but he added terror to it. A month before they moved, his older sister and protector, Zuli, had departed for the beginnings of her stellar career as an affirmative action baby at Harvard, and now that Langston was unable to shelter in her shadow, his parents had made it known that they expected Big Things of him, too. As if Zuli's abandonment of him were not enough of an insult, his father's commanders, scrutinizing their top-secret global strategies, moving pieces on their colossal chessboards, had once again decreed an exodus for the Fleetwoods. From Fort Bragg, North Carolina, they had journeyed to Ansbach across the ocean, and there Langston was again to be an outcast, doomed once more to roam the hallways of a new school for a purgatorial term, alone and unseen. He braced himself. As an army brat he had never lived anywhere for longer than three years. This had all happened before.

This time, though, rescue—or had it actually been a little cosmic joke, a curse in a blessing's guise?—came far more quickly than he expected.

In the first week of his eighth-grade American history class, Langston Fleetwood and Damian Garrow were seated side by side. The teacher, a halting, bespectacled figure whose shaving misfortunes daily made it appear that he had been attacked by vicious kittens, sweatily stammered out a joke to put everyone at ease—something about slaves and Old Virginia and the motive power of taxation; the humor required a graduate education to unravel. Langston can't remember the joke now, but he remembers how he and Damian, two black boys clumped together by the fate of the alphabet, glanced at one another in shared incomprehension and outrage, as if to say, *Slaves—he's makin fun of slaves?* The expression on Langston's face almost precisely mirrored Damian's expression. Somehow they knew this, though neither, of course, could see his own face at that moment.

While Kitten-scarred fiddled with stripping the plastic from the new textbooks, Damian and Langston smiled—the innocent, heterosexual boy's equivalent of flirting, to be transformed with advancing age into gruffer and warier variants—and then they fell into an increasingly arousing conversation about the cover of the *Jaws 2* novel Langston had impudently brought with him from home. *The teeth, lookit the teeth on that thing!* they whispered and, *I know someone who got bit by a shark, a friend of my dad's and he went right into shock and doesn't even remember how he got out of the water* and, *Yeah, and I don't blame the shark, that girl looks like somebody* I'd *fuckin eat*. At which Langston, unable to keep it down, giggled.

Damian passed Langston a note across the aisle. In the hieroglyphic scrawl, Langston made out, *Can you get drunk on wine?* Langston, who had never imbibed more alcohol than his mother gave him on New Year's Eve, wriggled his hand in the air and pursed his mouth into an expression which answered, *So-so*. "I prefer beer," he improvised—but, since Damian knew a German place that, like many such places, happily sold wine but not beer to American minors, that was what the two of them ended up getting drunk on.

This tack (lying) having borne such promising fruit, Langston soon made a practice of it. Langston did, after all, have a native talent for fantasy and invention, for endless rumination on elusive dreams. At first he put this talent to use with a degree of reticence and modesty: only half lies and untraceable lies, to the effect that yes, he had played first-string JV football back in Bragg, well, he *started out* second string, but he was so good that . . . and he'd had this wonderful girlfriend, Vanessa, yes, beautiful name, huh?, Vanessa (the endowments and personality of whom closely tacked those revealed in photographs and interviews of Pam Grier in *Right On!* magazine) used to put out all the time for him, she loved him so much she never said no and he really, really missed her.

Of course Langston's lie was small fry, as lying goes, and no taller a tale than many another spun daily among Langston's classmates. To hear a sizable proportion of the adolescent male population of Ansbach's combined junior and high school tell it, those three-tiered buildings were veritable temples of erotic celebration, sacred sites where young black and brown and white bodies discovered one another in the damp dark of basements and in the pink and ruffles of girly-girl rooms decorated with posters on the wall of Snoopy and Shaun Cassidy and Leif Garrett and Michael Jackson. "Two girls got fucked in this storage room," the tale-spinning stud of the moment might say, pointing to a mattress in a dark ten-by-twelve-foot cube that he felt to have been rendered seraglio-seductive by such accoutrements as a cheap imitation Oriental rug, a lamp that appeared to have been taken from a Barbie doll townhouse and blown up to human size, and a stack of withered magazines. One was left to imagine the mouthwatering details.

Such stories were bread and butter to Langston. He knew these accounts to be unreliable, but he cherished them anyway. In their fancifulness they resembled and took on the luster of myths: not altogether believable, of course, but superior to reality and revelatory of some truth that no account of reality could articulate. Whether his own embellishments of the truth were believed he couldn't be certain, but they didn't seem to hurt, as, little by little, he was introduced into the hallowed social circles lorded over by the star athletes in the ninth and tenth grades, and even met one or two seniors.

Although Damian, dangerously, seemed a dissenter. His half gasps and affirmations as Langston would tell Tales of Vanessa ("Really?" "Damn!") often seemed transparently patronizing, and there were too many moments Langston would catch Damian throwing a smirk over his shoulder or down to his feet, as though sharing his unexpressed contempt with an invisible compadre with whom later he would gleefully backbite. Damian had a way, even with, or most particularly with, the unwavering quality of his attention, of appearing to regard Langston's excitement about sex stories with an arrogant air, an indulgence that felt much like a gentle pat on the head. It was as if Damian were one of the Enlightenment *philosophes* the history teacher so admired. Only the ignorant believed that lightning flowed from the hand of a bearded fellow making sport at the top of a mountain. Only the superstitious marvel at the boasts of boys in locker rooms. Those of more mature mind know better. Those with experience *know*.

Damian Garrow was the only child of a stern, burly master sergeant with stunning dark wavy hair and sallow, faintly African features. The master sergeant and his lovely young wife had adopted Damian shortly after they married, when Damian was eighteen months old. But not long thereafter the young wife soured on the demands of her sudden family. Hell broke loose when, at dinner one night when Damian was six years old or so, Damian innocently inquired after the "things" that the master sergeant's lovely young wife stuck in her arm when the master sergeant was away. The lovely wife, who had in months prior taken to wearing long-sleeved sweaters day and night and complaining about chills, and who put the boy down for his nap when she took her afternoon constitutionals, simply stared. As the story emerged, Damian, unsettled by his stepmother's silence, tried to jog her memory by mentioning the

"Mex'can" fellow with the "big ears" who came by to play as well. After much shouting and endless weeks of sullen silence, the lovely young wife became the lovely young divorcee, with only a token payment of alimony to show for the many, many pains of belonging to the Garrow family.

Relentlessly critical, fanatically perfectionist, Master Sergeant Garrow revenged himself upon the world by demanding inhuman services from Damian. He insisted that the boy, no matter his tender age, learn to cook, that the boy clean the apartment within an inch of his life, that he never bring home a grade lower than a B, that he wrestle in the winter and pitch baseball in the spring, and that he obey all commands at all times with Benedictine humility. Any duty performed to a lesser standard than demanded met with a commensurate punishment. They made an odd pair, this father and son, as they left wrestling matches together in the master sergeant's Volvo, Damian's small, dark head bowed against the backdrop of his father's massive shoulder.

Of course Master Sergeant Garrow couldn't control Damian when the boy was out of his sight, and outside the master sergeant's domain, Damian was vibrant and adventurous. He had that attractive power that nature and magazine blue-jean ads endow to precociously robust young boy-men. In the hollows of Damian's cheeks beneath his cheekbones the shadow of a very young beard already grew at age fourteen, and Langston was envious of the dangling length between Damian's legs that he spied in locker room glances.

Damian was intellectually able, friendly if perhaps too tenaciously competitive, and, despite his occasional arrogance, he gave his friends the sure sense of his absolute loyalty to them. Just don't ask Damian how he felt about anything you could have feelings about, and don't count on him to stick up for you or try to make you think he still respects you if you even look like you might start to cry. Damian wouldn't ridicule you, but he was himself the sort who would recount without a waver in his voice a harrowing story of walking inside the door of his home one afternoon and being attacked by the master sergeant. In full fatigues, Damian would say with a blank smile, his father threw him to the floor and yelled, "Wrestle! Wrestle!" This went on, Damian said, for five minutes before his father finally relented. Then, standing tall while, at his feet, Damian's lungs heaved and his muscles burned, the master sergeant delivered a critique of Damian's Greco-Roman technique.

Langston remained dumb when told of these horrors, reflecting back to Damian what Damian projected out and therefore seemed to desire: an attitude of resigned impenetrability that, even at thirteen, when the charades of manhood usually are not so well practiced, would not deign to ask for comfort or sympathy or admit to anything so sodden with femininity as hurt or fear.

In the privacy of his thoughts, though, Langston fastened upon Damian's misfortune with a secret gleefulness that was far from stoic. Damian's terror-filled home life made Langston's own struggles with his father look like a 1950s sitcom. The more Langston could conjure in his mind the image of being wrestled to the floor by two-hundred-plus pounds of muscle and unremitting hatred, and the more keenly he imagined he could taste the salt of the dust layering the floorboards as his father's hand forced him down, by just that much more Langston and the lieutenant colonel seemed a father-son couple haloed by rays from heaven. The colonel often approached his parental duties like a sentry at a correctional facility, true, and he may have called his son "spoiled" or "sissified" from time to time, but he never laid a hand on him.

Perhaps owing to having experienced the laying on of hands, or some other experience he had not described, Damian seemed to possess a knowledge of something, painfully acquired, closely kept. The intensity of this—his knowing and not ever saying what he knew—drew Langston to Damian as to a beacon. Though it rankled and outraged Langston, Damian's benevolent contempt for Langston's sex stories tantalized him. It hinted at the possibility of some experience that outstripped all the seemingly limitless pleasures and powers of the sexual congress Langston yearned for, some way of entwining one's body and soul with another that vaulted from the realm of the sexual to the super-sexual, the meta-sexual, the ultra-beyond-hyper-orgasmic-answer-to-life-sexual.

That the tension of Eros ran between the two boys like a hot pipe behind drywall was undeniable. This seemed particularly clear, and in retrospect particularly poignant, on one late winter afternoon of 1981, when there was a bright sun aloft in the sky, an event that one does not take for granted in the month of March in Germany. Damian and Langston skipped their last two classes, sprinted out from the doors at the end of the hall where the science classes were taught, and ducked into the faux-marble stairwell in the building across the street. They panted and jumped at every sound in fear of truant officers that did not exist. After a cautious interval, they peeked outdoors and then took boldly to the sidewalks to make an exhilarated trek to the PX, where they liked riffling the record bins in search of the few records whose names they could recognize from the Top Twenty Albums list in Colonel Fleetwood's weeks-old *Jet* magazine.

That day they could not contain or restrain themselves when they saw the cover of an old album that each had heard but never owned, glistening in plastic: a tousled heap of orgiastic male limbs, heads, and torsos, auburn- and cinnamon-colored, sepia and ginger. They fought over it until they found another copy, and after each bought one, they ran all the way to the Fleetwood duplex to keep in shape. Then they repaired to Langston's upstairs sanctum, where they chattered at high speed about the album, about the group Foxy, about nothing much, about something for which they did not wish to select a name.

The static of the needle along the slick rim of the record heralded it, and with the optimism of youth they leaned forward to listen. To the brutal jackhammer, jackrabbit, jacking beat, and the call to which they longed to respond: *to get off! to get off! to get offf, to get—get off!* After one playing and a half, Damian was up. He snapped his fingers and pumped his lean brown hips—wildly, Langston felt, unsettlingly—but in perfect time to each insolent beat. Soon Langston followed, matched him, performed his own more modest inner and outer gyrations. They sang the words. *(Sensuality excites my mind) it makes me GET OFF/ (if I were you I'd get a good perspec-tive) on how to GET OFF!*

That night Langston slept badly, and to make himself sleep he masturbated several times more than his usual nightly ritual of twice. That night Damian probably got a whipping with the master sergeant's paddle for his tardy arrival home. Probably nothing special, no more painful or brutal than was the custom in Master Sergeant Garrow's dominion.

Although—maybe not.

At first things went along just as they had. At school Langston and Damian told a covertly jealous Dillon all about it, and between the three the beat and lyrics became a little anthem, the punch line to every joke, so that if Mrs. Beattie in English class said that she loved the musical *Camelot*, Dillon might whisper, "It makes her get! off!"; or if some haughty girl who routinely snubbed them kept to her routine, they might flick their tongues and pelvises at her, and recite, "If I were you I'd get a good perspective, on how to get! off!"

This bliss (it only seemed so later) lasted for a week.

There was an explosion early the morning Damian was absent from school, with the mysterious consequence that the power in both Katterbach and Bleidorn Kasernes had gone out. Rumors traveled up and down the stairwells of a terrorist attack, of the return of the dreaded Red Brigade. In Dillon's building a Soviet preemptive strike in the form of an electromagnetic pulse was mentioned. The end result was that school began three hours later than usual, after power had been restored. But, owing either to missed buses or fear of the rumors or indifference, a third of the student body didn't show up. Damian was one of the no-shows. Langston and Dillon cursed their poor luck and consoled themselves with the anticipation of the story Damian was sure to tell them the next day. "He probably went and got high with those German guys he knows, and then they went and bought a whore," Dillon said. Langston thought this an unlikely (though exciting) scenario, but Dillon was curiously insistent upon it. "His dad's at work, he doesn't have a mom, he can do anything he wants," Dillon said.

But Damian didn't come to school the next day, either.

Langston and Dillon called Damian's home during lunch period. There was no answer. Another day passed, and Dillon called, and then another day Langston called. No answer. On the third day the gym teacher, who had been their wrestling coach during the winter, announced that Damian had been withdrawn from school, a fact confirmed by two other teachers. Langston and Dillon were bewildered. They called Damian's number repeatedly but vainly. The phone was never answered, as if Damian's father had gone, too. Dillon, more forward than Langston, pestered their teachers, but received only shrugs and sighs.

Langston's parents liked Damian, so he was finally able to convince his father to call Master Sergeant Garrow at his job. In the abbreviated and scrupulously civil conversation that followed, the master sergeant informed the lieutenant colonel that young Damian had gone back to live with relatives in Mississippi, and there he would remain.

This fact—strange, unaccounted for, as mysterious as the doings of scruffy-bearded terrorists in the shadows—settled upon Langston and Dillon gradually, at a slow creep. At first Damian's seemed an unlocatable absence. Without a word or cause to name or to blame, his unsigned departure teetered on the edge of inconsequentiality. Yes, Damian wasn't there, but then track practice (for Langston) and baseball practice (for Dillon) were still there every day, and the girls they tried to rap to were there, and the hallway radiators they warmed their butts on each morning and used as a perch from which to gossip about passersby were still there, too. It was almost as if Damian had never been there at all, and looking back on it now, Langston remembers how soothing and familiar this initial feeling was: having left so many friends over the course of his short life, Langston was by then adept at amputating need, at skipping lightly over memories. Friends came, friends went. Presence and absence were, in the end, more alike than unlike. Both states reflected the irrevocable distance between people that would make itself known early or late, the emptiness that lay between you and them whether they were there or not.

But this time proved to be different. There was something special about Damian, in both presence and absence. Langston began to detect, swimming all around him and clamoring to pierce his defenses, a keen and deep loss, deadly and invisible like the molecules of an airborne virus. Damian's absence changed, it transmigrated. It became Damian's disappearance—

and a nastiness, a disquiet, came to linger around the master sergeant's "back to Mississippi" phrase.

Langston wasn't old enough to be knowledgeable about the exigency and capriciousness of grief. He could only account for his feelings in more elliptic, embroidered fashion. He would retire to his room and sit upon the threadbare cushions of the chair, with the door locked, and survey the way that everything in his sight hung, dangling and dissipated. Repeatedly he set a record upon his turntable and sang the lyrics of an old song that had long escaped his attention.

I really wasn't caring / but I felt my eyes staring / at a guy who stuck out in the crowd / He had the kind of body / that would shame Adonis / and a face that would make any man proud / I wonder why (he's the greatest dancer) / I wonder why (that I've ever seen). Langston held the album jacket in his hands and studied, while he sang, the faces of the honey-complexioned sisters, their cordial expressions spiced with a slight hauteur of sophistication, of knowledge.

So Langston listened and he sang, and so he spent his evenings: Sister Sledge and fretting about the cold, dreaming of going back to the world.

Langston feels the twangy pangs of nostalgia and loss, celestial notes struck on harp strings. Damian, in the few encounters they've had since they met one another again on Telegraph Avenue, shrugs when Langston asks about what happened. "I went back to Mississippi," he says, and shifts the conversation—always frustratingly brief in any case—toward less weighty concerns. Langston has tried to ask, what happened *after* that? Damian's responses make Langston think the Mississippi story is as much a lie as he always believed. "I came here," Damian said once. "Isn't the Bay Area great?" And the other time he cryptically and infuriatingly said, "You never really know what happened at any given time until way after the fact, do you? It's too soon to know yet." Followed by a shrug.

Langston thought but didn't say "bullshit" at the time, but now he wonders. He thinks about how he may never have put Damian's absence behind him, about how it may have kept growing, spreading like lichen on his mind. It isn't over, and never was. Maybe there's a corner in his psyche from which emanates the heat that warms half his thoughts and fantasies, and in this corner the spotlight falls on an album cover and a record player playing over and over tunes masking secret truths and abstruse formulae. Maybe until the mystery is solved, Langston's every move is no more than an offering at the altar of memory: a libation of fresh tears and new salt for old wounds. Maybe everything repeats.

Langston's hand rests very lightly on sleeping Azaril's warm thunder thigh. Azaril shifts again; his head falls backward against the headrest.

Langston gazes out the window. The clouds travel thick, like buffalo, and their fleece masses like the dense foliage of an elaborately sculptured English garden hedge. The clouds teem with shape and vigor, with magic and life. A break in the white and gray, like a parting between great cliffs, reveals a vision of night blue, a mouth of twilight, dazzling in its dark glory. A white tuft of cross-shaped cloud cuts across the blue, its thin arms like raised swords.

Langston takes *Hex* from his bag and puts it in his lap, and it almost seems to hum with a heat of its own.

In his dream, the clouds become longer and flatter and blacker. Lightning curls around them, like fire licking at the edges of a photograph.

A girl stands at the bottom of a hill in the midst of a forest, looking at an empty road on a summer day. Her hair is almost white, her color wan, but these marks of maturity blend incongruously with the rest of her: she's small, of dangerously fragile make. Her smile seems so big it might tip her over. And then a shadow slips over her body, slips over her like a hood, and takes her.

While, somewhere betwixt heaven and earth, two mature and powerful women float—not physically, but in spirit. Reginia Jameson Wolfe and Roan Gillory, each in her own peculiar way, peer into the crystal globes they carry within, searching. Think of them as cartographers and chronographers, and that each in her fashion and for her own ends looks to chart another point in time and space. They look for the source from whence their hopes and dangers come, the answers to their questions. So far in this landscape of psychic time they can descry only the mountains, where light flows like a swift stream over the highest peaks, and, below, glimpsed in the chance parting of sulfurous mists, a dark, dark patch of forest that gives off from afar the unquiet, sleepy aura of pregnancy, of something waiting to arrive.

On a plane that leaves Miami three hours later, tracing the identical flight plan for John F. Kennedy Airport, the pursuit of which Aunt Reginia warned hunches against the window and nuzzles its ear against the inadequate pillow lodged between seat and cabin wall. He has been watching closely since the four young men left Wessex House, and, though now hours behind them, he is confident that patience will be rewarded, and so has no trouble sleeping quietly until the plane lands.

Part 2
SEXUAL HISTORIES

New Haven, Connecticut
shortly thereafter

9

New Haven, around midnight

Langston frets, waiting for the others to go to sleep so that he can complete the second part of his nefarious plans.

It's Langston's second hotel room in almost three weeks. Looking around the room at the floor-length heavy drapes that glint a faded gold on one side and an oatmeal-ish gray on the other, at the two boxy beds and the tall coffinlike television armoire with its one sticky door, and at his sagging, somewhat beaten luggage, the complete tableau framed by straight-line boxy walls and a stucco ceiling, Langston swoons for a half second with business traveler's vertigo: a shaky off-centered feeling, the sense that he might be some fungible commodity that passes its days packed in a box being shuttled cross-country in the darkness of a train car—as though life has become one long, attenuated visit tinged by constant anxiety about a return trip both depressingly imminent and endlessly deferred.

Nothing's gone particularly well since they landed. A late deplaning at JFK, an interminable delay at the luggage carousel that allowed Reynaldo and Quentin to get into another argument, the lengthy wait for a rental car, and the lengthier journey on Interstate 95, clogged by road repairs, managed to sink all of them into a wordless funk. By the time New Haven's skyline came into view, even Quentin had run out of bitchy complaints and convoluted stories. Langston tried to sound a cheery note—"They have some good pizza in New Haven," he'd said—but no one offered so much as an "oh" as the car glided onto exit 46 and banked softly down through the camouflage of treetops and late-summer foliage hiding the streets below. They had watched the city sprawl out around them in stuporous quiet, as if absorbing a bitter defeat.

Then sleeping arrangements worked out badly, with the worst possible pairings. Mrs. Gillory's generosity means they can easily afford two adjoining rooms in a hotel conveniently proximate to Yale campus. So when they checked in, Langston worried, *How can I possibly get him to share the bed with me here?* It didn't occur to him that they might not share a room at all. But Azaril barreled his way into one of the rooms, and, before Langston could follow him, there came Reynaldo, slipping around Langston and flopping onto the bed in the blink of an eye it took for Langston to shift the weight of his hanging bag on his shoulder. Langston tried to give Reynaldo a surreptitious pump of the eyebrows to let him know he was trespassing, but then there Quentin was pushing Langston from behind and saying something coarse to the effect that since "the boys" had already decided which room they preferred, "we girls" were stuck with the other one.

It all sorted out so swiftly and smoothly that Langston could see the fingerprints of Fate in the matter—or, perhaps, something more sinister, like maybe Azaril is deliberately keeping his distance. Azaril's been a little weird ever since Aunt Reginia blurted out that stuff about Langston being in love with him. Langston's been wanting to pull Azaril aside and feed him a line: "You know—this is sort of embarrassing" (little laugh) "—and you may not even remember because it was so offhand and not even important" (shrug, make a squinty face) "—but you know when Aunt Reginia said I'm in *love* with you? Well, when a psychic uses the word *love*, you should always translate *loosely*. The picture they see may look like *love* to them, but they don't *know* what that picture means to the person they're reading. What she *meant* was that we're really close friends."

But that kind of conversation could go a number of different ways, and he might end up hearing something he doesn't want to hear. Besides—why bother with all the drama of confessions and confrontations, all the hand-wringing and rigor of having to maturely process one another's feelings blah blah blah, when you've got a magnificent love spell working for you, a work of sorcery handed down from the great hoodoo master Marie Laveau of New Orleans herself?

Langston gets excited again thinking about it, and can't stop himself from stealthily peeking at the photocopy he's got neatly folded up in his front pocket. "The words must be spoken in a high tower," he reads below the crease in the paper, and he ponders the provenance of this strange little addition to the spell, for surely prior to the building of skyscrapers there were no towers in New Orleans. Langston calculates giddily, like a little boy working out which Christmas gifts he'll get from the meager clues he can glean from his parents' facial expressions and the excessive length of time they spent supposedly buying groceries, that perhaps this last requirement is a survival of some French medieval recipe for sorcery that, in the convoluted, often unfathomable process of theft and exchange that gestates human cultures, somehow became sutured to the bastardized, vadoun practices of black freedmen. Or perhaps it recalls the nocturnal activities of a Catholic noblewoman of Aquitaine or Navarre who secretly practiced the black arts in hidden rooms in the castle of her ancestors. Or maybe you could trace its origin to stories told by traders in a Yoruban marketplace, stories that had come out of Mali and Songhay describing wondrous deeds occurring in the Mameluke minarets of distant Cairo.

Langston tucks the paper away quickly when he hears Azaril's voice drawing near. "What do you think?" Azaril says—he has a very serious, almost grim expression on his face, but to Langston he looks sexy and powerful striding in, not unlike, perhaps, Mansa Musa himself, the handsome king of Mali about whom Arab commentators wrote ejaculatory, adoring accounts.

"About?" Langston finally responds, but he already knows, he only wants to hear Azaril talk, see that marvelous mouth moving—how amazing this spell is, it's working already, it's like X, it reveals layers and shimmers of beauty you couldn't see before! Azaril is of course referring to the debate that's been raging in the other room between himself, Reynaldo, and Quentin, each of whom seems to be struggling to figure out how you behave when embarking on a psychic quest. Do they expect to find that Damian is *with* Sergeant Master Garrow, that he came to him or was kidnapped by him? Or is it that Garrow will know where Damian is because Damian is his son and they're in contact, or because there's some mysterious connection between father and son? Should they call first, or just visit him in his place of business? Shouldn't they conduct an Internet search on Garrow's name and see what comes up?

Langston tries to settle things by putting on the appearance of the sage initiate he would like to be. "When it comes to following these psychic hunches, and visions . . ." (He adds the vision bit to make sure they remember that's *he's* psychic, too.) "My aunt says you just have to follow your best instincts. Don't be wed to any specific plan. Just take a deep breath, and do it."

Azaril is skeptical about this haphazard approach, but before he can object, Quentin bursts into the room. "What'd you say?

We're going to call Mister whatsis, Damian's daddy, first thing in the morning?" There is a trace of anxiety in Quentin's voice.

Langston is rummaging through his travel bag. "Yeah . . ."

Azaril sucks his lips into his mouth and throws up his hands. "Whatever. If that's a plan . . ." He waits, thinking that now would be the time for Langston to start trying to mollify him and for him to start resisting being mollified—but Langston excuses himself. "I really need some air," Langston says, shrugging on a jacket. "I'll be back in a bit."

"You'll be OK? You don't want somebody to come with you?" Azaril asks; his tone is begrudging and exasperated, but it masks a peevish sense of hurt.

Ordinarily Langston is an eager rider on the little ups and downs of the miniature roller coaster of Azaril's unspoken needs, and might be expected to at least pretend offense at the idea that he's some child requiring adult protection, but tonight he's just too excited. "'Bye," he tosses behind him as the door slams shut.

Marwick Hotel compares poorly in every way to the vibrant color and beachside glamour of Wessex House, and as he skates over the hellish hallway carpeting to the elevator, Langston appraises it with disgusted pity. The walls of the hotel are dark and dead and dull-thud brown, as if the hotelier had burrowed a tunnel in dry wood or modeled the place on runs in a rabbit warren. The lobby is heavy with an atmosphere that makes you think of a highway rest area toilet indifferently sponge-wiped and given a puff of expired perfume. The disapproving face of the desk attendant who checked them into their rooms an hour earlier complements the decor: faded lipstick, sagging cheeks, a hairstyle reminiscent of 1985. Her eyes briefly widen when she sees Langston (my God! a black man!), then narrow down to malignant recognition. "You have your room key with you?" she snarls as he nods to her. "Since we have *rampant* crime here"

(Langston gathers from her tone that the crime is his fault), "the doors are locked every night after 9:00 P.M.!"

Langston feels grateful once he's out of there and the sky is above him, offering its baptismal cobalt cleanliness and calm. In his pockets he fingers the room key, and along with it, a small package wrapped in tissue paper and saran wrap.

Six peppercorns, a small vial of ink, and three cubes of beef bouillon. He also has some lumps of sugar doused with cologne in a separate little bag tied with ribbon. Before they left Miami, he'd slipped the cubes into the pocket of the light jacket Azaril had brought with him, then retrieved them while Azaril slept on the plane. He'd purchased this ragtag before leaving Miami, after checking *Hex* four times to be sure, and now, to get the final ingredients, he'll stop by an all-night convenience store so that he can complete the second half of the spell.

In a way these kinds of weird-vibe exchanges are good, Langston thinks: the more he and Az fail to connect, the more fractured their communication, the better and sweeter and more triumphant the moment of conquest will be. The anticipation of it makes his groin pulse, makes his hips feel suddenly loose and pantherishly powerful. Everything seems so possible now. "Magic," whatever that is, exists; magic happens. Langston has seen the unsettling evidence of it in Mrs. Gillory's room, felt it with *Hex* thumping hip-hop rhythms as it sits in his hands. Magic is the impossible rendered possible, magic is freedom from what can't be and can't be done. Magic might even be freedom from the inhibiting limits of who you've come to think you are, who you've been told you have to be. Magic might be the permission Langston's been waiting for to be truly fabulous.

The hotel is sandwiched between a pay parking lot and New Haven's downscale mall. Across the street lies the Green, the city's concession to a New England charm it otherwise relentlessly resists, a two-block expanse of grassy, slightly dilapidated park presided over by a holy trio of smallish, no-nonsense churches that turn their backs upon the proud fairy-tale castle spires and turrets of Yale's Old Campus. Langston takes to a path cutting through the park, feeling ridiculously cheerful, and he nods capaciously to a bedraggled homeless couple who are picking quietly through the sere contents of a shopping cart patterned with vines of rust. He crosses the street and walks beneath the dark red brick and high windowed walls of the freshman residences, with their air of dusty carrels and high-piled books and their dour Anglo-Saxon names: Bingham, Welch, Phelps, Lawrance, and Farnam, the recited litany of which used to make Langston shudder with a palpable recognition of how alien and foreign was the world he had entered in his terrible first year at Yale. Then, smiling a bit at the memory of his disempowered youth, he turns west along Elm Street. Battell Chapel looms up to his left. Several groups of students are about, clumps of pale white folks with heads of tousled hair, dressed in shapeless sweatshirts. Three really young kids with soiled faces carrying skateboards pass by. Each notes Langston in the same way—quick, unconscious check for danger, followed by bored dismissal.

The incongruity between what he knows to be his magically radiant fabulousness and the way everyone looks at him makes him wonder if he's dressed unfashionably—but then he's in New Haven, after all, and to be out of step with the fashion of New Haven is a bit like being unfashionable in Soviet Russia. New Haven has the feel of a fallen city, though the height from which it has plummeted probably wouldn't breast the lower branches of your average tree.

Now, what they *need* in this little bitch of a place, Langston thinks, is—hmm, how about a sun god? An Apollo to worship. Bring some sunlight into these dark doleful streets, sprinkle white sand over the mud on the shore, tint the water bluebell-blue, and invite the rich and wrinkled to come spend their declining years in a northeastern oasis of semitropical warmth. Apollo would do it; he'd fix things right up. All he'd need is a little sacrifice—of a few virgins, maybe. Apollo *nuevo*, tall and brown-sugar brown, with long blond dreadlocks and a tiny, tiny scar above his eye . . .

At the convenience store nestled among shops on Broadway, Langston thinks that the clerk disapproves when he buys a small bottle of corn oil and a large self-service coffee. Certainly the clerk has to be suspicious when Langston returns three minutes later and puts the cup into the microwave and sets it on high for twenty seconds. The cup feels warm inside Langston's hands; he caps it and takes a plastic spoon just for pretend. He smiles on the way out, feeling both ridiculous and mysterious, empowered with secret knowledge. On the sidewalk, he glances at the puddle of fresh coffee that laps the curb and checks the cooking oil in his cup to determine whether it has a slight fizz.

Memory moves him confidently down the street to the two archways beneath the wide, two-story turret squatting above the entrance of the Law School, and through the locked front doors—he dawdles, rummaging in his backpack for a nonexistent key, until a quartet of students arrive, unlock the door, and, after glancing at him, let him in. He travels down a faintly echoing high-ceilinged corridor paneled in blond wood, then up flights of wide, flat steps cold as marble that climb to the third-floor library, where, as he recalls from his days as a scruffy undergraduate checking bags for stolen books for six dollars an hour, ambitious students develop eyestrain parsing the majority, concurring, and dissenting opinions of circuit judges and justices—yet another kind of magic, of course: words that make what they say happen in the world. Langston strolls with exaggerated casualness by the library, imagining that nonchalance might slow his rapidly accelerating heartbeat.

He moves a little faster past the dark doors of the professors' offices. The hall curves left, but to the right there is a dark stairway that rises above the library's main floor. He'd have been OK if he'd run across other nocturnal prowlers downstairs and in front of the library, but if he's seen here it might look suspicious. Especially when he reaches a door at the top of the stairs and begins to pick the lock with his Visa card.

It should be easy, unless the lock's been changed; the Law School has recently been renovated, and where once it had the gloomy, decaying air of a Hollywood rendition of the castle in *Wuthering Heights*, it now seems to Langston disorientingly trim and fastidious, like a health club for corporate managers. Nine years ago there was a brief period when Langston came to this floor once or twice a week for secret dates. The law student whose high derriere he had followed up the stairs was Cliff, a robust, broad-shouldered man-about-campus with a basketball player's build, a high-profile family name, and an earned reputation for womanizing. Evidently Cliff had taken note of Langston's conspicuously dilatory and worshipful searches of his bag at the library door, and one night, very late, he'd loitered in the hallways until Langston's shift was done, and, with an inviting tilt of his head, summoned Langston to follow him to his lair. There were never many words spoken during the few weeks this went on, and Langston had very little info about Cliff other than Cliff's reputation. The only facts he had access to were that Cliff's coloring all over his body was an even cherry black, that he always carried a tin of mints in his pocket, and that he liked to have Langston lie on his back on the floor of the Law School handball court so that he could lower his fleshy buttocks onto Langston's face.

Langston shivers at this memory as he negotiates a large, shadowy room of cluttered desks and file cabinets. He can recall Cliff's musky odor, the smell of it imprinted for hours afterward on Langston's upper lip. Cliff's smell was rich, coarse, like—

A sound. Langston hears a sound, behind him.

He stops, breathless.

The sound does not repeat. Langston considers the possibilities. Was it a step on the stairs beyond the door? A rodent's claws skimming across the tiled floor? Or was it the noise of settling that buildings make, the way they seem to groan as if trying to rouse themselves to life?

Langston, heart tapping, drops into a low crouch. He waits.

A minute passes. Nothing. There is a sound, finally, somewhat unlike his memory of the earlier noise, and it seems clearly this time to be nothing other than the building settling.

Langston breathes and stands up. He moves on with renewed stealth, each light step an experiment in action and reaction: step, stop, wait, listen. He reaches an alcove where a small doorway is cut into the wall. He lingers again for a moment, listening, before he bends and passes through the low arch to step lightly onto the floorboards of a handball court. After the cramped, dark journey of the last few minutes, its high ceiling and empty space feels like a cathedral. A shaft of moon glow angles through a high window in the tiny glassed-off spectator's gallery above. He needn't risk turning on the light. The moon provides enough illumination for Langston to write Azaril's name on a scrap of white paper.

He tries to read what he's written. The letters look crooked and misshapen. Child's letters, baby writing. Here he is, an academic in training, wishing someday to be respected as an intellectual, and he's scribbling the name of his beloved in the dark in the closest thing to a high tower that he can come up with on short notice. What would Carolyn Halperin, the classicist and queer studies guru at Berkeley who'd taken him on as an advisee, think of him if she could see him now, stripping off his belt and wriggling out of his pants on a dark handball court like a little boy about to masturbate in a closet?

Langston sets the cup of warm oil on the floor, pulls off the pop-top, and spills the peppercorns and bouillon cubes in the oil. There is a brief sizzle as the peppercorns dance in the liquid. Next he pours in the ink, and the desultorily fizzing surface of the oil clouds.

Langston strips off his shirt. He hesitates a moment—if someone were to catch him now, it would be horribly embarrassing—then, with a quick, brutal move he sloughs off his boxers. He breathes: big inhale, slow exhale. Somehow being naked makes him begin to feel better. In nakedness there can be no artifice; for the magician (and that's what he is now; no one can say different), stripping serves to symbolically remove doubts and hesitations, cast away all obstacles lying between the visceral soul and the soul's powerful intention. Magic exists, Langston reminds himself, thinking of Mrs. Gillory. Magic happens.

Langston positions himself in the spear of light from the window. The drama of it, the blue-gray sheen spilling down his torso, shellacking his skin like a polish, the murky darkness of his groin like some dense center of power, the shadow that leans across the floor behind him like the revealed shimmer of his secret self, make him think he can sense a surge of what must be magic warming the bottoms of his feet and tickling its way up the ladder of his spine. Hurriedly he ties a red ribbon around his waist. He slips the paper with Azaril's name on it into the oil, and then he ties six tight knots along the length of the ribbon that trails from the first knot at his waist. He recites—he starts once and finds his voice too timid, so he begins again, speaking as loudly as he dares, endowing his voice with the grave inevitability of distant thunder, "In the name of the saints, and of Hecate, and the shade of Marie Laveau. By the seven words Christ said on the cross. With two, I look at you. With three, I see you. By the names of the Father, the Son, and the Holy Ghost, let Azaril Shahid-Coleman come and be set at my feet."

Sign of the cross, and done.

Being who he is, of course, the doubts flood in the minute he starts putting his clothes back on. What if this is one of the apocrypha? What if the love spell is a fake?

Nah. Like Aunt Reginia says: You know. You smell it, taste it, see it. Langston's got a quiver in his bones. He's been feeling it shimmy up and down his spine each time he takes that grimoire into his hot little hands. Oh, yes, he knows: something is coming.

And it's got love written all over it.

Hotel hot and horny: at that very minute

Many blocks away and six floors higher, Azaril, sunk in dream, suddenly kicks out sharply with his left foot. The movement yanks the tucked sheet from beneath the mattress. Cold, he turns over and tries several positions. A feeling like heartburn reaches up from his groin. Azaril grinds himself into the mattress, as if trying to scratch an itch, but the heat blooms and spreads, it thrusts roots into his feet. Like a writhing snake it winds and curves until it finds his navel and circles it like a lasso. Azaril scratches, flings off the sheet. Eventually he falls asleep again. But his sleep is not restful, and his morning erection will be fiercely red and painful.

Reynaldo, undisturbed in the next bed, dreams the dreams of angels—or devils, depending on how you interpret the Scriptures with regard to the matter of sex. Despite being twenty-six years of age, Reynaldo's dreams are so good that they're wet. A large discharge of seminal fluid stains the sheets of his bed, the whip-tailed sperm cells wasted, all dressed up with no place to go.

In the next room Quentin has been fighting sleep. He waits anxiously for a soft knock at the door or a turn of the lock.

In his disquiet and restlessness he goes to wash and apply an avocado-paste mask to his face. He is piqued but not stimulated to satisfaction by the incongruous reflection he sees, at once haggard from lack of sleep and transformed into something demi-divine.

Unmollified, he exits the bathroom, puts his ear to the door between the rooms and then to the door to the hall, checks the curtains, and then settles into the bed nearest the window to watch one of the late-night Showtime soft-porn movies. He undoes the drawstring of his pajama bottoms and fiddles perfunctorily with his growing penis. The only satisfaction: while the movie's no good, the blond guy starring in it used to be a soap star before he decided to try to make it in Hollywood, and the evidence of his making it is all there on the forty-inch screen: bigger muscles and nicer teeth, a much-improved haircut, and the opportunity to parade around in a very flattering loincloth for ninety minutes, scowling and growling and clipping hedges with a vengeance as he follows the orders of an uppity hourglass-shaped mistress who just aches to boink him.

There is a price to be paid for stardom, certainly, but then look—once you're there, you can do and be and look like almost anything.

Hotel hot & horny (2)

South, at the tip of North America's toe, Roan Gillory wraps her body around one of the beveled wooden posts at the foot of her bed, peering through leaf-framed night at the TV screen that has miraculously appeared in the cradle of one of the big-leaf maple's lower branches. She hasn't yet been able to coax the remote from the hands of the baby rhesus monkey squatting on the black plastic casing of the screen, so she, too, is forced to endure Showtime's *Savagestroke: Lady Chatterley's Lover VI*. The close-ups of the actress's heaving bare breasts and the actor's armor-plated stomach do not provide much of a distraction from all the buzzing, ribbet-ribbeting, clacking, heeing, hawing, and occasional bestial roaring, however. She gives the rhesus the finger and threatens to donate it to a cancer research lab, but irritation exhausts her, and soon Mrs. Gillory's chin is striking the lower swell of her clavicle and she lapses into comatose slumber.

She does not notice the dog padding up to the bed with its head bobbling on its neck as if it does not quite know how to manage the length of its nose; nor does she know that it takes the corner of the mud-spattered bedspread in its jaws to pull the cover over her exposed flesh. In her dream, she is transformed by the light of the half-moon into a cat, and she possesses delicate porcelain fangs and black fur that triangles back from the top of her dainty whiskered nose. She passes away dream hours licking the black luxury of herself, tasting the fragrant petal softness, longing for piano-player-length fingers and opposable thumbs so as to run them through her hair.

At some point—the sequence of events lacks clear metered progression, time melts and loops, the now circling back to embrace the then, and everything that happens seems to fall in upon everything else that happens, as if collapsing into an event horizon—at some point she knows that a hunter is following her. Sometimes far off and sometimes near there is a clashing of steel, a firing of volleys, the stench of burning wood, the tramp of heavy boot bottoms doing violence to shrubbery and crushing slugs underfoot. Now, then, she finds herself settled on her haunches at a roadside. Trucks and sedans, buses and twin-engine propeller planes dash by at sound-speed, following one upon another nose to caboose. The hunter bears down upon her, brandishing his scimitars, his spiked garrotes like dog collars worn by obese submissive women at an Exotic Erotic Ball, and his pearl-handled derringers loaded with silver bullets. At the worst moment, when the blades dance near her face and the bite of steel is imminent, and the smoke of belching firearms fills the air, when the knowledge of certain death wrings all the air from her dream-cat lungs, she thinks—*but this has to be a dream, you're not supposed to die in a dream*—she's rescued by an ebony saint in a loincloth. He boasts an upper body chiseled from Michelangelo's marble. He smiles at her cat-self, spreads his arms to the sky with a sword hilt grasped in either palm, and the long thin blades of the swords shine. Far away and very near, the sky is a dark lagoon-blue smudge, the horizon lost in a surge of sea spray like a curtain from top to bottom of her sight: a storm is coming. A wound opens in the clouds, like a toothless mouth filled with rainbow red and orange. Go through it, the ebony saint tells her. Or so, when she awakes, she thought he said; in her dream she is a cat, and does not understand or care to understand the prattle of mankind, be they saints or sinners. *Poo poo poo poo poosh boo bee booo* was all she heard: a kind of faux French.

Pissoir, at the same time

Back at the Law School, Langston dumps the paraphernalia of nefarious dark arts in the trash and goes to a restroom on the second floor. He's happy. He can feel waves of desire and desirability emanating from his body.

So strong is this feeling of invincible beauty that he almost laughs aloud when a guy enters the bathroom from behind him and saunters over to stand at the urinal next to his. Even though Langston can't see him, he knows the man's every move is attentive to him, his slow steps and stance a careful but unmistakable invitation; he knows without seeing that the man's eyes are fastened to the slightly swollen shaft in Langston's hands, and he's sure without doubting that the man is unzipping, and his hands—large hands, surely—are burrowing inside, fondling and tugging, and that soon the man's breath will shorten and the pace will quicken, that everything in the little universe the two of them alone share will go still and quiet like the forest when a bear enters—everything but the sewing-machine stutter of the man's hands.

It's a marvelous knowingness Langston feels, a heady, mindless, can't-even-feel-your-feet-on-the-floor joy like the highest high of a drunken evening's first buzz. He toys with looking up, flashing a brilliant smile, or leaning over to sweep the man's torso with a hungry, wide-eyed look. Just to find out how far their silent flirtation might go. He doesn't want to encourage the guy, and yet he does. The indecision is delicious. He relaxes and lets a stream of urine flow. His bladder is full and it seems to take sweet forever to empty.

From the hall outside he hears voices. Langston feels the man's attention withdraw from him for a moment, can sense him turn away and then return to Langston again. Langston's still peeing. He laughs again, more softly. He's not interested right now, he decides, he's saving it for Azaril. But it's pleasant to be cruised this way. Langston's eyes shift to his left—just to take a little peek, see what's being offered.

He glances into a void. No body, not even a dickhead or a hairy hand or beckoning finger. The man is standing too far back. He is behind Langston but near enough that Langston can smell his breath: which smells sour and acidic, like wine that hasn't been aged. And at the limit of his peripheral vision Langston makes out a dark shape and big dark legs clothed in what seems like black mesh.

Langston tries to dredge up some kind of smile and begins to turn his head around. He freezes, suddenly aware of his exposure, his vulnerability, and he turns sharply back to the wall.

An animal sense tells him that he is not being cruised but stalked. He can feel the man's eyes on him, a fixed stare that no longer seems to caress and lap him, but feels as if it's flaying the skin from his back. *Zhhp*. The sound of rain pattering on the heavy denim of Langston's jeans. Has he missed the bowl and peed on himself? Langston goes rigid. The flow of his urine stops, the muscles of his upper body tense.

A slither of warmth hugs the prickly skin of his ankle as the piss seeps through. Langston zips up sloppily and, out of fear or courage, whirls to confront the man.

The bathroom door swings back and then a little forward on its hinges, like a broom sweeping across the floor. The single stall's door is open, the dark army-green cubicle empty and serene.

Langston's breath returns to him. He waits, listening. There are sounds, but none are near or distinct. He thinks he should go but is afraid to move. Then his curiosity gets the better of him. He hurries into the hall, searching. No one. The voices both he and the man heard earlier have sped away.

Outside on the street, too, he finds all is still, so quiet that the electric hum of the streetlamps burrs like the heavy sound of crickets. He feels foolish and humiliated, breathing at the foot of the steps below the main doors that stand recessed in the darkness of two wide arches behind him, when he hears sounds: low voices, emerging from his left, on the other side of the arch.

An entrance is there, built into the south wall. It can be reached by a short stone ramp built over a concrete ditch—the

Law School's moat—and it is guarded by a heavy gate. Langston knows the entrance well, having used it years ago on occasion. Probably these voices are just some law students, he thinks, and he wonders with irrational hopefulness whether one of them might be tall and broad-shouldered with a hand spread the size of a sweet potato pie. Langston takes a step beyond the stairs onto the sidewalk, just to hear better.

"What did you find out?" Langston thinks he hears one voice say.

"Not much. Too many people around. I couldn't get to him safely." Deep voice, clipped intonation. Irritated. "You?"

"He's up to something. He *used*." This voice is somehow fuller and calmer, like a dam that checks and dissipates the swelling anger of the other voice.

"So you were right. And if . . ."

The voice drops too low to be heard, or perhaps the other one is speaking now. Langston senses that they're moving, hears, or feels—fears? He doesn't really know if he hears what he thinks he hears. Are they walking away, back into the courtyard beyond the gate? They shouldn't be, because it's almost always locked, and he'd have heard the gate open. Do they know he's there?

Langston tries to hold his ground. Since he can't go back in now that the main doors locked behind him when he came outside, he should just try to look casual—

He strains to listen, but picks up only the drone of the streetlights. Again he feels that his senses are leading him awry, that his imagination is leading him astray. Does he detect the scuff of shoe soles on concrete? Dread overcomes him: surely they know he's there.

Langston steps backward and stumbles slightly as the back of his heel clips the lowermost stair. He hears himself gasp, then freezes.

Two dark oblong blots like the nubs of the fingers of a huge hand stretch across the sidewalk, heading toward him from the left.

He turns, runs up two steps, he sees the shadowy door several feet in front of him, dim and grim and shut. He hesitates. He desperately flings his body against the wall of the arch to lose himself in the blackness. Clip-clop, clip-clop: multiple pairs of hard-soled shoes advance into the light. Langston shuts his eyes to pray, wishing he had *Hex* with him; he wouldn't be afraid then, oh no, he'd find a spell and whip it on them.

The darkness under the arch grows darker.

A sound like mingled song and laughter blusters into the shadows looming behind his fused eyelids, slicing through his fear, like a beam from a lighthouse. Clear voices rise and fall in the misty night air.

"Oooo," somebody is saying.

Langston opens his eyes. Two steps below and a yard or so away, three milky white girls in silver bomber jackets and black bell-bottom slacks locked arm in arm cruise by, their hair in sloppy ringlet swirls pressed close to their skulls, platinum, Coca-Cola, and orange sherbet. Three pairs of lips, muddy henna red, oval and arch and grimace, and blow out rings of laughter like smoke. Langston stares.

The girls pause slightly. He sees the platinum one grit white teeth that all seem to be canines when she spies him hunched beneath the arch.

"Why are we going this way?" she says as she turns to her girlfriends, and then turns back toward him as they pass. "I'm not feelin this vibe over here, OK?"

"I think he was fuckin the fwuckin wall," another says—perhaps the platinum one—and then they all croon, "*Oooo!*" and burst out laughing. He can't see them now, just the hem of their shadows slipping away beneath the streetlamp.

"Niggas sexin up walls, some ho and her pimp—nothing but freaks out here tonight."

"Yeah, and you one of 'em, bitch!"

"I know thass right!" one says as Langston steps down from the dusk beneath the recessed arch and feels his feet settle, safely, on the sidewalk.

They laugh as they flow out of sight. Langston takes a quick, fearful look into the shadows of the south wall entrance. He searches the street. He sees nothing. Only partly relieved, he starts walking at a swift pace for a few steps, all of his senses and attention focused behind him. When a trail of breeze whips by his ears, he breaks out into a trot that becomes a run that becomes a sprint in the direction of the hotel.

A gleaming police car, white and racing-striped in a blue that meanders and swims in Langston's sight, passes through an intersection like a fairy-drawn pumpkin coach just as he catches sight of the Green, and it is only then that he slows. He can't see the faces behind the gray glass, but a blur of ghostly color and the imagination of shiny metallic pistols make him remember where he is and what he is doing. He casts a look over his shoulder and sees two women cross the street, as if they have been watching him suspiciously and have decided he's dangerous.

After that Langston tries to act as if he's taking his time, though everything in him tells him to sprint back to the hotel, which suddenly seems appealingly homey, its paranoia and redundantly locked portals now welcome armor against the vampires and werewolves that prowl the night. As Langston walks, he questions himself and doubts his questions. The territory he's traveling now is full of possibilities, the unsettling and terrifying as well as the marvelous. If magic exists, could those men be pursuing him, could they be connected to Damian's disappearance?

By the time he arrives at the Marwick's shabby entrance, he's convinced himself that things may not be so dire. There's at least the slight possibility that he's simply jumpy because he's spent the last hour calling upon eldritch powers. He sighs, willing himself into a fragile bubble of relaxation, and then spies a tall, big-busted woman almost a full block away, walking in his direction. He hadn't noticed her before. She turns into the entryway of a posh apartment building, answering the jovial greeting of a mustachioed man in a trench coat who exits as she enters. She disappears—presumably to the safety of triple-locked doors and shuttered windows, to the welcome comfort of lots and lots of lights splashing the walls, flooding the floors and bringing civilization to the cobwebs.

Langston breathes, turns the key, and pulls the door shut behind him.

10

First thing the next morning

At some point before the sun rose, while they all lay fitfully asleep—Langston dreaming of vampires lurking at urinals, of werewolves baying calmly at the moon, their howls strangely lulling and therapeutic—clouds stole across the lush, blue-black sky and buried it under a heavy quilt of suppurating gray. The sky huddles over the city now, unmoving, hoarding light and warmth, and a pervasive humidity puckers the air.

Langston, Reynaldo, Azaril, and Quentin troop along the edge of the Green on the way to their group's first bona fide detective interview (Langston's second, technically, since he had a chat on the phone with Mr. Garrow before the others awoke): a meeting with a Malachai Reynolds, who apparently knew Damain's biological father. They find themselves writhing and wriggling in their light jackets and chapeaus as moisture leaks from their armpits down the sides of their arms and crawls below the neckline of their shirts across their chests, as if cockroaches were playing dodge-the-light on trails between their hair follicles. Langston shakes himself as he hears Reynaldo demand again, "But if they said, 'He *used*,' how could they be talking about you?"

Reynaldo's tone is as strident as his stride is decisive, that rolling, deep-through-the-knees slight-dip-of-the-shoulder pigeon-toed bowlegged walk of the cute street thug. Langston can see a trace of crystallizing carbon dioxide emerge from Reynaldo's mouth as he walks beside him.

"*Using*, thass a drug term," Quentin agrees from behind.

"Maybe I didn't hear them right . . ." Langston mumbles, though of course he knows he heard them perfectly well, and he has a guess as to what "used" referred to: magic. But he can't reveal this. The notion of casting spells seems like an almost intolerable indulgence on this gray morning, when he looks about him and sees telephone linesmen, street construction workers, and delivery men double-parking their trucks as they go about the practical, mundane, and necessary acts that make up the kind of daily living from which his long vacation has set him adrift. The impression of solidity they give off, of material bodies engaged in tangible acts, makes Langston cringe at how selfish he has been, exulting in fancies. Damian is missing, could be hurt or even dead, and here Langston is, rubbing his eyes, sleepy and fuzzy minded because he's been up late casting a love spell.

"It doesn't make a real difference. You're safe and sound. There's no real evidence you were being *pursued*." Azaril's tone ambles between distracted and annoyed. "Maybe if you were doing something at the Law School that could have been *mistaken* for drug use . . ."

"He was just taking a piss!" Reynaldo thunders. Then looks at Langston. "Right?"

Azaril waves Reynaldo's defense of Langston away. "I want to hear what Langston learned from Garrow, so I can understand what's up when we talk to this Malachite dude."

Langston seizes the opportunity to change the subject and tells them about the phone call he made to Garrow's office this morning. "It was a lot easier to track him down than I thought," he says. "I called the Payne Whitney gym, and they knew exactly who he was, because even though he hasn't worked there for a couple of years, he's running for city comptroller now."

"What's that?" asks Quentin.

"Money man," Reynaldo puts in, rubbing his thumb and fingers together. "A comptroller audits the city's accounts."

Although you'd think it was prefect of the Praetorian Guard from the way he told me about it, Langston is thinking. He tells them that Garrow seemed to recognize Langston's name and place in his adopted son's past immediately—almost, if one were being paranoid, as if he'd been expecting to hear from Langston. "Oh, yes, the colonel's son, you played baseball—no, no, forgive me, forgive me, you were on the wrestling team with him, am I right?" The formal diction had thrown Langston off. He'd expected a rougher tone, a hint of abusiveness, street swagger tempered by the iron shackles of military manners—this part he doesn't mention, for fear that someone (especially Azaril) might detect an ever-ravenous fantasy sharking in the depths below such an admission. There was certainly a manly richness in the way Garrow sounded over the phone; he spoke in a deep and chesty voice that fairly bristled with copious body hair and flexed meaty forearms. "You know, I am running for city comptroller this year," Garrow told him, and if there had been any hesitancy in Garrow's manner until that point, it fell completely away then. He spoke, Langston thought, with a great measure of pride about how he'd left the army and acquired an accounting degree, worked in various positions for Yale, then got his MBA, and now was posed to become a mover and shaker. When Langston gingerly broached the subject of Damian, Garrow shifted from resonant pride to an edgy vigor. "I haven't heard from him in *months*," he huffed. "You've been in contact with him? He never said." (That figured.) Langston was about to give Garrow a modified version of Damian's disappearance when Garrow said, "You know, he has announced himself as a bye-sexual."

Langston's silence at that point must have discomfited Garrow, and surely it was the politician in him rather than the gruff master sergeant of old who'd dived into the empty soundlessness on the phone line to say, "Don't get me wrong! It's not his fault. His father, he was not exactly—"

"So you knew Damian's real father?" Langston asked, thinking: *now we're getting somewhere.*

"I knew *of* him. One of these crazy lefties—he even had some ridiculous name I guess he thought was a code—Credence Gapstone. Yeah, he was mixed up in what-all, we don't know. Weird sex. Probably dealt drugs, they say, because he had a lot of money for a black man without a job, you know. He skipped town after killing somebody, evidently. Typical. The mother was this, well, *disturbed* young gal who was hooked on something narcotic. The father probably was her dealer. She was a whore, so you can see what kind of forebears the boy came from. One day she stepped in front of a bus. The child was left for adoption when no relatives came forward. Liz and me, we wanted—I wanted—a family right away, so we applied. Nobody else wanted him. Nobody they'd let have him, at any rate. He was in the care of the state for months. The papers'd made it a big sob story, and people were screaming on the one hand that these damn lefties should take care of their children, and then on the other that the lefties shouldn't be allowed to have custody of an innocent. An innocent. Sounds funny, don't it? Damian innocent."

Langston asked him what he meant.

"Well, you know, the way he, uh, you know, ran away." Garrow paused, no doubt drawing on his acquired politesse to dress up an unsavory assortment of facts. "Of course I told your daddy and all that I'd sent him away. But he ran away. Sent some detectives after him. They didn't find anything. Then he calls me out of the blue, three, four years later, and wouldn't give me a straight answer about anything he'd been doing. Not that I couldn't guess. You know what that boy was into."

"What?" Langston had asked, a bit mischievously, expecting Garrow to have to struggle with describing seamy "bye-sexual" orgies.

"Oh, you know. Witchcraft. All that—" and Langston could have sworn he heard Garrow shiver—"all that magic and sorcery stuff he always did."

"Did you ever hear of a book called *Hex?* Or own it?" Langston asked him. But by this time Garrow seemed to have lost interest, or moved off into a reverie of his former years, maybe, because he seemed eager to finish the conversation. He hadn't heard of *Hex*, but he had some advice. "If you're really serious about digging all this old history up, one person you might talk to is old Malachai. Craziest leftie of them all. He and Credence Gapstone used to run in the same crowd, I believe. You ought to know about old Malachai since you went to Yale. All you undergraduate types fawn over him and his I-was-a-Black-Panther lies. You can find him wasting his time and government handouts over on Howe Street. Tell him I sent you. That'll give him a laugh."

The boys mull over this information. The magic stuff freaks Reynaldo out, and Quentin says he doesn't know whether to believe it or not. "Oh, I definitely believe it," Azaril says. "I happen to know Damian was into stuff like magical ceremonies." Azaril basks in the heightened attention that suddenly flows toward him. "We talked about it a couple of times. Not about disappearing into thin air or possessions, but he was into wearing amulets he told me were magical, and he did chant and perform little rituals, I know that."

"He told you this?" Reynaldo asks blankly—the flat tone might be an indication of jealousy.

"Oh, no, I've seen him actually do it!"

Azaril senses Langston beside him, in a quiet that seems to exhale plumes of sulfurous steam. Azaril clears his throat. "He showed me once," is all he says.

Langston speaks very, very gently. "I wish you'd told us about that earlier. I had no idea that Damian did anything other than burn bad incense and wear a lot of cheap New Age jewelry he bought on Telegraph Avenue."

Azaril doesn't say anything.

"Well, so: we've got two stories now, Quentin's and Mr. Garrow's, both associating Damian with occult or paranormal phenomena. Then there's your tardy corroboration, Az, so that makes two and a half storics." Langston pauses briefly to give his dart time to find its target. "Plus, our encounter with Mrs. Gillory, who's connected to Damian through *Hex* somehow. We still don't know if my aunt is right, if Damian's father ever had the manuscript in his possession—since evidently what she meant, even if she didn't know what she meant, was that Damian's *biological* father was the one who had the book, since Garrow clearly doesn't know a thing about it."

"And then there's you bein' chased, or pissed on," Reynaldo observes earnestly, though his assessment brings a high cackle from Quentin. "You know what I mean. Didn't your aunt say something about pursuit? Somebody lookin' for Damian, too, maybe?"

Langston feels a ripple of fear pass over him, remembering last night. "I dunno. I thought she was speaking metaphorically, but—I should ask her . . . I hope old Malachai can help. Although even if he knew this Credence guy, it may be too much to ask that he remember Credence carrying around a bound manuscript almost three decades ago."

"Garrow could be lying about not knowing the book," Reynaldo says. "He sounds kinda fucked up. And didn't he used to abuse Damian?"

"He is fucked up," Langston agrees. "But I believe him about *Hex*. He was definitely uptight talking about Damian, but he would've been happy to pin *Hex* on him. It would support his negative view of Damian and make him feel he was justified in being a strict father."

"I can't believe Damian had to grow up with that," Azaril says feelingly.

Too feelingly, for Langston. The ache of envy seems always to surround and halo Langston's thoughts about Damian, like the low buzz of tinnitus: in some ways Langston had even envied Damian his father; he had suspected, darkly, that perhaps having an openly evil father rather than a covertly unpleasant one like his own had been responsible for Damian's masculine confidence and cool. Damian has always appeared to Langston as the Langston of the Road He'd Be Too Chicken to Take, the other twin of some Dumas-like adventure tale who suffers the castigations of imprisonment and harrowing escapes but emerges at the end as the beautiful prince, beloved of all, while Langston, unhappily endowed with a lesser strand of the family's divine DNA, slips back into the mediocrity that he defines. Garrow, at least back in the old days, was *sexy*—since isn't evil always a little bit sexy?—and so Langston can't really stop himself from dreaming about what it might feel like to have mean Daddy Garrow's hands handling his flesh, those sirloins flush against his flesh, the smoldering warmth of large daddy palms rubbing, pressing—spanking? All right, it's immoral or at the very least amoral to get the quivers fantasizing about a child abuser. But it's not so bad if the molested child is in his thirties and scheduled to take his oral exams next June, is it?

"Hey!" Azaril snaps his fingers. He directs his words mostly to Langston. "The woman who corrected *Hex*, her name was Verity Gapstone, right?" Langston nods. "Well, this guy who was Damian's real father, Garrow said his name is Credence Gapstone, right?"

Langston stops, his mouth open. "Yeah . . ."

"So there is definitely a connection between Damian and that book," Azaril says.

"But Garrow said the name was a fake."

"Doesn't matter. There's still a connection. You don't make up a name like Gapstone from out of nowhere. And maybe it wasn't a fake name."

"Shit," moans Quentin. Ever alert to impending discomfort, he is the first to notice drops of rain spattering the shoulder of his jacket. Uselessly, hc shakes the moisture off him with manicured fingers that knob at the knuckles as if bruised. "Eww. I hate getting wet."

The others note the rain spots as large as beetles on their shoulders and rapidly accumulating on the front of their jackets. An elderly black man, gray like his fuzzy handlebar mustache and dapper in an Italian vest and creased white shirtsleeves, takes advantage of their checked stride to navigate around them on the sidewalk. He shakes his head in sympathy as he looks at them and up at the sky. "Ain't finished with us yet," he says. "Gon be a ugly one."

11

Old Malachai and the warlock's revenge: near noon

Old Malachai, as each successive generation of left-leaning, quasi-Afrocentrist Yalies since 1978 have called Malachai Reynolds, isn't such an old man. He's heading toward sixty-five and will reach that high-water mark fourteen days and eleven hours after the arrival of the New Year—and sixty-plus, Lord knows, isn't particularly old by medical standards in the twenty-first century. But the way Old Malachai sees it, age is only indirectly a function of time and body. Growing old amounts to an increasing susceptibility to being the victim of theft: little things stolen in the midnight hours, so that you go to bed with two eyes of perfect 20/20 perspicacity and find come morning that five of your points have been ripped off and the optometrist can't rate you higher than 20/25 no matter what lens he makes you try on. What his brothers back in Lousy-ana used to enviously refer to as "girl-gettin hair," black and radiant on a proud Africanate head and on a fine, trim chest—stolen, and replaced with gray changelings not possessed of a hint of charm. Memories of names snatched away under cover of darkness, leaving other folks' names to do double and sometimes triple duty, so that next thing you know you call your own grandchild by the name of a cousin who died in 'Nam. And memories of events just become slush somewhere in a sewer in the basement of your brain, so that when an old girlfriend says, *'Member when we went down to so-and-so and did that and met him?*, all you can dredge up is a feeling like chewing on a clump of cold grits.

If it's not outright theft, it's creep that gets you. Creep: like a mission that started out being a rescue and ended up as a war. All these little gremlins of the gray netherworld creep up on you, gremlins that are fang-fingered so they can surgically pry choice pieces of your soul and body away, and gum-mouthed so that when they eat you up you won't hear the crunch of their mandibles and awaken.

There was a time when Malachai could open his shirt in public and proudly puff up his chest so that you could feel his beating heart and thus understand that you were in the presence of living history. I *was* a Black Panther, he could say to the young folks, I carried a gun, I gave food to the hungry, I challenged the pig. Of course, this shining chest of medals owes its luster to the spit polish of revisionist brag, but there's a little bit of truth in it, and since most of those who know better are dead or have moved away or feel guilty because they were busy watching television during those days, he usually gets away with it. And when those days had passed, he could say, puffing himself up even more to help the girlies tip completely over in their inevitable fall for him, I didn't fade away, hell, naw, I kept up the struggle. I taught students without benefit of classroom or degree, I helped run political campaigns and led a drive against drugs in our neighborhoods. I've known every governor of Connecticut since 1978 by his first name, can call him up in Hartford and have my say; and the mayors of New Haven and presidents of Yale come calling at my door, invite me to their homes for dinner where I charm their wives. I milk the system, and when the cow won't put out, I slap its teats around to teach it a lesson.

"I used to be a *crazy* nigga, I used ta be *fine*," Malachai told a hot-to-trot Donna Summer-y young thing he met at the Black Church at Yale last Sunday. It shocked him to hear it coming out of his mouth—what had made him voice the thought aloud, what had the fucking conversation even been *about?* And the faintly repulsed look of pity and scorn and wait-till-I-tell-my-girlfriends anticipation she put on her face when he said it—that was downright ugly.

Today, Old Malachai sits on his stoop pondering his life. The gloom of the sky and heaviness of the damp, breezeless afternoon air presses on him. Every time it sprinkles, he thinks about getting up and going inside, but he sits there, not quite able to decide, or having provisionally decided, not quite able to muster a movement. He feels sluggish, his muscles worn out. He almost finds it difficult to breathe, and his thoughts are thrashing awkwardly through dark water—bad memories, old anxieties—at the moment Langston, Reynaldo, Azaril, and Quentin arrive at the black wrought-iron gate that borders the front yard of Malachai's modest Howe Street brownstone.

"Malachai?" Langston ventures.

Malachai snaps to attention and immediately stands, senses alert for FBI, for jealous husbands, for larcenous gremlins and ghosts. He grunts answers sourly, squinting at them. "Uh?" As his sight returns and the fuzzy figures before him become distinct, he reads the surprise in Langston's face. After all these years one thing he's still able to do is smell a Yalie from three yards away. He relaxes. "Oh. You caught me napping. Gettin' to be like a old bear when I get woke up from dozing off." (*Ugh—that didn't come off right.*) "Well, come on in, come on in. Watch that gate, now, it'll stick on you," he urges them, and gives them a broad smile as the manners his mother lashed into him with a sapling branch from the yard forty years ago begin to surface.

"Good afternoon, brothas. What can I do for you?" he says, then points a finger pistol down from his height of six-feet-six at Langston. "Hey, now, brotha! I believe I recognize you!"

Langston, overcome by a wave of bashfulness, grins like an idiot. Malachai reminds him of the men in his mother's family, the Jameson boys, a formidable conclave of wits, rakes, and malcontents from north Florida in whose presence Langston invariably feels like a country squire in the court of Louis the Sun King. Malachai's body posture is just like the Jameson boys', his humor and speech and elaborate greetings just as foreign and mysterious.

"Let me look at you," Malachai is saying. "See, I don't forget a face. Ain't none of my young black brothas and sistas that don't stay in my mind. You from Yale, huh? Came to some meetings on, um, Rodney King?"

Langston nods—"Mmhm, class of '92." Malachai makes an exclamatory sound. "Welcome back, brotha, welcome back. What you been doin with yourself?" Langston pauses—the pause seems thunderous to him, fretful with all the embarrassment that inevitably floods over him in the presence of such men—and then he launches into a fumbling, incoherent outline of his PhD project. "Good! Good!" Malachai quickly interjects when Langston takes a breath. "We need to be *everywhere*, I know that. Especially these days. You know that damn board of trustees of yours is meetin' to consider a motion to water down affirmative action at Yale? I'm telling you, my brothas"—he glances at Reynaldo and Azaril—"The storm is rising. It is surely rising." Malachai shakes his head and discovers, like an unexpected island of high ground in the midst of floodwaters, a warm feeling of contentment suddenly radiating from his core. "So, you just visiting, passing through, or on business?"

"Business, in a way," Langston says. "We'd like to plug into that famous memory of yours for a couple minutes. We're looking for a friend of ours who's gone missing. We have some information that suggests he may be with his father. Unfortunately, we don't know his father or his whereabouts, since our friend—his name is Damian—was adopted by another family some years ago. But we've been told that our friend's biological father used to live in New Haven around twenty, thirty years ago, and was a member of the Panthers when you were. His name was Credence Gapstone. Do you recognize his name, or remember him?"

Ghosts—ghosts flying up in front of Malachai's face out of nowhere.

Malachai swats at the air as if at a buzzing fly. He coughs and puts his hand to his chin. "Credence, huh . . . You know, young brothas, my memory's not like it used to be. I lose track of things. . . ."

"He's supposed to have left New Haven around 1970," Azaril adds helpfully.

Malachai's face twitches as he looks at Azaril. He seems almost skittish. He says nothing for a long moment, then slowly begins to smile and wag his finger in the air. "Oh, oh . . . yes, uhmm-hum, yes. I do recall Credence. Tall brother. Dark. Very dark. Yes, I do vaguely remember him." He grins. "'Course, y'all got to understand that quite a few folks was going around callin theyselves members of the Panther Party when they didn't do much but talk a good game and try to lay hands on some firearms. Some of 'em didn't even do that much, but just let on like they was members years later when nobody's around to say different. See, there was quite a few unrecruited recruits swarming around for a few weeks after John Huggins, a local boy who was a bona fide member, got shot out in California. A rival black group done it, 'cause they were workin for the police.

"You might know the history. Huggins' family was from New Haven, and lot of us knew them or knew somebody who knew them. At the funeral the cops came in and took pictures of John's body and everybody who came to pay their respects. Made a lot of people mad, outraged—me included. I wasn't no Panther, till that happened."

He pauses, keeps a smile on his face while he considers whether he is straying into dangerous territory. "A bunch of folks joined up then—I believe Credence was one of us. He wasn't from 'round here, I don't think. But he worked for this fella had a business or something here, and so Credence, he just got mixed up in things going on. And really as I say, more people talked about joining than really joined. There was an inner circle of real Party members, the folks that hung close around John's widow, Ericka, and the people they trusted, and they ran the New Haven chapter of the Party, and then there was the folks who did some of the work the inner circle ordered. And then there was us, the fringe. We fringe—now I did get further inside later—we participated, but it was like this thrill at first, you know. To stand up to the man, not like them sissies down south gettin hosed and beaten and shit: that's the way we thought, then. My crowd was young. The Panthers was young in general, but I think us folk on the fringe—they called us the Cats, you know—we was especially young."

"Do you know what happened to Credence after he left? Or why he left town?"

Malachai stares at the ground and then puts his hands in his pockets and shrugs. "Naw. Can't say I have the slightest idea. I didn't know the man all that well. Unless my memory fails me, which it could, you know." He laughs.

"Would anyone else around here remember?"

"No. No. I don't expect so. I don't think old Credence was a dedicated member, like I said. He coulda been fly-by-night." He shakes his head and shrugs again. He begins to walk forward toward his gate, herding the boys along with his movement. "Sorry that's all the help I can give you. You know, they say old people's memories ain't necessarily bad, but that all the information just gets stuck in a traffic jam. The older you get the more you got too *much* to remember. It kinda all starts to run together. Well!" He slaps Langston on the back. "Good to see you again. I always love a visit from my young protégés. You are the future, my brotha. Brothas. Don't forget that. One day the people will rise up. There will be a revolution! A real one. Not like this what they call *terrorism* folks do now'days. We all depending on you young people."

He speaks with the fervor a man at a pulpit, but as he does so, he opens the gate and stands aside to usher them through. If his hands were electric cattle prods he could not get them to leave fast enough.

Once they are safely through, he shuts the gate, and then figures he ought to say something nice. "Y'all hungry? Turkish Heaven, that place right cross the street? It don't look like much, but they cook the best falafel and baba ghanoush you find outside of Istanbul. James Baldwin told me that himself."

Langston, his body flush against the cold iron of the gate, reaches into his backpack. "You wouldn't happen to remember if Credence ever carried around this book, would you?" He says this with his best hypnotic charm.

Malachai looks at *Hex*. Because Langston is pushing it at him, he takes it in his hands, gingerly. He turns the first couple of pages and glances at random pages near the end, then hands the book right back. "Naw," he says.

The four are several feet away, ambling slowly, when the sudden snap of Malachai's fingers splits the air. "Fellas?" Very mild, smiling. "I did—" Malachai's fingers play at the hair on his chin, clutch at the bridge of his nose between his blinking eyes—

"I did just remember one thing." He hadn't wanted to speak, not really, but here he is doing it, anyway. *It's the ghosts, them gremlins*, he thinks, *got to be those motherfucking gremlins*.

Malachai hesitates, then exits his gate. When he hears it shut behind him, he feels a chill wriggle up his spine. He coughs as he draws near to the young men.

"Ah . . . I don't know if it'll be any help, but . . . well, one time I remember I was with this other fella fooling around. Casing the city courthouse. We were considering whether or not to blow the courthouse up, because at the time they had Bobby Seale and was gon put him on trial. And, uh, Credence was there, too. It was late at night, and we drove by the courthouse, kinda circlin, you know. 'Course we didn't know anything about blowin anything up, we didn't consider the *seriousness* of it, we was just—you know, everything just started to feel like it was possible in those days. Never mind we didn't so much as have a book of matches in our hands at the time.

"Well, some cops pulled us over, took us out of the car, frisked and cuffed us, and then drove us around town in the squad car. We hadn't done nothing but look at the courthouse, but I guess that was enough of an offense. The whole time they was yellin at us. Like, 'Nigger! What you doin out at night? Nigger, your black mammy put her big juicy lips on my dick last night!' Shit like that. And they'd hit us with their clubs or pistol-whip us every time they said something.

"I was so mad." He laughs. "I actually started to tear up. Not from pain, just from, you know, fury. The third fella was up front, and me and Credence were in the backseat, and the cops was on either side of us. They had they hands on our necks, like a choke. When tears started comin out my eyes, those motherfuckers laughed. I wanted so bad to kill them. But then they just beat me more, you know, like they knew I was mad.

"Seemed like all four of 'em wanted to get they licks in," Malachai says. "The driver, he was turning around to smack me with his hand. I do believe I coulda been beat bad enough to die or at least to pass out. And I might *have* died, except for Credence. He was right beside me. I couldn't exactly see him anymore, because blood was in my eyes. But I could feel the side of his knee pressed up on the side of my leg. His knee felt warm. It was downright hot, to tell the truth. Hot as an iron. Pressed up on me. And I found the feeling of it to be kinda calming like. One of those strange things that happen, you know. Things was so bad in that car, I mean I thought I could be dead before it was over, and it just seemed so crazy you know, one minute you looking at the courthouse, twenty minutes later you gonna die in the backseat of a cop car. The only good thing was Credence's knee. I put all I had of myself, balled it up, and put it into that spot on my leg where the side of his knee was pressed. And you know, it was like after I did that, I didn't feel any pain. They was hittin me, but I didn't feel it. Can't be true, I know. I *must* have felt it. But I didn't recognize the pain anymore. Least I don't *remember* the pain. I remember his knee. It was like he healed me. And, you know . . . I believe that's what he intended to do."

Malachai breaks off. His eyelids flutter softly, then he revs up again, his words spin out rapidly. "Don't make sense for me to have forgot about that. But it took you askin the question to bring it back to me. I hadn't thought about that shit in years. I never did get to thank old Credence, though. Didn't pay him back for helping me out."

Langston reaches up to place his hand on Malachai's shoulder. "Is there anything else you remember?"

Malachai nods uncertainly.

Reynaldo joins in. "Why don't you let us buy you a falafel?"

They cross the street, Langston's hand still in place on Malachai's shoulder, and now Reynaldo's arm is lightly placed partway around Malachai's waist. Malachai's eyes are shut. He doesn't exactly relish being seen led down the street like some gibbering old widow by young studs. But somehow he does feel he needs help at the moment, somehow he has a fierce need to cling to a railing to keep from plunging over. He finds himself biting down on his teeth. It must be the guilt, he tells himself. The guilt over what he did to Credence.

Malachai's eyes are shut for only a few seconds. When he opens them, he's crossed the street and stands on the sidewalk across from his house. His house looks very far away. Malachai can't see it clearly; he knows it's there only by memory. Disgusted with his body and its failings, his gaze wanders off along a short two-block street that runs east-west to Howe's north-south.

And sees a ghost. A ghost attired in a black leather jacket and dark shades and a large felt beret that slants across his dark forehead. The ghost is hiding, obscured behind the honeycomb mesh of a screened-in porch that dwarfs a spindly white house halfway down the block. The ghost is hiding, but Malachai sees the ghost as if the sun were out and haloing it in a spotlight.

The ghost is staring at Malachai.

And he's much bigger than Malachai remembered.

How could it be him*? Almost as if he* knew *I'd be talking about this, almost as if he's here with these boys, but how could they be with* him*? What has he told them?* Alarm and confusion catch in Malachai's throat.

The gods intervene: the swollen sky shudders and bursts. The storm has arrived.

One heartbeat ago, Ajax, the ten-month-old Rhodesian ridgeback puppy that Mr. Aziz, proprietor of Turkish Heaven, purchased to protect his business from burglary and harassment, lay prone beside the entrance to the restaurant, his long legs splayed in a leisurely stretch. Ajax has known his neighbor Malachai since he left his home on a Connecticut breeder's estate to become a sentinel, and catching sight of him—and unwilling to remain both motionless and wet—the dog suddenly rises and begins to trot toward the tall, rich-smelling pack member who sometimes dispenses chicken-flavored treats he keeps for his grandnephew's pit bull.

Malachai's attention is on the ghost in black who watches him impassively from behind mirrored shades.

Ridgebacks are a strong breed, lean and well muscled, with skeletons of adamant and crushing jaws. Ajax, perhaps miffed that one of his pack is ignoring him, or perhaps responding to some unheard command or mysterious canine instinct, breaks into the loping ridgeback dash that helped his ancestors keep pace with lions and lets loose with a bark of such blood-chilling, lion-cowing menace that Langston drops his hand from Malachai's shoulder and turns. Mr. Aziz, cooking in his kitchen, is so startled by the sound that he lets a heavy cast-iron skillet slip from his grasp, and boiling oil showers the blue flame burning on the eye of an old industrial stove. A grease fire erupts on the stovetop; within a minute it has blackened three feet of the ceiling and charred the flesh of Mr. Aziz's right hand; he falls to the floor screaming for help.

When Malachai hears Ajax bark, he jerks away from the ghost in black leather. (The ghost doesn't move from where it stands, but slowly its head cranes upward. Its shades come to mirror the clouds, unshaped and indistinguishable now like piles of dung.)

Within a minute: within a minute it's almost done.

Ajax sprints at Malachai. From four feet away, enraptured with the delicious power and speed of his own limbs, the puppy takes a great bounding leap and launches his ninety-plus pounds of bone and sinew into the air. Frantically Malachai pushes his hands out to ward Ajax off. Too late some instinct warns Ajax that he has no open ground on which to land. He tries to scramble for room as he comes back to earth by turning his side rather than his snout and chest toward Malachai. But gravity flings Ajax against Malachai hard, and he crumples as if the compacted freight of two full ten-gallon trash cans had been hurled at his body. In the curious chemical action of memory, Malachai recalls very clearly and sharply what it felt like for the deputy's fist to strike him as he sat in the back of the car. He flails and plummets down—it's only a few feet, but it's as if he's been tossed from the top of a building—into the stream of filthy water flooding like the violent birth of a new sea into the gutter.

As Malachai's shoulder makes contact with the asphalt, the barrage of rain begins to flash down in scythes, in a fierce, lacerating torrent. The street's sodden gutter walls cannot absorb the intensity of this new salvo; they give way like so much cardboard, as does a portion of the street itself, which has been pushed to its limit by two successive winters of unmended potholes and fat spikes of concrete-cracking ice. In a few instants the intersection becomes a quagmire of mush, an oozing, sucking hole that groans aloud as it drags all within its grasp into thick, torsioning reams of silt and raw sewage below.

Ajax, gifted with youth and animal strength, manages to claw his way up and hold fast to the curb, which suddenly has become the outer rim of a new gate to hell. Langston and Reynaldo, scattered by the force of Ajax's landing, struggle to regain their balance.

Malachai, plagued by gremlins and the visitation of a ghost, falls off the curb.

~

(Payback, Malachai is calmly thinking. He has endured so much, suffered so acutely and so often, that there is a part of him numb enough to be lucid now, as he heaves for air, as everything in his body struggles upward. Or do these thoughts come later, after he's dead? *Ain't nothing going on here but some payback*. The past has a way of creeping up on you. You lie down with a dog once, and eventually the fleas will eat every bit of you away, even if it takes decades.

Payback: the past repeats itself. The black ghost, a heavy figure like a slab of lead, its familiar square face obscured by the black shades it wears on this dark day—demon eyes: the gremlin eyes you see when you wake in the depths of the night and catch them at their work—its solid ghost-body seeming to soften and melt at the edges behind the rain-smeared porch screen. The tiny wet wires make the ghost's body glow in black. Light spirals across the dark, makes the face seem to smile, seem to mouth words: *This time*—you *pay*.)

In the downpour, through squinting eyes and with hands at their brows to shelter their faces, Reynaldo and Langston observe this scene. Reynaldo's arms wave uselessly at the vision of Malachai's head, several feet away, as it slowly circles and then rapidly sinks into a great roiling pus of mud: like the tip of a banana before its last moment of solidity in the blender. Langston considers leaping in to rescue him. Seconds flee while he considers. Vaguely, he is aware of Azaril and Quentin screaming, and then he finds himself kneeling beside Reynaldo, who is lying flat on the soaked concrete, his arm outstretched across the muck toward where Malachai is—where Malachai was.

Reynaldo and Langston turn from the scene in horror—it is the sucking sound that repels them, the sound that probably is sifting mud and concrete but makes them think of bones squeezed so hard marrow spurts like blood. They see dark figures—sundry would-be rescuers and tragedy hounds—running through the rain toward them. The people race past a decrepit white house, its spectral colorlessness like a maw of emptiness or an omen in the sweltering noontime dark. Like lab rats in a perpetual state of skittish shock, Reynaldo and Langston watch people yelling at them, demanding to know whether they need help, demanding to know what has happened, who has fallen. They watch as clouds stoop down upon their heads and quake with the fury of their barely bridled power.

And they watch a lone stocky figure in black clothes and heavy boots and an oversize cap emerge from behind the porch screen of the white house. This figure weaves deftly through the crush of people being drawn toward the sinkhole as if tugged by the gravity of a collapsing star: looking as incongruous as a delicate butterfly floating against the wind of a storm. Reynaldo and Langston watch the figure's back receding from them, and little by little it dwindles into the endless, shifting gray.

12

Phone calls: mid-evening, the Marwick Hotel

There is something of a taunt in the way the wind tosses pellets of rain against the hotel window, something mocking and mean in it. Having manifested as a divine wrath that afternoon, the passing storm now sputters, blissfully unmindful of the damage it has done, its few plaintive drops like a shedding of crocodile tears. Langston, Reynaldo, Azaril, and Quentin huddle in the room Reynaldo and Azaril share, dumped across the beds or slumped in the chairs. The television whines while Quentin, seated at the table by the window, thumbs a deck of cards, shuffling and reshuffling in an attempt to perfect a con he hopes one day to take to Vegas. Quentin passes a weary shrug of a look across the table to Langston, who sighs and catches a glimpse of Reynaldo's eye as Reynaldo looks up from the bed when he notices the two of them acting as if they're about to speak, and then Reynaldo glances over at Azaril, who doesn't lift his head from the pillow, but glares at Reynaldo.

Azaril is thinking: *the Hardy Boys never had to deal with anything like this.*

Langston looks at the clock, sees its hour hand edging toward eight. "I should call Aunt Reginia," he says quietly.

"Good," Quentin sniffs. "She the one who got us in this shit."

The phone rings several times in Key West before Reginia answers.

"Hey!"

Silence.

"It's Langston!"

Reginia mutters some response. Langston can hear music blaring in the house—Sly and the Family Stone, from the few distinct lyrics he can pick up. "Uh, is this a bad time? You told me to call in before nine."

"Mmhm. I was listening to my music, though. . . ."

"Some big stuff has happened. It's important. We could use some advice."

Pause, then an exasperated sigh. "OK."

Langston can feel her distraction as he recounts his conversation with Garrow. "Yeah, yeah," she keeps saying. When he talks about his run-in at the law school bathroom, her "yeahyeahyeahs" become slightly more animated "mmhmms." He gets a "So that's it," when he tells her the common last name of Damian's father Credence and *Hex*-emender Verity. The story about Old Malachai and his untimely demise, though, completely shuts her mouth, and before he reaches the tale's end, Sly and the Family Stone are cut off in mid-song. When Langston finishes the story, Reginia charges into action. "Oh, that is just *ghastly!* That is ghastly!" She presses him for details: did they see anyone else with Old Malachai? What time of day was it exactly? What was the temperature and the color of the clouds and how were people acting on the street?

"Well . . . Reynaldo and I were talking about it, and we both saw a big guy in a black leather jacket running away from the scene." Listening, Reynaldo makes a face. "Well, not exactly running . . . huh? I don't know, it was hard to see well. Just a big guy, thick, kind of like a football player, wearing some black leather, a little hat, some boots."

"He had on shades!" Reynaldo offers.

"We think he had on shades."

"Oh, my. My, my, my, my, my." Reginia sighs again. "Just ghastly. Well, it's plain to see now."

"What do you mean?"

"Oh, it has the plain stamp of witchery on it. *Man* witchery. Poor Malachai's accident has that funky man-smell on it, like what you'd sniff in a bachelor's bathroom when he hasn't cleaned it for six months. Yes, that's plain as day. Sunglasses in the rain with a heavy cloud cover. Hm. Sometimes folks put dark glasses on when working with nasty spirits, so as not to go blind in the glare of the hellfire. I mean, it's not *actually* hellfire, of course, that's just a conjuring metaphor, but the nasty spirits do sometimes like to play with bright fire, you know, so when performing a summoning work, a practitioner of the art might wear shades. Or, he could just be concealing his identity. As if someone might recognize him . . . hmmm . . . well, so a warlock is stalking you, Langston."

"Stalking *me?* A warlock?"

"Yes, a warlock. Don't act surprised. I warned you about pursuit, didn't I? You're looking for someone who melted into thin air and your aunt is an oracle. Yes, sweetie bear, a warlock is after you. Now, the PC thing is to say that warlocks don't exist as such, just witches. But even if it's just cuz of a hangover from seven seasons of *Bewitched*, I always liked the term. Witches are from Neptune, warlocks are from Uranus, I always say."

"But why would a warlock be after me, and why would he kill Malachai?"

"Because that's what adds up. It has to do with your little friend Damian. He has stirred up quite a mess, evidently, and you're in the middle of it. We've had our troubles down here because of him, too. We had a couple more Castro sightings.

That's been a joy for the papers. Yesterday I took a little trip over to South Beach and your hotel to see what I could see—you know, find out if I picked up any vibes, and maybe see if I could sniff out this Gillory woman you told me about last time we spoke. I found the place crawling with cops. Somebody seems to have ordered a mob hit on the hotel and shot out half the third floor. Two people got flesh wounds—which is pretty lucky, considering the extent of the property damage. I couldn't get inside the hotel, but the situation didn't feel right, you know. I saw ethereal footprints heading away from the place outside the police cordon—red ones. The prints ran right to the ocean, so there was nothing for me to follow after that—you can't track anything when it crosses the sea—but somebody's sorcerous hand was deep in whatever went on up there at Wessex Hotel. It wasn't about no drugs or gang wars or any of that foolishness folks were talking about. It was like a show crime or something: somebody just wantin to serve notice, or draw attention. Maybe he wanted to draw the Gillory woman out?"

She pauses, thinking. "I don't know how or why this warlock got on your tail, but he is there. He went after somebody or something in Wessex Hotel, and he took out a supernatural hit on Malachai—possibly to stop you from getting information from Malachai. Though, truth to tell, that sorcery you're telling me about sounds like a revenge spell. He wanted Malachai to go down hard, like they had something personal against him." She sighs. "I warned you to look over your shoulder. This ain't a game of Clue."

"But—what can we do to protect ourselves?"

"I'm not sure. If this warlock is capable of calling down a cloudburst and opening up a sinkhole, could be that if he wanted to do you in, he could have already done it. And if the man who was beside you in the restroom was him or somebody working with him, your body could be swinging from a meat hook in a warehouse right now, and your entrails lying on somebody's table so they could read it for information. . . . No, this warlock doesn't want you dead. Not yet. It seems more like this show-crime stuff. Like maybe he's *testing* you. Trying to provoke you."

"Why? For what?"

"We'll have to see. Maybe he thinks you know something he doesn't know? You 'used,' they said. That could mean they think you're using sorcery yourself."

"This isn't making me feel very good."

"I'll help out as best I can. I'll meditate. Maybe he's floated something out there on the spiritual Internet that could give me a clue. Of course, if he knows that *I* am involved, he won't have been foolish enough to be that obvious." She blows heavy air into the receiver again: Langston can see her massaging her brows and shaking her head. "I guess maybe I can get hold of some acquaintances of mine up that way from the old days when I used to dabble in this kind of mess. Oh, Lordy, Lordy, Lord. I told you I did not want to get mixed up in any magic mess! Look. You keep a sharp eye out. Warlocks like this usually use the ancient tools—storms, dogs, bright lights and/or darkness, a fire. A sword, maybe, or a knife. Stay away from those things. Stay away from anything that, you know, smells funky, and anything old."

Langston sees the others looking at him fearfully, and realizes that his own expression must be terrified. "But . . . isn't there something more active we can do to protect ourselves? Staying away from bright lights and darkness—how bright? How dark?"

"Listen. *Activity* is not the best course of action here. Long ago I studied with a practitioner of the arts, and he taught me how to fend off an attack, psychic or physical. The trick is just to be *still*. You do not act on the fight-or-flight instinct, but you reroute that basic, animal energy into a radiant stillness. As in: once, when I was living in a not exactly top-line neighborhood, this ugly fellow called himself breaking into my house to rob, rape, and kill me. *Get on the floor, you black bitch*, he says to me—their kind will always fall back on ugly cliché, which means the racial ones. Well, I was reading a book, sitting in my chair beneath my reading lamp. So I didn't move when he came running in there smelling like manure and saying his mess. I just didn't move. At all. He screamed and screamed, lunged at me, even fired a bullet at the wall. I didn't move. He started to sweat, started rubbing his eyes. I was so still, time stretched out around me; time yawned and took a nap. I didn't move. Finally, so-and-so fell out on the floor, weak as jelly, crying and blubbering. I took him right down to the police station—I put a dog leash on him, since that was the only appropriate thing I had available. The police station turned out for him to be just a way station on the road to a hospital for the criminally insane. See, the way it works is this. I in my stillness became a kind of screen on which all his personal ugliness was projected, all his fears so awful that he could never bear to look at them, his pain so deep he never could feel it. That will knock somebody out, every time. The more fucked up you are, the easier you are to manipulate. I drove the man bonzo. That is a trick my mentor, the wizard Winston Arde, taught me.

"So don't be so quick to run around doing this and that. Try staying calm. Observing. Reflecting. 'Course, I know you, you're like your mama, can't stop running your mouth or quiet down the thoughts in your head."

"Is she saying anything about Damian?" Azaril asks from the other side of the room.

Annoyance ripples through Langston's fear. "Azaril wants to know what do we do about finding Damian?" It takes an effort for him to overcome the petulance that makes him want to just stop talking and hang up. "After Malachai, we have no way of finding Damian's biological father, short of trying to get Damian's adoption files open or something, and we don't even know if they would have much information on the natural father. I guess we could find his mother, but . . ."

"Oh, Langston." Reginia's exasperation returns, and Langston can hear the stereo volume crank up again. "What kind of detective are you? Avenues are still available. What you are doing is not so much *finding*. It's not like trying to locate a missing necklace. You're working on instinct, collecting impressions. You take those and what you do is put together a *narrative*. You've got a middle and maybe even a beginning from Garrow and Malachai, and you've got a part near the end—namely, Damian taking a teleportation hike, and a warlock slipping from out of the woodwork to do you harm. Be open to anything that comes your way, even if it seems totally unconnected. Don't be surprised if the answers walk up and announce themselves with a handshake. If I were you, I'd keep a dream journal, too. Sometimes the roving unconscious picks up things the rest of the mind won't pay attention to."

Langston's silence makes Reginia suck her teeth. "Look, child. Damian's father was involved with some pseudo–Panther Party cell, right? So take that and run, because you know you probably could find information on it. FBI were swarming New Haven in those days. Check out the COINTELPRO files."

"Ohh, I should have thought of that. The FBI's sabotage of the Panthers . . ."

"Exactly. They might have had informants in Damian's father's group."

"But the Freedom of Information Act takes so long. You have to apply, wait. . . ."

"You have a sister in high places. Zuli is the Law Enforcement Poster Babe. I believe she has a calendar out that's a best seller among cops. The black ones, anyway. What's that kind of power for if you can't use it to cheat and bend the rules for your own family? Call the gal up."

Langston squirms. "Zuli? . . . I don't wanna go getting her involved in all this. . . . It wouldn't even make sense to her."

"Oh, all right, Langston, all right. *I'll* call her up. What did that Gillory woman send you up there for anyway? She could have paid me the money, and I'd've had the thing solved already."

"Oh, shit!"

"What now?"

"Mrs. Gillory! Her room is on the third floor of Wessex House! Do you know who was hurt in the shooting?"

"Like I said, Langston, I wasn't allowed inside."

"Fuck. Excuse me. I better call her."

"So just like that you're going to hang up?"

"Well, I thought we were finished. And you seem sort of busy, so . . ."

"Oh, I see. So Mrs. Gillory could be in trouble, and suddenly now you're interested in whether you're interfering with my private time."

"Aunt Reginia. This is important!"

"Do you realize you interrupted me during a Sly and the Family Stone moment? Even my never-listened-to-a-word-their-mother-ever-said children know not to disturb me during a Sly moment."

"I'm sorry, Aunt Reginia."

"Will your being sorry give me back my moment?"

"It will if you get off the phone and get back to your moment."

"Oh, so now we gettin smart-ass. Well, all right, Mr. Detective, you make your important phone call to Mrs. Gillory."

"Thank you, Aunt Reginia."

"Mmmmhm."

"I love you."

"Mmhm."

"I worship you."

"As well you should. 'Bye."

Langston hasn't yet hung up the phone before Quentin and Reynaldo hurl demands at him. "What did she say?" "Are we in danger?" "What you talkin about, a *warlock?*"

Langston ignores them and takes his cell phone into the room he shares with Quentin. Quentin and Reynaldo crowd the doorway between the rooms until he waves them off. He dials Mrs. Gillory.

"Yes?" she answers. Somehow in this single syllable she manages to convey a dire threat.

"Mrs. Gillory, it's Langston! I'm so glad to hear your voice! Are you all right?"

"*Mr.* Fleetwood. Where the fuck are you?"

"I'm in New Haven, as we planned."

"Yes, but where can you be reached?"

"We're at the Marwick Hotel, room 549. Here's the number."

She makes him wait while she fetches a pen. "Now, why didn't you call me before? You didn't stop off on the way, did you? Have you gone on some puerile escapade with my money? Have you been sex-club-hopping or bathhouse-hopping or whatever young homosexuals do nowadays?"

"Mrs. Gillory."

"Never mind. I don't want to know. Just see that you put some portion of my money toward completing your task. I am not a charity fund. Have you found your friend and his father?"

"We haven't located them yet. Mrs. Gillory, my aunt tells me that the hotel was shot at."

"Oh yes, that. I was asleep. The police could have proved troublesome, but I concentrated on the matter and managed to convince them to ignore my door in their search. The bullets left holes in my far wall and broke the glass of the windows, naturally, but the holes have since filled up with moss and the windows have grown back like a lizard's tail. Isn't that a bit of a marvel? There are some advantages to this magic business, after all. If I still have a bit of it left when this is all over, my household help will become obsolete. If and whenever I return to my home, that is—which would be all the sooner if you get about your business, my darksome young detective. I shall be expecting better news when next we converse."

"Do you have any enemies, Mrs. Gillory?"

There's a pause. "I have a husband. It would be redundant to have enemies."

"OK."

"Do you love me, Mr. Fleetwood?"

"Uh . . ."

"Well, it doesn't matter. I simply thought it would be amusing if you did. If you *had*."

Langston can't say anything.

"Good night, dear (click)."

Quentin and Reynaldo go at Langston again, and he's rapidly telling them everything when his phone rings again. They stand looking at it.

Langston picks up the receiver wearily. "Hello?"

"Langston?"

"Aunt Reginia?"

"I've got one more thing to tell you."

"OK."

"You foolin around with that book?"

Langston hesitates. "What do you mean?" he half whispers.

"I *mean* are you trying to work sorcery?"

Langston glances over his shoulder. He turns away from Quentin and Reynaldo in the doorway. Quentin's stare especially seems threateningly perspicacious. "Well . . ."

"Because if you *are* messing with that book, then you have managed to get something going. That shows you have some native talent—that's not a surprise, you're my nephew. But I don't like it. I believe the backwash of the spell may be affecting me—maybe because I've had the damn book sitting in my basement for so long. I asked myself: why am I listening to Sly and the Family Stone? See, because I do not listen to Sly and the Family Stone unless I am pining after a man I have lost. Lost my first true man-love while I was listening to Sly. And then that red-boned Negro didn't like no kinda pop *except* what? Sly and the Family Stone. And I have not listened to Sly for nigh on two years. Suddenly last night I couldn't get the melodies out of my head. Had to cancel an appointment with a rich simpleton that don't have a future worth talking about, but the woman pays well and I hate to give up a check—all because I couldn't think straight hearing all that music. So why Sly now, I asked myself. And it started me tingling like I tingle when I mess with that book."

"Huh, well, that's interesting. . . ."

"Let me tell you something. Despite Verity Gapstone's efforts, that book is eighty-nine point nine percent full of junk. But the junk is mixed in with true stuff, some of which Verity never even checked out fully, and some of that unchecked true stuff has real effects. Although often not the *intended* effect. OK? So watch it. If you've done it once, *do not do it again*." She pauses to let some carbon dioxide escape from her lungs. "Especially not those love spells. They are the worst. The absolute worst. Understand?"

"Um . . . OK."

"Well, all right. Get off my phone."

"Wait."

"What?"

"Hypothetically speaking. How long might one of those love spells last, if you cast one? What would be the unintended effects?"

"Those are big questions, my dear. If you're reckless enough to mess around with what you've never bothered to properly study, it's like getting in the cockpit without—oh, what's the use of a lecture, anyway. I'll say this. There is no way of telling what the unintended effects of a potent love spell will be. And there's no telling how long it will last. You just have to ride out the mess. Does that answer your hypothetical question?"

"Well . . ."

"Good. You be sweet, now. And careful!" She hangs up.

Langston lets the phone stay in his hand for a bit before he goes to hang it up. He feels nervous and embarrassed, so that he can't quite bring himself to look at Azaril, who has now joined Quentin and Reynaldo as they all trail into the room. "Did I hear you mention the Freedom of Information Act?" Reynaldo starts while Quentin commandeers a hotel stationery notepad to write down all the relevant info—until he is hijacked by the shrill ring of a cell phone.

"Jesus," Reynaldo says. "It never stops."

"It could be my grandma," Quentin says as he puts down his notepad and starts searching for his phone. But it's Langston's. He walks over to just inside the bathroom and, aware of being observed, tries to keep his voice low.

The others watch the muscles of his back tense and listen to a series of *ohs!* and *OKs!* At length Langston shuffles back into the room looking rather damp and wilted. There is a braced-for-trouble hesitation in his tone when he says, "That was an old friend of mine, Galen. I called him when we first got in, cuz he knows everybody here, and—anyway, he throws this big party every year and he's invited us. Are you interested?"

They all look at one another. Reynaldo raises an eyebrow.

Azaril is first to speak up. "Fuck, yeah, I wanna go."

The others look at him in surprise. His attitude—and indeed, the way his mahogany fingers pass like the scuttling legs of a crab over the mound of his genitalia as his tongue takes a savoring pass over his lips, strikes them all, Langston not least, as belonging in the realm of improbable conversions, as if Nixon were pledging fealty to communist China.

Quentin caps his pen. He smiles. "Just what the doctor prescribed. I *love* mischief."

Two hours later, a large white van with broad, tinted windows rolls to the front doors of the hotel. A portly bald man releases the door locks and motions the four of them inside the heated interior with a jerk of his rotund head. "Oh, OK. Drama," Quentin says approvingly, and Reynaldo and Azaril are impressed, too, especially when they see that the van has three small TVs with DVD players mounted on three swivel arms for each of the three rows of bench seats. "Oh, this is nothing," Langston says. The fleet of rented vans and door-to-door service, he assures them, are mere appetizers for what awaits: Galen's parties are famed for the breadth of pleasures that they offer for the sampling, from the prosaic to the perverse.

Langston is chewing on his fingers. Everything seems off somehow. *Be open to everything*, Aunt Reginia said. So maybe it makes sense to be going to this party. (Although it doesn't. A man has just died, been killed by a spell—there's a warlock chasing them—it doesn't.) Maybe it's not doomed to disaster. Still, portents, signs are everywhere—legible, if one has the eyes to see and the faculty to decipher the code. From the window of the van, Langston can see spiders dance along the rim of a cracked concrete drum under the streetlight beside the road. They are black as black Indian eyes and black India ink, these spiders (Langston counts six), they see the world eight different ways in shades the wise, mournful color of dusk, and their red jaws wait to snatch up the unwary. Langston ponders the meaning of this augury as he rolls his body into a comma in the backseat. As the nephew of famed secular oracle Reginia Jameson Wolfe, Langston ought to know something of these matters.

"So what's up with this Galen dude?" Reynaldo asks. He's in the seat next to Langston's—again, the strange and mysterious work of the seating gods—and is sedulously trying to work himself into thc frame of mind for a party. "How long have you known him?" Reynaldo asks Langston.

"Ever since college," Langston says, deliberately vague. It's horrible, he thinks, that he has reached the age that when talking to a magnificent beauty like Reynaldo he must suddenly be delicate about accurate knowledge of his age for fear that it might make him unattractive, or incite in the younger person some unbearable attitude of pity. "All the gay people pretty much know who the other gay people are. The out ones, anyway." He speaks as if he's still in college and is due to arrive at a keg party at any moment.

Reynaldo's lovely face skews. "Is it possible he's involved with the warlock?"

"Galen?"

"He knows you. You called him when we got in, so he knew you were here, right? Maybe he's the one who had you tailed."

The noise Langston makes sprays saliva on his chin. "Galen's brain extends no farther than the perimeter of his crotch. He's not involved with a warlock, unless he's fucking him. Believe me."

Reynaldo regards Langston watchfully, but doesn't press his speculations further, and turns back to his TV console.

Galen is dear to Langston, but Galen unnerves him, too. Galen has, ahem, a little *habit* for romancing, bedding, and falling in mad mad love with men of darker persuasion. He traces his ancestry back to a family of Yiddish-speaking cobblers who made their living in pale, semipolar Poland, and his sexual preferences begin, as journeys of desire often do, far, far away from the source of the desirer, at the mouth of the Nile with dark-as-darkness Africans of the Original Nubian stripe. His lusts and romances then wend their way through dusky Latinos (no fats, fems, or anglicized Argentine types, please), travel on to the Indian subcontinent (here as elsewhere, the closer to Dravidian the better), and make a circular sweep to encompass big Turks, the more delectably dark run of Arabs, and a smattering of Filipino, Thai, and Indochinese beauties. The border of this endlessly erotic country is patrolled by a robust, foul-tempered Sicilian with a very deep tan. Beyond that boundary Galen cannot find anything to make the blood rush to his penis and his brain at the same time.

Galen's predilection has origins as murky and mythic as the source of the Nile, and no amount of psychotherapy can find it, whether thrice a week with a drug-happy Freudian or a combined massage and tête-à-tête session with a neo-Jungian who sat cross-legged on a mat and sipped sake. As he closed the door on the heavy resin of incense in the neo-Jungian's office for the final time, the realization that even if he could find a satisfactory explanation he would never be able to dampen his desires or subject them to conscious control struck Galen as an epiphany of general implication. Galen said to himself: beauty is beauty, and

I yam what I yam. He had come out once, but true happiness demanded, as for the fanatical Christians, coming out a second time, this time to announce more idiosyncratic and thus more accurate truths. Whereupon, being a scandalously wealthy sophomore at Yale in Morse College, he decided to throw an extravaganza. Galen rented a mansion in the countryside and meticulously arranged for a program of entertainment designed to encourage among his guests an ethos of unadulterated license that would, in its sheer excess, obliterate political and intellectual anxieties. Mere seconds after the party came to an official end and he had wearily closed the doors on the last departing fellow libertine, recollections of the party entered the realm of legend. Under considerable pressure he hosted another and another event, until by popular demand the party became a twice-yearly affair that continued even after Galen graduated in his fifth year and gained admittance to the English department to study for his PhD.

Langston can tell himself this version of Galen's life because it is the version Galen himself tells. Galen will let you know his story for the asking, sexual obsessions and all. "I feel no guilt," Galen is apt to say, meaning that he has overcome the discomfort of being a sexual, racial, and class interloper by almost daily confessing his trespasses: frequent confession becomes confident assertion relieves shame shakes loose creativity and reveals self-love.

"I feel really weird," Langston confides to Reynaldo, trying to make up for giving him a curt answer before.

Reynaldo nods, his eyes on the TV. "We've gone through some weird shit today." He pauses, turns his full attention to Langston. "I had a funky dream this afternoon when I took a nap. It started out as one of those school dreams, right—you know, where you're s'posed to take a test in a class you realize you skipped all semester. But then it got all dark in the classroom, and there wasn't anybody there. Except you."

"Me?"

"And then the teacher was there, and he was this big, muscular guy with a white face—like it was powdered, and there were black lines around the eyes and the nose and the mouth. He was sort of hovering over us. You were screaming. Then the darkness broke. There was a big blue light, like in the shape of an X, or a cross. That was when I woke up."

Langston gazes deliberately out the window; he has the sense, unsettling and shiver-producing, that if he looks at Reynaldo he will not see him in the flesh, but as an apparition plucked from the vision he'd had of him days ago on the floor of Redemption. Is this what the life of a psychic is like, where the boundaries between dreams and substance flow into one another like watercolors on a child's construction-paper canvas? "Maybe it was just a nightmare," he says hopefully.

Reynaldo's lips fold into his mouth. "It seemed like a warning, maybe. For me, and for you, too."

Langston cannot remark upon this. *Be open to everything—and be careful*, Reginia said. His eyes fall uneasily upon Azaril. He doesn't like the quiet way Azaril is sitting, as if he were gathering himself, husbanding his resources in anticipation of . . . what? Azaril's carnal presence is like a case of hives, Langston decides: oh so very delicious to surrender and scratch-scratch-scratch, but you know it's not good for you and you know you have to do it anyway.

13

The party: around ten o'clock . . .

Galen Scott Fiss's party is held in a great house on a hill in the Connecticut countryside. The van takes a narrow private road that winds upward through a battalion of pines and oaks graced by a few European elms planted fifteen years ago in homage to the arboreal past, before the blight, when New Haven's sobriquet was the Elm City. The riders, of course, see the trees only as the headlights bring them briefly to life, before they dissolve again into almost abstract blackness. At the hill's summit the road dips down into a shallow, broad-rimmed cup, where a majestic four-story manse with muscular wings stands, colored Spanish Mission sandy in the light and mercurial gray in the afterglow, appearing in the dark like an island lifting up its peaks above a rolling, open sea of lawn ringed by tall trees. Bright but gentle lamps, inventively angled at various points above and within the lawn, illuminate the smoldering orange, red, and saffron leaves of the trees.

The estate, a gesture toward the architectural marvels once occupied by English aristocracy, and very faintly reminiscent of Blenheim, was built by a svelte, leather-loving pop singer who, his days of glory having passed, expected to spend the twilight years of his beer-gut forties and beyond in the comfortable seclusion accorded to abdicated monarchs. Unkind fortune struck him with an AIDS diagnosis very early in the epidemic, however, and after the seven-week confluence of a deeply satisfying conversion to Buddhism, the release of a Greatest Hits CD that went platinum, and a short but epochal battle with a colony of cryptosporidium that had laid claim to his intestines, he perished. His will gave his newly christened property to one Vanessa Soames, a longtime friend (and, many cynically pointed out, fellow junkie), who had at that time just embarked upon a miserable career in performance art that involved the onstage recitation of haikus in the original Japanese (of which she had no knowledge) and an auto-strip-search meant to echo slavery and the indignities visited upon enemies of the FBI during the sixties. Thankfully for audiences throughout the northeastern corridor, the pop star's last will and testament brought her to her senses. The sudden gift of life amid sumptuous mortgage-free surroundings and the prospect of well-nigh unending highs laid bare to her the subtler, stronger needs that had led her to pursue fame and narcotic bliss in the first place. She saw that at the bottom of the well of her plans and schemes lay remnants of a self dying a slow death of thirst for the intangible things promised a soul when it incarnates in a human body: a home to belong to, the love and esteem of others. The pop star's bequest gave Vanessa the tangible twin of that home for the soul that she hadn't known she missed so deeply, the outward trappings of esteem, the extravagant material proof of someone's love. Grateful for this revelation, she decided she ought in some way to pass it on to others, by creating for people a space where all needs and most desires are satisfied, so that her visitors might also be enabled to decide what was truly important to them. She took this mission as a divine calling. In its service she acquired modest wealth, marketing her home as a retreat for the management divisions of rich corporations, for artists' enclaves, Buddhist meditation groups, sports teams in need of group therapy to improve their win-loss ratios—and, of course, the twice-yearly Fiss bacchanal. And she became serene. Like the royal Hindu adherents of raja yoga she was released from the niggling problems of bodily survival to become conversant with the deepest mysteries of her true self.

She retained her performance name, however, and the house has for almost fifteen years been known simply as Destine's.

Destine greets them at the door attired in an ankle-length wrap of richly-reds and gushy-golds (her Rising of Autumn ensemble) that twines about her waist and body like a sari. Gray frosts her ropelike dreadlocks, and there are two gold teeth in her gracious smile as she ushers in her guests and points them toward the coatroom. She stands not quite five feet tall, but she's buxom in her diminutiveness, and Langston, last to enter, notes that in his absence these past years she has also purchased a pair of violet-colored contact lenses.

As far as Langston remembers, Destine has always been as pleasantly impersonal with him as with anyone else, but tonight she holds on longer than is her wont when she clasps his hand in both of hers. When he has given his coat to the nose-ringed, shirtless coat-check boy, he's surprised to find Destine behind him. She rises on her toes as he turns and tugs the lobe of his ear, and says quietly, "Watch out for your friend in the black shorts"—meaning Azaril, Langston assumes.

"I sure will," he says reflexively, as if what she's said is just a banal party pleasantry, before the meaning of the words dawns on him and he stops. But Destine by now is occupied with another guest. Langston hovers for a moment, considering whether there's any good reason to ask her what she means, when he finds himself drawn along by an impatient tug of Reynaldo's hand. He looks around for Azaril and catches a brief glimpse of his delectable right buttock sheathed in black before the sight is swallowed by the mountainous visage of a big, red-faced, bespectacled boy in a skirtlike scarlet T-shirt that brushes his knees. To Langston's immense discomfort, the boy winks and flashes a slurring smile as he moseys by. Destine is lost in the shuffle. In any case there's too much traffic flooding the mind and senses for anyone to ponder any single mystery very long: "late-supper service is on the second floor, sir, but please know that there are over sixteen different plates of hors d'oeuvres circulating on this floor, and of course there are several full-order bars. The first two cocktails are on the house; after that, full price." (The waiter stamps both Langston's and Reynaldo's palms.) "One hot chocolate with Godiva liqueur, please, Ariel. . . . Charles—oh, right, *Caliban*, watch that lamp! He can be so clumsy. . . ." "I can't believe he almost broke that. Destine would have a fit. That lamp's from Bali, you know, and it's supposed to bring good luck to all those whose light it touches. . . ." "No, he did not stuff his stuff like that, did he, girl?" Reynaldo gets shouldered by a woman with attitude etched in the worry lines around her eyes and mouth. She's shouting, "Goddamn all you Yale wenches! I *said*, God-*damn* all you intellek'tial motherfuckin Yale wenches! Ain't there no nasty bitches in this motherfucker that just wanna FUCK?" Someone finds a way to usher Miss Girl upstairs—somebody spilling way out of her white suede halter, which naturally catches both Reynaldo's and Miss Girl's attention. Langston, an old hand at negotiating the Fiss zoo, tries to get Reynaldo to follow him to the source of the pulse of music that now and again makes the floor and walls tremble.

Reynaldo holds back. "Where's Galen?"

"Oh, you can't find him at these things," Langston says. He pops a pill from the little stash he brought with him.

Galen appears behind Reynaldo. Lanky, Langston's height. Pale with black hair down to his shoulders and trim-shaven brushstrokes of black hair beside his ears, beneath his nose, around his lips, and on his chin and jaw. Like many of those whom he's hired to serve the pleasures of his guests, Galen arrives upon the scene sans upper-body attire, but he concedes to modesty by having shaved his copious body hair and adorned his virginal new skin with a million silver necklaces, rings, bracelets, and metal armbands. His pants are skintight alligator.

"Langston, *girrrl!* Whusup? I thought you was gon be shady and not come!" Hug, hug, kiss, kiss. "I can't come to New Haven and not see *you*. . . ." "Please, Mary, you're here for the menz, not me. . . . This is Aloysius—at least that's his name for tonight." Ridiculous laugh. He gestures toward a burly black guy with a thick neck and the buttocks of Life (you can see them clearly, as he has been kind enough to wear a G-string; the crotch pouch conceals a coiled anaconda, and of course Galen wouldn't have it any other way). Aloysius nods without smiling.

"Meet my friend Reynaldo. . . ."

"Hello, pleased you could come to my party, Reynaldo." Wink, wink.

"Hi . . . Hey, Aloysius."

Nod with a smile, this time.

"So what's up, Galen? You look fabulous, as always. But . . ."

"This is the problem with old friends, Aloysius, they refuse to let you get away without dealing with your *issues*. OK, if I must tell you, my professor broke up with me." ("Oh. This was the guy from U Chicago you were dating last time I saw you . . .?") "Yes, yes, of course it was him, I'm not a complete whore, I don't change men every thirty seconds. I do fall in love with some of them, you know." ("So what happened?") "After his post-doc was over he dumped me—called me up and left a *message* on my *voice* mail, how fucked-up is that. And I liked him. I actually did." ("I'm sorry.") "Whatever. I'm back to what works, honey." Galen whispers, "Nothing like paid escorts," and gives Aloysius a smooch. "You also may have heard that there was a new bombing attack in Tel Aviv, on a department store." ("I think I did. . . .") "My great-aunt lost part of her leg there. She was visiting. Now why she was in one of those rinky shopping centers—! So I'm having a fabulous September!" ("God, I'm sorry, Galen. . . .") "All right, girl. Gotta swing. I'm paying Aloysius by the half hour. Get as many lickies as you can, sweetie, that's what the party's for—you did tell him the private rooms are on the attic level, right?—and call me before you leave town, OK? We have to inject caffeine and hash over old times." Kiss, kiss, hug, hug.

Langston watches Galen disappear. "So, anyway, that's Galen. It's hard to imaginc him involved with anybody being disappeared, isn't it?" He turns and finds Reynaldo gone.

Langston frowns. Few things are quite as intolerable as the petty discomfort of being alone at a party. Where's Azaril?

It takes fifteen minutes to track the errant boy down. Langston finds the love of his heart and loins in one of the house's numerous lounges, which appear to be situated at regular intervals as rest stops along the journey from revel station to revel station. Billy Strayhorn plays softly from speakers built into the lounge's pink-and-fuchsia wall, and Azaril is squeezed up on the end of a wine-colored leather couch with a dark, slim young woman wearing one of those insufferable Guatemalan vests and scads of neck jewelry. Her hair is short and curly, she has on shorts uncannily similar to Azaril's that reveal a great deal of lovely, shapely (but unshaven) leg, and she's cute in an unassuming, easy way. A big iron key hangs from a small ring in her left earlobe. The heft of it makes her head seem unbalanced.

Langston scoots over there pronto. It pisses him off, the way Azaril's got his big hairy leg pressed against her and his big body leaning out and over her, his nose to her nose. Why, they can see one another's tonsils, practically.

"Az!" Langston radiates a faintly acidic aura of casual flair. A martini he picked up earlier in his quest slowly turns in the fingers of one hand. "I *have* to show you the upstairs! Have you been stuck in this tired little room the whole time?" (Hmmm . . . maybe too bitchy.)

Azaril glances up, but his eyes return quickly to the woman. Her cleavage, is it? Is that what's got the cad mesmerized? Langston doesn't realize that a corner of his lips and one nostril have curled upward.

"Langston"—Azaril is still not looking at him, and she isn't either, rude ho—"This is Leah Francesca. Leah, my friend Langston Fleetwood. He went to Yale, too." So his words say, but to Langston, Azaril's tone sounds like he's telling him that Leah's panties are lined with velvet and Azaril's fingers are now at play there.

Leah—belatedly—smiles and extends her hand. She has the gall to have pretty eyes, almost as pretty as Azaril's. "So what is it that brings you guys out from L.A.? Not Galen's party, I hope," she says and laughs. Eyes back on Azaril.

"We're not from L.A." Langston speaks daggers, but Leah doesn't feel the prick of his blade, since she's occupied at the moment with the finger Azaril makes bold to twist in her curls. She gives Azaril's finger, and then Azaril's face, a haughty I-know-you-didn't look, and pushes him off—but gently, ever so gently, with a crooked smile.

Langston tries again. "We're looking for a friend of ours, a very *good* friend who's missing. He could be in serious trouble. He disappeared under very dangerous circumstances."

Leah seems to laugh. Langston's mouth opens in the expression of mock horror he has planned for the first hint of a faux pas on her part, and spins to Azaril for a sign of his outrage or at least his embarrassment at her gauche behavior. But Azaril still beams the same idiot smile, as if his expression were the mold for a plaster clown's face. Leah, too, seems to have paid no attention whatever to Langston's dire reminder. Belatedly she asks, "So, what are you, like, detectives?"

Langston wants to spit. He can tell by her tone that she's asking Az whether he has a big dick.

"Sorta," Azaril breathes. "Maybe you've seen Damian. Five-eleven, shaved head, very dark African American man, slim and muscular. Lotsa tattoos. Very striking, very good-looking—wouldn't you say so, Langston?"

"Mmhm."

"No, I haven't seen him. I don't think I'd miss anybody like that." She gives Langston a cursory and, he feels, rather too dismissive glance. "Since being a detective is one of your talents . . ."

"One of my many talents," Azaril interrupts.

Leah tosses her head back and laughs, Mrs. Robinson in *The Graduate* style. "I did say *one* of your talents. Maybe I should hire you for my case."

Azaril talks to Langston while bringing his lips ever closer to Leah's neck and ears. "Leah wants to find her old family house in Spain. She can trace her ancestry back beyond the fifteenth century. Her family on her mother's side was expelled from Granada by the Inquisition in 1492, just for being Jews." Evidently this is an arousing fact, as he can't seem to stop himself from offering a couple of soft kisses to the nape of her neck and the end of her chin.

Leah brushes off these insistent affections (but notice the cleverness of her technique, turning her face away, ducking out of reach and warding him off with her hand raised in the universal sign for "Stop," then immediately returning, as if tethered to him by a string that snaps her back if she dares draw more than seven inches away—bitch). "You probably know that history," she's saying to Langston—speaking to him but not looking at him, of course. "My mother's ancestors wouldn't convert and left with nothing, except this key—" she flicks the iron drooping from her earlobe—"to their house in Granada the Christians took from them. They thought they'd be back someday."

"It's a thousand years old," Azaril says. It's sickening to Langston, the way the two of them seem to have already become synchronized. "She'd like to find the actual house, if it's still there. I say we should do it. Take her down with us to your aunt's house and have her do a reading of the key."

Langston gives them a glorious smile. "What a complicated family history, Leah! So what happened, then, did your family come to America directly, or end up in South America, or . . .?"

Leah doesn't answer, probably doesn't really hear the question. It's really a sight to see: Azaril swinging his big leg over Leah's knees and ramming his fat tongue into her mouth.

Horror and realization arrive in a single fierce instant for Langston: as Reginia warned it would, the spell he cast has done all the wrong things in the wrong way. It's turned Azaril into a sex demon, and it's turned Langston himself into a mean, jealous bitch. He wonders, as he blankly watches Leah's jaws work Azaril's tongue like she's chewing bubble gum, whether something like this might not have happened to Damian. A spell gone awry, an incantation fatally flubbed, and poof! Everything falls apart and you disappear, you melt into air.

"Don't you realize there's a warlock after us?" Langston almost shouts. But neither of the kissing duo notices.

"Langston, come here, please."

Destine has him by the collar of his shirt, so her entreaty isn't exactly a request, and besides she speaks uncannily like his grandmother sometimes did, in a similar I-shall-brook-no-nonsense-so-don't-make-me-beat-the-nonsense-out-of-you tone. As he lets himself be taken away, he considers doing something dramatic. Yelling out "There's Damian!" comes to mind, but that solution might be almost as unpleasant as the problem it would address, since in effect Langston would be surrendering completely to the idea that it's not him that Azaril wants or cares for. "Where are we going?" Langston demands, and takes a desperate look back over his shoulder.

"Shhh," she says, and leading him by the collar as if by the nose, she drags him down a long hallway. Langston feels dimly humiliated by the puzzled and derisive looks he gets as they plow through a thicket of half-clad teenagers (*God, how young and beautiful everyone looks*, Langston thinks, *and I'm so old now and faded*). Their destination is an elevator, and as the lift doors close and quiet settles over them, Langston straightens his shirt to distract himself from the anger and hurt that have their hands around his throat. Why not follow a crazy woman who's treating him like a piece of chattel? He's open to everything, right? He feels her looking at him and refuses to show that he's noticed, loftily keeping his focus on the relay of floor numbers on the indicator display.

They emerge on the third floor. Here the walls and floor do not tremble, but throb like a living heart in ecstasy.

"The ballroom floor's up here," Destine explains. "We knocked out I don't know how many walls. Like it? The sound? I think it's—cold. Clammy. Now back in my day, we could *party*. We changed the world by day, partied at night. They felt almost like doing the same thing. The same rhythm. Now, what do you have? I listen to this music and watch these people dance and I see a bunch of cold, clammy sad folks working hard to warm up. World seems old these days." Destine sighs. "This way."

Langston has barely listened to her. He takes a surreptitious peek over his shoulder as he stumbles. Of course, how stupid, Azaril has not followed him, and is likely—what? Seven, eight, nine inches inside Leah right now? Langston has no idea, having never seen it erect, which is a terrible shame, really; after all this time you'd think two friends would at least get to see each other's—

Destine leads him away from the ballroom, stroking his shoulders and neck with her hand. They trace a path through the labyrinthine hallways that seem always to be approaching and then avoiding the heart of the music. "Where're we goin?" Langston asks.

"To my room."

Dim emerald-tinted bulbs affixed high in the ceiling give off a light like that of those old mirrors that are so high in lead content they sink over the years into a catatonia of bronzelike rust and blotted reflections. The long passageway on the mansion's fourth floor shrouds in murk the partygoers who mill about, shadow figures Langston sees at an angle or sideways. The voices of these people are more hushed than on the floors below, and a deep pile carpet cushions the sonic throb of the disco-house music. A mélange aroma of strange perfumes and incense and varieties of plants it is illegal to smoke softens the pine-forest sheen of the air.

At the hallway's end, Destine turns a key in a lock. They enter a modest-sized room. Langston, through eyes no more than slits, sees a desk, two comfy chairs that face each other, an armoire, and bare walls. An extravagantly large Turkish rug covers the hardwood floor. It is cooler in the room than in the hall, almost cold, as air flows in from tall, wide-open windows. Conversation, laughter, and music drift up in distorted snatches from the lawn below. Destine pulls the windows almost shut but leaves them cracked, and with a yank on a dangling velvet cord, brings curtains patterned with arabesque designs to a close, cutting off the nocturnal light. A candle that looks as wide around as an elephant's leg burns fitfully in a shallow platter on the edge of the scrupulously well-ordered desktop. She drapes Langston across one of the chairs, practically arranging his head and limbs for him. He feels odd and ungrounded, breathless, as if he's been racing rather than walking. She's confused him with the route she's taken, he's unsure where he is. The music, when he hears it, seems to be traveling upward through the floor, not through the walls.

"Comfortable? Good. You just relax. Relax and listen." Destine looks at him. "That is, if you not so far gone you can't handle doing both at the same time." She laughs.

Langston can see the glint of her gold teeth, like signal fires on a hillside the night before a battle in ancient times. Something seems to want to warn him. He tries to rise in the chair, but softly, with the touch of a soothing—or aggressive?—lover, it seems to pull him low into the quagmire of its cushions.

Destine is watching him. She lowers herself into the chair opposite his. "I hear you been scouting some information about an old friend of mine."

Langston tries to look at her, but the view of her in the murk of the room is scumbled. All he sees clearly are her knees, vast and great somehow like the knees of a towering marble statue in the temple of a goddess. "I'm sorry . . .?"

"Malachai Reynolds is my very old friend."

"You knew Old Malachai? I mean . . ." He works hard to bring himself into clear consciousness. "I'm sorry . . . I guess you must have heard. . . ."

"Malachai and me didn't have no secrets between us." She speaks with quiet assurance. "Not much that passed through his mind and almost nothing that stayed in his heart that I didn't know or have some inkling about. We didn't waste lots of time, see, him and me. We didn't dawdle at becoming lovers, didn't come into this world as siblings or kissing cousins. Didn't bother with being best friends. We've already done all that. Way, way back we pledged ourselves to each other. You've heard of reincarnation, I expect. See, a long time ago Malachai and me figured it out—of course we wasn't Malachai and me then. Maybe we were philosophers together, or scientists. Monks or holy men, that's how I figure. Some way we knew we would be back, over and over again. So we pledged to rendezvous. Each time we meet. Each life. No matter how it would turn out, whether we was to end up fighting or fornicating, we pledged we would find each other. We decided to do this for comfort, I reckon, against the curse of being ignorant from one incarnation to the next. Got much more complicated as we went along. We thought we was doin something to cheat the gods, but turns out we was probably working their plan even by cheating. As it is always when you try to take matters into your own hands, I believe."

The room falls into deep quiet. Langston believes that he can hear the candle burning: a small, timid series of sounds like an infant trying to spit.

"Langston Fleetwood. I never heard that name before tonight, although—" She trails off, seemingly lost in the necessity of looking at him extra closely. "Thing is, when I felt you, when I touched your shoulder when you walked in, I got a hit. I knew you was the one who was asking my Malachai questions before he died."

A hit? She's psychic, too? "I . . . was there, when it happened, the accident," Langston ventures. "I wish . . . I'm very sorry about your loss."

"Oh, it don't matter," Destine interrupts him. "Accident, shmaccident. Who cares? He'll be back. What matters for us left behind is the tidying up. The unfinished business. Whichever one of us gets left behind always has that job. And something makes me think the tidying up involves you."

The air in the room is cold. Langston feels more confused than ever. He wonders if his disorientation is by design. The woman is like a snake, swaying before him, mesmerizing him for—the kill? But maybe she doesn't mean him harm. He has the sense that she's preparing him for something—sweeping aside the cobwebs of rational thought. Maybe she wants him to be confused so that he can be receptive. Reginia has told him: it's when you're blank, when you're exhausted or drugged or otherwise shifted a few inches outside the narrow lanes of habitual perception, that you really see, that you go galloping among the gods in the spirit world, hear voices, converse with the dead, peer through the veils into lost dimensions.

"What were you asking questions about Credence Gapstone for?" Destine's voice is rough, commanding. "Because Credence was heavy on Malachai's mind before he passed. He was heavy on my mind, and I had no reason to think about him, so I knew it must have been Malachai's worries, slipping into my mind. And I have been wondering all evening. Why Credence? Why now? And since no answer come to me, I know it's about the unfinished business."

"How did you—?" Langston begins, but then decides not to ask yet. "Credence is—or was—the father of a friend of mine who's missing. A guy named Damian Sundiata. It was kind of a long shot, but my companions and I thought finding Damian's father would lead us to Damian."

"Do tell?" Destine laughs. "What made you think that?"

Langston again tries to pull himself up to sit more properly in the chair and again fails. "Uh, well, my aunt told us

Damian's father was the key to finding Damian. She's kind of a psychic."

"Huh. I guess that explains the e-mail that came in tonight—one of those list messages, must have been thirty, forty addresses it was sent to. I recognized some of them. People I know from here to New York and Boston."

"A message—about Damian?"

"The e-mail asked everybody to keep an eye on four young men—and then it named you—who got a warlock on they tail. I didn't recognize the address it came from: ladyreadsthe-blues@hotmail. But now I guess that must be from your aunt. I figured something funny was up. What's your aunt's name?"

"Reginia Wolfe."

"Oh, yes. I know of her. She came to speak at a 'Buddhism and the Body' conference I attended over in New York. She knew a lot about Buddhism but claimed not to believe in any of it. Hm. Anyway, I asked Galen if he knew of anybody in town by the names in the e-mail. He did, and I told him to invite you to the party, so . . ." Suddenly she rises, slapping the palms of her hands against her knees. The violent sound makes Langston fearful again. "Well, it does figure that that child would disappear and be the cause of trouble, I reckon. Just like his daddy."

"You knew Damian's father? You know Damian?"

"Hm. Yes, I guess you could say I knew Credence Gapstone. Knew him in the biblical sense. Hm. As for Damian, I should hope I know him at least a little, seeing as how I bore him in my womb and brought him into the world. Named him, too."

Langston manages to push his head up a little higher out of the quagmire of the chair so that he can get a good look at Destine. He remembers all the times he's seen her before at Galen's parties, and suddenly her claim seems so credible, so unassailable, really, and he's embarrassed that he could have missed it.

The resemblance around the eyes and the nose, almost as if Damian had been wearing a mask like the Green Hornet's in the shape of Destine's face all his life.

"I met Credence in passing. Wouldn't have guessed from that little meeting we'd get as tangled up together as we are. But things happen like that. When I first come across Credence, I noticed him 'cause he was wearing some nice clothes. Very black clothes, all brushed and smooth and the buttons was polished. I was a D.C. girl, poor and not exactly fetching, you could say. Dark. Black wasn't exactly beautiful in them days, not yet. Oh, I was a hellcat then. I lived in a bar after my mother in her infinite wisdom threw me out. I helped clean up and serve drinks and fucked the owner so I could sleep in the maintenance room in the back. He was one ugly man. Blackhead dots all over his facc. He shoulda wore a sack on his head. Now, Credence, he was elegant. Sometimes Credence came to the bar I stayed in. I caught him lookin at me funny. Not like he wanted to screw me, though, and that got my interest. Third time he come in I bought him a drink. Turned out his nice clothes were work clothes, a uniform. He worked for some crazy old white couple that had a place in D.C., and they was there for a few weeks that spring. April of 1967. I just turned seventeen."

Langston tries to imagine her at seventeen: he takes his memories of Damian's face at thirteen, especially the structure of his mouth, the smooth depression of skin beneath his nose that flows into his upper lip, and gives him hot-combed tresses and a black girl's Farrah Fawcett flip on either side of the face like open folding doors. But this is an anachronistic construction, he realizes, since Farrah's hairstyle hadn't been invented in 1967 and Destine probably would have worn a natural.

"In those few weeks, Credence and me got to be friends, kind of. Started to go out to movies together, walks together. I figured he liked it that I didn't talk too much. Lotta men liked that about me. But he didn't try to screw me even with all the time we spent. Threw me for a loop. How you gon go out with a slut, pay for dinner *and* a movie and not try to screw her? We went out maybe three, four times, and nothing. Here I was, in what I figured was fallin in love with this man. I figured it was love 'cause I wanted to be in love, and because he was nicer to me, more gentlemanly, than any other man I'd met. So I'm in love, and he ain't out to get no pussy." Her laugh is cackling and muffled, almost internal. "Well, it scared that little girl I used to be. How was she gon keep the man? Never mind she hadn't managed to keep no man by sleeping with him, anyway. Seventeen and *confused*. Didn't know what to do with somebody calling themselves a friend. And hadn't ever even thought of a *man* friend. So I did what I thought was smartest. Got him drunk, used every trick in the book I could remember, and finally got him on top of me."

Langston's alert to hearing about this, and repulsed at the same time. The sex life of Damian's parents: on the one hand far more information than Langston needs to know; on the other—possibly a clue to Damian's own enchanting sexual appeal, a genetic preview of his charms?

"My dear, the earth did not move. I don't recall that the blankets even did." Destine seems to find the memory of this very amusing. "Next time I saw him he was all bashful and embarrassed. Cold, cruel, I was used to. But not all that bashfulness and shame he was acting. It was like he'd stepped in something on the street and was smellin up the place and everybody was lookin at him, that's how ashamed he acted. Well, I didn't like that. I let him have it. Called him seven kinds of names. So it turned out the result was the same as if he'd been one of the other ones who'd gone cold on me, because after I told him off in the bar with everybody watchin, I did not see him again. For three, almost four years. 'Course when I told him off I didn't know I was pregnant.

"If that had been the last time I seen Credence, I wouldn't remember his face today. When Damian was born, I had to try to remember him. At first I figured the child must be the ugly man's owned the bar, but the timing wasn't right. Damian was born in December, a few weeks early. After the birth I think I asked some folks about Credence, but didn't nobody really know him, and they didn't know where he was. By that time my mother had invited me back into her house, and the two of us got busy raising my little boy. Gave him two, almost two and a half good years.

"See, Bill Garrow, always assuming he knows everything, he wouldn't know about all that, and about those two almost three good years." Her laugh this time is louder and more explosive. "All he can think about is how when he heard about me, I was *acting* crazy. But by 1969, 1970, I *was* crazy. Credence was nuts, too. We was both crazy in love with the same crazy man, crazy Old Malachai. Credence got so crazy he left." She purses her lips, apparently in contemplation of the mysterious causal logic of this development.

"You were both in love with Malachai? So Damian's father was—"

"Funny. Mmhm. That's what we called them then, *funny*." She reaches up to dip her finger in the hot wax trickling down the trunk of the candle. "Not that he didn't sleep with gals from time to time, I guess. Don't know what you really would call Credence. *Bisexual* just doesn't sound right. Wasn't like he was two things at once or had one thing going on equally with the other. Galen, he'd probably come up with a good word for it. Galen likes to classify anything where sex is involved. I did think Credence would come back someday, though," she says, shifting gears. "To see his son."

"Do you know where—are you in touch with Damian at all?"

"Not one bit. It's a strange thing. Back when I was ignorant, I was a good mother. Then I was able to give Damian two, two and a half good years. But once the truth started to come to me—hm. Memories of Malachai and me together in other lives started to come to me. At first I didn't know what the hell was happening. I ignored the memories as long as they stayed in my dreams, but then they started coming at me, day and night. I couldn't barely hold a conversation no more. Drove me up the wall. Drove my mother to throw me out of the house again."

Langston emits a little murmur of sympathy; it's too easy for him, having seen waves crash over his head while standing on a dance floor, to imagine the plaguing terror of nonstop visions.

"After that—I just lost the mother feeling. I tried to hang on with it, but I was faking. He knew it. Children always know. I'd look at that sweet boy and couldn't even keep my eyes focused. Do you have any idea what it's like to start to remember past lives like remembering what you ate for breakfast? I took drugs, you know, to ease the craziness. Just made it worse. I had come to New Haven by then, following these hallucinations that kept drawing me toward Malachai, and I was hooking for a living. Things got so bad, to the point where one day I stepped off a curb on Whalley thinking I was stepping into a mountain stream to cool my feet and ankles 'cause it was so hot. It was not a hot day in New Haven, I'm told. I got hit by a bus—knocked flat and put into a coma for a few days. After I recovered, while I was still in the hospital, I decided to give Damian up. Haven't laid eyes on him since that day. And it might be the best decision I ever made in this lifetime, for him and for me."

Langston sighs. "Malachai made it seem like he didn't know Credence all that well, but you say Credence was in love with him. Do you know what happened between them? I mean, you say—you *were* deeply connected to Malachai. Maybe there's some clue, something that would help, in the real story."

"Could be." Destine bends from her chair and takes a match from a lower drawer of her desk, strikes it, and adds its flame to the wick of the candle—needlessly, it would appear, since the candle has been steadily burning since they entered the room. "You never leave an experience like that without some kind of hangover, see," Destine says. The tone of her voice is stronger now, as if she'd been working up to this point all along and is no longer sidetracked. "One thing that has stayed with me forever is that to this day I am still fascinated with them. Drugs. You could say I have a love for 'em. So now I study drugs 'stead of takin 'em. I know about all kinds, especially hallucinogens. I have acquired as much pharmacological knowledge as your doctor—if not more, because I like to learn about the *weird* stuff."

Langston perks up.

"I don't know if you care about animals or pay attention to them, but if you know anything about dolphins and whales, you know that their brains are as big or bigger than humans' brains. But since they're creatures of the sea, their brains are devoted to different things than ours are. A large part of what goes on in they heads has to do with making sense of sounds, so they can use their sonar to navigate underwater. You know, they find they way around by what's called echolocation—they shoot sound waves out, the waves hit something and travel back as an echo. But it's a much more complex and sophisticated echo than any ordinary echo. So this hippie marine biologist out in California who's a friend of mine became very fascinated by this. 'While back, he developed a process where he could synthesize some of the organic chemicals he found in the dolphin and whale brains. Mostly this was for legit research purposes, but being as drug-happy as myself, he took some of these chemicals, and tested them with human brain tissue. Then he took what he could keep from the dolphin chemicals without doing brain damage and mixed it up with hallucinogens: LSD, and some 'shrooms. He took the compound and buffered that with some other stuff—and what he came up with was this."

Destine reaches into a tall, thin wooden chest of file drawers beside her chair and produces a small vial. It is shaped like a tiny genie's bottle.

"What does it do?" Langston asks. While theoretically eager about the possibility of sampling a new drug—although he realizes he should be more careful, even if this is Damian's mother acting as dealer—the viscous liquid in the bottle disturbs him: especially its color, a queasy mixture of periwinkle and a color that reminds him of a miniature swamp of regurgitated asparagus that had given him a minor trauma when he'd seen it as a ten-year-old.

"I won't take it myself, so I have to rely on reports. What my friends who've done it all agree is that if you drink the stuff it gives you a sensitivity to sound. Kind of like a sonar intelligence."

Langston isn't following.

"This stuff—he calls it En-*dolphin*, ha ha ha—enhances hearing. While it's in your system, sounds become the major way you experience the world. It's 'spòsed to be a helluva trip. From sounds your brain creates every other sense. You begin to see a picture, you smell what is in the picture, you can touch it, even taste it. Your brain creates a whole world, rich, complete, detailed, just from hearing something."

"Huh. Well . . . I don't think I . . ."

She nods, as if having anticipated his objection. Langston recognizes suddenly how choreographed their interview is, how she must have thought about it, planned it out. "The most interesting part is that the sensitivity of these chemicals in the human brain is especially triggered by the sound of the human voice," she says.

"One friend of mine had his wife just read stories for him. She read from *The Thousand and One Arabian Nights*, she read Brothers Grimm fairy tales and whatnot. He told me he could *see* the metaphors, he could touch and smell them. He'd hear the word *east* and the Old English root that literally means the direction of the sunrise hangs onto the sound of the word like an echo vibrating around it. He said he could see light rays jump out from behind the peaks of a mountain, he could feel the smallest shift in heat on his skin, like a cold night had ended. He could smell and taste flowers in the meadows on that mountain beginning to open. Just when she read the sentence, 'So he went east.' Ain't that something?"

Langston eyes the vial doubtfully. "That's freaky. . . ."

"I'd like you to take a hit."

"Oh . . . I really don't think I should."

"We don't think there're any big side effects. Only six or seven people have done it that I know of, but believe me, we are very thorough in my little drug investigation group. We run blood tests on people for new drugs." She presses the vial into his hands; he holds it gingerly and squeamishly, as if it were a human body part. "They say with this, you come down faster than if you were doing coke or Ecstasy, and apparently it leaves you less drained."

"But—why do you want me to take it?"

"It'll help you get what you looking for. I want to tell you the story of Damian's father. And I want you to do more than hear it, I want you to experience what I have to tell you."

Prudence would make him refuse, but Langston has a fascination of his own with drugs and precious little backbone when invited to partake of them. Perhaps, he thinks, he's an addict after all, like Destine, and addictions are the modus operandi of all those visited by intimations of other lives, other worlds. Of course, the prospect of brain damage is not appealing, but . . . it may help them find Damian, so why not?

Destine helps pull him up higher in the chair. At Destine's command, he puts the vial to his lips and briefly sips. The taste is bitter, part vodka and part battery acid, and it stings as it streams down his throat. She instructs him to swallow it all and hands him a pair of old, dilapidated headphones that Langston worries may have such ancient circuitry that they'll give him a shock. He flinches as he feels the cold leather press against the rims of his ears.

In the silence, waiting for the drug to take effect, Langston begins to get suspicious again. From somnolence and confusion his mind has taken a leap forward, rapidly formulating and discarding analyses and decisions—it may be that Destine knows he's been talking to Malachai because she's working with that warlock. Langston recalls Aunt Reginia's warnings about the tools of warlocks: beware of anything old, she'd said.

His eyes are closed and he opens them slightly, to sneak a look at Destine. She's pretty old. He reaches up to remove the headphones—let's just end this farce right now, he decides.

But somehow he keeps missing the headphones. He raises his hands to the place his ears have been all his life and grabs hold of air. He laughs a little to himself: the little hit of X, the drink he had earlier, they must have drained him more than he imagined. There's something funny, too, about the smell of that candle. . . .

But his hands patting here and there in the gray darkness sweep past, over, behind their targets again and again. He begins to panic. He can't find his legs, either, or his stomach.

Now his face. His face is gone. And then he cannot even feel his hands.

Langston can't see. The room is pitch-black. He's lost his

bearings, all spatial sense has slipped away. Destine is a vampire; she has drained him, sucked him dry. She's run off with his body, with his touch and smell and sight.

A blast. A huge explosion, or at least it sounds like an explosion, like thunder and napalm, like a concert amp in a stadium blowing out. The sound flings him out. He falls. He can't make sense of what has happened, but he is convinced he has moved. He is on the floor—possibly. Sound—there is still sound, the only tangible thing that remains. If there is sound, he can scream. His thoughts call fruitlessly for a response from his throat, his tongue and lungs.

The darkness lightens, and something resembling shape makes its way out of the shifting gray: squiggle lines, like the graph of a tectonic tremor, waves that he can see but that seem both to chart and at the same time to *be* palpitant sound, wildly vibrating, then shimmering, wavering, clarifying:

There is a man—no, a woman, very tall, very powerful. Langston cannot see anything, but the image of the big woman makes itself clear in his thoughts. My God, is she tall. She has an ugly, ugly look on her face—no, a sound on her face. Her face is a sound. He cannot quite describe it, can't get a handle on what's happened to his perception—but it's kinda cool, once you adjust to it. He can see by hearing: the heartbeats of several people, but some—two? Exactly two heartbeats come through strongest. The sounds make a picture of the tall woman's face. It's hideous, as if someone has taken each half inch of her skin and filliped that half inch between thumb and forefinger so that her face is a map of lines, lines like scars. Oh, OK: wrinkles! That's what wrinkles sound like. And then her teeth, he can hear them gnash, and it's like a huge house sinking into the earth, but sped up, louder.

Awright, awright, I'm not trying to hold out on you. I seen him, I swear to God. . . . Someone's voice. A little man, with bristly hair like a porcupine's; his heart beats rapidly. *You fucking better have, you little motherfucker, you better, because all we need right now is one good excuse to carve you a new asshole. . . .*

The word *asshole* pushes out of her chest with a muscular heave and glows, nucleated, a newborn life. Langston cannot follow: her voice sends him spiraling. Her voice is like wasps clustering together, beating out electric rhythms that give instructions as to the building of a nest beneath the awning of a porch. Hearing her, hearing all that vibrates and echoes in her word, Langston is mesmerized, captivated, it is as if he were watching two cars collide in slow motion and every shard of glass had a name and a life history of its own, and each corpuscle of blood and striation of tearing muscle were a separate universe teeming with galaxies. He makes an effort as if to lean in closer, to hear more, to sweeten the rush of the high, and is startled by the result: the woman's voice dissolves, frays, shatters, and in its place Langston perceives its component parts; it is no longer words or flesh but energy, energy for which all forms are merely masks. Langston hears a sound no human has claimed to have heard in recorded history: that of electrons singing around the nucleus of an atom, like a chorus singing a Gregorian chant in a cathedral the size of Canada with walls that carry the echoes of their reverent voices to the stars, the sound of quantum particles hip-hop staccato rapping as they dip and dive and fizz in and through the atmosphere of the woman—no, they are not *in* the atmosphere of her, they *are* the woman herself—

"*Langston! Langston!*"

His attention shifts. He moves or thinks, and the electrons, the quanta, the woman and the little man disappear. The squiggly waves rush up again in his mind's eye.

"Langston? Can you hear me?"

This sound has no origin. It is bodiless, everywhere, immanent: godlike. He follows the waves as they flow forward and backward. He finds that when he focuses upon the waves, their movement slows and they begin to take shape.

"Langston, it's Destine."

Her name clinches it for him. Suddenly out of the mire in his mind he sees her, standing nearby in sharp clarity outlined by a halo of light.

"You're disoriented, I know. If you can, close out everything but the sound of my voice. Nothing you hear right now is as important as my voice. You are still in my room with me, listening to me. You hear only me, only my voice. All you're doing is listening. Easiest thing in the world . . . that's better. That's better . . . OK. You want to know about Credence. I'll tell you about him. I'll tell you what Malachai didn't tell you before he died. Listen very carefully to the sound of my voice."

Instinctively he resists, as Destine's words blare like an air-raid siren in his ears, every syllable and intonation three and four times its normal decibel level. Indeed, each part of her voice seems alive and distinct, as if it were several voices combined in one, and the resultant sound is as gross and multifarious as the insistent, unwelcome touch of many pairs of hands. But try as he might, he can't escape. The sound has a compelling power. With surrender comes something new, a different awareness.

Yes, it is indeed Destine speaking to him, it is her voice. But it's not quite her cadence. The tone is lower, and in place of her dignified calm there is a tremble of animation and the gravel of a masculine voice. Destine is imitating Malachai, precisely, uncannily. Speaking as he would speak. But if at first Langston wants to laugh, thinking she's doing a stagy impression, the performance soon becomes a channeling. It is the drug, of course; no imitation could be so exact.

Langston can see Malachai beside him in the front yard of his brownstone many hours ago, and he listens, awestruck, as Malachai rises from his quagmire grave, silt and mud flowing down from his body like streams of blood cascading down the body of a Christ. The resurrected Malachai gives vent to the words he could not say when he lived.

"I'm gon tell you the truth now. What was on the tip of my tongue to say, what I was gonna tell you, before—before he got me."

Who? Langston wants to ask—but reduced as he is to an invisible ear now, he has no voice.

"As I look back on the days when Credence and me ran together, I have to question the seriousness of our commitment. *My* commitment. Shit, I didn't know what I was in for. I'd had cops on my ass before, but to have cops on my ass like that! And the truth is we wasn't even no Panthers, not for real. We wasn't nothin but hangers-on. No different from a bunch of girls runnin around after the drummer of a rock band or some shit, frankly. Even that much involvement was too much for me. The meetings we went to was too much, all that talk they was talkin, all the walk they expected us to walk. Organizing the masses. Recruiting. Planning, plotting, shouting. Sneaking. At least that part I knew about, the sneaking. I figured I was down for some sneaking. Well, some folks was involved in helping get weapons and they occasionally had me help get guns and stock 'em. Scared the shit out of me. I was not a serious revolutionary. Didn't know what that meant. Guns was something you used to hunt rabbit back where I came from, not to carry around on a street or hide in somebody's aunt's basement. Revolution—fuck. I wanted some pussy. I wanted to look good in them clothes.

"But the Party, even being a hanger-on to the Party, offered something different. Almost everyone around me was just as much a coward. They called our little group the Cats instead of the Panthers, and I know some brothas resented it, but it was cool with me. 'Cause if shit got too hot, I wanted to party. That's what you think of when you think of a 'Cat.' Some smooth clothes, a good line, good shit to drink and smoke, fine ladies on your arm. And I wasn't a complete fool, 'cause the fact is there was a lotta pussy to be had even if you was a Cat just associated with real Panthers. Gals looked up to you, thought you was a star. And sistas in the Party was supposed to give it up as a duty to the revolution—and a couple of 'em actually did it.

"So that's what I was about. After the first few times, they didn't give me no weapons to hide. But they gave weapons to Credence. Credence was serious. Devoted. Committed. Or so it looked like. Later on, they said he was a FBI spy. Even then, even though they gave him dangerous stuff to do, they must not've liked something about him, because the inner circle, they didn't let him get too close. Maybe they was even trying to set him up. Anyway, they kept him at a distance, so de facto he became a Cat, too.

"I liked him from jump. I guess I admired his seriousness, just because I knew I damn sure didn't have it. It got so I wanted him next to me, like if I had him next to me, the courage he had would rub off. Like him being there would fill up the hole I felt in my own heart.

"I liked corrupting him, too. Gettin him to come get high with me, run some women with me. Talk him out of talking about politics all the time. I wasn't very successful at first, but after that time when we was almost killed by them cops, when he saved me by puttin his leg up against mine . . .

"Well, next thing I know we were tight, and the brotha is coming to meet me wearing some gold boots and some pants. I mean, you needed to see those pants, now! Tight as hell. Tight as a mother, like on his ass and his legs. And then there was this, there was this *patch*—! Not like a patch you stitch on, more like a stain, or something painted on or woven into the fabric. And this patch was over his stuff, you know. His—between his legs. And the color, well, you'd have to see it to believe it."

Langston does see. A memory, perhaps, plucked from his own thoughts, or a vision crafted from his own imagination, like an image from the kinds of dreams he has when he drinks tequila: strange people he's never met in the waking world but knows intimately in the underground reality beneath the bed-covers, strange towns and cities and landscapes somehow familiar, arrestingly detailed and alive—

From the sound of Destine's voice channeling Malachai's voice, the echoes paint a picture that Langston can see though his eyes are shut, though he doubts the existence of his eyes. It is as vivid as a sunset on a cloudless horizon, this image of Credence's pants: a slim, supple torso and slender legs in tight cloth cut from soft velvet, its color a beatific azure like the robes of a Madonna in a Fra Angelico: tight pants that bulge and that blush at the crotch like a blooming chrysanthemum.

"Well, shit, a man wearing some pants like that—you either strip him and put them on yourself or take the man out. So we went out. Had a *blast*. Crazy time. I didn't know that motherfucker could drink and smoke like that. We did the town. It was a beautiful thing. It really was. I can't remember having a better time with a friend.

"Naturally before the sun came up, I had to find me some pussy, as a chaser for the good time we'd had. Credence came right along with me. I called up my hos, and they gave me the usual runaround women will give you when they know what you really want. It turned out wasn't nothing to do but hook up with some ladies of the evening. I happened to know a few that weren't too street, 'cause I figured Credence wouldn't fly with anybody too skanky. We took them to a hotel room in the nice part of town, got attitude from the bellboys and shit, but we didn't care, we was high as kites. And then up in that room we got down to business.

"Everything went just right: I was on my bed with my girl, he was on his bed with his. I was having a good time, a real good time. It's not so strange, you know, to have as good a time as that and want, need, to share it. I could remember my brothers talking about how they didn't never want to see another man taking care of his business with a woman. One of my brothers, he was supposed to be what you'd call the freak, the wild one, well, he admitted he could see two women gettin down, but other than that, he didn't want to see. Anything else, thass faggot stuff, just faggot stuff. That's what they'd say. But they hadn't been out with a friend on the town like Credence and me. We had been together the whole night. We had been through shit together, with them cops. And it wasn't like just 'cause some ho had her legs wrapped around my back that I was just gon forget he existed, you know? He had to be a part of it. That's what I was thinking. Not like I wanted anything *from* him, or *of* him, you know? I just wanted to *see* him. Make contact.

"So I'm on top of my girl and we gettin to it, and I hear the noises from the other bed, and it's dark in there. So I look over, just to see. And what I saw was Credence looking at me. Right at me. The most intense damn look I ever seen. Just about freaked the shit out of me. I wanted to see him, but I didn't expect for him to be looking at me like that. Like some goddamned wolf. And then he saw me seein him, and then look like the moment we saw each other looking that something came over him, and water came into his eyes. Look like a tear come rolling down his cheek. I don't know if it was sweat, you know, comin off his forehead, except I don't believe he was workin all that hard up on that gal—I kept my eyes to myself after that. Just thinking about it almost made me lose my shit, and the girl was lookin up at me like, well, you gon come, nigga, or not. So I just got it over with as fast as I could.

"I didn't know exactly what was up with Credence. I didn't want to know. Credence wasn't about to let me off easy, though. Soon as those girls were out of that hotel room, he was up next to me, looking at me. Right up next to me. Like he was gon kiss me or something. I laughed, tryin to play it off, said, 'Get off me, man, you drunk.' He stood right there. Told me he had a secret to tell me and begged me not to share it with a soul. I didn't want him to tell me a damn thing, and I told him just that. But he kept pushing. Making me uncomfortable. So finally, just to get the negro to shut up, I swore I'd keep it a secret. And then the boy didn't say nothing. With his eyes locked on my eyes I felt like I was being hypnotized or some shit. He reached down and put his motherfucking hand on my dick. On the whole package. Firm, like. I guess he was waiting to see what I would do, because he just kept lookin at me, and didn't move. But I was sorta hypnotized. Couldn't move. I don't think I really wanted to move. He bent down on his knees and put his mouth on it. It was disgusting, I was disgusted. But—for someone to want you that *bad* . . .

"I let him do it. And he was enjoying it. And when you enjoy something, you know, you good at it. After he finished—after I finished—I felt embarrassed, and I think he was, too. On the other hand, I could tell something was freer in the way he was with me, some new contentment or zip or something. Made the rest of the night look like he'd been depressed the whole time. He insisted on walking me home. Like he was escorting me home after a date, or something. He hugged me at my door, looked at me that intense way, and I had to admit to myself, something about his openness, in the way he hugged me, touched me. Made me kinda feel like there was something in me that wished I could be that vulnerable, you know. Made me see how I wished things coulda been different between my brothers and me back when I was comin up. Not different *that* way—those niggas was so ugly not even a gay would want 'em *that* way. But I wished we coulda been closer. And I never knew I wished that before. So Credence hugged me, and it made the whole nasty thing OK. Maybe I was just drunk, but I was OK with it. Wouldn't have been no trouble at all from me about it. It would have been our little secret."

Malachai—Destine—falls silent. Langston hears the hiss of the candle, like a cat issuing a warning. The room feels (sounds) like a dark cavern, a great emptiness in the middle of nowhere. Nothing seems to exist, except her voice, and Malachai, the outline of a ghostly form shivering around in and through her.

"But shit was happening. I didn't know it, but there was a split among the real members of the Party. Cleaver and the folks who said they followed Cleaver wanted to get more militant. Then in late '69, Fred Hampton from the Panthers in Chicago was murdered by the police. Cleaver wanted to retaliate. Shit, *I* wanted retaliation, long as somebody else's neck was on the line. It was all about to go to hell, man. It was about to blow up. Some crazy ass in the New York chapter was trying to get the folks down there to take violent action, had them planning to blow shit up. It turned out this New York brother was a plant from the FBI, and that he was trying to undermine the Panthers' whole project. We Cats didn't know it, but we had a plant running around right under our own noses right here in New Haven. He never did get to the inner circle, but I guess he figured he was going to cause some trouble somewhere with somebody. He called himself Oliver. Big, strong brotha. Handsome. He had that charisma, that magic you *wont* your black leaders to have, you know. I didn't care for Oliver 'cause I knew he was gettin all the pussy I couldn't get, or gettin what I could get but gettin it when I wanted it so that I had to wait.

"At a meeting Oliver got up and started talking about how he was with Cleaver. Armed retaliation against the state was the only way, he told us. The state had declared war on us, and it only made sense for us to take the battle to the doorstep of the oppressors. He rattled off some Marx, some Fanon. He had everybody in that little living room hot under the collar. Claimed he was ready to lead us if Ericka Huggins and them couldn't. I was sitting there shivering, literally shivering. All that talk was scaring me. I was ashamed of how I felt, but I was scared as shit. Credence noticed it and put his hand on my shoulder. I should have known better than to let that go on, should have known somebody was going to see the way Credence looked at me. But like I say, I wasn't no revolutionary. Oliver scared me so much I didn't even think about nobody seeing Credence's hand on me.

"But Oliver saw it. Turned out he'd been waiting to catch Credence and me in the act. I noticed him watching us while he talked, and my shivering stopped cold. I have never in my life known a more malicious bastard than that Oliver. He didn't say a word, but just by the way I saw his mouth twist when he looked at Credence's arm around my back, I knew he knew. He dredged up all the shame in me, made me feel disgusting. I threw Credence's hand off me. I think I may even have pushed him. And right at that moment, Oliver started in talking about how we were going to need to be ruthless. 'We have got to be strong,' he kept saying. 'We have got to purge ourselves and each other of weakness in all its forms.' That old line, you know. 'We can't afford to be soft,' he says. 'We can't have any *backsliding*, any *counterrevolutionary* milksop whining, we can't have no Unca-Tommin' sissy behavior. Anybody who can't be strong does not belong here. Anybody who is too weak, anybody who is infected with the white man's diseases has to leave, because we are a nation at war.'

"Oliver was a powerful speaker. He had that goin for him. And like I said, he was a handsome, strong-looking brotha. And while he was saying this, he kept looking at us, back and forth, from Credence to me. Of course, people in the room started noticing this shit. Finally Oliver got quiet and walked over to where we sat. Everybody in the room turned our way. 'I know one of you is weak,' he said. 'I know one of you pretends to be with us, but you're a liar.'

"I just knew he was gon call me out. I would have done anything in that moment to get out of there, I was so scared and horrified at myself. But Oliver didn't want me. He wanted Credence. Next thing I know he'd grabbed Credence by his collar and started screaming. 'I saw you! I saw you! I saw you *on your knees* with a old white man's dick in your mouth!' Well, it was quiet for a second. The Cats was just sittin there staring. Didn't nobody know what to say, even what to think. They was just shocked, and waiting for Oliver to tell them what to do. Credence was so shocked himself, he couldn't even deny what Oliver accused him of. Oliver kept screaming at him to admit it, and everybody was just staring, not doing anything, and Credence did the worst thing he could do, which was to start bawling. 'He's my boss, he's my boss!' He was whining. 'He's rich, and he gives me money I put into the Party!'

"Well, wasn't nobody having any of that. The Cats started to get ugly. Started acting like they had some claws and some fangs. 'Oh, so you a bitch, huh?' Oliver said. Which was a vicious thing to say for all kinds of reasons, because what he meant was that women in the Party was s'posed to be prepared to sleep with the enemy for information, you know. So he said, 'If you're a bitch for the Party, why'd you sign up as a man? You not a man, I know that. You just a Uncle Tom bitch, huh? Then we'll treat you like a bitch.'

"So Oliver slapped him. With a open hand. Slapped him again. He started to beat the mess out of him. Before I knew it, a couple of the other men were holding Credence down, and then they joined in. People was standing up, and all the emotion of the moment just boiled over and they were saying 'kill the motherfucker' and crazy shit. There were women in there kicking Credence's ass. Somebody looked at me like, you his friend, what do you have to say? Before I even knew what my mouth was doing, I was hollering and pointing at Credence like he was some creature from Mars. 'Goddamn! He tried to suck my dick! I thought he was drunk, but the mother tried to suck me! He tried to get me up in bed with him!'

"That was all it took to finish Credence. I gave him a punch myself, in the stomach. Somebody started talking about how we should take the traitor out to the woods and burn him, but that didn't go anywhere, thank God. Cooler heads prevailed. I'm ashamed to say mine wasn't one of them. The truth is I would have gone along with anything to keep my place right then. I would have done anything—anything—to make sure I belonged. I had to be a member of the tribe.

"You know what I mean? It's like that. Don't nobody try to tell me it's not like that. White folks be thinkin we all so cool together: 'Look at how them niggers stick together,' they say. They see some fools playing basketball and slappin high fives and think we just go together naturally, like the brothas we call each other. But it's not like that. It's not easy to belong. You got to work at it. You expected to pay some dues for membership. You expected to make a sacrifice—and if not, you better talk a damn good game. Membership doesn't come for free. That night, I was up against a wall, the way I figured it. It even cross my mind that, damn, I wouldn't be gettin no more pussy if I was associated with a faggot. So Credence was gon be my sacrifice. I decided that in a manner of seconds. That's who I was back then.

"We ended up throwing Credence out the house. I believe I even felt righteous about the shit, like he deserved it. He was beat up and bloody. For all I know, bones might have been broke. I saw him from the window as he staggered off. He tripped and fell facedown on the ground. Must have fallen so hard he smashed his nose. Some heifer come up behind me and put her hands on my chest, started strokin me. There was still commotion going on, and Oliver was bringing the meeting back to order—son of a bitch—but me and this gal slipped into the back row and in about three seconds slipped into the bathroom and fucked. I fucked her standing up, 'gainst the wall. Fucked her so hard she had to tell me to stop, and that made me feel all better. I wouldn't be surprised if there were a few others slipped off, too, later that night. When the meeting was done, Oliver was just grinning at me. I figured that meant he approved, I was one of them again. What it really meant was that I'd helped him do the Cats in.

"The last I saw of Credence was him facedown in the grass. Few months after, we figured out old Oliver was working for Hoover. Seems COINTELPRO wanted Credence out because his employer was in fact rich, and was in fact willing to funnel money into the Party through Credence. Credence been his valet for many years. That whole scene was the end of the road. The Cats never did go through with any armed retaliation. The police kept coming after us, and the Cats were through in another year or less. The real Panthers—well, you know what happened to them.

"Then come to find out later that prostitute I was fucking in the hotel room knew Credence, and had had a baby by him years before. She got hit by a bus and after that tried to go clean, gave up Credence's child for adoption. She became a good friend of mine.

"And I didn't never get to apologize to Credence for what I did."

Langston feels he can hear the candle singing to him in the quiet black that falls, like the curtain at the close of the show. It has a voice like the bells and drums of a dirge.

"If you see Credence, I want you to tell him for me. Tell him I know the wrong I did him, and I'm sorry."

~

Gallows. Langston sees gallows, a crook of wood, and rope and a trap door, he hears the crunch of a neck breaking, feels the air stir on his skin as he looks up from the ground to see the body swing—just before Malachai, the feeling and sound of him as if he were present in the room, fades.

Destine's voice is her own again when she speaks, near, resonant, powerfully filling the altered space. "To me the funny thing is that I was so gone when Malachai brought me and Hester up to that hotel room that I didn't even recognize Credence. Even when they said his name. My son's daddy, I didn't notice him. I don't think he knew me, either, because he didn't pay me much mind. Both of us only had eyes for Malachai. I was thinking about having Malachai hold me, how it was gonna feel to have him inside me. How I'd feel to feel him with my hands. Folks these days like to ask me how I ended up being a ho. Even now got me a little Yale feminist girl who wants to write my story, and she keeps asking me about that part of my life. I tell her it's not all that complicated. My visions made me come to New Haven to find Malachai. Once I found him here, I had to stay. I didn't have no job, I did have a child to look after, and had no money left." Destine sighs.

The sound of the sigh is billowing smoke on the stage of a magician's show: white, heavy with mystery. It leaves a soupy fog silence in Langston's thoughts. Blankness overtakes Langston, the visible waves he could perceive before now become little more than thin, evanescent lines traced by a stick in still black water. They make a soughing noise like a gentle tide. He is aware of Destine at his side, breathing gently.

To his surprise he finds that he can feel his hands again and he can move them; he touches his chest and his face, feels the warmth pulsing at his throat.

"You—" His own voice is a jolt to him; it seems unbearably loud. He struggles to find the words. "I . . . appreciate what you've told me. But is therc anything specifically that you might know, through Malachai or your own memories, that could point to where Damian or his father could be *now?*"

It takes her a long time to answer. He listens to her breath recede, feels her suck in her stomach. He wonders if he may have offended her. "No. That's all I know, what I told you." She hesitates. "I have to go now, and see to my guests. The drug will wear off in about fifteen minutes, maybe less. You'll be fine up here until it does. If I were you, I'd enjoy the high I have left."

"What do you mean?"

"Just expand your range. Go 'looking' outside this room with your ears. You started doing that when the stuff first kicked in, remember, before I asked you to listen to me? Try it again now, it won't be so overwhelming this time."

"But . . ."

"You can find something to interest you for fifteen minutes. Go ahead. There probably isn't a soul in this house you can't eavesdrop on with that stuff running around in your bloodstream."

She leaves him. The door closes behind her, the latch clicks into its slot, and the echo of it in his ears is ominous, final. He hears the emptiness of the room grow larger. Clumsily, as if the myriad threads of his normal perception have been bound and fused and become a hand with a thumb three times its normal size, he gropes about the room. He glances off the wall and the desk. Over and over he tries and he errs, until he begins to understand. Narrow he has to become, like a streaming wisp of smoke, small and fast. He bounces waves off the boundaries of the room, finds the door and its lock, and slips through its thin, jagged keyhole.

Outside at last. Images, tastes, smells, textures come tumbling over him. At first they seem hollow, like the sound of a song recorded in a garage. There are too many of them to sort through, an incoherent jumble of sonar waves bouncing back and forth between him and them: ice cream melting on warm skin and sliding into the crevices of a navel, someone talking about their mother and how she used to make him dress up when he was seven, chewing and swallowing, endless chewing and swallowing and the rumbling acidic churning of stomachs. It's horrible. The silence would be better.

He thinks of Azaril, and then suddenly as he thinks of him, he hears Azaril's voice speaking to him. *So, should I come over there and study?* he hears him say, and then recognizes it as a memory of their countless evenings together. The memory makes him happy, in a small, sad way. He holds on to it, tries to summon the sound of Azaril's voice back to him.

The squiggle lines of sound vanish. The hollow outlined images of too many fragments of too many people drain away, as if suddenly flushed into an unseen sewer.

What is left is still dark, but more clear, more stable. Langston perceives two shapes, black silhouettes against the background of a dim light. They seem to be in movement, but the movements are slow and give off a faltering echo. He reaches out to them, moves in closer, drawn in by the heat of their bodies, the glow that shimmers around them. They seem to lie coiled together in the soft red heart of a fading coal. He realizes from the presence of one kind of sound and the absence of another that they are naked human bodies. The smell of two kinds of flesh: two hearts both thumping, their warmth rising. It is as if he can hear the heat of their flesh, low, hot flames, their cells pulsing as they greedily lap balmy draughts of oxygen, energy spiking and then its barely contained pressure releases, flooding through muscle, blood, and skin.

Please? Lemme put it right up next to it, I'll just leave it there, I won't put it in, how about just the tip, ohhhhhhh. . . .

The words Langston hears and the words in his memory are in the same voice. It's Azaril.

The moaning sounds belong to that girl he was with downstairs.

Langston tries to withdraw, but in his anger he spins out of control. Like a handful of dust tossed to the winds he is flung again from thing to thing, sound to sound, racing around the room to butt against the walls. He sinks into the strata of a rug and becomes lost in the jungle of its dense, twisted fibers; crashes in the louvers of a closed shutter like a frightened moth and is confused by the rays of moonlight, their many colors, blue and cream and pale gold, streaming through. A voice in his mind whips him around again. *And then on the* upper *floor, we have the private* bed*rooms. . . .* Galen, with an annoying smirk.

Thrup.

A strip of leather striking the skin of the palm of someone's hand?

A moan, this one sharp and hard.

Ah. Oh. Thrup. *Ahh. Oh!* Thrup. Thrup, thrup, thrup. Thrup! *Aaaaaah!*

Langston is aware suddenly not of sound or sight but touch, feel: air like tiny bubbles, tiny fingers tickling. A sudden, violent flare of heat. Discomfort.

A movement like the fall and surrender of sighing, the two bodies sighing into one another, the breath of one flowing beneath the skin of the other. Then, almost indistinguishably, a tightening. And then the sensation of power—power and pleasure, the pleasure of power and the power of pleasure in their naked wordless forms.

A leathery, rubbery pulse of heat that throbs, sinks, and pushes wide—

My God. My God, my God, my God. (While along with her, as if he were her, he grips, tightens, pulls the weight and movement of the body above down. Up they lift, Langston and she together, to meet Azaril plummeting down. . . . The pressure of him bearing down on her—them—the delicious scrape of the coarse body hair, a cross between sand and an animal's pelt. It undulates across the endless expanse of her/their flesh. . . .)

"Oh, baby . . ."

Baby, Azaril says, and in the timbre of the word there is a vibration that tells a thousand stories. *Baby*, he says, and the rush of information that floods Langston's brain makes him realize that there is indeed something more mortifying for him to endure: dream images, whole cycles of dreams like Hindu epics, layered one upon the other, fire at once, and Langston experiences, knows, seeshearstouchestastessmells it all: he knows suddenly, fully, as if they were his own, that there are two secrets Azaril possesses. Both have to do with sex; both have the smell of sweat, the silky, sticky touch of fresh male ejaculate all over them: for to Azaril (as to Langston—they have this in common), sex is the door to the secret self. Sex is the language in which the things about himself that he loses in the workaday world are spoken—needs tearful and fragile that have no name and no voice and, like remains in a buried sarcophagus, would crumble to shapeless dust if exposed to light and air.

Oh, baby.

The other secret—Langston is sure of it, he recognizes the vibration of the little packet of memory trailing along behind the syllables of Azaril's groans like tin cans roped to the fender of a Just Married car, recognizes the vibration because it's so much like the tremor of similar thoughts in his own brain: the other secret has to do with Damian.

Langston tries wildly now to wrench free. He knows what's coming. It is a nightmare that he knows is a nightmare but that grips his mind and won't let go. The echo of the word rings in his thoughts, and he hears Azaril's mother telling him, "You're not too young to know this. When you make love, you must always try to engage all five senses at once—and always finish your pleasure away from the *source* of pleasure."

So that when Azaril felt Damian's finger snaking through the hair on Azaril's belly—when the smell of the cologne behind Damian's ears mingled with the smell of Damian's saliva mixing with the smell of Azaril's own saliva—when his tongue had baptized the stubble on Damian's left cheek—when he heard Damian's whisper in his ear—he counted, and having counted, he at last relaxed the lids of his eyes that had been so tightly, tightly shut, and allowed himself to look: on the glory of the body on top of him. And whispered, "You can fuck me, if you want."

In their private room in the attic above the fourth floor of

Destine's house of pleasures, Azaril reaches orgasm, and his thrashing and moaning is of such a fervor that it excites Leah to the first good orgasm she's had in three months.

⁓

The room Azaril and Leah share abruptly disappears.

Langston is in a hallway. The effect of the drug is dwindling. The sounds and their images grow duller. He finds himself in a hallway that he recognizes; far down the corridor, the entry to Destine's room lies hidden from ordinary sight, tucked away in an alcove. Slowly the sonar waves bounce back to him and dimly he sees it: yes, that looks familiar: the suit of armor, the old pirate ship's clock, some girl tripping on acid and X at once licks the mahogany wood paneling. Click—a lock rolls back into a cobwebbed slot. An old room, hasn't been opened in years, feelssmellslooks like—Destine. She is leaping upward, standing on the balls of her feet. Langston can hear her heart, can hear sweat rivering gushing over her skin. *You won't you* won't, she is saying—or the sweat is saying, the fusillades of blood pumped wildly from her heart are saying: *I know it was you*, she is saying. The words bounce against one another, become choral. *You killed you killed you killed you killed* you *killed*—

Malachai—

Beside her, looming, is a hulking shape.

A shadow? Or just—shadowy. Langston can't hear-see it. It's a blur of nothing: a hole in the living sounds of the room.

But he does hear the knife. The sound of the machines that fashioned it glimmer-echo on its surface, and the air slipping over the blade like a rent sleeve as it plunges in a downward arc (one side of a perfect oval; the knife's fall is a pencil stroke, the movement a collage of action and image) conjures sparks thrown off by whirring metal wheels in the knife's past, the knife's—

being? Somewhere in the knife there is a tiny consciousness, glacial, involute: like a tumor with teeth inside it, tiny tiny tiny incisors cut cut cutting—it—

That's blood. Langston hears blood vomiting, then spilling, sliding down the slope of a slender ankle lying twisted on the floor.

Did she scream? Langston didn't hear a scream. How could she not cry out, with her whole body, the cells, the vessels, the blood shrieking like that—

Destine lies upon the floor, the contents of her femoral artery soaking fast into the rug. Langston hears her breath, weak, drifting, a dust of snow on a mountainside, a dust of snow falling away from the sharp angles of a goat's cloven hooves. She—her spirit?—is running away, running away in bounds and leaps, up the mountain . . . her spirit fleeing her body.

The shape stands over Destine. Bits of sound now leak through the cloak of its silence. Langston hears breath, rough like an animal's tongue. The man, if it's a man, lifts the knife, which seems vibrantly alive now, vampirically vivified, it has grown, or seems to have, long as a forearm. The man shape cleans the flat of it on thick cloth. He hovers over her body for a moment. Then suddenly he turns and drops into a crouch, swings the knife outward. Langston tries again to focus, to bear down on this male creature, see him.

Then the man stops. Another shape has joined him. This one is clear, its sound a sharp clean whistle: an emergency broadcasting signal brought to life. Tall, shapely, with slender shoulders and supply muscled legs that glow inside the generous slit of an ornate evening gown—feels like, sounds like—it is the same woman Langston had seen arguing with a scrawny little man when the drug first took effect.

She speaks to the hulking shape, and he rises from his defensive crouch, he relaxes. A light dawns around him now. He is not as lucid to Langston as the other, but he has become radiant, blinding almost. Something about this man speaks of lions' manes, of kings and prophets and the dreamed-of liberator. He is a tall man, big and handsome. Familiar.

"She pretended not to know anything," the big, now-bright man says. Langston attunes himself to the vibration of the words. They give him nothing more; it is as if the man were veiled in a blond aura. But the aura is not steady: like the image on a television screen when the roof antenna is blown askew by the wind, it flickers and breaks before it reassembles, flickers and breaks again. "She said I was Malachai's killer. As if she knew, as if she was there today."

The warlock.

"I felt something. Watching. Him. He's still here, isn't he? She's hidden him—"

"Down the hall," the other—the woman—says. "There's an alcove you can't see from here, and a door that's locked. I checked."

In the last sputter of the drug's power, Langston hear-sees her clearly, hears and sees the waves of malice radiate from her skull, hears and sees the creak of her knee-high leather boots as they rock back and forth on the floor. It's him. She's a he. It's the guy who stood beside him at the law-school urinal, who pissed on the floor while he stood behind him. It's the woman who stepped into the lobby of the apartment building near the hotel.

There is a nasty expression on the drag queen's face. Now there can be no doubt: she's on a hunt, and she's hunting Langston. She is leading the big bright man. They are coming.

The big man with the drag queen must have known Langston was with Destine, and that was why he had attacked her. If they find Langston, having killed Malachai, stabbed Destine, they might do anything.

The image fades, and with it, the drug's effect. Langston opens his eyes to see, and tastes a dry film on his tongue and in his throat like paste. He whips off the headphones and moves toward the door.

It opens. The drag queen—ebulliently attired in a marigold minidress—grins ferally at him. Behind her appears a bald dark man with the juiciest finest damn lips Langston has ever seen and shoulders that threaten to push back the doorjambs. The man's sumptuous damp brown eyes looking at him check all movement, dissipate the flow of time.

The vision—an angel of apocalypse—speaks. "Langston."

For a moment, perhaps longer, Langston is still. Fear makes Langston's heart pound in his chest, in his arms and wrists, his temples and throat. His legs dematerialize, transported to some other space-time; he cannot feel the weight of his feet on the floor. He thinks of his Aunt Reginia: *I in my stillness became a mirror. . . .*

Maybe it's working because no one does anything for what seems like forever, and then the drag queen's grin devolves into something crenellated and ugly, and she takes a heavy step forward, her arm raised either to grab Langston or strike him—when someone down the hallway screams.

"Destine! Destine! She's been hurt!"

Langston turns and runs. There is another door, on the other side of the room, and he bolts through it to the corridor beyond. Here as elsewhere, there are people leaning and lounging against the walls. They squint as he dodges to avoid tripping over them. "Call the police! Call an ambulance! Destine is bleeding to death!" he yells out. Everyone stares. No one moves—until they get shoved aside or feel the cleats of a pair of boots brand their legs as a wild-ass woman running even faster than the guy she's chasing goes by. As she passes by, shouts of surprise and anger begin to fill the corridor.

One by one, as if in a chain of explosions, expertly timed by some terrorist's clever mechanism so that each follows the conflagration preceding it like an echo, Galen's party guests start to lose it. Raised voices, running feet, dishes skidding off tables and shattering, folks slipping down unexpectedly on the hardwood floors and chipping their pelvic bones, phones ringing and the noise of cell phones being turned on and dialed. Langston, breathing hard and with knees rising high like a champion sprinter, keeps up his exhortations, trying to yell loud enough to be heard over the chaos. He wants to make certain Destine gets the help she needs; he's heard of cases like this, and he knows she hasn't got much longer to live.

Each time he swings into a new corridor or bursts onto the scene of a lounge adorned in satin and smoky lights, he scans before he gathers speed again: he does not see Reynaldo or Quentin anywhere. And he knows where Azaril is.

Langston comes to a stop and catches his breath where one hall the length of a train station lobby meets another hall perpendicular to it. He is thinking of which way looks more likely to take him outside when he hears what sounds chillingly like a rebel yell out of an Alabama nightmare. Over his shoulder, he sees the drag queen 150 yards or so away and bearing down fast. That mirror trick seems to have made her very angry, maybe driven her mad. He doesn't see the warlock.

Langston goes left.

To the left there is a large formal dining room that once sat forty-plus. Now it is divided into small rooms arranged in the dizzying, frenetic pattern of a Moroccan street market. Wisp-thin sheets and heavy carpets, each printed or stitched with elegant Oriental designs, border the passageways and the cubbyhole chambers. Moaning, ooohs and ahhhs, and long, triumphant ssssses fill the air and the place smells like a locker room.

Langston banks against one rug, swivels against a cordon of sheets. He trips into the midst of two women about to go at it. He remembers the face of one of them: the woman who was god-damning Yale political wenches and looking for someone to fuck when he first arrived. Her jeans are down to her ankles as she lies spread-legged on the floor with the other babe slithering on her belly and licking along her inner thighs, headed home. "Be gentle with me," she's saying, and she bats her eyelashes, "I ain't done this kinda shit before. . . ." That's when they see Langston.

"Run! There's a murderer loose in the house!" he yells. Somehow he evades their curses and gets to the other side of the room, and he emerges into territory he knows from memory: this small vestibule, with its little dome like the roof of a chapel and a small, stork-legged table where the deceased rock star's framed photograph stands, is near to the servant's kitchen, and that's near a back door. . . . Behind him, he hears someone's voice get loud: "I *know* you not bumpin into me, white girl!"

The servants have already vacated the kitchen, and Langston can hear the soles of his shoes strike the floor as he runs. He emerges into the night air and finds the back lawn and driveway beginning to throng with honking cars as the caterers and other one-night hires with little loyalty to Destine mill about trying to find rides. Langston weaves and dodges between them. On the front lawn, party refugees are massing together in confusion, while white lights and red sirens machete through the black forest hugging the long road up to the great house. Langston stops. There's nowhere for him to go, except into the dark web of forest surrounding the house. Trapped. He searches fearfully for the drag queen, but she doesn't show. How could she have hoped to escape notice, chasing him like that? It's all so insane.

Then three police cars and two ambulances arrive, parting

the crowd in two. Paramedics and some of the policemen head toward the mansion doors. The remaining rescuers endure a verbal pelting from the crowd as they begin sealing off the house with reams of yellow tape and herding the injured into the ambulances and the uninjured into armored police vans.

"There're too many of us for them to arrest everybody. We can make a break for it. They won't even notice."

Langston turns and looks at the warlock beside him.

Mesmerizing. *Being a man with so gorgeous a head, he is just naturally someone you'd want to give good head to.* This thought comes to Langston, as lucidly, precisely, and incontestably as a quadratic equation. Then words and thoughts both founder, dashed upon the rocks of a strange, perfectly satisfied emptiness that cannot conceive of the need for something as clumsy and attenuated as language. Langston breathes deeply, deeply, into the tips of his toes and to the top of his head, the taste of the air a pure elixir. His ego is gone—or if not gone, cannot be found. *He's mesmerizing me.*

Then he thinks—he hears, it is the drug, one final spurt, the last dregs—Aunt Reginia:

"Watch out! Watch out for all this sex, this sex and sexualitee thing!" she is saying, her voice as strong in memory as it was nine years ago, when Langston shocked her in the midst of a phone conversation that had begun to founder on the subjects of end-term exams at Yale and Reginia's inexplicable decision to plant some rutabagas. "I'm gay, Aunt Reginia," Langston had told her. He'd had to claw the words from his unwilling throat.

"*What!*" Reginia had thundered—which, by the time she settled down, became, "Well, now. I would have thought that I could *see* that." She got a good deal louder and happier once she got going with the sermon.

"I said, watch out, now! Sex will fool you. It wants to make out like it's about the body, but it ain't about the body. The body is an instrument. The body is a vehicle. Sex is a medium. See what I'm saying?"

At the time he didn't.

"Think of it like water. You put sugar in water and it becomes sweet. Put salt in it and it's salty. Water isn't alive per se, but all kinds of life exist in it, and even those that don't live in it need it. Water can hold you up, and it can drown you. See? You bring love to sex and it gives you love. You bring anger, the will for power, the need to dominate, and that's what sex gives you back. What you have to be clear about is distinguishing the medium the thing floats in from the thing itself. It gives love, but it is not love. It gives power, but is not power. It gives shelter, but it ain't shelter. Neither the object of sexual lust nor the sexual act has any intrinsic properties. Get it? Another way of putting it is like that joke, you know, when you're a child at breakfast and they watch you pick up the Log Cabin's maple and say, *Why don't you have some pancakes with your syrup?* You see what I'm saying? You'd be thinking that you like pancakes when what's really going on is that you like the sweet taste of syrup."

"So, sex is the pancakes," Langston had said.

"No, foolish. Sex is the syrup. And you are *pouring* it over what truly nourishes you. See? All of which is to say, don't be too sure about this sex, this homosexuality thing. Because the truth is—you never know."

"Come with me, Langston." The warlock's voice weaves itself below Reginia's—he has been talking all along, Langston realizes, his blandishing vocables a filigree twining itself in and around Reginia's syllables in Langston's memory. Now the warlock surfaces to seize control, rewrites her voice as if overtaking it via viral code, the way one dance-floor track swallows the one previous, drowning the recollection of it. Reginia's bass tamps down, rendered inaudible, only the scraps of her melody filter into aural range; the warlock's powerful bass dominates, a steady, implacable thunder.

He keeps saying it. "Come with me." Langston's body buckles to the words, compelled as it is by the beats on a club floor.

Oliver!

This man is Oliver!

Langston remembers Malachai-by-way-of-Destine, remembers her body, bleeding on the rug. He swerves—he can't exactly turn, can't pull himself completely away from the man, from his spell—and with a cry shoves his way through the bodies around him. The man calls after him, his voice hoarse as he tries to whisper and shout at the same time, "Hey! Wait!" But Langston is like a prairie dog, darting for empty spaces in the crowd. He offends several peoplc before he crashes headlong into the dark blue chest and black leather belt of a policeman.

Langston is dazed. He sees the policeman, with his dark eyes and heavy, dark eyebrows as if cut from a black panther's hide. Italian, he must be Italian, look at that big, beautiful nose—Langston's out of breath and it's an effort to speak. "There's a woman . . . Destine, she . . . her femoral artery . . ."

The policeman grasps Langston by the arm. "Get in the truck, fuckhole!" he says and pushes Langston into the hands of someone else, who in turn pushes him into a big gleaming truck, a sort of cube on wheels, where stoned and drunk fellow partiers sit in two grim rows.

"Evenin," someone greets him amiably. But Langston cannot see who, with all the bodies streaming toward him into the dark van from the light outside, shadowed faces and apish shapes tumbling beside him, their movements seeming to mimic jerked marionettes.

Down at the station, Langston and his cohort are led along a row of barred holding cells. A few demand their First Amendment rights, their Mirandas, their lawyers and cell phones back, pronto, but the policemen pay them no mind. Langston has had a sensible terror of corrupt police brutality and the hell-pits of jail all his life, but he feels relieved. At least he doesn't see the drag queen or her tall accomplice. In the cell he slumps down with his back to the mildewed wall and tries to keep his eyes open to watch his cell mates, all of whom look to be party guests. He worries about Destine, but from what he overhears no one seems to know anything, and he is afraid of asking too many questions and drawing attention to himself. When at last sleep comes—a version of it at least, reminiscent of slumber during transatlantic flights, where he's always tenuously conscious of his body being situated in some alien, confining space—Langston runs from variations of dreams in which he attends Azaril and Leah's wedding to dreams in which he walks along a dirt path running beside slanted houses that seem always in danger of tottering down on top of their picket fences, while a dark angel beckons him to come, come and picnic in the shadow of the falling houses.

At about 11:00 A.M. the partygoers in Langston's cell are all summarily released, with the same grim cheer and lack of explanation with which they had been detained. Langston is sore in his back and butt and legs from sitting up against the cold wall of the cell, and sore in his head from the drugs. Crankily he asks the fellow he presumes to be the desk sergeant whether they have arrested a Reynaldo Cavazos, Quentin Shaw, or Azaril Shahid-Coleman. The desk sergeant takes a full twenty seconds before he denies that any names have been taken.

Langston looks around for a bit, sees no one he knows (he dimly and nastily hopes to find Leah, looking makeup-less and sallow). He goes outside.

The very act of walking unmolested by an enraged drag queen or enhanced by drugs seems incongruous to him after last night, too banal an act for a life that has gone so very, very crazy. The morning is cool and brisk, the sky golden like a ripening apple. It takes him a while, but he is finally able to find a taxi that will ferry him. He would prefer to close his eyes as they drive, but the cabbie is a loquacious man of Middle Eastern origin who enjoys practicing his English. First he asks Langston if he's been in the drunk tank, and where was he drinking, and by the time they reach the Marwick Hotel, Langston learns that Destine arrived at Yale–New Haven Hospital having lost eight pints of blood. The ER physicians pumped ten pints into her cold, gray body and managed to revive her. "She had no pulse! They say it's a miracle," the cabbie says.

To Langston's halting query about the status of a crazed drag queen, the driver gives a blank rearview-mirror stare. "It was all a big drug fiasco. They might gonna charge that black lady. And the president of Yale, becausa all the students, hoo, he's *hot*. Says it lucky ain't nobody killed. They gonna crack down at the university," he says and hunches over the wheel giggling with glee.

14

Marwick Hotel, room 549, 11:45 A.M.

No one is at home. Both rooms are gray with shadow and stillness. The maid has made the beds and tidied the rooms. There is no evidence of the others ever having come back.

Langston sloughs off his clothes, slips on a fresh pair of boxers, and with his eyes closed throws his arm down over the side of the bed and rummages in his bag. He takes a pill from an inside pocket, looks at it, and then swallows it down dry.

Marwick Hotel, darkness

Langston rolls over a couple of minutes later.

More weird dreams. He felt like he was sinking in them, like his dreams were a sinkhole in his mind, drawing him down into filth. He could smell the stench clawing at his legs from below, his lungs would soon fill with silt and wet asphalt, with gravel and dog feces and pennies too worthless to be kept; already he felt the tickle of sand grains skipping down his throat.

Langston struggles up and looks at the clock. It's 5:30 P.M. Five hours since he lay down, not a few minutes. The room is gray and sunless, the curtains drawn tight. He feels as if he is wrapped in whorls of cloth made from spun valium, in blankets of anesthesia. The disorientation is acute, sensuous, physical. The door to the next room is shut. The place reeks of tobacco—Quentin smoking in their nonsmoking room again. Langston is too tired to wake up and too afraid to fall back into those dreams. He forces himself free of the sweaty sheets, an effort that seems worthy of Atlas, pulls on a sweatshirt over his T-shirt and briefs, and trundles over to the door. He puts his hand on the knob, hears voices, and puts his ear to the wood.

"Did I hear you say you used to walk the streets, Quentin?" Followed by an uncomfortable cough. Azaril.

"Walk the streets?"

"You know. Turn tricks."

"I think I may have *mentioned* that I was for a brief period a hooker, yes."

"What was that like? You must have run into men who wanted to do a lot of deviant shit."

With all that's happened, they're still talking about sex. *Men*.

Langston begins to twist the doorknob. He hears Azaril's distinct laugh.

"Lemme ask you guys something I always wanted to know. Does it feel different, I mean, is it more exciting, to get a blow job from a guy who has a goatee?"

In all the time Langston has spent with Azaril, he has never quite heard him speak this way. The whispery, conspiratorial tone, the uncontained, exuberant excitement. Langston gingerly cracks the door open and looks: Azaril, seated beside Quentin. Azaril, grinning from ear to ear like somebody who's eaten a tray full of hash brownies, dressed in exactly the same black clothes he wore last night. Langston sees Reynaldo and Quentin opposite one another at the table by the curtained window. Reynaldo has on a tank top and little shorts that show all the brown bulges and ripples of his physique. Quentin wears a robe cinched tightly at the waist, and with his elbow on the table he holds a cigarette between two fingers with such affected effortlessness that it seems to levitate in the air.

Quentin and Reynaldo look at Azaril, and then at each other. "Well, yeah, it's different . . ." Reynaldo offers.

"So is there more stimulation? Like, you get the tongue and the mouth and the throat and the feeling of all that on your package, but then you also get the hairs of the goatee tickling you, too?"

Reynaldo seems a bit flustered. Quentin steps into the breach fearlessly. "Depends on how far he's going down, what position you're in, and how long the goatee is. If you're just sitting up in a chair with your legs spread, that's one thing. Standing up, fucking his face, that's another. Sixty-nine's different from that. Also there's the quality of the hair. Sometimes that does more than tickle. It burns."

Langston can't stand it. He means to open the door but ends up flinging it open, and it slams against the wall.

"I cannot believe—" Langston can't believe he's saying this, that the words are leaving his lips, that his voice is so shrill. "I can't *believe* you're talking about this."

Azaril looks stricken, a boy caught with chocolate-covered fingers after his mother has warned him to leave her cake batter alone. "Lang! How're you feeling?" he says, rising from his perch on the edge of one of the two beds. "You don't look good."

"Are you OK?" Reynaldo asks, giving Langston a keen look. "Come and sit down."

"I'm fine, I'm fine," Langston says.

"Drink some water, man." Reynaldo has bent over him, a glass in his hand. Langston distractedly mumbles thanks and takes a sip of the tepid stuff as Reynaldo passes the back of his hand across Langston's forehead before he settles upon a diagnosis that he finds reasonably comforting. "You didn't get mixed up in all that shit at the party, did you?"

"I did. I did an experimental drug that Destine gave me. It—it and her—told me a lot about Damian's father that we didn't know."

"Destine? Really?" Reynaldo says excitedly.

"And then this man who I never got a good look at attacked Destine, and then a scary drag queen who was working with him came after me with a knife. The police came to break up the party and put me in jail." He can't help giving his recitation a little whine.

"We heard all about that," Azaril says. "What did Destine say about Damian?"

"Well, she's his mother, for one, and . . . oh, it's so complicated. What do you care anyway? You're in here talking about blow jobs and goatees and shit when Destine's been stabbed and people are in fucking jail."

"Langston, try some carrot juice," Reynaldo interjects. "Carrot juice is *good* for when you've been fucked up—"

Azaril's look of bafflement infuriates Langston even more. "How is it exactly that this question about goatees and blow jobs came to mind?"

Langston hears himself screaming. Is it possible he's actually screaming?

Azaril glances briefly at his companions in crime for help, but Reynaldo shifts in his seat and looks out the window to pretend he's not listening, while Quentin keeps his gaze low, studying the table's woodwork.

"Well . . . I don't know. I was . . . You remember Leah? She was saying that I should grow a goatee, and . . ."

"And that made you envision getting a blow job from someone with a goatee? Or were you picturing giving one?" Langston now has his hands on his hips. In this moment, he is every inch his mother, though both would be horrified to recognize it.

"No . . . She was going down on me and . . ."

"Oh, my God!" Langston screams. "Damian is probably *dead* for all you know and you're talking about this?" He storms back out of the room and slams the connecting door. Everything seems out of kilter as he moves: his feet not solidly pacing the floor, the wrench in his shoulder as he flings the door like a sensation pitched at him from afar that he watches for a while, an abstraction in the air before it lands and he actually feels the weight of its impact.

Azaril's dark tan reddens to copper. "What was that all about?"

Quentin would like to answer—he is eager and ready and excited to answer, the theories are bubbling up over the edge of his throat and lubricating his tongue, he is thinking, *should I start with Explanation A, but no, that's the good one, save that one for last, start with C.* . . . But Langston opens the door and pops his head in. His skin seems to be glowing, his eyes stare straight ahead.

"Could I see you for a minute, please, Azaril?"

Azaril gives Quentin and Reynaldo a helpless glance—Reynaldo ducks the appearance of complicity and stares ahead; Quentin smiles like a nurse ferrying dire news in an oncology ward.

Azaril shrugs and gets up, a puppy going to take his spanking like a good dog, tail sweeping the shanks of his back two legs and head lolling dolefully between the front two. In the room he goes instinctively to the trussed-up curtains and unties them, to give matters a lighter tone.

"Hey, I'm sorry, Lang," he says. The muscles of his face struggle with the urgent need to express both empathetic sorrow and a protective sheen of boyish I-didn't-do-nothin innocence. "I didn't realize what happened to you. I'm sorry I left you alone at the party." He pauses, clears his throat, then plunges in. "This doesn't usually happen to me, you know, meeting someone out of the blue like that. I don't know, it was like I was on fire last night. It was crazy. We didn't even notice all the madness going on in that house until the police were searching everybody's room." He stops again, waiting, but Langston says nothing. "But hey, Langston, you'd love this girl." Langston massages the palms of one hand. *Why does he say my name like that, as if there'd be any confusion about who he's talking to? Like saying my name is some sort of intimacy. . . .* "You didn't get to spend much time with her, but Leah's amazing. She's warm, she's genuine, smart, down-to-earth. I don't know if you pay attention to women—I mean of course you do, I mean maybe you don't notice the way a—the way I do—she's a major hottie. And she understood so much about me! You know, the race thing. I don't usually even tell people about it. And her own background is amazing. Did I tell you about this key she has . . .? Oh, yeah. You know, I was thinking of asking her to help us out with our mystery. She knows New Haven really well, and she's got great instincts."

Langston prowls the space between the two beds. "What about your girlfriend back home?"

Azaril frowns, trying to buy time. "Kelly? She's not my girlfriend. We only dated a few times."

Big pause. Langston glares at Azaril. "And what about me, then?" He's screaming again. This time it feels right.

"You?" *Come up with something quick*, Azaril tells himself. If he had a cat-o'-nine-tails and an altar to kneel on, he'd scourge his back with welts. "You mean . . ."

"I *mean* what about me being in love with you! You came with me to Miami knowing I'm in love with you, you sleep in one bed together with me, you're here *with* me, and the first thing you can think of to do is to go out and find some ho to hump!"

"Langston—how dare you call her a whore—!"

"I said *ho!* Ho! Even punk-ass suburban white boys know how we use *ho!*"

Langston feels a little guilty. But it's too late to stop now. The train has left the tracks. "We're here to find Damian, not on some sex tour! Don't you care about Damian?" He throws his hands up in the air. "And I bet you're in love with her! You're in love with her!"

"Lang. Maybe I knew on some level that you had a crush on me, but . . ."

"Aunt Reginia *told* you I was in love with you!" This is lightning from the hand of Zeus himself—or is it Hera, in this case? "But you just ignore it! Not one word to acknowledge it. And to top it off, you had to go and fuck the bitch? Oh yeah, you can have a crush on Leah, you can have a crush on Damian, but oh *no*, not me!"

Azaril feels as if he has just stepped into a wind tunnel, testing Mach 12 speed. Some glib response is being cobbled together in the synapse fire of his brain cells, but his body and soul writhe in agony and resentment. A big dose of shame, too, that really makes him furious. To contain the motion he retreats for a moment of steeling: ears plugged, eyelids soldered shut, chakras padlocked. He tries to bellow, see if a warning shot across the bow will cool things down long enough for him to think. "What difference does it make, Langston? I had sex with her! What's wrong with that? It's just sex! You can't draw conclusions about what it means! Maybe I was just horny!" He wants to say more, but runs aground the second he realizes that he's already said something he didn't plan on saying and doesn't actually mean.

Langston's gone syrupy now, smiling in a truly hideous way. "It sure as hell means *something*. When you've been my 'best friend' for I don't know how many months, and you never put your dick anywhere in or near my body, but you can't keep your pants unzipped after spending ten damn minutes alone with Leah."

Azaril gives no sign he's heard. His face is flat—the mere outline of features, dark patches and bars like the Shroud of Turin.

"It means something," Langston insists. "It's a cement. It's a seal of some kind. You belong to Leah now in a way you never allowed yourself to belong to me. That makes what's between the two of us become less. Sex changes things, everyone knows that." He stops, gathers himself. The train, having labored up the side of the mountain taxing the strength of its little engine that could, now becomes an express, screaming as it pierces the bright air on the way down. He realizes that he's really not behaving as he would like to. He also realizes that he has no choice. There's a conundrum in this dilemma that makes all the gears of his intellectuality and analytic acumen seize up, so that all he can do is react, react, react. "And Damian. I *know*. I saw you . . . with Damian!"

Azaril gives no sign. Maybe his lower lip retreats into his mouth a little.

Langston wants to draw blood. He can't stop. "Yes, it means something all right. It means that you're a—!"

But thinking about what it might mean sends an unexpected feeling surging up from Langston's gut and through his chest that is soon to become either a wail or streaks of saltwater running down his face. Of course, it's extremely bad form to cry in front of somebody whose pants you want to get into before you ever actually manage to get into their pants. So he goes to busy himself with clothes he's dumped in the dresser drawer.

"Lang . . ." Azaril is plaintive. He moves in Langston's direction, arm extended.

Langston waves him away. It is far too easy to say, "I don't need your pity, Azaril." Of course, he would love Azaril's pity; it's just that he doesn't want to admit how afraid he is that pity is all he's ever going to get.

There is a part of Azaril that cannot bear to know he has caused Langston pain. Sure, you live, you do, you cause other people pain. That's part of life. But to have the fact you've caused someone pain sit in front of your face so that you can't turn away and pretend? That's unbearable. Azaril would like to run away from their relationship, Houdini himself free of its adhesive entanglements to fly away. Still, he intuits the importance of this particular corner of his psyche now stamped with Langston's name in red ink like a massive paw print. He knows he has to tolerate it, give it room. Within limits, that is. On a good day, on a clear day, when Langston doesn't have the temerity to *demand* something from him, Azaril can see those limits reassuringly far off, a thin, blue-green line spied from a mountain summit. At the moment, however, the limit reveals itself as if drawn in heavy black marker: it has a width and depth of several fathoms, and it's coming in fast for a crash landing.

He ought to be firm, in a reasonable, caring, kindly way. But the situation is unsavory. The two of them screaming, Langston standing there in a sweatshirt and tighty-whiteys—it's like some dreadful scene you watch play out in a trailer park. *Why should I care?* Azaril fumes, finally summoning up some lightning and thunder of his own. Azaril's head snaps up and his tone is as harsh as Langston has ever heard it (but his eyes are wide and round as if electrified by a stun gun and then laminated in a glistening sheath of moisture). "Langston, look. This is your shit. You want to act like somebody's betrayed wife? Fine. Find yourself a husband. I'm not him. I'm straight! And I *don't* know what you feel about me. Maybe we can talk about it sometime, but right now? I don't care. I can sleep with, or fall in love with, or have a crush on whoever I want to. You have no right to scream at me because you don't like my choices. You have no rights in these matters that I have to respect at all."

Langston stands still. He takes a long time to answer. The only thing that comes to his mind is, *Don't quote* Plessy v. Ferguson *to me, whitey,* but this has very little bite and quite possibly would sail right over the boy's head. So he waits, arranging his sweaters underneath his short-sleeve shirts. When finally he has it together, he first goes to the door between the rooms, remembering to breathe into his groin and stomach so that he doesn't totter. He can feel Quentin and Reynaldo loitering nearby on the other side. Now completely possessed (as he ruefully recognizes) by the righteous indignation of his mother, he pushes the door open wide so that Azaril can exit. (Keep your other hand on that hip, girl.) As wickedly as he can manage, eyes narrowed and blazing, he fires, "You know something, Az? The thing between you and Leah isn't even real. I cast a love spell on you, you—!" He thinks of several insults and discards them. "Do you have any idea why I did that?"

Azaril is stunned. Not by Langston's histrionic nastiness (scratch a black man and you'll always find some species of diva lying in wait beneath the surface—years of close observation have taught Azaril that). Not even so much by the concept that Langston mumbling some words over a candle could somehow have an effect on the complex biopsychological process currently called "falling in love": everything to do with being human is essentially chemical, isn't it? Love, too, is no more than a modulation of hormones, they say, the brain working in conjunction with cellular peptide receptors producing the body's own native brand of opium. Maybe there's no difference, ultimately, between a drug and a spell. The lesson of the placebo, after all, is that there's no great dividing line between a pill and a bit of persuasion. Bizarre things have happened that

Azaril can't explain rationally, so it's at least marginally possible that there are psychic energies floating around that can be manipulated in the physical world. So far he's coped by suspending his disbelief, trying to take it all in stride. But he's in vertigo now, and it's because a number of things that had not seemed possible before this trip suddenly, subtly, are possible, are happening: he's fallen in love in one evening more or less at first sight, he and Langston are having a catfight, he and Damian—and he might be a . . .

"Say something, Azaril." Langston's trying to calm down, but he sounds like some immensely authorial personage pronouncing a fiat. Just the sort of effect that's bound to make Azaril feel attacked, bristle, consider a retort, reconsider, cast his eyes down, and slowly walk through the door to the other room.

"Come on in here, baby," Quentin beckons. "You scared, huh?" Followed by an evil cackle.

Azaril kicks the door closed.

On the other side, Langston flinches. *That mofo has the nerve to get violent?*

Just then his cell rings. He seizes the receiver, trembling with fury. "Yeah?"

"Those aren't very pleasant vibrations I'm getting from your voice, young man."

Aunt Reginia.

"Oh, hi . . . uh . . . this isn't a good time."

"Don't you have anything you need to report?"

"Y-y-yeah . . . I'll call you later. In a couple hours."

"I see."

Silence.

"Langston. What's going on?"

"I don't really wanna talk about it. Azaril and me had a big fight. . . ."

"You broke up?"

Broke up? It sounds so formal. They were only friends. And then he remembers what Reynaldo said about friendships way back at Redemption, and he thinks of what it means for his friendship with Azaril to exist in the past tense. "Yeah, we did," he replies. He needs more strength than he would have imagined a moment before he spoke to hold back tears.

"I see." The stolid acceptance in her tone, the unpitying surrender to his report, makes it worse.

Silence.

"So your man has left you. Will you be able to continue breathing? Shall I send over an ambulance? A priest to administer the last rites?"

"I'll call you later, Aunt Reginia."

"Hold on, hold on. I need to tell you something. I pulled a card for you from my tarot deck."

Sigh. "I thought you didn't go for that mumbo jumbo stuff."

"Tarot is not witchery, it is a symbolic representation of the soul's journey. And I think it's more or less supported by chaos theory, if I'm not mistaken. You want to know what your card is?"

Despite himself, he does.

"Sixteen. The Tower."

He doesn't remember that one.

"The one with the really, really horrible picture of the building being struck by lightning and burning down. With all the people falling out of the windows upside down with their heads about to be crushed to pulp on the rocks below."

"That's very comforting, Aunt Reginia."

"Oh, sarcasm! Almost a sense of humor! Guess you not dead after all, huh?"

"Mmhm."

Silence.

"So what does The Tower mean?"

"In your case I think it would mean: at the end of chaos and tribulation, you will find perfect clarity."

"Clarity would be good. Wouldn't be enough right now, but it would be good."

"That love spell is messing with you, I bet."

Long pause. "I think it may be."

"All you can do is ride it out." She breathes audibly through the silence. "But are you all right otherwise? Are you in danger?"

He tells her, leaving out far too much, he knows, about Destine, the drag queen, and the warlock. "Out there in the yard, I almost couldn't move. It was like a spell he was putting on me . . ." he mumbles.

"It *was* a spell, no 'like' to it. And you're more susceptible precisely because you're busy messin around with that damn love incantation. That foolery opens up all kinds of channels. Opens holes people can reach through, tunnels nasty things can crawl down. Haven't you ever heard of possession? You were lucky to break free of his influence."

"But why would the warlock be after me? It seemed almost like they were going through Destine to get to *me*—"

"I don't know, I don't know. But it makes me nervous. He doesn't want you finding Damian, I see, but . . . stay sharp! This is no time to get distracted with all your little dramas. I'm going to need you to check in more frequently. Twice a day at least. Call me late, or call me tomorrow."

After she hangs up, Langston sees the red bulb on the hotel telephone handset flashing. Mechanically, he dials to listen to his message. Something seems to be crackling, then, "Mister Fleetwood! Whatever is that noise? It's as if they recorded a vacuum cleaner! What sort of establishment are you staying in that cannot provide a decent voice mail system in the twenty-first century?" There is a gap—filled by a sound not unlike a vacuum cleaner—as if she were waiting for an answer. Then abruptly, "Mr. Fleetwood, I have somehow or other managed to transform my toilet into a bowl-sized version of the Everglades. It is *highly* inconvenient to clear away the Spanish moss and bend back the topmost branches of the cypress trees when one squats for a pee! The incessant chirping of those damnable little tree frogs and the finger-length alligators going at it at night is simply unacceptable, Mr. Fleetwood, simply *un*acceptable! Call me! No, don't call me! Call me if and only if you have something solid. I cannot bear the idea of answering that phone if all you're going to give me is twaddle. And, Mr. Fleetwood. Hurry!"

Langston falls across his bed. He thinks he hears the faint reverberations of laughter in the other room. He can't sleep. So he gets up.

15

Around 7ish that evening

"Sounds wretched." Galen commiserates with his buddy Langston over fresh-wrapped sushi and boysenberry-strawberry smoothies—Galen's own gourmet concoctions. For dessert, a bracing cup of obsidian espresso will be served.

Twilight has settled over New Haven with a cornflower blue sky. Galen's apartment overlooks the street behind the Payne Whitney gym, and while the two friends eat and reminisce in his breakfast nook beside a large window, they can see a few autumn leaves ambulating over the asphalt toward the gutters, and—more picturesque—a couple of stallion white boys in Boola-boola regalia making their way home after a weight workout (note: two pairs of hairless, ivory thighs, glistening; one Clark Kent jaw and a red-cheeked scowl, and the first hairs of a flaxen goatee).

Langston, having taken up so much time talking about himself, now asks Galen about the scandal over his party. "Oh, please." Galen rolls his eyes. "They've threatened me the last three years in a row. Things aren't what they used to be around here. There were cops I used to *invite* to the party, remember! You'd think with poor Destine hurt they'd have the manners to leave us be this time. But it will blow over. We're very good at efficiently getting rid of the drugs. Nothing to worry about."

He rises and goes over to start fiddling with the espresso machine. Langston, watching not altogether idly, compliments Galen on the superb line of his latissimus dorsi. Galen laughs. "Don't think I don't notice you're trying to change the subject, girl." He comes over to knead Langston's shoulders with his large, hairy hands. "Sweetie, forgive me if I'm stepping on toes—oh, whatever, what do I care if I'm stepping on toes—what is this about, really? He's a straight boy. You're a grown-up gay boy. You read too much about ancient Athens and Rome. In today's world, these things always end exactly the way they did."

Langston quivers. Is it Galen's touch that's unnerving him? Is it that he can't bear to have someone offer him sympathy? "I know . . ." he says. But he doesn't. There is something he cannot yet name, cannot yet see.

"I think the issues are all mixed up," Galen comments. "There's Azaril sleeping with Leah. And there's Azaril sleeping with—maybe sleeping with, you don't even know for sure, you were high—what's his name, Damon?"

"Damian," Langston corrects him, and when he says the name he quivers again, more strongly this time, so that Galen can feel it and his hands flinch as if a current of electricity has run through Langston's body. Langston apologizes. He grabs hold of Galen's hands, suddenly not willing to let them go; he caresses them slightly, admiring the web of veins in the pearly skin, kisses them, places them back on his shoulders. "I'm sorry," he says again.

He realizes that he hasn't been thinking clearly. It must be the drugs that made him forget, the hangover must have buried it all under the silt and garbage of last night and yesterday, like the silt and garbage that buried poor Malachai. "Must be the drugs," he tells Galen—but he knows that it is not the drugs. It's the love spell, working its wicked way through his memories and emotions and actions, rewriting them, embellishing some and banishing others as it flexes its magical muscle, far more insidious, infinitely more subtle than anything science can devise. Perhaps the spell alters the subtle processes by which the brain correlates the myriad of data flooding it into a narrative, in which time is neatly arranged as past, present, and future.

"Where are you, girl? What do you mean, you forgot?"

But he hadn't forgotten. He just hasn't been lucid enough—imaginative enough?—to draw the connection till now. Now, maybe, it's clear again.

Damian had disappeared. Back to Mississippi, Sergeant Garrow had told Colonel Fleetwood when, on Langston's behalf, he'd inquired about Damian's whereabouts. "That's all he said?" Langston demanded, again and again hurling the question at his father in new packages—"I wonder if Sergeant Garrow meant that blah blah blah instead of going to Mississippi, do you think that's what he meant?" "But do you think he would just leave in the middle of the school year?" "Mississippi? The Garrows aren't from Mississippi, are they?"—to the point that his father had to do a Pontius Pilate on him and wash his hands of the matter.

"I don't know. Shit," Colonel Fleetwood said, and he had a way of saying *shit* that made you feel that a viscous brown glop of it was soon to come flying your way if you didn't back off. "You act like you in love with the boy," Colonel Fleetwood said.

Splat. Langston, despite the attempt to duck, took that missile of feces right across the eyes, and he was obliged to let it slide down over his cheeks and into his mouth and to swallow it unchewed. Too late he recognized that his father had been watching and waiting, weighing the evidence as Langston grew more bold and reckless, while each reconfigured question about Damian's whereabouts illuminated more and more of what

Langston truly felt. And now his father, ever vigilant against fault, his father who subjected his children's words and the thoughts the words concealed to stringent scrutiny much as a quartermaster subjects vacated military housing to a white-glove test, had caught him.

"You act like you in *love* with the boy."

In fact, as a matter of historical accuracy, Father Fleetwood did not repeat himself, and when the sentence left his lips he laid no special emphasis upon any particular word or words. Such was the elegance of his rapier attack, which Langston now appreciates much as a general must bow to the wiles of his enemy, as the Romans to Hannibal, Montgomery to Rommel. Having spoken once, the colonel need never say another word, because his dutiful son would take the words and repeat them to himself until they became so deeply embedded in the pattern of his thought that he would no longer hear the phrase distinctly or be able to identify its authorship; its contemptuous warning would become a reflex, as inevitable and inescapable as a glandular command. Such is the magnificent economy of all the enunciations of authority: it is, in fact, like magic, like spells, where words said by one human being profoundly reshape the thoughts, wishes, and actions of another.

The colonel, satisfied with having done his duty to protect his son from the scourge of homosexuality, turned his attention to other important matters: being strong; setting an example; running a tight ship. Langston was left to make his way through the evening with a boa of shame writhing up through his guts, swallowing his tongue in its mouth.

But, Langston muses with some satisfaction now, the iron hand of authority has space between its fingers like any other hand, and things slip through. Colonel Fleetwood had not reckoned on his son seeking and finding a rescuer.

It had seemed likely that, with Damian gone, his wrestling teammates Langston and Dillon would become estranged. Their shared devotion to Damian made them allies, certainly, but the fierceness of this devotion also preserved a dynamic of rivalry between them. While neither said an unkind word about the other, at the heart of matters they had long regarded one another with a slightly wary coolness. Each felt he had the stronger connection to Damian, and each looked upon the other as a more or less tolerable interloper. With Damian gone, there would be no need for any explicit decision that their trio could not be pared to a duo; they would simply drift away, Langston to his world and Dillon to his.

But their feelings for Damian proved stronger than they knew. It kept them bound, manacled together in inarticulate grief. Few days would pass without one of them conferring with the other about whether he had heard from Damian. The answer was inevitably no. For a time it was little more than that—waiting together—but this laid a foundation.

When it began to appear that the wait might stretch on longer than they had first believed, Langston and Dillon began to talk. This they did secretively. It would have been unseemly to share their thoughts with others. When they could sneak away, they drank wine in the old places Damian had led them to, and they speculated: Damian's father had tried to kill him and Child Services took him away; the same thing had happened to that Yarborough girl. Damian had tried to kill his father. Damian left to go live with his former stepmother—assumed by both of them, who had never seen her, to be electrifyingly "fine." Damian ran away and was now a street kid, snatching purses in Frankfurt and living in a haze of hashish.

One thing was clear. The official story was not to be believed. "Back to Mississippi," Dillon said with scorn, and gave Mississippi all his venom.

He did not say so, but the mockery in Dillon's tone comforted Langston. Dillon's tight anger had depth. It was a well of strength from which Langston could draw at need; in its manful certainty it could counterbalance the contempt of, "You *act* like you in *love* with the *boy*." In Dillon's sharply angled nose, cheeks, and brown eyes, each fired with the high color of indignation, Langston found an embrace that kept him from feeling alone.

And, there was that evening.

After wrestling practice, in the locker room, Langston pulled his towel across his narrow waist and walked out from the shower, weary and damp and looking forward to his mother's cooking. Dillon was there, as he usually was. There was nothing new in this, nothing to note about Dillon's unhurried approach to dressing himself. But that evening Langston came to a certain view of him.

Langston discovered or remembered something that he had always appreciated: the smooth, smooth white cotton of Dillon's admirable briefs—indelibly imprinted on Langston's consciousness, so that he can recall them now in idealized form as he remembers. And along with them, in a package with them, the cannily hairless and cream-colored legs—canny, you see, because their hairlessness and creamy complexion highlighted, allowed Langston to see, as if etched, each cord of muscle in Dillon's thighs, and to follow the supple rounded line of Dillon's calves.

Dillon's back was to Langston, and Langston's locker was near Dillon's. Dillon bent and began to struggle with pulling his jeans over his feet and then over his thick adolescent legs. Langston watched the legs and the low, narrow pouch of cotton hanging below the curve of Dillon's ass. And a bit faster than he had begun, he walked straight from the shower toward Dillon. Muscle rolled beneath the skin of Dillon's back as he straightened and tugged at the worn white waist of his blue jeans. Up close, Langston discovered to his shock—almost as a terror—that Dillon had a smell.

Langston paid attention to smells. The locker-room smell, stale, the rank socks worn one day too many, and the smell of combs and fold-out black-power picks stored in back pockets, and new underwear on baby-fat skin, and the stench of someone else's shit in the open toilet and his own sweet fart in the air. The odor of hair everywhere, on the shower floor and in the sink and plastered to the blue-gray surface of the mirror. The smell of an athlete before practice, an athlete at practice's end. Langston loved his smells, he could categorize them; he could taxonomize: but it had escaped him, he had not known before or he had not pursued the implications, until that evening, of the particular smell of a particular person at a particular time: that someone, another guy, could have a smell all his own. And that that smell could register in a certain way. That it could have meaning.

Dillon, up close, had a smell, a scent: soapy, fresh, fragrant. Turbulent. With his arms at his sides, dark brown hair bulged out from Dillon's armpits, and this, too—the way he stood, the white briefs and the armpit hair—together these had a smell, too.

Murderous. Dillon was the kind of guy, Langston thought, who could murder you.

Langston did not campaign openly to seduce Dillon. But he trusted, with some joy and a great amount of fear, that for the first time since Damian disappeared he was once again within the tow of a powerful locomotive force. Langston needed only to ruthlessly suppress the conscious knowledge of what he desired and to let his desire, thus unfettered, do its work for him. At times he would find, to his surprise, that he was staring at Dillon's crotch. And at practice and in class (but particularly in practice; since then, Langston has found that sweaty, drooping

Adidas athletic shorts are an aphrodisiac) he would wait—quite unconsciously, of course—until the exact moment Dillon felt Langston's eyes on him before he looked away. Langston might smile then, as if to himself, and he knew Dillon was watching him smile.

Dillon responded greedily to these advances. First he complimented Langston on his tight biceps, and Langston let that sink in for a lengthy, locked-gaze moment before he laughed and deflected the compliment with, "Not as nice as yours." Next Dillon went out of his way to have his arms full of books he obviously would never read, so that he could ask Langston, four feet away, to tie his loose shoelaces for him. Langston bent agreeably to the task, and by the way his head took its sweet time rising up after he was finished, Dillon knew that their friendship was taking on a rather different shape.

Dillon could scarcely be restrained once this knowledge came clearly to his mind; the opposite of Langston, he had only to recognize his desire before putting it to work. Since the two were frequently alone, it was not long before they stood toe to toe in the deserted boys' bathroom, an hour or so after a Saturday meet. Dillon stood perhaps half an inch taller than Langston, and for the first time they noticed this. "I always thought you were shorter than me," Langston said, and lifted his eyes upward like the whore he was swiftly becoming. Dillon did not respond, even with a smile, but his head tilted downward, and while one hand cupped—in a palm suddenly grown bear-size—the curve of Langston's skull where it met the top of his neck, Dillon's salty tongue burrowed between Langston's lips and into Langston's mouth.

So they kissed, and Langston, one eye open, could see the rough poetry of their image in the bathroom mirror. Outside the door they heard, one million miles away and a thousand years in the past, the sound of the coach and his assistant, talking down the hall. Langston had the feeling that Dillon was trying to ingest him, from the insistence of Dillon's tongue and the way he held Langston as if trying to enmesh Langston's body into his own. Langston, more and more in his element, worked by smell: he inhaled the warmth of Dillon's skin and the light musk of his upper lip and his hand dove straight past those pop-fly buttons for Dillon's dick. Its thickness filled Langston's grip. Langston felt himself awash with something. He felt he had reached a culmination, he was on the brink of some sort of transfiguration.

Then Dillon broke their kiss, let his head fall back, and closed his eyes tight.

"Oh, God," he hissed. "You're even hotter than Damian."

Then Dillon pushed Langston into a stall and latched the door and they did the deed—after, or during, the time it took for Langston to extract a few mumbles from Dillon to the effect of, Yes, he'd done this with Damian, too.

Langston's shock and fury propelled rather than checked him. Dillon stripped down his pants so he could stick that fat thing somewhere, anywhere, but Langston shoved Dillon down by the shoulders and fed him his balls. He meant it meanly, but Dillon's mouth was as tropical and questing below as it had been above. Langston groaned and jerked all over Dillon's knee the moment Dillon's slathering tongue expertly slithered between Langston's cheeks, and, dazed, he let himself be lowered to the floor and be folded over the open toilet seat while Dillon jammed two fingers, coated and recoated in a small pool of saliva, and then half the length and all the width of his dick, into Langston's ass.

Later Langston reached back there with his finger and gave it a gingerly touch. He could not believe it had happened, he did not remember how it had happened that the entry, though excruciating, was at the same time not unduly painful, and that despite the burning sensation in his rectum and the odd, constipated discomfort of it all, he had rode his ass back in time with Dillon's quick, every-which-way strokes. Langston even heard himself moan. The only sensation he remembered as pain was Dillon squeezing his shoulders as if he'd fall off him without the support.

Dillon came, and after a moment or so of collapse he stood, pulled up his pants, tucked in his shirt, and exited the stall. He was fixing his hair in the mirror when Langston finally emerged, fully dressed. Langston's stride was slightly askew, and he was afraid that he had suddenly been rendered incontinent and would be doomed to live out his years like his great-grandfather, who spent the better part of his days being wiped by a nurse. Despite this Langston managed a smile, which Dillon warmly if somewhat distractedly returned.

"Smells like butt in here," Dillon said and shook his head, then tucked his comb into his back pocket and blithely departed—leaving Langston to peer at the reflection of his newborn clone: its new face grafted onto the old, its bright new body, its unkempt clothes and lopsided Afro.

Dillon lived closest to the school and his mother worked at the commissary three days a week, so the Lawrence residence at lunchtime became the most frequent site of the boys' rendezvous. These were often not explicitly planned: it was simply understood, an unspoken pact, that they would get some whenever the getting was good.

The liaison was not without consequences for Langston. He had read the book of Leviticus and knew that God had decreed homosexuals should be killed, and this gave him pause. "The penalty is death for both parties," God saith, which was certainly awful, but it was the line, "They have brought it upon themselves," that troubled him most—especially since it came from his mother's Living Bible, which was replete with black-and-white photographs of young people of all races hanging out on steps in city squares and playing sports and holding hands and generally looking like the sort of fun-loving people Langston hoped one day to become, so that it was hard to believe that everything the book said didn't apply to him, right then, in 1981.

He promised God each time that he wouldn't ever do it again, but then Dillon would come looking for him, and if Dillon didn't make a move, he would go looking for Dillon. This seesaw of repentance and recalcitrance itself became limned with the shimmer of sexual excitement, its inexorable rhythm of hold/wait/circle, hold again, wait again, and finally, passionately, surrender became linked to the lure and pleasures of orgasm. He was far yet from knowledge of terms like "closet queen," and thankfully a couple of years away from having to consider the strictures of "safe sex," a concept that young, thirteen-year-old Langston would have found particularly baffling and mean-spirited. If, after all, you were going to commit a sin, if you were going to step off the edge of a moral cliff, what was the point in doing it safely? It was the lack of safety, the near certainty of condemnation and shame, that made Langston hunger for more and more and more. It was humiliating, to get fucked and like it and look forward to it, to throw himself with ardor at another male and find that he did not think about whether he had done it correctly, and that when he did what he did he thought about nothing at all. Shame and humiliation were fun; being closeted was fun; being unsafe was fun. They were the elements of a new craft. They were the habits of a novitiate. This turn of events had been prepared for him by forces beyond his ken, and if they were not quite the forces imagined in the laws and whimsies of various tent-dwelling desert tribes, then so let it be written, so let it be done, amen.

Sometimes Dillon—never quite predictable as to how, when, where, or whether his desire would ignite—personified these forces. More often, the memory of Damian stepped into that role, as smoothly and confidently as if it had been written for him, a Broadway vehicle for a comeback superdiva. Langston drafted this memory to slave for him, he sank his teeth into the image of Damian and shook it like a dog, he tore at it with the savagery of a cuckold: again and again he coaxed Dillon to tell him in detail what Damian had done with him and how often, and then, steeled by jealousy, Langston set about bitterly and joyfully to surpass him.

Now, Langston vowed, now I will fuck Dillon in every way known to man and do it thrice over, until by sheer volume nothing Damian touched in Dillon (and withheld from Langston) will not have been touched by me. It was as if Langston were going to lift his leg and spray so that no inch of Dillon's body did not bear his mark, too. He would undo Damian's undoing of what might have been.

The betrayal that spurred him on was not only sexual or romantic, and at base may have been neither. The keener loss was vague. It had something to do with belonging, the hope and promise of someday truly belonging. If Damian had not disappeared, if Damian had not crept behind Langston's back to seduce Dillon (well, that's how Dillon told the story, anyway), then there might have been a world where he could be in *love* with the *boy* and *act* it completely unashamed, then—. But *then* was a blank space, forever to remain incomplete. Nothing belonged to it anymore.

Gradually—perhaps no more than three weeks or more later—their affair petered out, lost its heat and steam. One imagines two horny boys, the indefatigable lust of adolescence, the allure of taboo and the satisfactions of secrecy, and it seems inconceivable, a waste, that the two of them shouldn't have been able to keep it up (as it were). Not at least without some bitter scene of guilt and blame topped off with vengeful heterosexual reassertion, or some teacher or parent or parent's friend happening upon their naked bodies postcoitally embalmed in sweat, followed by shrieks and the onset of scandal. Yet no such drama came to pass. Dillon's interest waned. They avoided one another. Perhaps, for both, the sex, no matter how nasty they tried to make it, no matter how dangerous, did not quite measure up, either to what they had known before or to what they had hoped to know. When they were together, somebody's cock up somebody's ass, panting and heaving and all that good stuff, after the novelty of it had worn away they were still in limbo, or in some other universe parallel to the real one, the one they truly desired. And the doorway to this better universe was sealed shut by the silence of a friend's disappearance, a silence made more awful by the echoes of memories and fantasy.

In June the school year came to a close, and Dillon, his father having been reassigned to the Pentagon, departed for a suburban home in Maryland. Dillon promised to write but didn't, and Langston promised to write but didn't.

Langston waited, steely, cold, impassioned, to hear from Damian.

Galen listens to this story with murmurs of lecherous approval. "Mm, sounds hot. I can't believe you were getting some at age thirteen, girl! I was like this shriveled-up skinny bookworm bitch, hiding in the library so nobody would make fun of me. I wish I had some hot Dillon type around to rape my ass."

"It wasn't as much fun as you think," Langston says. Lying, of course: it *was* that much fun. And also much, much more painful.

They lapse into an uncharacteristic silence as they watch the sky rapidly purpling, the last shreds of light imparting to the tower of Payne Whitney gym an ephemeral glow of silvery melancholy.

The Grad Ghetto, that same evening
In the first-floor bedroom of a two-story, wood-frame house on Avon Street that Leah Francesca shares with three other women, Azaril lies in bed awake.

The bedroom is small, the blinds battened against light because Leah can't sleep without the shroud of near-total darkness. Leah was next to Azaril a minute ago, her nakedness imprinted along the length of him from his nose to the top of his feet, but now she has rolled away, taking even her arms with her, so that in this queen-size bed that he and Langston wouldn't be able to share without constantly brushing against one another, he cannot feel her, and if he closes his eyes he might not even know she was there. So Azaril keeps his eyes open, fixed on Leah beside him: the muted blue tinge of the skin on her face and her exposed forearm, the hump of her body, unchartable in its wondrous curves and crannies beneath the blank sexless swells of the comforter. He could move across the bed, shuffle over there, just to wind his feet with hers, perhaps lay his fingers on her thigh, but he hesitates, not knowing whether she's one of those girls who hate to be touched while they're sleeping.

So he watches her. He ought to be tired, but he's not. Guilt tethers him to the waking world, restrains and incites him, both a bridle and a biting set of spurs. Guilt, his mother once told him, is nothing more than the experience of inner conflict between what you want to do and what someone else wants you to do. This seems to him unassailable gospel, and never more so than now. The problem is: what does Azaril really want? Guilt is also an aphrodisiac, and Azaril feels excited now, restive and tumid, a surge of blood and prickly nervous sensation pulsing into his groin.

He knows what he did tonight was, in a way, wrong, or at least unkind and therefore in some measure wrong. He refused Langston. And everything he refused to Langston he gave—and would give again, and more, if asked—to Damian. There is a stark unbending cruelty to that asymmetry, a wantonness and amoral abandon to the choices he's made, that feels both freeing and horrifying—as if he has become some obstreperous drunk tramping the city streets with his pants down at his knees, whizzing fusillades of piss at shocked and defenseless passersby. In one sense his fight with Langston changed nothing; it only revealed an undergirding truth that, once uncovered, means actual changes become unavoidable. He is free to give what he wants to whom he wants: that was always true. It's only now that the accompanying responsibility, to himself and to those he chooses and those he doesn't choose, makes itself starkly felt. The choice he's made thrills and devastates him. He has lost a friend. He's irreparably destroyed something, almost like an old and cherished sentimental possession, the last link to relatives long dead or traditions lost, though he's only known Langston for a short time. Though longer than Damian. Longer than Leah.

When he and Damian first met one another months ago—by happenstance, though with all the gravity and epochal decision of fate—Damian—he was prowling Cody's bookstore, they both were, Azaril to waste time, Damian probably to do exactly what he did, exactly what his life work seems to be: seduce. Azaril ordinarily kept his distance from dark, borderline burly black men with shaven heads whose muscles looked as if they were pumped full of anabolic steroids and whose hard expressions posted a warning sign legible on every continent: KEEP OUT UNLESS YOU WANT A ASS-KICKING. But this man whose name Azaril didn't know was smiling at him. Azaril was shocked by the sight. He could scarcely bear to look squarely at that smile without the usual protection afforded by viewing it from a distance, say on a TV commercial or in a magazine ad or a newspaper sports photo. Black men he saw on the streets never smiled; the set of their mouths almost never exceeded the narrow range between expressions of indignation, placidity, and purposeful contentment. Even Langston never smiled at Azaril the way Damian did. Langston, always guarded, always manipulating, weaving and bobbing around Azaril as if Azaril were a floating mine that might explode, gave him smiles that had a tentative, devious character.

Damian smiled, and Azaril felt instantly the ache of something he had never known it would be so sweet to possess.

Was that all it took to start the thing, this hard-to-say nameless thing between them? Azaril wasn't sure. He knew what it took to end it: what it took to end one phase and open up, with all the wild lovely fear and joy that accompanies all opening things—whether petals of new flowers on the first hot sunny day of May or moon-sheened gates of heaven—that was how Azaril had opened up, to the new phase, the new world, as yet uncharted.

On the last night they saw Damian, at some dark hour Azaril never checked the clock to ascertain, he had awakened, groggy. He needed to piss. He sensed, and then with a slow torso twist to the right actually saw Damian's body lying next to him. Smelled rich cologne. It was only for a millisecond, as Azaril pulled back the covers to go back to bed, only seen in the faint luminescence seeping through the tightly down-turned blinds, the shimmer of late morning falling like mist across his knees, in a tail of light across the bed. He caught a snapshot of—Damian's package.

He got out of bed, quickly, but in the next moment didn't know exactly why he'd gotten up. Out of habit, he went to the bathroom. Didn't turn on the light. Did he shut the door? He peed. As he was peeing he was wondering, in a mildly alarmed, sleepy, only partly sentient way, how he had ended up in bed with Damian. And then, instantaneously or simultaneously with the thought of Damian filling his mind, complicit and complementary to the heavy tang of Damian's cologne like orange rinds and fresh banana slices that blossomed lingeringly in Azaril's nostrils, Damian, in the flesh, in his body, was there. In the bathroom with Azaril. The bathroom door was closed.

Azaril remembers that he immediately started talking. He remembers he was holding his free hand out toward Damian, in the windowless yet somehow luminous bathroom, in which every polished surface, the commode and the washbasin and the tub and shower curtain and backsplash tiles, glimmered and shone with light that seemed perceptibly to quiver, in which the great square mirror was like a transparent door behind which lengthened a narrowing corridor wholly out of scale with the room it reflected. "I was having this dream," Azaril blurted. He may have been whispering. "I was in like a pyramid, in this deep hole, but I could see stars." Azaril remembers the feeling he had and the tone he heard himself speaking in: childish, as if he were a little boy and his father was there attending him in the bathroom to ensure he aimed into the bowl rather than splattered its rim.

Damian smiled at him. The same smile: promising a sweetness you had only to reach up and taste. "The pyramids of the pharaohs were built so that a diagonal tunnel ran up from the hidden tomb where the dead pharaoh's mummified body lay,"

Damian said, just as if he were Azaril's father telling him a story, "and this tunnel opened onto a view of the night sky. When the tomb was sealed after the pharaoh died, the pharaoh's soul was supposed to use the tunnel as a launching tube to streak up to the stars, so that the dead king could reach heaven and impregnate the goddess Isis. That way she'd give birth to the falcon god Horus, who was in each successive generation supposed to be the new god king on earth."

"So it's kind of like the tunnel was a huge phallus, and the pharaoh's soul was like a divine ejaculation," Azaril concluded. The enthusiasm that had overtaken him made him speak more loudly than he intended. He was experiencing some kind of rush, spasmodic, abrupt. An afflux of feelings: wishes, memories, a swift plunging enormity of sadness. He had never had a father perform such an act for him, stand beside him this way, companionably in the bathroom, at ease with him talking or doing the simple masculine things men do in the bathroom. The recognition of how much he had missed and how much richer his life might have been was overwhelming, lacerating. Not knowing what to do—and yet, in some quick instinctual way, knowing exactly what he needed at that moment, what he had to have—Azaril stuck his head out there into the darkness, into the interstellar chill of cold, vast space, and, like a Doberman diving for its quarry's neck, he jammed his lips against Damian's and opened his mouth and did it. He was still holding his dick over the bowl, and piss began running again as they kissed.

After that, a slapdash running together of various acts. No one act meant anything or did anything much for Azaril physically or sexually: the playful fraternizing of their tongues, liberal hands squeezing and pulling at pouch and nipples, fingers tangled in crotch hair, an eruption of madly thrusting frottage that left Azaril terrified and breathless, Azaril licking the taste of

Damian's cologne from his shoulders and neck as if shearing off a layer of skin and consuming it, eating the smell and the skin bearing the smell as if the combination were ambrosial sustenance—nothing of it seemed quite real or concrete. At no point was Azaril ever fully erect—not as he is now, stroking himself as he lies next to Leah and tracks the tiniest movement of her head on the pillow and the minute shifts in the depth and rhythm of her breath. What Azaril and Damian had done together was not sex as he knew it, not everyday hormonal lust. Admittedly there was great pleasure in the acts: the inescapable pleasure of merely being touched, the pleasures of being licked and lapped and handled, common to all such sensuous events. These were familiar pleasures, they were nothing new, but Azaril found himself fascinated, enthralled by them. The pleasure made him ravenous, made him demand more and more. It was a kind of pleasure he was not supposed to feel—or, at least, a source from which no pleasure was supposed to flow—and this delicious improbable presence where there was supposed to be an absence made everything he and Damian did seem magical. Some useful, perhaps vital secret lay hidden in the very surprise of that pleasure. The very fact of its being unexpected was a sign that truth lay there, waiting.

"A man in Egypt told me," Damian had said, "that the Egyptian gods were believed to have bones of iron, and meteors were supposed to be the gods' semen, shooting as fire across the skies. *Can you imagine that, Damian*, he said to me. He said, *To fight against the will of gods with bones of iron would be to hurl yourself against a wall that would break you. To love a god whose semen was fire would be to walk willingly into the arms of an inferno.*"

Damian's tongue traced designs in the hair and flesh of Azaril's belly, up, down, around, a pentagram here, a cross there. Damian claimed in fervid whispers that he was writing magical sigils in Azaril's flesh, signs of power; he claimed that secrets of eternal deathlessness, of resurrection and of reunion with the stars were inscribed in the tongue tattoos drying on Azaril's skin. Whether it was truth or nonsense, the strangeness of it all—the darkness of the closed bathroom and the appalling, illicit schadenfreude of knowing that Langston lay sleeping on the other side of the door; the mirror that recorded everything they did, that watched without judgment or reaction, as unmoved and seemingly as eternal as stars and sea—all of it combined to allow Azaril to imagine the disparate pieces of himself soldered together at last.

At some point the frenzy relented. In the ensuing lull, the two bodies parted. Azaril rocked on the floor, in the throes of abandoned love, enthralled with the cold clarity of the tile pressing against his bare ass, intoxicated with self-forgetfulness, moaning and pleading, "Shit, shit, shit." For a moment it was as though Damian wasn't there and wasn't missed.

"Shh. Langston," Damian said in a hoarse voice. And then Azaril panicked. They both froze, listening until they heard a gentle wheeze far off on the other side of the door. Breathing again, Damian grinned at Azaril in the darkness, a sly grin of complicity and lewd intention. Azaril waited: what magical thing would they do to one another next? "I'd love to stay with you," Damian had said consolingly.

Azaril's heart fluttered. Previously unthinkable insecurities began to toy with him. Was he a bad gay lay? Did he give the kind of blow job guys roll their eyes and tell worst-blow-job stories about?

Damian rubbed Azaril's stomach with his papery, corrugated palm. Azaril lay frozen, feeling that the smell of Damian was everywhere in him, permeating his body: he would never be able to escape it, nor would he have to make the choice to. "But . . ."

Damian tossed his head toward the door, not saying—perhaps not daring to say—Langston's name. "And I gotta go meet this guy for breakfast in about a hour, anyway."

Damian left Azaril on the bathroom floor with a strong hug and a tender pursed lip smooch that he left on the corner of Azaril's mouth like the impression of a soft, cool branding iron. That final taste engorged Azaril's senses with an almost inhumanly erotic aroma, expunging any trace of anger or hurt at Damian's departure. In the swoon of that kiss Azaril grabbed hold of his balls and brought his fingertips to his nose. The same. Damian had kissed him with the lips that had been imbibing Azaril's flesh, and overpowering Azaril now was the smell of his own pungent aroma. And the smell was indistinguishable, especially now, from Damian's. For Azaril the congruence was profound, its meaning obvious—obvious, at least, in an otherworldly sense, a kind of realization full of awe and relief. That delicious smell on Azaril's fingertips, overpowering, elusive, was in fact allusive of his secret blackness, of that part of his being bequeathed him by his father—exotic, foreign, unknown, and yet oh so heartbreakingly intimate. So close it beat in his heart, so close it ran out through his pores and mingled with his sweat, so close it lay unseen on the surface of his skin: his secret blackness.

To compromise the memory of that revelation, to taint what Damian had given him, would be a sacrilege. He couldn't explain this to Langston without hurting him further—though Langston seemed to know already, in that ultrasensitive way those who are betrayed always seem to know that they have been betrayed. But if Azaril'd given in to Langston's entirely mundane and prosaically romantic lust, if he even entertained that idea—he and Langston as *boyfriends*—he would be refusing the gift Damian had given him. Langston would never understand this. Langston, if Azaril told him everything, would insist that that night with Damian meant what Langston had long suspected. "I knew it," he would say, and, lying there beside Leah, the fluted tune of her soft breathing in his ears, Azaril can picture exactly the triumph that would light up Langston's eyes.

16

The Marwick Hotel, 10ish the next morning

The hotel room seems stifling to Azaril when he walks in, unnaturally cold and even sinister despite its veneer of comfort, like it's a prison cell for white-collar criminals. But the others don't appear to share his disquiet: Reynaldo and Quentin lie side by side on Reynaldo's bed, and Langston—lying back comfortably (and covetously?) on his elbows on Azaril's bed—meets Azaril's nervous greeting with a flicker of his eyes and a slight hardening of his jaw before he goes back to listening. Quentin is talking, and both Reynaldo and Langston seem to find what he's saying fascinating.

"I didn't sleep good, either. Had all these strange-ass dreams."

In one dream there was a big black man, he tells them. In the dream, Quentin was asleep in the room next door, or something that looked very much like the room, except that there was a bigger TV. And then the TV screen went snowy, and there was someone standing outside the door. It was a big black man, Quentin says, taller than a basketball player, heavier than a football player, you couldn't even see his face. When Quentin opened the door, the big black man broke the arch and the doorjamb as he forced his way in, and Quentin would have been trapped if the window hadn't at that very moment crumbled into ash, and a stroke of lightning whipped inside the room to lash the big intruder's feet and throw him down on his knees. In the rectangular hole in the wall where the window had been, Quentin saw a tall, slender figure floating, like a man made of wood, his arms spread out as if to welcome Quentin to leap into the foundation-less air.

"I looked out that window, and saw how far it was down to the ground, and it was like, two hundred and fifty stories," Quentin says, his eyes shifted away from them to the remembered depth of that impossible drop. "I wasn't about to make that leap, so I woke myself up."

They pile dream stories on top of one another: Reynaldo recounts the dream he told Langston about, where there was a big, menacing teacher with a white face and black eyes and black lips, and then a rescue by a cross with beckoning hands. Langston—omitting the detail of having seen both Quentin and Reynaldo in the vision—tells them for the first time about the dream he had way back in Miami on the night they went to Redemption, of the sky collapsing, and then a man with a muscular back appeared, his arms spread wide—

"Like the arms of a cross?" Azaril says.

Langston nods. The delicate companionable feeling in the room evaporates as soon as Azaril speaks.

"You guys couldn't sleep last night, either?" Azaril asks, stepping closer to his bed, as if to sit beside Langston. But the mention of last night makes Langston flinch, so Azaril stops at the foot of the bed.

"Mmhm." Quentin pierces the awkward silence. "Langston was tossin and turnin. I think I heard him moaning out somebody's name, who was that you was calling out to, Langston, Aza—!"

"Quentin!" Reynaldo says sharply. After staring Quentin down, he tells Azaril, "I couldn't sleep, either. I don't remember any specific dreams, though. I think I may have dreamed about Damian. Langston"—there is a nurturing solicitude in Reynaldo's tone and manner—"when you had that dream at the club in Miami, that was the night before Damian disappeared, right?"

"Yeah," Quentin agrees. "You were at Redemption real late, for the after-party. I was with Damian in Little Havana the next day."

"It has to mean something, us having these similar dreams," Reynaldo says. "Is it like, a warning . . . ?"

"The cross thing," Quentin says. "You think thass some Christian stuff? Maybe Jesus is talking to us."

"Damian's doing it." Azaril's voice trembles. "He's connecting us. It's his influence from—from—!"

"The grave," Reynaldo finishes for him.

"No," Langston says. "Damian isn't dead. Aunt Reginia would know. Anyway, we haven't *all* had these dreams. You didn't have any dreams about Damian, did you, Azaril?"

Tense pause.

"I did . . . have a lot of trouble sleeping. I was—remembering stuff about Damian," Azaril says nervously.

"That fits. Our dreams or our sleep, they've gotten synchronized," Reynaldo says, in a decisive tone that makes them all turn to him hopefully and that establishes him, for the moment, as their general. "The night before Damian disappeared, Langston got his vision. We're being tipped off. Something's about to go down. The warlock's already killed Malachai, and tried to kill Destine, maybe tried to get Langston. Maybe we're being warned that one of us is about to be—"

"Zzztt!"—Quentin, hissing. He makes a fiercely exaggerated pantomime of a beak closing, puts his finger to his lips, then urgently stabs the finger toward the hallway door with a grimace on his face.

The others catch the sound of feet tramping toward the room—perhaps feet in boots, heavy enough to make the floor whine a little with each step.

Azaril tightens up, Reynaldo the general rises—

There is a knock. Tap tap tap.

No one moves. No one breathes.

A manila envelope slips lizardlike beneath the door and shoots half a foot across the stubbed tentacles of the melon green shag carpet.

Tramp tramp tramp tramp. The heavy-booted feet start up again, then fade away.

Langston the scout bends down to pick up the envelope.

"It could be a letter bomb," Quentin offers.

Langston hesitates, trying to recall the telltale signs for Suspicious Mail enumerated in the post office's advisory—funny shape, no return address—and then he sees his name written across the face of the envelope and a printed sticker in the corner that says, "Office of the USA, Southern District of New York."

"Office of the USA?" Azaril is hovering behind Langston, his chin almost on Langston's shoulder.

Langston takes a step toward the door before he turns and says with a relieved sigh, "The United States Attorney's office. This is from my sister Zuli." He opens it. He sighs again, with less relief and more agitation. "It's just a short note. She has some information about Credence Gapstone that she thinks might be helpful, and wants us to come to New York this afternoon. She's given us directions of where to meet her—in secret."

"Oooh. Drama," Quentin says, with a flourishing bow of approval.

17

Nueva York

Langston, Reynaldo, Quentin, and Azaril go to meet Langston's sister in a bar called Vanity Affaire.

Quentin is making a big deal about leading the way. "I *been* to New York, now," he has said some two or three times already since the four of them disembarked in Grand Central Station from a zombifying ride on the Metro-North train. Before they can fully shake off the effects of commuter catatonia and let the grim semblance of rigor mortis fall from the muscles of their faces, he has them marching at a martial clip into the main concourse to dart up the flight of stairs to the bar and get a better view of the universe of hurrying humanity, the marble floors, the seventy-five-foot windows and glamorously restored examples of "Beau's Hearts" architectural style around and above them. He points out this and that archway with the ruthless fervor of a Nazi tour guide.

"Don't miss the ceiling!" he commands Reynaldo and Azaril, and while they reluctantly look up to the lit constellations mapped across the blue dome, Quentin forces Langston to pay attention to the details of why he knows New York and how. "Grandmother and me come here every other summer, for a week in June. She saves her Social Security checks and I pay the rest. Back when I moved in with her, I asked her what I could do to thank her for taking me in after Miss Maria Shaw threw my ass out, and she said she always wanted to go to New York City. So we been coming up here for 'bout ten years. Grandmother and I stay in the Helmsley Palace Hotel, Fiftieth and Madison, OK? And yes, Miss Girl, because I know you are wondering, I do have a connection that helps us stay there at a discount. A rich Italian I had as a customer for a while—*very* elegant man, real friendly—he helps me out. You know how it is. Rich white folks. You thirsty, Reynaldo? They got papaya mango carrot juice and all that gourmet, high-priced shit you like in the European market, down the steps, all the way across the floor past the central information booth, and to the right down the corridor. No, to the right!" Quentin sighs with the outrage of a mother on-her-very-last-nerve, then turns back to Langston. "I musta gone down to Vanity Affaire twice the other summer. Funny your sister would choose there. She's not family, is she?"

"Well, she's my sister . . . oh, I see what you mean," Langston replies, the presence of Azaril having left him very few nerves himself. "No, no. She's straight."

The constant irritant of Quentin's commands and guidebook recitations at least has managed to provide a veneer, if not a bona fide distraction, to divert them from the tension crackling between Azaril and Langston. The sullen I'm-just-pretending-you're-not-here moments alternating with Nothing-has-happened-I'm-fine fakery has them all feeling downcast and pessimistic, as if the loss of harmony between them is a bad omen they can't escape. And Reynaldo's dire interpretation of their dreams hangs heavy in the air.

Almost as soon as they reach the peak of the stairway at Christopher Street station near Waverly Place, they feel the early stirrings of autumn creeping under their clothes in chilly gusts, slipping into their underwear like fingers of ivy. The spires of the tallest buildings are sewn up in a layer of haze, arid dust funnels swirl up from the grates in the sidewalk. To the four of them, wading through the thickening silence, a sense of unease feels pandemic in the streets of the city. Where New Haven seems to flounder in the river of time and is almost medieval by the standards of brisk American progress and boom, Manhattan seems at the moment to have lifted itself above the foam of the rapids as if in a hovercraft, the citizenry crowded uncertainly at the rails, not sure whether they belong in the past or the future, whether recent glories are the last or more spectacular triumphs await.

As they walk along amid the jumble of the West Village, where shops and bars and restaurants cozy up to three- and four-story brick residences, and gym-toned and tony young urban blond professionals rub shoulders with mustachioed gay men widening at the middle and with the occasional skateboarding troop of sexually unidentifiable youth, Azaril distracts himself with moral indignation, chews on the idea that Langston—in addition to being a hysterical, needy, jealous bitch—has supposedly cast a love spell on him. Azaril's head turns in loops of fervor and experiments of panic—is it his own emotions that he feels, or is it some mumbo jumbo shake rattle and roll that's spinning him around like a puppet? He rehearses warnings he thinks someone ought to yell at Langston. That it's wrong to tamper with the emotions of others, it's so wrong it should practically be a war crime, and that apart from using another human being in a way that's sure to ruin your karma or your dharma or whatever, making people sex-crazy is especially heinous when there are diseases to worry about.

Meantime, Langston's got his own troubles. He ponders a spooky cell phone conversation he had with Aunt Reginia in the

New Haven train station fifteen minutes before the arrival of the 1:10 P.M. Metro-North.

She'd listened more or less unmoved to his full report about Destine and her channeling of Malachai, the surprising connection between Destine and Damian ("That's not surprising," she'd said maddeningly), and the attack of the warlock ("I *told* you to be careful," she'd said). He was long done with the report and was rattling off on other subjects—angst-ing about Zuli and how he felt intimidated by her these days, what with all her success and fame—when Reginia huffed, "You had a dream, didn't you?"

She'd sounded very grouchy, as if she felt he'd been deliberately failing to bring up the only important matter for them to discuss. "What do you mean? I always dream."

"But you've been having visions."

"Um, visions?"

"Child, don't 'um' me! *Visions*. Like the one you had when you were at that club." The words *that club* came out in the tonal equivalent of biting into a raw lemon.

Langston had felt unaccountably reluctant to talk about his recent dreams, almost ashamed, as if she wanted him to reveal his erotic fantasies. "I saw that woman again—the tall woman with the straight black hair, who was going up the hill? Well, she was going up the hill again, and her son was with her, and when she reached the top of the hill, the house was, like, cut in half or something. And then, you know how it is with dreams, or at least how you remember them, suddenly I saw the house again, but from the front, whole, except it was slanting like it was going to fall."

"Now that's the good stuff!" He'd had no idea what she was talking about. "And how did the slanted house and the house cut in half make you feel? What's your intuition about its meaning?"

"It felt . . . I felt like it was familiar. Expected. Dreadful. Like the bad thing you fear is going to happen but you know it will happen. The bad things that always happen."

His despair seemed to make her very happy. "Yes, yes, yes, yes, yes. Because this whole mess you are working through has something to do with *repetition*, and losses that occur again and again. Something or someone that goes missing and doesn't get found." (Feeling his heart leap, he tried to break in, "You mean we won't find Damian—?" But she kept rolling.) "*And* it's about the despair the loss drops you into. This woman climbing the hill, she's calling to you from across the void—and she is, of course, Credence's mother, Verity Gapstone, Damian's grandmother, the same woman who edited *Hex*. She felt the same despair of loss *you* feel. Right?"

Then he thought of Damian and Dillon, Damian and Azaril, the fresh humiliation of Azaril and that woman. He nodded dumbly to the phone. It had felt like his heart might break if he acknowledged it.

"Exactly. And that's the connection." Of course he hadn't said a word, but she understood. "Now this one you went into the fire with years ago, this Damian. I don't know him personally. But I know his kind. They're very powerful, those sex magicians. My red-boned Negro ex-husband was one. They leave a kind of resonance you can sometimes track. Like the spoor of an animal in heat. Yes, they are some stringent teachers, those men. The lessons they impart are not easy." She paused, making a brief sound like humming; Langston assumed she was lost in the memory of Uncle Dilbert, who like nearly every relative of his parents' generation, he finds difficult to imagine as remotely sexual. "You understand what this particular vision means, don't you?"

"Um . . ."

"Use your training as an analyst, Langston! Clairvoyance is one-third experience, two-thirds understanding what your experience is telling you. What this vision means is that the house is about to fall down, darling dear. Just like in your Tarot card, The Tower. Be ready."

Reginia hadn't had the time to get into what that meant, or so she'd claimed (since the volume on the TV he could hear over the phone shot up at about that time, Langston had the feeling that a particularly important moment was transpiring on her soap opera), but he frowns now, pondering it again. How would the house fall down? What was the house in this case? Did it mean that they were going to lose Damian for good?

Langston frowns just in time for Azaril to take a cautious look over his shoulder at him bringing up the rear and assume the frown has to do with him; Azaril flushes, pretends to have looked past Langston to the gay bookstore to Langston's right, and snaps his attention back to the pavement.

"Langston, where is your head?"

It's Quentin, field-trip(ping) schoolmarm.

"The bar is right here. Where you going?"

Vanity Affaire crouches low behind a department-store-style display window framed in multicolored glitter that creates a disco-ball light effect. In the center of the frame is a broad-shouldered and hip-endowed female mannequin whose cheekbones bear a resemblance to Kim Novak's. She's done up in fifties chic, in a hat like the upturned cup of a flower and a cobalt blue top and knee-length dress that molds to her perfect plastic hourglass dimensions, accented by a glossy silk white scarf worn low around her white neck and white gloves glistening with jeweled bracelets that reach up to her elbows. Kim Redux stands on slender heels and turns one toe out as if torn between dashing back in the direction from which she came or posing for the benefit of the bar's patrons. "She's having an affair, see?" Quentin explains as they file through the black door, and looking at it, they do see something in Vanity's plastic and rubber face, a melancholy secret wish seeping out of her painted, unblinking eyes.

The passageway beyond the door is narrow and curves downward with a grand balustrade, the sort of entry that announces one's presence without the worry of having to hire a butler to do it. At the bottom, the space opens out onto a roomy, semidark rectangular area spangled with hanging lights at the bar and at the various booths. It is dominated by a model's fashion show runway, where a few drag queens in training and too-sober homosexual tourists prance awkwardly to a reverberant techno beat that fades from memory almost as soon as it reaches your eardrums.

"It's early," Quentin sneers and goes straight to the mounted scrims that stand on either flank of the stage; vintage wraps, feather boas, flapper-girl skirts and the like lie in piled heaps, for customers with supermodel dreams to slip on before taking to the runway. "Nothing," Quentin pronounces.

Meantime Langston and Reynaldo have made a quick circuit of the bar and the booths. Langston doesn't see Zuli, so they slip into a booth to wait. Langston notices Azaril hanging back, as if sitting next to him would give him cooties; he rolls his eyes vigorously, and scoots across the fake leather of the booth to slam his thighs against Reynaldo's.

They sit in silence after ordering their drinks, Azaril brooding, Reynaldo contemplating and discarding several attempts at peacemaking, Quentin bored and throwing attitude to whomever he can capture in his sights.

Langston stares blankly toward the bar. His eyes come to rest on the bartender, a studly siren of chocolate color and sultry lips who has on a Diana Ross wig, circa 1968, and a tight, pink, short-sleeved sweater that draws attention to both the torpedo tits of his stuffed bra and his vein-rippled biceps, triceps, and substantial forearms. Langston watches, smiling a little to himself at the absurdity and beauty of the man's mismatch of attire and physique, and the inelegant way he tramps along behind the bar like a heavy-footed high school football player. It takes him a while before he notices that the bartender is staring back. Langston, embarrassed, smiles more broadly, but the bartender's expression doesn't change. Langston drops his eyes, looks up, drops his eyes and looks up again, and begins to fidget under the man's unrelenting stare. He's never been cruised by a drag queen before, and for that matter has never been attracted to one, but this one. . . . Azaril picks up Langston's discomfort and glances back over his shoulder to see what has Langston so distracted.

"What?" says Quentin, desperate for something to jump into.

"The bartender," Azaril replies. "He's so . . . I dunno, he's almost . . . kind of sexy." Azaril breaks into an involuntary grin.

Quentin gives him a condescending little chuckle. Langston cannot keep his jaw from stiffening. "You're just full of lovely new fascinations, aren't you?" he says, not quite under his breath.

Abruptly the bartender deserts his post and makes a beeline for their booth. Involuntarily excited, as if they are about to be visited by Diana Herself, they wait in wide-eyed awe as he comes to tower above them (nearly seven feet in heels). He introduces himself as Dalton in a haughty manner befitting one of royal blood.

"And your name is?" Dalton asks Langston with just a hint of attitude. Langston's somewhat stammering reply makes Dalton smile. "Langston Fleetwood? Your sister is Zuli Fleetwood-Hilliard?"

Langston stirs. "Yeah . . ."

"Then you need to follow me. She's waiting for you in the back room."

The others cast Langston a questioning look, wondering if Zuli is the kind of daring and heretofore unimagined species of woman to be found groping and slurping the goods in the dark back rooms of gay clubs. Dalton is already scuffing across the floor, so Langston hastens to follow, with Reynaldo, Azaril, and Quentin behind him. They pass the runway and the restrooms (marked MEN and SUPERMODELS) and a sign that says DIVA EMPLOYEES ONLY to enter a little cubbyhole of a room stuffed with file cabinets and a wheeled chair without a desk. A window at sidewalk level is opened at the top of the far wall, and they can see a procession of shoes pass—pumps and boots and sneakers and clogs and sandals—the almost rhythmic sudden grouping and thinning of them oddly like a migrating swarm of bees traveling in clumps and straggling trails. Below this tableau of urban nature Zuli waits.

Reynaldo, Azaril, Quentin, and Dalton hang back inside the door as Langston steps forward. "Hey, Miss Girl," Langston says, his voice involuntarily subdued, and then she rushes into his arms and grips him fiercely before they stand back and, in observance of Fleetwood ritual, get a good look at one another. A pair of full-moon glasses obscures Zuli's round, freckled face and soft features. She is dressed in a smart, conservative Donna Karan black suit that contrasts strikingly with an overhang of frizzy, ginger-colored 'locks that thicken and harden as they trail down to the bottom of her neck and then abruptly stop, as if Zuli's willingness to flout conservative appearance codes goes only so far and not one inch farther. Langston is surprised at how much thinner and smaller his sister seems to be, and then is annoyed with himself to realize that her image on a television screen has replaced his own recent memory of her.

Zuli strides forward to meet the others, and they genuflect without intending to, Quentin's and Reynaldo's eyes falling low and their voices getting mumbly, Azaril introducing himself as if on audition for a big-voice part in a Broadway musical. Zuli smiles with a warmth that appears to be genuine but remains removed, and as if in answer to a telepathic command, Reynaldo, Azaril, and Quentin drift uncomfortably back again to the door while Zuli and Langston move to the privacy of the far wall beneath the window.

"You look good," Zuli observes. "A little heavier, maybe? Naw, that's muscle. How long since I've seen you?"

"Oh, what was it? Christmas two years ago?"

"That's awful. Way too long. Sorry I made you come meet me back here. I intended to just wait for you at the bar, but then I had two queens coming up to get my autograph three minutes after I sat down. Isn't that ridiculous? I just hate to have people recognize me all the time—although everyone does since we prosecuted those terrorists—so I had Dalton bring me back here."

"You know Dalton?" Langston says, loud enough to get Dalton's attention—partly out of courtesy, partly so as to distract him from schmoozing it up with Azaril in the corner.

"Oh, yes, I know Dalton." Zuli smiles and raises her voice, too, offering her tiny hand as a gently irritated Dalton is forced to come over and clasp-and-kiss in a show of sororal affection. "Dalton and I met at the West Indian Day parade last September. Then I found out he works at Vanity Affaire, and since Baby and I came here one night I have *loved* Vanity Affaire—they do a supermodel karaoke here that you *have* to try. Dalton has been sweet enough to help me out ever since. We're going to get me an office back here where I can be incommunicado, aren't we, Dalton?"

Dalton, all grins, nods enthusiastically at this plan, which neither has any intention of fulfilling. "Your sister is the busiest human being I have ever known, Langston," he says, and flings in a lilt that reveals his Jamaican background. Langston, glancing to his left because he knows what he'll see, does not miss—or cannot miss imagining—the curiosity that the sound arouses in impressionable Azaril, the fickle son of a bitch. "And she is very highly sought after. We have to protect her so that she can get some rest."

Langston keeps his attention riveted on his sister. "I thought Baby was supposed to handle that," he says. He licks his lips as is his compulsion when mentioning his six-foot-six, 227-pound, coffee-brown Clark Kent sans glasses brother-in-law.

Zuli sighs—too deeply, Langston thinks, so much so that he is suddenly concerned for her. "I wish. I'm so busy with work and public speaking and traveling—they had me speaking up in Toronto two days ago, London two weeks ago—Baby and I barely see each other. I know you've heard how people keep circling around me asking me to run for Senate: Democrats and even some Republicans, and the Reform Party and the Liberal Party, too. I don't even know if I want a Senate seat, but I have to keep them all interested while I do a Cuomo and hem and haw." She breaks into a smile and her face dives in toward him as she whispers excitedly—"Meanwhile what I really want is to get appointed to a judgeship on the Second Circuit!"—the exact same expression Langston remembers from childhood. "At least I think I do, anyway. And then Baby with his practice and consulting for other doctors, and you know now he's getting called to be an expert witness on neurological problems for court cases, so he's building a reputation in that, too. I come home at night sometimes and almost have a heart attack, thinking, 'Who is that sleepin' up in my bed?'" She and Langston laugh (while Dalton takes his cue to sneak back over to Azaril). "Most black women of my education level worry about whether they're gon *find* a man. I got one, rescued him from a white woman, and still for all I know he could have fathered three children with the maid since I last spent longer than it takes to eat a meal with him."

Langston nods. He has always marveled at and been exasperated by this in her, the high, chirped words running at thrice normal speed, alarming self-revelation nestled in jokey self-deprecation and tacky self-promotion, flavored by a controversial dose of Race Woman pride (he has heard this boast about stealing Baby from a white woman several times since she married him three years ago, as if the comparative lateness of their nuptials—Zuli was thirty-nine—had to be explained and its embarrassment overcome by a narrative of triumph over daunting odds), each piece delivered with an intense attentiveness that makes it seem as if Zuli cares about nothing so much as his opinion despite the fact that she's going on and on about only herself. It's her unique charm, really, and why she has become such an appealing softy-lefty-cum-law-and-order pop-culture figure, perfect for a CNN afternoon talk show and breathlessly if rather disingenuously touted by media wags as possible for the presidency "someday." The star effect of it all is something that Langston adores and envies; he notes the way that his friends keep staring at her despite all the high-diva muscle-boy posturing and man-of-the-islands verbiage Dalton throws to distract them.

"Sounds like they're running you ragged," Langston offers.

"*Oh.* You don't know. Fame and power"—she pricks up the forefingers of both hands in a gesture that looks more like Nixon than quotation-marks—"is a drag. It's no *fun!* Do you know how long it's taken me to figure that out? Not like somebody couldn't have told me. But it just hit me, not long ago. Life is not fun. Now I know why people become corrupt. You figure with all this pressure that you're entitled to skim some profits, or accept some gifts, or at least make the taxpayers pay for your masseur's visits. Oh! Did you see me on the cover of *Time?* They didn't call you for a quote? I told them to. Well, that figures, because the article wasn't good, which is disappointing since I know the chick that wrote it, which just goes to show you that sometimes, these so-called sistahs—you know what I mean."

She sighs again, less deeply this time, having gotten it off her chest for this afternoon, at least. "Can we meet later for dinner? I mean, really late. Around eleven, maybe even twelve, child. I'll take you out to my new favorite restaurant, run by this gay South African couple, one black, one white. You'd love it. Just you and me. Not that it wouldn't be wonderful to meet your friends, of course, but we don't ever get to see each other alone like we used to." A strange look crosses her face, as if the thought, or some memory she hadn't expected, has pained her.

Seeing it, Langston, too, is pained. They were very close once. It seems so long ago, before she went to Harvard and he was dragged to Ansbach. The education she'd received there seemed to catapult her out of childhood, away from the family, out into the wide world she seems to conquer another piece of each time she takes a step. Whereas Germany singed Langston; it made him tentative and cautious.

He shrugs. "Sure. They won't mind if I ditch them." He could add: *and anyway, they're not really my friends*—but that would be ugly.

"Well," and now she rises up on her toes and takes a leather satchel from the top of one of the file cabinets, "what I have here is a summary of what I found for you."

The others, moved once more like chess pieces by changes in her tone and body language, break off their conversations and crowd near. "There's not much, but it was difficult to get to, actually. I had my poor assistant searching up and down through

FBI files, and you know how those Virginia farm boys can get about somebody combing through their precious reports. What we found were a few entries in the COINTELPRO files, logged during the early '70s when it seems the Feds were under the impression that Credence Gapstone was a mortal threat to the Republic. Gapstone was a servant, a valet, I believe, for Aden Rose, the wealthy heir to a robber baron financier fortune."

Langston makes a small hissing sound and shakes his head in a mime of laughter. "Gillory's grandfather. God. Shoulda known."

"What is cointelpro?" Quentin asks.

"J. Edgar Hoover's Counter Intelligence Program," Langston answers. "That's the nice name for it. Basically this was the group that conspired to destroy liberation movements across the country during the late '60s and early '70s."

Zuli nods approvingly. "Which would be right about the time Credence disappeared. According to what they dug up on him, Rose took Gapstone in as a young boy, maybe as young as six. The circumstances of their adoption of him aren't clear. He was raised in both Mississippi and New Orleans. His father died in a terrible accident—burned alive, it seems—and the son was raised by his mother. Her name was, what was it . . ."

"Verity Gapstone," Azaril says. Langston feels himself flinch a bit at the sound of Azaril's voice.

Zuli smiles. "Yes. You have a lot of this figured out already, I see. The grandmother, Verity Gapstone, was working as a—consultant, or native informant or something—for the Roses in a book they were writing about African people's magical rituals in the New World. We don't know what happened to Verity. She just seems to have disappeared. The Roses took Credence in, sort of adopted him, in a weird way."

"They adopted him?"

"Not officially. But Aden Rose and his wife saw to Credence's education, and took him with them as they traipsed around the globe spending their inheritances. I say 'weird,' though, because at some point he was actually *working* for them, as Aden's valet. And it gets even more complicated, as I'll tell you in a minute. Anyway, after Credence reached adulthood, he began to spend a considerable amount of time away from them, though officially in their taxes he was still in their employ. There's very little about him during this period—some modest properties he owned in D.C. and New York, another around the Great Lakes, some odd jobs he might have worked."

"But why was it that they even had a file on Credence?" Langston asks.

"The FBI became interested in Gapstone when he became loosely associated with a Black Panther Party chapter in New Haven. They had a mole or two in the chapter and figured out Credence's association with Rose—evidently Credence was taking money from Rose to give to the Party—and so the bureau set out to discredit him by revealing that Credence was gay and a white man's lover. Which apparently wasn't *exactly* the whole truth—good old COINTELPRO, never reluctant to twist the facts. From what they say, Credence was probably a victim of abuse. As soon as Credence was of age, or perhaps earlier, Rose—how shall I say it? Rose and Credence became sex partners."

Quentin interrupts with a loud "Yueucch!" that makes Zuli pause and gives Langston a weird chill: Reginia would tell him to pay attention to it, but he can't imagine what it means, unless maybe Quentin's experienced something like what Credence had to deal with.

Zuli continues, raising the level of command in her voice so as to censor further outbursts. "Rose did give Credence pretty lavish gifts during his adolescence and young manhood, including the properties Credence owned. According to servants who were bought off to inform on Rose, the sexual activity between them was going on at least until Credence was twenty or so. You can imagine how the agent in charge of undermining Gapstone used this information to stop Rose from giving the Panthers any money. When he was exposed, Gapstone fled New Haven and went out West. At about that same time, Aden Rose was killed. Gapstone was the natural suspect. Gapstone was caught running from the police up in northern California—dressed as a woman, interestingly. He was using all kinds of aliases. The agents suspected Rose trained him to do so, during those years his wife and he had Credence running around with them uncovering the secrets of the occult." She smirks—complicatedly, so as to suggest her disdain for both obsessions with the occult and for the agents and their theories, while maintaining an overarching sympathy for Credence.

"Well, the bureau wanted to 'talk' to Gapstone, so field agents from San Francisco were headed up there to pick him up at the jail when something bizarre happened. Somebody blew a hole in the jailhouse and blew up all the police cars parked in the lot. The police were all knocked out, some seriously injured—one of them died later, I think. Gapstone wasn't there. His body wasn't found along with those of the policemen. The field agents didn't witness anything that had occurred, but a couple of other men who happened to be incarcerated at the time also escaped. When they were caught later, they had different stories. One of them said a freak tornado swept Gapstone away—but there wasn't any corroboration for that from the National Weather Service. Another said a helicopter came and spirited him away, but that was considered an even wilder theory. Apparently no one could figure out what the explosive was, either. Gapstone hasn't been tracked down in the twenty-five-plus years since. He remains wanted."

She takes a breath while letting this sink in. "So that's it, more or less. I don't know what good that does you. Aunt Reginia told me you needed this info, but she didn't tell me very much about why."

She looks expectantly at Langston, but he chooses to ignore the implicit query. "You've remembered a lot of the story," he comments blandly as he scans the seven-page summary.

"I wanted to know exactly what my little brother needed COINTELPRO files for, so I read the reports. Had to make sure you weren't in any trouble."

"Are we?" Reynaldo asks. "In trouble?"

Zuli notices him and frowns. "Regarding Credence Gapstone and the FBI, I don't think so. I wouldn't expect to find him, if I were you. But there does appear to be *another* source of danger, perhaps serious."

They look at her with dread.

"Once I started looking into this, I got a call from someone I know in the FBI. He was the one who filled in the gaps. As it were. He wants to meet you." She shrugs at the look of alarm on Langston's face. "Couldn't be helped. I didn't expect you to bring your friends, I thought—" Her eyebrows arch as she glances toward the door. "Ah, here he comes, with his usual timing."

"Got here a few minutes ago. I thought I'd wait outside for the right moment," the man announces as he makes his entrance.

At that Langston turns to see, and frowns. Brown hair—no, nothing familiar about that clipped, militaristic cut. But the strange body, skinny stick legs, and a chest that looks almost inflated . . .

The man shakes Langston's hand first. "We've met," he says with a peculiar look in his eyes. "I'm Bill Paxon." No, Langston realizes, a twinge of fear touching him, it's not the expression of his eyes but the physical appearance of the eyes themselves: rheumy, silvery, killer-for-hire.

Langston returns Paxon's firm grip as if he were plucking a pan from the interior of a hot stove with his bare hands. "The hotel . . . in Miami . . ."

"Yeah!" Azaril agrees. "I remember seeing you in Wessex House once, talking to, uh, whatsername. . . ."

Paxon grins and laughs. "Luisa. Yep, I was doing my nutcase number at the time. That was a piece of work, wasn't it? You should have seen me, Zuli! I had your brother and this woman Luisa, my contact there at the hotel, completely fooled!"

Langston is beginning to get the drift. "He works for you, Zuli?"

"Bill doesn't work for me, although we've worked together in the past. The two of you being in the same hotel was a coincidence. *Mostly* a coincidence."

"I was in Miami on my own," Paxon interrupts, with a harrumphing, patronizing laugh. "I'm kind of semiretired from the bureau. I get called in sometimes to consult on old cases, which is how your sister and I are acquainted. Sometimes I follow up on some unsolved cases from when I was full-time. This particular case involved a fellow who used to work for me when I did a stint in COINTELPRO. Oliver Pierce was his name. He went sour on us around 1970 after he helped expose this man Gapstone. Informants will go sour sometimes, they're often pretty unstable characters. Ollie was more unstable than most, as it turned out. After he brought Gapstone down for us, it seems he became obsessed with him. Went on a one-man hunt for him. At the same time, Aden Rose was murdered. We didn't know Ollie was running after Gapstone, but Ollie was poking around at the Sonoma Country jailhouse Zuli mentioned when our field agents got there. He ran when they arrived, and they didn't catch him. That's when I was informed; Ollie had been my responsibility. So I tried to track Ollie down. He was almost as hard to find as

Gapstone. Pretty soon it became clear he was actively evading me. He left the country for about ten years—we didn't find out what he was doing, but he spent some time in Europe and in Africa. I retired in '85—figured Ollie was gone and that was that."

Zuli shakes her head. "Bad guess. Having read a bit of his file, I could have told you that man was the type who wouldn't give up."

Paxon shrugs. "You may understand him better than me. Anyway, a year or so back, completely by chance, I happened to spot Ollie when I was vacationing in Miami. He was bigger and stronger, and he carried himself more confidently, but I knew it was him. I believe he saw me when I saw him, because as soon as I could get my kit together to go after him, he was gone.

"Since then I kind of keep tabs on Miami. A few weird things have been happening that seem vaguely tied to someone of his description. Best I can figure, he goes by the nom de guerre of Sunder Rex these days, but I never had the time or resources to really track him down. When the shit hit the fan with the Castro sightings, I had a hunch he might be involved, and I happened to be in the South, so I flew down there to check it out."

"You tailed Sunder to Wessex House?" Azaril asks.

"He'd been seen in Wessex House, that same night I met Langston, and maybe before." Langston feels a ripple of fear pass over him. "Then when I got wind that Zuli's office was scrounging up old files about Sunder from way back, well, I called Zuli up."

"The man who talked against Credence at the Black Panther meeting was named Oliver," Langston says quietly. "Why do you think Oliver, or Sunder, has something to do with the Castro sightings?"

Paxon's nonplussed reaction seems less deftly pulled off this time, more clearly exaggerated and artificial. "Those

Castro sightings—damnedest things. I can't prove any connection between Sunder and Mr. Castro's mysterious resurrection. But like I said, my contacts have associated Sunder with some weird incidents. Strange thefts from museums or university archives. Ritual orgies in which apparent participants reported lost time or garbled memories, consistent with the idea—unproven, I have to admit—that they may have been kidnapped and given the date rape drug. Possibly murder. Evidently he even runs a prostitution ring. The police haven't connected the dots, but I think Ollie—Sunder—is at the center of it."

"Why?" Zuli asks.

"Because when he came back into the country many years ago, he sent me a little note. To taunt me. In the note he said he'd discovered some 'power' source during his travels, and that he was going to use it to make people like me pay. He said he was going to become a magical terrorist." Paxon pauses for reaction. He notes that Zuli and Dalton have querulous looks on their faces, and that the four boys do not. "My superiors at the bureau were concerned that Ollie might have become involved with terrorist cells abroad and was back in the country to do mischief. Naturally they weren't very concerned about the 'magical' stuff. They thought maybe he had chemical or biological materials. Eventually they decided there was nothing to it. But for myself, you know, times being what they are with terrorists, and knowing the connection to Aden Rose, and Credence Gapstone's mysterious disappearance . . . Well, my guess is that it requires some kind of resources to pull off those Castro appearances. Castro shows up several places, appears to be flesh and blood, then isn't. Causing panic is a terrorist's goal, and the Castros accomplished that, didn't it? I wouldn't rule out something that could go under the category 'magical.'"

"Oliver's the warlock my aunt warned me about," Langston concludes. "And the one who—it all connects."

Paxon lifts an eyebrow. They can almost feel him restrain himself from asking further questions. "Very possibly," he replies carefully.

"But you said Sunder was seen at Wessex House? Why would he be there?" Reynaldo asks.

Quentin clears his throat. It is the first time he's made a noise in a while. "From what Langston's told us"—he casts an almost prayerful glance Langston's way—"Aden Rose's granddaughter was staying in the hotel. Roan Gillory."

"Oh, right. Shit," says Reynaldo.

"Did you know that, Mr. Paxon?" Langston asks. His eyes are narrowed and his eyebrows pinched together.

"I did later. Didn't know that night. You all know as much as I know, maybe a lot more, looks like. If we could sit down right now and—"

"What's Sunder look like?" Reynaldo interrupts.

Paxon hesitates, watching Langston closely. Then he offers Reynaldo a sympathetic smile. "Now that you ask, the main reason I came down here was to show you a picture so you can tell me whether you've seen him." He pulls a manila envelope from the inside pocket of his jacket. "This was taken on a street in a suburb outside Miami. Not very good quality, but it's all we've got."

Reynaldo squints at the picture, then makes a noise. "Lang, come take a look."

Azaril moves close to peer over Reynaldo's shoulder with Langston.

"You think . . . ?" says Langston. "It's pretty fuzzy. . . ."

"But it was fuzzy in the rain, too," Reynaldo points out. "We saw this guy. In New Haven, after Malachai's accident. If it was an accident."

"You're sure?" Paxon asks. They nod. "Tell me about this accident, then. The when, where, and what."

While Reynaldo tells him, Langston gets ahold of the photograph. Is this the same man who stood beside him outside Destine's, who made him almost fall to his knees?

Paxon starts pulling his chin. "Hm. Ollie knew Malachai Reynolds. They were in the New Haven Panthers' auxiliary group together. So it could have been him you saw. Wouldn't surprise me." He looks at his watch. "Unfortunately, I have an appointment across town." He smiles at Zuli. "Took longer than I expected to get over here from Jersey. When are you young men leaving New Haven?"

Azaril and Reynaldo mumble contradictory answers ("Tomorrow"; "We'll be there a while").

Paxon behaves as if he's been told what he needs to hear. Smiling, he plucks the photograph from Langston's fingers. "I'd like to stay in contact with you. Through Ms. Fleetwood-Hilliard, of course. I think we can be very mutually beneficial to each other." He waves the manila envelope at Zuli. "See ya, Zoo. As always, a pleasure."

Zuli shakes Paxon's hand, and clasps him by the elbow. "Thank you so much for coming, Bill." Langston churns with embarrassment. Surely she knows how suspect this will make her look in his friends' eyes. "And for being so helpful. I know you wouldn't ordinarily be so free with the information you have." She does not say what her manner makes apparent: I owe you one. Recognizing the sacrifice she's making for him, Langston feels doubly embarrassed—at his silent reproof of her chummy behavior, and at the chary, distant way he's been dealing with her. He notices that it's only when they can no longer hear his steps in the hallway that Zuli exhales.

"This guy worked to infiltrate and undermine liberation

movements by people of color, and he fucking wants us to work with him?" Reynaldo fumes.

"We still didn't get a definitive answer," Azaril says. "Why is this Sunder guy a danger to us?"

"He's dangerous enough to suck Malachai down into a hole in the street that wasn't there two seconds before. He stabbed Destine, and he tried *something* on me," Langston reminds them. "He thinks he's some kind of magical terrorist. He has connections with everybody we've found, and at one time he was looking for Credence himself. I think it's pretty obvious why and how he could be dangerous."

"I knew some shit was gonna come down," Reynaldo murmurs —then apologizes to Zuli for his profanity.

Zuli takes Langston's shoulders in her hands. "You want to tell me what's going on now, for real?" Langston feels himself soften beneath her touch. He begins to speak, and then an electronic squeal interrupts. Zuli withdraws to open a purse that sits on top of the file cabinet. Her cell phone is roughly the size of a book of matches. "Oh, shit. That's my secretary. I told her not to call unless . . . Shit. I'm gonna have to go now, too." She has already moved off into another realm. "Langston, we're definitely on for dinner tonight, aren't we?"

"Yeah," Langston answers, feeling slightly dazed.

"You be careful till then, all right? I mean it. Call me on my cell around ten." She hugs him again, quickly and efficiently. "Reynaldo, Azaril, Quentin, it was a pleasure to meet you. I hope I can get to know you a little better the next time you're in New York. Have you been to any shows? You should definitely see if you can get some late tickets or standbys for tonight's performance at the Public. I know the artistic director, and whatever he puts on is *always* fascinating! Tell you what, have Langston call my secretary, Delilah, she'll be able to wrangle you some seats, OK?

So sorry I have to run! Love you, Langston!" Zuli smooches her brother, then smooches Dalton. "'Bye, honey!"

As her heels clip the tile in the hallway, they hear her call back, "You all be *careful!*" And then a high-pitched string of indistinguishable words as she issues commands into her cell phone.

18

En route, fifteen minutes later

Manna, Quentin promises, is a restaurant that offers every sensual pleasure you cannot otherwise experience except in multiorgasmic sex. Langston, Reynaldo, and Azaril meekly follow him there through the byways of SoHo—the sights of which distract them momentarily from the vague sense of imminent peril. Shaped by sleek modern buildings bristling with glass and steel and old warehouses and apartments girdled by nineteenth-century cast-iron catwalks and fire escapes, the district seems to be a state of being, ever in fashion-magazine pose and attention deficit disorder motion at once: it is populated by an endless armada of designer clothes boutiques that make their siren call to wealthy tourists' wallets with the shimmering circus colors and synesthetic textures on display behind windows that mirror you in them, rendering the clothes and paraphernalia of couture more solid than you, who are, of course, too insubstantial to afford them: *pay up and we will make of you a thing fabulous*, the leather pea coats and thousand-dollar denim jeans and carnation lizard belts with big flat virile buckles tell you with a wink; adorn your neck with this jewelry from Madagascar, stare in worshipful silence at a gallery of white-sugar-canopied lemon bars and nectarine tartlets in our gourmet grocery. SoHo seems like a swank grand Hollywood premiere spilled over onto the streets and solidified in brick; like an otherworldly hipster's haunt, the walled inner city of a town in Renaissance Italy, updated and transferred to Superman's Krypton.

Quentin expertly navigates the thicket of bodies that travels the sidewalks. No one's talking. The westering sun has transformed the late-afternoon autumn air into an unexpectedly humid, soupy cauldron. At a stoplight, Quentin looks to ascertain that they're all in line, then stares off over the top of their heads. "Uh, wait a . . . do y'all mind if I run to a restroom?"

There is something a little queer in his face and voice—the other queer: as in strange, palpably so, queerness that squirrels the hairs on the back of your neck. It is as if Quentin were asking a different question altogether, one far more portentous.

But Langston, dreamy and distracted, is reminiscing about his sister and how he once had her all to himself and how that mirage of ownership once seemed the most important thing in the world. Reynaldo is busy watching the high serve-a-three-course-meal-on-it ass of a chocolate-tasty black man pass by, glance back, keep walking, and glance again. Azaril fails even to shrug.

Quentin flashes them a slightly discomposed smile, and dashes back down the block.

"This is Manhattan. Where does he think anyone's gonna let him use the restroom?" says Langston as he comes to his senses.

He speaks to Reynaldo, but Reynaldo is preoccupied stripping off his shirt to let his glistening, hairless upper bod (he shaved his chest last night) breathe in the warm sun. The heat on his back feels luxurious. The contrast between bare flesh and the snow white of his jeans emphasizes his modestly protuberant buttocks and the shapely sweep of his thick legs. Langston takes in the sight of the man. An open smile spreads wide under Reynaldo's nose.

Kind of a big nose, Langston notices for the first time. Slightly, ever so slightly hooked. "We should prob'ly be careful," Langston says. "This Sunder guy is definitely after us. I don't know what he planned to do with me at Destine's party—"

"Langston." Azaril's hand is on Langston's shoulder. It is the first time they've touched in a few days.

"Mmhm?" Langston casts half a glance's worth of attention toward Azaril, but continues to face Reynaldo.

"I wonder if we could—"

Suddenly Quentin is there.

"I just realized something," he says. "I misremembered the address. Manna ain't in SoHo. I guess I got it confused cuz it has a SoHo feel to it. It's up a few blocks, below Washington Square." His tone is very grave, almost hushed, but the pace of his speech is hurried.

"You made us walk all the way down here for nothing?" Reynaldo barks.

"Sorry." Quentin's expression is unusually downcast.

The shift back uptown seems to dispel the delicate three-way détente between Reynaldo, Langston, and Azaril, and silence falls over them again as they follow Quentin's rapid strides north. Langston hopes that Azaril will tell him what he started to say, and Azaril hopes that Langston will ask what he was going to tell him, and both of them figure that if the other one doesn't say anything, they'll just wait for the right moment to come and speak up.

A few blocks farther on, they follow a broad white-lined lane that cuts between the two street corners. Langston sees ahead of them a small herd of people emerge from the double doors of a theater stuffed between a curio shop and a convenience mart. The crowd turns directly toward the four almost in unison, coursing like a river rounding a sharp bend.

"They hold actors' workshops there," Quentin says, perking up. He gestures toward the theater's doors, plastered with posters of a film star—his tousled hair, intense stare, and grizzled chin circa 1988, it looks like. "You see it all the time on this actor's show on cable."

Langston nods. He tries to breathe away a surge of claustrophobic panic as the four of them become engulfed and are brought almost to a standstill while a couple hundred mostly white actors-in-training stream past. They keep coming and coming, their eyes peering toward the horizon where marquee lights illuminate their names and where they will have their pick of gowns to wear at the Tonys. Some see the slightly disheveled and partially disrobed foursome in their midst. A frisson of the small crowd's momentary regard—mild contemplative interest, ephemeral desire—passes electrically through their bodies. Langston quickly gets bored with being jostled and walking at so slow a space. His annoyance and resignation are mounting hand in hand, when suddenly, as if a soap bubble has popped, there is an empty space beside him. Quentin's gone. Azaril and Reynaldo, too. Somehow Langston's lost all of them in the crowd.

Something—a habit of impracticality, of looking for signs rather than material substance—makes Langston look up at the sky. A ponderous, ship-length wedge of cloud inches across the sun and mutes its brilliance. Langston comes back down, vaguely dismayed.

The street is empty and as chilly as San Francisco in August. It is as if the sun, and the world, have melted away.

The spell bewitches each of them, in almost exactly the same way:

The street is clear. The sunlight is muted. Langston perceives people moving in the periphery of his vision, to the extreme left and right, and he sees the rosy glow of late afternoon. But in the center of his vision it is gray and quiet, as if someone has thrown a cloak over the block. A cadre of autumnal leaves skips along the edge of the sidewalk, rising and falling at the pace of a sewing machine needle. The rapidity of their movement is out of sync with all else. Langston can't feel the wind that makes the leaves march. The air is still. Into this hollow of darkness arrive—appear? like Damian, who faded into nowhere, they seem to arrive from nowhere—solid presences who disturb nothing as they appear, who appear as if they have been where they are forever, obelisks of Egypt from the dawn of recorded history that suddenly loom up in the adventurer's path as the mists of sand dissolve. As if it is Langston who has appeared in their domain, not them in his.

Five cops. Tall. Wide through the shoulders, mountainous through the chest, narrow in the waist, long and lean in the leg, their uniforms are Mexican morning—-sky blue. And everything on them glitters: the buttons on their shirts, the buckles on their belts, the badges on their breasts, the straps slanting down from their shoulders to their holsters, and the visors that jut out like arrogant chins from their caps.

Reynaldo misses much of this. He is taken by their faces: settled on thick necks are square-cut jaws and short handsome noses, bushy mustaches and big blue eyes, all set in smooth, lineless skin like the white and gray of Arctic ice. The five cops each have a gun in one hand, a nightstick in the other. Their tall bodies and bright white faces shine in the low-burning light on the empty block. They advance as one, swift footfalls barely touching asphalt, like the paws of a bear skimming wild grass as it gathers speed for a charge. They cock grim smiles as they cock their pistols.

Langston runs down a list of names of black men shot by New York police in the last decade, and Azaril and Reynaldo stand and stare, and Quentin hears them all say in low, laughing voices, "I got your Damian right here."

The guns fire, and the nightsticks crack across their skulls. As they sink to the ground, they see five rows of white incisor teeth grinning down at them beneath a fringe of blond mustaches.

19

Below

It is the pungent smell of the chalk that slowly forces Reynaldo awake. Salt burns his eyes as they flutter open into a world of crepuscular whiteness and vague shadows. Has he been crying?

He is on his back, in a dark room with a low ceiling. His arms are rigid at his side. His head is surprisingly free of aches and pains, given that the last thing he felt was a truncheon coming down across the back of his skull. The sound of dripping water pit-pats behind and before him. Whatever it is that he lies upon is cold. The feeling of it on his back makes him shudder, makes his flesh prickle. This is a place you would imagine rats nesting in, seething together in a chaotic morass of feeding and fighting and fucking, a place where a million rat dramas play out in the dark. Reynaldo does not know it, but he is several feet below the floor of the theater he had begun to walk past an hour ago.

"This one's up," a voice says.

"All right," says another. Reynaldo tries to lift himself up and feels his torso strain against powerful straps. He can just manage with a maximum of effort to lift his head. There is a figure—Reynaldo can see him from his waist up—a tall and burly man, with black circles around the dark, denlike sockets of his eyes and with a round face smeared in heavy chalk.

"Who are you?" Reynaldo spits out. "Let me the fuck out of here!"

The man slaps him across the mouth. The slap is heavy, delivered with the full weight of a powerful arm—and, Reynaldo believes from the feel of it, at least a soupçon of sadistic glee. The worst of the pain fades quickly, but the shock does not, and Reynaldo, trembling, hesitates to speak again.

A few feet away, Reynaldo's cry shakes Langston awake. He, too, lies flat on his back, bound with his arms lashed tight to the contour of his body. Langston hears the shouting, perhaps hears the slap as it scourges Reynaldo's face, and he stirs groggily, slow and reluctant to rise into consciousness, for he instantly remembers the row of white picket-fence teeth and the mustaches like the beards of a blond woolly mammoth.

For a moment it seems even worse than he feared: the two men standing on either side of him, their arms folded, are ridiculous clowns out of some hideous dream: blank faces corpse gray and lice white, with skin that seems to peel like flaking crust or the curled tatters of decaying paper. *Are these the cops?*

One of the two men standing beside him speaks. He is not so stout or roly-poly as the other, whose gut hangs over in his long-sleeved white shirt like a sack of Santa's goodies. Langston is instantly terrified of the big one, of his sloppy, bestial obesity, fearful that he'll feel the man's brutish strength turned upon his body, so small and helpless now. He is grateful that it is the thinner one who speaks. This one is muscular, in fact chiseled, and in the chalk and white clothing he looks downright Michelangelian, hard, as if he were hewn from marble. In another context Langston might lust after or feel intimidated by his perfect proportions. And in fact Langston does feel slightly, just slightly, aroused at the sight of the man so near to him, towering over his prone body. The feeling is involuntary, Langston hates it; he can't distinguish between the slow build of terror and the first stirrings of arousal.

"Langston. Be calm. We mean you no harm."

A brazen falsehood, clearly. Still, the man's tone is soft, very kindly indeed, and Langston clings to its promise. His breath slows and deepens a bit—and this, too, feels involuntary, as if the man were pushing buttons to activate different physiological responses.

"Don't worry about police. There aren't any. I apologize for duping you with that particular illusion. It is an especially distasteful choice for me. But it was the best I could do under the circumstances. The vibrations one works with in New York, you know," the man continues. There is very little emphasis of any kind in his words. He might be reciting the alphabet, so even is his tone. "We didn't even strike you with nightsticks. That was also an illusion. You were chloroformed."

"What's happening? Where are the rest of my friends?" Langston is surprised by the moderate volume of his own voice. It is incongruous, speaking in café-conversation fashion with a man whose face is smeared with chalk, while strapped down on a table like a dangerous inmate in a psych ward.

"Near. They are near." The man seems to loom nearer as he speaks, though Langston does not hear or see him move. The man hovers above, as if his body were the trunk of a tree growing from roots set deep in the table where Langston is bound. "Do you know who I am?"

Langston knows. It's him. The man who stabbed Destine, who stood beside him in the yard and whispered in his ear, and has been, Langston suddenly realizes, whispering ever since. The man's voice now does not announce a new presence, it merely lifts a low stream of white noise to fully audible volume. Langston strains against his bonds. The only part of his body he can lift is his crotch.

"Good. No need to waste time, then." Langston wants to say something, but the warlock's voice seems to fill Langston's body; it seems to occupy his every cell, to overtake him. His vocal cords are dead.

"Do you know the formula?"

Langston stares up at the white face.

"Do you *know* the formula?" The emphasis falls through the dark, dank air like a crack of thunder, like a heavy slap.

Langston shakes his head vigorously. His abdomen, the only other part of him that is free, shakes with his head: his body will do the work of the words he cannot find.

As his head falls back to the cold, hard surface, Langston sees the big man with the big belly lift his hand into the air. The palm is white, white, white, so that the life-line and love-line and heart-line are crevasses of white; it is massive and unreal, a plaster prop from an old movie set. The hand rushes toward him. It will hit Langston's face.

Langston tries to scream, but nothing comes out.

"Wait." As if a tiny arrow from a child's archery set could divert timber as it falls from a treetop—but it does. Langston doesn't feel the blow he's bracing for, and when he can open his eyes again, he sees not the Evil Hand but teeth curved into something resembling a smile in the white face of the warlock. The smile distorts the beauty of the man's face, as if human emotion was not meant to be expressed in the medium of that flawlessness.

"You puzzle me, Langston," the man says. "You advertise to your friends that you fancy yourself an expert on occult matters. You cast spells in secret rooms of old buildings, and the shimmering glow of the spells' effects is like a yellow mist of pollen dancing in the auras of you and your companions. Your aunt is a powerful practitioner, all the more dangerous since she hides her face behind the silly title 'psychic.' And you have allied yourself with a witch who has powers no one has ever before witnessed."

He pauses. Langston sees a dark protuberance emerge from his mouth—he wants to scream out: *is it a slug? A snake?* He feels like he's lost his mind. It's the man's tongue, licking his meaty lips. Langston tries to speak. His crotch pumps in the air. Something about the warlock's presence. He is responding to it, in Pavlovian fashion. What is this man doing to him?

"And yet," the warlock continues, "all reports indicate that you know nothing. You carry that book *Hex* around with all of its useless spells as if it were a treasure. It's as if you don't know how to contact Damian Sundiata at all."

Now Langston is slamming his buttocks against the hard surface beneath him in a desperate cry to be heard. Why can't he talk?

"You cannot talk because I have taken the lie from your mouth. It's a weak spell, but a serviceable one. I cannot make you tell me what you know, but I can be certain that you won't tell me any lies."

"I DON'T. Understand."

The surprise of speech makes Langston suddenly lie still. The silence that follows is frightening. Langston waits dumbly for a blow from above.

The warlock responds with his mild recitative tone. "Do you know the formula for breaching the wall to the other side and calling back Damian?"

Langston wants to shout his denial—but he can't.

The warlock nods. He licks his lips. He has made a decision. Langston does not know how he knows this: it's as if he sees a clear and tangible sign, as though the air changes color from dark cellophane to bomb-warning red.

"I'm sorry it's come to this," the warlock says. Despite the melodramatic shift in mood-ring colors that Langston's probably imagining anyway, the man's demeanor becomes even more measured. The pace of his words is slower yet, and his address is courteous in the courtly sense; he is a diplomat in the halls of a foreign monarch, delivering the message of his faraway sovereign. "As a rule we like to remain in the background. We find the shadows, the margins, more commodious to our work. But now. Now you're trafficking with our enemies. You are trafficking with your own enemies. Oh, I know you believe they've been reined in, so to speak. Your sister works for them, and you believe that she's grown powerful among them. But Paxon and his cronies are not the kind that can be controlled. Even Malachai and the whore who calls herself Destine now; they are idiots, but they are not harmless. They are not trustworthy allies. You don't know what these people are capable of, Langston. They have done and can still do some truly horrible things. I know. I used to work for them, too. I once was their prize darky." He sighs, a loud, troubled noise. "Now, since you have fallen into their orbit, we can no longer wait. We have to intervene more directly."

"What do you mean?" Langston blurts—but at the same time he wants to stay quiet and just listen, listen to the man's voice, which was at first so soft and is now so deep and strong and sonorous. Everything is out of whack, off-kilter. Nothing makes sense. Why should he be at once so terrified and vaguely aroused, and yet feel so free, so at peace? It has something to do with the man's voice. The voice is playing Langston, using him as an instrument. He is weaving a spell, he is conjuring.

"I never meant your friend Damian any harm, either." *Listen,* Langston tells himself: *listen for the lie.* "He also didn't believe me. The two of you. In some ways you're so clever. But you never know who your friends are, do you?"

Reynaldo makes a noise of frustration in the darkness. Langston hears the sound of flesh striking flesh, hard.

"I met Damian many years ago, of all the strange coincidences, while he happened to be traveling in Egypt," the warlock says. "He was probably no more than fifteen at the time, but very knowledgeable in his way. I've a tendency to draw lost young people to me and to include them in my work, and when I saw him wasting his hours in the streets of Cairo, I thought it likely we might be of use to one another. As it was, he was already there under the wing of another patron. You know the type: one of those white men who prey upon young dark flesh for their own pleasures. I tried to offer Damian another way. He said that he was interested in magic. I told him I knew a great deal about that subject. He didn't trust me, though, and ran away. I pursued him. You may imagine my surprise when he demonstrated a far more potent feat of sorcery than any I myself could perform. Still, I was not as surprised as he might have wished me to be. I had seen the aftereffects of a like phenomenon before, in a little jail far up near the northern California coast, when Credence Gapstone disappeared."

He stops again. Langston, looking up into the cold white expressionless face, has the sense that the man expects him to say something in response. After a moment or so, the man picks up his conversation again, as if he had never ceased to speak. "Yet I didn't discern until very recently that poor old Credence was Damian's father. The family resemblance is clear once you know to look, but in the abstract . . . Strange, isn't it? I was not as sharp as I needed to be in those days.

"It surprised me to find out so many years after our first meeting that, without any intention or design on my part, the very Damian I had once known had come to Miami. Once I was told he was in the city, and then later once I was told that he had disappeared and under strange—yet familiar—circumstances, the bits and pieces of the puzzle began to settle into their places.

Disappear once or twice on me, I'm as foolish as anyone. Disappear a third time and I begin to know what I'm up against.

"At first, Langston, it was my intention to simply keep watch on you until the time came for you to see fit to cast your summoning spell and bring Damian back, or join him. But despite my best efforts to nudge you along—stalking you, frightening you, destroying that old faker Malachai Reynolds in your very presence—nothing yet seems to have shaken the truth out of you."

He sighs again. Langston sees in this last sigh black storm clouds streak the red tint in the air: now the color he sees wafting through the air, the color of the air itself, even after he blinks to make it go away, is a bright, bright, palpitating orange.

"Do you know the formula, Langston? Are you so clever that you've been able to hide it?"

Langston tries to speak again. He stops straining when he notices that the warlock isn't even looking at him, but is staring off beyond him, as if he does not expect an answer. The blood hue of the air deepens. Langston feels the small stirrings of a sob in his chest.

"You're familiar with the practice of sacrifice, of course."

Langston hears himself whimper. He shuts it down immediately, praying that it sounded like a gasp. The warlock smiles down at him. His white teeth are white stakes in the white, dead soil of his face. "Since I didn't see Damian kill so much as a fruit fly when he made his dramatic exit from Cairo, I can't hold out much hope that this sacrifice will prove effective. But as you surely know, there is no substance that seals a pact with the spirits as well as the fresh blood of an innocent human victim."

"Please don't do this," Langston says. Somehow he's found the man in himself that can beg. "Please don't. It won't do you any good. I swear it, if you kill me, it won't help, I don't—!" But something—the spell, bizarre though it seems—will not allow him to finish.

The warlock looks down upon him. In the madness of circumstances, Langston could believe that those two eyes were a mother's eyes, wide and loving, peering over the edge of his crib. What has this man drugged him with?

The warlock cups his hand between Langston's legs.

Langston, against his will, without knowledge of his mind, lifts his torso, offers himself to the gently tightening grip.

"No! Don't!" he screams.

The warlock bends low and touches the lobe of Langston's right ear with the tip of his tongue as he whispers, "The lynchers knew what they were doing when they cut these off, didn't they?" He squeezes hard and breathes a steamy sigh of satisfaction as Langston screams. "Such tremendous power these grant. At least potentially."

Langston shuts his eyes and bites his teeth to keep from crying.

"Blue, ungag the last one."

Langston hears some scuffling behind and to the right of him, followed by a short series of painful gasps as somebody spews out carbon dioxide in bursts and gulps down oxygen.

"Your name is Azaril, isn't it?"

Langston's heart quivers. He would open his eyes to see, but he's afraid. He waits for Azaril's response, but it doesn't come.

"Is he well? Check him, Blue. Once again you tied the gag too securely. It *is* this one that Damian really cares for, isn't it? Isn't that what you said, Quentin?"

Langston's fear alchemizes into confusion.

His head jerks up and his eyes fly open as he tries to get a good look at the face of the betrayer. There is only the warlock, watching him as if in observance of microscopic activity in a test tube.

Langston hears, farther back, Quentin answer in a tiny voice. "Yeah. That's him." Then loudly: "And fuck you, Sunder."

"Only an idiot wouldn't have figured it out eventually," says the warlock. His tone is still maddeningly mild.

"Quentin, you fucking *punk!* You fucking motherfucking whore shit fuck!"

Another slap falls hard on Reynaldo's mouth.

Quentin, in the shadows, covers his face with his hands. The noise he makes is hard to make out. He could be crying, or laughing.

"Az!" Langston calls out. "Are you all right? What have you done to him?"

For a moment still there is no answer. "You have leave to speak, Azaril," the warlock says.

"I'm fine, Langston. Don't worry about me. I'm fine."

Langston can tell immediately how much effort Azaril has expended just to say the words without shouting or sobbing uncontrollably. "And what about Reynaldo, how is he? I can't see him. If you've hurt him . . ."

"I'm here, Lang," says Reynaldo. He risks another slap, but it doesn't come. Perhaps Blue perceives what Langston hears: the ring of abject submission in Reynaldo's low, careful tone and in the terseness of his reply.

"You fucking son of a bitch, Quentin. You set us up!" Langston cries out in frustration.

Quentin keeps to the dark. He is leaning against a cold wall. He wants to say something, but a gesture from Sunder silences him.

Sunder speaks as if there have been no interruptions, as if, in fact, everyone around him were merely the seamless burnished quadrants of a mirror before which he was practicing a speech. "Finally I understood. I figured it out. When Quentin told me everything he'd witnessed, everything that had passed between him and Damian when they met and Damian disappeared, I went back in my memory to that day in Egypt and saw it again as if for the first time. I had been thinking that this force was at Damian's and Credence's command, that they summoned it, as I might summon some minor spirit of the ether. But it isn't like that. Oh, no. These disappearances occur only when Damian or his father is in danger. In Miami, somehow, some force, some god on the other side—these are mere terms of art, you realize—*knew* that Quentin had alerted me to his presence and that I was coming for him. Quentin didn't realize the significance of the man he'd begun to flirt with, but when he described him, when he described how this Damian made him feel, I knew. I knew immediately. So I was coming to find them. Quentin had arranged for us all to meet, in much the same way that he arranged for all of us to meet tonight. And then—Damian was gone. It was the danger to Damian, the immediate danger, that must have triggered the response of—whatever, whoever *It* is.

"If, therefore, you, Langston, cannot or *won't* give me the formula for breaching the wall to the other side, my hope now is that if I pose a very great threat to the friends Damian cares for most, It will try to rescue you as It did Damian."

"Stop fuckin around, Sunder!" Quentin barks. Something catches in the sound of his anger; something held back, as if he's swallowed bubbles.

Sunder shrugs him off. "I had also hoped you would see this coming when you saw our faces, Langston, so that I wouldn't have to go this far. I'm certain that you know that the ancient sorcerers of the Near East chalked their faces when they were about to sacrifice a victim. Quentin tells me you study the classics, the old stories."

"Azaril, since you are about to die, you should know something of the tradition. Shall we tell him the story of Zagreus,

Langston?" the warlock says. As he speaks, they can hear his excitement building. His calm melts away, replaced by a grasping eagerness. "Born of Persephone before the world knew winter, the child Zagreus, wondrous, beautiful, the glorious offspring of glorious gods, was hidden in a cave in Crete, where he was under guard lest he be discovered by his enemies. But the guards were traitors. To make themselves assassins they covered their faces in white gypsum, and they beguiled the boy with toys and with the sound of their clashing shields and the glint of their knives. So doing, they enticed little Zagreus to crawl into their midst. When he was in the middle of their circle, the playing child, his heart light with trust and love, looked up at their cold white faces and their dark eyes and sharp blades. So their faces looked, without smile or frown, as they sunk their knives into Zagreus's tender divine flesh and tore him apart limb from limb. The young god was later reborn, his heart placed into a gypsum figure whom Zeus brought to life." He pauses. "I doubt that you, young Azaril, will be similarly resurrected."

Langston twists helplessly in Sunder's grip. "Don't do this," Langston says. He tries to speak in a level tone. "Obviously if your spell prevents me from lying, and I can't tell you I don't know what the formula is, then maybe, in some subconscious way, I do—hey! Maybe the love spell I cast. Maybe the love spell is—!"

"Red, Blue, join Green at Azaril's table. We'll begin, gentlemen, by stabbing Azaril in the stomach, then we'll cut out his heart—in the fashion of the Aztec priests, you'll no doubt recognize the technique, Langston. Then we shall take his hands and feet and his ears and tongue. While you're carving Azaril, I'll take Langston's potent little gonads. If nothing has happened by then, we'll finish in true sacrificial style in the hopes that the gods will respond. At that point, Red, you'll split Azaril's head open down the line of his nose, and last I'll offer up Azaril's brains with Langston's balls. Do you think that will please It, Langston? I hope that It will come from the other side to save your friend before any real damage is done. On the other hand I've never done a human sacrifice before. I'm somewhat curious to see how it will turn out."

"Look, if you're gonna do it, then just get it over with, just get it over with, I can't stand . . ."

Azaril's voice is a gravel-strewn whisper. Tears dribble from the clenched corners of his eyes. Langston knows they are there; he can picture them without seeing them. They glisten on Azaril's face, they tremble like tiny creatures. Azaril's unvoiced thoughts are much the same: hurried, one atop the other, in horror of their own existence. *Do it! Justfuckinkillme! I do love him he told me that he would always be there for me he'd always be able to take care of me I didn't even know what he was talking about I knew he fucked around with magical shit I didn't understand, I just knew I loved him.*

Something drastic is called for, yet in this direst of all emergencies, Langston's state of frenzied panic and paranoia miraculously dissipates, and he finds himself enveloped in an unnatural calm. There are no tears in him as he listens to the revelation of what he already knew, not even the threat of tears. And there is no fear, either, only a perverse ripple of laughter, which he has to clench in his chest lest it run free: it's all too *too*, somehow, the white faces and their icy half leers, the leather straps like props from an S and M porn film, the gothic echo of the water as it falls in Chinese-water-torture drops to the floor.

Calm. How utterly mysterious, Langston thinks, are the properties of calm. It is a force all its own, an element deserving of a place in the reckoning of the ancients and the periodic table both. In calm it is as though a second pair of eyes detach from their hiding place in Langston's forehead and rise in a helium balloon to a vantage point above, where they can observe the whole scene. He sees Sunder, enveloped in his own aura of calm, but colder and more blind than Langston: Sunder does not see any of them. Sunder sees only his desire. Langston can see Sunder's lieutenants, and though they are embossed in white, he knows at least one of them: the tall hairy man who'd pursued him at Galen's party dressed like a woman (Green); he does not know the thin one (Blue) or the fat one (Red), but seeing Red now towering over Langston's body as if reluctant to move over to Azaril, feeling his lust to murder, sensing what crawls in his thoughts as he leers at Sunder's hand on Langston's genitals, Langston is unmoved, unafraid. Langston can see Reynaldo, seething and cowering at the same time, and he knows that Reynaldo is wrestling with the vague conviction that somehow he is the one to blame for this. He can see poor Azaril, sobbing manfully, the stream of his thoughts running with thin prayers to a God he'd never before had the courage to believe in, wondering about his mother and whether she felt this way on the brink of death. Langston can see Quentin hiding in the darkness, his body shaking, his thoughts rocking between fury and fear—and something else: hope, clear and star-bright. Hope for what?

"Look," Langston addresses Sunder, and a tinge of command, of power, irradiates the word. His body, and his voice, feel his own, now. "You think I'm some sort of magician. Maybe you're right. Maybe I know more than I think. But one thing that's sure is that if you know me, you know my sister is the U.S. attorney, and that she'll have the whole FBI out looking for us if we don't meet her later. And I don't even want to think of what Aunt Reginia will do to you, or Mrs. Gillory. But you should think of them. Think of all three together coming after you."

Sunder's grip relaxes marginally. He takes his time before answering. "Possibly. But that possibility doesn't change anything.

I want that spell. I want the power Damian's disappearances bring. I will offer yours and Azaril's blood and brains to open my own gateway if you won't open it for me. Whatever your coven does, it will be too late. Choose now. Do you know the formula? I don't believe you do."

The warlock in whiteface releases Langston's crotch and lifts high his dagger. There is no strain in the tendons of his thick bodybuilder's arm as he moves, and his expression is impassive, his face as still and mysterious as the moon. The dagger's point hovers above, in perfect alignment with Langston's groin. Five feet over, Blue, Red, and Green lift their daggers likewise.

"Yes, kill him. Kill us both." From his vantage point in midair above the warlock's head, Langston hears himself say this. He wonders what he means and why he says it. He detects a slight alteration in the color of the air: from orange to a faint daffodil yellow.

The knife falls.

A phone rings.

Everything—time, movement, everything—stops.

"What is that?" demands a wrathful Sunder. "What *is* that?"

The ringing continues.

"It's a phone," Quentin says.

"Whose is it? One of these damn boys'?" Sunder's anger makes the knife move a little in his two-handed grasp. The tip of the blade shivers six inches from Langston's groin.

"My phone is off," Quentin says. (So much satisfaction in his tone. What is he doing?)

Scrambling noises.

"Uh, here it is, down here with these boxes." A new voice. Red, probably. "It's just one of those old phones, those rotary phones, you know . . . um. It's, uh, not connected."

"What did you say?"

The phone bleats, bleats, bleats.

"He said it's not *connected*," Quentin says venomously.

"Hand it to me. Hand it to me!" Sunder puts the dagger down. Its pommel lies on the table, at the edge of the reach of Langston's fingers.

"Hello?" the warlock screams into the phone.

The reply makes Sunder drop the receiver.

A sonic boom very much like thunder rattles the chamber. Langston hears Sunder's breath catch, feels Sunder's body twitch, like a mouse the split second after it's caught rooting through the garbage.

A voice, hoarse and yet loud, bursts free from the phone and thumps against the walls.

"Release Langston and his friends, now. If you release them unharmed, we'll tell you where the man you seek is, and how to find him. But if any of them are hurt, you will become our enemy, and we'll never rest until we've killed you. I, Reginia Jameson Wolfe, and I, Roan Gillory, swear to this by any god and all gods, whether of hell or heaven, or of sea, earth, fire or sky."

Release me. . . .

The beat of an old house tune pushes into Langston's mind, but it is not the semblance of sound produced by thought, not merely the illusion of sound drawn from memory, but a real sound, as if, on some lower frequency unheard except by dogs and magicians, the walls and floors are singing. And the molecules of the air, too: and as they sing, Langston sees first blue, then indigo, then a violet like the sky swollen with rain and shot through with the setting sun, all spill across the yellow. And ignite.

The tables they're bound to split down the middle, the captives' backs sink into the broken edges of particleboard and wood. Their bonds slide away like little garden snakes fleeing for the high grass. On their tongues and in their nostrils they take in the petroleum smell of young olives crushed, and of wet mud on asphalt smeared over the ripped skin of a bare knee, and of burning leather and of strawberries baked in fennel, and old cold milk and cereal mixed with sewage. As if a war is being fought for the territory of their senses.

Above the fray comes the angel host of the Lord, in the guise of silvery spheres of light that go spinning across the room, shattering the darkness. But the darkness, too, gets a bit of its own: for there is a dark oval mass, larger than a stove and rapidly growing, that dangles above the floor—it almost appears to be an eye, when they look at it, a giant eye in which swim glassily the reflections of swarming azure pinpricks of light: like stars skating across an exploding sky.

A Klaxon—the mother of all Klaxons—is wailing. Langston crawls blindly in the darkness and the piercing light, crashes into bodies, cries out the names of his friends but can't hear himself or their answers. Something—an arm, he thinks—pulls him down.

When at last the Klaxon ceases and Langston's brave enough to crack open his eyes, there they are: Sunder, Quentin, Langston, Reynaldo—beside Langston, with his arm around his back—and Red, Blue, and Green, the seven of them all crumpled against the damp concrete floor of a small storage basement below a theater, surrounded by stacks of dusty boxes and locked file cabinets and folded chairs, their hands pressed over their eyes and ears and mouths as if they were a troop of performing monkeys.

"Azaril! He's disappeared!"

A voice carried on wind.

20

Zuli's apartment, Prospect Heights, Brooklyn, later that night

It was Quentin who called in the cavalry. Aunt Reginia has just informed Langston of Quentin's heroics via telephone—a real telephone this time. Langston reflects upon this revelation, just another in a bewildering series of revelations, while safe and warm in the domestic quiet on the second floor of his sister's brownstone. It's almost one in the morning. Zuli has gone up to her room, weary and relieved, and he doesn't expect to see her again tonight, though he can hear the voices of the television still, trailing down from the third-floor landing. Her husband is away in Japan at a conference, and she will sleep restlessly with the laugh tracks of Nickelodeon's reruns of '80s sitcoms tunneling through her dreams. Reynaldo is soaking in the tub of the guest bathroom for the second time tonight, and is likely as desirous of solitude as is Langston. Enough hours have elapsed since the table split beneath Langston's body and he watched a man he's been trying to tell himself is his best friend disappear into God knows what for Langston to recover from the numbness and begin to mull the thing over, to tentatively step out into the mud of the corral and try to saddle this latest and most bizarre of his experiences.

Langston and Reynaldo arrived at Zuli's house after an interminable and rather harrowing gauntlet-run through late traffic in the limousine Zuli sent to pick them up. Langston noted a neighbor across the street peek out from her window as the limo came to a stop, but when he and Reynaldo stepped out and proved not to be celebrities, the curtain of the window swung back into place. Inside the four-story building, there were soft lights and quiet music and food waiting on the dining room table. Zuli had evidently already been informed of some basic facts by Aunt Reginia and maintained the manner of a hospital nurse at first, handing them towels and assigning them rooms and checking to be sure that the thermostat was set at the right temperature. At dinner she couldn't stand it anymore and peppered them with questions. But she had to be satisfied with tidbits while Reynaldo and Langston sullenly wolfed Thai takeout and then scrambled up to the bathrooms for cleansing.

After his long shower, Langston had delayed going back down to give Zuli a full report. He'd wrapped himself in the terry cloth bathrobe Zuli had presciently placed on his bed and pulled the lapels of it up to his nose to get a quick whiff of Zuli's big ol' man of a husband, Baby. He hoped that being naked and warm and all covered up would ground him. Strangely he has found that what comforts him is to believe that he is the victim of a physical trauma. Being held captive on a madman's sacrificial altar is the sort of bad luck that others have to respect. No one can complain should he suffer deleterious effects, both psychological and physical. He'd be excused any number of weaknesses and character flaws for a while, riding on the crest of his victimization. He might, for example, say he has had enough, pack up, fly away, leave, let it all be just as it is, and who could blame him, who could gainsay his logic? Were *your* balls going to be severed from your body? he could ask anybody who called him a coward. Did *you* see your best friend swallowed up?

In truth he does not feel afraid, does not feel victimized—or even particularly mournful. For Langston there are worse matters to consider than almost being killed, which had seemed distant to him even when the threat was imminent. Langston knows things, Sunder said. Langston is powerful, Sunder suggested. This prospect looms up more threateningly than a knife's edge. What does he know, and when did he know it? Aunt Reginia has just told him a lot of things on the phone. The confusion of knowledge makes him feel light-headed.

"I mean, just to hear the thing *ringing*," Reginia had said to him minutes ago. He hadn't been able to follow her at first. Compulsively he had mashed the lapels of the robe to his nose. "Langston, are you listening?"

"Yes."

"Are you OK? Zuli said you didn't want to see a doctor."

"Yeah."

She'd paused. He'd felt dizzy. "Look, just so you don't fuss over it. Azaril is going to be OK, I'm sure of that. We'll get him back. He's—!"

"With Damian. I know."

"Right . . . you know?"

"Damian took him where he was, to rescue him. Like Damian's father, Credence Gapstone, took Damian, to rescue him," Langston said.

"Right. So you figured that out."

"Yeah, I got it." He'd sighed.

"Then what are you making all those noises for? Are you interested in hearing how I rescued your rusty butt, or aren't you?"

"Yes."

"Good! Well, see, my boys got me this durn cellular phone

two Christmases ago, not that I'd asked for one or saw the need, because I have never wanted a client, or anybody for that matter, ringing me up at all hours disturbing my private time with their little mess. I rarely use the thing. But today just on a whim I took it with me."

"Took it with you where?"

"I went to see your Mrs. Gillory."

"Oh!" He was still bewildered.

"*Oh*, is right. I've been meaning to go back, after I couldn't get in the first time because of the shooting."

"There was a shooting?"

"Yes, Langston. Don't you remember I told you about it before? Somebody—well we know who it was now, this Sunder creature—shot up the third floor of Wessex House and wounded two people. Of course in retrospect it's clear he was trying to stir things up, and see if Mrs. Gillory would react and maybe call down this 'power' he's so eager to have."

"Oh. Yeah."

"Yeah," Reginia said excitedly, as if Langston's maundering tone were an encouragement, "so I finally went over there and took the phone with me."

"You talked to her?"

"I did. It took some doing. I had the room number you gave me, but the door wasn't there. I looked up and down the hall. Room 351. Nowhere. So I went downstairs and asked the desk clerk, and he said, yes, the room is there on the floor it should be. So I went back up again, and since this time around I knew what kind of dance I was trying to crash, I looked for the room with my other senses. And then I was able to see it: the door, alone in a long hall with no other doors. Except, you see, this door and this long hallway were crammed into a tiny, tiny space right up against room 353."

"I don't understand."

"Spatial warping. It was like she'd taken a huge space and pinched it into a tiny one. Like if you had drawn a landscape on a sheet of paper and crumpled the paper up into a tiny ball. The landscape is hidden, but still there, and you know it's there. You see what I mean? You can smooth out the ball of paper and view the landscape. Which I did. So I knocked on the door. Didn't get an answer. Well, I know a few tricks, so I tapped the doorknob and said a few words in Ibo, and the door opened. Onto chaos. Absolute bedlam. Trees, grass, pythons, monkeys swinging from the branches, moss and heat, all of it thick as thieves—Lord. It was a mess."

"I've seen. Didn't I warn you about that?"

"You did. But you didn't prepare me for the reality. Let me tell you what I mean. I went searching around in there looking for this woman, and, Langston, I scraped up my ankles and knees on the thorns and undergrowth and whatnot! My boots were getting soaked from the mud and damp soil, and I took out my little Swiss Army knife thing, you know, and pulled out the spoon and started digging a little. Well, the soil was not a layer of dirt over a hotel room floor. I dug and dug with that little spoon, and the more I dug, the more soil I burrowed down into. Found bugs and worms and everything geology and biology class tells you you ought to find. Now, granted, I couldn't go too far with my little spoon, but Langston! It is one thing to have such a powerful psychic gift that you can project images outward that people who come within your ambit can see, touch, smell, taste, and hear. That trick is called *glamour*, or *throwing a glamour*, the way I was told about it, and that trick is not so different from getting a good makeover at the local beauty salon. But what I was seeing when I opened that door was not just glamour or projection, but the very thing it claimed to be. Those trees and gibbons and boa constrictors and what have you were real matter. And since I know that gibbons are not native to Miami and rooms in Wessex House are not zoned for usage as a zoo, that meant *energy* had to have been converted into the matter there. Or, alternatively, a piece of a rain forest had been transported right into your Mrs. Gillory's hotel room."

"Seems like a reasonable theory," Langston had said dryly.

"But it's not *reasonable* at all. To do something like that, my boy, requires some serious power. Virtually nobody I ever heard of who calls herself an arch-witch or high wizard or supreme grand guru yogi could claim to do anything like it. That sort of power has to have a source more powerful than the frail human body, and getting to that source is very difficult, indeed. You have to call on a god or gods, a demon or demons, or you have to do what any physicist will tell you that no one should be able to do for at least a thousand years. Remember what I was telling you about the Castro appearances?"

"Um . . . they could have been from parallel quantum realities, but . . ."

"*But* it should take longer than the life of planet Earth for tunneling between parallel realities to occur. It should—but not if you have the power to reach *at will* into the foam of space-time and manipulate the energies that bring universes into being. You have to probe down into the Planck length."

"The what?" he'd asked.

"Well, now, that is very complicated. Basically, there is a theory these days that the universe was not always a universe of the four dimensions that we know: length, breadth, width, and time. There were, according to this theory, ten dimensions, that is, six more spatial dimensions. In that ten-dimensional universe, all matter and all forces were unified. This was, however, an unstable arrangement, and at some point in time, it collapsed.

Our universe was born or created when the other six dimensions were broken off from the four we know. These other six curled up into some form, some *place*, that is 100 billion billion times smaller than the smallest proton—somewhere in the neighborhood of ten to the minus thirty-second power centimeter in size. And that's called the Planck length. To probe that infinitesimally tiny length you would need more energy than the whole Earth could provide. The energy necessary to gain access to the other six dimensions far outstrips nuclear bombs of any size and payload that we can construct. You'd need maybe ten to the nineteenth power electron volts, you know?"

"Uh-huh."

"Well, that much energy is impossible for us. But if you *could* probe down to those other six dimensions—our lost other, the part of what the universe is that's been left behind, out of reach—you would be able to access the unification of all universal forces. You could create wormhole tunnels to shuttle across the universe to galaxies no telescope or cosmic-wave telemetry could detect. You could travel backward in time. You could create whole artificial worlds. You could transmute particles of energy into anything you wanted. You could create a house from nothingness or flood the country at a whim."

Langston let the lapels of the bathrobe fall from his hand. "Mrs. Gillory can do all *that?*"

"I hope not. Roan Gillory ain't exactly who I'd like to have running the universe, thank you very much. Luckily—luckily so far—she doesn't know what the hell she's capable of doing. She has no idea that if she'd just had some idea how, she could have gone up to New York herself, in the flesh, and taken care of that nasty warlock toot-sweet. But the inkling that she could has got her scared to death, and it ought to. Mrs. Gillory has a tap into something—or maybe somebody—that has at command some measure of this power. I think she may be being used as a conduit. Or maybe her newfound power coming out of nowhere comes from this place at the Planck length. Maybe what she's been able to do, transforming her husband into a dog, bringing the rain forest to her hotel room and whatnot, is no more than an effect of the use of the energy to probe down into that tiny place of six dimensions. Like an aftershock from an earthquake, you know? Like a mushroom cloud or a massive electromagnetic pulse or nuclear winter. All bound up in this little somebody, five foot two and in need of a tan and some lip implants."

"That's frightening."

"It's scary, but it's not utterly beyond the pale. According to quantum theory, there is a very, very, very small possibility that at any given moment all of your molecules will suddenly overcome their natural stability and tunnel into some other locality. You could go to sleep somewhere and wake up adrift in the Atlantic. The probability of this is so small that you'd have to wait almost as long as the universe has existed for it to happen. But maybe that's not true down there, at the Planck length. Maybe if someone's using that energy, these improbable things can happen. Are happening."

"Like the Castros appearing?"

"Like that. Maybe the Castro apparitions are part of this aftereffect: just some interaction between tremendous excess energy and the historical chance that thousands of people happen to have their psychic focus on Castro. Maybe that's creating manifestations."

"And like Damian and Azaril disappearing?"

"Like that. Although I still don't know exactly how Damian and his father come in. . . ."

"But I don't get how you know any of this."

"It's a theory. When I finally found Mrs. Gillory, she was

laying up in a bed surrounded by mangoes and pineapples and kiwi, in her nightgown with a big-ass dog curling around her toes. In the middle of this jungle. The dog didn't even growl, but Gillory looks up at me and says, 'I've been ringing for days. For days and days.'"

Langston almost laughs. "She thought you worked for the hotel."

" I didn't waste any time with that. I introduced myself and didn't bother to ask any more questions with my mouth, I got right down to reading, because if anything has felt like a true emergency in all that's happened since you brought me this mess about Damian missing, it was walking into that crazy woman's room."

"And you found out what you've told me?"

"No, what I've told you is my theory based on what I found out—which, essentially, was that Mrs. Gillory has a barrier of immense fear in her right now, built up in her thoughts. And that she needs this fear, she must have it, to contain an enormous amount of energy that's within her. As much as she was trying to contain it, I could feel it flowing from her. I could see it: it was sunlight, the radiance of day suns and night stars, rising up, shining over the tops of and through the chinks of the battlements she's constructed in her mind and body. The jungle itself is a kind of barrier that she's thrown up to fend off the effects of—whatever this is. She's trying to hide, trying to control it, by removing the door to the room and the room itself from plain sight and from three-dimensional space. But it's all going to burst, child. Unless we give it something to do. Which, I figure, is to return it to its place of origin—where, I am very much convinced, we'll find your friends Azaril and Damian, and Damian's father, too."

"They're manipulating this energy?"

"I can't attest to that. I do know I felt something of Damian and his father in that room. Strong echoes of them. On Mrs. Gillory. In her, in a manner of speaking. And something or someone is there, too, that I couldn't identify." She stopped for a moment then, and mulled over the matter. "Yes, I think I was right from the beginning—if I do say so myself. It's all connected."

"So—but then, how did you find out I was in danger?"

"Oh, yes. After I read what I could of the woman, I told her what I thought. She didn't say anything, just kind of looked at me. I thought she might have lost it. No sooner do I start to explain than my cell phone rings."

"Quentin?"

"Exactly."

"How could he have gotten your num—oh. Unless he was looking through my stuff in the hotel room when I was away."

"Yes, that is a risk you run when sharing a hotel room with a person you don't know, isn't it? Well, whether by hook or crook, he had my number, even that ridiculous cell phone number I can hardly believe I ever gave you. When I got back home, I found out he'd called and left a message on my machine, too."

"So what did he tell you?"

"He identified himself, and then he starts talking really fast. 'I'm calling to warn you that your son is about to be captured by the warlock who's been stalking us. This man will kill him if Langston doesn't give him the information he wants.' And I said, 'Langston's not my son, he's my nephew'—partly 'cause I'm not so sure he's telling me the truth and I want to keep him talking. So I could listen to the vibrations over the phone and be able to read him, you know. I asked him how he knew what was going to happen. He hesitated and then told me that he worked for the warlock, and it was his job today to make sure the bunch of you ended up in harm's way. So I told him, 'Don't do what you've been ordered to do. Tell Langston and the others they're in danger.' He got agitated again. Said he couldn't do that, that if he could have, he would have. 'That man will do something awful to me if I don't follow his orders,' he told me. He said he'd seen him do some hideous things to people. He wouldn't even think about going to the cops. He figured that somehow I could help if anyone could, with my being a secular oracle (which, by the way, was not the title he used, dearie, so I suppose you've been calling me a medium or a psychic behind my back again). Well, I was in something of a panic, because I didn't really have a good idea of what I would be able to do so far away in Miami. I screamed at him, tried to bully him to take matters in his own hands. I demanded that he go find you and put you on the phone. I even threatened him.

"He got very calm when I did that. I think he's used to having people try to push him around. I felt him almost getting comfortable in my screaming at him. He spoke very quietly, so quietly that the first time I didn't hear him because I was so busy loud-talking him. He said, 'I have AIDS.' Which stumped me for a second,'cause I didn't know why he was telling me this, but I had that PC reflex, you know, like I needed to respect what he was telling me. So he says, 'Sunder said he would help cure me. He did some things that made me believe he could. But I had to help him to help myself.' Well, as terrified as I was, I have to say my heart went out to him. I can't tell you how many times I've been worried that you might get AIDS or even have AIDS—!"

"Aunt Reginia . . ."

"Well, I've worried anyway. And when I've thought about that, I've had to think about what I would do if you did have AIDS. I've thought about what lengths I would go to, what demons I'd strike bargains with. And to think of my own two boys—well, I couldn't keep hollering at the child then. He kept saying how he needed to go, you all were waiting for him and he didn't want to raise suspicions. I thought: a spell. I'm going to have to cast a spell, which I have not done in eight and a half million years. So I made him say the warlock's name, and tell me whether he knew his real name—which he did. I had him tell me where you'd be, exactly. And then he hung up on me.

"So then Mrs. Roan Gillory was key, because if anybody was going to have the raw power to make a spell work, it was her. I let her know that we didn't have any time to waste, and that she would need to follow my instructions to the letter."

"And they were . . .?"

"Never mind. It's too complicated. I couldn't trust that her raw talent alone was going to get me where I needed to be in one piece, so suffice it to say that we had to perform a little sacrifice on our end, too."

"Of one of the animals in there?"

"Well, one of the snakes slithering around—we had a devil of a time catching his butt, let me tell you. Nasty work, but it did do the trick. Grounded us, or something. Roan was able to boost my consciousness out into the—well, I don't know what to call it, the sorcerer's Internet, as it were. It's an aspect of the divine consciousness we all have in us—never mind. I was able to grab onto a portion of her power in the process. Distance and time are not such formidable obstacles in that kind of astral travel as they would be in the flesh. It did take a while to zero in on your location, because of course I had no mental picture of such and such street in the upper part of lower Manhattan, let alone the theater. And then once I found it, it took nothing at all to go down in that basement and kick up a nice ruckus—though I have to say if I'd been a smidge later than I was, you might currently be a castrato."

"Uh huh. So in a way, you were bluffing. You didn't know how to find Damian."

"Oh, I *know*. Ever since you told me about this, I've been

working on it, thinking about it, and having met Roan, I can see now how everything fits. I think. At least what I have is a good, solid hypothesis and theory. We just haven't tested it yet." She paused. "For the test, I'm going to need all of you back here with me, in Roan's room, along with that fool who just got through trying to offer your bodies up to his Gott-damn demon angels. As soon as possible."

"Sunder's going to be with us?"

"Yep. Quentin, too."

Langston remembers fretting a bit when she told him that. "So we owe everything to you and Mrs. Gillory. And to Quentin," he'd said brightly, to cover up his disappointment. "I wonder what it was that made him betray Sunder."

Reginia considered this for a moment. "I think he likes you all. When it came down to it, maybe he didn't want to see you hurt. There was a powerful vibration in his voice when we talked. I was trying to read him for all I was worth, because I wanted the information he had. On top of everything, or underlying everything, maybe, there's this thick, thick layer of loneliness in him. It's heavy. He likes to come off light, but he's got anchors tied to his feet. And he sees in you and your friends some hope to escape the loneliness."

"Yes," Langston said. He understood that well enough. "What can I say then, Aunt Reginia? I, all of us, we can't thank you enough."

Reginia seemed not to hear. "Ooh! How about the phone ringing to get the warlock's attention? Wasn't that a nice touch? I thought of a ringing sound because of the way that cell phone of mine had scared me so. The stuff about any god from heaven or hell, that was good stuff, too. Those old warlocks, they like that junk. Ooh, and how about my thunder? Was it scary? I've always wanted to do that, blow some wind and crack some lightning like a goddess on a mountaintop."

"I do seem to recall some sound effects, yeah."

"Well, how where they?"

"I'm sure they were good. It's all kind of a blur. It happened so quickly. And so unexpectedly and strangely . . ."

"Well, anyhoo. The whole mess left me with a migraine and put your girl Gillory right to sleep. But it did the trick."

~

Langston shudders. It all feels like more than he wants to know right now.

He wanders around the room looking at photographs. There on top of the dressing table, backed against the mirror, are he and Zuli, in Germany, when she came home for Christmas. They sit on the floor in front of the tree, its lights like white stars above their heads. Her arm encircles him maternally and his face is prickled with acne. In the photograph, they are both exactly the same color as the Black Madonna ornament that hangs from the bough drooping over Langston's shoulder.

Langston looks at this and feels almost that he wants to cry. For a moment he even tries, but all he manages to do is make his eyes sting a little. He wonders, blankly, whether Azaril is even still alive. But the question is an intellectual reflex, a trick of the mind. He already knows the answer, he knows it without Aunt Reginia's information, and this is unsettling to him.

He wanders to the window. The drizzle of a late-night storm mists the panes and makes the pavement of the street below shine like black shoes polished for Sunday morning. At the corner, a three-pronged streetlamp gives off the luminous haze of lit torches in fog. A skinny figure walks slowly by on the sidewalk, his head covered in a hood.

A knock on the bedroom door.

Reynaldo enters, in a plaid robe that sweeps his ankles,

smelling of soap and fresh moisturizer. He asks how Langston is doing.

"Fine," Langston says, taking Reynaldo in, the V of the robe and the line of his chest.

Reynaldo loiters near the doorway for a moment, unsure how to manage the space. He feels awkward. This is Langston's room, Langston is in a bathrobe, this is Langston's sister's house. He shakes his head, grins (he is fully aware of how dazzling is this grin). "It's fucked up, dawg, ain't it?" Langston shrugs, but cannot dredge up a grin to answer. Reynaldo shifts his approach. "You're worried about Azaril?"

Langston answers with a grunt.

"Your aunt said we'd get him back."

Langston responds with a grin, at the absurdity of the predicament and the strangeness of listening to Reynaldo champion psychic visions. "Right," he says. He sounds more coarse than he wants to.

Reynaldo continues more gravely. "Langston, come on. I know you're in love with him, but . . . I don't mean this bad, but face it, he's not all that. And he's straight."

Langston laughs. "Oh, yeah, straight. I guess that's why he fucked Damian." He is saying this, but in truth it's hard for him to get a firm grasp on the part of himself that really cares.

"But that was probably just experimental. I mean, Damian can charm anybody."

The look on Langston's face suggests he is less than pleased with this theory.

Reynaldo catches it, lowers his horns and hastily backs out of the china shop. "I'm sorry." He tries again. "It's always easier when you're telling other people how to feel and what to do. It's that I was just thinking about Quentin, and . . ." Reynaldo shakes his head. "I can't believe that motherfucker."

"That's funny. I was thinking of him just now, too," Langston says.

They look at each other. Reynaldo's frustration at his own dumb inarticulateness builds. He aches to bring parsimony to the moment, to say exactly what he wants to be said in exactly the right way. Then their shared look embraces something new: both see the other reflecting the smile he feels spreading on his own face. The smile expresses almost nothing of humor or happiness in it, just awkwardness. But it reassures them because they share it, and they savor it, knowing that this fragile communion will break at any second. But the smile holds. And holds.

Reynaldo moves forward across the room. Langston's fear and his penis rise simultaneously.

"Langston."

Like a cat, Zuli has soundlessly descended the creaking stairs and now stands beyond the doorway, leaning so that her head pokes inside. "Oh. Hi, Reynaldo."

Reynaldo wheels wildly to her. "Hi, Zuli!"

"I'm sorry to disturb you. I know you need your sleep." She hovers uncertainly—or deliberately, Aunt Reginia-style—saying something with silence. "But this might be important. There's someone who's been pacing outside my house for the last twenty minutes."

They stare at her.

"I hate to call the security people, or the Brooklyn cops, who're just itching to have me owe them a favor. But I recognize him. It's your friend. Quentin."

21

Zuli's house, 1:15 A.M.

In 1993 Sunder approached Quentin in the lobby of Leo Francis Hospital, on the afternoon when Quentin was discharged from the psychiatric ward. The ward, isolated on the top floor of the hospital, consisted of two brightly lit corridors, a row of rooms replete with World War I-era white canvas sheets hung from the ceiling to create the illusion of privacy, and creaking gurneys bearing howling patients. The ward had been Quentin's home for three and a half weeks: he'd committed himself after his mother, Miss Maria Shaw, discovered the tear-smudged copy of the doctor's report of Quentin's positive HIV test. Miss Maria Shaw, though somewhat addled at the time by acute symptoms of nicotine withdrawal, was lucid enough to deduce from the test that her only son was, as she had always suspected, a terrible sinner and was bound, as she had always warned him, for hell. She could not in good conscience allow him to remain in her home unless he reformed his ways. Quentin, never one to take well to ultimatums, ran away from home. His pride wouldn't permit him to avail himself of city homeless shelters, nor yet was his practice of on-a-need-or-pleasure-basis hooking sufficient to pay rent. Starved for options, Quentin recalled that his mother had once committed herself to the psych ward when he was ten (the episode was brought on by an acrimonious split with her common-law husband at the time), and that she had remained there for nearly six months, leaving him in the care of his grandmother. Miss Maria had emerged from her sequestration no less crazy than before, but certainly better fed and rested, so Quentin, in desperation, decided that it might not be the worst thing in the world to follow her example.

The ploy had succeeded only for a short time, alas—he really had no insurance to pay for an extended stay, and his depression was deemed insufficiently severe—and that afternoon, the accumulated strain of thrice-a-week art therapy sessions, the recognition that he was at last severed from the maternal tyranny of Miss Maria Shaw, and the knowledge that he still had no place to live broke over him like the end of a fever, and he cracked, then and there. By the time Sunder spied him crossing the lobby, Quentin was covering his face with his hands to conceal the fissures in his skin as they overran with tears.

Sunder worked hospital lobbies as a kind of ambulance chaser, a Valkyrie combing the battlefields for valiant, lonely souls slain by the brutalities of institutionalized care. He required recruits he could command in his own Ragnarok, his revenge against the white gods who had betrayed him; and Quentin, helpless, alone, carrying along a penis he swore had been shriveled by secretly administered drugs and which he could not make harden with the most outrageous, taboo-breaking fantasy, was very much in need of a mission and a commander.

When Sunder materialized in Quentin's midst, clad all in black like a gorgeous angel of death, his dark fingers corseted in double and triple rings of beaten silver, ivory, and gold, his smile like a flash of lightning in a storm, Quentin let his hands drop from his face and stared in awe and immediate, desperate love. He surrendered eagerly.

He interpreted Sunder's invitation to his home as a kind of business proposition, which gave him hope. One of the few unmitigated pleasures of his life pre-psych ward was his unmitigated whorishness, which had earned him a legendary reputation as fellatrix supreme, first in his home district and later among a certain unsavory stratum of bar-prowling, mostly married men in Miami willing to pay for a bit of expert Hoover action. Consistent with the self-absorbed grandiosity he had been taught by his mother's example, Quentin had worried that because he'd committed himself his name had been entered in Webster's new edition as a synonym for insane, undesirable skank-ho. As he stumbled out of the elevator, he was already deep in mourning: he would never again sidle his hips in a way that could make a fleeing criminal slam on his brakes, never again lift up his shirt to reveal his fat-free stomach as hard as granite and as smooth as a turtle's shell in a way that could make a potential john weep at the pain of his erection. No thought hurt Quentin more than knowing that this most potent of his powers—and the one surefire way to curry love and favor in the cruel wasteland of affection that is this mortal life—was now, by some cryptic act of psychobabble witchcraft and powdered drugs in his milk, forever denied him.

So when Sunder touched his arm where the nurse had, Quentin blubbered with relief. That Sunder wanted him and was willing to lead him despite all this made Quentin cast aside all caution. It even occurred to Quentin that night, riding along in the hushed black velvet interior of Sunder's massive BMW, that perhaps he was being escorted to hell; he considered seriously the likelihood that he would be trussed up and raped by Coke bottles and cock-ringed by barbed wire, end up beaten, slashed, and tossed aside. But it didn't matter. As long as he could be in the arms or the service of a man who wanted him.

Yet Sunder neither touched nor harmed Quentin. Not for some time. He took the boy to a large, nondescript house in a development full of such homes in a suburb countless miles from anywhere that Quentin recognized. The garage was as shadowed and sepulchral as Sunder's car, the house Spartan, lean as a racing hound, its one nonfunctional attribute a sweeping Hollywood staircase of the sort that Lana Turner might have ushered into the images of myth had she descended it in pearls and black velvet, with a long trail flowing behind her. Quentin loved the staircase and treated it as a shrine when he followed it flight by flight up to the third floor and to his small, spare bedroom.

That first evening, Sunder fed him. He scooped up hot chicken pot pie with a ladle from a bowl as wide as a dog-food dish and held it to Quentin's mouth and bade him sup. Quentin savored the aromatic steam, felt it suffuse him; and he understood and accepted the buttermilk pie crust, the rich, soupy broth, the soft carrots and melt-in-your-mouth chicken as a kind of seduction.

Vaguely Quentin recalled his grandmother reading fairy tales to him and his siblings when they were young while his mother was out in the streets: "So the moral of the story is don't go up in no stranger's house, and if you do, don't ever, never eat his food!"

"You won't die of AIDS, my boy," Sunder had said to him that night, punctuating the declaration with the sort of laugh one uses to demonstrate contempt for an absurdity: as if to say, "The sun does not fall into the sea, my boy."

"Each morning and evening, you should shower," Sunder said then. "When you do so, you should think that the gifts of the gods are raining down upon you. Can you do that for me?" Quentin waited for Sunder to describe the erotic denouement of the scenario: was he to pretend to be a virgin sacrifice in some crazy sexual rite? He was ready. But Sunder only reached over and wiped Quentin's mouth with the hem of the napkin he had tucked at Quentin's neck, then pushed back his chair and excused himself.

Quentin wondered if his benefactor was a Jesus freak. He looked for signs of this but found nothing revealing. The kitchen was well stocked, and hidden in a black cabinet there was an enormous television that received three hundred channels via satellite dish, and a stereo system and scores of contemporary CDs, all of which Quentin would have been happy to steal. There was no car in the garage, but there were bicycles, and he could easily call a cab if he wanted to leave.

But he had no place to go.

Every few days a pair of women came to give the house a furious cleaning. They spoke a language Quentin could not recognize and cast their eyes floorward every time he spoke to them in English or his juvenile Spanish.

Each night Sunder arrived to feed him, and asked his favorite question. "Did you remember this morning to think of the gods' gifts while in the shower? Don't forget tonight before you go to bed."

Quentin became deeply suspicious of the showerhead. He tried not taking a shower one night, as a protest, but found himself so discomfited by the smell of his own funk that he bolted from bed at 4:00 A.M. and gave himself a proper douching. He loved the bathroom, his bathroom, its black marble and elephantine mirrors, the shower stall itself, as big as a bathtub and smoky black sprinkled with moony silver. But he took the showerhead apart and studied it, finding nothing. He began to leave the door to the bathroom open and the glass doors of the stall ajar and let water spill out on the spotless floor, so that he could breathe fresh air and get out quick in case the pellets of liquid transformed as they fell to the tile and erupted upon contact into Zyklon B gas or acid. He had heard something about how the Haitians used a potion made from toxins taken from fish or toads or lizards to turn a man into a zombie, and he worried about that, too. Although he could find no evidence of toads or lizards or fish in the bathroom, he found some evidence of them in the yard. He studied the little bottles in the kitchen spice rack. He was convinced he would be killed, but resigned to it, too. Not quite happy about it, but relieved.

Though life of a sort did seem to be stirring despite his resignation: he found, bit by bit, that his erection was coming back.

So at dinner one night, Quentin, once again being hand-fed something delicious from his bowl, this time a rich concoction of cream, potato, and roasted garlic, decided to speak up. "What did you mean, I won't die of AIDS?" He tried to serve up the question with attitude, curling up the sounds of the words with contempt—but his lips kept smacking for one last taste of the broth drizzling onto his shirt.

Sunder made no move and did not change his expression, but it was the moment he had awaited. He replied with serene force. "I know of a power that can defeat illness. A place where AIDS cannot exist, and where absolute law rests in the hands of the good and justice reigns. This place is perfect, and the power it grants is absolute. I know something of how to reach this place. And it is not heaven. You need not die to arrive there."

Sunder had intuited (or found out by use of some other, less natural faculty) the right word to use. *Place*. No BS about antiretrovirals and vaccines, protease inhibitors, baboon bone marrow or acupuncture regimens, expensive fool's gold that in Quentin's admittedly less than rigorous research didn't do anything but make you sick with side effects and stave off collapse for a few toxin-soaked months. There was a *place* that Quentin could go. Since the time that he was old enough to walk around the streets where he lived, and old enough to walk the streets that surrounded those streets, and the streets beyond those, Quentin had known that he was meant for another place. A glamorous place that lurked somewhere off the map of his knowledge. This place is not paradise exactly, but might be understood as a kind of anti-Shangri-la, where rather than peace or contemplation, a quality of unrepentant ferocity and high, gaudy spectacle hold sway.

As Sunder spoke, weaving a spell with his words, stitching together the net to snare his quarry, Quentin's old desire sharpened and became less vague.

"I know young men like you, Quentin. You think Miami is the end of the rainbow and the top of the world. You think the only problem is that you don't have enough of it. That you don't possess it in the palm of your hand. You think poverty and lack are all that keep you from paradise. But Miami is nothing to the place I speak of. I'm talking about a City of Delights and a City of Glamour, where streetlights are like the moon and want of any kind is no more troubling to treat than a hangnail. There, no species of beauty whether natural or man-made is unrepresented, and no pleasure known or unknown is forbidden or unavailable. There, palatial homes with verandas the size of an airplane hangar overlook views of radiant twilight. No one is poor. In such a surfeit of wealth, both material wealth and wealth of experience, no one could be. There is no pain in this place, no loss or death, only endless pleasure and ever evolving and expansive style. It certainly isn't Miami, and it isn't heaven, either."

Quentin sighed. He knew the place well: the metropolis of his dreams. He beheld it now clearly, its arms like those of a mahogany goddess outstretched to welcome him. He was so moved he let something he'd never before heard himself say (and has never heard himself say aloud since) slip out. "Oh! And are there dragons there? Beautiful, fierce, powerful dragons?" Quentin likes dragons because they're big, gorgeous, breathe fire, take no shit, like pretty jewels, and live forever.

In Sunder's delivery there was then a slight hitch, like an automobile that gives a tiny hiccup before it hurtles into gear. "Yes," he said. "This power knows no limit, Quentin. Dragons such as none the world has ever seen. Of a kind."

Sunder explained to him that night that he had once met a young man in Egypt named Damian Garrow, and that this fellow had given him a glimpse into this Other City, and the smallest taste of its infinite power. He described what he remembered of Damian to Quentin. The look of his eyes was dreamy, his lips parted as he spoke. Quentin wondered whether Sunder was in love with this Damian.

It was Sunder's plan to bring all people who had been oppressed or hurt to this place and to use its explosive energies to exact vengeance upon the governments that had betrayed them. "I understand your hurt," Sunder said in a voice that was a whisper and tickling touch, like a feather tip swirling down Quentin's spine. Quentin felt naked. He felt aroused.

"What can I do to help?" Quentin asked. He had already placed his hand on Sunder's knee, was already hungering for his palm to grip Sunder's massive thigh.

Sunder remained very grave. "I would like you to collect information for me. With your talents." As he said the word, Quentin's penis surged with blood, hardened into something larger and more sensitive than he could remember possessing. "Particularly information having to do with—magic. You'll know what I mean when you see it."

"Yes," Quentin agreed, to whatever it was Sunder was saying, whatever reason he had for saying it. He performed a bit of sorcery of his own then, a telepathic push, communicated with the new light in his eyes and a noticeable flare of his nostrils.

Sunder responded lazily, like a lucky gambler who has won the pot so often that even while the casino manager counts out his winnings he is spying out in the distance some more impossible game, some rarer prize. He left off feeding the boy and motioned him over, whereupon he gruffly unclothed him. He bent him over the table, freed his desultorily tumescent prick from his pants, and pushed the boy's head down so that he could lap at the bowl like a dog while he got what he'd been begging for.

Quentin, thrust back and forth, toward the bowl and away from it, felt that the kingdom had come. He didn't want to clean himself up, preferring to retain the feel of his benefactor on him. "The feeling of you, every speck of dirt you left on me, every drop of sweat and cum on me and in me. It'll be like a cradle for me tonight, rocking me to sleep," he said, overwhelmed almost to incoherence by his gratitude.

Sunder insisted Quentin shower anyway.

Standing with his back to the wall in the hot, needling spray, Quentin opened his eyes and looked up to see liquescent pearls tumbling toward him. The pearls beaded on his skin, and like perfect crystal globes they shone with dream visions of purple-towered dragon cities, the images billowing like banners in the wind, like sunlit scenes on a shore viewed from beneath the undulating waves of the sea. Then the drops seeped into his flesh, or slid away and disappeared.

So Quentin signed on with Sunder and his little band of magical terrorists. Sunder gave Quentin instructions and sent him out into the world. He told Quentin to return to live with his grandmother. Once or twice a month Quentin was summoned by a phone call and a gypsy cab to the house out in nowhere, and if Sunder was happy with Quentin's reports, he put him facedown on the uncarpeted floor and sometimes even on the mattress of what used to be Quentin's bed and serviced him. Sunder no longer fed Quentin, but he stayed with him through the night at least, and didn't seem to mind that Quentin rose in the wee hours and snooped around, looking through the stuff of the new guy who lived there, who was always mysteriously absent.

This arrangement, peculiar though it was, provided Quentin with a safety net and a purpose. But there were a few runs in his stockings, he admitted in his darker moods.

Quentin missed hooking just for pleasure, for one. He had taken up drag performance as a substitute, like a smoker downgrading to chewing gum. It thrilled him to get up onstage, and he took very naturally to the clothes, the sashaying, the attitude, and the adoration, not to mention the makeup, but drag lacked the element of service, the satisfaction that one is vitally and urgently needed.

Then there were the stories about the drugs, protease inhibitor stories, new antiretroviral rumors, vaccine and interleukin-2 gossip. The new hope unsettled Quentin. He had become wed to a vision of two possible futures: in one he would perish, miserable, decimated, and unmourned. In the other magic would intercede, and he alone of his generation would survive the carnage, he alone would have possession of the Secret of Life; he would be a marvel to scientists and theologians, be feted, even worshipped by primitive tribes; he would have his own talk show. Sunder encouraged Quentin's belief in the second future. At times when Quentin suffered an acute need for reassurance, Sunder drew a pail of water and professed to prognosticate based upon images that floated upon the surface of the water and that invariably suggested favorable outcomes.

But too many friends Quentin had known but had avoided for years, too many friends who had acted far more afraid than he ever permitted himself to feel or whom he had witnessed beginning to decline, arrived unexpectedly in his midst, and he couldn't fail to note their ease, their eyes alight with newfound health. They were like signs, like whispers from heaven. Possibilities he had imagined closed were reopened, and choices loomed that he had no desire to make.

One night he found himself walking toward Leo Francis. He could feel his penis shrivel the closer the doors and the word ADMITTING approached him, but he walked on. He ducked in and then sat sheepishly in the emergency room lobby, just sat for hours, silently, his hands cupped tight over his crotch. Finally a nurse who had been scowling at him since the beginning of her shift approached him to see what his business was in the hospital. "This is not a homeless shelter," the nurse admonished. Quentin raised his eyes to her and dry heaves shook him up and down. The nurse scurried to get help and he bolted. At his grandmother's that night he was afraid he might hurl himself from his second-floor bedroom window. By morning he was again swaddled in the familiar blanket of denial.

In this marginal state, supported by a net checkered with holes, walking in tattered pantyhose, Quentin instinctively put himself to the task of Finding a Man. Enter Damian. Cute—no, not cute, *hot*. Worldly. Smart. Maybe even a little bit of money, or at least he acted like it. Talkative: Quentin liked a man who talked. A very familiar name—but no, his last name was Sundiata, not Garrow. Still, the coincidence, small though it was, gave to Quentin's Damian an air of mystery and power. If these qualities were not enough for Quentin to love him, then the matter was settled when Damian started to talk about Egypt. And a big, handsome, scary black man he chanced to meet there.

(Quentin called Sunder up immediately. "I've met him," he said, almost as if he were lording it over Sunder.)

The most important characteristic of the Man You Keep When You Find Him? He's capable of disappearing into thin air.

When Quentin saw Damian disappear, he saw the pearly gates of his private dragon city swing open. Quentin's hopes were instantly rearranged. To hear of the disappearance was one thing; to behold it firsthand, another order of revelation altogether. The power no longer seemed to be in Sunder, but independent of him—at the very least in Damian, but perhaps even beyond Damian, elsewhere, and accessible to someone not in Sunder's power.

Quentin's insight was confirmed when he told Sunder what he had seen. Sunder's control was shattered; he could not conceal his excitement, his surprise, or his fear. Sunder demanded to be told again and again in detail what he had witnessed. Quentin acceded to Sunder's commands about how to approach Damian's friends and what to say, but his mask did all the talking. The real Quentin, the needful Quentin, as soft and flabby as cooked lobster meat, was breathlessly plotting.

These are the little facts that Quentin needs to tell Langston and Reynaldo.

On the first floor, the living room leads to a short hall that widens into a foyer, and Zuli, with thermal house slippers on her feet because she's always cold, takes the distance in long strides. While Langston hangs back in the living room, she punches in the gate code and the door code on an illuminated column of numbers set in the wall. Then she swings the door open, and a thin brume of vaporous raindrops blows gently across her feet.

"Come in, Quentin," she calls out.

Quentin comes to stand in the middle of the living room, tracking the rug with wet shoes. His pants are soaked and he wears a navy blue nylon pullover with a wide hood that cowls his face like a medieval monk emerging into sunlight after days of meditative retreat in dark catacombs. Zuli half circles him, makes a comment about how he's soiled the rug, and then, to Langston's surprise and relief, takes hold of his shoulders and gives him a quick, brutal pat-down just as she's seen her law-enforcement community buddies do. She's too embarrassed to say, "He's clean," but she sort of nods to Langston before suddenly conceiving the urgent need to heat water for herbal tea, a decision that will remove her from the scene while permitting her to hear everything that transpires.

"I don't remember you wearing that," Langston says as he helps Quentin shrug off the pullover.

Quentin frees himself from the tangle of nylon. "Sunder gave it to me," he says, eyes wide and looking straight at Langston.

"Did Sunder tell you how to find me?"

"No. Your aunt did." There is the sound of a spoon hitting the floor in the kitchen.

Langston grimaces. "Why are you here, Quentin?"

Quentin doesn't think he'll be able to get away with trembling hesitancy and choked tears, so to compensate he launches in like a man taking his first swing of a bat too heavy for him. "I wanted to apologize." He pauses, stares down at the carpet. "I was wrong, I know I was, it is awful what I did. And I can't never make it up to you. I'm sorry, I'm real sorry. I understand you for hating me. The truth is I didn't mean anything by it, you know?"

Something about the way this mea culpa concludes with a question brings an unexpected smile to Langston's face. But he can't think of anything to say.

"I really didn't want to hurt anybody," Quentin blurts. He pauses, seeing some hardness pass through Langston's expression. "Not even Azaril. Honest. I . . . Sunder helped me when I needed it. He put me on my feet, way back when I come out the hospital. He said he could cure me. . . . Your aunt told you? Anyway. I did the best I could think of with the time I had. He told me then what he'd decided he was gon do after we went to Vanity Affaire. I tried to get him not to, but he doesn't listen to nobody. I tried. . . ."

"I know you called my aunt." Langston looks behind him, until he sees Reynaldo standing on the stairs. "We both know."

Quentin nods gratefully, even smiles a little.

Langston begins to fidget. "What will you do now? Are you going back to Miami?" He is about to add, *like we are*, but restrains himself. "With Sunder, I mean."

Quentin fidgets, too, glancing around the room. He does not look back again at Reynaldo, however, not after the first time he sees him on the stairs. "I can't trust Sunder right now. I don't mean he would do me harm. He's not thinking about me right now. He's so full of thinking about how he's going to get everything he's been working for. Anyway. He's ugly to me now. After what he did. And he left this evening."

Langston briefly raises an eyebrow.

Quentin feels a flash of annoyance. He takes a step as if to start pacing, then remembers the dirty soles of his shoes. He makes a sound that combines sucking his teeth and a groan. "I wish . . . I want to be with y'all. Even after all that went down. I know you don't want me to. Maybe if I was you, I'd feel the same. I don't know, though, maybe not. I know what it is for somebody to be down. Desperate." He gazes at a vase on the mantelpiece. "You can put me in handcuffs if you want."

Langston laughs despite himself.

"I want to be with y'all. Listen to me. I don't say things like this. You know I don't say things like this."

"I know you don't." As with his laugh, Langston makes the sound, is aware that it is himself speaking, but feels the words as a strange sensation, like the release of a knotted muscle beneath a masseur's hand. He watches himself approach Quentin and sees his own hand rest on Quentin's shoulder.

"I don't hold it against you, Quentin. I . . . just don't." A familiar awkwardness and reflexive fear comes back to him. He turns away. "And if my sister's OK with you staying, that's OK with me. We're leaving tomorrow anyway."

They both listen for a word from the kitchen, but hear nothing.

"I'm sure it'll be OK," Langston says.

Quentin rushes forward and flails his arms around Langston's back. "I appreciate this. I'm so thankful, so thankful."

Langston demurs. "Oh, that's OK. . . ."

"No, it's not OK. Cuz see, I didn't like your ass when we met. And to be really honest, I didn't like your ass *before* we met. Damian talking about you like you was the sun and moon, like you was all that with a napkin. But now you stick up for me, you forgive me when I need it the most? Oh, Langston! I'm so relieved to know that you are my brother."

The sharp whine of the teakettle breaks them apart. Langston, less eager to escape the clinch than he would have thought, goes to the kitchen to check things out with Zuli and feels incongruously that he could almost skip the length of the living room. He returns a moment later with instructions about the small room at the other end of the hall from Reynaldo's and his own, where a plump little daybed shares space with boxes of documents and dusty shelves of ten years' worth of *Federal Reporters*.

"I'll show you where the towels are," he says.

The stairs are empty on their way up, and the door to Reynaldo's guest room is shut. But Langston retires for the night feeling pretty good about himself.

22

Philosophy in the boudoir, 3ish A.M.

No sleep for Langston. He has taken a sleeping pill. No discernible effect. He has tried to conjure masturbatory fantasies, surefire ones that'll get him off fast and rocket him into sleep, but no go. He has tried tallying facts, as in: *I am due back at school. I am missing classes. Will the department reimburse me for my travel if I change my itinerary and don't tell them?* He thinks of Leah, and how it is his duty to call her and tell her that something has happened to Azaril.

Langston picks up the phone and dials without looking at the illuminated buttons.

He waits while the ringing repeats.

"Hello?"

Reginia's voice cheers him. "I knew you'd be up."

"Langston. It's near four o'clock."

Langston can hear voices and the faint strains of music. "Are you watching one of your movies?"

"Mmhm."

"Which one?"

"Wait, I like this . . . Oh, shoot, I missed the best part of it. Uh, *A Place in the Sun*."

"Oh, is it the scene when Elizabeth Taylor and Montgomery Clift are dancing together at his uncle's party, when they say they love each other?" He wonders if she can psychically read his true motive for calling her simmering beneath the chatter.

"Why did you call, baby?"

"I feel stupid bothering you about this . . . I don't want to keep you from your movie. . . ."

"Don't worry about it, child. Your sister called me not forty minutes ago."

"She did?"

"We are a family of night owls, my dearest dear. She called to fill me in on the goings-on. Of which there are a few, I gather." She pauses. "So you forgave Quentin. I'm happy to hear that."

"You are? It was the right thing to do, then?"

"Oh, Langston, don't ask me for a *reading* at five o'clock in the morning! I just meant that you forgiving Quentin shows growth. It shows character. Now, if you could forgive your friend Damian, too, and then a host of other folks lined up behind him—I should say, *men* lined up behind him—then we'd be getting somewhere."

"Speaking of Damian, Aunt Reginia," he says desperately, "there were things that that warlock—that Sunder—said that I . . . He said I know how to contact Damian."

"Uh huh."

"He said he put a spell on me that prevented me from telling a lie! Is that possible?"

"You're asking me that question—you, the man who cast a powerful love spell from a book of fake spells? You know that love spell worked so well that even though I figure it's mostly worn off, a coupla times now it's been like I can't distinguish you and Azaril from one another. Psychically, I mean. Like you're both humming the same tune, beatin out the same rhythm. Your vibrations are nearly identical, sometimes."

Langston is elated and horrified by this. "Then . . ." He swallows. "Sunder *was* able to cast a spell that prevented me from lying? Which means that when he asked me if I knew the formula to contact Damian, and I couldn't say no, it was because I do know—how could that be?"

She takes a while before responding. He can feel her, weighing what she'll tell and what she won't. "Sometimes," she says, drawing the word out to a ridiculous length, "you know things you don't think you know. Simply put: magic works in the realm of the subconscious and unconscious."

"You're not telling me everything."

"What's to tell?"

"Aunt Reginia, I need you to tell me everything. I feel like—like I'm at a turning point. There's a decision I need to—that I've made."

"Decisions are good," she answers noncommittally.

"I've decided I want to be like you."

"What do you mean?" She suddenly gains some vigor. "You don't want to become a woman, do you? Because that's too far out even for me. Your mama would flip out—"

"*No.* I mean, I want to be a—a magician, or whatever." This is greeted, as he expects, by silence. "Tell me more about how you got to know about sorcery. I know how your gifts came to you, but how did you acquire the skills?"

Reginia's tone acquires an edge. "Look here. Listen to me. It's not like that. It's not that easy. It's not fun and games, what you're asking for. You think this Azaril boy sneaking off with Damian's thrown you for a loop? Honey, you don't become what I am or Sunder is, or even what Roan Gillory is, by denying that kind of pain, but by affirming it. Indulging it. Sucking it up like a milkshake through a straw."

Langston hesitates. "Uh, OK. But what about—how do I find out what I know but don't know that I know? You know what I mean. How do I figure out how to contact Damian?"

"I'm telling you, child, but you're not listening." She starts talking as if she's reading aloud to a child. "Remember back in my kitchen when I said about how I could see Damian all over you? Because of what your relationship with him was, and the way it changed—I won't say it ended,' cause relationships never do end—because of that, there was always and remains an incompletion. An unsettled energy between you. Like a tether, glowing, if you look at it. Because of the *desire*, see. In that sphere of desire, in the energy you create between yourself and another person, a form of knowledge is created. Knowledge of you. Knowledge of the other person. See what I mean? That *wanting*, that mixed-up-with-sex-no-matter-how-infrequently-you-get-it thing. Did you and Damian do the do?" Reginia asks.

"Huh?"

"Come on."

"No . . ."

"But you got close. You built up that desire."

"Yeah . . ."

"Then between you, you made something. You generated some knowledge. A connection. And maybe because of who the two of you are, your erotic and magical potential, you generated some very powerful knowledge and energy."

Langston lets this sink in. In the mirror above the polished counter of the dressing table, he sees his mouth hanging open. His eyes bloated and sagging from lack of sleep, his shaven head looking balder than ever, his skin the skeleton-less burlap of a scarecrow's head on a stick. His whole face, slack and stuporous.

Reginia, delighted by the evidence that true learning has occurred (teaching is most satisfying when the student just plain shuts up, she's found), rolls merrily along. "You know, I have tried to assimilate the wisdom of Buddhism and Vedanta, and it does make sense. The sages asked: What is the root of unhappiness? What is the cause of the anguish of the heart, the pain of the soul kept from its true flourishing? Desire. For in desire you have hidden a part of yourself from your own powers of perception, and foolishly you look outside, searching for this missing part. And so you get into a mess of trouble, because what is missing is not missing and therefore cannot be sought and found. Solution: look—then go—then be, inside the self. The abnegation of desire. Crystal clear.

"But, see, as a Westerner and an African American, we have so many blocks before us in the assimilation of this knowledge. We've been kept from so much—we were created as Negroes just so there could be somebody kept away from all the things that people who weren't Negroes got to have—it just seemed like I couldn't make that Buddhist thing work for me. Or so I thought. And then I figured out that it ain't necessarily so that desire is a *block*, a handicap. The crucible of our learning and coming to be and contributing to the cosmos is simply different from the folks in the East. As Aframericans, to have experienced a fierce negation from without, from a power outside our ken, and to take that negation inside yourself and believe its lies, to experience it as betrayal from within—well, it just makes a voluntary abandonment of the ego quite a conundrum, see. To abandon desire seems to be about abandoning justice, abandoning our right to be and be let be, and to be heard. Of course, this being betrayed and seized was ultimately productive of wonderful, world-conquering cultural forms (soon to be galaxy-conquering forms; mark my words, I have seen the future, and come the era of interplanetary travel, black folks will be kicking some butt, culturally speaking). We know that, we see that.

"But in the matter of spirit, there are still other lessons which have yet to be brought from seed to flowering plant. I have come to believe that we of all folks must travel *desire* of various kinds, in order to reach another place—a different place from that of the Buddhist sages. We can't simply pare away desire, because we're not meant to do that. We're meant to employ desire or transform desire in some other fashion. And that's what you're doing. That's your sorcery. Working with desire."

Langston grasps to work through what she's telling him. "I think I see . . ."

"See if this helps. Everything in the cosmos vibrates and is a product of vibration—at least, that's how far we've gotten in theoretical physics these days. All matter, all life is energy, little components vibrating to their own unique and basically universal rhythm. All energy wants to move—create and destroy, build up and break down, coalesce and separate. But the object is the same: to connect, to give off, to receive, to exchange energy."

"Everything is a moving particle," Langston says. It's a relief when he can follow at least some of what she's saying.

"Yes. (Remind me to tell you later about superstring theory.) *All* energy is movement, and all movements can be characterized in a fairly simple fashion that even your dumb cousin Vernon Fleetwood can understand: you move toward something, or you move away, or you try to do both simultaneously (usually unsuccessfully for us sad little mortals). On Earth, the movement of energy in living things is governed by genetic code, or by instinct, or learning. And by desire. So we might call these movements desire, the opposite of which in human beings might be simple disinterest and ambivalence. From acts of desire in the past we find our history—our genetic history through the desire of our forebears, all other history in the form of our cultures: our stories about life and about ourselves, our everyday practices and beliefs. Given this kind of theory, the problem is not desire itself, since desire is movement. It is not only the 'natural state' of the Cosmic All but the very defining characteristic of the cosmos, the *thing* which makes all things, which *is* all things.

"So that's my spiel. The gospel of desire."

Langston doesn't respond for a while. Reginia seems content in the silence—or rather, content in the movement of images across the screen in her bedroom, as *A Place in the Sun* plays on. "You astound me, Aunt Reginia," he finally says.

Reginia chuckles. "I know *everything*, sweetie. Ain't no deity in my life but the Holy Trinity Triple Goddess: Me, Myself, and I."

"But how do I use what you've just told me? You said that you have to suck up your pain, affirm it, to gain magical power. How does that connect to what I know about Damian? I don't get it. . . ."

"You've always had the potential. I've seen it. Your mother has, too. Now this warlock has seen it. It's partly the gay thing, I think. And how that orients you toward desire, and makes you experience in a certain way the depths of desire unfulfilled. That sets you up nicely to walk the wild side with folks like Gillory and the warlock and me. Not that this list provides you with the most encouraging sort of company—which you should duly take as a warning."

"Can you . . . take me through the first steps? Walk me through it?"

"You don't even know what you're asking me to do. Walk you through what?"

"I don't know."

"Hm. Well, that's the right answer, anyway. All right. Is your door closed? Will you be disturbed?"

"Hold on." He sets the phone down, then comes back. "I've locked the door."

"All right, then sit down foursquare if you aren't now, with both feet firmly on the ground, and your back straight, but relaxed."

"OK."

"Shh! Listen. These words are a spell. Hear them as sounds and listen to the words, but don't puzzle over them, just let them in. And above all, keep breathing deep . . . in through the mouth to the groin . . . out of the nose . . . in . . . out . . . in . . . out . . . in . . . out . . . in . . .

"Listen.

"There is only one being, one existence, and that existence is God. The Universe. The first energy. The one and only energy of all the Universes, first cause of the Big Bang and Over-Heaven and Under-Earth and All-Night and All-Light. You and every other thing are a component of that one existence. You are that existence as a tiny, tiny fragment, and you are a microcosm of that existence as a whole. As above, so below, and so you and your life are like God: you have only one life, and that life has stretched through all time and space. You have lived for all eternity. On Earth you have lived for all the time that Earth has existed, a million, million lives that are small pieces of your one life. The life you live today is similar, broken down into small pieces. This action and that one, this thought and that one, that year, that month, that day, hour, and minute and second and millisecond and nanosecond.

"Now. A piece of your life just flew past. It happened, and it remains with you as you leave it behind to move to another moment, and it was always here.

"If you would live your life as something other than a fragment, you must begin to see and understand this. And in order to understand this, you must become engaged with where you are, what you are doing, and how horrible it is.

"Your life is a horror. How do you know this horror? How do you measure this horror? By your desire.

"You wanted to be embraced by your father, wholly, completely, unconditionally. You were not. Nothing can change that. You were not embraced. You wanted to be taught by your mother how to get your father to embrace you. You were not taught. Nothing will ever change that. You seek embrace from every man you meet and teaching from every woman. You are not embraced. You are not taught.

"That boy—Azaril. You love him. You want him. You need him. You want him to make it right for you because you need to have it be right, and then you can love him and love yourself. But though he loves you and he needs you, Azaril does not want you. And he never will. He never, ever will. He will not embrace you and he will not teach you.

"You are a homosexual male in a place and time when homosexual males are shunned. It doesn't matter if every man may want to be as you are, or even if they don't want to be as you are and just want to be embraced, that doesn't matter, either. It doesn't change anything. They still won't embrace you and they won't teach you, because they don't know any better how to do it than you do. They'll tell themselves it's because you're a homosexual, but even if you know that's a lie, nothing changes, because they actually know that they are lying. They, too, look to women to teach them. And the women ain't gon tell 'em, either, because even though we know more, we don't know much. And even if you cry and scream and holler unfair and become a serial killer and murder the weak, this truth will never change, never alter. No matter what you seem to do, your life is a horror.

"To know this, to accept this, to feel this, to live this truth—that is what it's like when you first come into power.

"When you roll around in desire like a pig in his filth, when you do it till you can't stand it. That's what it's like to first decide that you can become a sorcerer. You begin to understand how so little that you believe is true, and how so much of it is intended to control, limit, harass, and ultimately destroy you. You begin to see how so much of what you want—how much of your wildest dreams!—is really so tiny, so minuscule, so insignificant compared to the bounty and possibilities of the Universe of which you yourself are a part and which you can call at need. And once that's done, once you've peeled off those layers—knowing that you will never fully be aware so long as you are confined to this existence, you understand—you can take another look.

"And then you begin to see how your life is a joy, a great, bountiful flowering of every good thing under the sun. Then you will see that you were never alone, that you were always, in every moment and in every way, embraced. Your father embraced you. Your friends embraced you. Your lovers embraced you. Your enemies embraced you.

"Then. *Then*. Then you take the next step."

She blows a long breath. "So that's it. You've started."

"But, how do I know? How do I know what the next steps are?"

"How do you know what freedom is? By the small, certain conviction that speaks again and again in your thoughts, telling you that what you are experiencing, what you are living now is not freedom. How do you know love? You do not know love by its joy. You know love by fleeting moments of contentment, but not by joy. You know love and you know freedom because you sense them, hovering somewhere in some other life just out of reach. So how will you know what steps to take to become a magician? You will know by your desire."

Part 3

THE MISSING

Miami, Florida
Two days later

23

Miami, afternoon

The sky that domes the city of Miami when they return is like the walls of a candy brothel, awash in cartoon colors of rosy pink and Sleeping Beauty blue, shot through with careless smears of honeydew melon and streaks of fluffy Santa Claus white. A penitent hush seems to have brought a degree of calm to the doings on the ground, however. On the streets there are signs of collective hangover and repent: soiled banners overflowing trash cans or fought over by scuffling stray dogs, abandoned bandstands teetering precariously on corners like drunks sleeping off a binge.

Departing the airport, Reynaldo goes his own way once it is decided when the three of them will rendezvous with Langston's aunt and Mrs. Gillory. His thoughts are largely occupied with what he's reading in the papers—ongoing investigations of the Castro sightings with speculation running rife; yesterday a mass ceremony conducted by a trio of famous Babalawos to banish the evil ghost of Castro from American soil; plans for a Victory Flotilla, in which hundreds of well-heeled exiles will sail back to Cuba in glorious white yachts to symbolically bring freedom and the joys of capitalism to their long-benighted brethren. Apparently his father is considering joining the Victorious Ones, his mother tells him on the phone. "Why, I don't know," she says. "He certainly doesn't have enough money to fit in with that crowd." "Probably he thinks there'll be a lot of free booze," Reynaldo says. Celia Cavazos laughs, wildly, loudly. She's glad her son has come home safe; now there will be someone in the house she can talk to. She promises that she'll have a feast waiting for him.

Quentin crosses Reynaldo's mind here and there, which makes him uncomfortable, but he's used to the sensation and stuffs it down as he has learned to do.

Reynaldo crosses Quentin's mind once or twice, too—but so as not to get all knotted up with guilt feelings and composing imaginary letters to Emily Post about the etiquette of making up to people after you've betrayed them to a warlock who planned to carve their hearts out, Quentin tries to imagine himself in a scene: a triumphant return to his native land, a Miami reminiscent of *Ivanhoe* and Elizabeth Taylor glory days, and he some African prince robed in the silks and sashes of decadent European aristocracy, burying his face in a handkerchief powdered with snuff as he awaits the arrival of his opulent Cinderella-esque carriage. As it is, Quentin must take the bus home to his grandmother's, since no one has been generous enough to offer him a ride, or cab fare.

Langston has a long, lonely cab ride from the airport. He's headed for lunch, alone, and then to the Wessex. In the backseat he hugs the right-hand passenger door, fetally affixed to the wall of a brown leather uterus. The air-conditioner vent spews a chill breeze over his face, which makes his eyelashes flutter. Or is it the effort of holding back tears that makes him shut his eyes? Azaril's absence, the unoccupied space to Langston's left where he imagines Azaril would sit, is a shimmering ghost.

Makes sense, Langston thinks. This all began with ghosts: the ghost of Castro, running from a mob down Calle Ocho, and the ghost of Damian, who in some ways has always been something of an apparition. Odd repetitions, unnerving symmetries—these are proof of the intelligence of the Universe, the gods toying with us, inviting us to share the joke in a language of signs in which each emotion, each experience, is like some bewildering alien glyph written in invisible patterns in the air.

The first step in deciphering the glyph is figuring out what he really feels: not sad about Azaril. Not afraid of failing to find him or Damian. Not feeling emotions exactly, but not numb either: more like he's dwelling somewhere deeper than emotions, traveling briskly but without hurry along some cool Styx-like undercurrent somewhere in his chest. He's calm again, as he was at the moment of epiphany in Sunder's clutches. He's completely capable of taking anything the universe dishes out. Is this what it feels like to start down the magician's path? *You will know by your desire*, Reginia had said. And she'd made it sound like the last thing you were likely to feel would be a sense of calm, like contentment would be something you'd have to fight for and earn. He was supposed to start with the dark stuff, wallow in his worst fears, delve into his hurts and his rage.

So he gives it a try. From his vantage point on the Styx, seated comfortably in the prow of his tiny magician's scull, which stirs the black briny waters of his unconscious the way a rake passes through a thick carpet of dry leaves, he looks at himself and meditates on what Reginia said about his father, about men and his unfulfilled desire to be embraced.

When he thinks of his father he feels love, but that love is in suspension, a pendulum at an impossible moment of equipoise, the muscular flurry of a sprint arrested in midstep. Nothing Langston desired of his father got much farther than the pit in Langston's stomach where the hunger for his affection churned. Which possibly is what Reginia meant: in that hunger and emptiness, like a pot of salted water brought to the seething edge of boiling, lies the heat of his power.

Langston learned early not to approach his father in a childish or foolish way, not to babble about matters of little consequence or demonstrate out of exuberance some silly playground skill he'd acquired. Any such disguised plea for affection invited ridicule—or perhaps, astonishment at the temerity of the request; Langston's grandfather had died when his father was very young, so perhaps the demand for love seemed like a demand for a Rolls-Royce and private jet from his father's point of view. When the two were together, even if no word passed between them—and mostly no word did—it was as if his father were reciting Langston's inadequacies: all the ways in which Langston was too little or too much, a baby, a bum, a fool, a faggot, a burden, and, in retrospect, perhaps even a threat. He could tell that his father didn't like him, because with Langston's mother and sister Daddy could be a sweetheart. Langston could hear his father, dove-cooing with his mother inside the closed bedroom door. For Langston's sister his father had yet another voice, patient and even indulgent. He still talks this way with her, though Zuli is in her forties.

Of course all childhoods are fraught with disappointment and the inevitable wrench of abandonment. Langston knows his indictment of his father and his childhood is not true and it is not false. Its greatest flaw, perhaps, is that it lacks scope. Fathers and sons together can make the universe a narrow thing, no wider than a shotgun corridor in a rickety house built on stilts. Taking a more compassionate view, Langston surely knows that as for him, so for his father, and so for Langston's father's father and for his great- and great-great-grandfather before him. In the course of time, confined between the hedging walls of their narrow universe, the Fleetwood men have come to learn harsh and unpleasant lessons about how to hold a family together: with rope, chains, whips, and a big dick and/or all their metaphorical and psychic equivalents, just as most of them had been kept and held by their White Fathers after they were hurled onto the shores of the New World. At intervals, as each Fleetwood man trudges along the endless length of the shotgun corridor, he will cast a wistful look back over his shoulder. Wasn't there some other father, there across the water? A father or a whole village of fathers who held you close when you were afraid and set you free when you were ready, in some paradise back yonder? Or was that father the one who sold you into slavery?

The Wessex

"Business is down because of the shooting, right, that's no surprise, but other than that, things is finally under control here," Luisa is saying. "Especially now that that crazy heifer Gillory has checked out. You know she'd be buzzing us all the damn time, hollering about how slow room service was, and demanding they leave the trays outside the door. We were like, ma'am, you have to sign for your food! Of course, she never would, mean-ass bitch that she was. She didn't even officially check out or pay her bill! Not that it matters, because we have her husband's credit card number, but we think maybe they broke up and that's why she left, in a huff or something, because after a while nobody ever even saw him anymore, not that anybody was gonna cry about that, seeing as how he was trying to feel all the women up."

Langston smiles generously, neglecting to inform Luisa that Mr. Gillory is now a dog and that Mrs. Gillory has not in fact departed the hotel but has only shifted her room into another dimension.

"It's so cute you all came back here," Luisa observes. She is perhaps more focused on Reynaldo's cuteness than anyone else's.

Reynaldo walked in a half hour after Langston arrived, and he stands nearby, far enough away to avoid talking, close enough to hear everything.

When Reginia arrives, she appears all in red. A silky red blouse flares wide around her neck and at the ends of her sleeves, matching in perfect vermilion tone her soft red velvet bell-bottom pants and slender crimson-dyed calfskin boots. The effect brings out the copper tones in her dark skin, and with her height and commanding full-figure curves she might be an Afro-Indian queen, the kind who emerges clad in a leopard loincloth to greet the Great White Explorer in colonialist fables. Luisa, who has an eye for these things, decides she looks like a shapely and bounteous glass of rich claret.

"There you are," Reginia says, all out of breath. "I'm sorry to be late. I visualized and visualized an empty space, but the parking gods were not with me today." There is a forced jocularity in her smile and tone as Langston introduces her to Reynaldo.

Langston notes that she isn't wearing any jewelry, and that she carries a small black hip bag. He tries to be polite when he notes that his aunt looks . . . different.

She throws her hand to her hip and says with a prideful grin, "If you have to know, I've been fasting for the last several days. Don't I look cute without the water weight?" Very seriously she looks around, giving Luisa a dubious once-over. "Are we all here?"

"Luisa's not part of this," Langston says. "But there's still Quentin. I guess . . ."

"Quentin's already here," Reginia interrupts. "I picked him up on the way and he decided to go right upstairs. They should both be here by now." She heads for the elevator.

"Both?" asks Reynaldo.

"Yes. Sunder, the high and mighty warlock himself, is here as well."

Reynaldo looks at Langston and shrugs, which Langston translates as Masculine-latin for a bit of fear he expects Langston to share, some buck-up encouragement for both of them, and a lot of resignation.

"Don't worry," Reginia tries to soothe them. "I can protect you. We're gonna be safer doing this with him rather than having him hunting us down and messing it up while we're at it. And since he knows a lot about this, he might even be of help."

As the elevator door slides closed on the four of them, Reynaldo says, almost in a whisper, "We're finally gonna get Damian. Hard to believe."

In the hallway, leaning against the empty wall space between room 349 and 353, they find Quentin picking at a small zit on the corner of his nostril in dramatic avoidance of Sunder's baleful glare. Sunder, like Reginia, is monochromatic, a portrait in obsidian from his T-shirt to his padded motorcycle pants and motorcycle boots.

"So you decided to go traditional, I see," Reginia says. Rather surly, she sounds, like a person greeting her ex's new spouse at a mandatory social. She stands a foot or so shorter than Sunder, but she comports herself in a way that demonstrates she more than meets his measure.

"Red?" Sunder sneers.

"Your rings," Langston says. He is surprised to hear himself speak, but the memory tugs strongly at him: the dagger clasped in Sunder's two hands, poised above Langston's abdomen, the hands much like the dagger's handle, glittering and metallic, with so many rings on the fingers they had seemed fleshless, prostheses shaped from ribbed gold.

Langston cringes when Sunder glances back at him.

"Yes," he says. "You have to go cleanly into the nether regions." Sunder eyes the two young men at Reginia's tail in turn. "Why didn't you have them dress appropriately?"

"The what region?" Reynaldo blurts. In contrast to Sunder's assured, level tone, Reynaldo sounds belligerent. He has moved forward to defend Langston.

"Don't worry," Reginia interjects. "We won't be seeing any 'nether regions' unless I have to put my foot up Sunder's backside for trying to scare you boys. And I didn't ask them to dress up, Sunder, because I didn't want them to arrive here any more nervous than they already are having to share a room with a man who for the last few days has been trying to kill everybody they talk to."

Sunder seems to rise up on his toes, and his voice shakes with repressed anger. "I did not *kill* Destine. That was an unfortunate—loss of control. And Malachai deserved exactly what he got. Do you know these boys are working with COINTELPRO—"

Reginia gets up in Sunder's face. "Are you here to work, boy, or not? I agreed to let you come only on the condition that you wouldn't start trouble. Are you reneging on your agreement?"

Sunder's reply is in a slightly less level register. "Don't pretend with me—girl. You're not doing me any favors. You need me, if this is going to work."

"*Are* you reneging on your agreement?"

As she looks up into his dark eyes, her chin seems ready to pierce Sunder's Adam's apple like a spear. The others feel the strain between them. Langston wonders what he'll be able to do if Sunder, a huge, strong man who can bring down storms and open sinkholes in concrete, attacks his aunt.

Finally Sunder folds his arms and looks away, his mouth drawn tight in disgust.

"That's not good enough," Reginia says quietly, the satisfaction of victory making her face tight and conspicuously smileless. "I need to hear some words."

At that Quentin, the only one who can see Sunder's face now, flinches. But Sunder, with an effort made visible by the way the muscles of his back throb through the cotton of his black T-shirt, manages to turn back to the woman and say the words. "I'll keep my vow."

"I'll keep my vow, what?"

"I'll keep my vow—Mother."

"Better," Reginia says, and then, turning to Langston before he can say anything, "It's just a term of art, honey, don't get scared you're related to him." She begins to rummage through her hip bag. "Since you're so very necessary and all, Sunny, you do the honors. I need to save my strength."

Sunder grumbles, but reaches to place his palm high on the corridor wall. Slowly he moves his hand along the wallpaper and leans close, like a picklock listening for the telltale click of a safe combination.

"What's he doing?" Reynaldo demands.

"Shh!" Sunder whispers. His movement ceases. Perfectly still, he shuts his eyes, and his lips part slowly. After what seems like minutes he moves, only to place his other hand lower against the wall. "Roan Gillory," he says softly.

The change is hard for them to follow, as if a breeze had stirred a pond, and the resulting ripple on the surface of the water carried away the reflection of the cattails bending over the bank and of your own serene face leaning over to savor the view. As the reflection returns and you and your image are one and the same again, the plain door to the late, unlamented room 351 appears, evenly situated between 349 and 353, exactly as God and the architect of Hotel Wessex intended.

Mrs. Gillory opens the door and ushers in her awaited guests with manor-born grace. She is attired rather unfortunately in what looks like a traditional sailor suit, floppy pants with a floppy top complete with a sweeping V neck, wide, flat, hoodlike collar, and the characteristic bandanna tied loosely and hanging low around the neck: all twilight blue. "I couldn't find anything in my closet that was appropriate, so I tried whipping something up. I daresay designer patterns are not very easy to create from thin air," she says apologetically as she hugs Reginia.

Reginia gives Mrs. Gillory a peck on both cheeks. "The important thing is that what you're wearing is comfortable, dear," Reginia says.

As the others trail in (Mrs. Gillory notes Sunder's behind with an interest visible in all the features of her face), only Langston reacts with shock. "What happened here?" he shouts, looking around at the two queen-sized beds, the television set in the open bay of the entertainment center, the nightstands and the table and two chairs and the little dog sniffing aggressively at Sunder's pant leg.

"Mister Fleetwood! How grand to see you again!"

She clasps him into her thin, diminutive body, trailing a finger from his ear down his neck, over his shoulder and along the length of his arm. Then she gestures happily at the mundane confines of her room. "Marvelous, isn't it, to have brought it all back as it was? I have your aunt to thank. She has given me a bit of help in focusing my little *gifts*. I do hope you appreciate the fact that your Miss Jameson Wolfe is a very remarkable woman. If I didn't loathe appearing to be gaga, I should say that I have rather fallen in love with her." She leans close to him and cups her hand near his ear. "One is almost tempted to go the way of the lesbians." Her finger comes to rest in his belly button after tracing the ridges of his stomach muscles.

Langston wriggles away. "So she helped you use your . . . abilities . . . to clear out your room?"

"Oh, Mr. Fleetwood! Before your aunt came, I had sweat pouring off my body, and it was not a sight to see. If you could see beneath this—this tunic—you would see that I have become almost a stick figure! I would have wasted away, I think, had dear Reginia not come along and helped me restore the air conditioner and everything else. But I may be swallowed up into nothingness yet. And all of you beautiful people with me. We might pass eternity in the mouth of an angry, hungry god. Not very pleasant to contemplate, is it?" She sighs. "Well, one way or another, it will all be over soon. Promise me that when this is all over, if we survive, that you shall join me in a wild ride in a convertible. A red convertible. We'll have the top down and I shall wear goggles and twirl a parasol in one hand and steer with the other. I'll be Zelda and you will be my F. Scott of the River Niger. We'll hear the sirens of the highway patrol screaming over the whip of the wind as we go. Will you promise me that?"

Perhaps delirium is a side effect of wielding the energies of the Planck length, Langston muses. The image of the two of them riding together is not a comfortable one, but, being an agreeable fellow, Langston assents. Mrs. Gillory nods in satisfaction, though she looks very sad. "If only we could find a convertible with a running board. That would make it perfect."

"I'll need the book, Langston," Aunt Reginia says.

Langston removes *Hex* from his bag. He doesn't know whether it's his own excitement at work, but the book's red cover has a faint sheen like sweat, and it seems to hum in his hand.

"So there *are* real spells in there after all," Reynaldo says.

"A few," Reginia answers. "In code."

"How do you know what one to use?" Quentin's eyes eagerly

follow the book from Langston's hand to Reginia's, but his tone is skeptical.

She doesn't answer as she begins to leaf quickly through the pages.

"Won't there be consequences to our doing this?" Langston asks. "Explosions or strange phenomena have accompanied the use of the spell before, right? And you told me that the energy required to tap into other dimensions was more powerful than the sum total of all the energy available on Earth. How could . . .?"

"It's dangerous, yes. But remember what I told you long ago. In all phenomena there is a spiritual component. We're operating here not according to physical principles only, but by the laws of metaphysics. There will be fallout, but Sunder and I will channel it."

Sunder hovers near Reginia's shoulder, greedily drinking in the book's words as they speed by. "The effect ought to be no worse than it was in Miami a couple of weeks ago," Sunder says. "Some mass hallucinations. Perhaps a small explosion." He shrugs.

Reginia loudly taps a page. "Exactly as I guessed. There are six spells here that Verity Gapstone corrected. Each of them is for bringing your loved one to you. Well, let's get this mess started. Lord, I hate me some sorcery gobbledygook," she mutters.

"But I thought after I tried one you said it was a bad idea." Langston tries not to notice Quentin and Reynaldo turning toward him.

"We're not doing the one you screwed up. We're using the words that are in common to all six. The greatest number of spells in the world have to do with getting laid and getting rich. You start to bring them together, isolate the common summoning agent, and then have a source at your disposal like Roan's raw power. . . ."

"But I think this won't be sufficient," Sunder interrupts. "My feeling is that the number is eight, not six. We'll need two other components. . . ."

"I know, I know. Please. Eight. It's covered. You and I, Sunder, will handle one of the missing components (I'm sure we can make something good up), and Langston, you'll handle the other."

"What?"

"We'll also need to use two talismans just to keep it all kosher."

"And there are two people missing, too . . ." Quentin says, getting the hang of it.

"Exactly," Reginia says. "Now. Talismans: Langston, you've got something of Azril's, I mean, Azaril's?"

Langston's still wrestling with the idea that he's supposed to provide a missing spell. "Yeah, not really *of* Azaril's. I went to see this girl Leah in New Haven before we left. She and Az . . . had become friends. She was upset about him going missing, and she asked me to borrow this key she wears as an earring. Said it's a good-luck charm. Really it's her family heirloom, and wasn't all that lucky, but Azaril was so into her—"

"Oh, goody. A key's just the right symbolism. And Quentin, you've got something of Damian's?"

Quentin reaches inside his big black bag and produces a ball wrapped in cellophane. He unwraps it and dangles a pair of black Calvin Klein briefs from his thumb and forefinger.

"You stole those from Damian's suitcase?" Reynaldo says.

That these are the first words Reynaldo's actually spoken to Quentin since he called him a whore shit pig of a traitor is not lost on Quentin, who considers this last accusation simply a repetition of the former. "Damian *gave* these to me when we were hanging out."

"You musta been doing more than hanging out if he was giving up his underwear," Reynaldo shoots back.

Reginia clears her throat. "Let's keep those young minds on the matter at hand, please? Sunder, if you could seal the room for us—nothing fancy, just a basic keep-out-the-noise mumbo jumbo thing will do, don't want to waste your strength. Roan, if you could draw the curtains, and then take that canine and lock him in the bathroom, please, before he starts barking and defecating and what-all. I want all of us to form a circle. I think we should sit, so let's do that. Go cross-legged if you want, but keep your knees lower than your waist, and you shouldn't be right up on one another, but you should be close enough to hold hands and feel the body warmth of the person beside you."

"What are we expecting to happen when we do this?" Reynaldo asks as he shoves one of the beds hard up against the wall.

"Quentin and Langston, put the key and the underwear in the middle of the circle. And Reynaldo, sweetie, come sit by me." Reginia settles to the floor, *Hex* in hand. Reynaldo remains motionless, so she talks to him as she continues to gently wave him over and pat the space on her right. "We're not doing anything that we 'shouldn't' here. We're not calling down any spirits or invoking Satan or celebrating a goat god. This is what practitioners might call a working. We're coming together to focus the energy of our minds and bodies, and then we are simply going to *follow* Roan's power to its source. No more or less. Think of it as an exercise in creative visualization or a group meditation. Now sit your little behind down."

The tone of her voice does the trick more than anything she says, and Reynaldo goes to sit by her side. "For your own good, shut up and stop thinking," she tells him.

Langston gently nudges Quentin so that he moves over and allows Langston to sit on Reginia's left. She takes a plastic bag and hands it to him. "Take out one and pass it around."

Langston takes a small clump like a cutting from a branch of a bush and holds it to his nose. "What is it? Looks kind of like ginger root, but the smell . . ."

"It's horrid," says Mrs. Gillory, next to Quentin. "Like a prisoner kept in a small dark place for years and made to perspire."

Reynaldo winces. "Stinks like a horse's breath."

"Ooooh," Quentin says excitedly. "*Drogas*. I bet this shit'll really make you trip." He dabs at the coarseness of it with his tongue.

"Don't eat it yet!" Reginia warns. "It takes years to find that stuff. It's died out everywhere but the Amazon interior, and I'll be damned if I'm gon cough up three thousand dollars for another hit. Anyway, it's not a drug exactly. But when we take it, it'll help make us more labile. More open to perception."

"A hallucinogen?" Langston asks.

"In a way. When I tell you to, chew on it, and keep chewing until it's completely gone. Don't stop even if your jaws are tired." She looks over the open pages of *Hex* again, then pushes it away from her toward the center of the circle. "Are we all ready to do this working? Roan? Reynaldo?"

"I'm ready," Reynaldo says softly. Mrs. Gillory twirls her index finger in the air.

"Sunder."

Sunder rises from the circle. For the last minute or two he has been sitting with his eyes closed, his large, ox-muscled body still. He reaches inside his shirt (the boys can't help straining a bit, to see the broad slab of hard chest Sunder briefly exposes), and from a sheath slung low on his side he pulls a knife. It is polished and silvery, the blade like the slim hourglass figure of a silhouetted model, and markings inlaid with gold ride down to the pommel.

Langston and Quentin slowly shut their eyes, but Reynaldo watches while Sunder walks around the circle. His feet scarcely seem to alight upon the carpet. His eyes are open but unfocused, though he makes no misstep, and he holds the knife out in front of his chest. As he walks, he makes a noise, gently rhythmic, a clucking noise, almost like the dim echo of the far-off beat of a drum.

Reginia begins speaking. Her words run in and out of the sound Sunder makes as he walks, never overlapping him. "We are calm," she says in the lightest of calms. "This is standard procedure. Mere occult science. We seal the circle. We focus. We cleanse."

Reynaldo feels suddenly as if warm water were trickling down his back and over his chest. He shivers in the unexpected pleasure of it, and his eyes fall closed.

"This is standard procedure, mere occult science. Old and new. Nothing and everything. We breathe, and from each of us flows the breath of spirit. Calm, everlasting, cleansed. We breathe, and from each breath comes the small, mighty magic that forms a dome around us. As above, so below. To the side of us and behind us, and below us and between us, this breath flows. Flowing. Feeding us. Focusing us. Freeing us."

The sound of Sunder's noise broadens. Reynaldo hears it settle opposite him and peeks to see that Sunder has returned to his position in the circle. But the sound continues. He thinks he hears it from Reginia, and maybe from Quentin, too. It is a hum, a low drone, a rise and fall of surf.

"Now this," Reginia speaks, her words again in collusion with the chant rising around them. "This small thing, this mighty thing, only standard procedure, mere occult science. We are free. We are open to that which is now and always was. It flows down to us from above. Through the tops of our heads, flowing like the waters of a fountain. Consciousness. Wisdom. This flowing meets another that comes from within. The light of each of us like the light of sun and stars and moon, flowing out to meet the flow that rushes in to kiss it.

"Langston."

He trembles.

"Make your sound."

His sound? He has no idea what she's asking him. He sits, trembling, dumb. Sunder's chant is like the loud cry of crickets outside a backyard tent in the dark. The one sound he can think of to make is to ask the question, *What sound should I make?* Is that against the rules? The drone seems to fill him. It makes his skin hum. Is there a tune, running low and sweet below that pulsing din? Then he remembers the last time his skin felt this way. At Redemption in Miami, when he had his vision. The drums, the bass, the darkness. *Release me.* . . . And before that, too. With Damian, years ago in Germany, in Langston's room, they danced, the two of them, but it seemed that there was something in the room larger than the couple they were. It seemed, if only he could remember it clearly, as if for a moment the roof went transparent and the sun was a milky hole in the sky. And there was something—someone?—there with them?

"Langston, make your sound."

Langston opens his mouth. He thinks he will sing, *to get off, to get off*. But no words issue from his throat. Only a sound—a cry, pure and piercing.

"We hear," Reginia says, effortlessly matching him. "We speak in the tones and rhythms of all things. This small thing, this oh so mighty thing, only standard occult science.

"Now this. From the east, we call to us that which we know always was and is. It comes on the wind. It lives in the breath. The spirit of Spirit. The gateway to the source."

Langston feels a breeze across his neck. Then a force like strong wind pushing him fore and aft. The sound around them deepens, begins to echo, as if it were contained in a great dome. His own cry continues as if it no longer needed his breath to sustain it.

"This is our purpose. To seek our lost friends along whatsoever roads they have tread, and to find them. There is no obstacle before us, no hindrance in our path, no delay in our success. We know this, and it is done. We see the road before us. We see a broad road, and it is paved with stones. Smooth, old stones, gentle to our feet. They sigh like cushions as we pass over them. Around us we see the green grass as it was in the mornings of our youth, and we smell its fragrance, fresh, new. In the grass we see the trees, tall, bounteous, guardians who will guard and guide our way. We hear their leaves singing to us of the path, telling us how it winds and where it leads. Behind the trees in the bright light of the risen sun we see the lush hills of far countries, with their secrets and their treasures and rewards for the fearless traveler. And there to the hills of far countries our path will take us. That way we will go.

"Roan, you take the first step. Ease into it."

Roan Gillory raises her hands above her head. It is an awkward gesture for her, as she does not know, really, what she's doing, but it seems appropriate for a witch to make some kind of gesture, so she does. She would make a sound, hum or cluck like Sunder and Reginia have been doing, but she feels silly. She begins nervously to laugh, and then feels the electricity surge through her.

"Oh!" she gasps.

Reynaldo, lullabied to a state of near sleep by Reginia's words, has been watching the breeze tickle the blades of grass in the field in his mind's eye. All at once he feels the bottoms of his feet grow warm and tingly. He shakes them to help the circulation but finds that the feeling intensifies. In the vision in his thoughts he looks down at his feet to find that the path beneath them is softly glowing.

"Now the power is raised," Reginia announces. "We six hold it together. The power is raised and it flows around us and through us. The power is ours to command. We walk the shining path of the power at our feet."

Each of them can hear the breathing in the room: their own, and the breathing of the people on either side of them. As one they inhale and exhale. (*How did that happen?* Quentin wonders. But he likes the feeling: each time they draw breath, he can almost believe himself to be rising, floating from the floor. Each time they exhale, it's as if the space around them expands like a gently inflating balloon.)

Reynaldo, mesmerized by the pretty picture so vivid and steady in his thoughts, breaks the hush to say, "Wow, that was really nice. I can still even see the field. Did you get the info you needed, Reginia?"

Someone laughs unkindly.

"Shh," says Reginia. "We're not finished yet. Take the root and put it in your mouth and chew. Keep chewing until every bit of it's gone."

The bitter gasoline-like taste on their tongues makes some of them stir and lose their rhythm. They hear Reginia urging them on, her voice ringingly clear yet somehow indistinguishable from Sunder's chant and Langston's strangely ongoing cry, as the two disparate sounds rise and fall, rise and fall, rise and fall.

Reynaldo listens, he tries to listen, tries to remember to breathe and to chew. Far away he hears Reginia calling to him. *Don't listen to the words*, it sounds like. *Just breathe.* She is not near. He believes he sees her in the distance, and moves to close the gap.

The weeds along the path lick his ankles as he goes. The sun is high in the sky, the trees are tall and grand. At the foot of the hill he looks up and sees a great green slope. Reginia calls to him from high up. He hesitates, but the wind pushes at his back and he ascends. He finds it easy to climb the hill, for the path is paved with rough-hewn stone that winds ever upward, like a stairway cut into the outer wall of a ziggurat. He looks behind him. Already the plain and the path he had trod is far below, tiny as the course of a river viewed from the window of an airplane. A dark head and dark limbs follow him up the face of the hill, two flights down, but the figure has no face that Reynaldo can see. It is Langston, he decides.

Hold my hand, she says. Reginia is beside him, and they are together at the summit of the hill. *I know this feeling,* Reynaldo says. His thought or his voice (he cannot distinguish) sounds lazy to him, feels like summer and the buzz of a lawn mower or the slow propeller of a flight overhead. *I know this feeling,* he says. *I am asleep, I am dreaming.*

The hill's summit is grassy like the plain far below at its feet, but it is flat and oblong. Pine trees mark its edges, and their branches reach across the summit to one another and form a partial canopy overhead. Reynaldo can see the blue sky above him as if through a skylight or the oculus of an observatory. *What a wonderful dream,* he murmurs, for the pines are evenly and widely spaced around him, and the effect is like that of a wonderful home with huge floor-to-ceiling windows of wafer-thin glass panes. Other hills spread out below, and the gray and white tops of mountains, and the shimmer of a mighty sea radiant with color and vibrant light as if it has swallowed a blue sun. He stands—where? In the Parthenon upon the Acropolis? Houses flow down from the summit over the slopes.

(*Wait a minute, wait a minnit. . . .*)

"Ohhh, shit! Iss kickin in! I really see something! I see a—" Quentin's face and form fly at Reynaldo like the whirling colors of an acrobat.

(*Waitaminnit, this can't be. . . . Where has she taken us? I'm gonna throw up. I'm gonna blow. I'm breaking up, I'm breaking up!*)

"Shhh, shhh." Reginia. "Don't think. This is nothing, a mere landscape of the mind. We are traveling only in thought and dream and the stuff of hallucination."

"Thought and dream my ass," Sunder grumbles. He is there, too, his form black and massive like a bull, its hoof raking the dust as it readies its charge. The excitement in his voice makes it squeak. "Gillory transformed this place, she switched it over to something else, she *moved* us in space and time as easily as ripping a plug out of a socket!"

"Shhhh!"

(*Hold my hand.*) Reynaldo tries to back away, but Reginia's grip on his hand is like an iron lock. It is as if, little by little, their hands have become fused, and not only their hands, but their arms and legs and feet move in perfect synchrony like the well-oiled wheels of a locomotive. Liquid, the six of them seem together, each seeping into the one nearest him or her, each flowing in the same stream.

(*Thought and dream.*) A whisper, echoing. (*Thought and*—)

"Jump!"

She pushes him, and they jump through the window between the trunks of the trees. They hurl themselves into nothingness, into an airless void of bright, cruel white.

Reynaldo screams. Langston laughs and screams. To him it seems that they have left the center of a perfect balloon, and now they careen against its rubber walls and fall, sucked into its neck. Twisting and falling and flailing they turn around and around and around. Quentin shouts in exultation. Sunder joins him. Their voices condense into a long, keening howl.

Langston feels himself and all of them shrinking, tinier and tinier. The sky of their little world breaks open, shatters like glass.

Everywhere is falling everywhere, as in the long, slow snowflake descent from a cliff's edge at the end of a nightmare.

—∞—

(Outside, in the waking world usually ruled by Euclidean geometric shapes and semi-Newtonian physical laws, traffic comes to a violent halt on several South Beach streets as an endless stream of nude gnomes leap out from hotel windows to take to the pavement. No more than two feet tall, bearing beards of Old Testament length, bowlegged, pale as Swedes in winter, their genitals tucked into tidy flaps of hairy skin like a kangaroo's pouch, the gnomes wriggle and wedge their way between cars and buses in packs as if being chased by the bulls of Pamplona, ululating the gibberish sounds of an inhuman language. Hundreds of the little fellows make a mad lemminglike dash for the sea. Taking Superman dives off the sand—and kicking up a tiny storm of spray in the process—the exodus collides with and then melts into the surf. The gnomes' phantasmagoric presence in the ocean turns the foam along a ten-mile stretch of coast a flagrant shade of purple.

More disturbance attends the appearance of Martin Luther King, Jr., Robert Kennedy, and Malcolm X doing a can-can together in salmon-silver spacesuits on the stage of a Miami theater during a touring Broadway show. There, things degenerate quickly—the rush for autographs, an onslaught of interviewers from the local news shows, pushy historians who aren't afraid to give a sharp elbow to an old lady if she gets in the way, and of course a few skeezes who materialize out of nowhere to try to get up on stage and fornicate with the performers right then and there, as well as four rednecks who, upon hearing of this second coming, barrel downtown in their pickup trucks carrying loaded rifles so that they can finish the job Sirhan Sirhan and company appear to have failed.

The general melee will end an hour from now when the police crack a few heads and the dancing trinity reaches its finale: as the song ends and they raise their legs for one final triumphant kick, first Martin then Robert then Malcolm (scowling, and with hair more brightly red than was his norm) float up from the stage to the ceiling like balloons to go pop! like three weasels. Their exploding bodies shower the onlookers with gold coins. The gold coins will themselves become daffodil petals in a few days, but not before several people have cashed them in for hard currency.

Later, informed of the consequences of his channeling work, Sunder the warlock will shrug. "It could have been worse.")

24

In between

Langston's mother, Carol Jay Jameson Fleetwood, didn't raise any fools. But she didn't raise any poets or writers, either. No matter the tumult of her daily life, no matter the misfortune of being an officer's wife and thus having to host luncheons for all those horrid racist wives of white officers who would have liked to have her as a maid, and despite the even greater misfortune of trying to transport the idea of her own pastry-catering service from dreamland to reality—despite all that, she managed to clear a space each day to read her children poetry. She read to them as they tossed and turned in their liquid fetal dreams before they were born, she read to them as late as when Zuli was in the seventh grade and Langston was in the second, while they fidgeted and did everything under the sun but pay conscious attention. She read them Emily Dickinson, Elizabeth Barrett Browning, Lord Byron, Percy Bysshe Shelley, Countee Cullen, John Keats, Samuel Coleridge, Robert E. Hayden, Pablo Neruda in the original Spanish, and of course Langston Hughes.

"I might not make it to the mountain with you," she would tell them sometimes, "but I have a dream today, that one day your names, my little children, will stand alongside the immortal list of the men and women whom I've read to you.

And that you'll win the Pulitzer Prize or the Nobel." She encouraged them to set themselves apart in their rooms with a new ballpoint pen and a ream of blank paper for what she called "creativity time." Only she and the Lord (and perhaps a good psychic) know how deep was her disappointment when neither child on any of many occasions "created" much more than doodles, graceless drawings, or, at best, a rambling diary entry with all the good parts heavily crossed out so they wouldn't get in trouble. By the time her son elected of his own volition to read fifth century BC verse in the ancient Attic Greek, she was already too defeated in her hopes either to be an artist or to mother one that, apart from being proud of her child and knowing he would do well blah blah blah, she felt a vague resentment, seeing as how she herself had had to forgo graduate school in English literature to get married and save Zuli from bastardy.

It might therefore be some consolation to her, now when she is a docent at a college in suburban Philadelphia and teaching an erratically attended course on nineteenth-century American poets, that her one and only son, upon being cast into the nether regions of the nonspace of parallel universes and the Planck length, perfectly recalls a stanza from an English translation of the thirteenth-century Sufi mystic poet Jalal ad-Din Rumi, which she must have read to him more than two decades ago:

The body is a device to calculate
the astronomy of the spirit.
Look through that astrolabe
and become oceanic.

Langston did not know two decades ago what Rumi meant.

Now, whenever now is, Rumi's mystery arrives as if from

thoughts far distant from Langston's, like the light of Venus reflecting the rays of the sun in the evening sky, a part of his world but extraneous to it, and the riddle's meaning is quite simple: Langston has lost his body.

All of them have, if in fact all of them or any of them still exist and Langston is not completely alone. He is adrift, formless, limbless, senseless. He cannot move or even prove the existence of a physicality capable of moving, or find a point of reference from which he could move, other than the tiny echo of his thoughts hitting against themselves like the tap tap tap of a Ping-Pong ball bouncing. When the panic passes—there is no accounting for how long this succession of emotional states takes (how can he experience emotion without hormones, enzymes, a heart?): this now and this after, this past and that future, it's all a dupe, a concoction of his thought—he decides he can meet the challenge. The memory of Destine's drug anchors him; he tries to imagine this experience is like that one.

But this time he not only can't see, but he can't hear. His location—if you can have a location without a body—is one of utter and absolute darkness, empty unbounded silence.

Yet rich. Rich somehow. Not with the waves of sound. But resonant, with a force he cannot name, a kind of rhythm attuned only to extrasensory perception. This is not black like a void, but black like the soil of a riverbank. There is something at work here, Langston thinks. A presence.

(Az?)

But another presence answers. It is new, alien, and yet disturbingly familiar. Langston feels suddenly blanketed, enveloped in a luxurious and esurient embrace, gathered by something so vast and encompassing that Langston, his meager thoughts, are as nothing before it, are finally and utterly crushed within its endlessness forever.

They all know it now that it chooses to reveal itself. Damian's father, Credence Gapstone.

Another country, at ten to the minus thirty-third power centimeters.

Minds can only categorize it as a voice, though auditory stimulus of any kind is lacking, and they can also imagine it as an image free of visual template: blackness lush and opulent. Words clean and seductive. Words like warm arms, outspread.

Come to me.

The voice vibrates on its special frequency, in its special place, which is every sound, everywhere.

Join me.

From the formlessness rushes a sudden flood. Behold: light. Then, cloud and misty rain and the diaphanous stars and nebulae of a distant galaxy. The rush of sensations like a wave cresting seven floors above their heads, the boundless world suddenly above and around them. They lie pinned to the bottom of the ocean floor, looking up at a breathtakingly enormous watery universe.

The tempest draws back. Before the semblance of their eyes are arrayed tableaux, richly appointed in props and painted backdrops, dense in detail of sound and sight, which pass one by one on a stage as capacious as the Great Plains:

Langston and Leah embrace one another in a hospital bed swept by the flutter of gauze draperies and the whisper of breezes zephyring in through the open doors of a veranda. From an egg culled from Langston's ovary and an unnamed donor's generous draught of sperm, incubated together in Leah's warm womb, the two women finally see their first child born, a little colored boy whom they will name Azaril. Quentin, a baronet become wealthy by canny investments in the slave trade and from the profits of a tea plantation in the wilds of Ceylon, lives in a grand manor in Lyme Regis by the Sea, and his house is full of harem wives and princelings and bastard children with whom he romps in his bedchambers by the light of the sickle moon. His wife, Sunder, lectures him on sins against God and in vengeance seduces the town's Catholic priest, with whom she ruts in the prickly hay of an abandoned barn at the edge of the Undercliff. Reynaldo takes up a propeller plane into the blue sky. As it climbs, its new coat of paint winks at the undiluted sun like a winsome country lass gathering sweet berries in a spring field. Reynaldo coasts upon the winds for an hour or so, singing songs to the birds, and then drops his load of bombs on a quiet Ethiopian village whose men have all gone off to battle and whose women and children die with shrapnel slicing through their bodies, including young Reginia, a ten-year-old cattle herd who cried this morning because she could not be a man and go kill enemies like her older brother. She frowns in a face half-smashed by flying debris and snorts blood out of her nostrils. "Gott-damn alternate realities," she grumbles before dying. Reynaldo, Langston, Roan Gillory, and Sunder driving in a rusted chug-a-lug gunmetal Ford pickup truck in the backwoods of Mississippi on a cloudy night see a flurry of white forms on horseback rallying toward them. "The Klan!" Roan screams, and wishes aloud that her hair were blonder, her features more 'Merican, and her foreskin hadn't been clipped. But then a soft cone of blond light lifts them and their truck up into the clouds, and soon they realize they have been kidnapped by a UFO, flagship of the Reconnaissance Fleet from the Dog Star, Sirius.

The pressure of images mounts and mounts, whirls and whirls.

"Gott-*damn* these alternate realities!" Reginia demands order. She, at least, is herself, one and indivisible. The others feel tied to her like Odysseus lashed to the mast.

I ain't God, I'm just godlike, Credence answers. *Try this.*

Now they see a seething latticework of jeweled strings and bubbles. They see the alternate realities from which they've fled, like bulging and shrinking shapes in a lava lamp. They see a house leaning on one side and furniture flying. *From my dream,* Langston thinks—or says or otherwise communicates, as Reginia answers: *It's simple, in this nonspace or superspace apparently ruled by Credence and all things Gapstone, Verity's memory is a living echo—*

Langston, Reginia, Sunder, Reynaldo, Quentin, and Mrs. Gillory surf the electrical currents coursing through the gray matter of Verity Gapstone's brain and alight upon the corpuscles streaming through the vessels of her limbs. They see themselves, circled in a sandy, covelike version of Mrs. Gillory's hotel room, staring back astonished at the body of Verity that they inhabit, as the black horizon darkens unevenly in patches: storm clouds sail in, blowing west. They see Verity, sitting forlornly in a pool of blood that whirls around her feet.

Sensations drench suddenly recovered senses: they can breathe!—and they awaken to limbs and eyes, ears, a nose, the simple comforts of solid things: they see a couch with a quilt bearing geometric Christmas trees stitched into its panels thrown across the cushions and a coffee table, the wood chipped on the knobbed legs; a stove or heater, looking vaguely to Reginia like a great squatting metallic toad, stands to the left, and a bricked-in fireplace lies behind it; on a tall stand is a vase of fake flowers, faded and somehow dark in the evening light flowing through two windows in a wall behind them. They can smell a heavy, watery aroma, both clean and dirty: mustard greens cooking. Hanging on the wall to the right of the unused fireplace is a calendar with a biblical scene—blond angels blowing trumpets before the crib of a blue-eyed babe. Below the triumphant cherubim and above dates scratched out as if in a countdown is printed DECEMBER 1951.

Not Mrs. Gillory's hotel room.

They are sitting on a chair; their buttocks feel cramped, as if they've been sitting for a long time unable to shift to a more comfortable position. The rug beneath their feet is bright red, the painter's red of cardinals perched on a branch against a backdrop of snow that makes the color more red than red is in reality. The red is a splash—no, a *pool* of vivid color in a room composed entirely of browns: the walls are brown, the couch and table, the three people looking at them. The rug's pooling red makes them think of sinking into blood, drowning in his blood. Of course only oxygenated blood is truly red. All of his blood would be dry now. *What does burnt blood look like?* they wonder in unison. And alike they feel the genuine intellectual puzzlement of the question, the terrible anger beneath it. The grief at its bottom.

This doesn't feel like the parallel realities. It feels real.

Each of them, all of them together, are a five-foot-ten woman, their dark skin suffused with a strong tint of rose, with a lean chin and ample round cheekbones, heavier eyebrows than seems properly feminine, large brown eyes and straight black hair (with one thick strand of gray) bound back in a braid. Langston knows who they have become; he has seen her before, in his visions. Verity Gapstone.

Verity—this conglomerate being who believes herself to be Verity Gapstone, though Verity does not know there is a gap in her knowledge of herself at this moment as surely as there is a gap in her name—waits uncomfortably in the chair. She waits for her husband's boss to come and tell her how David died.

The air outside the window crackles. An orange light flares across the sky, as if lightning seared the sunset for a moment.

Black ashes drift through the window. There is the smell of burning. . . .

What the fuck. Damn, that was—

It's Verity's memories, and Credence's memories, Reginia tells them, *they rope us in, we step down into the moments in time that keep repeating for her and for Credence, the places in Verity and Credence.*

But Reginia's not satisfied with the way things are going, and kicks and screams (while the others try to express their rage despite experiencing the astral equivalent of vomiting), until, like Daddy building a dollhouse for his little girl on Christmas Eve—a wall here, a roof there, one neat division followed by another—Credence orders things so that it all begins to make sense.

25

Where oh it's that woman again it's WAIT we're getting it in order now this happens earlier than what we did—

It is December 1951. A strange time for tornadoes.

This time (Langston has been here before, has been this woman, is now her again) Verity runs up the hill. She jumps over thin broken trunks of young trees downed in her path and crashes down in pits that cover her feet in mud. She plows through the whip and bramble of weeds that clump like shaved-off shocks of nappy hair or lie horizontal to the ground as if bulldozed. When she encounters a black cable lying in the mud, Verity slows and catches her breath. Then she takes the long way around; such hazards drive her off her path, but she's thankful that there aren't as many live wires here as there are in the more thickly populated neighborhoods. As often as she can, she carries her son in her arms; the going is faster that way. When she tires—more and more now as the hill climbs—she drops him to the ground and pulls him after her. He mewls and complains. "Oww, Muh! My hand!" Verity grips harder (*hurting Quentin, who inhabits Credence's hand, and making Reynaldo, who is a wire lying in the path, spasm with electric pleasure*). She takes hold of Credence's wrist and yanks his arm fiercely if he needs the encouragement. She finds herself screaming at him. "Shut up, Credence!"—and then a wave of guilt makes her say, "Just hurry, please."

Usually when she's angry with him she calls her son by his first name. But not today. He shares his first name with his father. She's so afraid David is dead that she just can't bear to say the name aloud: as if by not speaking it she can keep David safe, she can suspend him in some safe bubble in time and maintain intact the thread by which his life may be dangling.

Del White told her that he'd seen the roof of Waterbury's Ice cave in. He said he'd seen it crumple like the top of a fallen cake, "like the roof wasn't nothin but paper, like it wasn't *nothin*," he'd said. Verity had wanted to slap the stupid slack-mouthed awe from his face. And then Sam Dewberry came over, with a ream of blood spilling over his forehead and running down between his eyes and over the ridge of his nose, where it split in two and trickled out on either cheek. His hair was ragged, full of hills and declivities like the outline of a mountain range, and yet he was handsome, Sam Dewberry, there was a severe glory about him like a prophet's. He had the look of a bleeding messiah standing in the doorway of her house, and he'd said, "You cain't go down to Main Street. They blockin off all that area 'cause too many buildins is fallin down."

So instead of running downtown to Waterbury's, Verity's running up to Aunt Plennie's house—where David might be, where he has to be. (This is not completely irrational, though she knows it is not likely, either: her husband drives an ice truck; he needn't have been in the ice house when the roof caved in; he could be anywhere in town, even outside town; he could be at his aunt's house, which he loves as much as Verity does.)

The landscape around Verity looks—feels—twisted, as if somebody'd taken hold of both ends of the Earth and wrung it like a towel. It's after sunset on a winter's evening but the whole sky glows red, glows with streaks of smoky yellow and violent tides of orange and russet, like the raging interior of a stove.

By the road there is a silent girl, couldn't be much older than Credence is, who bends over a dark womanly shape on the ground. The woman's head and neck lie at a crooked angle that makes Verity shudder, and the woman's eyes and mouth hang open. The girl sees Verity and pleads with her for help.

Verity runs right past her, continuing upward, pulling Credence along. She thinks they may have kicked mud onto the poor woman's body, but Verity doesn't dare look back. She will not be Lot's wife. She will not tempt fate by looking behind her.

A few steps short of the summit, Verity stops.

Plennie's house stands as proudly as it ever has, untouched, impregnable, secure. The burning sky is just a crown adorning its regal beauty. Plennie's house is like the highest crag of a tall mountain that rises serenely above the storming clouds, like a finger reaching up boldly to touch heaven.

Verity sobs and sobs at the sight of it, relief flooding her, her frozen hope breaking into floes and coming to life again. She walks toward the house, carrying Credence with her, a last rush of adrenaline giving her renewed strength. *Thank you, God. Thank you. Plennie's OK, and David could be*—is—*David's OK, too.*

Someone touches Verity's shoulder. She sees Credence's eyes widen as he stares behind her. Verity turns her head very slowly. Should she look, or wait? It's bad luck to look behind you. Verity is about to turn her face to the house again, when out of the corner of her eye she recognizes Lin, Plennie's housekeeper.

Lin's presence chills rather than soothes Verity—a common enough effect where Lin is concerned, since Lin is the sort of person who makes people whisper. No one can prove to their satisfaction that Lin is a woman, though everyone, including

Plennie, presumes her to be: apart from the beaten-down hot-combed kinks on her head, Lin lacks other indicia of sex, having no hint of breast or hip curve, and sporting a thin growth of hair over a thin upper lip. No one knows what race she is, either. Everyone assumes she's black, but imagination might easily make her or him Egyptian, Arab, or Indian. Looking at her, at her rumpled, baggy pants, her cap pulled down low over her forehead, her inscrutable face, Verity has the impression of having carelessly stumbled into a bad omen. She freezes again, the spigot of her tears turns off.

Lin's fingers dig into Verity's shoulder.

"She gone," Lin says.

Lin's *gone* is full of *o*. It sounds like wind and moaning, like ghosts calling as they flee from light. Lin's face is clenched and shrunken, riven with folds of quivering skin that seem to converge on her mouth like a funnel. Her eyes mirror the red glow of the sky and she looks like a demon released from some cage in hell.

Verity turns away in disgust.

"I saw the wind take her away." Lin makes a choking noise. "I saw her fly through the air. And then I couldn't see her no more. She gone."

Verity rips herself free of Lin's touch. She moves on, staggering now as Credence's weight pulls her down. Determinedly she reaches the front of Plennie's house, meaning to take Credence in, to shut Lin out, to shut out the world.

Then she realizes how broken the world really is.

The north side of the house isn't there.

Half of Plennie's house has been sheared off as if by the stroke of a guillotine.

Credence (*now Reginia and Langston, hands joined*) shakes free of Verity's slackening grip and runs into the yard to gape. It's like a dollhouse. From the north side yard you can see inside several rooms, now that the outer wall has been ripped away: the living room with the couch and chairs still primly wrapped in plastic, the high-ceilinged den where the radio was but is no longer, the dining room, its table strangely bent and warped so that it seems to resemble the bark of an ancient tree, the kitchen a mess but seemingly whole. The three bedrooms that looked out on the north are gone, no identifiable trace of them anywhere in the vicinity. The bathroom sink and the tub lie sideways on the grass. Water—soapy water?—seems to be running in a continuous stream from the tub, as if it were right side up and overflowing.

Impossible. It's impossible. Verity shuts her eyes.

"It ain't over," Lin warns from behind them. "You know how it is with these storms. They always come back."

Credence begins to wail and tries to climb up his mother's legs, back into her arms.

~

Almost two years later: Verity Gapstone stands alone, at the edge of the sea on the rock-strewn white sand of a tree-sheltered cove. She feels wind throw stinging whips of salt spray across her bare arms and face. She feels the warm night air on the Caribbean island combust, feels its dark invisible flames heat the world around her and make steam rise from the surface of the sea. She sees the lightning and hears the thunder, and she shivers with a delicious emotion of combined fright and excitement as the first black pellets of rain soak through the worn cotton of her clothes.

Lin was right. They do come back.

A storm rides in from the east.

~

Verity looks at the door of the row house she shares—shared—with her husband, David, and David's brother and sister-in-law.

Langston, traveling through the corridor of Verity's optic nerve to the brain cells that sort out the undifferentiated waves of light her retina receives into finite shapes bearing the meaningful attributes of color, height, and depth, realizes that vision is never ruled solely by biomechanics and reason, but also by fantasy. Verity looks at the door, waiting for Mr. Waterbury, but what she sees is like something in newsreel footage of towns in Europe or on Pacific islands during the war, a landscape of half houses fragile as twigs, their frames and unveiled interiors twisted into terrible Cheshire grins. She sees something she has never seen before: the edge of some terrible creature that most of the time hides itself, suddenly broken through into her tidy little world. She sees God, in a moment of insomniac restiveness—or as part of the slow, cruel grinding of his plan for eternity—shifting his vast body a tiny bit, and the tip of his elbow nudges Jacksonburg and lays it waste.

Am I going crazy? Verity wonders (*and Reynaldo with her*).

A knock on the door. Mr. Waterbury, proprietor of Waterbury Ice—J. B. to clients and favored employees, among whom David occasionally counted—has arrived. Of course Verity already knows most of the story of how David died (Del White couldn't wait to tell her when she got back from seeing the devastation at Aunt Plennie's), and the important part of the story is clear enough—he's dead—but Mr. Waterbury has come to tell her anyway. His idea of a condolence. J. B. Waterbury considers himself a southern gentleman, and as such takes a paternal interest in the well-being of his employees, the white ones of whom he considers as sons, the black ones who deliver ice to black neighborhoods as nice boys. His coming to speak to Verity is like an officer coming to the home of a serviceman to report the soldier's death.

Mr. Waterbury's face dramatically widens at the part of his jaw below his ears, so that his head seems to be partially inflated.

He wears a heavily starched white shirt with roomy, tentlike short sleeves, and shit-brown pants smudged with multiple creases. The shirt meets the pants in a pregnancy bulge that erases all suggestion of masculine organs. Not a thing of beauty. Not a sight to have to look at, respectfully, quietly, while being told of your husband's death. News of death should be told by a messenger bearing the soothing gift of some kind of beauty: beauty of face or body, or dignity of carriage, loveliness of voice. Jehu is uncomfortable, and when Jehu is uncomfortable his whiny way of talking becomes a flimsy saw slowly serrating its way through dry wood. "Uh . . . Davey . . . that is . . . your husband, Miss Gapstone . . . he was . . . his bravery . . ."

Verity is a bitch*!: Quentin, approvingly, amid the thunderous gallop of Verity's thoughts.* A quiver runs through Verity's body. She tries to listen again to what Mr. Waterbury is saying.

It's a simple enough story. On that rainy day—yesterday, but an infinite stretch of time ago—ice deliveries weren't running smoothly. Schedules were not followed. David should have been done with his shift by four. The storms didn't sweep in until shortly before six. Ted Lumbly, who generally delivered to the two or three small islands of black neighborhoods on the north side, hadn't finished his route in the south. David, desirous of overtime because it's the holidays, volunteered to help him out. He was slow getting where he was going. And Mrs. Pope, the woman in the house where it happened, lived at the top of a steep hill. Most of the damage that the tornado wreaked in residential areas had been visited upon houses on the tops of the hills. Most homes in the valleys or on the slopes, like Verity and David's own house, had been spared. (There may have been tornad*oes*. Official reports had not yet settled on the number, since as news of calamities spread—a movie house destroyed, the balcony crushing the late matinee attendees in the seats underneath, windows of two department stores shattered and a rain of glass scythed down on the sidewalks and streets below—sightings of ominous funnels dipping down from the sky have multiplied.) Probably not long after or long before Verity saw the lights flicker in her own house, and heard Cissy make a strange noise and yell at Credence and her daughter Shirley to get down flat on the floor, David, hefting an armful of boxed ice into Mrs. Pope's home, navigating the scurrying children, must also have seen the lights flicker. A moment later he must have heard a sound like a train bellowing. Mrs. Pope reported that her house shook violently. Mrs. Pope, who knew nothing of tornadoes, only storms, said that she was astonished, because she didn't live near the train tracks, and hadn't heard any thunder or seen lightning in over half an hour. When the house shook, Mrs. Pope fell down. It continued to shake as David lifted her up.

"And then she said . . . it was like a mouth opened up and . . . just spewed," J. B. Waterbury says. "Fire everywhere." As in many other houses, the stovepipes of the heaters had been shaken loose by the beating the houses took in the maelstrom of wind. Mrs. Pope kept the fires in each of her three potbellied heating stoves running high. At least two of her small-scale infernos must have escaped their cast-iron hearths, and the small wood-frame house, not much different, Verity imagines, from her own, combusted. In the ensuing melee—about which Mrs. Pope's recollection of details is not comprehensive—David pushed Mrs. Pope and two of her girls out of the house. They tumbled down the porch steps into a wet, wild chaos of flying trees and the slats and posts of fences dancing down the street. Mrs. Pope's middle child, a boy, emerged from the house screaming, his back aflame. "And before Davey could get out, the *whole* house went up," J. B. says, becoming very animated. "In flames."

Verity's wicker chair nearly falls before gravity rights it, so strong and athletic is her movement when she comes to her feet. She goes to one of the windows in the wall on the back of the house. The window latch, which David has promised—had promised—to oil, sticks again. Mr. Waterbury insists on helping, though Verity tells him she doesn't need help. Impatiently she watches the blunt tendons in Waterbury's forearms work as he struggles with the recalcitrant latch and then with lifting the window that she mistakenly painted to the sill weeks ago. Mr. Waterbury's muscles must never show except under strain, he's so fat. Verity thinks of David's arms, the beauty of them. Until now, she didn't know they were what beauty is: a smooth valley cut slantwise from his wrist almost all the way to his elbows. The skin soft like something spun, radiant like something polished. She has never before thought, *I love this about him, his arms, what a glorious wonder his arms are—were*. But now she does. She does now.

It's winter but it feels like autumn outside the window. The sky is clear, a gray blue painted with languorous strips of gold. There's no trace of yesterday's tempest. The air against Verity's face is clean, the bite of it cool, like a plunge in water on a hot day. Cold waltzing with warmth. Exactly the invisible process that gave birth to the storm and tornado that killed her husband.

Verity shivers as a draught of arctic wind ripples over her and slips its tendrils below her dress. Some prickled sense, whether smell or peripheral sight or perhaps something she hears, makes her look directly above her. Where something hovers.

A strange light, not part of the sky, not part of the spectrum of sunlight. A glow hanging on the air like the stubborn radiant edges of coals left in a dark hearth. The light hangs, quivers as if alive. It seems to mold itself into, and then quickly lose, a vague shape. Later, in trying to describe it more accurately to herself, she'll think of it as a mysterious residue, the faint register of singed particles like burning dust that might travel on the breeze in the vicinity of a great fire.

Verity greedily sucks in a deep, strong breath. She reaches forward to touch the light.

"What is it, Miz Gapstone?"

The light flares once, like a setting sun as it drops beneath the Earth's edge and then dissolves.

Verity feels her body buckle, feels laughter and sobs bubbling in her throat: it was the fading aura of her husband's spirit, that's what it was, vaulting outward in the last gasp of its mortal existence. David has been here. He came to her.

⁓

Is that real, *Aunt Reginia, did she really* see *him what's* real?

When Verity returns to her family's home—

There's a rustle of confusion and disquiet inside Verity, as Langston, Reginia, Sunder, Reynaldo, Quentin, and Mrs. Gillory try to get their bearings.

It is spring 1952. Verity sits in the parlor of the house in New Orleans where she was raised. She blinks and looks around her.

"You all right, bitch? Look like you had some little fit."

Lin, indefatigably coarse and unpleasant even when she's nurturing, looms up before Verity. There is a cold practical vigilance in Lin's black eyes. A sheen of moisture glistens in the ghost of a mustache frosting her upper lip. The sweat is honestly earned, from the hard work that keeps Lin busy and feeling useful; and the vigilance has to do with the nature of the hard work, which has been taking care of a household of sick people. "Look like somethin hitched you up, like you went blank, like there was a bubble that burst in yo brain. Or you was seein haints. Or the devil stuck his hand up your dress, or . . ."

Lin will run through a list of diagnoses, a mantra of woes and fanciful illnesses that seem both to entertain her and to help ward off trouble: if she can list all the grotesque possibilities, there's a good chance none of them will turn out to be true. Or so she's explained it, though not for the first time Verity questions the wisdom of having agreed to bring Lin along with her when she returned to her family's home in New Orleans. At the time, the night after Lin had shown up at the doorstep in Jacksonburg and made her offer, it had seemed comforting to imagine Lin traveling back with her and Credence. Lin reminded her of Plennie, and Plennie of David. The Greyhound bus journey south and west, the mirror of the trip she'd taken with David and Credence only a year earlier, would be less depressing with three together rather than the two of them alone, unbalanced like a tripod table with the third leg broken off.

I don't trust this Lin chick, Reynaldo says—and straightaway finds himself looking at Verity through Lin's eyes, and feeling her/himself bite down hard on the nail of her/his index finger so as to chew away the excess growth.

It's true that Verity has needed all the help she can get. Raising Credence alone is a wearisome and strangely infantilizing task that often dispirits her, making her feel she's incapable of matching wits with a child. Going back to work teaching in St. Michael's Academy, a school for black children in which she is one of only three instructors neither white nor a nun, does little to inspire her. And there's tending to her father and her aunt Ida, both of whom are swiftly dying of cancer.

This last concern Verity typically ranks third or fourth among the trials of her daily life, though family friends assume that it's her chief burden. Tending to the ill, watching people you love wither and decay, is not a business for those who love logic and reason and are accustomed to making sense of things, or for those who find their greatest peace in the beauty of literature, music, and the young, healthy human body. Since these are the fundaments upon which Verity's persona is known to be built, no one has expected her to last very long, especially since she's still reeling from David's death. But despite this Verity's been holding up surprisingly well.

No one except Lin knows that Verity has been in steady communication with the unseen, with the incorrectly called "dead" who are not dead, but merely Missing.

The Missing speak to Verity. In whispers of thought, but low and clear, like the first song of the birds that call to you beneath layers of early morning dreams. The Missing tell Verity about the condition of the world. They remind her that all across the planet, in every place and every thing, something is always missing. Everything in the world, everywhere, is an amputee.

"Well, Goddamn cornhole me!" Lin again. Verity tries to focus on Lin and finds that looking at her is like looking at a mouse running from you: you see it, but it's raced away so quickly that milliseconds after it's gone what you're really seeing—its twitching body and repulsive rubbery tail—is the memory recorded by your eye, the lingering electrical pattern in the brain that merely represents what you can identify as a mouse. "That ain whas wrong with you, is it, bitch!"

"It isn't?" Verity says, not at all clear which of the various maladies or forms of demonic possession Lin has decided explains her affliction.

"Naw. Finally I got it. You tryin to walk in two places at once. You takin the *middle* lanes."

So this is when Lin decides to school Verity in what she calls The Actual Shit: magic.

When Lin comes to her for her first lesson, Verity is full of eager confidence. "And what is this?" she asks as Lin hands her an amulet—a dusty, dun-colored circular case, hollow and bound with a rusted clasp, its face inscribed with a faded sinuous design reminiscent of the universal sign for woman. "Is it a mojo bag? Are you a practitioner of hoodoo? Or do you" (and here she smiles broadly, and drops into a whisper) "practice the Left-Hand Path of Conjure?"

Lin fixes Verity with an unpleasant look. "Egypt."

"Egyptian magic?"

Lin nods.

"Ancient Egyptian?"

"Kinda. Some from round 300, some up to 1100."

Verity founders. "The year 300?"

"Yeah. Put that on."

"Really? But how do you know anything about spells from late antiquity?"

"Put the necklace on, heifer. What you think, you the only one heard of Egypt? I *know*," Lin says, and gives her forehead a vigorous tap—a gesture that Verity puzzles over, wondering if there is any ritual significance to it.

Lin leads Verity in conducting rituals for healing eye problems, for protection against fever, for driving demons out of their hiding places in the viscera of the body, for performing baptisms of fire; incantations to heal with a concoction of oil and honey, to make a woman pregnant, protect a woman from rape by rendering a man impotent, to attract the honor of one's superiors and stir the fires of erotic passion in one's neighbors. There are curses to bring down the powers of darkness and spells to make a dog stop barking or give yourself a fine singing voice.

Of particular interest to Verity are rituals for summoning the heavenly powers or suing for the assistance of a powerful ghost. At first Verity thinks she's on solid ground with these, when Lin's first spell begins with, "I invoke you, great Isis, ruling in the perfect blackness, mistress of the gods of heaven from birth." But soon Lin wants her to invoke gods completely unfamiliar to her: Baktiotha, Shafriel, Abrasaxax, Bainchooch, Bathuriel, and Yao.

"Are these names Egyptian?" Verity asks. "They don't sound Egyptian to me. Are you *from* Egypt?"

"Sure. Egypt, Mississippi. Shut up."

Another time when practicing a summoning of a thundering power called Petbe the Requiter, Verity asks, "Do you ever use this to—contact the dead? To talk to Plennie?"

"Naw. She'd just be sayin the same thing she always say."

Verity performs all assigned tasks, no matter how bizarre or unappealing, with seriousness, with vigor and integrity. She does exactly as she's told, and more. She adds to some spells vocal and physical flourishes of her own, adornments of her particular style; she makes her own amulets and creates her own set of invocations. Like the good and great practitioners of any art, Verity improvises upon tradition.

All to no avail. None of Verity's spells work. Unlike Lin, whose banishings and healings and summonses shimmer with barely checked force, making vases roll from their shelves in the house and causing rogue strokes of lightning to burn obscure designs in the grass of the backyard, Verity demonstrates nothing in the way of power. She can't even throw a glamour to successfully beguile butterflies, a practice that only involves dusting your arm with powders made from plant nectar and from crushed butterfly-wing glands.

After a few weeks, Lin's facade of stony confidence falls. "I'll be fucked."

It is a night of the new moon, and the two of them, having put Credence to bed, are out on the back porch charting constellations. Lin is evidently in an oracular mood. Verity trembles, almost on the verge of tears. "The thing is," Lin says at last, "you *see*. But don't nothin *work*. You don't work."

Thenceforth Lin banishes Verity to the public library of the city. Her new assignment is to copy out all the spells she finds from whatever source her gifted sight guides her to peruse. "Might as well use that schoolin in The Fake Shit for something," she explains. "You write good, and sometimes jus writin a spell is a ritual, you know."

Verity, proud of her learning and her mind, aggrieved by her failure, takes to this task with ferocity. She haunts the libraries when not teaching and not busy at home, and when these infrequent gaps overlap with the scant hours allowed for Negroes to use the facilities. She comes to know the librarians, who when they see her striding through the doors with a stack of notebooks and Dewey decimal notations in her arms either become apoplectic at her nigger presumption or smile indulgently and send someone to check that the carrel they've set aside for "nonsense" books hasn't been colonized by someone unaware of Verity's special status. A few times Verity takes Credence with her, and he helps her fill her notebooks with copies. And often, when he doesn't go to the library with her, she gets home in time to teach him the words of the spells that she likes. "Listen to me," she has him repeat, "listen to me today, you who listen; listen to my words, you who hear; incline your ear to me quickly; listen to the words of my mouth, that you may hurry to send to me, quickly and immediately, rouse for me mighty lightning-eyed Petbe who is in the abyss. Yea, shake yourself today with your power, Petbe lightning-eyes, who is in the abyss. Raise up for me great Sachlabari, that he may come and accomplish my heart's wish and fulfill the desire of my soul."

Verity teaches eight-year-old Credence spells and words of

power in the same way that she once read him bedtime stories: as entertainment, as drowse-inducing lullaby, and as covert moral lesson. Magic has become important to her, and she hopes that her son might one day find it of use. Her failure hasn't made her doubt what she knows about the unseen, only strengthened her conviction. Her newfound wisdom is this: *magic* is the word for a successful wish, as *fakery* and *charlatanism* are the words for an unsuccessful one. Verity, with the severity her students at St. Michael's fear, bitterly judges herself to be a fake and charlatan. If she were a true worker of the craft she wouldn't be unhappy as she is now, she would have the key to happiness in her hand. Verity realizes now what it is that all her investigations, all her scholarly assiduity are about. All of it begins with and returns to a single, heartfelt, unfulfilled wish: to bring David back to her, and restore, tangibly, without the distortion of memory or the strain of meditated belief, everything that is missing.

Nineteen-fifty-three.

A blustery evening in late July finds Verity approaching home from an easterly direction. The sky has partitioned, arranging the pages of time side by side, simultaneously legible. The setting sun leaves the skies above the end of her block aflame in layers of color: ruddy and effulgent rose crests below a melancholy rim of amber—is that the present, the now of time, or have we already turned away, the sun revolved into the sea, while the true present hovers directly over her head, where the flare of violet dims and darkens as the sun's rays rapidly retract? Behind Verity the stars that try to hide themselves during the day begin to litter a fast-growing field of indigo that seems rich with dark wisdom—a past that is always there, that becomes present and promises, eternally, its immense, unchartable future.

Verity's eyes seem to warble a bit in their sockets—eyestrain, no doubt, brought on by six long hours of poring over books in a badly lit corner of a library—and her hair has fallen flat in the wet air. Humidity is Louisiana's curse, the veins of the city slosh with atmospheric moisture as if besotted. But Verity likes it. She likes her clothes clinging to her skin, the constant reminder of her body. She likes the way smells linger on the air in humid weather—how the bite of cigarette smoke and the reek of garbage are more potent on evenings like this, and how ladies' perfumes designed to skip through the senses as a subliminal invitation become heavy, the rutting musk of estrus.

Musk? Verity scents perfume as she opens the gate of her fence and moves toward her front door. Lin opens the windows wide when she cooks, so you can always smell dinner before you see it. Tonight onions lie heavy on the air—and woman. Lin doesn't wear perfume, doesn't smell like a woman. Neither do Lin's running buddies, who usually stink of seawater and cigars. Instinctively guarded, Verity steps inside and crosses the dark foyer into the small living room bathed in twilight streaming through the tall, narrow windows.

She finds, as she expects, guests. The glow from the kitchen lights gives them a soft-focus spotlight. But Verity doesn't expect white people.

An older woman—clear enough from the gray hair, though her body seems youthful and fit, broad shouldered and broad chested, with a small waist and small hips, dressed in a blue shirt and khaki pants: dressed a bit like a man (Lin must love that)—bounces Credence on her knee. Credence is giggling and doesn't even notice his mother until the gray-haired woman smiles and greets her—too casually, as if momentarily confounded by the puzzle of how one greets a Negro woman in the Negro woman's home. A thin bald man, his clothing obscured by Lin's apron but his blue eyes blazingly clear, has emerged from the kitchen. Unlike the woman, he has come with the express purpose of greeting Verity; this is clear by the triumphant air of purpose with which he strides toward her, wooden spoon in hand. He stops short, smiles—his face is wan and thin, the skin of his neck latticed with faint lines of blue, but his jaw is strong and his nose is ramrod straight, fit for the profile of a presidential portrait.

My grandparents! *shrills Mrs. Gillory.*

Verity feels slightly faint for a moment before she takes his proffered hand.

The man bows. He actually bows. "Good evening, maestra," he says: deeper voice than Verity expects. "Aden Rose."

The woman's voice is also deep, but full of cracks where his is smooth. Cracks of pique, Verity gathers. "Oh for goodness' sake, Aden. She's not *Italian*, she's not *Spanish*. This is New *Orleans*. At least speak French if you're going to be pretentious."

Aden Rose's chin moves slightly in the woman's direction, but rather than looking at her he aims the expression of mixed annoyance and bemusement on his face toward Verity. "Forgive my wife, Mrs. Gapstone. Atalanta's difficult to tolerate, but ever since she bewitched me I haven't been able to get rid of her." At which Atalanta rolls her eyes. "And I hope you'll forgive us invading your kitchen this way. You were recommended to us by John Sante, at the public library, you know him?"

Verity does: Sante, a former Catholic become devout Methodist. Works nights, and likes her—perhaps for the wrong reasons. Very helpful. Usually.

"We don't like to arrive unannounced at a person's doorstep without bringing something to make our presence worthwhile, so, with Lin's permission, we're making fish soup Provençale—*soupe de poisson*, excuse me. Lovely recipe we've learned. They serve this in bistros in every little port town in the south of France. You see, Attie, I have my cultural references properly aligned after all."

"Yes, your pretentiousness is exactly on target. Congratulations. But do please forgive me, Mrs. Gapstone. I didn't properly introduce myself. Atalanta Rose, of course. Credence dear," she says, suddenly shifting her attention, "won't you show me your voodoo dolls?"

Aden smiles and lowers the volume of his voice. "Credence has been complaining about the stench of the garlic and fennel."

That bit about Credence showing Atalanta voodoo dolls (which Lin has given him, and ought not to have done) is about to grow a thorn or two on Verity's reply, when suddenly Lin has slid snakelike between her and Aden. "Sante sent 'em over here to talk to a *expert*." There's a quirk in Lin's mouth that's full of mischief and suppressed laughter. "They want you to tell 'em 'bout *magic*."

~

So begins Verity's brief but fecund association with Aden and Atalanta Rose, a pair of wealthy New York occultists who scour the hemispheres, thirsty for the most meager scrap of magical knowledge.

The three converse warily at first. Despite their show of gastronomic generosity and charm, the Roses are skeptical about whether Verity can help them. For her part Verity doesn't gladly suffer being doubted or tested, and a deep learning that passes itself off as instinct makes her recoil from sharing secrets with white people. But Lin allowed the Roses into the house, an unusual event no matter who the visitor; generally Lin is as welcoming as an ill-tempered Doberman. Unusual behavior in Lin is something to pay attention to and respect: often she's trying to teach you something by it.

The Roses show Verity a copy of their bound, unpublished manuscript, *Hex*. Verity peruses a few pages and instantly can tell them that several of the spells they've transcribed don't look right, indeed may be wrong altogether. They interrogate her about the specifics, and Verity responds with such robust confidence—her scholarly arrogance asserting itself—that they find themselves convinced. Without even asking for permission, Verity takes a pen and begins furiously making notations. Lin hovers around her, offering grunts or humming noises (approval or disapproval) each time Verity looks to her for corroboration.

"But why would anyone invoke the god Min for an erotic enchantment?" Atalanta demands as she reads Verity's notes. "Min governs storms, doesn't he? Storms signify destruction, wrath. Surely the theory behind a love spell would be that the caster of the spell gathers up all his psychic energy in a kind of great invisible *fist*, and uses it to *umph! grab* the person he desires. I would think—"

"No, no, no, you totally misunderstand the *metaphysics* of it!" Verity thunders.

The two women are getting on famously, which shocks them both. Verity generally would be cautious of speaking so freely with the nuns at St. Michael's, the only truly educated white women with whom she's acquainted. And though Aden has a romantic attachment to the colored people, Atalanta does not as a rule share it. She profoundly respects the darker races as peoples, as cultures, of course, but rarely likes them individually. Nevertheless, Verity and Atalanta find they have a similar propensity to enjoy the twists and turns, the thicknesses and entanglements, of theory. The practice and specific effects of spells and potions don't intrigue them nearly as much as the unspoken laws of the nature of the universe that spells and potions assume.

"Min is a god of conquest, who impregnates the spell-caster's object of desire with his divine semen, so that when the person bears the child, metaphysically speaking of course, she or he has been conquered, in a sense wed—"

"Ablanatanalba!" Credence shouts.

He beams proudly. Mission accomplished: nobody's been paying much attention to his voodoo dolls, but all eyes are on him now.

"Isn't that a palindrome?" Aden Rose says. He speaks proudly, as if Credence were his own son and had mastered some daunting skill of hand-eye coordination. "The same said backwards and forwards, right, Credence?"

"Obviously," Atalanta agrees. "And it's a word of power, isn't it, Verity?"

Verity's not listening. She's looking: at a tall, dark figure standing between Atalanta and Aden, his lower torso and long legs occupying the same space as the Roses' arms. His upper torso, broad shoulders, neck, and head are clearly visible, though nothing of the shape blocks her sight of the dining room wall directly behind him. The figure moves only a little but seems to carry himself in a dignified way, and Verity is certain he is handsome, though she cannot make out features since he seems woven from shadow. His hands rest on the shoulders of Aden and Atalanta. Lamplight seems to pierce his ethereal substance and beam through the dark slits of his eyes—yet somehow, she knows, his eyes are deeply sad.

David?

Quick as a mouse scuttling from view the light slides away, and there in the flesh Verity sees little Credence, his arms straining as he reaches up to catch the Roses' hands and climb up on the table to see what all the fuss is about. She wonders that she hadn't heard him singing until this moment, because in loud joy (now that he has everyone's attention) he's belting out a rather scabrous little tune the neighbors' children must have taught him.

"Verity?" Atalanta repeats.

"Did you see, Lin?" Verity whispers.

"What? Big Credence?" Lin says loudly.

Aden and Atalanta stare in bewilderment.

Ah. Verity's seen the shadow of her son as a grown man. She has had her first bona fide magical vision—or her second, if what she'd seen from the window of the house in Jacksonburg wasn't something she'd observed with her naked eye, but with second sight.

It's clear, then, that Credence, or Credence's spirit, is bonded in some way to Aden and Atalanta.

Verity's renewed curiosity about the Roses warms the rest of the evening. While they spoon bowls from Aden's fish stew (he complains that he forgot the orange zest, and that the quality of the redfish and bluefish he bought at market could be better, but really, it's delicious) and sally through Verity's supply of rum, they thrash through everything: theosophies and cosmogonies, the origins of all the pantheons of gods, the various mystical traditions of the East. Verity marvels at the breadth of the Roses' knowledge. For that reason alone she could like them. They know so much more than she's learned in her library surveys of the spirit world, which the conversation sometimes makes her feel are unforgivably dilettantish. Mostly, though, she feels the pleasure of the exchange, the way it lightens her spirit even as the rum lightens her brain of its cells. In the midst of debate about animism, drunkenly, almost with enthusiasm, allowing the coziness of her intellectual congress with them to lay a dizzying thrill-seeker bridge over the canyons of grief and fury she might otherwise tumble into, Verity finds herself revealing it all—everything, even things she doesn't ever voice to Lin because Lin always seems to know already: she tells Atalanta and Aden about David, and her father and her aunt, about her mother who'd left her father and died in the Detroit riots of '43, and about her theory, her belief: about the Missing, and how no one dead is truly gone, how the unseen persists in full measure with the seen, how the whole world *looks* and feels like an amputee torn from its other half, but it isn't, it isn't true.

There is a silence when Verity finishes.

Atalanta reaches out to grip Verity's hand. An adult touch. Not like Credence's touch, not soft, not grasping, needing, but worn and grooved with its own life. Lin rarely touches Verity, as if to do so would break some taboo, compromise protocols of respect to be followed between housekeeper and home-owner, teacher and student. Perhaps this is why the feeling of Atalanta's hand makes Verity tremble, makes her sway on her bridge and peer down over the slender rope rail. She thinks of David and of that other form of happiness that she's missed: his body, its heft and aroma (cedar, from the trunk she kept his clothes in, and the paprika of his sweat): beside her, hot and greedy inside her.

"I am so very sorry for your loss, Verity. I sometimes believe human life is like living under some kind of scourge. Only the spirit lasts. To lose one's husband, the father of one's child . . ." Atalanta shakes her head. "But, my dear!" she says, shifting abruptly back into the known. "Your theory reminds me of the Day of Return!"

At this, Lin, quietly shelling pistachios as is her wont after dinner, comes to attention.

"Oh, it's magnificent," Aden enthuses. "Kind of a variation on the Brazilian religious custom of honoring the sea goddess Yemanja by sending offerings out to sea. Yemanja's very vain, so usually they're supposed to send soap and mirrors and combs to her. That way she keeps the seas calm for the fishermen."

"I've heard of that," Verity sniffs, distracted by the lingering imprint of Atalanta's withdrawn warmth across her knuckles.

"The Day of Return is different. Not just an offering to Yemanja, although I think she's part of it, too. They give all kinds of gifts, and it seems to be associated with some myth of slavery, best I can tell. The story behind it has a wall of storms dividing this world from the next, and a lost homeland on the other side of the storms. On the Day of Return, people give back to the sea from which they believe they came—historically accurate as far as that goes." Aden smiles disarmingly, as if he were wasting their time with something unworthy of discussion.

Verity looks at Lin, whose eyes are on her pile of pistachio shells but whose fingers aren't moving and whose chest isn't rising and falling with breath. A wall of storms? Could this be the same tradition as old Aunt Plennie's stories, the ones she used to tell Verity when she'd visit her to take baths? "Why does my theory remind you of this ceremony?" Verity asks Atalanta.

Atalanta shrugs. It's obvious. "Because the celebrants give back to the sea in order to ask for the return of what they've lost. They ask for the return of that whole world, Over There. I think of it as a ceremony for everybody's lost world. Our private Atlantises, our gardens of Eden. Our departed loved ones."

"We should take her," Aden says. He looks inquiringly at both Atalanta and Verity. "I mean, if you're going to do this job for us, help us with our manuscript—" He becomes animated. "You should see it, Verity. Hundreds, sometimes thousands of people, dressed up in the most fantastic ways, they mob the beach like mad, the water is filled with their offerings. Like something out of a fairy tale. They do it in August, don't they, Attie?"

"Where?" Verity asks.

"The third week of August," Atalanta answers. "On a little Caribbean island called Yaruma. People from all around come to it, though."

"No shit."

Verity grimaces at Lin's coarseness. Lin chews a pistachio, knocking its hard but pliant flesh between her teeth noisily as she speaks. "I hearda that island."

They travel leisurely via the Roses' yacht, the *Roan*. For Verity there is a surprising luxuriousness in this, a disorienting sense of possibility she's never felt before. Owning your home, even having a live-in housekeeper as she's had for the past months, is an entirely different stratum of privilege; here on the water, with the Roses' cook below and captain above deck, the sun presiding like some ever-beneficent simple god who requires nothing whatsoever of his worshippers, it's as though Verity's climbed to a new plateau of existence, one she had never known existed before. It frightens her a little, this feeling, but she welcomes it for what it is: a new wind blowing.

While Lin—having the opposite experience of sea travel—lies under her covers in her cabin, and while Credence pesters the Roses with (it seems to Verity) a nigh infinite series of questions that fasten one to the next until they eventually become almost a chain, immobilizing and subduing them as he no doubt intends, Verity emends the errors of *Hex*. When this grows too tedious, she studies what little there is to study about the island of Yaruma in the books she's taken from the library. Yaruma, known for its slender, pristine white coasts, is a tiny, tiny possession of the

English crown among the Leeward Islands in the Caribbean. It lies a few miles south of Antigua and some twenty miles northeast of Montserrat. Little known, generally unmarked or even absent on the maps, Yaruma was once a locale used by shrewd sailors to conduct business without interference from the navies of England, the United States, and Spain. For a brief, swashbuckling period of its mostly somnolent history it became a market for pirates' trade; boats and small ships docked in its minuscule port or dropped anchor in the deep, deep fathoms of its coves, arriving and departing under cover of darkness. The capital, Libertytown, on the western side of the island, long the forgotten redoubt of a forgotten plantation state, was transformed in the years when piracy flourished, developing a reputation as a dangerous den of thievery, wanton murder, and wildly unchecked prostitution. The current population, numbering probably less than fifty thousand, consists of the descendants of slaves and slave owners and pirates and prostitutes, and a sizeable contingent of late-nineteenth-century emigrants from Antigua and Barbuda, who apparently left the neighboring islands or were chased out due to an obscure religious schism. Yaruma receives a notation in a terrible book published in 1930 called *Voodoo in Paradise* as the home of a peculiar variant of "Catholic voodoo" and the site of a strange "quasi-Ethiopianist" ritual called the Day of Return.

Present sources of income on Yaruma: food processing and the old standbys, rum, cotton, and sugar.

They arrive in the hours before dawn. "Perfect timing," says Aden.

Libertytown seems to run almost into the sea, as if determined to leave the humped hills behind it undisturbed. The air is chill, the cloud cover smothering. "It's so quiet," Verity says.

"No one's here, probably," Aden explains. "The procession

begins around midnight. The whole town empties. You could rob these people blind right now, if you wanted. If they had anything worth stealing."

He has them take flashlights and camping provisions from the boat. It would only take about an hour and a half to reach the eastern side of Yaruma, but Aden wants to be prepared, in case they arrive early, or the ceremony doesn't happen as planned. "I've been to three of these," he explains. "The Babalawos or Houngans often say conditions aren't right—the right kind of wind isn't blowing in, a storm isn't exactly close enough or far enough—and then you can end up on the beach for days with everyone, waiting."

He leads Atalanta, Verity, Lin, and little Credence through the town's abandoned streets, where doors to homes sometimes stand ajar, opened onto soft, eerily still dusky shadows of chairs and tables and beds within. They trudge past a firehouse and a serene green midtown square ringed with shuttered shops until they come to where Libertytown abruptly dies, becoming a thick forest that rises steeply up a duo of burly hills. "There's a road here, isn't there, Attie?" Aden says, with an uncertainty that makes Verity fearful. She doesn't like the dark, the bugs, the immensity of living earth out there that she cannot see (though Lin, happy to be on dry land at last, seems fearless enough). They follow cautiously behind him, and after a great deal of effort and sweating and Credence's excited whooping, they're high up and have emerged from corridors of shadow to be able to see the mulish clouds as they amble above the tops of the trees at the summit. "Look!" Verity says.

They're traveling a ridge on the north face of the hill, and below can discern the outlines of a capacious lane, so clear of foliage and brush that it looks almost white in the darkness. It winds along the base of the slope. "That must be your road, Aden," Atalanta says. "I knew this didn't seem familiar."

"What's that?" Lin murmurs.

As she speaks, they all see it: the outlines of the lane shift, buckling and reforming. What appears to be a road is actually rows and rows of people, many dressed in white or light colors, walking slowly and close together. A long thick line of thousands of mist-shrouded shapes trail below them. Occasional moonlight tears strips from the fuzzy gloom to illuminate yellow and red and purple colors like eruptions. The columns pass along the base of the hills down, down, down into a cleft between them that leads to—so Aden and the rest surmise, from the undifferentiated flat blackness of the sight—the Atlantic.

Like a biblical exodus, Verity thinks, and her excitement mounts.

It takes more than an hour to follow the path down from the summit of the slope. When Aden tires, Lin barrels ahead and leads them confidently along a rough sloping avenue of thick-boled trees whose shadowy branches curve like the tusks of mastodons. Soon the avenue dies away. Lin pushes along its trajectory into the largely pathless bush choked with growth. Verity carries a struggling and complaining Credence. Atalanta scrapes her ankle on a stinging plant and begins to grouse. "Just a little farther," Aden calls cheerfully from the back of the pack.

The land has begun to climb a little again when Lin turns sharply from the direction they've been following, and, to Verity's horror, walks straight over the side of a low cliff and drops out of sight.

Verity rushes forward, to find Lin, unharmed, on a bare plateau like a shelf in the slope of the hill, searching over the edge with the rays of her flashlight. They have emerged from the trees and brush and stand only a hundred yards from the base of the hill.

"Oh, I remember this. This is one of my favorite beaches," Aden says when he catches up. He points down, and Verity can see in the beam of her flashlight a narrow lawn of white sand, which shines as if it were dusted with kernels of ice. She can hear the wind whipping the waves beyond. The world has shifted during their dark trek. The sea that was below them seems to have risen, to loom up startlingly near.

"Breathe in the air. Can you feel it? The enchantment?" whispers Aden.

"Just as dawn breaks," Atalanta says. For once there's almost no trace of sarcasm in her tone. "Let's go down."

The mist and cloud cover of the night dissolve, and they see the hordes of worshippers and gawkers and celebrants milling on the sand, striding up in large gangs from the south and down in formation like a marching band from farther north. As they join them, they see old women, their heads elongated by high caftans of blazing white, and old men wearing the long-discontinued epaulets of uniforms and rusty medals of forgotten wars. In the laps of the old women who sit upon the shore waiting for the sun to break free from the girdling edge of the sea there are candied violets and tiny effigies of the saints, and jewelry wrought from the leavings of industry and fashioned painstakingly by their own hands, and portraits of loved ones whom they wish to see again: children dead, lovers lost, sisters and brothers murdered, forebears captured and sold into slavery in the past, and contemporaries whose time and bodies are held as collateral for debt payment by the enslaving sugar and cotton companies today: all are offerings to the Holy Virgin Mother, to Jesus the Risen and Moses the Lawgiver, to Allah and the Holy Spirit, to Yemanja and Olokun and Olorun, even to goddesses like Isis and Cybele, and some even to a deity called the Dragon Mother Ashrar. Devotees of all faiths both ancient and newly minted observe the Day of Return. These photographs and trinkets are gathered in beribboned canisters that are like the boats that the rich children for whom they cook and clean on Antigua and Barbuda and farther-flung places make to sail in their tubs: Verity can see, on the canister of the woman nearest her, the shape of a prow is there, if she looks closely, and a kind of stern.

Aden informs her that as a rule the men think themselves above such sentimentality. To be a man and observe the Day is to offer proof of one's craftsmanship, and so the old men come to the slender beaches in the darkness of morning, their hands laden with all manner of intricately reproduced models of ships: schooners, clippers, battleships, canoes, sculls, yachts, catamarans, and dinghies, even shapes that look like garbage scows piled with small heaps of burning refuse certain to engulf the model itself. Verity sees a large black model with a death's-head prow and ballooning black sails, with the red words SLAVE SHIP lettered in black-headed nails on the side; and Credence is fascinated by an ingenious model that resembles drawings of Noah's Ark, with little figures at the top carrying tiny umbrellas. They find, too, a disquieting model with great masts and sails, and small brown dolls suspended from wire attached to the masts, with manacles painted on their wrists and ankles—the dolls dangle as if frozen by the attention of their audience in postures of mid-jump, and as its maker tests the model by letting it bob for a moment on the slow gentle waves, the jumping figures bounce, performing a kind of grotesque ballet.

Not only the old are there to give offerings, but the middle-aged and the young, too, matrons and two different men claiming to be the mayor and several who say they are police, homeless cutpurses and slatterns of the alleys, schoolchildren, servants, shopkeepers, market-stall merchants, bankers, even West Indian sailors of the British Navy on shore leave (who come mostly to scout the pretty young women), and, in numbers that outstrip their proportion in the general populace and threaten to engulf the more respectable throng, a mob the others call abominations and nefarious sinners, attired outrageously in shirts without pants, pants that cling to their groins, codpieces from out of the olden days, sequined evening gowns, and red and purple caftans adorned with puffery and glitter as if to mock the solemnity of the old women's fashions. The abominations sport hats that have brims like the bottoms of ships, and each of them Verity asks tells her that by tradition they keep deadly secret what is hidden beneath the towers of those hats: speculation, most of it disrespectful, runs to flowery poems for "husbands" who have betrayed them for the love of their real wives, entreaties to bring the strapping young cane cutters who've rebuffed them under their erotic dominion, wishes for rich playboys in search of catamites, hopes to be swept away on the Day of Return to countries abundant with handsome and virile lovers.

More numerous than the abominations are the workers from the food-processing plants and the sugar-company employees, who arrive late. They troop in under the eyes of their shift captains and watchdogs, and bring, according to the whim of their employers, who own everything the workers possess, trinkets from the fields or from the rough weed-fenced cabins they share, in shapes made from paper or paper mixtures rougher in form even than the boats the old women carry. All know what the workers give, even their masters who permit them to come (or cannot prevent them): they offer tokens of their hearts, silent cries for a freedom and self-mastery they dream floats out there beyond the Mists, beyond the walls of time, in that other world lost to them and their forebears centuries ago.

At last the sun, as if reluctantly waking from watery sleep, lazily shakes off the fetters of the horizon, and a call goes up from the gathered crowds—not so much a shout or a word, but a murmur deep and wide and dolorous and resonant as the sound of the waves slashing against the sand at their feet. Verity shudders to hear it. She is surprised to find tears on her face, and on many others' as well, when, like seals returning to the sea, the folk wade out into the surf until it thrashes their knees. The water gets deep fast; less than a few yards out, tall men are almost to their necks. The thousands lift their gifts up to the rising star and then hold them out toward the sea. And then they all set their gifts upon the unsettled surface of the ocean, set them as they would set babes into rocking cradles, and swiftly then they turn their backs and come back to the beach. Not until their feet are free from the lapping of the water do they turn again and look upon what they've given away and cannot, on peril of death and madness and the condemnation of all the gods, take back: there, all across the water, for miles up and down the coast, far as man or woman can see, the little ships, the little boats, the hats, the tiny rafts, the boxes, bobbing, bobbing, an armada of miniatures afloat on water swiftly turning blue from black, the sun casting its light slantwise across their fragile assembled bodies. At first the flotilla seems to lie becalmed. Perhaps, like the first couple in the old stories, the ships fear to be sundered from the hands of their makers, or like the Argive ships assembled to lay siege to Troy the offerings are stymied by a contrary wind blown by an angry deity. But slowly the ships make their peace with wind and wave and begin to push away. Slowly, then faster, and yet faster still. Verity can imagine them being tugged by invisible tethers held by a nation of receivers in wait across the trackless miles.

Finally—hours later, with the sun moving toward its height—the last offering slips over the horizon and is gone.

"Fascinating, isn't it?" Aden says. He hasn't spoken in hours, it seems. "You'd think the Day's offerings just get nibbled by fish and gradually sink and get digested by the ocean, or come back with the tide. But I've been around these waters after, and don't see any. I mean—nothing. And they never seem to wash up, either. So where do they go, then?"

Verity dries her eyes. She grabs hold of Lin's elbow. "Do you think we should have sent something? For Plennie and David? I thought about it, I just . . ."

Lin's wiping her cheeks, too. She looks small and old in the morning light, stripped bare somehow. "Maybe you should," she answers. Lin lets her eyes rest on Verity's, linger and float on and in the depths of them. She touches Verity on the arm and squeezes. And then she turns her back to the sea and begins with thousands of others the slow trek up the narrow path toward the road between the hills.

But Verity stays a while longer. Deciding.

So where do the offerings go, then? Someplace, obviously. They don't just—disappear. Everything is conserved: matter, energy. Likewise, as she had learned, the dead. Surely, too, these offerings, these tiny ships.

("What if *you* the one lost?" Plennie had wondered.)

They go back. They are *pulled* back. By the Missing. Through the wall of storms that curtains this world from the old and new worlds always waiting alongside it.

All her life—which is all she knows and thus all the world there is or ever was or will be—can be described as a preposition: by, in, through, to, of, for. She needed to see the offerings and the ceremony to understand this, she needed something visual and psychic to anchor the intellectual realization in her true place of knowing, but now she feels it, now she can *work*. Everything, all her life, exists as, is, between states, between moments, between worlds, and tethered to both the point of departure and the intended arrival. Living in and living as a corridor, a passage:

you never really arrive anywhere. Always she passes back and forth from one into the other, like the tiny ships, released from a loving hand and bobbing forward, fast or slow, over and through the medium of passage. The medium through which she travels is the world, as it appears; just as the sea is the wake of the tiny ships' movement, that which seems to carry you forward or backward but which is also what you create by moving.

And as you arrive noplace in particular, you go (or can go) everywhere, for noplace cannot be separated from anyplace. The connecting threads are not only between everyone, but between all times, all places. All is movement. Moving is what everything is; all.

This is what Plennie had meant, what she'd been trying to reason out.

"It ain't over." Lin, warning from the past. "You know how it is with these storms. They always come back."

Verity makes her decision. She has known for years now that she would have to test her theory—ever since David, since she saw him glowing bright, making gold fire of the winter air above her head. She required only the right laboratory, the proper conditions.

The time is now. It will be tonight.

That night, white sand beneath her feet, Lin at her side, awash in cold, flogged by rain, the heaviness, the presence, the blackness, falls upon Verity, gathers her in crushing arms—

What the fuck Damn that was Hey Rey you were in Lin how was

26

Credence Gapstone arrives in Los Angeles in June 1971. (*But what happened Where oh it's him now It's Damian's father*) It is a new decade, and thus, as the six of them know from the vantage point of a future Credence cannot imagine, new experiments in ways of living, new music, new political alliances are beginning to bob up above the waters. Credence's life, too, will change. He is blind to this, as he is blind to the many discordant layers of consciousness that inhabit him as he settles into a taxi. He is blind to all futures, since his mind, his heart, as if arrested in a seizure, seethes with the pain of the recent past.

Credence has come to L.A. like other pilgrims to the Great West, seeking freedom. The plane ticket and the weeks of indolence he expects to enjoy will cost him a good chunk of the money Aden Rose gave him (he wouldn't call him *Mister* Rose now, no, never again). He spends a portion of the money on a few days in a beachside four-star hotel. The bellboys think that he may be an actor. There is an ethereal beauty about Credence that leads them to imagine he is exotic. He is tall and slender, his color dark in a way that doesn't threaten but allures with the promise of mysterious knowledge locked in its depths. His large eyes look almost inflated, childishly wide with amazement and sadness both.

Credence passes most of his vacation in his hotel room, grieving for the life he'd tried and failed to make with the Panthers. There are Panthers here in L.A., too, but they're at war with police more barbaric than the cops in New Haven, and at war with another black group, as well. The whole thing disgusts him, so much so that he doesn't want anything more to do with black people. He lies when he tells himself this, lies still more when he carves the words like a motto into the table in his room and giggles in satisfaction to think that someone will read I DON'T WANT NOTHING MORE TO DO WITH NO GODDAMN *BLACKS* and fear that a race war is coming. He lies because what he really means is that he hates Malachai Reynolds, and he hates the Panthers and the so-called Cats and Oliver. But he hates Oliver least of all. Oliver at least *won*. Mostly he hates himself for loving all the people who had given him so much cause to hate them. He recognizes this truth already, even as he carves the words, even as, like the prim, well-trained valet he is, he brushes the flakes of wood from the table with his hand and ushers the evidence of his sacrilege into a wastebasket.

On the fourth evening of his stay, Credence begins to discover that grief isn't a vaccine against going stir-crazy, so he takes himself out of his room and ambles down to one of the beaches that lie at the foot of the hotel. It takes great effort for him to bear the glances of fellow beachgoers, to bear the glare of the setting sun and the palpable sense, like stilettos pricking his skin, that he is naked to the world, that everyone knows him for the hateworthy thing he is. At last he finds a quiet spot. He collapses to the sand and tries halfheartedly to bury his legs in it. He's surprised to find himself getting cold. Isn't this supposed to be warm, sunny California? He reaches for a newspaper somebody left pinned beneath a rock, figuring he'll cover himself up like a hobo and then maybe he'll be carted off by the police and sent to a secret labor camp and there finally end it all. He wrestles a while with this scenario, trying to decide whether it's dire enough. Then, as he struggles to keep the flimsy newsprint sheets from flying off on the breeze, in the darkening twilight he catches sight of an upside-down name lying across his chest.

"Millionaire Writer Found Murdered. Occult expert Aden Rose courted danger, police say."

Credence snatches the paper off him. The story is finished in three slender paragraphs: Aden Rose was strangled to death outside a highway truck stop, where he'd apparently stopped on the way to one of his residences in New Haven, not far from his alma mater, Yale University, from which he graduated in 1918. No witnesses have as yet come forward. Rose's wife, Atalanta, disappeared in an Atlantic storm while flying a plane two years ago, and thus his sole inheritors are a grown daughter, Anne, a son-in-law, Roland Ansley, and a granddaughter, Roan.

The news spins Credence around, makes him feel, in one instant, that a world that has already in the past few days thinned to a gossamer tissue of regret is now wholly unreal, no more dense than a plume of smoke. The thought of Aden lying on the ground at some truck stop, Aden's neck that was already shriveled and gullied by age now wrung and twisted like a rope of taffy, his corpse growing cold on an unlit pyre of cigarette butts and greasy burger wrappers and dried piss, dizzies Credence: it gives him such a warm surge of perverse satisfaction that he almost can't be certain he didn't commit the murder himself. He'd wished it to happen, many times. But the warmth fades rapidly. It's too easy for Credence to imagine how it must have been for Aden, meeting his Maker at the violent hands of another.

The night Credence and Aden parted ways was the same night the Cats exiled Credence. They'd "found out"—like people didn't already know from the way he talked and how he conducted himself—that he was "funny." Why all of a sudden did they have to call him out like that? And then Malachai had to get manly, and start talking about kicking his ass to teach him a lesson, and then had done so much talking about it that he couldn't get out of the situation without throwing some punches and kicks. Credence could have fought back, but he'd just lain there and taken it. He could have stood up, shown them a thing or two of what he'd learned in all those years of traveling up and down the globe. Some capoeira, maybe, or some hapkido. But he just lay there, and it was almost as if he watched it happen: the fists and the boots and the folks gathered close around the way dogs do when they chase down the weak one who smells of fear, the shouting, clapping, hooting, the panting so loud in his ears it sounded orgasmic.

Pulped and discarded like some old jack-o'-lantern that's served its purpose, Credence had staggered, limped, and crawled all the way back to the house he was staying in, more than twenty blocks away. The pain was so *large*, so everywhere and everything, that his mind went soft as slush, and, purged of all articulate thought, a part of him watched, without judgment, with approval even, the few people he passed who shrank away when they saw him, as if the blood running from cuts on his face and body were the marks of some terrible contagious disease. By the time he made it to the house, he actually had begun to feel diseased. Wasn't it in fact a kind of disease to be unloved by the people whom you wanted to love you? Wasn't it at least a bona fide curse? He'd wondered what his mother might have said about this, if she'd lived to see it; she'd had a penchant, a gift really, for explaining simple emotional states as if they were the consequences of sorcery: if he came home from school distraught because the other children had teased him for his big nose (which was like his mother's; he knows this from the photos he's seen in the old house, not from memory) or because they'd said he talked like a girl, his mother would tell him not to worry, it wasn't his fault. She'd say something like, "It must be that I mispronounced the third line of a spell I cast this morning. You got caught in the fallout of a bad incantation." And then she'd have him recite the spell with her correctly, so that all the unhappy events would be erased and all the bad feelings would go away.

But then she'd been killed, or run off, or drowned, and he had no one to help him conjure away the pain.

Now, long after the initial spasm of fury at Malachai has passed, Credence can't say for sure whether he's cursed. But that night a week and a half ago he was almost certain he was. Collapsed on the bed watching Aden Rose scurry between the bathroom and the bedroom with bandages and tourniquets and water and painkillers, the despair and rage of living under that scourge had bubbled up and made Credence let the old man have it.

"You fucked it all up, you cock-suckin son of a bitch," was how Credence started off. The words were coming from elsewhere, pumped into him and through him via intravenous tube. "You put me under a curse, you animal! You go poking around in black folks' business, running around the South and the Caribbean when folks got lynched for talking the wrong way to white people, hunting up *magic* and *spells* and bullshit for some asinine-ass book! Fuck you! You took me away from my home and my family! My people! Now look what's happened!"

The tears that he didn't want to come came anyway, and they stung the cuts on his cheeks, and each grimace, every emphatic movement of the muscles of his face as he cursed broke the new scabs. "I'm nothing!" he shouted. Credence pulled himself up from the bed just enough to pound on the frail old man with his fists. Aden stumbled backward, then came forward for more, determined to daub the cuts with a cloth drenched in hydrogen peroxide. Aden kept his eyes somewhere far away from Credence's face.

"I don't belong to anybody!" Credence sobbed.

When Aden finally spoke, he spoke almost as if he were a clergyman offering counsel, as if his responses were merely another form of ministration. "Your mother asked us to take care of you, Credence. She—she—she left us instructions, a note. She must have expected to die. She may have been ill. She knew not all whites are bad, Credence. Otherwise why would she have chosen to tell us her secrets as she did? She helped us enormously, and in return she asked that we help you."

"Help me? Help me by what, making me your slave?"

Carefully Aden stripped Credence's bloody shirt from his wiry frame. He dabbed and delicately caressed Credence's cuts and bruises.

"Oh my goodness, Credence, you were never a slave," he said. "You dishonor your ancestors even by saying that. What might your grandparents or great-grandparents say, I wonder?"

"What the hell was I if I wasn't a slave? I was seven years old when you took me and by the time I was twelve you had me ironing your clothes and dressing you in the morning! You had me carrying your valise, running behind you like some circus monkey!"

Aden shook his head and made a clucking sound. *Tsk, tsk.*

Credence would have struck him again then, but when he tried to lift himself up, his stomach felt like it might spill open.

"Don't be cruel to yourself, Credence." Aden had had the gall to get queeny. "You were seven when you came to live with us. Don't tell me, my dear, that you were a servant. Did Atalanta and I take our servants with us to China? Did we take Cook to the

Congo, or bring Jessie to Vietnam or to the parties in Rio we took you to? Did they travel with us to the Argentine in the winter? No, they did not. And you were paid, my dear. As any parent gives a child an allowance for contributing to the household, in that very manner we paid you for the little valet duties you performed. We set aside money for your college education." He added reproachfully, "Which you have never used."

"And does any parent push his teenage child into a closet full of clothes when his wife isn't looking and sneak feels?"

Though it caused him physical pain, Credence smiled to see Aden flinch backward as if struck.

After a minute the old man's chin stopped receding into his neck. He tugged Credence's pants down while Credence lay there unresisting, watching Aden's trembling attempt to maintain an expression of ironic detachment on his face. Then Aden reached into the first aid kit he'd laid on the bedside floor and began patiently to unwrap a roll of gauze around Credence's thigh.

"You molested me," Credence said slowly.

Aden kept his eyes on the gauze. Credence tried to see what Aden was seeing: the creamy white softness of the bandage hugging Credence's dark muscular thigh. Was the sight beautiful? Magical? The words that came from Aden's mouth sounded dreamy, mesmerized.

"If you're referring to our arrangement, I'd hardly call that molestation, since you've made it clear how repulsive you find me and have extorted considerable sums of money from me for each intimacy." He clipped the gauze strips together, rather too tightly.

"You know I'm not talking about that," Credence said through his teeth. He kept his voice low, enjoying the sight of Aden's trembling. "I'm talking about all those *kisses* I didn't need that kept coming my way from the time I was fifteen. Those so-called hugs that meant your hands got to go anywhere you pleased. I'm talking about those dry humps in the poolhouse when Attie—!"

"Credence!" Aden shrieked.

"You thought I forgot, didn't you?"

Abruptly Aden stood. Credence looked at Aden. It was like looking at a scarecrow with its rags worn away and the sticks and stuffing beginning to show.

"I *thought* that you had a better memory!"

"You molested a boy!"

Aden's eyelashes fluttered. "That boy—who was not little—" he started speaking rapidly then—"that boy who was in his *late* teens—you were seventeen as I remember—and it was a *yacht* not a houseboat—that boy was a *man* when he and I—when we made *love*. Which is more than I can say for what I do with the man the boy has become."

Credence had lunged at him and it was as if Aden had kicked him in the gut, as if he'd shoved a hobnailed boot completely through his flesh. But Aden hadn't touched him; it was the pain from the beating, like a scythe slicing peremptorily through his entrails—or maybe it was more the memory of the pain, awakening dulled nerves to shrill attention. He fell and hung over the side of the bed, afraid to move. Aden tried to help him back to the mattress, but Credence cursed at him with the little breath he had left and slapped Aden's legs so often that Aden eventually left. From his almost upside-down position at the edge of the bed, Credence listened to the rattle of keys and then heard the front door close. When the car engine's rumble faded, he walked himself back up the mattress with his hands and then lay crosswise, exhausted and seething.

In the morning when he awoke, Aden's car was still gone. Credence took whatever money he could find and then caught a bus to the New York City airport. He packed light, except for the heavy book his mother had bequeathed him. He almost left it in New Haven. The Roses had presented *Hex* to him on his tenth birthday as a great gift, the legacy of his blood. He'd been expecting something like a treasure map or the key to a secret vault, but it was only Aden's and Atalanta's stupid book, *Hex*, which they'd already made him half memorize. They'd used their own copies to teach him to read, thinking, probably, that it was something a little boy would find dazzling and adventurous. But he'd hated it, sensing it to be a toy they had given him out of their narcissism, a Bible of their writ intended to invite his worship of them. Even at an early age he had rebelled, aggressively bored by their idea of what magic was. But this copy had his mother's writing in ink and dark pencil all over it, margin notes and emendations in a nearly indecipherable hand. One piece stood out bold and clear on the page facing the title page: FOR MY SON CREDENCE, WITH LOVE ALWAYS FROM VERITY, AUG. 20, 1953. As he weighed it in his hand, it suddenly became necessary. *Hex* was untainted by Aden's hypocrisy; it was a piece of his past that hadn't been fully corrupted. It was real, a real hex for escape and rebirth. He'd put it in his bag, and its 551-page girth slid in among his few other belongings and lay there unobtrusively, lighter than a feather.

On the plane to L.A., Credence considered going underground, maybe becoming a revolutionary all by himself. He could do it. He had numerous skills. He was a man of wide experience, having done and seen what few men dare. He'd traveled partway up the Amazon, he'd made camp for a few nights in the Arctic, wrestled ruffians in the alleyways of corrupt Old World cities, beaten back a few feet of tropical jungle with a machete, sailed four seas and crossed two deserts. Surely somehow those experiences could be put to use—perhaps in the theft of FBI documents, or the assassination of right-wing politicians? For money he would blackmail Aden. Make the lies Oliver told the Cats true, and let the old shit find out what extortion really was.

Now, as Credence reads the article briskly detailing Aden's death, he finds himself feeling helpless, battered. Malachai's betrayal, Aden's betrayal—which, in a horrible way, is also his mother's betrayal: his whole life. God has made it his divine hobby to ensure that nothing and no one Credence believes in ever proves worthy of his trust.

Still in a daze at checkout time the following morning, Credence packs up his little bag and makes his way out to the freeway junction. In the blazing Southern California noon sun, with little more than a pack of cigarettes, the last load of his cash and a sack of toiletries, a change of underwear and shirts, and a few mementos, including *Hex*, Credence strips off his shirt, unlatches the top buttons of his Levi's as he had once seen crazy Atalanta do back in the late fifties (when she must have been at least as old as the century), and sticks out his thumb.

The van that slows to pick him up after the first hour and forty minutes is full of reprobates and creeps, as he more or less expects and more or less desires. After they've fleeced him for his share of the gas money, he gets consigned to the cavelike cubby in the back, where he hunches into a small space of bench seat cushion and shuts his eyes, his hands clutched tightly around the straps of his bags. He can't sleep, though, and so ends up miserably counting drops of sweat as they trickle over his brows and fall onto his cheeks. The other denizens of the dark van—three guys, one of whom is black, and one woman—stare openly at him. He wants to scream at them, make them feel what he feels, make them hurt and suffer and grieve. But he keeps quiet. One thing he's learned. You never know when you might be lynched.

~~~
~~~

The still waters of the southern San Francisco Bay lie flat and low to the coast, like a shimmering blue-gray carpet spread over a ballroom floor that stretches away for miles. You get the feeling that you could step onto its surface in your tap shoes and have a dance. Foothills and junior-grade mountains elbow one another for space to give the bay its undulating contour as it leaks south after passing through the Golden Gate.

It is early summer, and the sun-baked hills are colored in the glorious browns and yellows of a desert, sloping up and down, jutting in and out like the shoulders of a pride of lionesses submerged in the cooling water. The effect, here on the heels of one of the world's most fabled metropolises, is of a grand desolation, turned inward to the dreamy contemplation of monkish solitude. Indeed it could make a monk of you, this view: between the high, bright, white sun and the quiet off-blue water, you could live a life naked to the sight of God, washed clean by the salt brine of the sea: or so Credence imagines.

In the back of a dust-shrouded 1966 van that creeps through traffic crossing the Dumbarton Bridge, Quentin and Sunder doze, Sunder's head having fallen back and to the left to rest on Quentin's bony shoulder. His mouth is open and he snores softly, while Quentin's eyes dart behind his shut lids and his fingers twitch like the paws of a dog chasing rabbits in its sleep.

Or is it Quentin? For a moment it is someone else, for a moment Quentin is right beside you watching Sunder, but then it might have been Mrs. Gillory or Reynaldo or Langston, except that all of them look like a slim white guy with a long face and a scruffy beard and showing a thatch of curly brown hair that makes a diamond shape between his svelte pectoral muscles and across his upper belly. Leaning on him is Reginia, but possibly also Azaril or even Quentin all over again; together they form a black guy with a football player's neck, around which is tangled the cheap metal chains of two necklaces that culminate in a plaster-mold crucifix and the ankh.

Credence, glancing back over his shoulder, tries to recall their names. The white one is Thomas? Terence? The black guy—maybe *he's* Thomas—but there was also a Ronnie, maybe he's Ronnie. At each stop they all shift positions. While Credence approves of the democratic principle in action, it makes him get everyone confused.

Credence turns back to the windshield and the view of the mountains and the sea, trying to focus his attention. The one whose name he has no trouble remembering, Costas—looking a lot like Reynaldo—drives the van with the window down and his shirt off, which lies damp with sweat on the floor below the accelerator pedal and the brake, not far from Credence's feet. Costas has hairy arms and tree-trunk legs, and his big body overflows his seat so that he is almost pressed against Credence, who's riding semi-shotgun while an emaciated chick named Angel (Langston?) nods in and out of slumber on the window side of the passenger seat they both share.

Credence, unintentionally, unavoidably, keeps inhaling Costas. Credence squirms each time Costas shifts to get more comfortable and an invisible puff of Costas's odor floats over from Costas's armpits, and from Costas's crotch jostling in his loose Bermuda shorts, to detonate in Credence's nostrils. Overtaken by the big Greek's smell, called again and again to it against his desire, Credence (like Langston, as Langston) tries to classify it. Costas's sweat smells like an opened jar of cooking spices, bay leaf and oregano dried and crumbled years gone by, with a dash of chili pepper and caked cayenne. Like an old jar pushed to the back of a cupboard, its glass cloudy and gray, its contents brown as mud and as rich. One of Credence's favorite books is *Peyton Place*, and there is a line in it that has always puzzled him, where the snooty Anglo-Saxon meanies in the New England town deplore Michael Kyros as "that big, black Greek." Now Credence understands: and he looks, bedazzled, at Costas, and drinks deep of him, savoring his memory of the words.

"How you get the name Credence?" Costas asks.

"My mother gave it to me," Credence answers breathlessly. "It's a family name. It's really my middle name, and if I'd been a girl I woulda been Verity, but . . . it's a family name."

The big black Greek nods. "Costas is my father's name," he says. "I been staying with my cousin for a while, but now I am going to work for my father's brother in San Francisco. He has a restaurant."

"Sounds like you have a good family tradition, too." Credence says this with a twinge: he has no family, and really has never had one.

Costas smiles. He reaches out with his big hand with dark hair sprouting toward the knuckles and grips Credence on the shoulder. He keeps smiling. It seems that the mention of family has almost brought him to the verge of tears. His hand stays on Credence's shoulder, and the smile stays on his face, frozen and sad.

Credence imagines Costas on a soccer field in the midst of a team huddle, imagines feeling Costas's hands on his shoulders, holding him, being held up as he pants with exhaustion—he can't help himself, he knows fully well that he's making a mistake, *another* mistake, but he can't help it—men: they're an addiction. He hallucinates Costas's sun-browned feet and brown legs flashing over green grass, and his brown, brown torso and limbs as he leaps high at the flying ball and scissors his mighty legs into the air; he sees himself cooking a lamb and tomato sauce dish he and the Roses had in Greece for Costas, when he returns from a day's labor ravenous for more than one kind of sustenance.

Credence, lost in love again, shakes his head. Bombs explode in his nostrils. Oh, well, he decides. He will not become a solo revolutionary, nor will he be a monk, but it's all worship, in one form or another.

It is a revelation, this ride. Langston, whose name, appearance, history, and memory is that of Credence Gapstone, feels a surge of hope in Baghdad by the Bay, detects in the breeze flowing in off the cool sea the scent of a sweeter destiny. He beholds an almost-familiar horizon in the sight of the great, vaporous mountains of fog that creep each July evening over the Twin Peaks to enshroud the city in a dome like a mirage of winter: San Francisco seems the mysterious radiant outline of the home country Credence has long dreamt of but never in all his travels seen. It is salvation, this ride in a rickety van, drunk on pheromones and gasoline fumes, a toxic, ecstatic brew that conjures for Credence (for Azaril, for Reynaldo) the experience of emerging from a dark tunnel into heavenly light. Once across the bridge he can look back and smile, even laugh, in the wry, amused, indulgent way one laughs at a child who keeps stumbling over the same rock and each hour wails anew for Band-Aids to patch up the same cuts in his flesh: *there on the other shore lies my pitiful former life,* Credence is saying. *How very overwrought and silly and precious it was* (as he draws deeply again on the aroma of Costas).

(But what about my grandfather? If Credence didn't kill Aden, who did?)

Roan's assertion of individuality is like a power saw gnawing through the trunk of a tree—all at once the scene tilts, wavers, and falls, the crash rumbling through their collective being. In the gloomy blankness that follows, another consciousness takes shape, another scene rises up to swallow them all.

Turncoat. Traitor to his race. Killer. Warlock. Sunder Rex first has occasion to reflect upon the possibility of taking on such titles, adding them to his name like a string of abbreviations announcing the acquisition of degrees of depravity, on a summer afternoon, in a locked room in a safe house he's taken great pains to reach without being seen by his fellow Panthers. His name is Oliver Pierce, but the FBI agent calls him Ollie.

Ollie, traitor to the race. When the FBI agent recruited him, he called Oliver *friend;* he called him a *patriot*. Oliver never had friends before—ever. He suffers, someone once told him, from some kind of sociopathy. Does it matter to a person suffering from sociopathy that he is a traitor to a social group? Would it matter if such a person were a traitor to the FBI? Oliver ruminates on this as he listens.

"It ain't gon be nuthin but a thang to let everybody know that you been working for da Man, Ollie," the man—The Man—says. The agent is enjoying himself; he enjoys coon talk. It makes him feel hip and free and full of power, Oliver guesses.

"And not just da Man, da Man's Man. When Uncle Sam tell the world, looky here, Ollie Pierce is my boy, what black man in the whole damn country gon call you his soul brother? What sweet black sista will let you 'tween her big old thighs when they find out you a traitor to the whole race?"

Oliver can tell how much the agent relishes the sound of *her big old thighs*.

Fine. Let them prod him. Let them see what sort of man they're dealing with. "Why are you threatening me?" Oliver asks—cool, cool, utterly unruffled, in the same tone he'd use to ask someone why they put ketchup on their scrambled eggs. "I've done my job. I've done everything you asked."

Oliver's mission was to infiltrate a cell of the Black Panther Party, a group he was told and believed was manipulated by

Communists and run by criminals, and help reveal them to the American public for what they really were. He was to talk a lot of Mau-Mau nonsense, quote Lenin and Mao, make himself important, or if not important then at least loud and often heard. "These crooks are just itching to kill somebody or blow something up," one of his FBI friends told Oliver. "All we want you to do is give them a good target."

But Oliver has begun to waver, and the agents know it. "You like strutting your stuff too much," the agent tells him. Oliver doesn't admit it, but it's true. He likes it when the men and women in his group listen to him, watch him, argue with him. He likes the way he has suddenly become attractive. He likes the women who prowl in his wake and who sometimes throw themselves at him. He ridicules the group to the agents, laughs at how they are mere hangers-on and would-be radicals who orbit the Panthers but lack the courage to land on the home planet. "They're just gophers," he snorts when making his report. But at the same time he has become attached to the Cats. And slowly, little by little, he has begun to believe some of what they believe. Is he a weak-minded man, as his uncle always said? He puzzles over this, tries to explain to himself how he could so easily be brought to change his mind. Is it that the story the Panthers and their ilk tell is a story of heroes, of courage and duty, having its own sense of law, order, and justice? He has always appreciated a good heroic tale. He has a powerful imagination. His masters in the bureau do not understand this about Oliver. No one understands how important Oliver could be, how intelligent he really is.

"I understand," the agent who always says he understands says. There are two FBI men whom Oliver meets or speaks with: the one who likes to talk black and the understanding one, whose eyes have a filmy sheen that make Oliver wonder if the man is blind.

"Listen, no one can say that the black man hasn't gotten a raw deal in this country," the understanding one says. He looks pained. "But these boys are mixed up with the wrong people. A lot of the money your friends are getting comes from a fellow named Aden Rose, for example. Now, we have reason to know that this old man is a terrible pervert, and that he has been sexually abusing one of the members of your group, this Gapstone fella you've mentioned. We have evidence that shows Rose makes this Gapstone fellow do all kinds of degrading, disgusting sexual favors for him in exchange for the little bit of cash he contributes to the group. And listen to this. We tapped the Rose sumbitch's phone."

The agent depresses the button on a cassette tape player. Oliver admires the organization of these meetings, the crisp fluidity with which they are carried out like the well-drilled synchrony of a marching military band—each psychological weapon at the ready, never more than an arm's length away. The sound of the tape is clear and undisturbed by static, as if they'd persuaded Aden Rose to come into their offices and speak directly into the microphone of their recorder. And who knows? Maybe that's exactly what they did.

It goes on for half an hour or more, a long string of bigoted invective and hatred so elaborate that it becomes a kind of giddiness, a joyous delirium. Apart from all the references to niggers, jungle bunnies, coons, shines, etc., a reference to Charles Manson especially catches Oliver's attention. "Now, Charles Manson," the voice on the tape says. "He had the right idea. I say somebody of will and courage ought to follow his plan. Commit some atrocity and blame it on the darkies. That'll let decent white people know what kind of animals we really have living in our midst. Start the race war we all know is coming, but do it now, before the damn monkeys get educated and start buying arms from Russia. The outcome'll be bloody, I know, there's no getting around that, but we know who'll win it. We've got the numbers, after all. And the smarts, Goddamnit."

This is enough for Oliver. He knows that he is being manipulated and that this voice on the tape the agents claim to be from a tap on Rose's phone could be anyone—could be one of the agents themselves, even the understanding one. But Oliver's knowledge, conscious or unconscious, of the extent of the manipulation overwhelms him. Suppose it *is* true? And even if it isn't true, doesn't the very fact that the FBI could conceive of a lie like that suggest that they've considered going through with just such a plan? Maybe they *are* going through with such a plan. And even if none of that is true, it's probably true that they're right about Gapstone and Rose. Hasn't he felt there was something funny about Gapstone, something about him that was a little on the sweet side?

Oliver knows for the first time that the stories he's read about the forces of evil in their dark towers, the stories he's heard from the Panther Party and the ideologues among the Cats, the stories he himself had been told by the FBI to tell—all of it—are true. There are sinister forces at work in the world. They lurk behind the curtain, they creep under cover of darkness, they draw maps of poor neighborhoods so as to make assassinations and concentration camps more efficient, they rule the universe and no one ever gets to see their faces. These two men alternately threatening to expose him and inciting him to take action—mere flunkies, gophers, the cold tip of an enormous iceberg of evil. Of course he is being manipulated. Of course he is.

At the next Cats meeting he is shaking with hate. He hates them all, as much as he hates the FBI, as much as he despises his uncle back in North Carolina, his stupid aunt, his flighty, useless mother. He watches Credence Gapstone while somebody takes the floor, talking half nonsense, half disturbing truth. Credence sits close to Malachai Reynolds, very close to him. They're practically snuggling, Credence with a pleading look in his eyes like some whoring bitch off the street.

Oliver stands up. It is only when he reaches the center of the room that he stops shaking, and as everyone's eyes come to rest upon him he feels his hate alchemize into power. The strength of everyone in the room, their regard and respect for him, flows into his body, making him as hard and as beautiful as diamond. He preaches them a sermon of his own devising, taking what he's learned from the FBI who have made him a traitor and taking words from the Panthers and from his reading. There are miracles in his words. He tells them about what it is to be strong and how contemptible it is to be weak, and they, afraid of weakness, dreaming of strength, believe him. He knows that he has to wield their power for them, that he has to show them what it is to be strong by showing them how to despise weakness and destroy it, wherever it is, whatever its forms.

"Somewhere in this room there's someone who is weak. He's pretending to be one of us. But he's a liar."

Somewhere in Oliver there is a flutter of pity as he walks over to where Credence sits, clinging to Malachai's arm. The feeling in his chest as he strides over to the two men is tremulous, tiny, soft. His hatred, therefore, grows all the greater; when he makes his accusation, when that idiot Malachai plays right into his hands, he beats Credence without mercy, liking to see Credence bleed, liking the feeling of flesh giving way beneath his fists.

~

Oliver relives the moment as if it were today, the look on Malachai's face as he joined in, and the look in the eyes of Credence's bloody face, the shrill sound of Malachai's screaming like some creature from Mars. He remembers it, and puzzles over the memory and its effect on him, after he strangles Aden Rose's corpse. The moments seem to be of a piece, the acts without distinction. Beating Credence = murdering Aden Rose. Oliver doesn't understand what put the idea of committing these acts in his head, but he has a theory that the energy that flowed into him that night in the meeting was so powerful that it has given him the drives of six men, given him the capacity to exist simultaneously at different locations in space and time, endowed him with a mind that calculates faster than a computer.

Otherwise, how could it have been so easy? He staked out Rose's house after the meeting, assuming that Credence would go to him to lick his wounds. He told his superiors nothing. He did not work for them anymore. He hadn't yet consciously made the decision to leave, to betray the agents as he had betrayed his own people, but as with the first betrayal, he knew what he would do before he told himself that he would do it.

Oliver followed Rose as he left the house in the predawn hours. He propositioned the old man in a truck stop bathroom off the highway. He scarcely knew where he found the words or the way to do it. At first it disgusted Oliver when the old man followed him into a copse of trees behind the stop and knelt on the damp ground. Oliver unzipped and held the back of the old man's head, revolted by the touch of his bare head and the tuft of lank white hair hanging near his neck like some tumorous growth. With the other hand Oliver reached into his jacket and—whipping his penis out of that disgusting aperture and smiling as if he were going to feed it to him in one deep thrust—he shoved a stuffed sock in Rose's mouth, as far into his throat as he could get it. The look on Rose's face was fascinating and horrible, his feeble struggle—feeble but magnificently animal, unvarnished in its ferocious determination to hang on—was exhilarating to watch and to so contemptuously defeat. He'd lifted the old man off the ground by the neck as he'd tightened his hold on his larynx. It enthralled him to see how strong he had become. Who was he? Whom had he become? Oliver felt—feels—wild with power.

Now Rose is dead. Oliver wishes now that he'd let the old man service him to fruition first, before he killed him, to make the humiliation of his enemies more complete. And then he thinks: but what if I do it now? Won't the coroner know, and when the FBI eventually finds out, won't they bc humiliated, too, because they will know he did it, and he is their boy? The thought makes him fuck with relish. There is nothing that stokes lust about the old, pale, just-dead body, nothing truly erotic. Unless the simple physical violence of the act is sufficient to summon Eros to witness the event, unless—yes, the thought comes to him as a revelation, there *is* something deeply, powerfully erotic about bludgeoning fear itself, for that is what he is doing by fucking the body of the man he's murdered, he has bloodied the fear within him, he is impaling the fear of the powerful—white men, rich men, government, all of it—on the haft of his cock. His friends at the FBI had wanted Rose killed, but they'd wanted the Cats or better yet the real Panthers to do it, not him. When at last they find out what he's done, they will know that he is dangerous, and that he has betrayed them. They will not know, though they'll be forced to speculate upon, the nature of his newfound power. They will not know, though they will rightly fear, that he has become greater than they. He has become his own secret agent.

With that thought he spills the last of his old self through his meatus into the dead cavities of Aden Rose: his vessel of rebirth.

He can discern no flutter of pity within him now. Weakness cannot penetrate him; it rolls off him, slight as raindrops sliding off a pane of clear glass. This is his first true act of magic, for in murder and rape of the dead, Oliver Pierce disappears forever. No wave of a wand and mumbled word, no artful harmonizing of smoke and mirrors could have accomplished it better: Oliver Pierce is gone, and Sunder Rex, secret agent, terrorist, warlock, stands in his place.

Thus Sunder Rex (Roan Gillory, Reginia Jameson Wolfe, Langston Fleetwood) learns that if the art of magic is anything, its root can be found in the density and concentration of the ego. To cast spells effectively, a man must be greater than himself, more powerful, more present than the puny collection of flesh and water that he is made to be at birth. To kill effectively, a man must be at least twice himself, so that he does not murder the part of his own being that is the same as the person he murders. He must be certain that there is a sufficient quantity of himself so as not to be extinguished in the act of extinguishing others. "I am twice myself," Sunder Rex says every day to the long mirror in his Black Room to his other self, the creature whom he guides to do dark deeds in the service of a greater good. "I am double-souled, I am God and man together, *ka* and *ba* and all that lies between."

For the warlock who accomplishes this it is as if the bullets of karma bounce harmlessly off his chest. He strides through the world, ordering it as he wills according to his own justice, without consequence to his next life or peril to his immortal soul.

And all such a man needs to shrug off Slave forever and become Master is a source of power.

If Roan Gillory has a response to this knowledge of the man who, somewhere back in a hotel room in Wessex House, now clasps her right hand in his left—whether of outrage, or fear, or understanding—it disappears and is lost, as the travelers rapidly plunge headlong into another scene, scatter themselves into other parts. . . .

27

Credence Gapstone washes dishes in the cramped kitchen of the Arkilitis family's tiny restaurant, but nothing about the menial work dispirits him. Not the fact that people treat plates and glasses they don't have to clean the same way they treat public toilets, nor the fact that the only horizon he sees most of the day is a grimy wall of faded tile and dirty grout and an autographed photo of Aristotle Onassis mounted in smudged glass. Credence finds portents of joy in the filth, finds delight even in the froth and foam of the soap that withers the skin of his hands and sometimes gives him scratching fits in the middle of the night. The Arkilitis diner is the place where he and Costas are together. The presence of love in Credence's life, the steady, routine, everyday glow of a love as inexorable as sunrise—but never taken for granted, because like an early riser he's always awake to *see* the sunrise, feel its warmth on his face—this kind of love makes all the ugly things in the world mere prelude to glory.

When the nightly cleaning is done and the seats of the chairs lie on the tabletops, Costas locks up the restaurant, and then he and Credence climb into bed together in the small room they share in the family quarters on the second floor. There is no sex, but at Costas's initiation the two kiss goodnight—aggressively, and at ever-expanding length. And after Costas's snoring has softened to a rumble like the passage of a distant train (stirring in the layers of Credence's memory the fear of the onset of a storm), Costas's limbs, lost in dream, tend to rove and find themselves in the oddest nooks and crannies of Credence's passive but cannily well-positioned body. Credence has come to believe that if he were to undergo surgery the doctors would smell Costas's sensuous reek wafting up from Credence's own internal organs. The kiss, the nocturnal groping, and the fact that Costas showers only in the morning when the sun is streaming through the bathroom window, are enough to make Credence feel that each night he and Costas consummate a marriage.

On Sunday afternoons, after Costas returns from church, the two often take a stroll through Golden Gate Park together and watch the ducks and turtles in the ponds, and the horses as their masters take them through their paces along the wide dirt paths beneath the trees. They sit on benches and talk about politics, and Costas spies in open-mouthed dismay and envy on the young hippie types who writhe in the grass waging battle for the sexual revolution. Then, on Monday evenings, sometimes late on Fridays or Saturdays, Credence and Costas get drunk. Costas always gets more soused than Credence and makes crude comments about women and their body parts until he passes out. Credence has to help him home, undress him, and put him to bed. And then Credence lies on the sheets, waiting for Costas's hands.

In this static perfection, like a bubble in time and space, Credence feels he is at peace. But the thought creeps up on him from time to time that there is a serpent in every Eden: since he is not highest on the short totem pole of dishwashers in the Arkilitis' restaurant (and indeed has only been hired on as a courtesy to Costas), Credence does not always work and is not always at Costas's side.

When he is alone, Credence window-shops the finer clothing establishments and reads newspapers from foreign cities in the library to test his spotty memory of the languages Aden taught him. Sometimes he likes to find dark corner bars in the black neighborhoods in the Tenderloin and the Fillmore where he can talk to men whose hope for the day begins with their noon whiskey, and he can charm lost women who know immediately that he's not a local and like to speculate on the origin of his accent. "I bet you from one of the islands," she says when he's doing his best imitation of the French, and with his acquiescent nod they both enter into a pleasurable conspiracy that transports them far away from the quotidian worries of other bar patrons and sometimes even blossoms into an afternoon of romance: wildflowers picked from a vacant lot for her hair, a new lipstick, a quiet moment of repose on their backs, side by side on the hill of Alamo Park that overlooks downtown and the Bay Bridge on a clear day. Occasionally an awkward but vigorously attempted roll together on somebody's mattress in which they both feign climax.

This last diversion, when it happens, tends to leave Credence unsettled. He stares at himself in the mirror, if there is one, or in the reflection of the window, if there is one, and he inspects his body, overcome with the feeling that it does not belong to him. Unconsciously he investigates his penis and testicles for abnormalities. After this has happened twice—and after he feels similarly disoriented and revolted at the conclusion of an unexpected encounter with a slender, pock-skinned, slatternly youth leaning in an alleyway on Polk Street who had charmed Credence and then charged fifteen for the charming—Credence begins to think he knows what's unsettling him.

What, after all, had been the lesson that the Roses had taught him as they dragged him from place to place all over the world like so much luggage? What had been their gift to him? The knowledge that in a new place you could be whoever you wished, because you had no history that anyone could tie you to, and yet everything in your new world—the landscape, the people, the culture—was rich with histories in which you could become immersed. "You must think of the past as chains, as weights dragging at your feet," Aden had lectured him.

"I don't think that is at all right," Atalanta corrected him. When Atalanta contradicted Aden, she did so with force; Credence remembered her fingers tripping through the air as she spoke, flung out with each new thought and then returning again to her thin lips as she settled again into contemplation. "You should tell him"—she did not usually address Credence in the first person; Credence took this to be an indication of her disapproval of her husband's attachments to young black boys—"You ought to tell him that the power of the past over us is a natural and necessary phenomenon, if a trifle tedious."

Then she turned to Credence, glaring. She spat out her words with the emphasis and sentiment of a spray of machine gun bullets. "History is a form of gravity, dear. It is fundamentally a *weak* force compared to electromagnetism or the other forces. If you want to fly, you simply must be moving quickly enough to break free of it."

Credence had thought her pompous at the time, though as always he found her stylish expressiveness admirable. But that day, this day now, as he leaves the darkness of the alley where the youth is still counting his money (Credence paid in ones, since that is the denomination in which Mr. Arkilitis pays him), he feels he finally has the gist of it, and recognizes both his mistake and his salvation. He must follow his first aim in leaving New Haven, unconscious though it was, to purge himself of all that has gone before. The problem with his plan to become a revolutionary is now clear, for that choice had a reference to his past, to Malachai and all that Malachai had promised and refused him in the end.

Credence understands this now, and his way is certain. Piece by piece he strips his past away as he walks north on Polk Street and turns east, heading toward the upper reaches of the Tenderloin and the borders of downtown and Union Square where the Arkilitis diner sits next to a hotel-turned-apartment-building. It is a mental exercise, for of course he cannot leave the past behind so easily. But there is a power in it, he can feel the power when he decides that never again will he allow himself to speak or think the name of the man who rejected him, nor the other man who betrayed and used him. He will forget them, unmake them; and so remake himself.

On the corner of Bush and Taylor, Credence waits for the stoplight. Two men are standing next to him. Their tones are abrasive, contemptuous, full of bravado. "Motherfuck that." "Gott-damn ass-wipe, like he know some shit. . . ." "*I* will be the sonbitch who carry this motherfucka, iss only about you and me and maybe Carlton, that weak-ass faggoty—"

Credence turns to look at them. One is sallow and slight, with a rangy, cheetahlike body with a dog's big-nosed, wide-cheeked head slung low between shoulders that pop up from his blue silk shirt like doorknobs. The other is taller, built lean and strong like a farmer, bearded where his accomplice is smooth, with a long, hard jaw and a wide nose and classically framed brows that combine to make him look like a movie idol. His skin is brown with deep red tones that border on orange, and his close-cut curly Afro is naturally auburn.

"You the man, Dilbert, I know that. You'll set it right," the cheetahlike one says, without much conviction.

"Fuck," red-boned Dilbert grumbles, but by now he has noticed that Credence is watching him.

Dilbert (who, if you look at him and blink slowly enough, might look a lot like Reynaldo) studies Credence's stare for a moment, trying to read it. Finally he says, "Hey, you look like you from around here. You know where a brother can get a good cut and shave?"

Credence doesn't answer the question. He has let his hair grow wild since he left New Haven, and it has begun to lengthen into ratty-looking tufts like the great shaggy mane of a woolly mammoth. Costas's uncle makes him wear a tight net over it when he washes dishes even though no one else in the restaurant has to. Costas's aunt keeps insisting that he cut it, and he keeps lying that he can't find any barber in San Francisco who knows how to cut a black man's hair.

"Are you a musician?" Credence asks.

Dilbert is puzzled, but he smiles. "Yeah, how you know? I'm with the Blacknotes. Both of us." He gestures toward the cheetah, who shifts uneasily from foot to foot. "We playing at the Fairmont tonight. You like jazz?"

"Love it," Credence says. "How long are you engaged to play?" He can't help licking his lips.

That Thursday night Credence's shift is over early—or, rather, he leaves early, skipping out for an extended break to complete his urgent errand. After washing himself up, Credence lifts Costas's uncle's sharkskin jacket from his closet in a rare moment when Costas's aunt doesn't have her eye on him, and skips out. He carries *Hex* in his hand, nicely wrapped in brown paper: the last token, the last piece to be divested. It takes some doing to get into the hotel without being accosted by every bellboy and doorman looking to impress the supervisor with his attention to hotel security, but when Credence finds his way to the club below floors, he settles into a quiet corner seat and sits unmolested, bobbing his head to the band's last set.

At the end of it he approaches Dilbert, who lingers at the piano with an exhausted and satisfied smile on his lips. The red in Dilbert's color is like desert clay in the dim illumination of the hotel club.

"I recognize you," Dilbert says, slightly taken aback. He looks dubiously at Credence's hair.

"You were astonishing. I didn't hardly notice the others. It was like you were a one-man band."

Dilbert smiles his puzzled smile again.

"I have a gift for you." Credence shoves *Hex* into Dilbert's hands. "Please accept it as a token of my esteem for the loveliness of your playing."

Dilbert turns the thing over and over, perusing it from each of its sides as if it were a miniature Trojan horse, but he does not refuse the gift or give it back.

When he looks up from it, Credence has already mounted the stairway.

⁂

Later that night, sleeping in a hotel downhill near Union Square, Dilbert finds he cannot sleep. He struggles to extricate himself from the unfamiliar tuck of the bedsheets, turns on the nightstand lamp, and begins reading *Hex*, which has been lying next to the phone, humming while he's tried to sleep.

⁂

Meanwhile, Credence, satisfied that he has ensorcelled Dilbert, discovers that hexes have a way of backfiring. So enraptured is he by the fantasy that he is on the road to freeing himself that he's almost seen walking up to the diner by the two policemen whom he belatedly notices questioning Mr. Arkilitis. They're interested in the location of a black man wanted for the murder of millionaire Aden Rose.

It is 11:18 P.M. on a Thursday night in early autumn, when Credence realizes he is a fugitive from the law. He leaves the name Credence Gapstone behind and becomes Thomas J. Waterbury, a name he plucks from the air, culls from the flotsam and jetsam of memories he cannot escape.

Time speeds. Maybe Atalanta was right. Reginia, Roan, Sunder, Quentin, Reynaldo, Langston, Azaril or the shadow of Azaril, and the presence that guides them, tumble through flat-screen television-like vignettes played out around them, in which they perform key roles:

Credence (each time a breeze strikes his face, he looks like Roan) in a store located in what appears to be a run-down warehouse, with bad lights and jumbled inventory spilling over floor displays like the jungle interior of everyone's kid sibling's messy room. Credence creeps into the dressing room, where it looks as if mice have been trying to build a nest in the corner, and tries on stocking hose, a bra that he needn't overstuff to get the right effect, and a narrow pair of black heels that will simply have to do, and the cutest dress, powder blue—it's amazing how darling it is. It's like one of the dresses Mrs. Kennedy once wore. Credence has never before thought much of dressing up in women's clothes the way bona fide sissies do; it never had any appeal for him. Or did it? Now, perhaps, the new him, the un-historied him, sees in this dress something that beckons him on to a freedom he'd never quite allowed himself before. Oh! And a pillbox hat! He'd always thought them ridiculous and impractical. But that, too, seems to be a kind of freedom: impracticality. Whimsy. Even in the face of old and too-familiar dangers.

Credence neatly folds his purchase, dresses again in his old clothes, and hides his face behind large glasses with lenses as transparent as windowpanes. His expression is set so that he appears neither too happy nor too glum as he pays the woman at the checkout counter. He's certain she does not even look up at him. . . .

Credence on a bus (the more he sweats, the more he resembles Quentin), so nervous as he scans the passengers aboard with him that he cannot enjoy the sight from the Golden Gate Bridge of the channel of Blue Bay as it passes by the Presidio, the golden Marin headlands, Sausalito and Angel Island. "A suicide's paradise," Credence hears the pensive man in the seat beside him comment. The man's eyes are bugged, which makes Credence even more nervous. "You know they take off the side of this bridge. Like the Wright brothers without the wings." He laughs. "I hear one drops a day. May I ask your name?" Credence had thought the man's eyes were bugging with fear, but now he knows they've inflated with fantasies of getting some. "Cissy Plenniford Davenport," Credence blurts without thinking, and tries to give each of the three mythical names the impact of a slap. But he knows that the man will probably turn him in, just as Costas did. . . .

Credence (slim and dark but shorter, somehow, as if he were an amalgam of Credence and Langston) in a car he has stolen from an elderly white couple who left the passenger door unlocked in the parking lot of a roadside restaurant. The car has no air-conditioning and it seems to get hotter as he journeys farther north, so he loosens the pins in his wig and laughs with huge, unexpected joy as it scoots around on his head when he leans toward the open window. . . .

Credence, wriggling out the bathroom window of a room in a cheap motel as a trio of cops burst in (the half of him above the waist that the cops can't see is a dead ringer for Reynaldo). At first the cops are in deadly earnest as they wrestle him down and grind his nose into the grime of the cold, unswept floor, clubbing him to answer his every squirm of discomfort. But the sound of grunts and scuffling soon gives way to hoarse giggles like gusts of steam from a hot pipe. Are they getting off on his cries of pain, distorted as they reverberate against the echoing tile, or the sight of a six-foot black man, skin dark and glistening with sweat like a chalkboard that's just been washed, slithering and flailing around in a torn blue dress that rides up on his taut runner's thighs encased in nylon and gives flashes of two layers of tucked tiger-striped bikini briefs beneath?

Credence trembling, alone in a county jail cell in rural northern California.

He didn't even need to tell the police his name. They had to have been forewarned, then: he's coming, they must have been told: the black murderer wearing a two-piece powder-blue number that went out of style half a decade ago.

This is the funny kind of situation that reminds you of how absurd life can be, the way the most meaningless bits come back unnoticed, as if you'd tossed some bit of trash off a boat years ago and then you see it again one morning, bright like a diamond in the sand at the tide line. Nothing so ephemeral and girlish as sartorial changes ought to mark the gateways between epochs in one's life. (But those dresses *were* beautiful back then, weren't they?) Fashion should never influence one's choices in life—not a man's choices, at any rate, and hasn't he proven his manhood, against all the odds? But the funny thing is, he'd left the country not long after Mrs. Kennedy began smiling into the camera wearing dresses a lot like the cheap knockoff he's wearing now (where was his pillbox hat?—they'd *taken* his pillbox hat?). Of course he hadn't skipped the border into Canada because of Mrs. Kennedy's dresses. She was wearing black by the time he left. It had been the beatings and murders in the South that drove him away, and the war, too. Still, when he came back a couple of years later, fashion played a part: he was enticed by photographs of handsome black men in tight black pants and black leather jackets with their fists raised high; they'd looked to him like messiahs, giving orders to the waters of the Red Sea.

But that promise, too, had been flogged to death: the clothes torn from its body, the skin stripped from its flesh, the flesh pared from the bone, its blood jagging everywhere like the streaks of a child's red crayon paying no respect to line or boundary.

In a windowless cell of cement unbroken even by anything as poetic as a shadow, Credence Gapstone sits without the benefit of a chair, bed, or bench, awaiting doom. All he has to distract him are his discomforts. His blue dress fits him poorly, the cotton rim of the sleeves biting into his slender biceps. The hose chafes his slender legs. During his arrest, they'd initially stripped him of his wig and the dress, but later the sight of his lanky, tight-muscled figure in bikinis with rouge on his cheeks that matched the pattern and color of the two purple bruises swelling beside his left eye seemed to disgust them, so they'd given the dress back, giggling and smirking. They never laid a hand on his pantyhose.

Now, what is it about a black man in a dress? Is it all that funny, really? So very hilarious, so incongruous that you have no possible response other than to double over holding your stomach and let the tears roll from your eyes? Many black folks hate the image even while they laugh; they look upon it as if by wearing one you had stepped up on the parapet of the fortress and waved a white flag of surrender. Yet neither black nor white can shake completely free of their fascination with the picture of it: always it stops you, the bulges and ripples of that dark sprinter's physique tucked into something soft and frilly. It reminds him of how Aden and Atalanta's neighbors used to stare at him in his cardigan when he was sitting in the garden—as if there were something subversive about the image of a robust young black man seated beneath a gazebo, sipping lemonade and wearing cashmere. . . . But here he is again, thinking about clothes.

Credence shivers, he blinks. He cannot control his blinking. There is a single lightbulb screwed into a hole in the ceiling. It's always on, though it gives off little in the way of useful light. The bulb has not been placed above him by accident; he suspects it is an instrument of subtle torture, and it's only the beginning.

He hears one of the deputies say something. He's heard men talking all along, of course, and phones ringing through the air, file drawers slamming shut and shoes galloping, a swirling, muffled hubbub of giddy mumbles. But he hasn't been able to make out anything distinct, until now.

He realizes this is because they're saying something that they want him to hear.

"They're coming."

He peers up at the bulb.

Not much time is left. What do you do when you see the end coming, you see the shadow of it widening like a hungry mouth as it approaches, when you know—wishing you didn't, hoping you're wrong, pleading *not yet, not yet*, wondering if that little persistent nudging desire for immortality we all share is a prophecy or a joke—what do you do if you know, this act is your last? Repent your sins, bid your good-byes, pray? There's no one left for Credence to say good-bye to, and his only sin, as far as he knows, is one of gullibility. As for prayer . . .

His mother had made him pray with her—or chant or cast spells, it was all the same—at night before he went to bed and in the morning before he washed his face. There were dozens of little incantations she asked him to recite with her. Verity knew spells and prayers for blessing breakfast and lunch, for walking north on the street, for walking south, for the silent, expectant moment before you made a wish. Simple words, cheap as moonshine, moving in their way, but faded away and forgotten almost as soon as you said them, like one of those ditties the blues boys would throw out to the club crowds to pass the time.

But Credence finds now that the memory of praying beckons to him, and that here at the end rather than being compelled to review his whole life in a flash, he's drawn inexorably back to a long discarded part of himself, a small corner of his past. The boy he once was comes back to him, unexpected, as if passing by for a final look-see just so they can shake hands, maybe plant a comradely kiss on each other's cheeks in farewell. It's strange and sad for Credence to realize that, even when you're a couple of years short of thirty, even in a span as short as that, the old selves don't travel along the path with you, stuffed in your duffel bag shifting about companionably with the rest of your gear; instead they fall away, cast aside like a child's dolls to mold and mummify in the tall weeds, and they leave behind just a snippet, just a tip broken off from something larger.

"They *say*"—his mother often taught him prayers in this provisional way, as if she didn't know whether it was safe to tell him, or didn't know whether she believed her own words—"They say this is a prayer to bring you exactly what you want no matter how forbidden. It will make those who shun you welcome you, set you free of any fear, open any doors to you."

It isn't easy after so many years to reconstruct his mother's face or her body—her color, the lines of her face and exact shape of her nose all vary as he tries to grasp them—but music cuts a lasting groove in the brain. With no trouble, with no more than the breeze outside the high, tiny window in the wall opposite his cell for his melody, he remembers the rhythm in her voice as she prayed in his ear, a rhythm like soft tapping on a drum, the words so simple:

Cracked is the back that once was broken; great is the price once paid. Mighty are the words yet to be spoken, true is the promise now to be made. Listen to my words, you who hear; listen to the words of my mouth: rouse for me mighty lightning-eyed Petbe who is in the abyss . . .

As he listens again, the feel of her words in his ears, so he speaks: each word as she said it, each sound as she made it, until the end.

. . . Ablanatanalba.

His breath spent, he sags. The prayer, or perhaps the burden of memory, has taken something out of him, and he drops down upon the concrete floor. He feels a touch more sadness now, a more present sorrow welling deep in his chest, and perhaps, maybe, a bit more calm. As he lies there breathing, his thoughts slowly evaporate. There is nothing he can do. But at least now that truth doesn't panic him. Instead he feels suffused with a watery cool, a gently rueful contentment. Maybe that's the magic of the prayer: just giving you permission to give in to it, whatever it is—the wanting, the knowing you don't have what you want, and the generosity not to blame yourself but just let it be.

Does he hear a car outside, coughing as it makes its way up the hill to the jailhouse?

FBI men, that's who they'd send after him, J. Edgar Hoover troops with briefcases packed with cattle prods and barbed ropes and electrodes to affix to his testicles. Let it be, then. In his mind's eye he imagines death coming to him, in the white robes of a church choir and with a gladiatorial smile on its darksome face, hovering high above, then slowly descending, like a leaf rafting on the air. *Yes, death, take me now,* he thinks, and he stretches his body out flat in surrender.

The explosion—of what kind no one will be able to say, for it leaves no trace of gasoline or dynamite or any substance known to the science of the period—levels the trees on the walkway outside the jail and shakes the jailhouse foundations as if the building is no more than a milk carton set on twigs. All the doors fly open, the bars of each cell snap and crumble, the walls tumble out onto the grass or sink into the soft earth like toast into a toaster. The alarm bell, the file cabinets, the gun rack all shake and shiver and shimmy five feet from where they stood, falling apart in the process. Looking at the powdery remains of the bars and walls there on the broken ground, smashed like graham crackers, the other three prisoners (drunk tank occupants, plus one smart-mouthed youth who owns a Harley) find themselves free.

Credence stands. A gust of air lifts his ten-dollar dress above his scarred knees. Barely able to hold himself up in the wet heaviness of the air, he hobbles over the line where the bars of his cell used to be, and—through the wall that isn't there anymore—sees a shallow swamp of blood collecting around the shiny boots of a deputy as he lies slumped over a mangled hunk of wood that had been his desk. A pillbox hat, pristinely blue and innocent as a newborn babe, lies in a declivity in the hunk of wood, inches from the reach of the deputy's fingers. Credence catches sight of this tableau as if it were illuminated by a brief lightning flash, a still photograph awash in floodlights in the midst of a dark, hazy blur. And for a blink of a moment he feels vindicated.

Then, amid balloons of smoke, beyond a door that clings to the exposed skeleton of its jamb, he sees outside—trees in flight, their earth-caked roots trailing behind like tentacles; grass and weeds and mud spinning like the blades of a fan; three police cars trampled into misshapen flatbeds that skim across the parking lot and the lawn, careening off one another in a game of bumper cars. His limpid sense of triumph vanishes. His brain, moving rapidly into arrest, appends a misnomer to what his eyes record. "What is it?" he screams. "What is it?" the echo comes back to him (the other prisoners? he sees them—darkly, scraggly shapes moving in off-kilter poses like figures of the risen dead).

But there is no it. *It* is the world bursting apart at seams he never knew existed. The sky is the color and texture of oatmeal, and from everywhere and everything, from the pitching earth and the broken walls, from the very pores of Credence's own skin, comes a howling. The epic, unruly sound is like a choir harmonizing its terror, and like a clattering, as of the iron wheels of a train, or great gears pushing and grinding and sparking against one another.

Beneath the inhuman ululation the barefoot prisoner in Jackie O circa 1961 detects something else: not a sound, but a subliminal sensation. The prickling caress of invisible droplets before a downpour—as if, above his head, there is a vacuum strained to the point of bursting under the pressure of its own hollowness, a bloated nothing, ready, eager, grasping. Sucking, sucking, sucking for something to fill it.

And he knows—in a message telegraphed to him by a memory from childhood, the recollection of a light he saw flash over the dark, rain-swept crest of hills the night his mother died—he knows that it is he who summoned this thing-that-is-not-a-thing. And that it is coming for him.

The others flee, are allowed to flee, while the thing calls him to it, reaches out with what might be wraithlike fingers and arms and claws. He sees—or thinks he sees—great, grinning gateway teeth; they flicker azure like the flame of a burner on a gas stove.

Death?

As he lifts his arms to signal his final surrender, a sudden funnel of windless wind comes to scoop him up from behind and jerks him into flight. He banks against pillows of air and shuttles among the flying trees. He could swear the tree trunk barks bear an expression of clenched terror. Terror rises in him, too, as his body ceases to be his own to command, and, apart from his limbs spun this way and that and the screeching in his ears and the trilling dance of ghostly cilia across his skin, he feels his heart inflate, his brain begin to bubble. He thinks of clothes, again: in that empty, golden plain more silent than dreamless sleep he always imagined death to be, he never thought he'd be wearing a dress. He thought he'd be naked, a glorious kind of naked, that he'd have the nude Olympic body of a sun-toughened warrior. Funny, to think that in death you'd acquire a better body than the one you possessed in life.

Into the maw of the thing he goes: is it hell, or is it heaven?

If he had control of his body, he would smile and shake his head at the easily legible signs of his own delirium. It can only be a trick of wish and memory, a phantasm crafted from the phantom stuff of desire.

Probably just death, looking funny.

Meantime, like a second or third show playing simultaneously on a television set, the colors and voices mingling, characters moving in and out of each other's programs, commercial jingles ringing over moments of tragic silence, the six of them see, feel, experience: Sunder Rex, still pretending to be the late Oliver Pierce. Sunder has just been informed of the death of Aden Rose. He has been informed, too, that the deputies of a northern California sheriff's office have captured Credence Gapstone, the prime suspect in the murder. Sunder receives this news solemnly, with the quiet satisfaction of a manly professional who has admirably acquitted himself in the performance of his duties. He asks polite questions, inquires, in a detached way, after meaningless details. The agents congratulate him, dismiss him from the meeting. They seem surer of him now.

When he leaves, he drives straight to the airport in New York. He packs nothing except money. He takes a flight to San Francisco, acquires a car, and drives northward like a madman, stopping for nothing except to fill the tank. Something is pulling him. Curiosity? A strange kind of vengeance? But his urgency is not anchored in emotion, not led by clear desire. It is his other self that leads him, that guides him and inhabits him and possesses and consumes him. And when this other self sees the crumbled jail, the crushed cars, the townsfolk mobbing the site and children running wild with excitement, when it beholds through Sunder's wide eyes the arrival of four black cars gliding up the hill like the barrels of longneck pistols and observes sixteen black doors swing open to reveal sixteen white men with very square shoulders wearing very serious expressions on their faces, when it hears those men tell the townspeople there were no gangs, no Russian infiltration, no subversive action of any kind, only a freak weather system, and hears them answer the question, "But what about the black man in the dress?" with, "He was carried off by rogue winds and probably dashed to death in the woods"—then Sunder's other self suspects that he has briefly found, and already lost, the source of power he craves.

Time slows.

Credence never fully understood what happened to him, or where he went. Was he lacerated, bisected, disemboweled by the grinning teeth like towers of blue flame? Did he vaporize, the way they do in science fiction movies? He feeds the impressions of his experience to Reginia, Langston, Roan, Sunder, Quentin, and Reynaldo, but they reel from it, recoil as he did:

In that Dark on the other side, in that bodilessness and senselessness which they have all now experienced, Credence floats, floated, a consciousness without anchor. In the waiting Credence figured that if he wasn't dead, he must be near to it. Was it the anteroom to Eternity? He was not himself anymore and yet he was, or at minimum he retained the sharp memory of a Credence Gapstone, and that person seemed to be buoyant in the vacuum of outer space, a bubble of nothing more substantial than name and memories. But if it was outer space, then it was one of those lightless patches between far stars, murky and unbeautiful. And if it was outer space, how could he be warm? For however slender his existence and wherever he now was, there was immense warmth around and about him, meadows and hills and sprawling hippodromes of it, endless galleries of hearthlike heat, as if in those caliginous depths he had become a gnat, a mite living on the surface of a vast topography of living, breathing flesh. A vast body in space. At times—moments of dithering wonder that seemed to repeat and stack one upon the next, till his sense of time became more vertical than horizontal, his sense of space inexpressible in three dimensions—he came to understand or to imagine that he had been transported in death to a new, nonincarnate life where he was a kind of sentient particle of dust nestled in a constellation without visible stars, and that, at the same time, his new home was as a parasite burrowed in the folds of skin covering a great full belly, a stomach slowly undulant like an exotic dancer's and yet reaching farther than the edges of a galaxy: that he lived on a body and he lived in a blanket of stars and dark matter, he was at once in heaven and deep in the black molten bowels of the Earth.

The living warmth never abated, but the silence, too, was large, an intricate, systematic emptiness, parlors and honeycombs and museums of blank quiet—until (and he could not say when, since once it happened, all that had happened before was extinguished in the new, a new now that erased all memory of the past and dreams of the future, and he could only recollect it as a point in time, an event, now, with Langston and the others crowded in his mind, tugging straight the untied whiptail frays of the densely snarled sphere of his thought)—until: sound moved across the Black.

The sound—and he listened for an eternity, not believing until he had no choice to believe—was of waves sighing against a shore, rising up and rolling forward to die and then be born again. It sounded like the sea. The sound was the sea—a sea. He could hear the bleat of gulls. Somewhere—above him, below him, to the left of the point at which his consciousness rolled adrift?

He could not reach the sea, or if he did, he did not know he had arrived. But he began to understand that the hiss of spray as water thrashed against rocks he could not see was not formless sound. It was language.

It said: *My son. My son. My son.*

That was how his mother came to him, his mother who had always been there, who was a part of that Dark, and who was it, as he was and is.

Verity embraced him, made him know that he was hers, that he was strong and wonderful, filled him with the pure elixir of her unwavering love as you would fill a balloon with your breath.

Then she sent him back. As she pushed him, she said, in a voice that was the chorus of rain striking earth, the metallic warble of lightning, *Son*.

Bubbles winking in and out; there, here, and in a twinkling gone. Gases colored the hot pink of flamingoes. Shiny bulbs with the startling heft of planets dangling inside them. At first they look to Credence, experiencing them again, like strange stars, a new galaxy, but then they look like huge beings, things with no faces but that move as if possessed of limbs; then they look like both.

Whatever it was or they were and are, the sight of them made Credence remember sight, and brought all of his consciousness back to him in one flash of terror at the unknown. Suddenly he did have a body, and his body was thrashing about, a weak swimmer in the grip of an undertow. In one panicked effort he tore himself free and discovered, as if he had spun 180 degrees in a room half shrouded in utter darkness and the other half illuminated in the unfiltered light of noon, the world he remembered:

The interior of a room with walls painted in sparkling blue and adorned with runny watercolors of horses and clowns and smiling, round yellow balls. There was a dresser and a two-shelf bookcase that stood on a desk, and a low bed with lots of large pillows on it—amid which lay like a pampered sultan a sleeping boy, no more than seven or eight years old.

A boy who saw Credence looking at him and at first shyly waved, only to grow troubled as he watched, for this was no good fairy from the picture books but a bloated version of a human, like a face squished against the glass of a locked window, like the body of a goldfish struggling against the invisible, incomprehensible limits of its tiny world.

The boy ran from his room, his small whimper doubling and trebling until by the time he reached his father it had become a piercing howl. The boy's father swatted him once on the arm to shut him up, and then swatted him again for making things up.

Credence watched the scene, unable to enter it. He knew at once that the boy being called Damian was the son that, in life, he never knew he had.

28

No one knew, but there were two Damians.

No one, that is, until now, here in the great waiting room at ten to the minus thirty-third power centimeters, where Langston, Reginia, Roan, Sunder, Quentin, and Reynaldo learn the truth at last, where Azaril has already been wallowing in it, and where the man-become-entity Credence Gapstone, so long tossed to and fro by waves of time and space, is reminded again as if for the first time.

Nobody knew before because nobody had been there to see both Damians. He tried to give them clues: the many piercings, for instance, and the tattoos of rayed saffron and scarlet suns glimmering above the backs of scorpions, and the winged dragon coiled around his waist with his belly button clasped between the serrations of its teeth. The change of name from Garrow to Sundiata, signifying his rejection of his past to embrace the heritage of a heroic warrior, was a clue. But even the people who thought they knew him considered these changes mere affectations. They missed the deeper transformations, beneath and beyond the dazzling tapestry of nomenclature and epidermis.

The first Damian is scarcely alive. The roving consciousnesses in the great nether space at the Planck length sense this: they feel themselves drawn like psychic simulacra of vultures to circle above the half-dead body of the young boy Damian.

The first Damian is a toddler who lives a fragmentary, water-torture existence, a limbo in which he perceives himself surrounded by the dead and haunted. Damian (that is, Reynaldo, or Langston, or Roan, now) does not remember the first Damian's mother well, except that when the image of her comes back to him, she appears like a still photograph in gray and white. She is not beautiful and not ugly. Her chief characteristic is her immobility, the certainty she conveys that she will not be moved by earthly considerations. She bears her son absolutely no ill will and just as much love as she can spare. She has greater concerns, and these are of such magnitude that a little rusty-butt boy-child bawling and screaming for succor cannot begin to measure up. Even as early as age two and three, his mother's absence is like a throbbing ache for the little boy. He feels hollow, emptied out, as if the bones of his skeleton have been sucked of their marrow and the only flow in his veins and arteries is of wind, a hot desert wind stirring sand and nothing else. Of course as a child he lacks the language to name his experience in this way. He has only the sensation of his hand thrust into hers, and the icy bloodlessness of her touch that jolts him like a shock and a shiver both.

The other women—later he will come to know that they are mostly either whores or nurses—do what they can to help him, but they, too, are otherwise occupied, and their affection is not unlike what they might bestow upon a stray puppy. They keep him fed and give him a place to sleep comfortably, and provide him with a few trinkets to maul in the various disheveled fleabag rooms they or their pimps rent. Mostly they keep him out of the way. "Your mama is very, very ill," the women tell him—cooing, making the bad news a lullaby. "She is feeling very, very poorly." When they deign to console him, they tell him ghost stories. It doesn't make much sense, filling a child's head with nonsense about gamy corpses risen from the grave with smashed noses and voices like howling wolves, but ghost stories feel to Damian's young mind inherently truthful, their fancies as factually solid as the sight and sound of Mommy and Daddy that other children his age consider the pillars of the universe. Somebody early on, maybe even his mother, had told him a ghost story, slipped it to him like an injection of heroin, and perhaps because he was in need, because he had neither blood in his veins nor mother's milk in his stomach, he became addicted to the intimacy he could wring from the promise of a return from death.

Perhaps the element of revenge in these stories appeals to him. *Deny me now,* vows the ghost-to-be, *but there will come a day when you will regret it.* The first Damian looks forward to the day he will become a ghost. And sometimes, when he sees a tiny version of himself twisted in the glassy reflection of his mother's eyes, he thinks he may be a ghost already.

Master Sergeant Garrow is of course more inclined to stories from the Old Testament than to superstitious old wives' tales, and he and his new wife both endeavor with the highest of motives to moor their adopted son in the rock-solid Word of the Christian faith. But Damian, child of the dead and haunted, pupil of whores (who know the little death) and nurses (who know the big death), slips from the grasp of his parents' teachings like a slender grass snake. He peppers the nuns who teach him catechism with questions about the Holy Ghost, a being whom he finds terribly fascinating. One evening he embarrasses his father in front of guests at Sunday dinner by announcing that Jesus Christ is a ghost, or else how could he have returned from the dead? The first Damian's adoptive mother, Lydia, tries in her halting way to intervene, but Master Sergeant Garrow—when stern appeals to reason and threatening frowns and warnings of a hellish afterlife fail to alter the child's position—ends up having to resort to the instruction of the belt, albeit with great reluctance.

Already a weak child, stunted by early years of malnourishment, the first Damian does not in the first years of his tenure among the Garrows weather his beatings well. Sometimes it takes him a couple of hours to feel himself walk as he had walked before the beating, and sometimes it takes too long for the scabs to harden enough to allow him to sit without breaking them and feeling stung. Nevertheless he is satisfied that he deserves punishment and that his father means the best for him. He is flawed, after all, and deeply wrong. He can never identify or predict his transgressions, but he pores painstakingly over all he does that arouses others' ire so that he might find the basic fault at the very core of his being.

The first of the two Damians strives mightily to become his father's son: tougher, leaner, meaner. When he can beat some of the other boys up, he thinks he can almost see the master sergeant's face floating in the sky above him, his eyes and mouth warm with pride. Yet if he sees his father's face smiling in the sky, he never sees such a face in the flesh. No matter what he does, no matter Lydia's appeals, the master sergeant frowns until he finds something that isn't perfect, and only then is the master sergeant happy. If Garrow feels pride, even at his own accomplishments, he never lets anyone know it. In the furnace heat of Garrow's dissatisfaction the proud floating face in Damian's dreams dissipates. Finally it, too, becomes a ghost.

The second Damian is, of course, born from the ashes of the first. A ghost is his midwife.

Damian is seven, and it is a stormy night. The lights are out in Damian's room and the master sergeant rages through the rest of the apartment destroying things—framed and mounted prints, silvery faux-crystal glasses, a hand-carved Bavarian dollhouse and all the little dirndl-wearing dolls, the transistor radio, each piece of the incomplete china set. Damian tries to sleep but he can hear them shattering, everything that bitch liked or bought for her own. Mrs. Garrow is soon to be Mrs. Garrow no more, having let it be known via airmail that, despite the fact that the allotted year of their trial separation is but four months old, she wants a divorce. Damian doesn't know how he knows this. The master sergeant didn't tell him. Damian seems always to know things he ought not to know. He knew of Lydia's affair before Garrow knew. Maybe it's the ghosts, floating around him, whispering.

The colors of Damian's room are pitch-black and smoky gray, the colorless colors of shadows, with only the *crack!* of breaking china to illuminate the gloom like lightning flashes. Damian lies on his back with his eyes wide, so that he will not be too much surprised if Garrow comes into the room. He's glad that Lydia isn't there, because he likes Lydia. He wonders if maybe she and the brown man she liked to play with will get married and have a daughter, and then someday Damian and the daughter will get married, far, far away from this place. The master sergeant won't be invited.

Little Damian dreams up scenarios: telling the master sergeant by phone that he is not invited and please just send money; writing the master sergeant a letter in which he tells him that Lydia's husband was more handsome than he and stronger besides, then hiding in a closet of the apartment while the master sergeant reads the letter and gets so angry he breaks all the windows and makes his hands bleed; arriving at the door with Lydia's husband with his big arms, and two bodyguards behind them, to hand the master sergeant a manila envelope inked in big black letters: "YOU ARE NOT INVITED, *p.s. you are fired you asshole*."

So enraptured is Damian by these visions, the joy and excitement of them, that at first he doesn't notice the strange shape that materializes in his room—well, *spiritualizes* or *ephemeralizes* might be better terms: a wispy, distorted, see-through phantom rustling in the dark air, its face bloated as if diseased. When he does see it, Damian waves without thinking.

The apparition makes no response, other than to continue the slow undulation by which it seems to curl in upon itself, as if it were paper suspended in a gently flowing stream.

Damian waves and waves, and the ghost doesn't respond. He begins to get scared. It's fine that there's a ghost visiting him, but for it to dangle there without saying anything feels like a threat. Holding his breath, Damian steps tentatively from his bed. He wants to be strong, decisive, like his father. But the ghost is between him and the bedroom door, and he wants to get out without being swallowed up. So he makes a dash for it, just escaping a right-leaning ripple of the thing's misty arms, and as he flings open the door the bottled terror of the moment spills out and he screams and begins crying.

These tears and his babbling description of the floating specter in his bedroom do little to endear Damian to the master sergeant, who is embarrassed to be caught shredding a pile of his wife's winter slacks with the broken edge of a shard from his wife's totaled glass lamp. Yanking off his belt, he swats Damian impatiently ("I'll give you something to cry about!" etc.), and, that duty done, orders the strange and perversely recalcitrant boy back to bed.

Given this reception, Damian isn't greatly reluctant to do as he's told. On his way down the hall, Damian feels his fear of the phantom recede, replaced by the slow burn of his anger and shame and the echoing throb of pain that lances his buttocks.

There's something new about the rudely uncommunicative ghost: it looks like it's moved. It hovers now by Damian's bedside, and a light that Damian had not noticed before burns through it. He climbs into bed, and in doing so has to climb through the ghost. It's a reckless decision to mix solid flesh with ectoplasm, and part of him suggests just sleeping on the floor rather than risking it, but Damian feels reckless tonight, because of his anger. Usually his father is right to spank him, but not tonight: there really is a ghost. Maybe the ghost calls him, maybe its silence speaks words Damian always needed to hear. He discovers that there's warmth in its light, a kind of tingling.

Damian can't stay afraid while that light touches his body. He sleeps easily with the ghost shining by his bed, as easily as if he were being rocked in a cradle.

When he wakes in the morning, the sting of his anger and shame is gone. Damian dresses himself that morning, and he feels happy as he goes about a task he usually dreads, feels happy even while surveying the holocaust the living room used to be. He does not see the ghost, but he feels certain that it is still there, beside him, above him, tingling beneath his skin. He is certain, too, that it always will be.

The child who has his or her own personal ghost has got it made. Langston realizes this and envies it as he experiences Damian's body and Damian's consciousness. And it makes sense, it explains Damian completely, this spectral presence. To feel that at every moment of the day, no matter what you do or how poorly or how well or how differently from everyone else you do it, that invisible arms enfold you. To be certain, truly certain, in mind and body both, that you are not alone and won't ever be alone, ever, ever again. Heaven. It's heaven.

This is Damian's secret knowledge, the truth that his friends Langston and Dillon and Azaril and Reynaldo and Quentin and so many others want Damian to give them: there are two worlds, and Damian knows it. A ghost walks beside him, with him, within him, and it tells him things, even though he can never hear it speak. The most significant of these missives from the Great Unseen are two: I am your real father, and one day, when I find the way, you and I will be together again.

Knowing this, having and hoarding this knowledge, Damian is freed. Master Sergeant Garrow was able to break the first Damian; but the new Damian is impervious to harm, impervious to control. He plays by his father's rules, but this is just a stratagem in the waiting game, for no rules of any kind really touch Damian or sway him.

Daddy Garrow notices the new streak of passive obstinacy in Damian after the destruction of the living room (it's always a mistake to let anyone see you lose control), and believes it the kind of challenge he can meet and master. Damian's body develops rather swiftly all of a sudden. Garrow solves this problem by pushing Damian into sports, to harness his troublesome new energy. Yet it is soon apparent that physical precocity is not the root of the problem. It's not the growth of his body, it's something occurring on a psychic level that he can do to you without even looking at you. The boy tends to arouse desire. His presence is subtly rattling. Garrow doesn't himself want the boy in any truly sexual sense, he's no pervert, for heaven's sake, but even he is not so immune to temptation that he misses the shift in the air, the distinct change in the charge of free-floating electrons that accompanies his son's arrival in a room. For a long time Garrow puzzles over the question, but cannot get further than the vague realization that Damian is tugging at him, tugging at everyone he meets. As if between blinks he calls to them by pursing his lips and obscenely wiggling his curled serpentine tongue. Damian seems without a single word or gesture to remind Garrow of something he's forgotten. Damian seems to chide others—chide, or tease them.

It's a threat. Garrow clamps down, issues strict curfews, polices Damian's room for porn magazines. When Damian hits thirteen, Garrow becomes obsessed with the suspicion that Damian is boinking his neighbors' wives. To combat this possibility, Garrow performs surprise inspections, dropping by people's homes unannounced at times Damian is supposed to be at practice or in school. The neighbors find Garrow's behavior unsettling and begin to think that the divorce has deranged him, but Damian endures these indignities with a detachment that seems infuriatingly to border on bemusement. He complies with the rules, never complaining.

The truth is Damian doesn't care that much about sex. He enjoys it, but he's not very driven by it. Very early in his life, perhaps when he was living with his mother's fellow prostitutes, he sensed that sexual appetite, sexual need, opened a way into people that allowed him to enter. He doesn't feel the compulsion to traverse the threshold—he has his ghost, after all, so what would he truly need from others?—but often he does, anyway. An insatiable curiosity leads him. Damian wants to find out if other people carry ghosts with them, and if they don't, what they feel like without ghosts. He wishes, in a sense, to be the ghost that others lack, however briefly. The feeling of being everyone's private ghost, everyone's sexual savior, becomes a sublime pleasure that pulls him back to people again and again; it endows his earthly life with meaning and mission, this task of transmitting the healing of the spirit through the climactic ejaculation of his seminal fluid.

No one frustrates or intrigues him more than those few who refuse his ministrations. Why should anyone refuse such an offer?

Why choose to live a life uninhabited by something greater than yourself? When the ghost came to him, Damian let him in. Wouldn't everyone else do the same?

Langston Fleetwood, for example, is a mystery. (*Langston, riding the tides of Damian's memory, thrusts the tip of his consciouness above the waves.*) In Ansbach they are drawn to each other. Soon after they meet they become linked, almost fused—almost. Their joining is inexorable and yet inexplicable, for their backgrounds and outlooks seem to be widely divergent. Langston is a child of privilege, and from Damian's youthful and still somewhat provincial perspective, a child of wealth. Langston's father, Damian once hears the master sergeant gossiping, is a big-time colonel and lawyer, with patrons in the Pentagon and the esteem of the commanding general of the U.S. Armed Forces in Germany. The Fleetwoods had never been slaves. The name Fleetwood rings with the sound of locks barring the doors of polished-wood-and-leather private clubs, the sound of ice cubes in tall tumblers of lemonade sipped on the veranda, the sound of servants bowing and scraping; Langston's airs have the scent of new-minted money and a rose garden on a sunny suburban estate.

Most important, there are no ghosts hovering about Langston's head—none, at least, of the beneficial kind. Sometimes Damian can look at Langston and see him as if from afar. What he sees in those moments is a huddled figure on an empty windswept ledge, two trails of frozen, crystalline salt tears like white ants running from eye to chin. Damian would like to approach that sad, lost creature as he has approached so many others, in the aspect of a quick-fix messiah. He would like to apply the salve of his magical saliva to Langston's open wound, to enfold Langston in a hug so hard and sure it would leave marks on Langston's psyche that would last forever.

Something is askew that prevents the enactment of this familiar drama. Langston refuses to be saved. And Damian—does Damian refuse to save him? Years later Damian can take a look back and tell a tale threaded with themes that were invisible to him at the time. He can parse out the differences between them. Langston, that's easy enough: an unruffled, serene exterior that masks a chasm of fear, a hidden valley where wolves prowl and dragons lie in wait. Damian himself: friendly, sympathetic, empathetic, passionate, but so calm, so imperturbably calm and removed beneath it all; his true self resides in another world behind the curtain, a site from which he channels the Damian everyone (except Garrow) loves. Even so, such a pairing ought to be complementary. Far from being night and day or oil and water, they should be more like two pieces of a disassembled puzzle, easily snapped snugly together.

Instead, they become antagonists. They pretend it isn't so, but several months after meeting, Damian knows—though Langston doesn't—that they are foes, wary of the other's successes, vengefully delighted by the other's humiliations.

Damian charges at the matter head-on. He doesn't understand the rift between them, he can't locate how or when it occurred, but he resolves to do something dramatic about it. He gives Langston one last chance. "Let's skip this afternoon," he whispers to Langston in algebra II, giving the invitation all the libidinous power at his disposal, practically blowing the words in the boy's ear. Langston lights up. Damian's sure he has him.

Damian takes Langston running with him, running together over the wet meadows that separate family housing from barracks, and under cover of the pretense that they're racing Damian brushes his hand near Langston's, lets his breath fall on Langston's neck. In Langston's room Damian uses the music to weave his spell. He traces sigils of beguilement in the air with the sinuous dance of his hips and the rhythm of his snapping fingers, he sings along with the lyrics in a voice that Langston was meant to hear as a lullaby and a seduction. . . . *Sensuality excites my mind—it makes me get! off!* Damian sings, but beneath the words, under his breath, discernible only if you record Damian's singing and then play it at twice the speed backward, other lyrics lurk. *That sly come-hither stare . . . it's witchcraft*, and a message: *get off. Get off the rag.You know what I mean. Get off that stupid little drama about how alone you are.*

Damian watches Langston dance, listens as Langston sings. There is no way he can fail. He dances around Langston, dances at Langston. He gyrates, undulates, oscillates, bobs, weaves, flounces, struts, zips, zooms, humps and pumps. If he wetted his finger with a slathering kiss and snaked it between the sweating cheeks of Langston's virgin ass, or let his tongue trace a helix or a pentagram from Langston's navel to the erect and oh-so-sensitive nipples of Langston's chest, he couldn't be closer to him. Damian waits for Langston to fall, quivering, into his hands. He waits to imbibe the taste of his conquest, waits to lap Langston's flavor and feel it mingle with the liquor of the drool coating his own tongue.

And Langston dances. He smiles. Dances and keeps on dancing. Oblivious? He can't be. But as Langston dances and dances, never quite retreating and never advancing, either, Damian upon closer inspection of the shivering boy he'd spied on the edge of a cliff perceives a fine golden mesh encasing Langston's body, and discovers to his shock that he can hear another incantation throbbing underneath the beat.

I am rubber, you are glue.Whatever you say bounces off me and sticks to you.

Damian leaves in a huff. It's late and he's missed dinner and he's in trouble, but he stops by Dillon's place and coaxes him into the basement so that he can fuck the taste of defeat out of his mouth. This stratagem does not prove satisfactory, but at least he comes if he fails to orgasm—and Dillon's plenty satisfied, so that helps. In school with Langston over the next couple of days, Damian tries pretending he hasn't been rebuffed. There are still flashes of opportunity: Langston sings with him, laughs with him, as if their stunted intimacy were something more than a failure. Damian enjoys it, but his enjoyment gives way to puzzlement and the conviction that he's being teased. He can't bear it.

There's a young guy in junior high school next door named Davey Mendez who's become enamored of Damian, and Damian turns to him for comfort. He brings the kid over to his room—that's the first mistake, but with Langston dancing and smiling, smiling and dancing through his thoughts, Damian can't be expected to think clearly. He figures he'll warm Davey up as he's warmed up others, with a little ritual he's pieced together from Marvel Comics, involving a knife, blood, oaths, a chalk-drawn circle on his wrestling practice mat, and an Earth, Wind & Fire song.

That night the master sergeant catches Damian for the first time: he bursts in on them when they're chanting, chanting nonsense, really, the kid's just keeping up with Damian and Damian's just making stuff up, words that sound cool, snippets of Stan Lee spells invoking the eternal Vishanti and Munnopor's mystic moons, and the truth is all they're doing is undulating to the music of EW&F, a little "Fantasy," a little "Serpentine Fire," and they're yodeling, kind of, as they try to match the falsetto vocals too high even for their choirboy voices, they're not doing anything really bad (though it's true their knees are touching as they pump their hips in the air, and neither has a shirt on, or pants, either), no, the bad stuff happened earlier—

But it's like a torrent, the way it happens that night, or like being down at the bottom of a well with the sun staring down to burn out your eyes and cascades of water pushing you down, down, down flat until you can't breathe or move. Daddy Garrow, false father, changeling patriarch, is more fiercely insane than he has ever been: he flings Davey Mendez aside, tossing him from the circle by the wrist the way you'd flick a fish from a boat by its tail, and he screams—actually screams, like a girl in a horror movie, when he sees the tiny trickle of blood across both boys' palms, and the other streak of blood, a scarlet crime that runs lengthwise and dribbles into spots like a messy exclamation mark on the backside of Davey Mendez's small white briefs.

Mendez runs. Damian fights. He's never fought before, only endured, but tonight he fights, as if infected by Garrow's frenzy, and they go at it, the battle both have been waiting for, their biblical and Homeric struggle. Damian thinks he might win, for a moment he does, he has Garrow nearly pinned in the circle, he sees something loosen in Garrow's eyes, a shift in Garrow's body, he has seen it in his opponents wrestling, he might be seeing it now—and then Garrow corrals him, entraps him so completely and successfully Damian feels that Garrow must have been toying with him. Garrow picks him up—he is nothing to Garrow, less than a doll, less than that—and now he will be flung against the wall, he will be beaten.

But instead Garrow collapses. Damian has stolen a glassful from Garrow's carafe of wine in the refrigerator, and now the tall tumbler glass jerks and falls, and berry red smacks against the black plastic covering of the mat as if one of them had spat it.

Damian looks at his father, lying on his back, twisted sideways across the center of the smudged circle. Garrow doesn't seem to be breathing. Damian breathes deeply and rapidly: he feels terrified, relieved, elated. And then the room grows unbearably hot, the sweat wrung from both of them as if they've been bursting with unshed moisture, and Damian begins to cry, because he knows: *This time he's coming to get me*.

But his guardian ghost does not manifest in the flesh. Instead it speaks through Garrow. Garrow's lips move and his tongue ponderously forms sound, but the words and voice are not Garrow's, but the ghost's. It is an obscene sight, a terrible sound. "I'm your daddy," the Garrow-ghost says. "Do you want to come see me?"

Damian hastily packs and runs away, without thought or worry for his destination. Hearing words more tender than have ever been formed on Garrow's tongue is the confirmation Damian needs to reject Garrow at last, finally and utterly, all that he needs to realize he can't stomach another day in Garrow's presence. He trusts in his real father to rescue him.

In the meantime, he knows he can rely upon his other charms, which is to say that he can depend upon the kindness of strangers.

Most helpful is a broad-minded German doctor named Andreas Neufeld, who spies Damian reclined on a Munich street corner using his backpack for a pillow. Dr. Neufeld is a Berliner, in Munich for a few days en route to a holiday in Morocco. He stops and offers Damian a meal and a bed. Damian knows exactly what Dr. Neufeld is offering, but Damian checks with his ghostly father, shrugs, and climbs in. He is surprised to discover that he's both right and wrong about the good doctor—right as to the doctor's proclivities and tastes, wrong as to the terms of the offer, which, as it turns out, was made more or less out of the goodness of Dr. Neufeld's heart, no strings attached. Neufeld delays his holiday to arrange for Damian to accompany him in his travels to Morocco and Egypt.

Trouble follows them to Egypt. An unfortunate chance event,

a maleficent configuration of the planets perhaps, or the consequence of a quantum probability equation that no science on Earth can yet calculate—*something* not wholly coincidental brings Damian and Sunder, his real father's nemesis, face-to-face.

Sunder Rex (i.e., the late Oliver Pierce, here in the cosmic waiting room sandwiched between quasars and nanoseconds very much a dead ringer for Quentin) is traveling in Egypt. He's found in his escape from the United States that his ability to become fluent in other languages has blossomed, and he has put this and his other unexpected talents to good use as he journeys the world studying insurgencies and acts of so-called terrorism, sometimes even participating in them, though always as a kind of low-level mercenary, so as not to become so involved that he loses his objectivity or gets diverted from his true purpose. In Cairo he's spending an indolent afternoon cruising the bazaars when he happens upon a young man, clearly American, clearly too young and inexperienced to be ambling about in a foreign land alone. Ripe for the plucking. Something familiar about him, too—but Sunder's not able to place the resemblance for years.

Sunder proposes to buy the young fellow a drink and dinner, even to provide him with a place to stay. To which the boy demurs, much as Sunder expects. Sunder, having become jaded in the ways of these seductions, probes gently but unwaveringly. When he finds that the boy harbors a keen interest in anything that can pass as occult, Sunder has the hook that he needs ("Ah, you are interested in the pyramids. Well, I can tell you *much* about the pyramids. . . ."). He decides, over a lengthy meal in a quiet cafe where he can be certain almost no one is a native speaker of English, to tell the youngster how he became a warlock.

"I left Oliver between Aden Rose's buttocks," he concludes. He smiles for the boy's sake.

The boy blinks, but holds up admirably, except that he can't stop looking over Sunder's shoulder.

"And now that I've told a secret of mine, why don't you tell me one of yours. This man, this German physician whom you are traveling with and who you claim to be your parents' friend, does not know your parents. And Damian Sundiata is not your real name," Sunder says. He cannot conceal his amusement and swats down a buzzing fly with the feral good nature of a fed lion flicking his tail.

"It is so," Damian retorts.

Sunder laughs. Immediately he sees that this is a costly miscalculation, for the boy leaps up from the table and dashes from the café—cleverly tipping Sunder's plate into his lap as he makes his exit.

Sunder leaves piastres on the table, dabs his fingers in the sauce spilled on his crotch, and licks before racing after the boy.

The chase presents him with very little challenge. Sunder knows the whimsical dance of the Bab Zuwayla quarter's medieval streets well, having been resident there for over a year, and Damian of course knows the streets and their dips and pirouettes not at all.

In Damian's flight back to the markets of the casbah, the one landmark he has any clear relationship to, he gets confused. Perhaps the incense, which wafts through the streets in a dozen different dizzying varieties, enchants him. Sunder can almost believe that his power is at work, controlling the young man by his own will, for he could not have planned better than to find Damian as he does with his back turned in a dead-end alley, with crumbling, boarded-up buildings on either side.

"I'm here to help you," Sunder says—but the thrill of the capture gives his manner a heavy air of menace.

Imagine Sunder's surprise when he's cast to the cobblestones by a sound like a freight train thundering over the rails at full speed. When he beholds the thirteenth-century facade of one of the buildings slide from the building like a falling curtain, and when the very air bulges and rips open before his eyes as if a fist had punched through thin plastic.

Damian—whose expression, Sunder notes, is not exactly one of fear—cannot be located when the smoke and debris clear.

Sunder abandons the search after a few hours. He departs Egypt reeling, haunted by the knowledge that once again, he has witnessed and lost what he seeks, and haunted, too, though more vaguely, by the memory of the boy's face and the sharper recollections that his features evoke.

Damian doesn't disappear, however. With the clear-headed quick thinking one would expect of a boy who has a private ghost, he uses the noise and commotion as a diversion and hightails it away. Upon his return to the hotel room he shares with Dr. Neufeld, he announces that he would rather leave, that, indeed, he is absolutely going to leave, immediately, with or without the doctor. Dr. Neufeld remains unflappable, undeterred in his apparent determination to support Damian no matter what he chooses to do. As his business in Egypt is mostly concluded, he offers to take Damian with him to Turkey and to India, and then back with him to Berlin, where he sets Damian up in a bedroom of his apartment. He demands neither rent nor sexual favors. He seems content to look at Damian, as if studying a sculpture reclaimed from ancient wreckage, and to listen to him, as if to the labyrinthine riffs of an obscure school of jazz.

Dr. Neufeld's generosity proves not to be unique in the annals of Damian's encounters. When Damian leaves Germany at the end of the summer (he decides he ought to continue his schooling, and fears doing it in Germany, where Garrow might somehow be able to track him down), he falls almost immediately into the clutches of an MIT professor and his wife with whom he shares a row of seats on the transatlantic flight. When the couple have seen to his enrollment in high school and put him up through six months of his freshman year in exchange for some nominal work around the house and the unaccountably scintillating pleasure of his company, off Damian goes again, this time under the aegis of a forty-year-old elegant black Chicago man who runs a company that performs traditional African dance and tours all over the country. A year or so later he stays with a lonely woman in New Mexico grieving the loss of her family in a car wreck, and so on, and so on. Along the way Damian finishes high school; learns to dance and to speak fluent Spanish; acquires a brown belt in tae kwon do; once in a great while—when between patrons—whores for money; and at all times plays Waiting for Daddy, a private game played across two universes, the high points of which are commonly marked by mysterious outbreaks of bad luck, ghost sightings, and peculiar explosions in the vicinity of his father's attempt to break through.

Damian keeps faith in his eventual reunion with his father by counting down each day that passes in a calendar the New Mexico widow gives him when he turns seventeen. She made the millennial calendar herself, a fat book full of blank unlined pages she's dated and decorated with pretty ink-and-crayon drawings of scenes from the book of Revelation, including three of the four Horsemen of the Apocalypse, and a heavily tattooed and hairy-legged version of the Whore of Babylon (who bears a resemblance to the drunk driver who killed the widow's family).

The widow tearfully explains when proffering the gift that she's counting down the days until she will be swept up in the Rapture and teleported to heaven to reside safely with her husband and children, while the rest of the wicked world perishes in the fires of its sin. Damian takes this to be a propitious omen, for, given the bedlam he's seen in Egypt and elsewhere, he, too, has reason to believe that when comes the day of joyous reunion with his father, the world will be rocked with cataclysmic change. In the meantime, Damian ventures about spreading gospel, though his ministry is of a more physical nature—but, he would have insisted if asked, with the intended effect of spiritual salvation. Perusing the notations on each marked day in the Apocalypse Calendar, we would find that over the years, between his stay with the widow and his departure into thin air during a celebration on Calle Ocho, Damian sleeps with—ministers to—several hundred men, and over fifty women.

Langston Fleetwood, naturally, is not the most pressing of concerns in the progression of these events. But neither is he wholly forgotten.

When Langston stumbles upon Damian in Sproul Plaza that day, halfway around the world from their first meeting and last parting, Damian beholds Langston's jangling, sleep-deprived eyes and he knows him instantly, recalls everything about him. It is as if a god has rolled back the waves from the shore and parted the sea. Langston the pharaoh, his onetime brother, stands at the edge of the sand on the other shore, and the spears of his armies glisten in the sun.

In each crisis, they say, there is an opportunity, and there it is, Langston Fleetwood from out of the blue, eyes wide and stammering his insistence that they once knew one another. Damian sighs, looking out over Langston's head at the walls of liquid, churning night, the fishes' eyes staring at the gap in the world, the green, crushed bones of animals and wrecked ships scattered across his path to the other side, and thinks: *It is time to cross over, to get to the bottom of the matter at last.*

He flashes Langston the sort of smile Langston gave him that night long ago when they danced, and goes home to think about it.

The key, Damian decides, is Dillon, the third of their trio. Damian has almost forgotten him, but Dillon was much like Langston, brimming with the force of need and desire. But unlike Langston, Dillon swam with the tide. Dillon let whatever forces ordered or disordered his life have their way with him.

What had made Langston different? Dillon and Langston were reasonably similar except in the inconsequential details like gait and ways of speaking, and the minutiae of their boring biographies. Except, of course, for that one thing. The color thing—Dillon being a white boy and all, Langston being what's supposed to be the opposite. They were not culturally different, really; Dillon was a white boy who'd hung out with black boys for as long as he could remember, and so the two were not much different in that respect than boys of a certain age and of similar economic class raised in two different parts of town.

Langston's difference from Dillon lay in his expectations for himself and for the world, which, while high enough in that educated American professional's way—where you aim to be "the best" in your field and rake in the green, you want to marry well, live comfortably, contribute something to the community, and maybe someday get your fifteen minutes of fame—were nevertheless not expectations that soared. A leash, as on a falcon's neck, kept Langston's hopes tethered to the Earth. Back in Ansbach, when Damian, frustrated with Langston and furious with him for no good reason he could identify, offered himself to Dillon out of the blue, Dillon took hold of the gift firmly, not from desperation, but with the confidence that he deserved whatever good came his way. Langston possessed no such confidence.

What happens when you don't belong to the group that already doesn't belong anywhere else? What happens when you're not at home in your family, not at home in your neighborhood, not at home among your own? We all know (Sunder knows best of all of them): equal parts desire and rage. The craving to belong and be alike—a craving like a jones, spinning you around, playing you ruthlessly, it's got you doing things you don't even know you don't want to do, going places you don't need to go, just for that fix, that fabulous high, of being at one with the all-powerful Them, be They the rich, the beautiful, the witty, the smart, or the boys on the corner chugging forty-ounces with the elegance of seraphim sunning on their winged backs in a bank of cumulus cloud. The desire to be alike, bound like the stars of Gemini to its equally irresistible twin, versus the rage to be apart, unlike—a frenzy that if coupled with telekinetic powers would make us lay waste to continents, would rocket us out into the emptiest corner of the night sky where we would shine alone, without the crippling need for air, water, or the insidious gravitational tug of other bodies.

That was (is?) Langston.

Got on Damian's nerves. Reminded him of something. The old Damian. Ghostless, motherless, fatherless, bereft. Where Langston and those like him were concerned, Damian had the bodhisattva's problem that the sages don't talk about: when you know you're not alone, don't all the people who just keep insisting that they are alone kind of piss you off? All that toil and worry about belonging—just get the fuck over it, please. How could you be a Fleetwood, whose ancestors were never slaves and whose fathers were officers and whose mothers didn't do heroin and weren't crazy, and *still* be parentless and ghostless? It is Damian and Langston who are too much alike.

But what about me?

A clamorous, tectonic shout rocks the nether universe.

It's the other five of them, wriggling free of each other to demand personal satisfaction now that they realize Langston's hijacked the narrative. (*What about* my *relationship to Damian? What about* my *powers? What about the powers I want to have? What about the disappearances?*)

Reginia, the role of band leader thrust upon her, tries to get them all to harmonize and stick to the main tune.

And then what happened? she demands, and grabs the whole place by the scruff of its neck (psychically, of course), and makes it cough up the goods.

One would think—

One would *think*—but Damian's not doing much thinking these days, at least not the sort of thoughts that we recognize, i.e., words and pictures in rapid transit like a *Ben-Hur* chariot race taking place on a German autobahn. Since he arrived in Miami with Azaril and Langston a few days ago, Damian's brain feels like it's emptied out, like it's left the solid state behind and entered a phase between liquid and gaseous wherein he neither calculates according to private agendas nor fully reacts to outside stimuli. He processes virtually nothing, yet neither does anything escape his attention. Everything is action, everything is experience: as he moves, the bottoms of his toes seem to soak in floods of information from the simple sensation of being pressed against the sole of his shoe touching the Earth. At rest, the mere act of inhalation makes him feel that he has taken a leap from a peak of the Andes, that he is spinning on an axis like a top, that he is in the throes of an orgasm pulsing to the rhythm of high tide, all at one time.

He thought at first that it might be all the drugs. Usually he's something of a horse where narcotics are concerned; a stew of ketamine, Ecstasy, and liquid acid chased by Herradura Silver tequila shots couldn't rattle him much more than a gin and tonic would rattle the rest of us, because his ghost is always there to steady him. But this is different. His ghost is there, always is, but something other than his invisible friend seems to steer his actions and perceptions. He cannot name it, nor does he care to; his only response to its capture of his body and mind is to obey, happily and without reservation.

This Guide has brought him to Quentin. Skinny fellow: strange and bitchy, but compelling. A tissue of faint magenta radiance around him that sparkles like a jeweled lattice collar of Elizabeth I when he smiles. Damian met Quentin at the bar in Redemption. He should have been preoccupied with this hot Cuban piece Reynaldo, a glorious new being he'd been jostled against two days ago while craning his neck to watch a float pass by in a parade downtown. When Damian looked at him, Reynaldo had a gold and white halo shimmering over the crest of jet-black hair on his head. And not only there: around his neck, and on his wrists, and hula-ing his waist, too. Damian, in love for the seventh time that afternoon, made a date with him, and they'd been playing with one another for two days. But then, rather than getting some more of what he suddenly couldn't get enough of (and giving more of what he could never get enough of giving), Damian got mesmerized by Quentin's terrible drag performance.

Ray-something-or-other melted in Damian's mind (the whole pocket universe can feel Reynaldo's ire flash across the memory, transforming the scene into a black-and-white negative for half a millisecond). Damian flirted with a cute, tanned, goateed blond boy who took a fancy to his tattoos, even made out with him, but Damian knew it was the bad drag queen he was there for, knew it though no sentence formed in his thought declaring it so.

When Quentin spoke to Damian at the bar, his southern accent put Damian on a playground swing: flying backward into the delicious fright of something you can't see, kicking forward into the sky, higher and higher, the ballooning of your stomach making you giddier and giddier. Quentin asks Damian to spend tomorrow afternoon with him. Damian says OK—though he remembers he was supposed to spend some time with Reynaldo, and he's aware of Azaril and Langston somewhere out on the dance floor.

But Quentin's important somehow. Each of his tricks, everyone who needs Damian's touch, gives Damian something in return, so Damian decides he'll go with the flow, see what Quentin has to offer.

So why, as they stand shoulder to shoulder amid the early afternoon crowd that has made a park of Calle Ocho, why, amid the haze of sounds—the men and girls and boys and women laughing, their hands where they shouldn't be and wouldn't be but for this extraordinary moment in history, like the end of the War, when the soldiers grab hold of women they've never seen before and won't ever see again and celebrate as we all wish we could celebrate always, with loose tongues thrashing around in the mouths of the beautiful, with our bodies nuzzled up urgently, naked with need, against those we desire but from whom on any ordinary day we shrink in fear, and here in the noon sun on the street where Castro's death was first announced it's like that, Damian can taste that frenzy of license in the air, and it's all around him, the hissed words full of teasing and innuendo, the hips and breasts slapping at the air made thick by sweaty proximity, and the band on the dais choreographing it all, drumming out a beat (five fast beats *boomboombboom boomboom*, four long beats *boom boom boom boom*) with horns crooning an exuberant strut—why, why amid all this, does Damian no longer perceive the soft lift of Quentin's accent, why does he hear nothing other than the incessant ringing of Quentin's cell phone?

Shrill metallic warbling. Over and over.

"It's ringing again," Damian informs Quentin. His own words sound harsh to him, like trash-can lids slamming over the delicate heights of an aria.

Quentin pulls the small silver contraption from his pants pocket. The face of it gives off a tepid greenish glow that wriggles over Quentin's cheekbones.

Is Quentin trembling?

"I'll just walk out of the crowd for a few minutes so I can answer," Quentin says, palming the phone.

While Damian waits, no sound penetrates his thoughts. Just that ringing, over and over.

And it seems hotter than before.

No, it's not Quentin who's trembling. It's Damian. He brings his hands together. They cannot remain still.

Quentin comes back. He looks annoyed as he maneuvers through the shifting labyrinth of couples and triples. When Quentin reaches Damian's side, he half shouts with a shrug, "My grandmother. Checkin up on me."

But when he says this, Damian's forehead throbs, right in the center. Like a cobra lies coiled there and suddenly begins to unfurl its cold, scaly length.

Damian wonders why he's trembling—oh, yes, there's no doubt Quentin is lying. Damian knows that face, it is like the master sergeant's face, and Langston's face, a face whose skin is stretched taut in an effort to conceal the muscular twitches that accompany plotting and dodging. But why should it matter that Quentin is lying when they all lie, what danger does Quentin's lying do? Damian wonders if Quentin, who has taken his hand, notices him trembling.

Damian, just because he must do something, decides he'll call Reynaldo. He gives Quentin a little consolatory peck on the cheek while he pages through his phone's directory, then dials. "Hey, Rey." Damian can't hear Reynaldo's response. There's an enormous amount of static. "Hey, hear that?"

Boomboombboom boomboom . . . Boom boom boom boom.

Maybe everyone else sees flames explode behind the band. Dimly, Damian is aware that what others see is not what he sees. His Guide tells him this. He doesn't trouble himself with the discrepancy. His mind is full, his brain sizzling, liquefying, collapsing in genuflection to what he sees: the sky, the whole world split down the middle, as if darkness were cleaved by a butcher's blade, and from the rend between spills dancing entrails of light.

Damian knows his father is there, though he is surprised, because his father's arrival has never felt this way before. Before, he would see this sight, or some unsettling version thereof, and he would behold it from a secure vantage point, frightened by it, perhaps, but apart from it, as one stands at the outer limit of the tide watching the tumult of the waves, or at the Earth's edge, peeking over into the fatal depths of a canyon. Between you and the revealed majesty of Nature there is a demarcation, the humbling certainty that says, there before you is God uncloaked, and here inside your skin is an overly bold child whose time has come to be gently chastened.

But not this time. There was never more than a wink that separated Damian from the unnatural, supernatural force that he believes is his father, never much more than a child's shaky faith in fairies and Casper the Friendly Ghost that it *could* be true.

Now that gossamer curtain of safety falls away. As if a playground swing travels an arc without limit, up, up, and away, and in the frosty reaches of the exosphere he realizes that the wide leather thong that held his buttocks is no longer there, the chains that braced his hands have disintegrated. And now—

In the frothing coils of light and dark, in the black sea above and storms of blue stars below, there is a figure, immeasurably tall, unsolid, much like the soup of brightness and liquid and gas and color in which the figure appears. The figure wavers, like a curl of fire. It has no face, for so ardent an emotion as this figure expresses would in an instant make a mere nose, mouth, and eyes combust and crumble to ash.

Yet it seems to have arms, and they are outspread in a stance recognizable as welcome.

29

Yeah, yeah, yeah say Langston, Reynaldo, Quentin, Sunder, Roan, and even Credence, shrugging their collective shoulders within the never-never land of Damian's memory.

Having been there done that, they want more. More thrills, more sensations, more knowledge. Like: the scene spritzes, a TV screen in high-speed remote control surf, and then there is Sunder, his dark bulk balanced on the tip of his toes as he holds the pulsing throat of a scrawny man in his grip, and Sunder watches the fear spread from the man's eyes to his groin, sees the sweat blur the swastika tattooed on the man's shoulder, and finds this panorama of sights so sweet that a surge of testosterone rattles him to his very core, so he waits, waits, waits—such regret that it has to end—until finally he twists the knife and lets the hot blood spray over his hand and up his arm. Like: Reynaldo's tongue lodged in Damian's throat, Reynaldo's thumb turning pirouettes in Damian's sphincter, Reynaldo holding Damian aloft with Damian's legs wrapped around Reynaldo's high, hairy ass—they tumble to a mattress of disarrayed sheets that smell of Reynaldo's funk, there is a demonic leer in Reynaldo's wide-open eyes, he doesn't close them when he kisses. Like: what it's like to have money, money, money, so much that if you liquidated every holding and got it all in cash you couldn't find enough space to keep the stuff, not if you slipped bills between every two pages of every book in your voluminous Alexandrian library, stuffed wads into winter-coat linings, hid briefcases of it under the floorboards, papered the cathedral walls of your Bavarian castle with it and wrapped the silverware sets with layers of it stapled together. What it's like to have an itch, and a fantasy about relieving that itch, and just order it up, presto, then forty-seven minutes after you've unplugged the phone and dismissed the servants, there he is, big n' rough n' tall n' mean with Mandingo endowments and endurance, the better to endure the whipping you give him across his back with the leather-padded whip, the much better still for him to revenge himself upon you, tossing and slapping and ramming and stroking and anointing you exactly as you said you wanted—and never mind the bill. Like—

(*Who wanted* that, *which one of you nasty little sons-of-I-don't-know-what wanted to . . .?*)

The cascade of mockery that greets Reginia's attempted occupation of the moral center almost overwhelms her. It's gone too far. They've stayed too long.

All right, then: evidently these sex-mad, kill-happy sickos are not aware of the divine Reginia's power, or how irked she gets when swine misuse the limitless powers of the spirit, so she's gonna show 'em.

The universe swirls and churns. From its nothingness, from the raw, mushy dough of suspended consciousness, a hurricane springs. *How?* Roan's cry can be felt above the fray, a whine in their thoughts as she is yanked from revisiting Damian's story (she happened to be Dillon, and found the experience of being a randy young wrestling stud rather stimulating). *She's seized control*, Sunder shrieks in answer, as the cosmic funnel vacuums him up (but he's grateful, as variously being drafted to inhabit

Damian's sphincter and playing the part of the Nazi youth he killed proved none too pleasant).

We're blowing this pop stand—unmistakably Reginia, grown as large as an ocean liner in the pictures of their minds.

Boom-shaka-laka-laka-boom, Langston hears, or feels the vibration of the universe attuned to its sublime beat, stars and planetary orbs shaking like tambourines, *boom-shaka-laka-laka-boom.*

He denies it, surely this schoolgirl pom-pom chant can't be the incantation. But the sensation or illusion of sensation is undeniable as he perceives himself lassoed away from the naughty pleasure of being a Mandingo hustler rummaging through Mrs. Gillory's orifices. He feels himself circling. Then he notices that it is himself he feels, that, indeed, pieces of his body are reattaching to his consciousness like pieces of a designer ensemble tossed from the wings of a stage onto a mannequin. His left foot, right eye, and third finger on the right hand all at once, then the shoulders, the eyebrows, the chin, gastrointestinal system (gross), buttocks, the other eye, all accumulating faster and faster as if he were being spun into consommé by a gigantic cotton candy machine.

Dad! someone screams.

It's Damian. Damian is there with them, not just in memory. And Azaril. Does Langston feel Azaril there with them, too?

In the no place, the now place, where they all are, Reginia, Langston, Sunder, Mrs. Gillory, Reynaldo, Quentin, and Credence—

Crushing arms of night and deep fathoms gather her in. . . . Verity rises from darkness into a rich humus blackness punctured by a pinprick of brilliant light that, as she notices it, spins toward her at the speed of lightning flicking from heaven to sea. And now she sees where she is, as she stands floats walks swims:

It is a gargantuan port, with a sky so tall the sun crowning it seems to be more distant than Sirius though its brightness is twice that of Sol, and with a crystal blue sea that plunges downward to what must be the center of the Earth. Ships, tiny, tiny, tiny as infant fingernails, tossed and taken by the waves, and ships larger than mountains, with hulls so massive they rake the seabed beneath as though farming the soil, ships shaped as hats and bowls and in the likeness of cigars and saucers and birds of prey, ships in the form of city spires and cathedral domes, wild horn-backed elephants bearing litters ships, ships of thick-skinned steel and of milky amoebic fluid, galleons and royal barges and aircraft carriers and triremes, ships that quite clearly are built to travel through space on solar winds or by riding the waves thrown off from exploding stars or to flipper under water or ride storm clouds or to pass through solid rock or dimensional walls.

Ships that look, that quite clearly are, human bodies: skin, bone, chemical, electric, soul-powered.

(and there is Plennie, Daddy and Aunt Ida, Lin captaining *one of the rock-ships; and there—there—is David—)*

Towering over these human figures, encasing them in translucent membranes like the skin of jellyfish, are massive versions of the man-sized flesh creatures, bestriding the waters and airs of the port as though they are colossi marching sentinel at the harbor of an ancient city. Verity, entranced with these ghostlike giants, bends farther and farther back to catch the look in their pond-sized irises, only to see her own face, big as three houses abreast and as thin as vapor, at the same moment bending toward her with an expression of beneficence that Verity cannot entirely see but that she can feel, as though she were a pup newly arrived from the womb, and the gentle canine-loving owner were surveying her from unguessable heights.

There are hundreds of thousands of the ships, human and quasi-human and otherwise, thousands of millions of them, maybe more, far too many to count: all bearing trinkets, jewelry, rings, candy, people, animals, viruses: offerings.

And passing, to and fro.

30

Mrs. Gillory's room, Hotel Wessex, Miami, Florida, midnight in September

On the floor. In a circle. Holding wet and slippery-slick salty hands.

They look around; see relief and exhaustion in the creases of the haggard flesh of everyone's faces. Their hair and clothes soaked—with sweat, with saline amniotic moisture.

Reginia, Roan, Sunder, Reynaldo, Quentin, and Langston.

Azaril, his arms around Damian. These two crouch in the circle's center.

Damian is wetter than all of them put together. There is a small pool rapidly collecting around his buttocks and feet. His whole body shakes, wracked with the seizures of the newly born. It's the first time he's had a body in a long while. His eyelids are clamped. To ward off the light? Maybe all the water comes from his tears. He is sobbing, wailing.

Langston imagines he understands Damian's trauma. Back there, in whatever state they were in, Langston knew what it was to be everyone all of them had ever met. It made him more afraid than he's ever been, but it was also more glorious than anything he's ever known. He felt for that brief, already fading moment that all the walls of the world had tumbled down, and there was no pretense anymore that he was not always, at every moment, in the entangling meshes of a network of thronging life. It was excruciating. He could neither bear it nor reject it.

Langston crawls from his place in the circle on all fours, unwilling to trust his reconstituted legs. He locks arms with Azaril, embracing Damian, too.

"There, there. There, there."

Uncomfortable rustling. Quentin and Reginia, who had been on either side of Langston, drop the hands of Roan and Sunder and Reynaldo, and the circle falls apart.

"I am not at all pleased."

Sunder is stationary, in Buddha pose. Perhaps a burning Buddha: mist, or smoke, trails around his elbows up past his shoulders and above his head like the living tubes of an opium hookah.

Reginia sags back to rest the top of her head against one of the beds. "You *ought* to be better than pleased. We have my nephew's friends back, safe and more or less sound. You've helped a man whom you betrayed years ago. And you have discharged the debt you incurred by damn near killing these boys. And . . ." She throws the book at him. "*Hex* is yours. Langston won't be needing it anymore. Right, Langston?"

Langston is watching Azaril slowly stroke Damian's bald head and fling away the sheets of moisture with gentle sweeps of his hand.

"Langston?"

Is it possible he doesn't hear her? Of course he does; his senses, working with a reassembled body though they may be, are operating with their usual proficiency. He notes the concern, the fillip of urgency as she calls to him. If anything, Langston's perceptual abilities seem enhanced by his resurrection from nothingness. But his attention, that subtle taskmaster that would sacrifice the lives of all its slaves to complete the pyramids, has other priorities: Damian is opening his eyes.

Reynaldo and Quentin approach the trio on the floor and

kneel down. Just as Langston once saw them in his vision, except that Damian is level with them on the floor rather than standing above them.

Damian's eyes open, and if like a newborn or a longtime captive in a dungeon he needs to adjust to the assault of visual stimuli, his gaze does not show it. He meets them steadily, levelly, each in his turn.

Damian does not speak. But he does not need to. In sci-fi flicks, the mind readers, the telepaths, are mutants and aliens and freaks of evolution. But maybe speech, after all, is merely the rough model of an antecedent telepathy. Maybe *homo erectus* spoke without speaking, composed poems without ever writing them down: he just looked at the hairy gal on the other side of the campfire, and looking back at him she shivered at the beauty of his description of the gibbous moonlight sifted through the ballet of flames.

For each of the four Damian has a message of gratitude. To Azaril he communicates simply, disdaining even the ostentation of a reassuring squeeze of Azaril's hand: we are brothers. With a bit more flourish he reminds Reynaldo of Reynaldo's native gifts, Reynaldo's worth even when he provides no support or service for others. *If things were different, you'd be the one,* Damian says—and though these words feel like Reynaldo's own thoughts, they come to him in Damian's own flowing cadence. Damian tells Quentin that they'll go somewhere special, do something fantastic, just the two of them. And to Langston he says, *You're my favorite.*

Two of them believe what they are told, two of them don't. Two of them have been told the truth, and two haven't. It doesn't matter—mostly they're all four getting the same communication, just by looking at him: to look upon Damian's face is to see that he's not quite of this Earth. His countenance appears to them like the surface of water stirred by the slightest of breezes—a pane made of liquid, and the liquid is dark, dark and yet mysteriously translucent.

In that opaque reflection they are jolted by an intensified version of one of those unsettling mirror moments—when you catch your visage and are brought up short, seeing you not as a face surrounding a zit or as a head of unruly or embarrassingly receding hair, but with the startling gift of total perspective. You see that you are not your thoughts and feelings. You become aware of yourself as others see you—limited, contained, a separate body moving through the world rather than through some elusive "experience." The vantage is godlike, for what stands before you is a strange, marvelous creature, produced from nowhere, as if from a magician's hat. And it seems as though all that is the self—the narratives, the justifications, the gallery of impulses bizarre and familiar and mostly forgotten, the wounds and scars, all of what you are today—is made lighter and more lambent, the mere product of practicing being you, a series of larks and gambits played out on a ghostly chessboard. The board's black-square-white-square repetition is the architecture of your daily experience, and the players are a pliable, plastic, variable Flesh trading moves with a changeless, eternal Spirit. Neither player gets the better of the other. There are no losers, or else, depending on how you process the facts, there are no winners. But the game is your life and the game is you.

Not that they can stand the revelation for very long. Reynaldo's the first to turn away, mumbling something about having to go to the bathroom, and then Quentin drops his eyes, and then Langston. But Azaril meets Damian's gaze and doesn't look away.

"Az, were you OK in—in there?" Langston ventures, touching Azaril on the shoulder.

"He should be fine. He wasn't in but for a couple days. It's dangerous only if you stay a long time," Reginia answers. She stands by at a discreet remove, a scientist immersed in the ecstasy of observing her experiment's data stream. "That's probably why Damian's having a little trouble speaking right now."

Moments pass as they watch Damian, waiting for him to speak. Mrs. Gillory takes her whimpering dog in her lap and strokes him, speaking quietly in his ear.

"Uh—Miz Wolfe!" Reynaldo dashes from the bathroom and whispers in Reginia's ear. "Do you think maybe that drug has, uh, side effects?"

Reginia's attention is focused on Langston. "Pardon?"

"Well, cuz I was urinating, and I could swear . . . I mean I know my own, you know, and . . ."

"Oh!" She brightens, and then answers so everyone can hear. "I forgot. That's a little gift. I hope you all don't mind. No feat is impossible at the Planck length, they say, and with all that abundant energy of baby universes and all the matter the energy could be converted to, I just couldn't resist the opportunity to do something, even a little thing, and it was on my mind because I had been thinking about when I was younger, you know, probably because of that damn love spell of Langston's—anyway, so: I gave all you boys an extra inch. Or two."

"What!" Quentin leaps up to go to the bathroom, and even Azaril turns away from Damian to look at her. Langston thinks, with a kind of precipice horror that prevents him from thinking beyond the syllables of the sentence: *My* aunt *has psychically handled my penis*.

"You may also notice that Roan and I have lost a few pounds and we've put on a few pounds in the right places, with a little nip and tuck on her wrinkles, too. It's a harmless way to expend excess energy. Granted it's a tad outrageous, but us witches and warlocks can't be about doing the Goddess's work *all* the time. We gotta have some fun, too." She raises her voice as everyone discreetly checks themselves and a growing murmur of pleasure ripples around the room. "Don't you agree, Langston?"

Langston's mouth mimics a smile. "I was wondering. If it's more dangerous there the longer you stay, what happened to Damian's father?"

Reginia gives Sunder a quizzical look

"Ummm, that's rather complicated . . ." Reginia says, gathering herself up in grand professorial fashion.

Langston, Azaril, Damian, Quentin, and Reynaldo sit on the floor like puzzled kindergartners.

"To get to the heart of the matter," Sunder harrumphs. "Credence Gapstone had no body. His body could not exist in that place without some form of protection, which he lacked. Only his consciousness remained. My own conjecture is that the place into which we have all recently traveled is a stable wormhole, a tunnel that penetrates and traverses space and time. It was most probably a constructed wormhole, built maybe by some extraterrestrial civilization in some way and at some time we could not begin to fathom. It might have been a mode of travel, or even a kind of ship of its own, in that it clearly converts matter into energy that can be more rapidly transported than matter, and binds together those who come into contact with it into a collective consciousness—perhaps originally the 'pilot's' consciousness. *Consciousness* is the key. Thought rules this wormhole, this ship. Credence had become that consciousness, and therefore he could, by thought, transport Damian to it. Likewise, Damian could transport Azaril. Hence the profusion of material figures that arise in response to thoughts. Like the Castro apparitions—the energy discharged by the ship as it passed, riding collective anxieties—"

"My view is that the Castros were tunneling in from parallel universes," Reginia interrupts. "We were positioned at a point where you could observe histories as they happen. Those scenes we were in were happening, right when we were living them, right there in '53 or '71. All times were one time. And all universes are one universe."

Sunder waves his hand dismissively. "Have it your way. In any case Gapstone spoke a spell that opened the door to this wormhole or the parallel universes because he had the thoughts in mind that acted like a key. He spoke the spell in the right frame of mind at the right time—"

"Oh, they're not going to understand that. Listen, kittens. A metaphysician understands that the Universe is not merely a wondrous physical construct made up of atoms and subatomic particles and populated with black holes and quasars and yellow suns and red giants and planets up the gazoo. Instead, in every form there is a Spirit which proceeds from a Single Force, and that Single Force is the origin of everything. Universal Law, the dictate of Spirit, responds to thought. This is the mechanism whereby we can understand Credence to have 'called' what I'll just refer to as the Other Space, which operates according to this mechanical metaphysical law. Verity probably also called it by using the storm on the Day of Return—somehow—she must have had more power than she knew—and so it is her spirit that has imbued the Other Space for decades, connecting its peculiar vibration to Credence and to Roan (through the Roses) and finally to Damian, and even to Langston and then Azaril (through Damian). *Hex* isn't necessarily key, though it helps. Ultimately, it's the connection to Verity and her descendants, and desire for reunion, that triggers the power. At this point Verity isn't much more than a sort of overriding sentiment in that between-space. And Credence will become the same, if he isn't already."

Sunder agrees. "And if her missing husband and father and mother were there, they're in the same state. If Credence remained in that other dimension, then he would remain in the same predicament he has been in for twenty years or more . . ."

"And continue to cause havoc every time he tried to get back with his son," Reginia says. "That's why Roan ended up being Mistress of the Universe for a while. Every time the Other Space conjoins with our little reality—"

"Every time the ship lands," Sunder corrects her.

"Whatever. It causes damage, the massive energy spills over—"

"The 'havoc' isn't so much of a problem, really."

"You say that only because you wanted to control the thing and cause the havoc you want."

Sunder rolls his eyes. "Reginia hijacked the energy of the wormhole."

"No one can say it even was a wormhole, Sunder! And this poor child Damian doesn't need to know all that mess, anyway. He just wants to know where his father is. See, darling, there was so much raw power associated with that Other Space we were in. To get us out, and rescue you, and get your father out, I had to—"

"She scattered him. She destroyed the 'door' to the wormhole and scattered all the excess energy as far and wide as she could scatter it, like someone pulverizing an asteroid and sending its pieces to plummet all over the Earth."

"Thank you for the dramatic reading, Sunder. But it wasn't as military a maneuver as all that. Damian, I'm sorry. I wasn't able to cobble together a body for Credence. It had been too long, and we didn't enter the place together and I hadn't protected him the way Sunder, Roan, and I saw to it we were all protected. Anyway, what I'm saying is that—"

"Your father only existed as consciousness imbuing the doorway to the singularity or wormhole. Excuse me. The as-yet indeterminate other-dimensional space. His consciousness now imbues the pieces of that doorway that Reginia flung to the ends of the Earth."

"OK." Damian's voice is loud and warbled, an effect of strained effort and long disuse. But apart from this his tears are gone, and he has about him a quiet reserve, a semblance, at least, of calm, as if despite everything he still feels and will never lack the feeling of a ghostly presence with its arms wrapped snugly around him.

"But where are these pieces?" Langston asks for him.

Sunder and Reginia give each other a look that mingles mutual hostility with a plea for help.

Sunder tugs at his wide, square chin. "That is rather complicated. . . ."

Think of Credence Gapstone as an ethereal meteor that crashes into your backyard garden. The typical flaming slab of celestial real estate would tend to strike Earth with homicidal vigor, like a thunderbolt from the blackened palms of almighty Zeus. The impact would have the force of many tons of TNT, cause maniacal tremors that ransack the globe in the form of earthquakes and tidal waves, send up dust clouds to cut off sunlight, and—supposing it chooses your garden for a landing strip—obliterate your house and you in your house. Thankfully the Gapstone meteor has no mass. It will not create an indentation in the patio furniture. The debris it kicks up is imperceptible to the eye, its tremors but lightly registered in the physical realm.

Upon impact the Gapstone meteor has the feel of a pure, free-floating emotion: an unvarnished need to connect with others. An unmitigated, unconditional, inarticulate love spreading through your house. The dog is spooked and even more neurotically clingy than usual. Spreading next door, across the street, and around the corner, stooping over the neighborhood like an invisible mushroom cloud.

Or think of the late Credence Gapstone as a weird alignment of off-kilter events. Real estate deals that gouge no one, inexplicable dips in the level of the median rent, zoning laws that somehow act as beacons for artists and for inexpensive fabulous restaurants, and for young trees that spring up everywhere. The result is that a number of key people in New York City, San Francisco, Miami, Lagos, Buenos Aires, Bangkok, Hong Kong, Berlin, Capetown, Bahia, Rome, and many points in between commandeer a derelict two-block park or a boarded-up store in a rundown strip mall or a vacant lot soon to become a sinkhole, reclaim a housing project marked for demolition, occupy the abandoned floors of a financial district office building that never recovered from recession, colonize a garbage-piled meadow off a lonely highway. In weeks, months, years, the strange inspiration that moves these people will bear fruit, will create from little or nothing other places. New neighborhoods.

The neighborhoods, according to Reginia's psychic scan, number about forty. There are very likely more, some not yet fully constructed. And there's no telling whether these magical locations are temporary or permanent, stationary or mobile.

"My father . . . is a part of all of these different places," Damian says.

Reginia nods. "The Yoruba say you get reincarnated as your descendants. Which is another way of saying that everything gets recycled. Everything that has existed always exists. All times exist in one form or another, in the same space as your time. And all universes are coterminous with this one. Your father has always been here with you—"

"I know that."

"He still is."

31

Miami Airport, six days later

In front of the lines for the self-check-in kiosk, Azaril kisses Langston good-bye.

"You're sure it's OK with the landlord for . . . us to move in?" Azaril asks.

Langston has just received Damian's hug, received it like a letter from afar, received its warmth and welcome, its evocation of past intimacies. His answer for Azaril is distracted.

"Yeah . . . yeah. I spoke to her. She's fine with it." He turns to Azaril with a shrug, his attention finally won. "My landlord loves me."

"Who doesn't?"

Langston smiles falsely to acknowledge this gallantry. He hears Quentin shift behind him, pulling Damian away.

"You got my new number, right? I gave it to you," Quentin is saying. "You sure? Nooo, see, that's what I knew, that ain't the new number, that's the interim number, you need—"

"You really want to do this?" Azaril asks. His voice has dropped to a more intimate level.

Langston nods. He watches Damian punching in numbers on his phone with one hand and seizing Reynaldo's waist with the other. When Quentin finishes bellowing the various digits of his various numbers (his new place, his grandmother's place, his cell), Damian pulls Reynaldo into his chest. Their hug is strong, almost aggressive. It is different from the way Damian hugged Langston.

"Well, if you ever feel like you wanna get married," Reynaldo laughs. "I'm planning a trip to Canada soon. . . ." The hair on Reynaldo's chest is a glorious sight in the unbuttoned channel that runs down the middle of his long-sleeved blood-red shirt. Langston appreciates that Reynaldo gets dressed up for farewells, and appreciates even more that he seems always to find a way to transform gentlemanly apparel into I'm-a-hottie wear. He thinks, *I* could marry Reynaldo.

"Because if this has to do with . . ." Azaril falters. "There's nothing going on between Damian and me. I mean that."

Langston smiles and lets his shoulders rise dramatically then fall in a pantomime of resignation.

Azaril insists. "I'm serious."

"I understand."

"You wouldn't leave because of something like that. Right?"

Langston reaches out, presses the veins in the back of Azaril's hands in his palms. "Call me when you get in."

"I'll drive your car out for you during Christmas break."

"That's not necessary, I can hire a service to do that. Aunt Reginia's got an extra car. . . ."

"Langston, I want to do it."

Langston's eyebrows rise and fall in a muted reenactment of his shoulder gesture. "OK."

"O*kay*."

Azaril turns, then rotates back on his toes. "You know the truth, right?"

Langston waits.

"That I love you?"

Azaril kisses Langston.

At first Langston is taken aback. Azaril's kiss is juvenile. Mouth wide open, chin high and head tilted back, red tongue slashing out impatiently with the sensual greed of a deviant altar boy kneeling to receive communion. But the kiss—perhaps the arms, too, encircling his back—overwhelms Langston. All that pent-up boyish delight, all that unabashed generosity—the lust? He can feel his aunt miles away shouting psychic warnings, but this is not the time for being sensible, being safe. He lets the kiss have its way with him. He throws his mouth and his body into it, opens wider so that Azaril ingests him whole, he surrenders everything.

When it's over, whenever it's over, Langston opens his eyes to see Azaril walking backward, his slim hanging bag thudding against his hip. He sees Damian's back moving rapidly toward the plane.

Azaril is waving and Langston watches his eyes, which skirt over Quentin and linger a moment on Reynaldo, then pass back to Langston.

"You're sure they're refunding your money back for the semester? Because I can go talk to someone!" he bellows, grinning.

Langston has no breath to answer.

They watch the two of them drift through the deserted security line. When Azaril passes beneath the arch of the metal detector, Langston almost feels that he should shout something, as if this were the moment in a wedding when the final opportunity for objections is announced. But he bites his teeth, and says nothing, waves weakly as they disappear into the strip mall of the departure lounge.

Reynaldo and Quentin bid their hasty adieus—Quentin with a sentimental tear globed in the corner of one of his eyes; he dabs at it with his new handkerchief when it refuses to fall. There is so much to do before moving into the house that Sunder has bequeathed them, seeing as how the old guy's let the place get a little run-down in the last year. They'll call Langston at his aunt's house next week to finalize plans for dinner at Reynaldo's mother's place.

"It'll be a big meal. I'm cooking it myself," Reynaldo says and squeezes Langston on the arm.

Mrs. Gillory strolls over and pats the same spot on the same arm. She has a new pair of driving gloves bunched in her other hand and she softly strikes them against her thigh. Her hair is unbound and the foundation of a tan dusts her forehead and nose.

"Let's have the top down all the way to Key West," she suggests.

Langston has no breath to answer, but he smiles.

In front of the lines for the self-check-in kiosk, Azaril kisses Langston good-bye.

32

Key West, early December

High season begins in south Florida.

The *Miami Herald* reports that local merchants dependent on tourists are worried by a number of unusual storms that seem to be heading north after percolating in the heart of the Caribbean, but at least, they say, all the bad press the city's been getting for the past few months has abated. MASS HYSTERIA bellowed the cover of *Newsweek* back in September, as usual doing its level best to whip up Middle American hysteria, this time with articles about widespread hallucination, violence, and debauchery in the first American city to be gripped by what one esteemed psychologist called a "psychological virus." "This kind of phenomenon may be worse than we ever dreamed terrorist attacks would be," the psychologist warned. The governor's and the mayor's joint efforts to contain the damage weren't helped by the appearance of Mr. Castro on a CNN satellite feed from Havana, alive though not so very well; the victim of an unidentified ailment, he had fallen into a coma and had been expected to die, indeed was pronounced brain-dead thrice, but had miraculously recovered. The talk shows couldn't get enough of the story of the city's collective insanity and flew every Miamian and their great-grand-cousin up to New York or out to L.A. to explain what they'd seen and generally make a fool of themselves on national television.

Congress frothed for days at the prospect of boosting its own ratings by passing some kind of legislation—didn't matter what, so long as it didn't cost anything, didn't offend any corporate contributors, and would show that it believed what everyone else believed but believed it better. A measure to chastise Miami for becoming "an American Sodom and Gomorrah" during its fortnight of madness passed the House but died in the Senate. Slapping revenue-generating south Florida on the wrist ("We are talking, sirs, about censuring a great American city near the home of Disney World," one influential legislator opined) receded as a priority when the medical condition of their colleague, the very senior senator of another coastal southern state, took a terrible turn for the worse. Said senator had fallen into a coma, but did not enjoy the luck of his old enemy Castro. Since the ancient, affliction-beset senator had been expected to fall into a coma for some years, this in itself was not terribly intriguing, but the unusual circumstances caused some consternation. The trauma that drop-kicked the senator into the grave via heart failure was the inexplicable appearance in the senatorial bedroom of a very large, very muscular, very naked, and very black man. "Lawd a mighty, Senatah, I cain't believe what Ah'm seein!" the senator's wife testified she'd said, at a Senate hearing hastily convened to investigate. No evidence was found of forced entry into the bedchamber, nor skin cells nor strands of hair nor even the depression of a big muscular toe in the carpet to corroborate her story, and as suspicion has begun to fall on the wife, whispers spread of a new scandal, one late-night talk show hosts and newsroom editors irreverently refer to as "Nekkidbigblackmangate."

Langston grimaces as he reads the latest story (the senator made a groaning sound in his hospital bed; observers thought it was the syllable "nig"). No one has had news of Sunder Rex since he surprised them all by offering the keys to his Miami home to the four of them. "Please accept these as tokens of my apologies," he said. Langston and Azaril didn't trust him, and refused, but Quentin and Reynaldo agreed. Langston has a suspicion that they're running Sunder's escort service from the house—otherwise how do they pay for things, especially with Reynaldo wining and dining all those pretty-boy models every other night and having to pay grad school tuition next fall? Langston dreads that someday they'll call and tell him that Sunder has come back and is threatening to kill them or something, but Aunt Reginia says she can't see it happening that way. "I think that damn warlock's found a way to use that damn spell," she speculates. "This senator mess—it's just for starters."

Langston leaves his desk and stands at the south window of his attic room. The light that streams in at midday bakes the floors and the walls, even with the air-conditioning. He ought to get curtains. Reginia has some in the basement, but he doesn't care for the colors, and he has been slow to purchase his own, complaining that he needs to husband the dwindling funds of his fellowship, especially since he is no longer using the money for an approved field of study. "I can buy you the curtains," Reginia badgers him. "We can work out our own fellowship plan."

He agrees, but then doesn't bring it up again. He doesn't want curtains just yet. He likes it when the solar rays heat his flesh, enjoys the feeling of being struck like a match.

He ought to study. *Prime Chaos*, *The Magick of Numbers*, *The Encyclopedia of Death and Dying*, *The Tantric Way*, *Dreamtime and Inner Space*, *Hyperspace*, *Tell My Horse*, and *Mules and Men* all lie half-finished at various sites throughout the room. He's agreed to have them done by the end of next week ("I don't want you to memorize them, Langston, just read them fast! Absorb!

Absorb!" Reginia exhorts him). At least he's finished *The Hermetica* (which doesn't count; he read it before, for his other degree), and the truth is he knows half the stuff already so it shouldn't be that big a deal, but . . .

He reaches for a cassette tape and snaps it into an old Walkman, and slips on his headphones. It's Quentin, dictating his aimed-for-Oprah's-Book-Club self-help best seller, tentatively titled *How to Seduce a Hottie*, which he has asked Langston to ghostwrite for him.

"It's all the same trip, child. Please, please sleep with me and in doing so prove it to me that I am wonderful, lovable, not guilty, right after all. We call that dee-ny-all and it is highly delusional, but it's a trip most of us share, so it gets a lot of reinforcement. And it ain't all bad, either. Even in these times, with AIDS still sputtering around and the sixty-third reincarnation of Mother Gonorrhea and Sister Syphilis waiting in the wings, even now I say it loud and say it proud: a little sex between friends don't do no harm. Stop. Grammar, punctuation, et cetera, et cetera."

Langston listens absently as he goes back to the window and opens it. He leans across the windowsill and takes a long drag. Impending rain flavors the late-morning air with the scent of harbors. By evening, if it hasn't rained, the coming storm will color the sky salmon. *Wish you were here*, Langston thinks with a wry twist to his private smile, and pictures the words on the back of a postcard that features the shadowed skyline of Miami's downtown framed in soft orange, like the ruins of a dead civilization on Mars. But who would he send the postcard to?

Langston feels an ache that is familiar. Like a hollowed space, a hole in his heart, an arrow through his gut, et cetera, et cetera. Such clichés and metaphors lie about the finality of it all. He would like to think he is finished, done for and defeated at last, that now he will retire to the upper room of some quiet hotel in a bucolic country and knit at the window while regretting lost loves and drinking sorrow in the bitter draught of his unsugared afternoon tea. Dillon got Damian, Damian got Azaril, Azaril got Leah and Damian. Over and done, splat, finished.

But the ache is its own undoing—it makes him restless, it makes him *feel* rather than surrender, makes him think about what could have been and might yet be. The truth is that, no matter how stark the defeat or how complete the conquest, there will always be something in him, perhaps in everyone, that squeals and hammers with its tiny fists like a baby, that nettles and nags and pushes to move. If history is like gravity, as Aden and Atalanta supposed, then desire is an irresistible kind of velocity, expanding outward with the vigor of a newborn universe, pushing forward to shape new planetary bodies, new histories.

He turns from the window, headed toward Reginia's copy of *The Hermetica*. There's that one part he should read again; the translation from the ancient Greek isn't right, he's sure of it. . . . Langston stumbles over one of the open brown UPS cartons full of his stuff that Azaril has packed and mailed for him, and thinks, *Ah! I was meant to find it*, because his original copy of *The Hermetica* is somewhere in this very box with other junk from the old desk.

Beneath a sheaf of promo photos of Eric Bana and Boris Kodjoe he bought in a Hollywood novelty store in North Beach he finds an old leaflet from Yale. Galen made it one night, using a *Vanity Fair* magazine ad and his computer. "Feel No Shame in Your Desire" it says in a banner headline arching over two half-clad underwear Adonises striving with a medicine ball. Galen would probably cringe if he saw it now. All that I'm-out-and-I'm-proud-we're-here-get-used-to-it stuff—so nineties.

Langston stares at the leaflet. He doesn't hear Reginia coming up the narrow stairway to his room, or her perfunctory knock before she storms in.

Reginia has to shout to get his attention.

(Quentin blares in Langston's ears, "A man ain't nothin but a man, children. And all you getting riled up about is some skin and muscle anyhow. Just pores, hair follicles, and striated tissue.")

When he finally hears her, the room is practically shaking with her screams. Langston, with his back turned to the door, feels as if the walls were talking.

"*Good morning!*"

Langston whirls. He slips off his headphones. "Morning."

"You're up early," she says.

"It's eleven thirty."

"Like I said."

She moves closer, and it is only then that she notices the droop in his expression.

She gently tugs the leaflet from his fingers.

"I'd use the word 'honor' instead of 'feel no shame in,' but same difference." Her lips turn upward into a wan smile. "Well, my dear. That is the other side of it, see. There always comes a time you have to let go. What you know in the marrow cells of your bones as a black child is how to make something beautiful out of suffering. That don't mean you should *expect* to suffer, or that anybody has a right to demand that you do. It just happens to be a skill you've mastered. But like any growing thing," she sighs, "you need to be about learning something new."

She hands the poster back to him, but he moves so feebly to retrieve it that she lets it fall to the floor. Lightly she brushes his shoulder with the tips of her fingers, the warmth of her palm. She has time to notice the flowers on the vine arching over the window before he speaks again. A maple yellow only a few days ago, they have matured into a burnt saffron color.

"Leah's going to move out there after she graduates in May. She, Az, and Damian will be living together in my old apartment for a while."

"Ugh. I don't even want to think about that."

"Mm. I do."

"Please don't tell me about it."

He won't: Langston imagines the layout of a whole house rather than his apartment, with three bedrooms instead of one, with stairs and breakfast nooks and crannies. He imagines the permutations and possibilities of sexy interconnections. Secret doors cut into the bookcases, underground passageways, glory holes drilled into the walls of adjoining bathrooms, identical doors in a nondescript hall so that one can stumble drunkenly into the wrong room on the right night.

"I talked to Roan this morning," Reginia says. "Things are OK in Philly. She's keeping her husband as a dog at least part-time, so there are still some issues for the two of them to work out, as you can imagine. Luckily she doesn't have enough power left to do more harm than that. But she's thinking of buying a place for herself down here. She wants to become one of my students, too."

"Oh, God."

Reginia shrugs. "It could be fun. And she'll pay a lot." She notices that Langston's face looks livelier and congratulates herself. "You know, she's still talking about funding a psychic detective agency. I told her I'm not interested in fieldwork right now, but you—maybe even your friends . . .?"

"Ugh. That's something *I* don't even want to think about."

"Well. In time."

"I don't like loss, Aunt Reginia."

"No one does. It's not easy."

"I mean that I don't accept it. I don't approve of it. I read an interview with James Baldwin once. It was all about him being gay. He said that the pain of it was a matter between him and God. He said he was reconciled to living the life God made him live, but he said he had told God that when Judgment Day came, they would both be at the Mercy Seat—and God would not be the only one asking questions."

"Jimmy Baldwin said that? Huh. That's a good one. I'll have to use it sometime."

"I don't care about the being gay part. But I think I've got a thing or two to tell God about this loss mess. People leaving you. It doesn't suit me."

"Well, good for ya, baby. Better you than me. I don't think I'd touch that one. I for one am glad that redbone is split, for example. Are you gonna eat? Michael's made brunch."

Langston looks skeptical. "What is it?"

"What a rude question, Langston. Pancakes. And he'll drown them in syrup. I keep telling that child he'll rot his teeth out, but you know how that is."

"I know."

Come nightfall, Reginia insists that Langston walk out with her to the beach to watch the storm come in. Langston considers this frivolous and quite possibly dangerous, but his complaints trickle away once he begins to enjoy the whippets of air streaming across his face, the gusts that press against his chest and push him back or nudge the small of his back and push him forward. By the time they reach the beach, they are both feeling very feisty. They push each other—Langston responds tentatively at first to Reginia's ruthless shoves before he realizes that roughness is permitted—and when they've had enough jousting they collapse, their heads at catty-corner in the dry, prickly sand.

They vie with one another to name the look and meaning of the clouds spilling over the moon-straddled horizon.

According to Langston, the clouds are candy, wet and dripping, begging for a child's taste, a candy mauve darkening to amethyst. Reginia sees something simpler and more majestic: purple like the robe of an Aquarian Age king. . . . Ah. Agreed: purple, and pregnant . . . well, yes and no: they are bloated like toads, these clouds, they are swollen with abundance, with bounty, they are fat and lazy grapes or rich dark cherries, ripe for plucking, ripe to burst.

Yes, they can both agree to that.

And oh! How they cannot wait for the sweet, sweet wine to rain down.